FORBIDDEN PLAINS

Petronella van Zyl, daughter of generations of Boer farmers of the South African plains, finds her life altered irrevocably the day she discovers love on the banks of the nearby Vaal River—with Marcus Cohen, Jewish *Utlander.*

Marcus is everything that her dour, resolutely Calvinist parents are not. Rich and sophisticated, Marcus is a city boy who knows less than nothing about farming—and more than enough about loving a woman.

But Petronella's family—most of all, her strong, stern-willed Mamma—will never forgive her for loving a Jew. Abandoned by their families, cut off from their faiths, Marcus and Petronella survive the test of their love only to be cruelly separated by the exigencies of the Boer War, at the mercy of their new British overlords. Their eventual reunion, a dream come true, poses new sacrifices as Marcus grows increasingly committed to the Church that's replaced his lost Jewish faith.

Left to her own resources, Petronella must carve a life for herself and for her children from the same soil upon which she was raised. Facing a stormy relationship with her firstborn child, mirroring Petronella's own with her

(continued on back flap)

(continued from front flap)

stubborn and autocratic mother years ago, Petronella will have to make some hard choices before her love and her life are restored to her.

Far Forbidden Plains, a stirring and emotional saga, is memorable for the breadth of its canvas, the richness and originality of its characters and the many human tragedies and desires it encompasses. Set during the years when the English and Afrikaners became bitter enemies, it also traces the seeds of South Africa's troubled history.

Janet Young Photography

CHRISTINA LAFFEATY has written an epic historical novel that uses the stories and experiences of her youth in the Afrikaans community in South Africa. Petronella's farm, Jakkalsdrif, is one of the farms where the author spent her childhood, she and members of her family living through many incidents similar to those described in the novel. Moving to England after marrying at nineteen, she began writing after the birth of her second child. She lives with her husband in Cornwall.

St. Martin's Press
175 Fifth Avenue
New York, NY 10010

FAR FORBIDDEN PLAINS

CHRISTINA LAFFEATY

FAR FORBIDDEN PLAINS

St. Martin's Press
New York

FAR FORBIDDEN PLAINS. Copyright © 1989 by Christina Laffeaty. All rights reserved. Printed in the United States of America. No part of this book may be used or reproduced in any manner whatsoever without written permission except in the case of brief quotations embodied in critical articles or reviews. For information, address St. Martin's Press, 175 Fifth Avenue, New York, N.Y. 10010.

Library of Congress Cataloging-in-Publication Data

Laffeaty, Christina.
      Far forbidden plains / Christina Laffeaty.
         p.   cm.
     ISBN 0-312-03337-0
     I. Title.
PR9369.3.L325F37   1989
823—dc20   89-30511
                                  CIP

First published in Great Britain by Hodder and Stoughton.

First U.S. Edition
10 9 8 7 6 5 4 3 2 1

In memory of Mammie.

This book is also for a little girl I once knew.

My friend Judith Murdoch convinced me that I possessed the material for this book, prodded me into writing it and then sustained me with unstinting encouragement, constructive criticism and moral support while I was doing so. But for her, the book would never have been written and I owe her an enormous debt of gratitude.

AUTHOR'S NOTE

During the period covered by this novel, the Dutch language in South Africa was gradually evolving into what later became Afrikaans, with growing variations in spelling, grammar and pronunciation. To avoid confusing non-South African readers, I have kept the spelling of 'Dutch' as simple as possible until, in the later part of the novel, Afrikaans had officially replaced it as the country's second language.

Although Zulus in the Transvaal would have been outnumbered by people of the Sotho and Tswana tribes, I have adopted artistic licence and created a Zulu family as part of the story. For the Fanakalo used I have drawn upon my own knowledge of this lingua franca, confirmed by a booklet of terms issued for use in the South African mines, and while there may be inaccuracies I have tested the terms on a black South African who has little knowledge of either English or Afrikaans and she understood me perfectly.

After 1884, and until the Peace of Vereeniging in 1902, the official title of the Transvaal and Orange Free State combined was *de Zuid-Afrikaansche Republiek*. Again, to avoid confusion I have referred to the Transvaal and the Orange Free State as separate republics.

Statistics invariably raise problems in that sources rarely agree, and for that reason I have used rumours existing at the time and passed on by word of mouth to give some idea of the strength of fighting forces, inmates of concentration camps and other numerical data. It has never been established, for instance, how many Boer men, women and children died in the concentration camps but official estimates vary between 18,000 and 28,000.

For the section of the novel dealing with the concentration camps I have relied heavily upon case histories compiled by Miss Emily Hobhouse during the Anglo-Boer War. Born in Cornwall, she became aware of the plight of the inmates of the camps and despite being arrested and deported from South Africa, she fought so tenaciously for reform of the camps' administration that her name is revered in South Africa to this day.

Finally, readers might be interested to know that the inspiration for the Benz Voiturette car featured in this novel came from a vehicle of the same name which was imported into Pretoria by Messrs J. P. Hess and A. E. Reno in December 1896 and was later publicly displayed there. It was subsequently sold to Mr A. H. Jacobs of Johannesburg, a coffee merchant, who used it for advertising purposes until it was accidentally destroyed in a fire.

Part One

1

Because it was Sunday, Jakkalsdrif shimmered under the Highveld sun in a state of suspended animation. Even the crickets were too somnolent to make more than an occasional, desultory noise.

Privately and defiantly, Petronella decided that Sundays were a bore. But sacrilegious as she knew the thought to be, it was hard for her to believe that the rest of her family were feeling uplifted by the observance of the day of rest ordained by the Almighty. Petronella studied them as they sat on the verandahed stoep of the farmhouse, hoping to catch a stray breeze.

Pappa's main function of the day was long since over. Dressed in his best moleskin trousers and jacket, his full beard neatly trimmed and brushed, he had held morning service for the family and their servants from the nearby *stad*. As always, Petronella had had to think hard of something else to stop herself laughing, because the Catechism sounded so funny when delivered in Fanakalo. Pappa preached in that hotch-potch of dialects for the benefit of some of their older servants who had never learnt to master Dutch, for it was important that the word of God should be spread even to the humblest and most ignorant of His creatures, Pappa said. Petronella could speak Fanakalo well enough, and normally she did not find it funny. It was only the atmosphere of solemnity that made it sound absurd.

But the servants had long since returned to the *stad* to observe the Sabbath in their own way, and now Pappa had the choice of reading the Bible or discussing politics with her elder brother Johannes. He took it in turns to do both, and she guessed that Johannes was secretly counting the minutes until he could ride over to the farm of Dorothea Becker's family for supper.

As for Mamma, she seemed incomplete, somehow, now that lunch was over and long hours of idleness separated her from the preparation of supper. She looked uncomfortable in her Sunday gown of dark-blue cotton bombazine, her bulk squeezed into the confines of the stink-wood chair which had belonged to her grandmother and which had been brought all the way from the Cape by ox-wagon, trundled up and down mountains and ferried through rivers by the early Trekkers.

In spite of her size, Mamma was an active woman, always on the go, making soap or candles, butchering and drying beef, preserving fruit, supervising the servants as they went about their household chores. And when she did sit down she was always busy with her sewing or her knitting or crocheting. But not on Sundays. Mamma would never admit to such blasphemy, of course, but Petronella was sure she must find the Sabbath a great trial. Now, those strong, nimble fingers of hers twitched restlessly as they lay in her lap, as if idleness made them nervous.

Fourteen-year-old Gideon was looking longingly at his Mauser, propped against the railing at one end of the stoep. Petronella guessed that he was itching to clean and oil the gun, but of course he could not do so because it was Sunday.

She rose from the bench with its seat of latticed rawhide and went to perch on the verandah railing.

"Petronella," Mamma said sternly, "get down from there! You're too old to be swinging your legs like that!"

"Let the child be," Pappa countermanded, and went on talking politics to Johannes. "There's trouble coming, and soon. The British won't give up until they've tried – and failed – to annex the two Republics."

Johannes nodded. "They're after the goldmines on the Rand, of course."

Pappa's eyes flashed with passion. "Of course! Cecil Rhodes knows precisely what he's doing when he stirs up unrest among the other *Uitlanders*! The biggest mistake we ever made was when we allowed that modern-day Babylon to spring up, with its gambling and drinking places and its disgusting trollops – " He stopped abruptly, as if he had said something he hadn't intended to let slip out.

Petronella's interest had been caught. From her perch on the railing she demanded, "Pappa, surely you can't mean Maria Trollope and her family? What have they done that's disgusting? And if they'd meant to move to Johannesburg she certainly said nothing to me about it when I saw her at the last *Nachtmaal* meeting."

Almost immediately, she realised that her question had caused a curious reaction among her family. Pappa was turning the pages of the Bible with great concentration, as if he hadn't heard a word she'd said. Johannes had coloured to the roots of his hair while Gideon gave a snort which he turned into a cough when Mamma glared fiercely at him.

"Even if they have moved to Johannesburg," Petronella protested, for she had liked Maria Trollope, "it isn't fair to call them disgusting! And if it's because Maria's great-grandfather was an Englishman from the Cape, *that* isn't fair either!"

"Maria's family haven't moved anywhere," Pappa said gruffly.

"Oh . . . Then who are those disgusting Trollopes in Johannesburg you talked about? Are they other members of Maria's family?"

"Distant relatives, my treasure," Pappa agreed with such a note of relief in his voice that she knew he wasn't telling the truth, but had gratefully seized upon the excuse she had offered him.

She recalled how he had stopped suddenly in his condemnation of Johannesburg, as if he had remembered what day it was and he had thoughtlessly used a bad word. A word which was meant to be kept secret from Petronella. Her suspicions were confirmed by the glances being exchanged, glances which excluded her. Gideon's face was almost puce with suppressed laughter.

"Trollope isn't only a name, is it?" she demanded. "It means something else as well. *What* does it mean?"

"It's a name," Mamma put in flatly. "That's all."

"No, it isn't! Even Gideon knows what it means, and he's only fourteen! I've passed my seventeenth birthday but *I'm* not allowed to know what it means!" She jumped down from the railing and went on heatedly, with resentment, "Why does everyone keep secrets from me?"

"Such nonsense, my little heart," Pappa said, looking up from the Bible, his usually stern grey eyes filled with tenderness. He stroked his beard. "How about singing for Pappa, hmm? *'Kent gij dat Volk'*," he began the opening bars of the national anthem of the South African Republic.

"I don't feel like singing," Petronella returned sullenly, tossing her long braids and walking inside the house.

As befitted one of the most prosperous farms in the Transvaal, the house on Jakkalsdrif had been built with careful planning. On each side of the wide front stoep was a gabled room; one was the bedroom of Mamma and Pappa and the other was the rarely used parlour where the harmonium had pride of place. Beyond lay the rest of the bedrooms which opened on to the side stoeps, and the kitchen and pantry led to the back stoep, with the enormous baking oven just outside. Petronella's room overlooked the fruit orchard with its peach and apricot trees.

She had occupied the same room for most of her seventeen years, and in that time little had changed. Apart from the patchwork cover on the bed, which Mamma had taught her to make, and the sampler reading 'Thy God Seest Thee', which she had stitched with less piety than boredom and pricked fingers, the room was very much as she remembered it from the days when she was a little girl.

The same marble-topped wash-stand holding a matching flower-patterned basin and jug; the same small mottled mirror on the wall which was only large enough for her to be able to see to braid her hair. Mamma said that mirrors encouraged vanity, and vanity was of the devil.

Petronella peered moodily into it now. As soon as she was old enough Mamma had taught her to scrape her almost silver blonde hair severely away from her face, and plait it into two neat, tight braids. Only for formal occasions like weddings and funerals and *Nachtmaal*, the periodic gathering of the Boers for the celebration of the Last Supper, was she allowed to pin the braids into a coil in the nape of her neck or arrange them in a coronet about her head.

She paid scant attention to her wide, long-lashed grey eyes or the neat golden curves of her eyebrows. She was counting her freckles in a spirit of childishly malicious satisfaction. There were eleven altogether. Mamma accused her of having gone bare-headed in the sun at some time or other, but she would fall down in a foaming-at-the-mouth fit if she knew how Petronella had really acquired them, and that she also had some on her upper arms and shoulders.

Her mouth set resentfully. She would teach them to share secrets which shut her out! She would go and do her own secret thing which would shock them half to death if they knew about it, and the fact that she did it on the Sabbath would make her revenge that much more satisfying and wicked. And if the Almighty struck her dead because of it, it would be their fault. Already she was beginning to feel like a martyr.

She would need an excuse to get away, however. On a normal weekday when Pappa and Johannes and Gideon were at work on the farm, and Mamma was absorbed in one of her countless tasks, it was easy enough to slip away unnoticed, and she always claimed afterwards that she had been working on her own bit of garden where she grew flowers.

But today Gideon in particular might decide to follow her out of curiosity and boredom. Johannes, she thought with derision, would be spending the afternoon in sprucing himself up and trimming his moustache before calling on Dorothea Becker.

Petronella thought for a moment, and then searched through the drawers of the tallboy which held her clothes. There was a spotted blouse which had become too tight over her bust, and which she knew Mwende had always coveted.

Armed with the blouse, she made her way towards the stoep but remained just inside the door when she realised that her parents were discussing her.

"Don't you think," Mamma was saying, "that it's time the girl had an *opsitkers*? Gerrit du Toit's mother told me, last time they visited, that he would like to call on Petronella Saturday nights."

"She's too young," Pappa said flatly. "She's only a child."

Forcing herself to keep a straight face, Petronella walked out on to the stoep. "I'm just going over to the *stad*," she told her family guilelessly. "I promised Mwende this blouse but I forgot to give it to her."

"Wear your *kappie*," was all Mamma said, picking up the poke-bonnet of starched white cotton which Petronella had discarded as soon as the sun moved from the front stoep.

Tying the strings in a bow under her chin, she set off sedately. But once she had gained the dry-stone corral into which the cattle were driven at night, and so was out of sight of her family, she sank to her knees and shook with laughter.

So Gerrit du Toit wanted to come calling on her on Saturday evenings! Petronella might not know what Trollope meant when it wasn't someone's name, but she knew all about the *opsitkers*. It was a candle, ritually presented to a grown-up daughter when a young man came to court her. It meant that she could, with parental blessing, sit up alone with him in the parlour after the household had discreetly retired, and the length of the candle indicated the favour in which the young suitor was held.

If Gerrit came to call, Petronella would make certain that the *opsitkers* was no more than the merest stub. She could just picture him, with his pimples and his pitiful moustache which refused to grow properly, trying to make conversation while his great Adam's apple wobbled nervously up and down.

They would sit at opposite ends of the sofa and look at the guttering candle, and probably pass the time in identifying the different insects lured by its light. Then, the subject and the candle exhausted, he would take his pimples and his wispy moustache and unhitch his horse and ride the twelve miles home. Saturday evenings with the *opsitkers* were supposed to make couples get to know each other better, but she already knew all she wanted to know about Gerrit.

Anyway, she was to be spared his attentions, thanks to Pappa. There were times when his insistence on seeing her as his little girl proved useful instead of irritating.

Petronella dismissed Gerrit from her mind, and removed her shoes. She hated them as much as she hated her *kappie*. Pappa made them himself, just as every other Boer fashioned shoes for his household, of the softest hide. These *velskoene* were supposed to be comfortable; far more comfortable than any fancy footwear imported from the Cape Colony. As far as Petronella was concerned, nothing could compare with bare feet for comfort.

Her soles were so tough that she could walk through a field of mealie-stubble or wade through a pebble-strewn burn without the slightest discomfort, and a thorn from one of the wait-a-minute trees had to be extremely sharp for her to feel it. She walked barefoot whenever she could, since no one was going to ask to examine her soles. But the hated *kappie* had to be worn, because the evidence would very soon scream aloud if she did not.

The mealies were standing green and tall in their rows, she noted. They stretched for as far as the eye could see, right down to the thick growth of wait-a-minute thorn trees which separated them from the meadows where the cattle and the sheep and the horses grazed. Another fence of thorn trees marked the banks of the Vaal River, their growth encouraged to prevent the livestock from falling in and drowning. Some way further along, the waters of the river had been diverted into tributaries which irrigated the fields and provided drinking water for the animals.

Near one of these streams the native *stad* had been constructed, and a permanent cloud of smoke wrapped itself around the beehive huts with their thatched or flat roofs of zinc sheeting. Petronella could smell its familiar odour as she made her way towards it.

Desultory thoughts slipped into her mind. She wished she had an older sister whom she could have questioned about the things which puzzled her. The matter of babies, for instance. Petronella knew that an Angel of God delivered them during the night, but how did the Angel know if a woman was married or not? Did he sometimes make a mistake? And how did one's breasts know that they were suddenly required to produce milk for the baby brought by the Angel?

She might have been able to ask Sarie van Tonder, who was nineteen and the daughter of their nearest neighbour, except that Pappa and Sarie's father had fallen out over the matter of some disputed land between their two farms, so that all social contact between the two families had come to an end.

Petronella shrugged the thought away. The smoke was beginning to sting her eyes as she skirted some of the disused and dilapidated huts. The Bantu people constructed their huts to their own designs, using materials supplied by Pappa. But because most of them feared the intrusion of evil spirits, they built them without windows or chimneys and with only one small doorway which one had to stoop to enter. Also, because it was the custom of many of them to abandon any hut in which a death had taken place, they were not constructed with any idea of permanence.

Through the smoke, Petronella could see the figure of old Bolih, leaning upon his gnarled stick, his blanket draped across his shoulders. No matter how fiercely the sun beat down, Bolih was never to be seen without his blanket.

"*Molo,* Nonnie!" he greeted her in Fanakalo.

"*Molo*, Bolih."

"*Hamba na kaya ka mina?*" he invited, pointing his stick in the direction of his hut.

"*Ayi, bonga*," she declined the invitation. She knew that it gave him great pleasure to press upon her a bowl of *magouw*, made from fermented mealie-meal, and tell her stories about the *Tokoloshe*, the supernatural creature in native folklore which was supposed to resemble a small man with a tail, and which lurked in rivers to drag young people into the water and drown them.

Knowing his disappointment, she explained that she was in a hurry today. "*Mina tshetsha. Upi Mwende?*"

"*Yena kaya*, Nonnie."

She thanked him and picked her way through the smoke and over the supine forms of sleeping mongrel dogs towards the hut where Mwende lived with her grandmother. Mwende was roughly Petronella's age, although the girl did not know the precise date of her birth. And because she had grown up on Jakkalsdrif she spoke Dutch, which made communication easier than the cumbersome Fanakalo.

Petronella knew that Fanakalo was a mixture of different languages which had originated among the sugar workers in Natal, and it had spread from there to the diamond mines at Kimberley and then to the new goldmines on the Witwatersrand and beyond. Pappa had told her its history, but all those places were just names to her. The furthest she had ever been from Jakkalsdrif was to Wolmaransstad, about thirty miles away Pappa said, but that had been soon after the town was established and she had been only a little girl at the time. As for Johannesburg, so often called Babylon by Pappa – well, even before the discovery that it was infested with Trollopes who were obviously too wicked for her to be allowed to know about them, that city had sounded so strange that it might as well have been in a foreign country. Petronella had been told that it was possible to reach it from here in one day provided one started early enough and changed horses frequently, but she couldn't imagine herself ever visiting it.

Mwende emerged from the hut just before Petronella reached it, for which she was glad. Courtesy would otherwise have compelled her to enter it and exchange polite formalities with the girl's grandmother, and Petronella was in a hurry to get away. Not only that but the hut would be filled with wood-smoke from the fire in its centre.

Mwende was of Zulu stock and quite beautiful, with high cheekbones and a light mahogany colouring and deep-set black eyes. She moved with such grace that she was able to carry a large calabash filled with water on her turbaned head for a considerable distance without spilling a drop of it. When Petronella was younger she had persuaded Mwende to teach her the trick, but it had ended with the water drenching her, and Mamma had taken a strap to both girls.

"I've brought you the spotted blouse, Mwende," Petronella said.

The girl brought her palms together once in a ritual expression of appreciation. "Thank you, Nonnie." She glanced at Petronella's bare feet and grinned. "If the Missus catch you with no shoes, you'll get it!"

Petronella tossed her braids. "She won't catch me."

"What if a snake bite you on the toe? You ever think of that?"

"Of course I have! I look where I'm going." Petronella turned away. "Tell your grandmother I asked if she was well."

As she picked her way back through the huddle of smoke-filled huts she reflected on the strange ways of their occupants. Because Mwende had been born before her father had finished paying the *lobolo*, or bride-price, for her mother, the girl had automatically become the property of her maternal grandmother. Mwende's parents lived in another of the huts with her younger brother Koos. It must have been a source of great regret to her parents when their first child turned out to be a valuable girl who would one day attract *lobolo* of her own. A boy would have been of no financial benefit to his grandmother. Had the Angel of God made a mistake? Or was he punishing the parents for something, or having a joke at their expense? So many unanswerable questions . . .

The afternoon sun was beating down fiercely now, causing Petronella's cambric gown to cling uncomfortably in damp folds about her legs. Oh, but it would be a relief, as well as a pleasure, to do her secret thing today! The thorn trees marking the bank of the Vaal River seemed to be dancing in the heat haze, and no breath of wind stirred the mealies in their fields.

By the time she reached the trees, perspiration was running down Petronella's cheeks. She crouched down, inspecting the terrain carefully. No sign of snakes or scorpions; just some industrious ants, unaffected by the heat, rushing about in controlled chaos and a dung-beetle pushing her unsavoury burden laboriously along so that she could lay her eggs in it.

There was a small gap in the thicket of thorns which Petronella had almost forgotten about until some months ago. She had discovered it when she was still a child, and allowed to run wild on the farm, to ride bareback any filly or colt she was able to catch and generally to enjoy her freedom. But after her tenth birthday Mamma had finally won her tussle with Pappa and had imposed all the restraints normally put upon Boer girls from a much earlier age.

Petronella had been confined to the house and to her bit of garden, where Pappa indulgently allowed her to grow flowers while Mamma snorted that flowers were no good to man or beast. Life had become a tame business of learning how to bake and sew and knit and pluck a fowl for the table, and other boring pursuits. And then she had suddenly remembered her secret spot of old, and had begun to steal away to it whenever she could.

Lying on her stomach now, she wriggled through the gap. A butcher bird flew up, startled, leaving his prey of a small lizard imperfectly speared on a thorn. He would be back later, to complete his task and hang the lizard thriftily there for future consumption.

With the wait-a-minute thicket behind her, Petronella had reached the area where the willows grew and dipped their green fronds into the water. Soft, moss-like grass covered the ground here, and the sun made a dappled pattern as it slanted through the foliage overhead.

She untied the strings of her *kappie* and placed it on the ground. Then she unbuttoned the bodice of her gown and stepped out of it. Her pantaloons and confining camisole of plain, unadorned cotton followed, and she folded them all neatly so that they would not acquire suspicious creases.

She moved towards the bank and began to wade into the river, gasping, shivering and then laughing at the ever-fresh shock of its coldness upon her skin. She knew precisely how far it was safe to go, for once one could no longer see the pebbles shimmering through the water it meant that there was a deep, treacherous hole beyond. When the water reached to her waist she took a deep breath and ducked down until it covered her shoulders. She was afraid to stay too long, for it was said that there were crocodiles in the river, although she had never seen one.

Reluctantly, Petronella left the water and returned to the mossy grass, lying down so that the sun could dry her as it shone through the branches of the willow trees. She felt refreshed and delightfully cool, but she was also filled with the usual mixture of guilt and pleasure her secret thing always inspired. What she had done and was still doing was wrong. One *never* took off all one's clothes at once, Mamma had taught her. Even when having an all-over wash, one did so in sections, re-covering parts which had been washed before starting on others. And at night, one kept one's pantaloons on until they could be decently removed under cover of the nightgown. One should not expose one's body and one should certainly not look at it, let alone take pleasure in it.

But there was pleasure in being totally without clothes, and in running her hand over the silky skin of her thighs. The faint blue veins of her white breasts reminded her of rivers and tributaries. Recklessly, she began to unbraid her hair. The hated *kappie* had its uses, for it would cover her clumsy attempt at plaiting her hair again later without the help of a mirror or a comb.

After the first shock of her appearance in their midst had passed, the riverbank dwellers began to resume their normal routine. The weaver birds continued to make their nests, which they wove like baskets. Petronella laughed softly as she watched them. The male constructed the nest with its intricate pattern, and every now and again the female came to inspect his work. If she did not approve, he was forced to dismantle it and remake it in the same place. Petronella could just imagine what would happen if human beings were to behave like that, with women ordering their husbands about!

A blue heron was using its long bill to spear frogs or fish in the river, its ornamental plumage making it appear like an animated, fancy feather duster. Dragonflies skimmed over the water and two frogs were calling to each other from opposite sides of the river, and Petronella wondered whether they were taunting the heron or perhaps monitoring its activities. There was a constant splashing sound of fish leaping in the water.

The Almighty didn't strike her dead after all, and she relaxed, her eyelids growing heavy. She stretched out on the cool grass, making a pillow of her folded arms.

She was roused from her doze by the instinctive knowledge that she was no longer alone in her secret place.

She leapt to her feet, and her first terror subsided when she realised that the intruder could not be an avenging angel sent by the Almighty, for he carried no sword and sported no wings. And the fact that he was a total stranger and therefore unlikely to betray her secret reassured her somewhat. Indeed, in spite of his undoubtedly and encouragingly human aspect, he might have come from a different world, so unlike was he to any man she had ever seen before.

He stood a little distance away, watching her. He wore the most outlandish hat of pale-coloured straw, and his shirt was not the khaki favoured by the Boers, but white. He was a tall, lean young man with brilliant blue eyes and dark hair and a clean-shaven face. And his shirt appeared to be of silk. A man with no hair whatsoever on his face, and wearing a white silk shirt! He might as well have been wearing a gown –

For the first time reality penetrated the complete strangeness of his appearance from nowhere, and Petronella remembered her own state of undress. She darted for her clothes, prepared to take flight.

"Please," the young man said, speaking in Dutch but with a strange intonation, and lifting a hand in a reassuring gesture. "You have no cause to feel fear, 'Juffrouw, or to experience shame."

Clutching her bundle of clothes, she blinked uncertainly at him.

He appeared to offer no threat, and she was filled with curiosity about him. Why did he speak in that unfamiliar manner? Where had he come from, and how had he chanced upon this spot?

The blue heron rose in its slow, cumbersome flight, with its long wings curved downwards, and automatically her glance went to the river. A white-painted boat had been pulled up among the reeds.

"You rowed across?" she asked the young man. "You are from the Free State side?"

He shook his head. "I traversed the distance between Johannesburg and Vereeniging on the back of a horse. My journey onwards from Vereeniging was accomplished by navigating the Vaal River in a rowing boat."

His way of speaking and his use of long words reminded her of a book full of spiritual messages which Pappa sometimes read aloud to them, but the manner in which he accentuated parts of some words and blurred others had an oddly mesmerising and exotic effect.

His gaze was travelling slowly over her. "You are beautiful in the extreme, Juffrouw."

"Oh . . ." She crouched down on her knees, still covering as much of her nakedness as she could with her bundle of clothes. She had been totally taken aback by his directness and his evident sincerity and by the open admiration in his eyes. No Boer, male or female, would have dreamt of calling her beautiful to her face. There had also been an implication that he found her naked form beautiful. Nudity was sinful and she knew it could give one personal pleasure, but it had never even entered her mind that it might be considered beautiful.

"When I first beheld you," he went on, "the word my imagination suggested to me was – *Lorelei*. Surely such a face, such hair, such a body could only belong to a creature of myth?" Her expression must have conveyed her bewilderment to him, for he added more simply, "The reflection which faces you from the mirror each day must reassure you of your beauty."

"It only shows me how to braid my hair neatly. There is a mirror in Mamma's room," she felt driven to explain, "inside the door of her hanging chest, but she keeps it locked. She says looking at oneself unnecessarily in the mirror is vanity, and vanity is a sin."

He spread his hands in a gesture which she found as unfamiliar, as exotically different, as everything else about him. "To feast one's eyes upon beauty and derive enjoyment from it – how can that possibly be to commit sin? Please," he changed the subject, "will you grant me permission to sit with you?"

"If – if you like." She was still clutching her clothes to her and everything – instilled modesty; common sense; Mamma's total horror if she were ever to learn of this situation – told Petronella that she ought to get dressed. But the thought of pulling her pantaloons on in front of him embarrassed her far more than her nudity did. Apart from its being an ungraceful, undignified act in itself, necessitating hopping on one leg, he would see where Mamma had made her patch her pantaloons with unmatching squares of gingham.

He smiled slightly, as if he sensed her inner conflict. Then he tossed his hat on the ground and pulled his shirt over his head, handing it to her.

She turned her back on him, put her bundle of clothes to one side and wriggled her arms hastily into the sleeves of the shirt which reached with some degree of decency to below her thighs. She had been surprised and overcome by his sensitivity, and his smile had revealed attractive grooves in his cheeks which whiskers would have hidden. She was glad now that he was clean-shaven.

What his face lacked in hair was made up for by his bare chest. She had not known that men had thick curly hair on their chests. She supposed she must have seen Gideon's naked body when he was a baby, since she was almost three years older than he, but if she had she could not remember it. Neither of her brothers would ever have dreamt of appearing in public, even at home, without their shirts.

She realised that he had been studying her equally intently. "What is your name?" she broke the silence.

He answered absently, as if preoccupied with other matters. "Mordechai Cohen." He appeared to recollect himself. "No, that is the Hebrew form of my given name, and not generally used. I have been too long alone with my thoughts, I suspect, or I would not have introduced myself to you by that name. Allow me, now, to make myself known to you as Marcus Cohen, 'Juffrouw – ?"

"Van Zyl. Petronella van Zyl." She felt bemused as she took the hand he offered her. "Which is your *real* name?"

"They are both real and rightful. To a few people only am I known as Mordechai, and to many others as Marcus."

"I see." But she did not see at all. How very odd it was that he should have two names, not used together but separately. Her brothers had also been given Hebrew names from the Bible, but Gideon's second name was Louis and Johannes's was Hugo, and they didn't go about introducing themselves by one name or the other as the mood or the circumstances dictated.

"You are obviously one of those *Uitlanders* who throw Pappa into such a fury," she said half-accusingly, "and that is why you speak such funny Dutch."

"I am one of those known to your people as *Uitlanders*," he confirmed. He looked at her, his blue eyes dancing in amusement. "I regret that you find my Dutch funny. The professor who taught it to me assured me that I had attained a high standard of grammatical correctness. It would appear that he was mistaken." The blue eyes, set in a perfectly serious face, were openly laughing at Petronella now. "Would people in France, I wonder," he mused, "consider my French to be funny? Would Germans laugh at me if I addressed them in their own language?" He shrugged, and even such an everyday gesture became eloquent and expressive when he made it. "Only of my Yiddish, it appears, can I allow myself to feel completely confident."

"So many languages!" Petronella sneered dismissively, angered by the knowledge that he had been secretly laughing at her. "Whatever is the need for them? Dutch is enough for anyone – and Fanakalo, of course."

"Do you imagine, 'Juffrouw Petronella," he asked gravely, "that the entire world speaks and understands and communicates in Dutch and Fanakalo?"

"Why, yes – "

This time he laughed aloud, showing those fascinating grooves in his cheeks. She stiffened at first and then relaxed as she recognised that there was nothing mocking or cruel in his laughter. It held amusement, indulgence and even something like tenderness. "Between the Chains, 'Juffrouw Petronella, you would hear a great many languages, but never Fanakalo, and only on occasion would you hear Dutch."

"I don't understand you. What do chains have to do with anything?"

"I will endeavour to explain." He moved a little closer to her. "When the ringing of bells announces the closing of the Stock Exchange at six o'clock, the workday has not been completed. How could it possibly be so when that is the time when from all over the world the cables are arriving – cables announcing the difference in prices in such places as London and the Continent? So, outside in the street the dealing is renewed in a specially chained-off portion, while buyers and sellers call out prices in voices loud enough to compete in being heard. This continues until late into the evening."

"But what do they buy and sell?" Petronella asked confusedly.

"Gold, naturally. And because of the special chained-off portion in the street the Exchange is often spoken of as 'Between the Chains', for a far greater amount of work is accomplished there than during High Change in the mornings."

Although she had understood the words he'd used, he might as well have been speaking in one of his other strange tongues for all the sense she made of what he had said. The only thing she had fully taken in was that he was connected with gold in some way.

"You are a miner?" she asked, gazing at him in puzzlement.

He looked amused. "The Cohens do not dig or blast for gold. We own shares in the mines or we deal in shares."

"And what are you doing here, Mijnheer Koen?"

"You cannot pronounce my name correctly," he observed in a teasing voice. "I think you will find Marcus easier to say. In answer to your question – I am taking a holiday. I was curious to discover how far I could navigate along the Vaal River in a rowing boat, and in so doing I have met some of your people. Yesterday, for example, I requested a family called van Tonder to sell food to me."

"They are our neighbours, but we are not on speaking terms with them. There's a piece of land between our farms which Pappa says is his, but Mijnheer van Tonder says it belongs to him."

"The Boers are strange people," Marcus commented. "They dislike and distrust *Uitlanders*, yet not once have they refused my requests for help or food and drink. They are more than willing to give, but they will not entertain the notion of selling. Strange people . . ."

"We are not strange at all!" she contradicted him touchily. "It is you who are strange!" Large chunks of Pappa's views, which she had heard so many times that she had stopped paying attention to them, returned to her now.

"You come here, you foreigners, in your thousands," she quoted Pappa, "and you start making demands as if the country belongs to you! You're not content with grabbing our gold to make yourselves rich; you want to bring President Kruger down and annex the free Republics in the name of the British Crown! You want to enslave us as the Cape Boers are enslaved – "

"It is the vote for which we are petitioning, 'Juffrouw Petronella, and your President persistently refuses to grant it to us."

"Of course he refuses! There are already almost as many *Uitlanders* in the Transvaal Republic as there are burghers, and soon you will outnumber us! If you were able to vote you would be running our Republic in no time and telling us what to do!"

"So angry," he murmured, touching her hair briefly, "and so beautiful. It would not please me that we should quarrel, you and I. So inform me, instead, of your life on the farm."

The cadences of his accented speech, as well as the reference to her beauty, had melted her indignation and she began to tell him about Jakkalsdrif; about harvest-time and how the ploughing always un-earthed many different species of poisonous snakes which had to be killed. She described the pall of anxiety which had enveloped everyone when an outbreak of *rinderpest* had been suspected among the cattle, and how they had rejoiced when the fear proved to be groundless. He listened intently but she sensed that he understood as little about her life as she had understood about what went on 'Between the Chains'.

She stopped talking, and silence stretched between them. Her glance fell upon the hair growing so abundantly on his chest. She supposed that Johannes and Gideon must be embarrassed about their chest-hair and that was why they always kept their shirts buttoned close to the neck. Marcus, however, seemed to be totally unself-conscious about his body hair. All the same, she looked away, staring into space, but she continued her fascinated speculation about the wealth of curls on his chest.

"Of what," he broke the silence, "are you thinking, 'Juffrouw Petronella?"

Impulsively, she blurted out the literal truth. "Of your chest, and that I should like to touch it."

His eyes darkened and an unfathomable look settled about his mouth. He had been shocked and angered by the impertinence and indelicacy of her reply, she decided with dismay. Mamma would certainly consider it to have been unspeakably shocking, but then she would have condemned utterly every single thing about this entire situation.

Petronella was about to tell him that she was sorry, that she must have been mad to say such a thing, when she felt her hand taken in his.

"The pleasure," he said, the unusual intonation in his voice more pronounced than ever, "will belong to me." He guided her hand so that its palm came to rest on his chest.

It was a most novel sensation, feeling the springy curls against her fingers. As she explored them she wondered if they ever grew so long that they needed to be cut. Her fingers encountered a small, taut circular ridge and her amazed examination disclosed a matching ridge on the left side of his chest.

Her eyes widened and her lips parted in utter astonishment. *He had nipples!* Of what use were nipples to a man? It was yet one more question to add to the long list of imponderable mysteries which exercised her mind, and she was about to ask whether he could throw light on any of it when his hand came up and touched her throat.

She felt it moving slowly, lingeringly, over her shoulder, down towards the valley between her breasts, moulding the silk against her skin. It brought a delicious sensation, and she thought that this must be how a cat felt when it was being stroked. She smiled dreamily at Marcus, and heard him catch his breath.

His hand moved, gentle still but more insistent, over the twin curves of her breasts. She shivered, instantly alive, no longer dreamily content but yearning for something the name and nature of which she did not know.

Murmuring something she could not understand and guessed must be in one of his foreign languages, he eased her down on to the mossy grass and leant over her. She gasped as his mouth took hers in an intimacy which she had never even imagined. A kiss, to her, had always been something which two people did briefly with pursed lips. But his tongue was making an insistent, darting journey of exploration inside her mouth, and instead of revolting her it seemed to set small fires alight throughout her being. And as he was kissing her his hands were unbuttoning the silk shirt.

His mouth moved from hers and lingered over her breasts, taking each nipple in turn between his lips while his hand slid over her flat stomach to the triangle of golden curls between her thighs. His fingers began to stroke and probe and caress until she cried out with the unbearable pleasure of it.

He moved his head, and spoke with his lips against hers. His earlier precision of speech seemed to have deserted him and it sounded as if he were thinking in one of his foreign languages and then groping for a Dutch translation. "You do not like?"

"I – I should not let you touch my dirty place – "

"Dirty place! Aai no! It is beautiful – beautiful!"

And then he did something which she would never have believed if anyone had told her about it. He parted her thighs and licked and tickled with his tongue the very core of her dirty place, engulfing her with ecstasy.

He moved away from her, leaving her lying there, quivering and pulsating. She did not see him removing his breeches, but suddenly he was beside her, rubbing his body gently and rhythmically against hers, bringing whimpers to her throat. He straddled her, and slipped his hands beneath her buttocks, drawing her knees up. Then something which was not his finger penetrated her slowly, and her muscles dilated in obedient, moist response to its incredible size.

This could not be real, Petronella thought. This great throbbing, drumming pleasure of moving apart and together in ritual sequence must be a dream. And just when she thought she had transcended the very heights of joy she felt herself jerking and dilating in an overwhelming explosion as the most incredible convulsion of sensations swept over her.

He had shuddered and grown still too. They lay together in a close embrace, their breath coming in gasps.

"Marcus," she managed at last. "What is it called – what we have just done?"

He drew his head away from hers, staring at her in shocked surprise. "You do not have a name for it, you Boers?"

"Boers don't do it. I didn't even know there *was* such a thing until you taught me."

"*Oy a broch!*" He struck his forehead with his fist. "It is not poss – " He broke off, his eyes searching her face. "Am I correct in thinking that you Boer girls ride horses, sitting astride and sometimes without saddles?"

"When I was younger, yes. Why?"

Looking stricken, he muttered, "It would explain why there was no pain."

The pleasure had been so intense that part of it might well have been pain for all she knew. She considered the subject irrelevant, and was about to repeat her original question when he thrust his hand through his hair and spoke in a voice filled with anguished regret.

"Petronella, forgive me. Mistakenly I interpreted your innocence as an invitation. I am more sorry than I could ever express – "

"What is it *called*?" she interrupted impatiently, quite unable to understand why he should feel the need to apologise for something that had been so utterly magical.

He gave a shaky laugh. "You are quite unlike any other young lady I have ever encountered. As to the matter of what it is called, my Petronella – there are many words for it. Some are technical and correct and others are euphemistic and often not at all correct. The word for it which I like best is *pleasuring*."

"So do I! Oh, I did like it so very much, Marcus! But why does no one else ever do it?"

His eyes rested on her in a stunned look. "Petronella, when you were at school did the girls not gather in corners and whisper about it?"

"I did not go to a school. Mamma taught me my letters and numbers, and Pappa taught me to read and write. No one else I've ever known has done pleasuring."

"Ah, but they do, Petronella. Married couples do it all the time."

"Not Mamma and Pappa!" she insisted, shocked. "Mamma would die at the very idea! And if Pappa knew about pleasuring, I'm sure he would call it a sin, and he would preach about it on Sundays when he holds his service for the family and our servants."

Marcus laughed, a sound between helplessness, continuing disbelief and dismay. "Petronella, every child that has ever been born in the entire universe has been the result of pleasuring."

"Nonsense! The Angel of God brings babies – "

"No, no, no! Attend while I tell you the truth. During pleasuring the man plants a seed and it grows inside the woman. That seed develops into a baby."

Petronella was silent. Once, years ago, she had wandered into the barn where a cow was calving and she had witnessed a good deal before Pappa saw her and sent her away. But never had she connected what she had seen with the birth of human babies.

She shook her head in slowly dawning understanding. "That means Mamma and Pappa have done it *three times*!"

Again he laughed, a tender sound. "Such innocence . . ."

She dismissed Mamma and Pappa from her mind and explored the mysteries of his body. That male instrument with which he had pleasured her was, after all, quite small. But as she ran her fingers over it she was astonished to see it grow before her eyes until it was rampant, proud and hungry.

"Aai no, Petronella!" he groaned. "It was very wrong of us – of me – to do it the first time and there must be no repetition."

"I liked it," she murmured. "I don't care if it was wrong. I want to do it again. And when the baby comes," she added recklessly, "I shall tell Mamma the Angel of God brought it!"

"You have no cause to fear, Petronella. There will be no baby."

"But you said – "

"I took care, and no seed was planted."

She did not understand, but she believed him. Experimentally, she closed her mouth over one of his nipples and sucked gently, and he groaned again, so that she knew it was something which gave him pleasure. She rubbed one leg slowly against his.

"Please let us do it again, Marcus."

He seemed to make a great effort in disentangling himself from her. "It is something which should be reserved for married couples only, Petronella."

"Then let us marry," she urged feverishly, "so that we can do pleasuring all the time!"

"Aai, *mein tiere*, that will never be a possibility." He was reaching for his shirt.

A terrible thought struck her for the first time. "Why not? Do you already have a wife?"

"No, but a marriage between you and me could never be considered or entertained. And Petronella – for the protection of your own name and reputation you must preserve the secret of the pleasuring between us."

He was shrugging his arms into the sleeves of his shirt. She knelt and kissed him, darting her tongue in and out of his mouth in the way she had learnt from him. He caught her and held her to him, but this time he would do no more than kiss her mouth. There was sweat on his brow and a look of desperation in his eyes, and she saw him gazing at his boat as if it represented escape.

"You can't just leave me like this, Marcus!" she cried.

"It is in the best interests of both of us that I should go quickly, Petronella."

"Let us just do it once more – "

"*Mein tiere*, listen. As I have explained to you, I took care. I do not believe I would be able to exercise the same self-control on a second occasion. Pleasuring, you see, is far, far better when there are no restraints, no need to take care."

She did not believe that pleasuring could possibly be any better than it had been, and she did not understand what he meant about taking care.

He was feverishly drawing on his breeches, as if he could hardly wait to get away from her. She followed him as he hurried to the river bank where his boat lay among the reeds.

"You should marry one of your Boers, Petronella," he called, using an oar to heave the craft away from the bank. "You should choose someone suitable and marry soon, and then you will discover how good pleasuring can really be."

She knew that she could never be content with a Boer now that Marcus had taught her the unashamed joys of the flesh. It was inconceivable that any Boer, with all the restraints he placed upon himself, would ever lead her to such heights of exquisite physical frenzy. She had tasted Marcus, and she wanted only him.

She wept bitterly as she watched him dip his oars into the water and row away.

2

Jakkalsdrif was the same, and yet everything was different. Petronella found herself dwelling now in a world which had been changed by Marcus.

She had gone to the river as a child, and returned a grown woman. Mamma seemed to sense the difference in her, without being able to pinpoint it.

"We'll have to see about making you a new blouse for Johannes's wedding," she said with a frown. "Something durable, but also pretty. Something to suit your age."

"And to make Gerrit du Toit's great Adam's apple jump up and down?" Petronella returned sourly.

"A man cannot help the way his Maker has fashioned him!" Mamma reproved, her voice sharp. "Gerrit is steady and hard-working, and one day he'll inherit the farm from his father. Of course he'll have his sisters to keep, but hopefully they'll marry. Yes, he will make a good husband."

"Then let him make someone else a good husband!"

"I don't like your tone, Miss!" Mamma rapped. "What has crawled over your liver lately? When you haven't been sulking, you've given me cheek!"

Petronella remained silent. Mamma could not know that she now viewed people through a different perspective, and that her attitude had become coloured by the acquisition of knowledge and experience.

When Johannes talked about his coming marriage to Dorothea Becker, for one thing, she no longer reacted with bored derision. She thought instead of plump, stolid Dorothea and of Johannes, so serious and so easily embarrassed, and she tried to imagine them engaging in pleasuring. It seemed as inconceivable as the thought of Mamma and Pappa ever having behaved in that way, and yet Marcus had said it was so.

A great hunger gnawed inside her, and because it could not be appeased she became moody and quarrelsome. If she had been less ignorant, she sensed with bitterness; if she had known what everyone including Gideon had deliberately been hiding from her, she would not have taken part so enthusiastically in what Marcus had begun that Sunday. She blamed Mamma and Pappa for the turmoil raging inside her; she wished she had never clapped eyes on Marcus, and at the same time she longed for him with a pain which was physical as well as emotional.

When Pappa fulminated against the *Uitlanders* she could no longer accept them unequivocally as enemies, for Marcus was one of them.

"What would be so bad about giving them the vote?" she argued with Pappa. "It isn't fair that they should never have any say – "

"You are ignorant, girl!" Pappa rarely spoke to her as sharply as this. "There is no question of their never having any say in how the country is run. The truth is that the question of the vote is nothing more than a smokescreen. The British Crown wants total control over our gold."

"And what do you think you are about, Petronella, poking your nose into politics?" Mamma scolded. "Go and help Mwende with the peaches!"

Sullenly, she went into the scullery. Mwende's brother Koos was picking the first of the early crop of peaches and carrying basketsful into the house, and Mwende was seated at the table, sorting the fruit.

Petronella pulled up a chair and began to help her. The blemished peaches were put to one side; they would not be wasted, but were destined to be cut into strips and dried in the sun. The perfect fruit was intended for a great orgy of bottling and jam and chutney making.

The early yellow peaches were hard and sour when one bit into them, and yet Mamma valued them far more than she did the later, freestone white peaches which were juicy and delicious but were useless for jams or preserves or for drying because their flesh was so wonderfully tender.

That is the difference between Mamma and me, Petronella mused. Mamma likes things that will last and improve with keeping; I want to gorge myself on what is perfect *now*. I suppose Mamma has decided that Gerrit du Toit will improve with keeping; he'll lose his pimples and become a hard-working, dependable, God-fearing man following in his father's footsteps.

But I want Marcus and I want him now . . .

She watched as Mwende set a huge copper pan filled with water to heat on the stove. The peaches would be dropped into the water as soon as it boiled, then quickly removed and plunged into cold water so that the skins could be rubbed off without marking the fruit.

"The Missus, she need a new pantry soon," Mwende observed drily.

Petronella knew what she meant. The pantry shelves were groaning under jars of fruit preserved in previous seasons; with jams and chutneys and pickled vegetables. Bountiful Nature gave, and Mamma preserved industriously, and the family was never able to catch up with the accumulating abundance.

"The wedding will clear a little space on the shelves," Petronella said. "Everyone in the district will be coming to the reception."

Mwende's beautiful eyes sparkled. "We start baking cakes soon. Already we make fat a pig and some hens for the wedding feast."

"Yes." The wedding was being brought forward because there was talk that Johannes might, at any moment, be served with a notice from his commando leader to join one of the small standing forces being set up in the Republic for security reasons.

Petronella knew that every male Boer, from the age of eighteen upwards and unless he were physically impaired, was automatically a burgher, and expected to undertake military duty when called upon. If the trouble which Pappa was always predicting should come, the menfolk would be required to offer themselves for service with horse, saddle and provisions, and join the various commandos to which they belonged.

So Johannes wanted to be married in case he should be sent on commando, and even though no one ever mentioned it Petronella's new-found knowledge told her he wished to try to father sons before he was sent away. Sons were important; they provided continuity and added to the prosperity of a farmer. And so there would be a good deal of pleasuring after the marriage –

At the thought, Petronella stood up with an abrupt movement. "Mwende, I'm going to gather some herbs for the Missus. Tell her if she asks where I am."

It was the one excuse calculated to soften Mamma's displeasure at her disappearing during a busy period like this. As well as keeping an overstocked larder, Mamma was also what the Boers called a *Ziekentrooster*, which Petronella did not really consider an appropriate title for someone like her mother, for it meant 'Comforter of the Sick'. Mamma did not comfort so much as bully the sick and force them to swallow her herbal remedies.

Petronella armed herself with a basket, and set off in the direction of the river. She picked *wilde als* and *balsem kopiva* as she went, cramming them into the basket. Mamma would have a fine old time later, infusing the herbs and extracting their sap, mixing it with raw linseed oil or turpentine or arnica essence for her remedies.

Far away in the mealie-fields, Petronella could see Pappa and the boys helping the farm-hands with the harrowing. If they noticed her at all, the basketful of herbs would reassure them.

The tranquillity of Jakkalsdrif and its bounteous plenty only seemed to underline her own inner turmoil and hunger. Partridges rose from cover and took to the air, and a *dik-dik* buck streaked through the grass, alarmed by her approach. The whole of Jakkalsdrif seemed to be saying – Here is food; here is abundance; take what you will.

And the one thing she wanted and hungered for was not to be had. How many times had she made this same forlorn pilgrimage to the river, telling herself that Marcus would have to make the return voyage at some time or other and that he might stop and wait for her to come to him.

She no longer took off her clothes and waded into the river when she reached her secret spot. The simple pleasure of feeling herself free and untrammelled and allowing the sun to dry her naked wet skin had paled before the remembered joy of pleasuring with Marcus.

Now, she merely sat down on the grass where it had all happened, and watched the river. She willed him to come rowing downstream, but he did not. Common sense told her that it was unlikely one of her visits would coincide with his appearance on the return journey, and yet she continued to haunt the spot whenever she could get away.

She was torn between desolation and fury as she returned home. How dared he create a need in her which he'd had no intention of keeping satisfied? She kicked viciously at an antheap, almost finding some relief in physical pain.

Mamma was irritable when Petronella arrived home, and only partly appeased by the basketful of herbs. She was busy cutting serrated patterns into the flesh of the whole peaches and then handing them to Mwende, to be steeped in a solution of salt and lime.

"I can't stop this until I have finished," she told Petronella. "The fruit will discolour. There's a *bredie* on the stove; see to it."

Petronella moved to the stove. Mamma kept a special iron cauldron for the cooking of *bredie*, and the appetising smell of the stewed mutton and spices and ripe tomatoes met Petronella's nostrils as she lifted the lid. She added more salt, and replaced the lid so that the food could continue to cook slowly in its own juices.

"Do some yellow rice to go with it," Mamma instructed. "And cook more than usual, because Johannes is going to fetch Dorothea back for supper."

As Petronella measured rice and raisins and turmeric into a pan, she reflected that life in the household was bound to change after Johannes's marriage. Dorothea would be coming to live on Jakkalsdrif, and she would be taking over some of the tasks as a matter of course, leaving Petronella herself with more free time.

Free for what? The thought sneaked up on her, and she bit the inside of her lower lip as hard as she could. Free to go on haunting the river with hunger in her heart and a throbbing ache in her loins? Oh Marcus, she seethed, you *vervloekde Uitlander*, why did you have to come and throw my life into such a mess of dissatisfaction and longing and rage and hopelessness?

Mamma was just finishing the preparation of the peaches in the scullery when Petronella laid the table in the kitchen for supper. The kitchen was her favourite room. The table and chairs were old, and had come from the Cape. They were made of yellow-wood which glowed like gold in the soft light of the oil lamps suspended from the ceiling beams. A huge dresser stood against one wall, displaying a blue-and-white dinner service which was a family heirloom and never used. A carved oak chest was pushed against another wall; it had been Mamma's marriage chest, and now it held the starched table linen.

Petronella stared at it. There was a similar, smaller chest stowed underneath the bed in her room, and since she was a small girl she had been stitching tray cloths and table runners and the like to store inside it. It had been something she had taken for granted; another chore forced upon her by Mamma, and she had never before consciously thought about its ultimate purpose.

Now, it symbolised the inevitability of her fate. Mamma would not rest until she had married *someone*, and Gerrit du Toit was the most likely candidate. That marriage chest of hers would finish up in his farmhouse some day, and she wanted to scream at the thought.

Pappa and Gideon came in, their hair still wet after washing at the pump outside, and moments later Johannes arrived with Dorothea in the Cape cart. Petronella studied her brother and his future wife narrowly.

What was it that had made them single one another out? Was there some magical spark between them which was totally indetectable to anyone else? It seemed hard to believe. Dorothea's brown eyes in her placid, plump face did not glow when they were fixed upon Johannes; they were gentle and submissive and reminded Petronella of those of a cow. The two of them seldom touched one another, and when they did it was as if they were no more than brother and sister. Johannes's hand would brush her shoulder as he pulled out a chair for her, and she would lay her fingers briefly on his arm.

They were talking about the wedding. "The Cape cart will hold no more than six people," Johannes was saying, "so we thought it best if only Dorothea's parents, ourselves and Mamma and Pappa rode to Doornboomstad for the church ceremony. It would be too much travelling for everyone to attend the wedding and then drive back here for the reception, and such an amount of traffic would also cover us in a cloud of dust."

"Yes, that would be the most sensible arrangement," Mamma said, and frowned. "I wish I could be in two places at once, however. Petronella has been so moody of late that I doubt if I could trust her to see to things here while I am away."

"I am sick to the soul of being picked upon!" Petronella cried, brushing angry tears from her eyes. "And I am sick of hearing about nothing but the wedding!"

"You are not too old, my girl, for the strap!" Mamma warned.

"Perhaps the child is sickening for something," Pappa sprang to Petronella's defence.

"*I* think she is jealous because *she* hasn't caught a husband yet!" Gideon jeered, and smirked at his own wit.

"I wouldn't *want* a husband like Johannes!" Petronella exploded, all restraint deserting her. "What does he know about anything but mealie crops or blue tongue in sheep or heart-water in cattle? He doesn't know what happens between the chains in Johannesburg, or that people speak languages like French and German and that some men wear silk shirts – "

"What nonsense are you raving about?" Mamma demanded.

"N-nothing." She looked down at her plate. Dear God, she had been about to give herself away completely.

"What was that about chains in Johannesburg?" she heard her elder brother ask, his voice restrained and hurt. "What kind of chains?"

"The gold chains the men wear with their silk shirts!" Gideon answered for her, and collapsed with laughter. "Are the silk shirts trimmed with lace, Petronella?" he gasped, wiping his eyes.

She glared at him, but prayed inwardly that no one would ask her to explain how she came to know anything about Johannesburg and men who wore silk shirts. She felt her prayers had been answered when Dorothea said with prim reproach, "I think you owe Johannes an apology, Petronella."

"Yes," she agreed gratefully, and looked at her elder brother. "I am sorry, *Ouboet*." She forced a smile. "Gideon, the little pest, was probably right. I am jealous because Dorothea is to get a tall, good-looking husband with golden whiskers, while Mamma has her heart set on Gerrit du Toit for me. And he can't even manage a moustache, let alone a beard to hide his pimples!"

Johannes accepted her apology with a forgiving smile, but Petronella might have known that Mamma would not be diverted so easily.

"Who told you about Johannesburg, Petronella," she demanded, "and the men of the place?"

Wildly searching her mind for a believable lie, she stumbled instead on a half-truth. "Sarie van Tonder! Before her father and Pappa became bad friends she told me about a visit they had made to Johannesburg."

Perhaps Mamma might have probed the matter further, but Dorothea took it upon herself to turn the subject and reprove Petronella for the remarks she had made about Gerrit.

"It is unwise and unkind to judge a man by his looks. It's character that counts, Petronella."

No, it isn't, she thought mutinously. What counts is blue eyes and dark hair and grooves in the cheeks which are not hidden by whiskers, and a mouth which can burn one's flesh and do wild, reckless, wicked things you would not even dream of, and which would make your cow-like eyes pop out of your head if I told you about them . . .

"Quite right, Dorothea!" Mamma said briskly. She turned to Petronella. "It's time you grew up, and began to recognise Gerrit's excellent qualities!"

Relieved that the subject of Johannesburg had been laid to rest, Petronella stood up and said meekly, "I'll go and bring in the milk tart, Mamma."

During the following days she found herself caught up in a frenzy of activities, so that there was no possibility of visiting the river. Apart from the normal cooking and baking which had to be done, and the peaches which Mamma was preserving and drying, there were the preparations for the wedding reception which Mamma directed with implacable efficiency. It was typical of her that she had bullied Dorothea's mother into agreeing that the reception should be held at Jakkalsdrif.

No corner of the house escaped an orgy of cleaning. The servants were constantly running out of polish, and then Petronella would have to make more, melting beeswax and mixing it with turpentine. Even when the work had been done Mamma watched fanatically for a speck of dust to settle anywhere. In the meantime, several different kinds of cakes had to be baked, and legs of mutton had to be cut into small pieces and the meat set to marinade in a mixture of vinegar and spices for *sosaties*. The marinade would not only flavour the meat deliciously but would also preserve it until the day of the wedding, when it would be threaded on to skewers and roasted over an open fire. A bullock and a pig were slaughtered, the carcases butchered and rubbed with salt and baking soda to keep them fresh, and yards of *boerewors* sausages had to be made, using the washed entrails of the pig as casings.

On the morning of the wedding, Mamma made a tour of inspection and declared with a frown that things would have to do. Petronella could not see how they could possibly attain greater perfection.

At first light that morning, Dorothea with her parents and a whole brood of her younger brothers and sisters had arrived on Jakkalsdrif by ox-wagon. In the ordinary way the wedding party would have departed from their farm, and the reception would have been held there afterwards. But Mamma had easily out-manoeuvred Dorothea's mother, a limp, ineffectual woman who had meekly agreed that Jakkalsdrif was more suitable and Mamma more able to cope with all the arrangements. Mamma had whisked Dorothea inside the house to help her get dressed for the wedding, while her own family hovered almost unnoticed in the shadows. Mamma, Petronella knew, would see to it that Dorothea became far more a van Zyl than she had ever been a Becker.

But Petronella had to concede that, largely because of Mamma's efforts, the wedding party looked extremely handsome as they prepared to drive to the village of Doornboomstad for the church wedding. Mamma had made Dorothea's wedding gown of white tarlatan and had lent her a head-dress of seed pearls, a family heirloom, to hold her veil in place, so that she seemed almost beautiful. Her parents were neat, background figures who blended in with Mamma, who looked quite grand in her best gown of blue cotton sateen, and with Pappa and Johannes in their starched collars and their shiny top-hats.

The Cape cart had been decorated with ribbons, and the two horses were bedecked with garlands of greenery and with flowers ruthlessly commandeered by Mamma from Petronella's garden. All the servants turned out from the *stad* to cheer the bridal vehicle on its way.

Guests were beginning to arrive and had to be offered coffee and buttermilk rusks while they waited for the real celebrations to begin. The veld stretched away into the distance, flat and uninterrupted, so that the bridal cart would be spotted on the horizon long before it reached Jakkalsdrif.

Some of the young men had brought harmonicas and one had arrived with an accordion, for there would be dancing later when the older guests had left for home. Gerrit du Toit was watching Petronella with sheep's-eyes and she was about to turn her back pointedly on him when she heard one of the other young men address him.

"A very strange thing happened a day or two ago. An *Uitlander* called at our house, wanting to buy milk and eggs. Spoke some kind of High Dutch."

"Is that so?" Gerrit returned vaguely, his eyes still on Petronella.

Marcus, she thought with thudding excitement. It could only have been Marcus. Her fingernails bit into her palms. If she had not been kept so busy with preparations for the wretched wedding, she might well have been at the river when he reached her secret place. Perhaps he had even spent several days waiting there for her, hoping she would come. But he had rowed on, because the neighbours to whom he had gone for supplies lived down-river from Jakkalsdrif.

A great tide of frustration and impotent rage surged through her, mixed with pain. He was on his way to Johannesburg now, and she had missed the chance of ever seeing him again. She could not even give expression to her feelings, for she had to remain pleasant and smiling, Mamma's representative and official hostess until the bridal cart returned.

She conversed and offered refreshments in what must have appeared to be a natural manner, for no one regarded her strangely, and all the time a cauldron of despair and rebellion was churning inside her.

"Well, Petronella," she heard one of the guests say, "you have certainly grown up to be a credit to your parents."

It was *Meester* who taught at the farm school which had been established four years ago. "However," he went on, "I have always felt you would have benefited from a few years' schooling. You have a quick mind."

"Mamma says I have been taught all the book-learning I shall ever need, *Meester*."

"I doubt it." He went on to tell her about her forebears, about Jan van Riebeek's colonisation of the Cape and about the Edict of Nantes which had caused her French ancestors to flee there, and then he spoke of her grandfather's generation who had trekked from the Cape into the wilderness to escape the British yoke. "You did not know all of this, did you?" he finished.

No, and I didn't wish to either, she thought sullenly. Why should I concern myself with dead people and a dead age? I care about here and now, and my here and now means no Marcus, and having to settle for Gerrit du Toit instead . . .

She heard a cheer going up, and realised with relief that the bridal cart had been spotted on the horizon. The festivities were about to begin.

The older guests left before the sun set, streaking the sky with gaudy orange and vermillion, and now the music started. By the light of the fires the young people formed a circle, linking hands, and wove in and out in time to the beat.

Johannes and Dorothea disappeared inside the house, their departure accompanied by teasing remarks whose meaning would have escaped Petronella completely if she had not learnt about marriage from Marcus. She threw herself almost frenziedly into the dance, twirling and weaving and constantly changing partners as demanded by the ritual of the steps.

From the direction of the *stad*, music was coming too; a harmonious blending of voices in a chant-like song which rose above the wail of the harmonicas and the accordion. The air was filled with the combined smell of wood-smoke and the lingering odour of roasted meat.

Petronella changed partners again and felt her hand clasped in Gerrit's, her hip touching his as they danced. Something stirred low down in her stomach, a purely automatic reflex, a kind of dim echo of what she had felt when Marcus touched her.

"It has been a wonderful day, Cousin Nella," she heard Gerrit say.

"My name is Petronella!"

"I know. But Cousin Petronella is such a mouthful – "

"Why do you have to call me Cousin at all? I am not your cousin."

She was glad she could not see his Adam's apple bobbing up and down as he protested nervously, "You know it is a term of respect."

"I do not want to be respected!" she exclaimed recklessly. "I want to be – " She pulled at his hand, drawing him beyond the light thrown by the fires, and forced herself not to think of his pimples or his moustache as she pressed her open mouth upon his.

He uttered a startled sound, and held her awkwardly. His lips remained pursed beneath hers and she forced them apart with her tongue, at the same time guiding his hands to her breasts.

He leapt away from her as if he had been scalded. "Cous – Petronella!"

"Oh, go to hell," she muttered, her voice thick with humiliation and anger and shame.

He reached clumsily for her, and she could feel him trembling in his eagerness to please, to make restitution. His tongue inside her mouth was not in the least like Marcus's had been; it felt large and wet and obscene, and his hands kneaded away at her breasts in a way which seemed to drive him to a pitch of excitement while the only sensation it created in her was one of physical discomfort.

She pushed him away so that he staggered and almost fell. Without glancing back at him she fled towards the house, keeping in the shadows so that Mamma and Pappa would not see her from where they were watching the dancing from the stoep. She entered the house by the back door, and went to her room.

It was only when she had closed the door behind her that she became aware of Johannes and Dorothea in what had been his bedroom and was to be shared by them from now on. It was next to her own, and probably because they believed themselves to be alone in the house they made no attempt to be quiet, and Petronella could clearly hear the creaking of their bed.

They did not speak at all until she heard Dorothea's muffled voice cry out, "*No!* Oh please, Johannes, don't – "

Her words were swallowed by a hoarse cry of pain and shock, and then Petronella could hear her sobbing softly, while Johannes muttered to her not to be a baby, that it was a duty expected of a wife.

Pleasuring, Marcus had called it. But Dorothea had found no pleasure in it, and Petronella knew with utter certainty that Gerrit du Toit would never be capable of giving her even a fleeting moment of pleasure.

She flung herself down on her bed and wept into her pillow for Marcus and for her own vast, painful craving which would have to remain unsatisfied.

3

The harvest was ripening in the late summer sun when Gerrit du Toit began to court Petronella officially. Pappa had been persuaded to allow her an *opsitkers* and she had fallen in listlessly with Mamma's plans for her future.

The courtship was much as she had expected it would be. Gerrit called each Saturday evening, and after supper the two of them were left ostentatiously alone in the parlour. She studied the portraits of her grandparents, lined up in their silver frames on top of the harmonium, as if she had never seen them before in her life, while from his end of the sofa Gerrit made the occasional observation.

"Will you miss me when I go on commando, Petronella?" he asked wistfully.

"*If* you go on commando," she replied evasively.

"Oh, there is no question about that. The British are spoiling for a fight."

"So you say. So everyone has been saying for as long as I can remember."

Gerrit lapsed into deflated silence, and a while later stood up to leave. She allowed him to brush her cheek with his pursed lips. Neither of them ever referred to that incident which had taken place on the evening of Johannes's wedding, and she did not offer him temptation or he try to take advantage of past intimacies. By tacit agreement, the incident had never occurred.

With a feeling of relief, she held the lamp aloft so that he could see to unhitch his horse from the verandah post before riding away into the night. A whole blessed week stretched before her during which she would not have to see him.

The next morning the usual Sunday service was held, with the servants from the *stad* gathering to squat on the stoep while Pappa gave his sermon. His prayers were no longer the usual submissive ones; he beseeched the Almighty to range Himself on the side of the Boers in the coming struggle, and prayed that the *Volksraad* of the Free State Republic should be moved to ally themselves with the Transvaal burghers against the British. Petronella wondered if the Almighty was getting as tired as she was of the never-ending talk about possible war.

The service and lunch over, the usual Sunday hours of boredom stretched ahead. They were all sitting on the stoep when a cloud of dust on the horizon heralded the approach of a vehicle.

"Now who in the name of heaven," Pappa wondered aloud, "would come paying a visit on the Sabbath?"

"Perhaps it's a messenger," Gideon exclaimed excitedly, "come to tell us that war has broken out!"

Johannes said shortly, "If war had been about to break out, we would have heard from our Field-Cornet."

Her elder brother, Petronella had noticed, seemed to await less enthusiastically than others the outbreak of any possible hostilities. Perhaps it was because there was no sign of Dorothea carrying a hoped-for son yet.

As the vehicle drew nearer, Gideon, who had the sharpest eyesight of them all, exclaimed, "Now what kind of a driving-contraption is *that* for anyone?"

Narrowing her eyes, Petronella could see that it was, indeed, a strange vehicle. Drawn by a single horse, it had only two high wheels, and both were positioned on the same side of the vehicle, one behind the other. It seemed impossible for it to remain upright, let alone be capable of being driven at such speed along the rutted track.

"It must be an *Uitlander*," Pappa summed up with hostility in his voice. "No Boer would be seen driving a thing like that."

The vehicle came to a halt a few yards from the house, but the driver did not climb down. Incredulity seized Petronella, followed by an explosion of erupting joy. *Marcus!* It was Marcus, whom she had despaired of ever seeing again!

She forced herself to remain where she was, instead of abandoning discretion and restraint and running to welcome him. Oh, he was as beautiful as she remembered him! She wondered why he did not alight, and then realised that he must be unsure of the welcome he would receive, arriving unexpectedly at a Boer farm, and he was probably trying to think of an excuse for his visit. He could hardly announce that he had called because of what she sensed to be the truth – that he had not been able to forget her either.

She thought swiftly, trying to invent a plausible reason for his arrival, because it was clear that he had not done so yet. "I've met him," she said aloud, making her voice as casual as she could. "His name is Marcus Koen."

"Koen? That's a Dutch name. No Boer would pay calls on the Sabbath, or drive such an outlandish, showy vehicle. And where could you have met him, Petronella?"

"He rowed up-river at the beginning of the year," she said glibly. "It was on the morning of Johannes's wedding that I met Mijnheer Koen. He came to the house, asking to buy eggs and milk. I did not know how much to charge him, with you and Mamma away, and he said he would come back later to settle his debt."

"Then why doesn't the fellow get down?" Pappa demanded.

"He can't!" Gideon laughed, slapping his knees. "If he does, horse and cart will clearly fall over!"

But Marcus got down a moment later without mishap to animal or vehicle, and Petronella threw discretion to the wind and hurried to meet him. She held out her hand, her gaze devouring him. The expression in his blue eyes was sombre, and the grooves did not flicker in his cheeks.

"Aai, Petronella," he said softly. "I committed great folly to come here, but my feelings compelled me."

"Oh Marcus . . ." With reluctance, she withdrew her hand from his and spoke in a swift undertone. "You came to the house earlier in the year, to buy eggs and milk. Pappa and Mamma were away, because my brother was being married. You've called today to repay the debt."

He nodded, and looked beyond her. She turned, to see that Pappa and her brothers had left the stoep and were walking slowly towards them, but they were more interested in the strange vehicle than in what Petronella might be saying to the stranger. Mamma stood in the doorway of the house, looking affronted, presumably because she had expected her nursing skills to be required and it was now clear that they were not.

Petronella introduced the men to one another, and Gideon broke the ice by questioning Marcus about the vehicle.

"It is known as a spider," he explained in that eccentric accent which lent a piquancy to the most ordinary statement. "By reason of its lightness in weight, and its high wheels which allow it to pass easily over obstacles, it has acquired popularity."

His manner of speaking and the long words he used caused Pappa and his sons to exchange startled glances. Then Johannes asked, "But how does the thing stay upright, with both wheels on the same side?"

"By reason of balance," Marcus replied. "Observe the two long poles on either side of the horse, and connected to its bridle. For more than one person, it is necessary for the passenger to sit behind the driver on his opposite side. Without the horse the conveyance has no balance." Marcus looked at Pappa. "May I beg your permission, *seur*, to set the animal loose?"

Petronella could tell that Pappa was struggling between his inborn urge to offer hospitality to any stranger, and suspicion of this man with his city clothes and his bizarre vehicle and his strange manner of speaking.

"Yes, go ahead, let the animal graze," he said after a moment.

Gideon helped Marcus to remove the poles which were slotted through a leather strap which the horse wore across its rump. As soon as the animal moved away with a flick of its tail, the vehicle tipped over on to its side with its wheels absurdly in the air.

"In Johannesburg," Marcus explained when the laughter had died down, "many people drive a spider."

Constraint fell again immediately. Mamma, who had come to join them, spoke sharply. "You are from Johannesburg, Mijnheer – ?"

"Koen," Petronella put in.

"Cohen," Marcus began and shrugged. "Or Koen, if it is easier to pronounce. Yes, my home is in Johannesburg, Mevrouw."

"Mijnheer Koen has come all this way," Pappa informed her with disbelief which he did not try to disguise, "to pay for milk and eggs Petronella gave him early in the year."

"We do not sell our milk and eggs," Mamma told Marcus flatly. "Anyone in need is welcome to have what we are able to give."

"If you please, Mevrouw, I dislike being in debt – "

"There is no debt. You owe us nothing." Petronella felt Mamma's eyes boring into her. "Why did you not tell us about Mijnheer Koen's first visit, child?"

"I – forgot, in all the excitement of the wedding."

No one said anything for a moment. At last Mamma broke the uneasy silence. "I am sure you would like something to eat, Mijnheer Koen, after driving such a long way. I can offer you sliced cold pork and some of my peach chutney – "

"I am a Jew, Mevrouw," he interrupted gently.

A small sound of shocked surprise escaped Petronella. She knew all about Jews from Pappa's sermons and Bible readings. They had murdered Jesus. She had never seen a Jew before, and had not imagined them to look quite like other human beings, let alone be beautiful in every way, as Marcus was.

Mamma recovered some of her equilibrium. "I understand. You people do not eat pork."

" 'The swine,' " Pappa quoted from the Bible, with the air of a man relieved to find himself suddenly on familiar ground again, " 'though he divide the hoof and be cloven-footed, yet he cheweth not the cud; he is unclean to you.' "

"And rabbits," Johannes contributed, flushing as everyone stared at him. "They don't eat rabbits either," he explained lamely.

"Come inside the house, Mijnheer Koen," Mamma said. "I'm sure we can find something for you to eat which is not unclean." But she bristled as she said it, as if her own domestic cleanliness had been called into question.

Marcus was taken into the seldom-used parlour. Petronella sat on the same side of the sofa which she had occupied last evening while she waited impatiently for Gerrit to leave. She was drinking in every detail of Marcus's appearance, so exotic in his light-grey matching breeches and jacket. Jew or not, he was back, and this time she would do everything in her power to keep him here for as long as possible.

"We know you do not consider milk and eggs to be unclean, Mijnheer Koen," Mamma said. "I'll cook some scrambled eggs for you."

"Please, do not inconvenience yourself," he protested uncomfortably. "A little bread, and perhaps some cheese – "

"It will be no trouble." Mamma left the room, and Dorothea went with her, and Petronella tried to think of a way of easing the atmosphere of suspicion and distrust which was almost tangibly emanating from Pappa and the boys. Before she could do so, Pappa asked, "Is it true, Mijnheer Koen, that the British are drafting in more troops from India?"

Marcus shrugged. "I have no knowledge of such concerns, *seur*."

"You live in Johannesburg." Pappa paused. "It seems strange to me that you've taken the trouble to learn Dutch."

Petronella knew what he was hinting at. He thought Marcus was a spy sent by the British. To anyone who did not know about the pleasuring, she conceded, it would indeed seem suspicious that he had made the journey from Johannesburg on such a flimsy pretext.

"Mijnheer Koen has learnt a great many languages," she told Pappa.

"Including English, I don't doubt," he returned pointedly, his eyes still fixed upon Marcus. "When do you go back to Johannesburg, Mijnheer Koen?"

"I am not a spy, Mijnheer van Zyl," Marcus told him with slow emphasis. "If you hold objection to a Jew being present in your house, then I shall sleep underneath my spider tonight and depart in the morning."

"These are troubled times," Pappa said gruffly, "and we need to be careful. But no man, whatever his race or his religion, has ever been denied the shelter of my roof. You will share Gideon's room and stay for as long as you wish."

"I am grateful to accept, Mijnheer van Zyl."

Another of those awkward, lengthy silences threatened, but Mamma created a diversion by entering with a tray bearing scrambled eggs and sliced bread and butter and some of her watermelon conserve, and Dorothea followed with the coffee tray. While the women set a place for Marcus at the table and busied themselves with pouring coffee, the men discussed neutral topics, such as the length of time it had taken Marcus to drive from Johannesburg and how often and where he had changed horses.

Petronella remained silent, her mind busy. How to snatch time alone with Marcus, that was the problem. Would Mamma find it suspicious if she were to offer to search the orchard for places where the hens had been laying away from the nests, and invite Marcus to join her? Or perhaps she could ask him casually whether he had ever seen a native *stad*, and when they had paid a token visit to it, they could slip away to her secret place by the river . . . The very thought set her heart beating thunderously in her breast.

But as soon as Marcus had finished his meal, Pappa ruined everything by issuing the invitation which was almost a ritual whenever a male visitor arrived at the farm. "Would you like to have a look at the mealie-fields?" he asked Marcus.

Petronella bit her tongue, and raged inwardly. What interest could mealie-fields possibly have for him, who was no farmer? He had not driven all this way to watch mealies growing! How could Pappa be so stupid? Surely Marcus would think of a tactful way of refusing the invitation?

But he hid whatever surprise or lack of enthusiasm he might be feeling and stood up. Petronella watched in hunger and frustration as he followed Pappa and her brothers from the room.

Mamma began to gather together the dirty dishes. "I'll manage alone," she said. "You and Petronella go and sit on the stoep."

Dorothea did not argue. She seldom argued about anything, Petronella thought. She just accepted.

Petronella's entire being was far too tautly wound for her to want to sit on the stoep with her sister-in-law. She excused herself and went to her room, staring at her reflection in the mottled mirror, loosening strands of hair from her pulled-back braids, allowing them to frame her face softly. She dared not loosen too many, for fear of Mamma noticing. She wished she could have changed into her best blouse and skirt, but that would have attracted suspicious attention.

She moved restlessly about the room afterwards. Oh, it was enough to drive anyone mad, having Marcus here on Jakkalsdrif and yet not to be able to exchange a few words with him in private, let alone –

Male voices sounded in the passage outside, and she sprinted to the door. Marcus must have been unable to hide his indifference to the mealie harvest, for they were back already!

She opened her door, in time to see Gideon disappearing inside his room, with Marcus at his heels. She coughed softly to gain his attention, and saw him turn his head.

Along the length of the passage-way, they stared into each other's eyes. *Tonight*, Petronella's signalled. *This is my room. Come to me tonight.*

He shook his head slightly, but even as he did so his eyes were signalling the crumbling of his defences. He made a slight gesture towards the interior of the room and she knew it meant: *When Gideon is safely asleep.*

She wanted to run like an excited child through the house, and tease Pappa by pulling his beard, and grab staid, dull Dorothea and force her to do a little dance right on the evening of the Sabbath. She wanted to be what Mamma called *uitspattig* – silly, noisy, exuberant, full of herself and of the joy of being alive and of knowing that Marcus would be coming to her tonight.

Instead, she walked sedately out to the stoep where Mamma and Pappa and Johannes and Dorothea were talking about Marcus. Pappa still suspected him of being a spy for the British, and he commented scathingly, as if that proved his point, "The fellow couldn't even tell us whether Jakkalsdrif's mealies are standing higher than those down Vereeniging way! Says he didn't notice!"

"What I want to know," Mamma fretted, "is whether I ought to tell him there's lard in the bread? And if my bread is considered unclean, then what am I to give the man for supper?"

"He is probably a spy," Pappa exploded, "and you women fret about a little bit of lard! Johannes, it would be just as well if you were to ride out tomorrow and see Field-Cornet Theron, and tell him about the man. Find out what he thinks."

Mamma stood up. "I'm going to fry some dough for supper. That way, I won't need to offer bread to anyone!"

Supper that evening was not a success. Gideon complained that the fried dough tasted peculiar, and made such a fuss about it that Mamma was forced to admit it was because she had used dripping instead of lard. Petronella's family looked uncomfortable and Marcus embarrassed, and no one enjoyed the fried dough which tasted aggressively of beef dripping, but everyone felt under an obligation to pretend otherwise and eat it all the same. Petronella told herself that she wouldn't have cared if the dough had been fried in rhinoceros fat. Marcus was on Jakkalsdrif and tonight, tonight, tonight he would be coming to her, and oh, the world was filled with colour and light!

She forced herself, later, to appear natural and normal as she said her goodnights and everyone retired to their rooms. Doors closed, and the house grew quiet. Outside, cicadas snapped and a bullfrog sang a raucous song. From the *stad* came the sound of a dog howling at the rising moon,

In her bedroom, Petronella unbraided her hair and brushed it methodically, trying to force calmness on herself with the slow, meticulous strokes of the brush. She would leave the lantern burning; she wanted to gorge herself on the sight of Marcus and not waste a moment of their time together in anonymous darkness. She put on her best nightgown and then took it off again. In spite of the fine tucks along the bodice, it was ugly in its shapeless cut. She would await Marcus with nothing hiding her body.

She stretched out on the bed, trying to assume exactly the same pose as the one in which he had first seen her, but after a while she turned restlessly on her side. Even the dog had stopped howling now, she realised. Every other living thing on Jakkalsdrif appeared to have gone to sleep –

Her mouth filled with the taste of sickening panic. Why didn't Marcus come? Gideon *must* be asleep by now. Marcus had decided not to come, after all. He was thinking about Pappa and Mamma, and about not abusing their hospitality. That must be it . . .

Her bedroom door began to open slowly and furtively. She would not allow herself to believe that it was Marcus, for she knew she would not be able to bear it if she turned out to be wrong. It must be the faulty catch again –

Then he was inside the room, the door clicking shut behind him, and her eyes widened as she saw that he was wearing a kind of belted coat made of embroidered silk. Oh, but he was exotic, this rare love of hers; just like the peacock they had once had on Jakkalsdrif!

"Petronella," he said softly. "Every day my thoughts have been of you only."

She stood up and went to meet him, her hair brushing her naked shoulders. "Oh Marcus, I was afraid I would never see you again!"

His glance travelled over her body, his mouth soft with desire. She felt a shuddering sensation in her stomach, a delicious surge of anticipation. He pulled at the belt around his middle and shrugged his arms out of the exquisite silk garment and then he stood before her, just as she remembered him. Slowly, they came together, his hands on her shoulders, and she could feel the tingling of her breasts as they brushed against the mat of hair on his chest.

Then he was kissing her. With his mouth still locked upon hers, he carried her to the bed, and she stifled a sound of ecstasy as he began to explore and caress in the way she remembered so well and had dreamt about so often.

She was drowning in pleasure. There was a magic in Marcus's fingers and in his lips which would have been enough, even without the final act. *That* was an incredible extra gift when she had already been brought to the crescendo of a dozen delights. They moved together, as if their bodies were part of the same entity, and when she finally arched against him he kissed her mouth to cut off the involuntary cry which rose in her throat.

He trailed his fingers along the flesh of her upper arm. "Aai, Petronella. We are the victims of an insoluble dilemma, you and I."

She might not have understood the words he had used, but she had been only too aware of the despair and defeat in his voice. *She* would not admit defeat. "You must ask Pappa if we may marry, Marcus! To begin with he'll refuse, of course, but – "

He interrupted her with a heavy sigh. "You understand nothing, *mein tiere*. You are such a child still. Your world – my world – " He continued in some other language, as if the stilted, learned Dutch he had been taught was inadequate for the emotion he needed to express.

"I won't let you go again!" she said in a fierce whisper.

"Ah, Petronella, it is not so – "

His head jerked up as the door suddenly crashed open with a violent sound. Petronella stared beyond him, at the tableau in the doorway. Pappa holding a lantern aloft, his striped nightshirt falling in voluminous folds around his legs. Beside him Mamma, with her hair hanging in two greying braids to her shoulders. And behind them, peering over Mamma's shoulder, was Gideon looking at the same time both avidly curious and scared.

For a moment Petronella's mind was frozen with horror. Then the horror became real, and not just images locked up in her mind. Mamma began to scream, and Pappa was shouting words he had never before been heard to use. Words which brought Johannes on the scene too, his face tautening as he stared at his naked sister and the equally naked young man scrambling from the bed.

A vicious blow from Mamma caught Petronella on the side of the face. Marcus had just shrugged on his wrap and was tying its belt when Johannes grabbed him by the arm and swung his fist at him. Marcus just stood there, making no attempt to defend himself, as if he had resigned himself to the justice of his punishment.

Above the noise of physical violence and rage in the room, Petronella heard Pappa's voice lashing at her. "*Harlot! Shameless Jezebel! You God-cursed little whore!*" Then he began to weep.

She tried to pull Johannes away from Marcus, but a glancing blow from her brother's elbow sent her sprawling against the bed. She became aware that Mamma had left the room, and heard Gideon babbling nervously to no one in particular,

"I thought he was a spy. When I woke up and he wasn't in his bed I thought he was snooping somewhere in the house . . ."

Marcus was still standing there, taking his punishment, making no attempt to defend himself. Then Johannes shouted, "What did you promise my sister, you Jewish bastard, to make her turn whore?"

Marcus's head jerked up at that. He drew back his fist, and struck Johannes with such savagery that the sound of bone upon bone was clearly audible above all the other noises in the room.

Gideon tried to go to his elder brother's aid, but Pappa shouted, "One against one! Even with scum like him we fight one against one!"

The impetus of their own blows was forcing Marcus and Johannes from the room, and Pappa and Gideon followed them, shouting their hatred and rage. Dorothea appeared briefly in the doorway, primly encased from her chin to her toes in a shapeless calico nightgown, and said, "How *could* you, Petronella, and on the Sabbath too!"

Then Mamma was back in the room, and shutting the door in Dorothea's face, and when she turned Petronella saw that she had the rawhide strap in her hand.

"You slut!" Mamma spat at her as she raised the strap. "What are we to say to folks when you spawn your Judaic bastard in nine months' time?"

Through pain and confusion and horror, Petronella tried to make sense of her words. Then she understood. Hoping to placate Mamma, she cried, "There will be no baby! Marcus took care – "

But instead of being relieved, Mamma's face twisted with revulsion and she brought the strap down on Petronella's naked body with renewed force. "Took care, did he?" she cried between blows. "And you understood what that means, of course! You trollop! It's clear that tonight was not the first time you have behaved like a bitch in heat! How many others have there been? Gerrit, and who else? Tell me!"

"No!" With her arms, she tried to protect her body against that cruel strap. "I wouldn't – not with Gerrit! Not with anyone but Marcus! Mamma, I love him – "

"*Love!*" Mamma bit the word off with revulsion, and made even more frenzied use of the strap. The last thing Petronella remembered, before her senses mercifully deserted her, was Mamma weeping as she wielded the strap, and sobbing, "Oh dear God, the shame you have brought on us all . . ."

It was dark when she regained consciousness, and for an instant Petronella was puzzled by the fact that she ached and stung all over. Then, like a river bursting its bank, memory came pouring over her in all its horrific intensity.

Marcus. What had happened to him? While Mamma was beating her she had become deaf to any sound other than the cracking of rawhide against flesh, and she had not spared a thought for how he was faring at the hands of her brother.

She rose painfully, and groped in the dark for the tinder-box, lighting a candle. Far worse than the physical wounds inflicted on her by Mamma's beating was the pain eating away inside her, for everything that had been beautiful and precious had been degraded.

She tried to think coherently. It was inconceivable that Marcus would have been allowed to spend the remainder of the night under Pappa's roof. And yet he could not have left Jakkalsdrif in the dark either; he would never have been able to find his horse among the others in the paddock, let alone have managed to hitch it to the spider. Even for someone accustomed to doing it, the manoeuvre would be far too complicated to be accomplished in the dark. And he could hardly have been in a physical condition to have attempted it. So, he was probably sleeping on the ground underneath the spider, ready to leave at first light.

She shook her head in a blind gesture of non-acceptance. Once he left, she would not see him again. He would never be allowed to return to Jakkalsdrif, and after what had happened she knew she would not be given any freedom at all. She would be watched, her movements monitored, and even if Marcus were to row up the river again she would not be able to meet him. Whether she could resign herself to his loss or not, she knew that life for her on Jakkalsdrif would scarcely be worth living from now on.

Moving as quietly as she could, she began to dress. Then she made a parcel of some of her clothing, and the sky was just beginning to lighten to a pearly grey when she opened her bedroom window and climbed out.

As she skirted the side stoep she could see the shape of the spider, with its two wheels in the air, and she expelled her breath in a sound of relief. She was picking her way towards it when she almost collided with Mwende.

"Nonnie!" Mwende demanded with surprise. "What you doing, this time of morning? Where you going?"

Petronella stared at the girl, the inside of her mouth dry. How could she have forgotten that on Monday mornings Mwende came early to stoke the bread oven for the week's baking? The girl could not fail to see her helping Marcus find his horse and hitch it to the spider.

"Mwende, I – I'm going away, to be married – "

"You not! Who you marry? Baas Gerrit?"

"Not him. Someone else. My Mamma and Pappa don't like him, because – because he is not a Boer. So I'm running away with him – "

"I tell your Mamma!"

"No, Mwende, please!" Unexpectedly, all the hurt of humiliation and rejection and physical abuse erupted in a storm of tears, and she flung herself at Mwende.

The girl held her self-consciously at first, and then she began to croon, "Ah, *tula*, Nonnie. *Ayikona kala. Tula.* Don't cry, my Nonnie."

Petronella drew away after a while, wiping her face on her sleeve. She gazed through tear-swollen eyes at the girl who had been her playmate when they were children, but from whom there had been a steady growing away as they both became older. But in one emotional moment the old bonds had been reforged.

Mwende nodded slowly. "I see nothing. I know nothing." Then she walked on towards the house, and Petronella remembered the many times, as children, when each had covered up the misdeeds of the other.

The sky was rapidly growing lighter as she reached the spider. As she had expected, Marcus was asleep in the shelter of the vehicle, wrapped in a rug. Probably because he was a good deal taller than Johannes, little damage had been done to his face, apart from a slight cut at the side of his mouth, and she guessed that most of Johannes's punishing blows had landed on Marcus's body.

She shook him by the shoulder and he groaned, sitting upright. "Petronella – ?"

"We must find your horse, Marcus," she said urgently, "and hitch it to the spider. In an hour's time Pappa and my brothers will be rising. We have to be away from here by then."

He was wide awake now. "What you suggest, Petronella, is an impossibility! You cannot leave with me!"

"I have to! I must! You don't understand what it would be like for me from now on if I stayed! You have to take me with you to Johannesburg, Marcus!"

"Petronella, it cannot be – "

She unbuttoned her sleeve and pushed it up, holding out her arm for his inspection. "Mamma did this last night, Marcus."

"*Grosse Gott!*" He shook his head, and sighed. "Come then, and assist me while I search for my horse."

"You'll take me? And we'll be married?"

"I shall take you," he confirmed sombrely. "But as to a marriage between us . . . Aai, Petronella. I can give no promise; no promise at all."

4

Petronella had dozed during much of the journey, but she awakened fully just as the sun was setting. As Marcus had explained, the balance of the spider could only be maintained by its passenger sitting behind the driver on the other side of the vehicle, and all she was aware of at first was Marcus's profile. Then she rubbed her eyes and gazed about her in disbelief and primitive fear. She might as well have woken up and found herself transported to another planet, occupied by a strange species with alien ways.

The spider was proceeding along a wide, frantically busy street. She could never have imagined it would be possible for so many people and so many vehicles to come together in one place. The scene reminded her of a disturbed antheap.

"What – where are we?" she demanded in confusion, and then gave a shriek, clutching at Marcus's arm. "We're going to collide with that wagon in front!"

"No, no." Marcus laughed softly, reassuringly. "We find ourselves in Johannesburg now. All who live here are accustomed to the pace of the traffic. It is quite unlike Jakkalsdrif, is it not?"

He was different here, she thought. Self-assured and confident. He seemed to have forgotten the doubts with which he had agreed to take her away with him. But then, he was now in his own environment, and she herself was feeling as confused and disorientated as he must have felt in her parents' home.

"It is not in the least like Jakkalsdrif," she answered slowly, staring about her. Impossibly high buildings jostled for space on both sides of the street. Many of them had up to three sets of windows, one above the other, and Petronella wondered what the purpose had been in building them so high.

"You, my Petronella," Marcus went on, "will convert and embrace the Judaic faith. When you have become Jewish we shall be able to marry."

She stared at him in perplexity. "One cannot *become* Jewish!"

But it appeared that one could. One took instruction from someone called a Rabbi, and in the course of time one was declared a Jew.

Marcus had thought the whole matter out during the drive to Johannesburg, and she tried to hide the fact that she felt both unnerved and outraged by the idea as he explained it all to her.

It was impossible to hold on to one particular thought for long, because so much that was novel and astonishing was going on around her. The last glow from the setting sun was just fading and two men carrying long tapers hurried along on opposite sides of the street, touching them to what appeared to be lanterns held up by tall iron posts. They instantly sprang into a brilliance far greater than any lantern of her experience, and she could not understand where the oil which fuelled them was stored. When she asked Marcus he laughed and said, "They do not function on oil, Petronella, but on gas."

"What is gas?"

"It is manufactured from coal – " He stopped, shaking his head. "No, Petronella. Chemical and technical information regarding the properties of gas would confuse instead of enlighten you. Accept it as part of the modern world, and accept also the electric light you will find in the house of my parents."

She said nothing. So they were bound for the home of his parents, where she herself was to be turned into a Jew. How appalled Pappa would be at the notion! She felt tears pricking her eyes, and dashed them angrily away. Pappa had called her vile names, and had done nothing to stop Mamma beating her, so why should she care how he felt about her becoming a Jew?

She became aware that they had left the busy part of the city behind them, and that Marcus was reining in the horse. Outside a large, imposing building with pillars and a good deal of wrought-iron decoration they stopped. Such bright light was streaming through the windows of the building that the scene was illuminated as if by day.

"Come," Marcus said. "We have arrived at our destination, Petronella."

She swallowed. "Is – is this – "

"It is my home, and the home of my parents."

She allowed him to help her from the spider, and gathered all her courage as she prepared to accompany him to the front door of the house. A black servant had appeared from somewhere and was taking charge of the horse and spider, and another servant dressed in clothes of almost ridiculous grandeur opened the front door for them when Marcus knocked.

Petronella was surprised, and further unnerved, by the fact that Marcus prevented her from entering the house before a curious ritual had been performed. Screwed on to the lintel of the door was a cylindrical wooden object which Marcus said was a Mezuzah. He touched it reverently and afterwards brought his fingertips to his mouth, and insisted that Petronella do the same. She obeyed self-consciously, feeling both foolish and out of place.

They stepped inside. The floor of the hall was not of wood, she noticed, but of some kind of fancy patterned stone, and she blinked in confusion at the multitude of lights sparkling from a strange collection of small pieces of glass suspended from the ceiling.

Marcus placed a reassuring hand on her arm as he led her through the hall. The door which he threw open revealed an even more splendid interior than the hall had been.

But it was impossible to concentrate on the furnishings of the room, for its occupants claimed her attention.

Marcus introduced them to her in Dutch as his mother and father and his sister Hannah, and then he switched to a language which she did not understand. She studied them, her heart sinking like a stone within her breast as she registered their alien quality which, in that moment, extended to include Marcus also. The fact that they addressed him as Mordechai helped to erect this invisible barrier between her and all of them.

His father was a stocky man with a prominent nose, a full beard and hooded eyes who spoke little, but left it to his wife to conduct a voluble exchange with Marcus. She had a high, shrill voice, and the light sparkled on the many rings which she wore on her fingers as she gestured with her hands. Occasionally, her daughter Hannah entered the discussion, and Petronella experienced feelings of both envy and pity for the girl. She was smartly dressed in a gown which Petronella supposed must have been imported from the Cape, and her dark hair was arranged in elegant curls which Petronella greatly admired. In spite of the curls, however, she was plain to the point of ugliness, with a squat figure and small dark eyes and the hint of a moustache on her upper lip.

Marcus touched Petronella's arm. "My family are unable to understand or converse in Dutch. My mother wishes you to accompany Hannah, Petronella."

"Where to?" she asked, alarmed and suspicious, feeling swamped by the strangeness of these people.

"She will take you to a bedroom," Marcus reassured her. "When you hear a gong sounding, it will mean that you must join the family for the serving of supper."

"Oh . . . Did you tell them that I am to become Jewish?"

He threw out his hands in one of those unfamiliar, oddly fascinating gestures of his. "Slowly, slowly, Petronella! Conversion to Judaism is a very serious, important matter – not only for you, but also for my family. So I must inform them carefully, and at the correct moment. Go with Hannah now."

Petronella followed the squat figure of Marcus's sister along the corridor, and stopped when Hannah did. A door was thrown open and Hannah's hand groped for something just inside the room. A moment later the scene was brightly lit as another, less ornate construction suspended from the ceiling flashed into life.

Uncomfortable and overawed, Petronella looked around her. Marcus's family must be very rich indeed, for all the furniture matched. There was a bed with a magnificent white lace counterpane on it, a tallboy, a wash-stand and dressing table and a hanging chest with a long mirror set into its door. Petronella stared curiously at matching small porcelain bowls with lids which stood on top of the dressing table, and wondered what their purpose might possibly be. Several pictures hung on the papered walls, but they were not of religious texts or family portraits. One depicted a scene in which ducks swam along a stream; another showed nothing but a tree, with fallen leaves scattered on the ground beneath its branches. What odd people Jews were, Petronella thought. Why on earth should they wish to be reminded of what a stream with ducks looked like, and what could possibly be interesting enough about a tree that one should have a picture of one on the wall?

By means of mime, Hannah explained to her that she was to put her clothes away inside the hanging chest and in the drawers of the tallboy. With an unsmiling nod, Hannah withdrew and Petronella found herself alone.

She unwrapped the parcel of her clothes and put them away. They looked pathetic and inadequate inside such grand furniture. She wandered nervously around the room, examining the objects inside it. There was a knock on the door and a black servant girl entered, carrying a copper jug. Without addressing a word to Petronella, she filled the jug on the wash-stand with hot water from the copper jug. She looked to be about the same age as Mwende but there any similarity between the two of them ended. This girl was dressed in a smart black gown over which she wore a starched white pinafore, and there was a similarly starched white cap on her head. She made Petronella a strange, bobbing little bow before she left the room, unsmiling and still without having said a word.

A sudden longing for Mwende, for Jakkalsdrif and the familiarity of home gripped Petronella by the throat, and she fought back tears. She moved to the wash-stand and poured water into the bowl, and removed her blouse. As she went to lay it down on a chair she caught sight of herself in the mirror set into the hanging closet. She gasped as she saw, for the first time, the full extent of the damage Mamma had inflicted on her with the rawhide strap.

When she had washed and changed she sat down on the chair to wait. Marcus's family, she sensed, did not like her. They didn't like her because she was a Boer. She was as alien to them as Marcus had been to her own family. But surely they would learn to like her when she became a Jew?

Her mouth was dry with nervous dread when she heard the sound which must be the gong of which Marcus had spoken. Timidly, she opened the door and crept along the corridor to look for the kitchen where supper would be served. Then Marcus appeared, wearing matching dark coat and trousers and a white silk shirt, and he led her into a room which could not possibly have been a kitchen. A long table covered by an elegant white lace cloth stood in the centre, but that was the only piece of furniture the room had in common with the kitchen on Jakkalsdrif. There was no proud display of china; no carved chest in which the table linen would be kept. There were a great many other elegant and polished pieces of furniture, the purpose of which she could not guess.

Hannah was already inside the room, and Marcus's parents appeared a moment later. Petronella felt wrong and out of place in her simple skirt and blouse, for Hannah and Mevrouw Koen were both richly gowned in what looked like satin, and they wore sparkling stones around their necks and in their ear-lobes.

Mijnheer Koen took his place at the head of the table, and his wife sat down on his right. Marcus pulled out a chair for Petronella and she took it nervously. His hand rested for a moment on her shoulder, strengthening her courage. Marcus loved her; he would persuade his family to love her too.

Mijnheer Koen said a prayer and afterwards his wife picked up a small silver bell standing on the table in front of her and rang it. A few minutes later three servants entered, carrying silver dishes.

Petronella thought the meal would never come to an end. There was nothing in the least familiar to her, and nothing which appealed to her taste. One strange, alien dish followed another, and she picked desperately at them, trying to create the illusion that she was eating some of it, and just when she thought that supper was finally over at last, the servants would enter with yet more silver dishes. Even the bread tasted unfamiliar and unpleasant, strangely sour and with aniseed baked into it. Had Marcus struggled just as hard, she wondered, to force down Mamma's fried dough on Jakkalsdrif?

"Courage, *mein tiere*," she heard him murmur, and she gave him a slightly unsteady smile. "Soon you will become more accustomed to my family, and they to you."

"Yes." For the first time, she was glad that his family did not understand or speak Dutch, for it enabled her to go on, "And there will be tonight when we can be together, you and I, and – " She broke off as he shook his head.

"No, Petronella. Not under the roof of my family. And they must have no suspicions of our relationship until the correct time has arrived for me to tell them that you wish to take instruction from the Rabbi."

"Oh . . . What reason did you give them for my leaving Jakkalsdrif?"

He looked slightly uncomfortable. "I have informed them that your Mamma beat you and ordered you to leave your home. I – was forced to explain to them that you showed me hospitality when my horse became lame, and when your family discovered I was a Jew there was a quarrel."

"It isn't fair to make my family sound so spiteful and petty and cruel!" she said angrily.

"But it was necessary. If you are to convert to Judaism – " He spread his hands in an eloquent gesture.

She understood. If she was to be accepted into his faith, she would have to appear pure and innocent. So there was not to be any pleasuring to make living with his strange, unfriendly family any easier.

The days which followed only sharpened her wretchedness and the feeling of being among alien people. Marcus's home was revealed to be even more imposing and grand when seen by daylight. It was situated in what Petronella was told was Doornfontein, the first of Johannesburg's residential suburbs. It was sheltered by hills on the windward side, and the houses were shaded by overhanging trees which Petronella was astonished to be told had been specially planted. She had never before heard of anyone planting trees other than those which bore fruit. They just grew naturally, or they didn't, and that was that.

A magnificent garden ran all around the four sides of Marcus's family home, and Petronella could not help being both deeply impressed and disapproving of the fact that no vegetables of any kind were grown. There were only flowers and vividly blossoming shrubs and short, velvety green grass which Marcus said was called lawn. There was also an artificial pond which made one feel cool merely to look at it. Mamma would have dismissed the entire garden as being totally useless, a sinfully frivolous waste of time and of labour.

On Petronella's first morning, Marcus's mother announced, through him, that they were to visit the town centre to shop for clothes for her. She would have been more excited about both the trip and its purpose if it had not been for an unpleasant feeling that Marcus's family were ashamed at the thought of any of their friends or acquaintances seeing her in the blouses and skirts Mamma had made for her.

But it would have been impossible not to be excited by the excursion. There was the fascination of the noisy tram cars and the excitement of being one of the crowd hurrying along either on foot or by every imaginable kind of conveyance.

They turned into Pritchard Street, with its many fine shops displaying every kind of female garment behind their plate glass windows. On the left was an establishment which Marcus said was called Mount's Bay House, and which proved to be very grand, selling drapery and clothing. But their destination was another large store called Thorne and Stuttaford. As they stopped outside it Marcus took out his watch and glanced at it, saying something to his mother. Then he gave Petronella an apologetic smile.

"It is necessary for me to attend the Stock Exchange now. You must remain with Mutti and with Hannah, Petronella."

"Do you *have* to leave us?" she asked in dismay.

"I have duties, yes. But tomorrow I shall show you more places of interest in Johannesburg."

Petronella's spirits revived a little, after he had walked away, when she found herself inside Thorne and Stuttaford, and she saw the amazing displays of clothing and of rich fabrics in glowing colours. Marcus's mother purchased lengths of material which were presumably to be made up into gowns for Petronella later, and she wished the woman had thought to consult her in the matter, for the fabrics were all in drab dark grey or brown which did not please her at all. Even though they did not speak each other's language, it would have been a simple matter to establish whether Petronella liked the fabrics or not.

When the three of them returned to the house she found that there was something different about her bedroom. The pictures had been removed from the walls, and the matching porcelain bowls had disappeared from the top of the dressing table. The white lace counterpane had been replaced by one of brown chenille.

She did not really mind. The pictures had seemed absurd to her; she'd had no use for the porcelain bowls, and she had been afraid of marking or spoiling the white lace counterpane. But she wondered why all the things had been removed and in the end decided that it must have been related to some Jewish custom.

A sewing woman had been sent for, and she took Petronella's measurements and pored over sketches of garments with Marcus's mother, again without consulting Petronella. Afterwards, the three of them had a cold lunch which was composed of items as unfamiliar to Petronella as last night's supper had been, and centred around pickled fish. She ate some beetroot and tomatoes and thought longingly of Mamma's *boerewors* and a slice of her crusty new bread glistening with farm butter.

Marcus kept his word, the next day, and showed her the sights of Johannesburg. There had been a long, voluble exchange with his mother beforehand, and Petronella feared the woman was insisting on accompanying them, but in the end she left the house alone with Marcus.

"Have you told your family," she asked him, "that I am to become Jewish, so that we may marry?"

"The time is not yet correct, Petronella. First, they must become fully acquainted with you."

"I don't see how that will ever happen," she muttered. "Apart from when you are present, and can interpret, they ignore me. When will you tell your family, Marcus? Next week? The one after that?"

He gave her a sad, troubled look. "It is a delicate matter, Petronella, and it requires caution."

She stifled her mutinous thoughts, and changed the subject. "Where will you take me tomorrow, Marcus?"

"Tomorrow, Petronella, I must attend to my duties 'Between the Chains'."

"Why do you have to work every day? If you do not need to work today, why must you work tomorrow?"

He sighed. "I am employed by my father, Petronella, and already I have taken many days of vacation. I do not work today because – well, I have told an untruth to my family. I informed them that I wished to take you to seek friends of your family in Johannesburg."

"Well," she said recklessly, "we could go on searching every day for those supposed friends, couldn't we?"

"No, Petronella. I cannot cheat and deceive my father in such a manner. You must be patient."

But patience was not part of her nature, and in spite of having been plunged into a totally alien world she felt beset by frustration. Friday was so strange that she sensed herself to be even more of an intruder than she had before.

The house was cleaned more thoroughly than even Mamma would have considered necessary, and when Petronella wandered into the kitchen she found Hannah and her mother examining all the fruit and vegetables, and ruthlessly discarding anything which showed even the slightest sign of bruising or decay. Petronella could understand this extreme insistence on perfection no better than she understood why a large joint of beef was soaking in a bowlful of water on the table, the water slowly turning a deeper pink. No wonder the meals were so tasteless if all the juices of the meat were wasted like this.

But it was the atmosphere, more than the domestic activity, which marked Friday out from other days. Candles in beautiful silver holders were placed on the dining table, and lit by Mevrouw Koen shortly before sunset. It seemed to Petronella to be a shocking waste that they should be lit before they were needed, but it was done with such ceremony that she concluded it was all part of being Jewish.

Marcus confirmed that it was so when he and his father joined the women in the room. Both men wore large, black skullcaps on their heads.

"The lighting of the candles commences the Shabbat," Marcus whispered.

She blinked at him in confusion, having been led to believe that Saturday was the Jewish Sabbath. She felt equally confused about the ceremonies which followed and which she felt excluded her and accentuated that she was an intruder.

After Marcus's father had said a prayer he poured wine into the extremely ornate glasses which had been set out on the table. Then he unwrapped a sharp knife which had been concealed by a cloth, and the removal of another cloth revealed a fancily plaited loaf of bread. Accompanied by chanting from his family he cut the bread into pieces and sprinkled them with salt before handing them to the others.

Petronella found herself unable to swallow the bread. She choked, causing a disturbance in the family chanting. Mevrouw Koen frowned at her, but there was nothing she could do to stop herself. Gasping and coughing, she ran from the room and left them to their ceremonies. A while later the taciturn black maid came to her room and offered her, without a word, a plateful of *mieliepap* with a fried egg on top which Petronella accepted gratefully, even though she realised she was sharing the servants' supper.

After that the pattern of her life changed subtly. On Saturday morning the Koens all set out for the Synagogue, leaving Petronella at home. She did not join them for supper that evening, for shortly before the gong sounded the black maid brought her a tray in her room. Petronella's surprise gave way to delight when she discovered that the dishes on it held proper food – *boerewors* and *sousboontjies* and bread which, although not as good as Mamma's, was not sour and full of aniseed, or else sprinkled with salt.

From then onwards all her meals were served separately to her in her bedroom. She supposed that it would be regarded as a profanity if she were to be served with Boer food at a Jewish table. The fact that Marcus's family were going to the trouble of obtaining for her the kind of food to which she was accustomed made it plain that he had not yet told them about the plan for her to become Jewish. She wanted to speak to him about it, but he was always working during the day, and now they did not even meet at supper. And most evenings, when he was not working 'Between the Chains', he went with his father to the Synagogue, which appeared to be a social meeting place for Jewish men as well as a place of worship.

The sewing woman had finished making Petronella's new clothes, and they were presented to her. She found them ugly and drab, but she forced a smile of gratitude and dutifully put them on. She felt somewhat cheered when she was also given some pretty, starched and frilled white aprons to wear over the gowns. Shortly after she had finished putting on her new clothes the unfriendly maid came to her room and spoke to her in Fanakalo.

"The missus, she has visitors. She say she want you to help pass them the coffee and cake."

Pleased and excited, Petronella stood up. She had been aware that, on most mornings when the Koen women did not themselves go out to visit friends, other women would call on them instead, but until now Petronella had been excluded from these social occasions. To be asked to take part now must surely mean that the Koen family were beginning to regard her as one of them. Passing coffee and cakes to guests had been something Petronella had often done for Mamma in the past; it was one of the duties of the daughter of a household.

To her delight, she discovered that one of the visitors spoke Dutch. It was a strange form of Dutch; in some ways similar to that spoken by Marcus but whereas he spoke it slowly and precisely and with his own exotic intonation, this woman's speech was rapid and assured and sometimes seemed almost outmoded.

"So," the woman addressed Petronella, "it appears that your people are determined to have a war."

"Are they, Mevrouw? I don't know much about the matter."

"They are demanding the withdrawal of British troops from their borders. Instead, the British are drafting into the country reinforcements from India and other places – " The woman broke off as Marcus's mother said something to her, and then translated, "You are to go and fetch some more cream from the kitchen, Petronella."

When she returned to the sitting room, Petronella addressed the woman again. "Why do you speak Dutch in such a strange way?"

"You must not address me, Petronella," the woman reproved her, "unless I speak to you first. And you must call me Mevrouw Grünwald."

"Oh . . ." Naturally she would have addressed the woman by her name if she had known it, but Marcus's mother had not tried to introduce her to any of the guests. And she could only assume that the custom of speaking only when you have been spoken to by someone older was another strange Jewish rite.

Mevrouw Grünwald relented. "I speak Dutch in a way which sounds strange to you, Petronella, because it is pure Dutch. I was born in Holland."

After that morning, Petronella's days sped by in a flurry of activity. She was kept busy, doing mending for the household or accompanying Marcus's mother and sister when they went shopping so that she could carry parcels for them, and whenever they received guests Petronella handed out coffee and cakes. And from Mevrouw Grünwald she received news of the war, which now seemed both inevitable and imminent.

Petronella began to worry about something which had never even struck her before. If she became a Jew, would that make her an automatic enemy of her own people, the Boers? She did not think she could bear that. She would have to ask Marcus about it.

But he was in his room, getting ready to go to the Synagogue with his father, and she knew he would not return until after she had gone to bed. She decided, rashly, to visit him in his room.

She knocked on the door, and entered. He was bending over the wash-basin, wearing only his breeches. He turned, groping for a towel, and came towards her. "Aai, Petronella, it is not suitable or wise for you to come to my room!"

"But I never see you, Marcus! Now that I am given my meals in my room – "

"Mutti wishes to show consideration, Petronella. She is aware that you do not find our *kosher* food to your taste, and so she arranges for you to be served the *trefah* food of the Boers."

"I know, and I'm grateful. But I shall have to get used to eating your kind of food when I become Jewish. Have you told your family about it yet?"

"No," he admitted. "We must proceed with caution."

"But Marcus, they like me so much better now! I can tell that they do. They are treating me as if I was already part of the family. You should tell them – "

"And *you* should remove yourself from my room, Petronella!" He took hold of her shoulders to steer her towards the door. She noticed that droplets of water glinted in the curly mat on his chest, and she was suddenly overwhelmed by the familiar hunger for him which was never far from her mind and her senses. She moved towards him, sliding her palms over his naked flesh, pulling his head down to hers. He crushed her to him, his mouth ravenous on hers, and she guided his hands to her breasts.

He lifted his head. "Petronella, no. Do not tempt me to pleasure you in the home of my family."

"Then let us tell them the truth, so that we may marry!"

He sighed. "There are so many things you do not comprehend. My family regard you only as someone who is without friends, without a home. They have given you a home, but for them to consider you as their daughter will require time and a great deal of planning."

"You're wrong," she insisted stubbornly. "Your mother already treats me like a daughter."

But he would not listen to any more of her arguments, and he forced her from the room. She gained the impression that he feared losing his self-control even more than he feared her being discovered in his bedroom. Mutinously, she decided to visit him there again in the future, since it seemed to be her only hope of seeing him nowadays.

But in the morning she discovered that a note had been pushed underneath her door. Written by Marcus, it explained that he had left for Kimberley to discuss the looming possibility of war with their family friend, Nathan Creager. "While I am absent," the note ended, "you must do all in your power to make yourself agreeable to my parents and my sister."

Petronella was desolate when she had read the note. She suspected that he had seized an excuse to flee because he had sensed her decision to haunt his room and offer him temptation. Anger warred with her sense of despair. It had been bad enough before, merely catching occasional glimpses of Marcus, but now she was to be deprived even of this, and he did not say for how long she would have to endure his absence.

As the days went by, misery and desolation threatened to swamp her. Winter had come to Johannesburg, and made her miss Jakkalsdrif all the more. The fact that it never rained in the winter meant that the dust from the mines was constantly being swept up by the wind into 'dust fiends' which blinded one when out of doors and covered every surface inside the house with layers of red grains of fine sand, no matter how one might strive to keep windows and doors shut.

On Jakkalsdrif, winter had possessed a beauty of its own. The air had a bright, luminous quality, and the frost outlined every single blade of grass or twig of thorn-scrub and made them glint in the sun like jewels before its heat restored them to ordinariness again. Winter in Johannesburg was merely dusty, uncomfortable and drab. Petronella wept bitterly at night with longing for Marcus and for Jakkalsdrif and Mamma and Pappa and her brothers.

Her only consolation lay in the fact that Marcus's mother seemed to be pleased with the way in which she made herself useful to her and to Hannah, and she had become so familiar with their daily guests that she knew precisely who took sugar in her coffee, and who preferred tea with lemon instead of milk. It was also a treat to be able to converse with Mevrouw Grünwald.

One morning far more visitors than usual arrived, and Petronella was kept so busy, fetching more cream and more cakes from the kitchen, that she scarcely had time to speak to Mevrouw Grünwald. Petronella had learnt that the woman was the Rabbi's wife, and she had been toying with the idea of broaching the subject of herself converting to the Jewish faith. Today, she meant to find the courage from somewhere to speak to Mevrouw Grünwald about it.

But during a lull in the conversation, the woman approached her and told her something which banished all other thoughts from Petronella's mind. The Orange Free State *Volksraad* had declared its intention to stand by the Transvaal Republic in the event of war. With the strength of the Boers reinforced in this way, there was no doubt left in anyone's mind that there would be a war, and the whole of Johannesburg was in an uproar.

Petronella was consumed by doubt and anxiety. She had forgotten, after all, to ask Marcus whether becoming a Jew would automatically make her an enemy of the Boers. From the way in which Mevrouw Grünwald always spoke, there was little doubt that the Jews regarded themselves as being enemies of the Boers. If and when war broke out, would Petronella be a traitor to her own people simply by being part of a Jewish household? She was about to put this question in roundabout terms to Mevrouw Grünwald when she heard a sudden buzz of excitement in the room, and she turned.

Marcus was home! He stood there just inside the door, with his father's hand on his shoulder, talking animatedly to his mother and some of her guests.

Petronella tried to hide her joy. She could not run to him and fling her arms about him as she wanted to. But she could, at least, demonstrate to him how thoroughly his family accepted her now, and that it was time to tell them the two of them wanted to marry. Simply seeing him so unexpectedly had supplied an answer to her own question. If becoming Jewish so that she could marry Marcus made her an enemy of her people, then it was a painful burden she was prepared to accept.

She poured coffee into two cups, and set them on a tray with small plates containing a selection of cakes, and moved with a smile towards the family group. He did not return her smile, but stared at her with a frozen expression. Puzzled, she hesitated, and then one of the other guests called her name, and she responded automatically. The guest wanted more cream in her coffee and Petronella had to put the tray down so that she could pick up the jug of cream and take it to the woman.

She heard Marcus shout something which could only have been a violent oath. She spun around. She had never thought to see such black rage in his face as he addressed his mother. He ignored his father, who was snapping commands at him, but turned his head to flay Hannah with furious words also.

Pandemonium broke out as the guests joined in the bitter, inexplicable quarrel. Petronella could understand nothing of what was being said, and she was totally bewildered and at a loss as to the reason for Marcus's rage. Why was he not pleased, instead, to find her wearing the clothes his mother had had made for her, their plain drabness softened by the pretty frilled white apron, and playing the part of a daughter by handing coffee and cakes to the guests?

Above the bitter, passionate outcries from the guests rose the sound of Marcus's mother's weeping. His father thundered something and gesticulated in Petronella's direction. The gesture had been a clear repudiation, and now at last she understood. Marcus had chosen the moment of his homecoming to tell his family that he wished to marry her, and they not only disapproved. They were passionately, inflexibly opposed to it.

Marcus answered his father in an implacable voice and turned on his heel. "Pack together your belongings, Petronella," he ordered. "You and I are leaving immediately."

"But what happened? Why did you become so angry?" She hurried after him along the corridor. "If only you hadn't started quarrelling with your parents, I'm sure they would have – "

He flung over his shoulder, "You do not comprehend, do you? Are you so blind and stupid, Petronella, that you failed to realise you had been turned into *a servant?*"

In total bewilderment and disbelief, she went to her room. How could she have been turned into a servant? Servants were black. Anyone who read the Bible knew that. Noah's son Ham had mocked his father, and as a punishment Noah had cursed him through Ham's own son, Canaan, saying, 'A servant of servants shall he be unto his brethren.'

The descendants of Noah's three sons, the Bible said, had populated the whole earth after the Flood, but Canaan's descendants had emerged as a race apart, and they had fulfilled Noah's curse: 'There shall be none of ye be freed from being bondsmen, and hewers of wood and drawers of water'. Everyone knew that. So how could a Boer girl possibly have been turned into a servant? It was quite ridiculous. She could only conclude that the Jewish Bible, which Marcus had told her was called the *Torah*, did not explain about the curse on Ham's son Canaan.

But all in all, she was not really sorry to be leaving this magnificent, oppressive house with its strange people and their strange ways. She made a bundle of her possessions and went to join Marcus in his room, where he was packing books and other personal items into the still-packed trunk he had just brought back from Kimberley.

He looked so grim-faced that she decided not to question him, but watched in silence. At last he closed the trunk and picked it up, nodding to her.

His father was waiting outside the bedroom door, flanked by several servants. Petronella stared in shock at Mijnheer Koen. His city-smart clothing had been torn to shreds, as if he had just been involved in a brawl. How could such a thing have been possible? Even more astonishing was the fact that Marcus showed no surprise or concern about the state of his father's clothes, but gestured brusquely to her to follow him along the corridor.

They almost collided with his mother, her face ravaged by grief. She was carrying a low stool, and she did not speak or look at either of them. A moment later she was joined by Hannah, who was weeping and carrying a similar stool. There was no sight or sound of the guests.

"Hurry," Petronella heard Marcus say, his voice drained of all expression. "We must rescue the spider before it is too late."

Too late? Too late for what? Uncomprehending, she lengthened her stride to keep up with him. In the stable at the side of the house he hitched a horse to the spider and after stowing his trunk and her bundle of clothing aboard it he helped her into the passenger seat.

He drove only as far as the street immediately outside his family's home and then he stopped, the reins held slackly in his hands. Petronella felt too unnerved by the strange blankness of his expression to ask questions. Instead, she followed his gaze.

The curtains were undrawn, so that she could see inside the house. In the dining room, a servant was draping a cloth over the mirror above the sideboard. Another ornamental mirror hanging on the wall of the sitting room was being similarly covered and so was any object bright enough to reflect an image. As Petronella watched this being done, Marcus's mother and sister entered the room carrying low stools. They could surely not be the same stools the women had been carrying earlier, and when Petronella rose in her seat for a better view she saw that something like a dozen of these stools had been arranged inside the room. Marcus's father entered, wearing a skullcap on his head, his lips moving as if he were chanting a prayer. He had not changed out of his inexplicably torn clothes.

A sound of shock was forced from Petronella. Mevrouw Koen and Hannah, their faces contorted with grief, had begun to tear their own beautiful, expensive garments, ripping the delicate fabrics as if they had no more value than cleaning rags. Then they went to sit on low stools on either side of Marcus's father, and as he prayed they wept and rocked themselves backwards and forwards.

Petronella swallowed hard. "What – ? Why – ?" she managed.

"They are preparing to sit *shiva*," Marcus answered her, his voice totally neutral.

"What does that mean?"

"It means they will soon be joined by my uncles and my aunts. For seven days they will remain seated and the men will pray and the women weep. The men will not work and the women will not prepare food."

"Oh." Her voice was small and bewildered. "But – why?"

"They are mourning the death of their son," he said colourlessly.

"But – you aren't *dead* . . ."

"In the hearts and the minds of my family I no longer exist on this earth." He moved his head, and gestured towards a courtyard adjoining the stables. "All that remains of Mordechai Cohen is to be burnt from their lives."

With a sense of unreality, she saw that servants were carrying out clothing, books, bedlinen, pictures and papers, and adding them to a pile which had already been made of such things as Marcus's desk and its matching chair and even old toys which were obviously relics of his childhood. Now she understood why he had hurried to salvage the spider.

"Because they made you choose," she whispered, "and you chose me?"

"Because I chose you," he confirmed. A muscle twitched beside his mouth. "I refused to admit it to myself, but my instinct has been informing me for a considerable time that I would be forced to choose, and there was only one choice possible for me to make."

He pulled at the reins and the horse began to trot along the street. She turned her head and saw a wisp of smoke curling into the air. The bonfire had been lit. Soon there would be nothing left to show that a son had ever been part of Marcus's family.

5

When they had reached the outskirts of the suburb of Doornfontein and Johannesburg city lay spread out before them, Marcus reined in the horse.

"I do not know where you and I will sleep tonight, Petronella," he said quietly, "or how or where we will live – tomorrow and in the future."

She stared at him in disbelief. "But Marcus, you are rich – "

He interrupted her with a hollow laugh. "Mordechai Cohen, the son of Joshua Cohen, was a rich man. But Mordechai Cohen is dead, and the ghost that remains has no capital, no employment and no friends. And with war coming it is not possible to find employment with those in Johannesburg who are not of the Jewish faith. So I must consider carefully how to make last the small amount of money I have with me – "

"We'll go to Jakkalsdrif!" Petronella put in excitedly. "We'll explain to Mamma and Pappa what has happened, and when they understand that *nothing* could part us they'll allow us to marry, and you'll live on the farm and help with the work!"

He gave her a grim smile. "You wish us to go to your family like beggars?"

"No, not like beggars! You say you are dead to your family and to all your Jewish friends. Why shouldn't you turn Christian?"

His head jerked up. He remained utterly still for a while and then he laughed again, without a trace of mirth. "For you it proved impossible to become Jewish. You believe it possible that I may become a Boer instead?"

"Yes, I do!" she affirmed recklessly. "And even if Mamma and Pappa won't forgive me, and won't accept you, at least they'll give us shelter and food until we have thought what to do about our future!"

Marcus shrugged, but this time it was not the exotic, almost flamboyant gesture which used to fascinate her. It was an expression of defeat. "Very well," he said. "We will proceed to Jakkalsdrif."

They drove as far as they could before nightfall, and then he announced sombrely that they would have to try to sleep in the veld. But it was still only early spring, and Petronella knew that the night would become bitterly cold and the dew relentless at dawn.

She saw the flickering of a light in the distance, and said with determination, "There is a farmhouse ahead. We'll stay there for the night."

"Petronella, I need to save the small amount of money I have – "

"They would not expect us to pay! The only thing is – lend me that ring you wear on your little finger, Marcus."

He removed the ring and she placed it on the third finger of her left hand, turning it upside down so that it appeared to be a wedding ring. As they approached the farmhouse she saw that it was little more than a *pondok* built of wattle-and-daub, roofed with zinc, and she wrinkled her nose. But it represented shelter, and it had also given her an idea.

A mongrel dog barked raucously at them as they drove up. The noise brought a solidly built woman out on to the stoep. In one hand she carried a lantern and in the other a Mauser carbine. She hung the lantern on a hook and awaited them, the gun raised in silent threat.

"Good evening, Mevrouw!" Petronella called out, and the Mauser was slowly lowered and placed on the stoep. Firmly holding Marcus by the arm, Petronella approached and said, "My husband and I are on our way to visit my parents on their farm near Doornboomstad. Our name is Koen."

The woman offered her hand. "Sannie Boshof. Come inside, Mevrouw Koen, while your husband sees to the horse. Excuse the gun, but I am alone here. My husband and my son left this afternoon to join their Field-Cornet on commando, and I am quite a long distance away from the farm homestead." A thought seemed to strike her, for she peered suspiciously at Marcus. "You have not been called up to join your commando, Mijnheer Koen?"

Quickly, before Marcus could speak, Petronella explained, "My husband is an *Uitlander*, Mevrouw. He was born in Holland."

"I see." The woman remained wary, but she added, "Come inside."

Petronella followed Sannie Boshof, while Marcus lingered to feed and water the horse. The house, for all its poverty, was painfully clean, the earthen floors meticulously swept. Petronella sat in the kitchen by the white-scrubbed table and watched as Sannie Boshof cut bread and set coffee on the stove to heat.

"I daresay I shall find that my father and brother have also been called up to join their commando," Petronella mused. "To which commando do your husband and son belong, Mevrouw Boshof?"

The woman gave her a narrow-eyed look. "Why do you wish to know?"

"I was wondering whether my father and brother would be with them."

"I don't remember the name of their Field-Cornet. Ah, here is your husband now. While you are eating, I shall make up a bed for you in my son's room."

"She thinks you are a spy," Petronella told Marcus, when they were alone. "As if anyone would forget the name of her husband's Field-Cornet!"

Marcus sighed, and shook his head. "Aai, I doubt that I shall ever understand the Boers. They believe me to be a spy, and a war is imminent, and still they are prepared to give me food and shelter." He dipped his bread in the strong, bitter coffee and she knew he was thinking of the sour aniseed bread which he would never eat with his family again.

That night they lay together in the narrow iron bed which their taciturn hostess had offered them, and Marcus pleasured her with a kind of desperate urgency which excited her and swept her along, even though she sensed that he was driven by something which went far beyond love or passion or desire. And afterwards, to her astonishment and dismay, he wept with great tearing sobs which shook the bed.

At first she was embarrassed, because she had never known a man to give way to such unrestrained tears before, and then she realised that he must be desperately anxious about the future. In spite of her earlier confident words, going to Jakkalsdrif was a gamble, the outcome of which neither of them could guess.

She tried to comfort him. "Marcus, Mevrouw Boshof has given me an idea. I suppose you've realised that she and her husband are *bywoners*?"

After a moment he became calm enough to ask, "And what is a *bywoner*, Petronella?"

"It is a – well, a sort of tenant farmer, except that you pay no rent. If you have no land of your own, you can ask a farmer to let you work on his land for a share of the harvest and grazing for your livestock. A *bywoner* generally builds a *pondok* like this one for himself and his family."

"So – our hostess is a *bywoner*. Of what importance is that to us, Petronella?"

"If Pappa and Mamma say we cannot stay at Jakkalsdrif, I shall threaten to ask the van Tonders to let us become *bywoners* on their farm. Pappa would hate that, because he is bad friends with Mijnheer van Tonder. There is a piece of land between the van Tonder farm and Jakkalsdrif which both of them claim, and because neither will give way it has become *uitvalgrond*."

"And what is that?" Marcus asked with a sombre pretence at interest.

"It means that the piece of land has become ownerless, and can't belong to either Pappa or Mijnheer van Tonder." She frowned. "I believe it could be claimed by an outsider. But because Pappa and Mijnheer van Tonder quarrelled about the *uitvalgrond*, Pappa would hate it if we were to become *bywoners* to a man with whom he is bad friends. Rather than have that happen, he will allow us to stay on Jakkalsdrif and marry – "

Marcus put his arm around her and drew her close to him. "Sleep now, Petronella. Tomorrow will be soon enough to worry about the future."

She buried her head against his chest, still tingling and throbbing after his pleasuring. They were right for one another; they belonged together. If Pappa and Mamma turned them away from Jakkalsdrif they would survive somehow. She could endure any hardship provided she was with Marcus. She smiled and yawned, and then slept like a contented child.

Beside her, Marcus found sleep impossible, for he could see his future stretched out before him, spent in the desolate wasteland of lifelong exile. Now that his anger had cooled, he could see that Mutti and Hannah could scarcely have been blamed for using Petronella as a superior servant. The fault had been his, for he had never been honest with his family. As far as they were concerned, Petronella was a friendless waif whose family had thrown her out because she had extended hospitality to a Jew, and to the Cohens, who knew little about those strange creatures the Boers, such extreme behaviour had not seemed improbable.

Mutti must have found it quite a problem to know what to do with this *shiksa* who had been foisted on to the household and did not fit in. So she had tried to solve the problem by having Petronella served with *trefah* food in her room, and by keeping her isolated from the family rituals.

And since Petronella herself had not objected to waiting upon his mother's guests, how could Mutti have foreseen that Marcus would object so furiously?

No, the fault of it had been all his own. He had not told the family about his plan that Petronella should convert to Judaism, and the reason he had not told them, he acknowledged now, was because he had known from the start they would never accept such a suggestion. It had been made clear to him, too, by his mother's guests, that none of Johannesburg's Jewry would accept Petronella.

If she had been anything but a Boer, it might have been possible. But the Johannesburg Jewry, themselves looked down upon by so many other races, despised what they regarded as a hotch-potch of semiliterates, an intermingling of Dutch, French and other assorted European races whose descendants called themselves Boers. The word itself simply meant 'farmer', which illustrated the poverty – culturally and intellectually – of a mongrel race of people who did not even have a suitable name by which to call themselves and so had adopted their predominant occupation as a means of identity.

No, as he had admitted to Petronella, Marcus had known all along in his heart that he had only two choices. It would have to be Petronella – or his family, his faith, and all that went with it.

Well, he had made his choice and she would never know, would never be able to understand, what he had given up for her sake. It was not only the question of security, and the wealth he would have inherited from his father, or the love of his family. How could he ever explain to Petronella what it meant to be a Jew? It went far deeper than faith or religious beliefs, and it was not something which could be sustained or fulfilled in isolation. It was an intangible thing, a mystical sense of belonging to an ancient, international brotherhood which had been bred in his bones and which he would have to replace with something else if he were to survive.

He sighed, his arms tightening about Petronella. He loved her; God knew he loved this beautiful, passionate, single-minded child. But for all her sharp wits, she was virtually uneducated, and he would never be able to discuss anything on a cultural level with her.

Well, the die had been cast. In his heart he would always be a Jew; in his blood and in his bones and in the very core of his being. But since he had chosen Petronella and his people had cast him out he would, for all practical purposes, have to cease being a Jew. His instinct was to belong, and so he would have to become a Boer, if such a thing were possible. He had recoiled from the suggestion at first, but common sense told him he would have to convert to Christianity so that he could marry Petronella, whether or not he could accept its teachings. There was no other way.

At last Marcus drifted into sleep, and he and Petronella were both woken up while it was still dark by the slamming of doors and the banging of saucepans coming from the kitchen. Marcus lit a candle and picked up his pocket watch, and saw that it was only four o'clock.

"Yes, well," Petronella explained, yawning, "Mevrouw Boshof has to make an early start, because she will have to do all the farmwork by herself." She twined her legs about Marcus's and caught his lower lip between her own. A loud crash came from the kitchen, as if Sannie Boshof knew what they were contemplating and was registering disapproval.

"She wishes us to rise," Marcus said, putting Petronella away from him.

"Well, I don't want – " she began, trying to reach for him again.

His anxiety to placate, to begin the task of integrating with the people whom he would have to make his own from now on if they would accept him, overshadowed his aroused desire, and he evaded her questing hands.

"Petronella, no. She has shown us much hospitality, in spite of suspecting me to be a spy. We must rise and offer her assistance."

But Sannie Boshof declined offers of help when they joined her in the kitchen. Her attitude made it plain that she wished them to leave as soon as they had eaten their breakfast of rusks and coffee.

About half an hour later, when the sky was growing rapidly lighter, Marcus and Petronella reached the crest of a hill and he reined in the horse. Below them in the veld to the left of the track a huge encampment of tents and wagon-laagers lay spread out. Smoke was curling into the air as camp-fires were being lit, and there was the restless sound of clinking metal as knee-haltered horses hobbled around the perimeter of the encampment, cropping at the grass. Above a large marquee fluttered the *Vierkleur*, the flag of the Transvaal Republic with its bands of green, red, white and blue.

"The commando!" Petronella exclaimed. "Mevrouw Boshof must have known it was encamped here, almost on her doorstep, and she must have known we were bound to stumble upon it. She thought you a spy, but even so she could not bring herself to refuse us hospitality."

Marcus nodded, his gaze thoughtful. "They are strange people, the Boers." The sooner he learnt to understand their ways, the better he would be able to adapt and fit in. An idea came to him with the lightning flash of inspiration, and he climbed out of the spider and helped Petronella to alight too, leaving the horse to graze. "We shall pay a visit to the commando."

"Do you mean, to ask for news of Pappa and Johannes?"

"That also." Marcus hesitated. "Petronella, I have decided that I will offer to fight with the Boers."

"No!" she shrieked. "It is not your war! Can't you see that this is our chance, that people will be crying out for *bywoners* to work their land while so many of the men are away? Why, I'm sure Pappa would beg you to stay at Jakkalsdrif and oversee the sowing and the harvesting!"

He tried to find a way of explaining to her his need to belong somewhere, and that it would never be filled if he were to exploit the coming war in the way she suggested. He considered pointing out to her that her parents were far more likely to welcome her back to Jakkalsdrif if she returned alone, and that there was far more chance of their being reconciled to their daughter marrying a Jew if that Jew had fought on their side during the war. In the end, he merely said,

"I am not a farmer, Petronella. I cannot remain a Jew if we are to be married, and if I am to integrate with the Boers then I must be prepared to fight with them."

She flung herself at him, kissing him in the way he had taught her, trying to seduce his senses and so persuade him to stay with her instead of joining the commando. But he remained implacable.

"We must go now, for I wish to request an audience with an officer. I have been suspected of being a spy, so perhaps I could in truth become a spy – for the Boers."

"But what about me, Marcus?" she wailed.

"We shall see. After I have had speech with an officer I shall, perhaps, take you to Jakkalsdrif and then return. We shall see."

There was a great deal of activity going on in the camp when they reached it. Horses were being fed and groomed; breakfast was being cooked over camp-fires and Mausers were being oiled. To Marcus, whose knowledge of military matters had been gained from history books, the scene was an extraordinary one; totally undisciplined and with no one apparently in command, and burghers sitting in groups, gossiping or indulging in horseplay. There was no formal kind of uniform, the Boers wearing their everyday shaggy moleskins, home-spun shirts and felt hats with their wide brims tilted towards the crown at one side. Among them, Marcus knew that he was an incongruous figure with his silk shirt and dark city trousers and coat.

Marcus, with the weeping Petronella clinging to his arm, approached one of the burghers who was staring at them. "Please," he said, "I wish to have an audience with the Field-Cornet."

The burgher studied him and Petronella in turn. While he appeared to consider it odd that such a strangely dressed man accompanied by a weeping young girl should have arrived at the encampment, there was no suspicion in his eyes suggesting that he thought they might be spies.

"Which Field-Cornet?" he asked. "There are half a dozen with their commandos at camp."

Marcus hesitated, and glanced at the marquee above which the Transvaal flag was fluttering. "Perhaps that one."

The burgher laughed. "That's General Joubert's tent. Come on, then. I'll take you to him."

Marcus found it all astonishingly casual. There was no form of protocol, no hierarchy through which one had to work one's way in order to gain the ear of the general. Any passing burgher could conduct one, without ceremony or prior appointment, straight to the tent of the supreme commander.

Inside, seated at a small trestle-table, was an elderly man with sharp, shrewd eyes, a prominent and fleshy nose and a flowing grey beard. He wore a black claw-hammer coat, and a semi-tophat trimmed with crêpe was being handed to him by a woman who appeared to be his wife, as if he were on the point of leaving the tent. She placed it on the table instead as they entered, and the burgher who had been their guide said with casual politeness, "Morning, General. Morning, Mevrouw Joubert. This gentleman asked to see you, General."

Marcus stepped forward. "My name is Co – Koen, *seur*. I desire to fight on the side of the Boers."

A loud sob escaped Petronella. He placed an arm about her shoulders and added, "This is 'Juffrouw Petronella van Zyl. When the fighting is over we wish to be joined in marriage. I am in the process of taking her home to the farm of her family, Jakkalsdrif, but if you would accept me I shall return here afterwards and enlist as a burgher."

General Joubert raised his eyebrows slightly, and asked, "Would you feel more comfortable, Mijnheer Koen, if we conversed in English?"

"You speak English?" Marcus returned with surprise.

The grey eyebrows rose higher in dry amusement. "Contrary to general belief," he said in English, "most Boers are not illiterate barbarians. Several of us have even attended universities in European countries. In spite of the name by which you have introduced yourself you are not, of course, a Boer. You speak Dutch far too correctly and formally for that."

Before Marcus could explain, Mevrouw Joubert moved to Petronella's side, and said gently, "Come and help me, my dear. I always accompany my husband whenever he goes on commando, but it can be lonely, sometimes, to be the only female among so many men. I am just about to broil some meat for breakfast, and I'm sure you and Mijnheer Koen would be glad of something to eat, also."

After the women had left the tent, General Joubert invited Marcus to draw up a folding stool and sit down. "Now tell me, Mr Koen, what your real name is, and why you wish to fight for the Boers."

Marcus told him the truth, leaving out only intimate details about his relationship with Petronella and the painful burning of his entire existence from his family's home and hearts.

"If I marry Petronella," he added in English, "I must become one of her people. Since I do mean to marry her, however long it may take to gain the consent of her parents, or even if we have to do it without their consent, I must throw in my lot with her people. Since that lot, at the moment, is to fight a war which is certain to break out within a few days, I want to share the fighting."

"Hmm. Do you own a horse, a Mauser and ammunition?"

Marcus looked at him in perplexity. "I assumed I would be provided with all the things I would need to be a burgher."

General Joubert smiled grimly. "You assumed wrongly. The *Krygsraad* cannot even afford to feed the burghers for long, let alone equip them. Each man must provide his own horse, gun and ammunition, and feed himself as best he can when our rations run out – by shooting for the pot, by relying on the generosity of wayside farms, or even by stealing from the enemy."

Marcus stared at him, dumbfounded for the moment at such a ramshackle kind of army. "May I ask, sir," he ventured at last, "what the strength of your forces is?"

"Combined with the men from the Orange Free State, our burghers number some sixty thousand men." He added drily, "The British Army, who will be drafting in regulars and volunteers from the Colonies in South Africa and from overseas, will outnumber us by an estimated two hundred and fifty thousand men. Do you still wish to join us, Mr Cohen?"

"I wish to be known as Koen from now on, sir," Marcus answered quietly, "and I will join you if I can solve the problem of obtaining a horse and a gun and ammunition. I have a little money, and I own a horse and a spider, but the horse has not been broken to the saddle. Also, I must take Miss van Zyl home to her family. When I have done that I shall return to Johannesburg and sell my horse and spider, and equip myself, and join you – "

"How good a shot are you?" General Joubert interrupted.

Marcus smiled wryly. "There have been few opportunities for sharp-shooting 'Between the Chains' in Johannesburg, sir. I thought my value to you might lie, instead, in my knowledge of languages. In short, by acting as a spy."

General Joubert regarded him thoughtfully. "You may be right. A Boer, no matter how fluently he might speak English, will give himself away in many subtle little ways. You, however, could pass as almost anything or anyone. A businessman whose train has been commandeered by Boers, and finds himself forced to apply for help at a British camp; an enterprising opportunist offering to arrange supplies of whatever a British encampment might be short of . . . Yes, I think you could be useful to us."

Marcus nodded. "So, with your permission, I will take Miss van Zyl home to Jakkalsdrif – "

"No, Mr Koen. Even if you are to work for us as a spy, you must still know how to handle a Mauser. We will be so vastly outnumbered that we shall need every pair of hands we can press into service. Miss van Zyl will be driven home in your spider by one of my burghers, who will then sell the vehicle and the horse for whatever it may fetch. In the meantime, a Mauser and ammunition will be found for you from among our burghers, and you will start to practise sharp-shooting as soon as possible. Tell me," he changed the subject, "do you have any preference as to whose Field-Cornetcy you wish to join?"

Little though he knew of military procedure, Marcus was still astounded by the question. He had assumed that he would be assigned to whichever officer's contingent General Joubert saw fit. "I am not sure," he answered cautiously. "Perhaps, sir, you will explain to me the organisation of your army, so that I may decide where I would best fit in."

As General Joubert went into details, Marcus grew increasingly bewildered by the haphazard methods of Boer military organisation. Each burgher, it appeared, belonged to a commando of men. The commandos themselves were divided into two or more field-cornetcies, and these again were split into corporalships.

"I suggest you try Field-Cornet Nortjé," General Joubert advised, "and see how you get on with him."

"Very well, sir." Marcus hesitated. "May I ask why you were so ready to believe my story? Boers, in the past, have suspected me of being a spy for the British."

"I saw the way you looked at Miss van Zyl, and I had also heard that Hannes van Zyl's daughter had run away with a Jew." General Joubert smiled. "I have no illusions that you are committed to the Boer cause, or that you believe in the justice of our case. You want to marry Miss van Zyl, so you want to be accepted by her people, and most of all you want to be accepted by her family now that your own have cast you off."

Marcus bowed his head. After a moment he changed the subject. "Will we be issued with uniforms, or must I buy my own?"

General Joubert laughed. "Every man's uniform is what he happens to be wearing, or what he has in reserve in his saddle roll." He stood up. "Now, I think I had better go and find my wife, so that you may prepare Miss van Zyl for the fact that she is to leave with one of my burghers for her family's farm."

A while later, after they had breakfasted on broiled venison steak, Marcus was bidding farewell to a weeping Petronella.

"Soon, *mein tiere*, we shall be united once more. This war, when it comes, will not last for long. A few weeks, maybe; a month or perhaps two. It could not continue for more than that."

How could it possibly be otherwise, he was thinking. How could a handful of untrained, undisciplined, ill-equipped farmers, unable even to afford uniforms or regular food rations, possibly hold out for long against the might of the British Army, reinforced by troops from the Colonies and the Dominions and other parts of their Empire?

The outcome was a foregone conclusion.

6

It was a beautiful spring morning, and Jakkalsdrif looked its best as the spider approached, driven by a young man called Andries Jooste. He had been chosen by General Joubert to take Petronella home because his family farm was on the way to Jakkalsdrif, and they had been able to spend the previous night with his mother and sisters.

Marcus's horse had been sold in Wolmaransstad, and a borrowed old hack had pulled the spider from there to Andries Jooste's family farm. They had passed many groups of burghers on horseback, their bandoliers strapped across their chests, their Mausers resting on the saddle in front of them, riding to join their commandos. The tension and suppressed excitement generated by impending war were evident everywhere.

In spite of the anguish of parting from Marcus, in spite of her trepidation and uncertainty about the reception awaiting her, Petronella's throat tightened with love for this land where she had been born as she gazed around her.

The ploughed fields lay quivering in the sun, waiting to receive and nourish the seeds of next season's harvest. The white-thorn trees were bedecked in tender green leaves, and a mimosa had broken out in frothy clusters of yellow puffs. A *korhaan*, its handsome feathers glinting in the sun, ran on its long legs across their path, oblivious to anything but the locust it had spotted in the grass.

Petronella's fingernails dug into the palms of her hands as the spider swept up to the house. Pappa and Johannes, she had learnt from General Joubert, had crossed the Vaal River into the Orange Free State to join General Cronje's commando. The fact that Pappa was away from home was unfortunate from her point of view. Pappa had never been able to stay angry with her for long; if he had been at home he would have scolded her and then embraced her, forcing Mamma to forgive her also.

But Mamma on her own would be a very different proposition. In many ways she was stronger than Pappa, more inflexible. Would she turn Petronella away? Or even reach for the rawhide strap again?

Petronella's heart gave an uneasy jerk as she saw that Mamma had appeared on the stoep. Her expression was totally inscrutable.

Andries Jooste helped Petronella down from the spider, and held her elbow as they climbed the steps of the stoep. He removed his hat, and held out his hand to Mamma.

"Good morning, Mevrouw van Zyl. I am Andries Jooste, and General Joubert asked me to drive your daughter home."

Petronella had discovered that it was already common knowledge even among total strangers that a Boer girl called Petronella van Zyl had run away from home with a Jew. Now, Andries Jooste was clearly waiting for Mamma to ask questions and demand an explanation, but she did not oblige him.

She shook his hand, and turned to Petronella, kissing her cheek. The gesture could have meant anything – or nothing. Mamma had never been given to extravagant displays of affection.

She sank down on to her stinkwood chair on the stoep, inviting Andries Jooste to sit down as well. She did not include Petronella in the invitation, but that again could have meant that her daughter required no such encouragement, or else it could have meant that Mamma was ignoring her. Petronella compromised by leaning against the verandah railing.

"Will you stay for lunch?" Mamma was asking Andries Jooste.

"Thank you, Mevrouw, but I must press on, back to the encampment. I have arranged to sell the spider in Wolmaransstad. If you would lend me a fresh horse to take me as far as my family's farm, I should be grateful."

Mamma asked no questions about the owner of the spider, or why the vehicle was to be sold. She inclined her head, and said, "Of course. Gideon will be home soon from checking on the ewes and he will choose a horse for you from among those we have left."

Petronella went to the spider, and lifted down her bundle of belongings. She returned to the stoep, and addressed Mamma uncertainly. "Am I – am I to have my old room?"

"Naturally," Mamma said in an even voice. "What else?"

Petronella went inside the house, and entered her room, a spasm twisting her face as she remembered that terrible scene which had taken place in it the last time she had occupied it. Now it was neat and clean, no echoes of passion or of physical violence lingering, and the sampler stared her accusingly in the eye with its motto – 'Thy God Seest Thee'.

She shivered, and placed her belongings on the bed. When she returned to the stoep she found that Mamma was there alone with Dorothea. Gideon had obviously come home and taken Andries Jooste out to the paddock to choose a horse.

Dorothea opened her mouth to say something, but Mamma spoke

abruptly. "Dorothea, take a basket and go and pick *wilde als* for me, will you? I think an infusion of it will do you good."

It was obvious to Petronella that Mamma wanted to be alone with her, and she felt her hands become clammy with nervous anticipation. As Dorothea left the house with a basket, Petronella asked hesitantly, "Is – is Dorothea ill, Mamma?"

"No," Mamma said shortly. "She needs to take care of herself, that is all." Her voice hardened. "It is not difficult to imagine what happened to you. With the war almost upon us, your Jew decided to throw you out like so much rubbish, and he drove you to the nearest commando camp where they requisitioned his vehicle."

"No, Mamma. It was not like that at all. Marcus and I left the home of his family together, because he had quarrelled with them. They would not allow him to marry me, and they forced him to choose between me and them – "

"*They* would not allow him to marry you?" Mamma interrupted, astonishment and outrage in her voice. "You were ready to lower yourself even further, *and they would not allow it?*"

"Mamma, you don't understand how it is. I didn't either, at first. Being Jewish is – is – " Petronella could not find the words to express something which she herself only vaguely sensed. "It's different. Oh Mamma, if you could have seen how Marcus's family behaved after he'd told them he meant to marry me . . . They tore their clothing and went into mourning. And they burnt everything – every single thing – that had belonged to him or had even been used by him. He says they have burnt him out of their lives and they think of him as being dead. He can't be a Jew any longer, so he wants to become a Boer – "

Mamma made a sound of shock and derision. "You can't choose what you are, or stop being it. No one can *become* a Boer, any more than one can become a Jew."

"No, Mamma. It can be done. At least – Marcus explained to me that there is a way in which I could have become a Jew. Only, his family would not allow it. So, instead, he has become a burgher, and he says General Joubert has agreed to use him as a spy for the Boers – "

Mamma threw her hands up in a gesture of disbelief and shock. "The man must be off his head! It's quite obvious to me that your Jew has thought of a clever way of spying for the British instead! He's an *Uitlander*, and all of them stand together with the British against the Boers."

"Marcus wants to marry me, Mamma," Petronella insisted. "He wants to fight for the Boers and learn their ways so that he can live among us as one of us."

"He never will be," Mamma said flatly, "and he'll never marry you as long as I have breath in my body. Now, Petronella, I want you to ask forgiveness for what you have done, not only from me but also from the Almighty, and I want you to promise never to see the Jew again."

"No," Petronella said with an open defiance which she had never before dared to display towards Mamma. "I am sorry to have grieved you and caused trouble for the family. But I am going to marry Marcus, even if we have to starve together, even if everyone else in the world turns their faces against us."

Mamma stood up. "In that case, Petronella," she said, her voice implacable, "you have made your bed, and you must lie on it. You are my daughter, and I cannot deny you food and a roof over your head. But that is all you will have unless you come to your senses."

She went inside the house, and Petronella sat there alone on the stoep, tears trembling on her lashes. It was clear that she was going to be as isolated here on Jakkalsdrif as she had been in Johannesburg with Marcus's family.

The extent of her isolation became plain after Andries Jooste had left again, and Petronella sat down to lunch in the kitchen with Mamma and Dorothea and Gideon. Her brother might perhaps have spoken to her if he had not been too embarrassed by the memory of seeing her naked in bed with Marcus, or too daunted by the attitude of Mamma and Dorothea, neither of whom acknowledged Petronella's presence by as much as a glance. She sat there, listening to the conversation which excluded her.

"I'm going to need more help, Mamma," Gideon was saying. "I've even got Mwende sharing the work of sowing the bottom fields with her brother Koos. Apart from the spring lambs which will be born any day now, two of the cows have calved, and I can't cope with the milking as well as finishing off the ploughing. Now that we have so few horses left, I have to use oxen, and they are cumbersome and slow."

Petronella cleared her throat. "What – what has happened to the men in the *stad* that you are so short-handed?"

Even the answer to her question was not directed at her, but woven into Mamma's observation. "We shall all have to put our shoulders to the wheel, with so many of the younger men in the *stad* going off with Pappa and Johannes to take charge of the spare horses and help transport all their equipment."

Petronella did not venture another question or remark. After the meal she stood up and, in silence, cleared the table, carrying the dishes through into the scullery to wash them. She had been wondering why Mwende was not in the house, and until Gideon had mentioned that the girl was helping with the sowing it had not occurred to

Petronella that life on Jakkalsdrif was going to be very different, in practical terms, with the men away at war. She decided to take upon herself tasks which would give her an escape from the house, and from the conspiracy of silence shared by her family against her.

After she had finished washing the dishes and put them away, Petronella picked up her *kappie* and went outside. She stood still for a moment, listening to a duet of love sung between the inseparable male and female shrike. They perched together on the spiky branch of a sweet-thorn tree whose scented white flowers filled the air.

"*Bokmakierie!*" called the male, hopping to another branch so that the sun flashed on his green feathers and yellow breast. "*Bokmakierie!*"

"*Kokkewiet, kokkewiet,*" sweetly replied his mate, cocking her head and displaying her black throat.

Lucky shrikes, Petronella thought wistfully. They chose their partners and there was no one to gainsay them, no one to place obstacles in their path. Then she watched as a sunbird perched on the sweet-thorn tree as well, dipping its long curved bill to drink nectar from the flowers, its long straight tail with its blue-green sheen stuck in the air. She sighed. Presumably there would be just as much consternation and hostility in the bird-world if a shrike were to choose a sunbird as its mate instead of another shrike. Like, it seemed, had been directed by nature as well as by man to stick to like, and woe betide those who sought to break this rule.

Her mouth tightened obstinately. She would not give Marcus up. Nothing anyone might do or say would persuade her not to marry him.

As she skirted the *stad* she saw old Bolih leaning on his stick. He greeted her as if she had never been away, and spoke to her in Fanakalo, grumbling that so many of the men of the *stad* had gone away that the women were having to help with the farm work, and so there was no one with time to brew *magouw*, the fermented mealie-meal which was one of the few pleasures left to Bolih. He did not seem to realise that a war was on the point of breaking out, and that the men had gone with Pappa and Johannes to help where they could in the fighting of it.

Petronella accepted his invitation to sit inside his hut for a gossip. The floor had been made of a mixture of pounded-up antheaps and ox blood, which gave a hard, clean surface. A fire had been laid in the centre but had not yet been lit, and she sat down on a bench which Bolih had carved himself and listened to his stories about the *Tokoloshe*, the evil being who lured young people to rivers in order to drown them.

As she left his hut later Petronella reflected on what a bitter home-coming this had been, with old Bolih the only person eager and willing to talk to her.

What had begun as an aimless walk, an instinctive escape from the house and an urge to renew her relationship with Jakkalsdrif, had brought Petronella to the lower fields skirting the Vaal River. She saw Mwende and her younger brother Koos, slowly walking up and down the ploughed furrows as they trickled mealie-seeds through their fingers, pausing every now and again to withdraw another handful of seeds from a small sack suspended on a belt around their waists.

Mwende had reached the end of a furrow and was turning to begin sowing the next one when she saw Petronella. She ripped the belt from her waist and threw it, with the bagful of seeds, on the ground and then she came running, her beautiful brown face glowing, her teeth very white in a smile of unqualified welcome and delight.

"Au, Nonnie!" she cried, and they embraced one another. "You home! You marry your man, Nonnie?"

"No, Mwende. Not yet." Petronella straightened her shoulders and stuck out her chin. "But I will." Her mood changed, and she grinned at Mwende. "Oh, I'm so glad to see you! I've missed you. Come, I'll help you with the sowing. Give me enough seed to fill my pockets and I'll do the furrow next to yours so that we can talk."

Koos greeted her more restrainedly, with a shy smile, and the three of them worked together. Petronella told them about Johannesburg, and while Koos tended to disapprove of and distrust such concepts as electric light, and gave it as his opinion that witchcraft had to be behind it all, Mwende was lost in fascination with everything she learnt.

That day set the pattern for Petronella's return to Jakkalsdrif. To escape from the house and avoid her family, who continued to ostracise her, she spent most of her time out of doors. Gone were the days when she was Pappa's precious little girl who had to be sheltered from such realities as calving cows, her only outdoor labours confined to growing flowers in her small garden. When the sowing had been done she learnt to milk the cows, and she helped with the harrowing once the mealie-plants had shown their green heads.

It hurt that no one ever asked her to do anything, or acknowledged what she did do. It was not that she wanted special recognition, for she was not the only one taking on new tasks. Mamma, while maintaining all her usual housewifely chores, was planting and sowing seeds in the vegetable garden with the help of two young boys from the *stad*. Even Dorothea was hand-rearing two orphan lambs. But by their attitude, her family were saying that it did not matter to them whether she chose to help or not, because she was there on sufferance and no longer part of them.

From the cryptic comments which passed between Mamma and

Dorothea, Petronella gathered that the latter was pregnant, and in the evenings they would sit together on the stoep and talk in low voices. Gideon, no doubt feeling oppressed by the exclusive company of females, would saddle up his horse and ride over to visit a friend on a neighbouring farm, while Petronella sat alone, isolated and lonely, missing Marcus with a great, aching emptiness inside her and wishing the war would end so that he could come and rescue her from her existence as the family outcast.

They received sporadic news of the war, usually by means of reports percolating from Johannesburg and spread by word of mouth. In that flat country, with no hills or valleys to interrupt the vista of the rolling veld, the old practice of sending heliograph messages by means of mirrors was revived, and almost every day mirrors flashed in the sun from some farmhouse or other, announcing that war-news had been received and inviting neighbours to call and become acquainted with it.

In this way they learnt that Boer commandos had already started to gather around Newcastle, Dundee and Ladysmith in Natal. A Boer column had pushed up to Elandslaagte and seized the coal-fields and also a railway station and a supply train on its way to Dundee.

Gideon fretted because he was too young to go to war; Mamma said grimly that right was on the side of the Boers, and that with the help of the Almighty they would smite the Amalekites hip and thigh, and Dorothea said she felt sure Johannes would fight to the bitter end and lay down his life if need be. She looked both smugly pious and resigned as she said it, as if she were making a personal sacrifice. Petronella remained silent and wished passionately and treacherously that the might of the British would quickly end the conflict so that she could be reunited with Marcus.

She longed for the sight of his beautiful face with those grooves in his cheeks and his blue eyes, for the sound of his piquant Dutch, for the feel of his hands on her body. She felt wretched and lonely, and more and more she was being ground down by the isolation in which she found herself.

She did not care whether Dorothea spoke to her or not. She despised her sister-in-law with her narrow views and her pious ways. Gideon's silence, too, she could bear with, for the gap in their ages was immeasurably widened by the gap in their experience of life, and they would have had little to say to each other even if he were not ostracising her. No, it was Mamma's implacable, flint-like rejection which hurt most.

In her isolation, Petronella turned increasingly to Mwende for companionship, and a new bond was forged between them. Mwende, too, was in conflict with her elders and the two girls spent much time in examining ways and means of outwitting fate and Mwende's grandmother.

The old woman wished her to accept as a husband a man who had offered eight oxen as her bride-price, and only the interruption of war had saved Mwende from being summarily forced into a marriage with a man whom she disliked, for he had accompanied his master on commando.

"He old, Nonnie Petronella," she brooded, her dark eyes flashing with scorn and passion. "He all wrinkled up, and he bury one wife already. He want mother for the children he already got, and to make more babies with me. I want – " She shook her head in frustration and despondency. "I don't want wrinkled-up old man."

"Perhaps," Petronella comforted her, "he won't come back from the war. Since he's old, he might get sick and die on commando. Or perhaps, without him to look after them, his cattle will die and he won't be able to pay the *lobolo* for you."

Mwende grinned, instantly cheered, and blithely contributed another callous possibility which might save her from an unwanted marriage. "Or perhaps my grandmamma she die, eh Nonnie? Then I go with you when you marry your man."

So the two of them hoped and dreamt and waited for the war to end, and Petronella tried to cope with the blank wall of Mamma's relentless, unfeeling repudiation.

After one brief shower early in the month, just sufficient to allow the seeds to germinate and thrust their tender green leaves above the surface of the soil, there had been no rain at all, and each day they scanned the sky anxiously for a sign of gathering clouds.

One night, after everyone else had retired, Petronella thought she heard a distant clap of thunder. It had been hot and oppressive all day, and since she had been unable to fall asleep in any case, she decided to go and sit on the stoep and watch the storm if it came.

She did not trouble to take a candle or a lantern with her, but felt her way through the house to the front door and on to the stoep. She leant over the railing, drawing a deep breath to try to detect the smell of approaching rain and listening to the cicadas snapping in the grass. A sudden sound behind her made her turn.

Her eyes had become used to the dark, and she could see Mamma's bulk squeezed into her favourite chair, her head in her hands, and slowly Petronella realised that the sound she had heard had been a sob.

Mamma weeping! Never, as far back as she could remember, had Petronella ever known Mamma to shed a tear in defeat or sorrow. But there she was, sitting in the dark, her face buried in her hands and her shoulders heaving.

Petronella moved towards her, touching her arm. "Mamma – has there been bad news? Has Pappa or Johannes – "

Mamma shook her head. "Then why are you weeping?" Petronella asked.

Mamma removed her hands from her face. "You – *you* ask me that? Do you think it gives me pleasure to treat you like a stepchild?"

Bewildered and moved, Petronella knelt in front of her. "Oh Mamma, let us make friends!"

"Then help me! Give up the thought of marrying the Jew!"

"I can't, Mamma," Petronella said helplessly.

"Why not?" There was genuine perplexity in Mamma's voice. "Is he rich, Petronella? Does he own land and livestock? Can he offer you a good home of your own?"

"No, Mamma."

"Then why? *Why?* Why him? There are other men, Petronella – "

"Mamma, I don't want any other man, but even if I did, do you think any young Boer would wish to marry me when everyone knows that I ran away with Marcus?"

Mamma was silent for a moment, and then she burst out, "I would rather you died an old maid than marry the Jew! In any case, you couldn't marry him until you've turned twenty-one, because Pappa would not give his consent."

"Mamma," Petronella said quietly, "if you and Pappa force me to, I'll live with Marcus as his wife until we *can* marry. But I don't think Pappa would be able to bear the shame of that, so he'll give his consent."

The deep sigh Mamma heaved signalled that she, too, believed Pappa would submit to the lesser of two evils. "If only you understood the grief you are causing with this obsession you have with the Jew."

"Mamma, I wish you wouldn't call him 'the Jew' as if – as if you were using dirty words. I can't give Marcus up. Even if I wanted to – which I don't and never will – I couldn't give him up. Not when he has already sacrificed so much for me. Can't you see that?"

"I can see only one thing." Mamma's voice had hardened again. "You might be able to force Pappa to give his consent, but if you marry the Jew you'll cut yourself off from your own people. Pappa and I will not lift a finger to help you. How will you live?"

"I've already thought of that. We'll become *bywoners*." Diplomatically, she rephrased the plan she had discussed with Marcus. "If no one else will let us build a *pondok* and work on their land, Mijnheer van Tonder will, because he is bad friends with Pappa and he'll know Pappa wouldn't like it."

"You'd sink that low!" Mamma exclaimed harshly. "*Bywoners* on the land of your father's enemy! Well, Petronella, if you marry the

Jew, Pappa and I will wash our hands of you, both while we are alive and after we are dead. You'll inherit nothing. All my personal bits and pieces will go to Dorothea, and so too will the Delft porcelain my grandmother brought with her from the Cape."

Petronella said nothing. The Delft porcelain meant far more than just pretty blue-and-white plates and soup bowls and meat dishes. It meant continuity, a family link stretching all the way back to the distant ancestor who had brought it from Holland. In its own way, being deprived of her rightful inheritance of the porcelain would be as great a repudiation as the actions of Marcus's parents had been in burning his memory out of their lives.

"And if you have children," Mamma went on inexorably, "Pappa and I will never see them or acknowledge them. They will never know the families of either their mother or their father. Think of that."

Petronella rose and went to stand by the railing again, staring into the night. Could Mamma not see, she wondered with despair, how useless all her threats were?

Because the more sacrifices were demanded from herself and Marcus, the more closely they would become bound and committed to each other.

7

A constant heat-haze rippled above Jakkalsdrif's waving fields of corn now that spring had turned into summer. Almost as predictably as clockwork, on at least five afternoons out of seven heavy clouds would build up, turning the sky cobalt blue. Suddenly, with a great fury, a storm would break and a brief, violent cloudburst would revive the hot and gasping earth. It would end as suddenly as it had begun, with a few distant flashes of lightning and desultory thunder; the sky would once again become hard and bright and clear but leaving plants and animals and humans and every other living thing refreshed until the next day.

News of the war still reached them on Jakkalsdrif in sporadic, unconfirmed reports, but no word came at all from Pappa or Johannes or, uppermost in Petronella's concern, from Marcus.

"We must," Dorothea said, shifting her increasing bulk in the chair, "trust in the Lord and go on praying for their safety."

They were all sitting on the stoep, trying to catch a stray breeze, for this was one of the few afternoons when it was clear a storm would not be building up. Gideon had been cleaning his Mauser, and as he leant it against the wall he said in a brooding voice, "I can ride as fast as Johannes, and shoot as sharply. And so can most of my friends. We wouldn't have lost the battle of Elandslaagte if the generals had allowed us to go on commando as well."

Mamma said tartly, "The day the commandos have to rely on the help of young boys not yet out of short trousers, that will be the day when we might as well hang out the white flag!"

Petronella, as usual, had been sitting apart from the others on the stoep, gazing towards the river and remembering another scorching hot afternoon like this one, when she had gone to her secret place and met Marcus.

An exclamation escaped her. "There are horsemen coming this way! They must have crossed the river at the drift, from the Free State side!"

For once, everyone forgot that she was an outcast whose utterances were to be ignored. Gideon sprang up and shaded his eyes with his hand as he watched the approaching horsemen, and Mamma heaved herself out of her chair.

"They're burghers," she said. "They'll be hungry and thirsty. I'll go and put the coffee on and cut some milk tart."

The riders were four men dressed in moleskin, their deep-brimmed hats casting their bearded faces into shadow, the sun glinting on the bandoliers across their chests. As they reached the house they dismounted.

Petronella was surprised and mildly interested to discover that Gerrit du Toit was one of the burghers. He looked older, leaner and harder, but she felt as indifferent towards him as she had in the past. Warfare or time had done something to stimulate the growth of his facial hair, for instead of the previous insignificant moustache he now sported a full set of whiskers.

He avoided Petronella's eyes and grinned at Mamma, offering his hand. "It's good to see you, Tant' Lenie." He introduced his companions, and they all sat down on the stoep to drink coffee and eat milk tart.

The four of them, it transpired, had decided to take advantage of a lull in the particular hostilities in which their commando had been engaged, and ride home for a brief visit.

"We're holding the British under siege at Ladysmith," Gerrit reported, "and the way things are going we'll keep them trapped inside the town until next Christmas!"

"What happened?" Gideon demanded. "Tell us everything! All we heard was that after Elandslaagte, when our commando there lost half their number and two of their big guns, the survivors joined up with other commandos and pushed towards Ladysmith."

Gerrit nodded. "Our commandos crept up on the town from every side. There are low kopjes ringing Ladysmith and we could see the British building their forts and redoubts there. They didn't have the slightest suspicion of our presence, let alone that we had them surrounded in a semi-circle from the heights beyond – "

Another burgher put in with a chuckle, "And they certainly never dreamt that we'd dragged a 'Long Tom' up Pepworth Hill – "

"What," Mamma interrupted with a frown, "is this Long Tom you're talking about?"

"It's a breech-loading Creusot gun, Tant' Lenie, firing ninety-four-pound shells at a range of up to ten thousand yards – "

"Never mind," she stopped him drily. "'Long Tom' will do."

"Well," Gerrit took up his tale again, "from our positions we could see right down into the plains below, and we knew they must have had some news of our presence when the British infantry began to move forward in wave after wave and firing at Long Hill – "

"This Long Hill," Mamma demanded. "Is that also a gun?"

"No, Tant' Lenie. It's the name of one of the heights surrounding Ladysmith. Some of the burghers had dug themselves in there. We were almost deafened by the sound of shells exploding on Long Hill. I can't describe the hellish sound . . ." For a moment he lost his acquired lean, hard look of a battle-worn burgher, and his Adam's apple worked, revealing youthful awe and remembered fear.

"Try," Gideon urged, his expression making it plain that he wished he had been present during the fighting and that the next-best thing was to hear it graphically described.

"Well," Gerrit countered, "*you* try to imagine the screeching and whining of shells, and the crack of thousands of rifles, and the horses joining in by screaming and whinnying!"

Gideon nodded, his expression of excitement showing that he was indeed picturing himself living through the scene. "What happened next? I'll bet the burghers on Long Hill gave as good as they got!"

"No. That was part of our strategy, you see. The burghers had dug themselves in so well that they presented hardly any target, and the fact that they didn't answer the fire at all rattled the British."

"Not nearly as much," one of Gerrit's companions put in with relish, "as it rattled them when they suddenly found themselves being fired upon from Pepworth Hill instead!"

"That's right!" Gerrit laughed. "And *Allemagtig*, if the mules of the British mountain battery didn't choose that very moment to stampede! The enemy were thrown into chaos, and the whole force had to surrender. The remainder of the British scuttled back into the safety of Ladysmith, where our commandos are holding them under siege."

Gideon sighed wistfully. "I'd give my right arm to be there!"

Mamma frowned at him, and addressed Gerrit. "Do you have news of my husband and of Johannes?"

"They are both well, Tant' Lenie, and send all their love." He stood up. "We had better press on now to our homes."

The four men offered thanks for the hospitality they had received, and almost as an afterthought one of them glanced at Petronella and said, "I have some letters for you, 'Juffrouw van Zyl."

Her heart bounced in her chest, and the blood thundered through her veins. The letters were from Marcus, of course. She did not care that Gerrit and the other burghers were staring pointedly into the middle distance, or that Mamma was glowering and Dorothea wearing her look of prim condemnation or that Gideon had flushed with embarrassment. The batch of letters was removed from a saddle-bag and she escaped to her room with them as soon as the burghers had ridden away.

"I cannot be positive that you will one day receive my letters," one of them began, "but I address them to you in hope, and also because it comforts me to do so. My love for you becomes stronger each day, my Petronella, my *harte-dief*. (I have learnt that word from the Boers. They delight to teach me their sayings and their slang, but I have to take care, for sometimes they tease me and teach me words that are not suitable in polite company.) Perhaps I will learn in time to distinguish between their slang and their curse-words, but I do not believe I shall ever learn how their minds function. They have an inflexible belief in their ability to win this war, in spite of the fact that they have so few men, so little food and scarcely any sources of supply. They swear to fight on to the finish, unto death itself. I do not share this ambition of theirs, and to you alone will I admit that I wish above all else for the war to be over so that you and I will be together once again."

The next letter he had written sounded a good deal more cheerful. "Today the sun shines and I have a feeling that *alles sal regkom*! (My friend Piet Nortjé taught that expression to me, so I know it is not something indecent!) I have shot my first blesbok and we shared it for our supper. Only when my hunger had been satisfied did I remember I had eaten *trefah* food. Biltong, of course, is also *trefah* but perhaps because it is dry it does not seem to be so. It begins to seem possible that I might change myself from a Jew to a Boer, but I have to confess to you that on Fridays I cannot prevent my thoughts from dwelling on the lighting of the Shabbat candles and on the blessing and the cutting of the *chalah*. But I am attempting to force myself to forget it, and on Sundays I join the Boers for the service of the Dutch Reformed Church, and I am also taking instruction in the Catechism. But aai, Petronella, my heart still refuses to do what my head dictates it must, and *believe*. Perhaps that will come, like the learning of Boer sayings and slang."

Another letter reported ruefully that Marcus had had no occasion as yet to act as a spy for the Boers, and that he could never hope to equal them as a sharp-shooter. "It is a fanciful notion, I know, but they give the impression almost that they were born on the backs of horses," the letter went on, "with a Mauser in one hand. I have to confess to you, my darling Petronella, that I am no longer convinced the war will end quickly. These people of yours possess a discipline which comes from inside. A British officer will order his men as to what they should do, while a Boer's instinct dictates what he must do and he does it without waiting to be commanded.

"We are now in the British Colony of Natal, but many people – despite being British subjects – are friendly towards us and disposed to help the Boers, so that they present us with food. Last Sunday I was baptised as a Christian," he added, almost as an afterthought, but he didn't go further into the subject of his conversion. "Today," the letter continued, "we are preparing to ride to Ladysmith where we plan to join other commandos."

Petronella put the letters away and went out to the stoep, where Mamma and Dorothea were still sitting. "Marcus's commando is also taking part in the siege of Ladysmith," she said.

Surely, she thought, the news that Marcus was sharing the same experiences as Pappa and Johannes, facing the danger of the final confrontation with the besieged British which must inevitably come, would soften Mamma's attitude?

But she did not react at all to Petronella's news, and instead addressed a pointed remark at Dorothea. Since that night when Petronella had caught her mother weeping, Mamma had resumed her implacable rejection of her daughter without showing any further signs of weakening.

"Marcus has been baptised as a Christian," Petronella tried again.

Mamma gave her a blank, impersonal look and stood up. "I'm going to collect the eggs," she told Dorothea. "The speckled hen has been laying away from the nest again."

Petronella turned back inside the house, fighting tears of angry defiance. Mamma need not think she would weaken either. She would put up with the repudiation and the stony silence for as long as she had to. Marcus, after all, was having to put up with a good deal more. There had been nothing to stop him from going back to his parents and telling them that he had given her up. He could have stayed safely in Johannesburg with them, aloof from the war, or even fled to Cape Town as so many other *Uitlanders* from Johannesburg had done. Instead, he was enduring a life of hardship and danger, often cold and wet and hungry, converting to Christianity and trying his best to learn Boer ways. For as long as Marcus could endure, so could she.

All the passion of her nature, for which there was no other outlet, she expended on work. She learnt more about crops and livestock during those wretchedly lonely months than she had ever learnt in the rest of her life as a farmer's daughter.

More and more small bands of burghers trickled across the Vaal River, wading through the shallow drift with their horses. Some had been wounded and were going home to recover; others were simply intent on paying short visits to their families, but because the drift happened to be situated on Jakkalsdrif's boundary all of them called at the farmhouse before riding on. None of them brought more letters from Marcus, but they all had news of the war to impart.

During the fearsome battle of Colenso, they reported, when the first attempt was made by the British to relieve Ladysmith, the enemy had suffered so many losses that they had withdrawn their whole force, and in the meantime Kimberley was also besieged by the Boers, and with battles fought at Stormberg and Magersfontein, there were further heavy losses for the British. Vastly outnumbered though they were, the Boers were excellent horsemen and marksmen and they blended so well with their sunbaked landscape that the British were discovering them to be a formidable enemy indeed.

· The New Year dawned, bringing with it a new century. The mealies stood high in Jakkalsdrif's fields, slowly turning a golden colour as they ripened in the sun; the sheep and cattle were sleek and fat and the future held great promise, for were the Boers not wiping the noses of the enemy in the dust? It could not be long before the British decided that this struggle was not worth so many ignominious defeats, and they withdrew their forces.

Mamma celebrated the beginning of 1900 by baking huge batches of sweet biscuits and by ordering a sheep to be butchered, some of the meat distributed in the *stad*, and the rest roasted for a family feast of thanksgiving.

One night in February Petronella was woken up by a sound like a cow lowing in distress. She jumped out of bed and hurriedly lit a candle. The sound had come from inside the house.

Outside her door, she found Mamma hurrying towards the kitchen, a lantern in her hand. For once, she forgot that she was not speaking to Petronella, for she said urgently, "Get the fire going in the stove and boil water. Dorothea's time has come."

Mamma hurried away again, and Petronella attended to the tasks she had been given, enormously grateful to have been drawn into a family crisis, even if it did concern Dorothea, whom she despised. She boiled water and carried it in jugfuls to her sister-in-law's bedroom, but Mamma would not allow her to enter. Gideon rose too, awakened by all the noise, but he soon found himself banished back to his room. This was female business, and he had no part to play in it.

Towards dawn Dorothea uttered a long, animal bellow, and a moment later there was the sound of an infant screaming at the top of its tiny lungs. Petronella went to stand in the kitchen doorway, trying to feel that she had taken part in a miracle of nature. All she felt, instead, was fatigue and a growing irritation with the baby's continuous screams.

The sun had risen when Mamma came bustling out of Dorothea's room. "It's a boy," she told Petronella brusquely. "Dorothea says you may go and look at him if you wish."

The grudging bestowal of this favour angered her, and she wanted to retort that she had no interest in Dorothea's brat. But knowing that it would be a mistake to reject this small olive branch, Petronella hid her feelings and went to look at her small nephew.

She found him quite grotesque, with his scarlet face and his angry slit-like eyes, but she murmured politely, "He is beautiful."

Dorothea gave a tired, complacent smile. "Yes. I am going to call him after my father."

Petronella said nothing. Dorothea's father was called Gabriel. It was a fittingly absurd name for an absurd scrap of humanity.

For weeks after the birth of the baby, women arrived by pony and trap from neighbouring farms to admire the infant and exclaim over him and to bring small gifts of knitted or crocheted garments to protect him against the cold of the coming winter.

Petronella did not share their adoration of the baby. It was not because he was the son of Dorothea, for whom she had no liking or respect, or even because Mamma was making such a fuss over her first grandchild while she was once more rejecting her only daughter. Petronella simply could not see what there was about the baby to make other women wish to hold him or touch his cheek or have him grip their fingers. Even Mwende regarded it as a privilege and not a chore to care for the baby whenever Dorothea was engaged upon some other task.

To Petronella, the baby was ugly and irritatingly noisy. She did not have the slightest desire to pick him up or hold him, and she experienced a feeling of revulsion whenever she saw Dorothea breast-feeding the infant, which her sister-in-law did with such exaggerated delicacy, even when there were only other women present, that Petronella would have found it laughable if she had not been so disgusted by the slurping, sucking noises coming from beneath the cloth which Dorothea had tied about her neck to hide both baby and breasts from sight.

Then other events began to overshadow the birth of Dorothea's son. More burghers crossed the Vaal River, looking drawn and weary, and reported that General Cronje had surrendered with almost four thousand fighting men after suffering heavy bombardment by the British.

This news threw a dreadful pall of anxiety and fear over Jakkalsdrif for both Pappa and Johannes had been serving under Cronje. There was no way of knowing whether they had been among the fallen burghers or whether they had been taken prisoner by the enemy. Dorothea went about with reddened eyes, her lips constantly moving in silent prayer. Mamma became more grim-faced than ever but carried on, doggedly and dry-eyed, with her chores, while Gideon fingered his Mauser wistfully, his expression revealing his burning desire to go and avenge whatever fate had befallen his father and brother. Petronella worried about their safety too, but a part of her mind gave thanks for the fact that Marcus had joined General Joubert and not General Cronje's commando.

Other burghers crossed the Vaal River, and brought news that, within a week of Cronje's surrender, Ladysmith had been relieved. Petronella blanked out of her mind completely the possibility that Marcus might have been among those who had fallen in the battle for Ladysmith.

It was now becoming clear to even the most obstinate optimist that the Boers could not win the war after all. Everything was going the way of the British. The Mayor of Bloemfontein, Petronella heard a visiting burgher announce grimly, had surrendered to Lord Roberts, and Lord Kitchener was calling on the Boers to surrender. No one at Jakkalsdrif expected them to do so, even though Petronella prayed silently that they would, so that Marcus could come back for her.

The harvest was being gathered in when they heard that the British had invaded the Transvaal, and that Johannesburg had been taken by them. The war was now on their very doorstep, and surely, Petronella reasoned, the Boers would surrender at last.

She had been out in the fields one day, helping Mwende and the other women from the *stad* with the last of the mealie harvest, and when she returned to the house she stopped in her tracks, staring at the stoep in disbelief. Johannes was home! He was sitting alone on the stoep, nursing his infant son.

Petronella ran up the steps to the stoep, crying excitedly, "Is the war over? Is that why you've been released? And Pappa – ?"

"The war is not over, Petronella." He gave her a sombre look. He seemed older, she thought, and he had lost so much weight that his face had a gaunt appearance. "Pappa and I had left Cronje by the time of his surrender. We didn't agree with his campaign and so we went to join General Louis Botha instead."

"Oh! And Pappa is safe?"

"Quite safe. I decided to come home for a short while and meet my son."

Petronella sat down beside him on the stoep. "Have you seen anything of Marcus?" She asked the question with some defiance, half-expecting a snub from her brother and a blank refusal to discuss Marcus at all.

Instead, Johannes said, "No, I have not seen him." He hesitated, and did not meet her eyes. "Petronella – " he began.

But whatever reproach he had presumably intended to deliver remained unspoken, for at that moment Mamma and Dorothea appeared from inside the house, flushed and excited, apparently having prepared Johannes's favourite dish for supper. They sat down, and

Petronella retreated to her customary position outside the family circle, listening to the conversation, knowing that any contribution she might make to it would be ignored.

"Matters are going badly for us," Johannes reported sombrely. "The British are occupying much of the Free State and they have driven us out of Natal. Lord Roberts has invited us to lay down our arms. A few 'hands-uppers' turned in their Mausers and surrendered to the British. But the vast majority of us have taken the oath of allegiance and we are determined to fight to the bitter end."

Gideon arrived home then from the village of Doornboomstad, to which he had taken a wagonload of harvested mealies to be ground into meal at the mills. He swooped upon his brother with disbelief and delight, and when he learnt that Pappa was safe and fighting with General Botha, he demanded minute details about the war. At the end of Johannes's report he said gloomily, "All the excitement will be over by the time I am considered old enough to fight."

Johannes gave a glimmer of a smile. "Don't be too sure, little brother. The British might think we are finished, but they will learn otherwise. We're planning to take to the hills and carry on guerilla warfare if we're left with no other choice."

The conversation turned to farm matters then, but Petronella noticed that Johannes did not seem to share their own pride and satisfaction in the good harvest. He cleared his throat, and then he explained the reason for his reservations.

"Farms in the Free State have been visited by British troops. They demand food; mealies and livestock for butchering, and also forage for their animals. Now that they have invaded the Transvaal and taken Johannesburg, they are likely to do the same here. Jakkalsdrif's good harvest is likely to end up in the possession of the British troops."

"I should like to see them try!" Mamma said with menace. "I can handle a Mauser as well as any man."

"Mamma," Johannes pleaded, "you must not resist if they come here, demanding supplies. They would take what they want in any case, and would do a great deal of damage besides. Promise me you won't resist."

"I can't, Johannes. You must know me better than that."

He sighed. "Yes. Pappa warned me you would take this attitude. I have a message for you from him. He says that if you can't bring yourself to contemplate giving in to the enemy, you must leave Jakkalsdrif so that you will not be here when they arrive."

"And allow them to help themselves to whatever they want?" Mamma demanded indignantly.

"You could take most of it with you, and go and join one of the women's laagers."

"And what are they?" Mamma wanted to know.

"Many women in the Free State, who like yourself would not entertain the thought of freely giving the British what they want, have packed up their families and as much of their livestock as they could take, together with all their valuables, and set out with ox-wagons to follow the Boer commandos."

Mamma gave him a sharp look. "Is that why you came, Johannes? To force me out of my home?"

"Yes, Mamma. It was mainly for that reason." He gazed out at Jakkalsdrif's fields, almost completely harvested now, only the mealie-stubble waiting to be ploughed back into the earth. "We have three wagons and enough oxen to pull them. One could carry the family and our personal possessions. A second could take the people from the *stad* with their belongings and the third one could be loaded with mealie-meal from the harvest and other provisions. We would take with us all the sheep and a milk-cow or two. The rest of the cattle will have to stay, I'm afraid, and we'll just have to hope most of them will still be here when the war is over. The British will probably take a few for slaughtering, but that cannot be helped."

Mamma sighed heavily. "If Pappa thinks it would be for the best, I suppose I shall have to agree."

Petronella's heart was hammering in her chest. If they were to follow the Boer commandos by ox-wagon, it was not in the least impossible that they might catch up with Marcus's commando. She had resigned herself, a long time ago, to the knowledge that he would not take leave and visit Jakkalsdrif, for he would sense himself to be unwelcome there. But if she were in the Orange Free State, part of a women's laager, and he learnt of her whereabouts, there would be nothing to stop him from coming to see her, because a women's laager would be neutral ground. Yes, the move from Jakkalsdrif was to be welcomed.

"You'll have to give us time to get ready," Mamma told Johannes. "I'll have to do some baking, and we must also butcher a steer and cut up the meat for salting and drying."

"I'll help you, Mamma!" In her eagerness, Petronella had forgotten that Mamma was not speaking to her and wanted nothing of her.

Mamma gave her the familiar closed, blank look of rejection, and began to discuss plans for the removal from Jakkalsdrif with Dorothea. Johannes's voice cut through theirs, as if what he had to say was important, and necessary for all of them to hear.

"Petronella," he said, "I have some news for you. I promised Field-Cornet Piet Nortjé that I would deliver a message to you."

"Oh . . ." *Marcus's Field-Cornet.* She waited.

Johannes looked away. "You know, of course, why General Joubert allowed Marcus Koen to go on commando?"

"Yes." She gave her brother a bewildered look. "He wanted to fight for the Boers – "

"He offered to spy for them." Reluctant admiration entered Johannes's eyes. "He infiltrated a British camp, posing as a Jewish diamond dealer just returned from a visit abroad, and said he wanted to get into besieged Kimberley to join his family. He pretended to speak only French and Hebrew so he was able to overhear much valuable information and pass it on to the Boers."

Petronella's eyes shone. "Does Pappa know that? Does he know how useful Marcus is being to the Boers?"

"He knows, Petronella," Johannes said quietly. "He also knows what I have to tell you further. Marcus became a shade too daring. He went back to the British camp one night and set fire to their munitions tent. It blew up sooner than he'd expected it would, and he was caught before he could get away."

Her heart felt as if it were being squeezed in the palm of someone's hand, and a paralysing numbness crept over her. After a while she managed through trembling lips, "Wh-what do they d-do to spies?"

Johannes looked away from her. "They shoot them, Petronella."

A roaring sound which had begun in her ears grew into a crescendo. She felt the floor of the stoep tilting underneath her feet, and just before she slid into a faint she had the impression that the railings were pressing down upon her.

When she regained consciousness, she found herself stretched out on the bench with her head resting on Mamma's ample lap. Something cold and wet was being applied to her forehead and for a moment she was filled with bewilderment. With a searing, unbearable pain she remembered.

Marcus had been shot. He was dead. Marcus, her exotic love with his languages and his silk shirts and his beautiful face and perfect body was forever lost to her. She would never know his touch again, never look into his blue eyes, see the grooves appear beside his mouth, listen to his voice as he pronounced long Dutch words in his own unique way, never be pleasured by him again . . .

She was incapable of making a sound, but a scream of agony was echoing through her mind. Above it, she heard Mamma's voice. "It was God's will, child."

Petronella stared at her. *Was it, Mamma? Was it the will of your own special God, because you had been praying to Him that it might happen?* She could no more utter the words aloud than she could give voice to the scream inside her head.

She felt a hand on her arm, and Dorothea's voice reached her. "Let me help you to your room. You'll feel better after you've been lying down for a while."

Violently, Petronella pushed her away. *Are you mad, Dorothea? How could I possibly feel better? How could anything in the world make me feel better?*

She stood up and began to pace the stoep, hugging her arms about her breasts as if the pain which racked her was physical, consumed by such agony that she was scarcely able to function rationally. She heard Mamma's voice again but this time it seemed to be coming from a long distance away.

"Cry, Petronella. Tears will help."

But she could not weep. The searing loss and anguish which engulfed her would not allow the balm of tears. She realised, suddenly, that she was banging her head against one of the uprights of the verandah railing and even though it produced a shooting physical pain she could not stop, for any kind of pain was preferable to the mental devastation which was consuming her.

Johannes grabbed her and forced her away from the railing. She sank down on a chair and stared blindly in front of her, deaf to what the others were saying, her eyes wide and fixed upon an image of Marcus lying dead and spattered with blood upon some sun-baked plain.

She sat there on the stoep until it grew dark, and Johannes came to guide her forcibly into the kitchen and made her sit down at the supper table. She stared in front of her, her food untouched. Now that nothing mattered any more Mamma was talking to her again, pleading with her to eat something, but she had retreated into a limbo from which she could not be reached.

Later, she did not undress for bed. She lay down, fully clothed, and gazed unblinkingly at the ceiling. The scream in her mind had changed to a monotonous, repetitive chant. *Marcus is dead. Marcus has been shot. I've lost my love. My love has gone. Marcus is dead . . .*

During the following two days an unconnected part of her mind knew that Mamma and Dorothea and Mwende and the other women from the *stad* were engaged in an orgy of preparations for leaving Jakkalsdrif. Soap was being made and so were candles. Johannes had slaughtered a steer and cut up the meat and salted it, and it was hanging, wrapped in muslin, suspended from the beams of the barn to dry. Gideon was checking the three ox-wagons and preparing them for their loads. Petronella knew all this but she took no part, and felt totally uninvolved. She sat down on the stoep and listened to the dreadful chant inside her own head.

On the afternoon of the third day Mamma tried to bully her out of the paralysing grief which gripped her. "You'll kill yourself, Petronella, if you carry on like this! You don't eat and you don't sleep. And what has happened to your self-respect, child? You have not washed since the day before yesterday, or changed your clothing, or brushed your hair! Do you have any idea what you look like? If nothing else, let Mwende heat up some bath-water for you!"

Petronella turned her head slowly and looked at Mamma, and uttered the first words she had spoken in two days. "Why?" she asked. "What difference would it make?"

Mamma began to speak again but Petronella was not listening. *Marcus is dead*, the voice intoned in her brain. *Marcus has been shot. I've lost my love* . . .

That night she did not even make the pretence of retiring by going to her room. She sat in the kitchen after the others had gone to bed, staring in front of her. The lantern light washed upon the blue-and-white Delft porcelain displayed on the shelves of the dresser.

It would not be passing to Dorothea after all. Now that Marcus was dead it would be Petronella's heirloom again. Her own bleak inheritance in a future which held no Marcus.

Without conscious decision, she stood up and moved to the dresser. She picked up one of the plates and hurled it against the far wall, and watched it smash into dozens of shards. Then she picked up another Delft plate, and another.

The sound of smashing crockery brought Mamma hurrying to the kitchen, a candle in her hand, her greying braids bobbing on her shoulders. Behind her followed Dorothea and Johannes, with Gideon bringing up the rear. Petronella barely glanced at them as she reached for another piece of Delft.

"Are you out of your mind?" she heard Dorothea scream.

"Dear God," Mamma muttered, "I believe she is."

Then Johannes thrust his way past Mamma and Dorothea, and placed one arm across Petronella's chest in a strangle-hold, while he prised another of the Delft plates from her fingers with his free hand.

"Petronella," he said, "listen to me. Listen! I hoped not to have to tell you this, but I can see – " He stopped, and then went on with emphasis, "*Marcus is alive. He wasn't shot.*"

She swivelled her head around slowly and stared at him. "You're lying," she whispered.

"No. I lied to you before, because I thought it was for the best. He *was* caught by the British, but they didn't shoot him. His parents might have cast him off, but a cousin of his – a man called Abraham Cohen – has some kind of contract to supply the British officers with wine imported from the Cape, and he intervened on Marcus's behalf. Instead of shooting him, the British agreed to send him into exile."

Slowly, Petronella recognised the truth in Johannes's eyes. Her mouth shaking, she asked with difficulty, "*Where?*"

"I don't know. Somewhere in Europe, or St Helena, or perhaps

Ceylon. The point is, Petronella, he can never come back to South Africa. That was why I thought it would be kinder to allow you to believe he was dead."

She groped for a chair and sank down into it, resting her head on the table and cradling it in her arms as she began to weep with great, gasping sobs. She felt Mamma's hand on her shoulder, and heard her murmur, "That's right, my child, weep. Get rid of the grief."

Mamma was wrong. She was not weeping for grief but for joy and hope. Somewhere in the world Marcus was alive. She would steal or cheat or even kill if she had to. But she would find out where he was and join him. Somehow.

8

A hand shook Petronella awake from the first sleep she had had since Johannes returned home. Her consciousness surfaced slowly, confused and disoriented, her head aching and her eyelids swollen and heavy.

The tears with which she had finally fallen asleep were still lurking weakly below the surface, and they filled her eyes again when she heard the song of turtle-doves coming from the orchard outside her bedroom; a sad, sweet sound evocative of longing and loss.

"Au, Nonnie," she heard Mwende's voice. "My heart is very sore for you."

She sat up, and found that Mwende had carried a tin bath into the room and had filled it with hot water. She tried to check her tears as Mwende came to kneel beside the bed, reaching for her hands. "Why *my* wrinkled-up old man not die?" the girl demanded passionately, her own dark eyes glinting with tears. "Why yours *babulala*, finish?"

Petronella gripped Mwende's hand, and her heart lifted as she reminded herself that there was still hope, still a battle to be fought. "My man is not dead. He is alive somewhere. Johannes lied to me."

"Ah, *jabula, jabula!*" Mwende exulted, and then frowned. "But why your brother lie to you?"

"He thought he was being kind. *Kind!*" she echoed with disbelief as she remembered the anguish and the torment with which she had been living.

Mwende shook her head and stood up. "The missus, she say you wash now, and put on clean clothes. If your man not dead, Nonnie, why you cry?"

Petronella wiped her eyes with the back of her hand. "They have sent him away, Mwende, to some other land from where he will never be allowed to come back to South Africa."

"What land, Nonnie?"

Petronella did not reply immediately. She swung her legs out of bed, and began to undo her tangled braids. Some time last evening, when she had become too exhausted for a few moments to continue weeping, she had questioned Johannes again about Marcus's exile. Her brother had said, "I don't think they would have sent him to

Europe. The two most likely places are Ceylon or St Helena, which are British possessions."

Europe, Petronella knew vaguely, was over the sea, and the place from which most of the *Uitlanders* came. That meant that it must be part of England, and a very long way away. Too far away for exiles to be sent to. She had never heard of Ceylon or St Helena before, but then there were many places of which she had never heard. She had not known of the existence of Ladysmith or Elandslaagte before the war had brought the names to the lips of everyone.

"I don't know what land, Mwende," she answered at last. "I think they probably sent him north. There are other countries in Africa, you know, which the British own. Marcus told me that." Her chin lifted. "Wherever he is, I shall find him. Will you help me to wash my hair?"

A while later, with her wet hair braided neatly and wearing a clean blouse and skirt, Petronella went into the kitchen, where her family were sitting down to breakfast. Mamma glanced at her with approval. "You look human now, child."

Petronella said nothing. She thought of questioning Johannes about Ceylon and St Helena, and decided against it. It was better that her family should not guess what was in her mind.

She heard Mamma say sharply, "You mentioned an oath of allegiance, Johannes, which many burghers swore. I thought you meant an oath of allegiance to Oom Paul Kruger, but several things you've said since have made me wonder. What is the truth?"

Johannes hesitated for a moment. "Mamma, you must try to understand. Lord Roberts was halfway across the Orange Free State, while Lord Kitchener's columns held the west, and three other British columns were advancing on us from other directions. We were caught in a trap. So when Lord Roberts issued a proclamation, inviting us to lay down our arms and take an oath of allegiance to British rule, we had no alternative. But it meant nothing. Apart from a few turncoats, the only arms we laid down were Martinis. We kept our Mausers and our ammunition back. It was a trick, to gain a breathing space, so that we could separate and regroup."

"Allegiance to British rule!" Mamma exclaimed, outraged.

"It meant nothing. It was a choice between taking the oath, or being sent to prisoner-of-war camps and then into exile. We have always sworn to fight to the bitter end, and *that* is the only oath which counts. You don't understand these matters, Mamma."

She sighed. "It seems not." As if to turn to something which she did understand, she addressed Petronella. "When you have eaten, I want you to help Dorothea and me to pack up the things we shall have to take with us to the Free State." With a sidelong look at

Johannes, she added, "Pappa was right. He knew *I* would not pretend allegiance to the British!"

"No," Petronella said, answering Mamma. "I won't be here to help you and Dorothea. I want to take the pony and cart, and visit *Meester* at the school."

At one time, before she ceased speaking to Petronella at all, Mamma would have rebuked her sharply for such defiance, and would have forced her to help with the necessary chores. But now she behaved with the slightly uneasy indulgence one displays to a bereaved person striving to come to terms with their loss. "Whatever do you want to visit *Meester* for, child?"

"I want to ask his advice about learning to speak English," Petronella lied.

Mamma and Johannes exchanged bewildered, anxious glances, and Dorothea's cow-like eyes almost started from her head. "Why do you want to learn English, Petronella?" Mamma asked helplessly.

"Because it might be useful." Petronella had her excuse prepared. "We might come across English soldiers on our way to join the women's laager, and then it would help, wouldn't it, if one of us was able to understand what they said?"

"Petronella," Mamma spoke gently, as if to someone not quite fully in possession of her senses, "we leave Jakkalsdrif tomorrow. Even if *Meester* were able to teach you English, how could he do so in one day?"

"Perhaps he could lend me a book from which I could teach myself." Petronella shrugged, and stood up. "Gideon, would you please hitch the pony to the cart for me?"

Her family, she noticed, were slightly wary of her, as if they feared another brainstorm such as that of last night when she had destroyed many of the precious pieces of Delft. Gideon looked at Mamma, who nodded briefly. Petronella was to be indulged for a while, it seemed. She had given expression to her paralysing grief; she had slept and washed and changed her clothes and broken her fast, and she was clearly on the way to recovery. But, for a few days, her irrational wishes were to be granted. So, while Mamma and Dorothea and Mwende and the other female servants laboured to pack up the ox-wagon and Johannes and Gideon supervised the gathering together of the small livestock, Petronella set out in the pony and cart for the schoolhouse.

She had to cross Jakkalsdrif's many acres to reach it, and she drove slowly, trying to imprint everything on her memory. The air already had a slightly luminous, autumnal quality to it, and the sun struck gold from the mealie-stubble in the fields and from the leaves of the rows of thorn trees and bushes which had been left undisturbed for generations and encouraged to form barriers, windbreaks and fences across the land.

She reined in the pony for a moment beside one of these fences and watched a *hottentotsgod* alight upon a branch of one of the hook-and-stab thorn trees. The moment the insect came to rest it remained motionless, having arranged itself so that it exactly resembled one of the dry leaves of the tree as it waited for some prey to step unwarily into its path. Other members of the species, she knew, had the uncanny ability to resemble a flower. No wonder the Hottentots had revered the insects as mystical, supernatural creatures.

Further along the row of trees, there was a sudden, scuffling sound and the next moment a vigilant *lammergeier* hawk which had been hovering silently in mid-air swooped and then rose with a flapping of its wings, a writhing field-mouse in its beak.

Petronella wondered whether they had *lammergeiers* and *hottentotsgods* in Ceylon or St Helena, and continued on her journey. In her mind she was slowly saying goodbye to Jakkalsdrif, because as soon as she had found out to which country Marcus had been taken, she intended joining him.

Already a plan had formed in her mind. Once they had joined a women's laager and she knew where Marcus was, she would steal one of the ox-wagons and sufficient supplies to get her to Ceylon or St Helena. Mwende, she felt certain, would gladly agree to go with her, and her brother Koos could probably be persuaded to join them too. Pappa had taught Petronella how to handle a rifle, which would give them protection against wild animals. But she did not anticipate much danger, for the roads to Ceylon and St Helena must be good or the British would not send exiles there. But she would need directions, and that was why it was necessary to consult *Meester*.

The school had been built a short distance away from the farmhouse, because as well as being the lay-preacher and the schoolmaster, *Meester* was also a farmer, but in a small way. He kept a herd of cows and grew mealies and vegetables, and there was never any lack of volunteers to help him with the ploughing or sowing or the gathering of the harvest. He would have gone on commando with the other men, were it not for the fact that his eyesight was so poor that, even with the help of thick spectacles, he was unable to see very far.

Petronella found him inside the schoolhouse. It was a simple building constructed of timber and roofed with corrugated iron, with two doors opening on to its verandahed front stoep. One room was set aside for older children, and another for those between the ages of seven and eleven. From Gideon, who had attended the school until his thirteenth birthday, Petronella knew that *Meester* took it in turns to set each age-group their lessons; while he was instructing one particular group in a subject the others were expected to get on quietly with work which he had set for them.

But now, the classroom normally occupied by older scholars was quite deserted, for with so many of the male servants on commando with their masters, any child old enough to be of use on the farm was naturally kept at home, and Petronella found *Meester* in the other classroom, where he was chalking the alphabet on the blackboard. Some half-dozen small children sat at the desks, making scratching sounds as they laboriously copied the letters on to their slates.

When *Meester* saw Petronella, he ordered the children to carry on practising their letters, and invited her inside the empty classroom next door.

"Is anything the matter, Petronella? We heard that your family are planning to cross the Vaal River and join a women's laager. Most of the other women with men on commando feel it is their duty to remain on their farms, come what may. It is not for me to judge who is right or wrong. These are difficult times."

She decided not to be drawn into idle chat. "*Meester*, I believe Europe is in England, and is over the sea. But where are Ceylon and St Helena, and how long would it take to reach either of them if one travelled by ox-wagon?"

Meester shook his head slowly. "Do you remember, Petronella, when you told me you'd had all the book-learning you needed? How wrong you were!"

"I know I am ignorant, *Meester*," she returned impatiently, "and that is why I am asking you to tell me these things."

He removed his spectacles, polishing them on his handkerchief. "Come here, Petronella," he said, adjusting his spectacles on his nose again. He led the way to a corner of the classroom, where a round ball with coloured markings on it rested upon a stand. *Meester* gave the ball a spin.

"This is a globe of the world, Petronella. This is roughly where we are." He pointed with his finger and with a nail of his other hand he traced for her the border separating the Transvaal from the rest of Africa. She stared at the ball with a sense of growing dismay. She had had no conception, before, just how vast the remainder of Africa was.

"The blue areas you can see," she heard *Meester* go on, "are oceans. You need only look at the size of the Transvaal Republic in relation to the rest of Africa to realise how vast those expanses of water are."

She was not concerned with oceans. Europe was over the sea but Johannes had said it was unlikely that Marcus had been sent there. "Please show me where Ceylon and St Helena are, *Meester*."

He peered near-sightedly at the globe until he had found an almost imperceptible speck surrounded by blue areas. "That is St Helena, Petronella. An island in the Atlantic Ocean." He spun the globe. "And this pearl-shaped dot at the foot of India is Ceylon. Europe is not in England, as you imagined. These are the British Isles, and this whole large area consisting of several different countries makes up Europe."

"*Oh God.*" She closed her eyes in despair and defeat. How pitiful of her to have imagined that she would be able to reach Marcus by ox-wagon.

Meester touched her arm gently. "Who has been sent into exile, Petronella?"

"Marcus Koen," she answered in a dull voice. Then she gave him a defiant look. "My betrothed. The man I intend marrying, exile or no exile."

Meester's voice was full of compassion. "It is no use, child. You must forget him. Wherever they have sent him – it might as well have been to the moon."

I shall not forget him, she thought fiercely. I shall discover where he is, and find a way of joining him. But how?

She still had the ring which Marcus had worn on his little finger, the one which they had used to make Mevrouw Boshof believe that they were married. She wore it on a ribbon around her neck. As soon as they joined a women's laager, she told herself, she would disappear and search for the nearest British camp. She would convince the soldiers there that she was the wife of Marcus and force them to send her to join him. She would claim to be pregnant and destitute; she would pretend that she had been the one who had persuaded him to spy for the Boers. She would tell any lie; sink her pride and beg if she had to.

Her resolve faltered as she remembered that she knew no English with which to plead or make demands or fabricate stories, and defeat almost engulfed her again.

Then she thought of the lie which she had told Mamma, and realised that if she turned it into truth it could become the weapon which she needed. "*Meester*, would it be possible for me to teach myself English? Are there books from which one could learn?"

"Not really, Petronella. But why do you wish to learn English?"

She had meant to tell him the same lie as she had offered Mamma, but involuntarily her glance went to the globe of the world, and he nodded with pity and understanding.

"Yes, I see. Ceylon and St Helena are part of the British Empire, and Dutch would not be understood there. It is clear that Marcus Koen has been exiled for life, or you would have reconciled yourself to wait for his return. But Petronella, even if your father were rich enough to pay for you to travel to either of those places after the war, do you really imagine he would agree to send you to join Koen in exile?"

She considered the question, which had never occurred to her before. Even if Pappa might be persuaded, Mamma would overrule him. But aloud, Petronella said, clasping her hands together, "It cannot cost so very much to travel to either of those places, or the British would not go to the expense of sending people into exile there. And when Pappa realises how impossible it is for me to live without Marcus, he will help me to go to him."

Meester shook his head. "Not if I know Hannes van Zyl!"

Stupid, stubborn old man! Petronella raged inwardly. What had it to do with him what Pappa might or might not agree to? All she wanted from him was the means to teach herself English, and not his opinions or his lectures. In her frustration and despair, she wanted to hit him. Instead, she forced herself to say humbly, with a catch in her voice, "I thought – if I could learn English – I might be able to find out where Marcus is, and write to him."

Meester sighed, and went to a cupboard, opening it and bringing out a heavy, leather-bound volume. "This is called a dictionary. It contains all the Dutch words, and shows you what each word is in English. But it wouldn't teach you how to put together sentences in English, or how to pronounce the words properly."

It *would* teach her how to put sentences together in English, she thought, and what difference did it make whether she knew how to pronounce the words or not? She would decide in advance what she wanted to say to the British, and she would look up each word and write down its equivalent in English. Aloud, she asked, *"Meester,* may I please borrow the dictionary? I shall look after it carefully, and return it to you when we come back to Jakkalsdrif."

He gazed at her for a moment, and then shrugged. "Very well, Petronella."

Any feelings of guilt she had about deceiving him, because she did not intend coming back to Jakkalsdrif or returning the dictionary, disappeared when she saw his expression. He was making it clear that, like Mamma and Johannes, he was indulging her in her bereavement. The dictionary would occupy her mind, he was obviously thinking, and by the time she accepted the utter impossibility of teaching herself English by studying it, she would have become reconciled to the loss of Marcus.

But nothing would reconcile her to his loss, and no force on earth would cause her to abandon her resolve to find him and join him. She thanked *Meester,* promised to convey his good wishes to her family, and returned to Jakkalsdrif with the dictionary.

She found that the loading of the three ox-wagons had almost been completed. Apart from Mwende and her mother and several of the more adventurous of the younger boys and unmarried young women, most of the people still left in the *stad* had decided to remain on Jakkalsdrif.

There would be game to shoot or snare, and there would be fish in the river. There would also be cows to milk, and if the British troops came and demanded animals for slaughter they were not likely to choose tough milk-cows when there were young steers to be had.

Koos, Mwende's brother, had also decided to stay at Jakkalsdrif, but for a different reason. He was afraid of crossing the Vaal River, more afraid of being dragged down to a drowning death by the *Tokoloshe* than of the British.

"I'll leave him in charge of matters here," Johannes said, as the family sat on the stoep, resting after their labours in loading the wagons.

Each of the wagons had its *voorkis*, a large space underneath the driver's seat, filled with their clothes and small personal possessions, and on the back of one wagon had been placed two *katels*, portable beds made specially for use on an ox-wagon. Johannes and Gideon would sleep on ground-sheets, wrapped in their bed-rolls, but one of the *katels* was reserved for Dorothea and her baby while the other was to be shared by Petronella and Mamma. Petronella looked up from the dictionary, in which she had finally discovered that the English word for *ballingskap* was 'exile', and reflected with some bitterness that she and Mamma would have made uncomfortable bed-fellows if her mother had an inkling that she refused to accept that Marcus was lost to her forever, and that she meant to go to him.

Mamma heaved her bulk out of her chair, as if on a sudden decision, and disappeared inside the house. When she returned she was carrying a small drum of caustic soda, which she added to the supply wagon.

"What do you want that for, Mamma?" Johannes asked. "You won't be needing it."

"One never knows. Since you won't allow me to take a Mauser of my own, caustic soda mixed with water would make a good emergency weapon if we are fallen upon by a band of British troops not content with plundering and looting the wagons of defenceless women, and they disarm Gideon. The threat of receiving a caustic soda mixture in the face would make even a coarse British soldier think twice before molesting Petronella or Dorothea."

"Mamma – " Johannes hesitated. "They are not as you imagine them. Many of the British soldiers are just bewildered, ignorant young men."

"How can you possibly say that? They came here, invading our country so that they could beggar and enslave us!"

"Many of the ordinary British soldiers, Mamma, had no idea what the war they were coming to fight was about."

"How do you know that?" Mamma demanded incredulously.

"Because I have spoken to dozens of British soldiers through interpreters. The Boers cannot afford to take prisoners-of-war, Mamma, apart from officers of rank whom it is important to remove from the field of war. We cannot afford to feed or shelter ordinary soldiers; we usually disarm them and after we have questioned them to try to discover the position of their troops, we set them free. I have learnt that many of them arrived from England, thinking of it as an exciting adventure in a sunny climate. They believed they had come to quell a handful of backward farmers armed with forks and pick-axes and a few rusty rifles. They thought it would be over in a matter of days or weeks, with hardly any blood spilt on their side, and then they would return to England as conquering heroes, with yet another large chunk of territory added to the British Empire."

Johannes's voice took on a compassionate note. "Poor devils, instead they found themselves faced with burghers who know every inch of their terrain, who can make themselves invisible against krantzes and kopjes, and who are not only deadly accurate with a Mauser but who also possess Creusot guns and howitzers and Krupp quick-firers and know how to use them. The poor 'khakis' saw their comrades dying hideously around them, with limbs shot off, and gaping, bloody holes where their stomachs used to be, and they realised they were fighting a real war for reasons they did not even understand."

Petronella gazed at her brother, half-mesmerised by what he had been saying. Johannes had changed, she thought. Part of her was moved to involuntary pity for the soldiers he had described, and another reminded her that those very soldiers had indirectly been responsible for Marcus's being in exile somewhere across the ocean.

Mamma frowned at Johannes. "If the soldiers do not know for what they are fighting, then why have they agreed to do so?"

"Because they are not like us, Mamma. They are not asked whether they agree to fight. They have to fight when they are ordered to do so, because it is what they do for a living. Others volunteered to fight because they have families at home who depend on the money they send them. I have seen so many young British soldiers who were bewildered and homesick and almost in tears when they learnt that they would not be sent to prisoner-of-war camps, but were to be turned free to rejoin their regiments and be sent back to bloody battle-fields."

"Mmm . . ." Mamma said thoughtfully, but she did not remove the caustic soda from the supply wagon.

Petronella had her own, secret supplies to pack. While Mamma was busy, preparing the last supper they would be eating at Jakkalsdrif for an unforeseeable time, she opened Pappa's side of the hanging closet in her parents' room and took from its floor the wooden box with its carved hollows, inside which were slotted a bottle of ink, several pens and a selection of nibs. She also found writing paper which Pappa used for his infrequent correspondence, and together with the dictionary, she made a bundle of it all, wrapped inside one of her skirts. These things were her passport to wherever Marcus was.

The sun was just rising the next morning when the three ox-wagons left Jakkalsdrif. All those from the *stad* who had elected to stay behind had come to bid them farewell.

"Now remember," Johannes told Koos, "if the British come, you must let them take what they want, and in the meantime, look after things as well as you can."

"Yes, Baas Johannes, I understand." He looked mournfully at Mwende, and Petronella knew that he doubted if his sister would survive the crossing of the Vaal River, where the *Tokoloshe* was lurking.

"*Hamba gahle!*" The servants chorused their goodbyes as the wagons prepared to leave, each with its strong span of oxen, and surrounded by the sheep and the few milk-cows which were to be herded by youths from the *stad*.

Petronella sat in the driving seat of one of the wagons. She allowed the other two, driven by Mamma and by Mwende, to go ahead before she cracked the long whip in the air. The skyline was painted with fantastic colours, and the mist rising from the Vaal River gave everything a diffused, magical quality of unreal beauty. A knot formed in her throat, for if she were to achieve her heart's desire and be reunited with Marcus, she would never see Jakkalsdrif again. Swallowing hard, she picked up the whip.

The journey developed its own slow routine. The wide, open, lonesome veld of the Free State stretched ahead of them once they had crossed the river by the drift, its emptiness broken only by an occasional small kopje or a giant termite hill, the monotony sometimes relieved by a springhare leaping in the air in front of their path as it dashed to safety, or by the sun glinting on a black mamba which had to be killed before it could spit its poison at man or beast.

On the second day a party of six burghers came riding to join them; they, too, had been visiting their homes in the Transvaal and were on their way back to their corporalship, and they slackened their pace so that they could keep the wagon convoy company.

Petronella itched with impatience at the slowness of the journey. Now that the oxen had settled into an accustomed routine there was little for her to do in the driving seat, other than crack the whip in the air at intervals when the oxen decided to baulk at their task, and she occupied her time by studying the dictionary which *Meester* had lent her, and by deciding on the composition of the note she meant to hand to the British at the first opportunity.

"*Mij man was naar ballingskap gestuur*," she wrote the opening line, and then consulted the dictionary for a translation of each separate word. The very first one presented a problem, for *mij* could mean 'my' and also 'me'. *Man*, surprisingly, was exactly the same in English, but both *was* and *naar* offered several alternative translations. She already knew the English word for *ballingskap* but she could not find *gestuur* in the dictionary. Turning the pages she chanced upon the word *gister*, and decided her own spelling must have been at fault. Thankfully, *gister* had only one translation; it meant 'yesterday' in English.

She experienced considerable difficulty in translating the rest of her note and it dawned on her slowly that the dictionary was an old one and still contained many Dutch words in their pure form, instead of the altered and simplified language commonly in use now. Yet another dilemma facing her was the wording which she should choose to trick the British into believing that she was pregnant. The English equivalent of 'I expect his child' seemed mercifully simple and uncomplicated and not subject to any other possible meaning. But would a British general or field-cornet, she wondered, be offended by such a blunt, indelicate term? It might be better if she used the common Dutch euphemism, the English translation of which also proved to be quite simple and unequivocal.

When she had finally decided on the wording of the note in English, she brought out Pappa's writing-box and carefully copied it down when they outspanned. Fortunately, the company of the burghers who were riding with them occupied much of Mamma's attention, so that she was not too concerned with what Petronella might be up to, seated on the *katel* in the shade of the wagon's canopy, and pretending to keep a watchful eye on Dorothea's baby while its mother helped to cook a meal over the camp-fire.

At last, satisfied with her efforts, Petronella cast an eye over what she had written. It made no sense to herself, but the words had all been copied from the dictionary, and even though she had undoubtedly made a few mistakes she was sure its meaning would be perfectly clear to any Englishman.

"My man was nauseous exile yesterday," she had written in her neatest hand. "She name is Marcus Koen. I have danger round with him to orphan. I is in the other time, and I have not benefit not. It was my debt that he spy worth."

She folded the note carefully, and put it away. It summed up her situation and her dilemma, and if compassion because she was pregnant and penniless would not move the British to send her into exile to join Marcus, then the fact that she had taken the blame for his spying activities would surely make them do so as a punishment.

Early the following morning, their small encampment was woken up by the crack of distant rifle-shots. Mamma, grey plaits bobbing, sat up and pulled away the canopy flap. From the *katel*, Dorothea's baby began to cry. Petronella struggled free of the bedclothes too and peered outside. The sky was pearl-grey, and etched against it Johannes loomed up. He and the other burghers slept in their clothes and Gideon, pretending to be a grown warrior ever on the alert, had been copying them. Now, Johannes was strapping his bandolier across his chest as he said urgently, "Mamma, I think there's trouble ahead. Get dressed and pack up everything, ready to move on."

The oxen had barely been yoked to the wagons and the livestock herded together, and all cooking utensils packed away, when two burghers came riding up to them, their mounted figures silhouetted against the glowing red and orange and pink of rising dawn.

"A column of British is on its way!" one of the burghers reported breathlessly. "There is a small women's laager not far from here, and we are riding to warn them to get to safety. You had best follow as quickly as you can."

Tension rippled through the convoy, but Petronella's had a different cause. Naturally she would do nothing to betray the Boers, but as soon as they were safe, she would get away somehow and reach the British column so that she could hand her note to its leader and be sent to join Marcus.

The wagons lumbered through the veld, and the armed burghers rode alongside slowly, keeping a watchful eye on the horizon. As the sun rose Johannes cantered to a nearby kopje, and mounted its ridge. He returned a short while later, and reported, "The British are some three or four miles behind us. I'd say there are roughly fifteen hundred horsemen, but fortunately they have a string of wagons with them and several guns, which will slow them down to little more than our own pace."

Shortly after noon, Petronella saw the women's laager coming into sight. It consisted of some fifty wagons and carts, with children playing among them and women cooking over camp-fires. At almost the same time as she saw the laager, a small corporalship of about forty burghers appeared from behind a krantz, and rode to join Johannes and the other men.

Petronella was able to hear the corporal talking to her brother. "We were on our way to rejoin our field-cornetcy when we spotted the British through our field-glasses. We thought we would stay and pick off as many of them as we could. The women's laager over there changes things, however. We can't risk involving them in a long-drawn-out sniping battle with the enemy. If we can get the women away to some safe place before the British arrive – well, let's go and see."

Mamma wondered aloud whether any of their acquaintances were among the women in the laager, but there was no time to find out. After the corporal had announced the coming of the British, chaos reigned within the laager. Poultry was run to earth and packed into coops, sheep rounded up and oxen yoked to wagons. Camp-fires were doused, children, pots and pans loaded up and hastily stowed on board, and they began to move off.

As the British gained upon them, the corporal shouted something to the burghers and they galloped away, streaking as fast as their horses could carry them across the front of the English advance and firing a few shots before falling back again out of range. They continued this tactic and Petronella understood what they were trying to do. They hoped to give the women time to get away to safety while they kept the enemy occupied and distracted.

But the oxen were too slow, and the dangerous ploy of the burghers futile. Now, the Boers could only hope to ensure the safety of the women and children by distancing themselves from them and drawing the enemy's fire. Petronella did not even notice, at first, that Gideon had also ridden away towards a line of kopjes among which the burghers had gone to entrench themselves.

The sound of firing was making the oxen nervous and scattering the livestock. There seemed to be no point in trying to continue onwards with the wagons. The women watched helplessly as the British halted, and a troop of mounted soldiers came at a gallop towards the kopjes where the burghers had dug themselves in. Rifle-bullets and shells were bursting hideously in the air, became sporadic and after several hours died down altogether from the direction of the kopjes.

British soldiers stormed the kopjes and reined in, their attitude signalling mystified frustration. The burghers, the women realised, had melted away into thin air on their horses.

A while later an English soldier came riding towards the women's wagons. He would, Petronella surmised, be coming to commandeer some of their stock, and she scrabbled for the dictionary so that she might attempt to argue with him on behalf of them all.

But to the astonishment of everyone, the soldier removed his helmet and addressed them in fluent Dutch. "*Dames*, I have come with a message from Captain Marshall. My name is Private Hendrik le Roux – "

"*So!*" Mamma's fierce voice interrupted him. "We shall remember the name! When this war is over it will go hard with hands-uppers and traitors like yourself, Hendrik le Roux!"

"I am a citizen of the Cape," the man defended himself. "It was my duty to fight on the side of the British."

"Your *duty*, was it? I have heard of many other Cape Boers who came to join the struggle of their own people in the Republics. So don't talk to me about *duty*, Hands-upper le Roux!"

Petronella saw that the man had flushed a deep red. "Those Cape Boers you mentioned," he told Mamma in a gruff voice, "are rebels. When they are captured they will be shot. And if I had decided to fight for neither side, the British would have interned me. Now, about Captain Marshall's message – "

"If, Hands-upper le Roux," Mamma said in a voice dripping with acid, "your English master's message is that they intend stealing some of our livestock, we are in no position to resist, since we are without arms."

Le Roux cleared his throat. "You do not understand, Mevrouw. Captain Marshall says you are to drive your wagons and your livestock to the British camp and join us."

"Certainly not!"

"It is for your own protection, Mevrouw – "

"The only protection we are likely to need is from the British themselves! Tell your Captain Marshall to fly to the devil!"

Le Roux hesitated, and then shrugged. "Mevrouw, I am afraid you have no choice. We cannot have bands of women and children roaming around in the veld. You are to come, immediately, to join us."

"And if we refuse?"

Le Roux made a gesture with his hands. "You would be forced to obey. Please, Mevrouw, I don't wish to have to tell Captain Marshall that you are a trouble-maker, so that he will have no choice but to keep you in confinement."

"Do you mean that we are prisoners?" Mamma demanded.

Le Roux looked uncomfortable. "You are merely being ordered, for your own safety, to obey Captain Marshall. Come now, Mevrouw, be sensible and persuade the other women to drive their wagons to the British camp."

Only the children wept as the wagons began to move obediently towards the British camp. The women stared stoically and grimly ahead of them, and Petronella guessed at the irony of their thoughts as they reflected that it was to evade the British that they had formed their women's laager in the first place. Now, however evasively le

Roux tried to wrap the matter up, they were prisoners of those same enemies.

They learnt, through le Roux, that they would be moved on in the morning under an escort of British soldiers to 'a place of safety'. But tonight they would be staying at the camp, and they were not to sleep inside their wagons, which were to be drawn up alongside the camp. Instead, the women were ordered to remove bedding from the wagons; they would be issued with ground-sheets, and were to sleep along the outer perimeters of the British encampment.

"Why?" Mamma demanded bluntly.

Her continuing contempt had finally caught le Roux on the raw, and he answered with equal, unvarnished bluntness, abandoning his defensive attitude. "So that, if your men who melted so mysteriously away into nowhere should return under cover of darkness with the intention of attacking the camp, believing that you are all sleeping on your wagons, you women would have one of two choices. You would either have to call out to your men, and so give us warning of their position, or else you would be the first to be killed by their fire."

Le Roux walked away, and Petronella looked at Mamma with fear and despair. "The burghers *will* try to attack. When they learn that the women have been taken prisoner, they will not simply ride on. Even if the others might wish to, Johannes and Gideon would never agree. Le Roux was right – we would either have to call out to them, pinpointing their position for the British, or be shot by our own men."

Mamma thought deeply, and after a while she came up with a plan, the only one which would successfully warn the burghers of the trap the British had set for them, and which the British themselves would be powerless to do anything about.

Mamma consulted the other women, and it was agreed that the families should position themselves around the outer edge of the camp in such a way that there would be at least one small child every yard or so. A roster would be worked out; at regular intervals during the night a child would be woken up and if it failed to cry spontaneously it would, regretfully, be forced to do so. The constant crying of children around the edge of the camp throughout the night would warn the Boers of the British plan. And the British themselves might be able to order many things, but even they would be powerless to order a crying young child to be silent.

Petronella's scorn for le Roux now equalled Mamma's, but she needed his services and so, while Mamma was occupied with the business of arranging a roster for the night ahead, Petronella went to look for the Cape Boer.

"Will you please take me to see Captain Marshall?" she asked.

"Why?"

"For reasons which have nothing to do with you!"

He stared at her for a moment, and then he nodded. "Follow me."

Clutching her carefully prepared note, she walked in his wake towards a tent which had been pitched in the shade of a lone sweet-thorn tree, ignoring the stares, both curious and admiring, of British soldiers as she passed. Guilt was warring with hope inside her. Her treachery and defection would hit Mamma hard, especially at such a time, when they were humiliatingly the prisoners of the British. But Mamma, she reminded herself, was only speaking to her now because she thought that Marcus was forever removed from Petronella's life. And Mamma would have Dorothea to comfort her, as well as the company of the other Boer women, while if the British captain agreed to send Petronella to join Marcus, she herself would face a lonely and unimaginable journey to a strange land. And Marcus *had* to come before everyone and everything else.

Captain Marshall, who could not have been very much older than Johannes, was seated inside his tent behind a trestle-table where he had been examining maps. As she entered with le Roux he rose politely, and said something in English. Le Roux answered for her, also in English, presumably explaining that she had asked to see the officer. After a further exchange between the two men, le Roux picked up a folding chair, set it up and said, "Captain Marshall has asked you to sit down. If you will tell me what you want to say to him, I shall translate for you."

"I don't need your help," Petronella told him stonily, proudly, and held her note out to the captain.

She watched him studying it. After a moment he looked up with a frown, and handed the note to le Roux. Petronella felt the angry colour creeping along her neck as she watched the Cape Boer's lips twitch. He put the note down and turned to her. "You had better tell me what your note was intended to say, because it makes no sense at all."

Choking back rage and humiliation, she translated her own note in a wooden voice, and heard le Roux make a muffled sound of laughter. He spoke to the captain, still with mirth in his voice. She was surprised to find that the Englishman did not share le Roux's amusement, but the look of pity in his eyes was almost as humiliating as laughter would have been.

Through le Roux, the captain told her, "Whether or not you really are married to this man Marcus Koen, and are expecting his child, it would be quite impossible for the British Army to send you into exile after him. If you could find out precisely where he has been sent to, and if you had the means with which to travel to join him, then it might be possible for the Army to give you permission to do so. But there are many exiles and many different places to which they have been sent."

Her lips firmly clamped together to prevent them from trembling, her colour high and her chin defiantly in the air, she turned and left the tent, clenching and unclenching her hands as she went back to the Boer wagons.

With dry eyes, she stared about her. Every single plan she had tried to forge to join Marcus had come to nothing. She might as well give up and try to forget him, as everyone had been advising her to do.

A picture of him rose in her mind, of his blue eyes looking at her with love and desire and the clefts creasing his cheeks. No, she would not give up! But what else could she do?

Learn English, she answered herself. When you can speak English, you will be able to ask questions. You will be able to discover to which country Marcus has been sent. And then you can go on to plan from there.

The logical person to apply to for lessons in English was le Roux. But she had only to remember the amusement in his eyes and his voice as he read her note to dismiss the thought immediately. Never again would she expose herself to ridicule by someone like le Roux, with pathetic attempts at expressing herself in English.

But the matter had to be left for the moment, and early the next morning the women's laager were ordered to leave, with their wagons, their possessions, their servants and their livestock, under a strong escort of British soldiers of whom le Roux was one, to be taken to this unspecified 'place of safety'.

They did not know for which part of the country they were heading, and le Roux was evasive when anyone tried to question him. Petronella could not believe that Johannes and Gideon would fail to persuade the burghers to come after them and attempt to rescue them from the British. Daily, she turned her head to scan the horizon behind them. On the third morning she spotted them, a scouting party of half a dozen Boers on horseback etched against the sky in the distance. For five more days the Boers tracked them but it became increasingly obvious that in that flat, rolling landscape there were going to be no opportunities for the Boers to launch a surprise attack on the British escort, and anything else would have put the women and children in mortal jeopardy. After the fifth day, the tracking party no longer appeared on the horizon.

The wagons continued to pass through interminable miles of flat, empty veld devoid of signs of human beings. Then, after a few days, they began to come across farmsteads which were blackened ruins, and which le Roux explained had been within the line of previous fighting. But he could not explain, or else declined to do so, the sight which met their eyes the next day. On another burnt-out farm lay the rotting corpses of hundreds of sheep, with vultures rising in an obscene black cloud from the carcases as they were disturbed in their feasting. The women might have concluded that some mysterious disease had struck the animals which their owners had not been there to eradicate in time, but the fact that many of the sheep had clearly had their throats cut argued against that theory.

As the convoy of wagons continued the journey, Petronella sometimes thought that anyone who did not know the truth and could ignore the presence of their armed guard of soldiers, might have formed the view that the women and children with their servants were all embarked on a protracted picnic. As soon as they outspanned in the late afternoon each day, the servants and children went foraging for fuel, and camp-fires were lit. Coffee was brewed, pickles and bottled fruit and vegetables were brought out, and some of the women would fry dough to eat with their strips of biltong, while others broke into their stores of rusks. Sometimes, when there happened to be a large antheap where they outspanned, it was hollowed out and a fire made inside it for the baking of bread.

But although they shared a common fate, each group of women had anxieties and fears of their own with which to occupy themselves, so that there was little social communication among them. They sat in family groups, surrounded by their own servants, like miniature households clinging to the known and the familiar.

, Mamma never voiced her fears, but Petronella guessed that she was worrying about Johannes, and fretting even more anxiously about Gideon, her baby, who had only just celebrated his fifteenth birthday, and had now gone to join a party of fighting men and would try to match and even outdo them in daring.

Dorothea, too, guessed at Mamma's thoughts, for she said several times, "Johannes will look out for Gideon. He'll curb his reckless streak."

Mamma merely stared fiercely ahead of her, and said, "I wish I had a Mauser, and not just a miserable little tub of caustic soda."

"Nonnie," Mwende whispered anxiously to Petronella, "what you think will happen?"

"I don't know, Mwende. I don't even know where we are. Oh, if only one of us could understand English, and listen to what the soldiers say among themselves!"

The thought brought an idea. After that, whenever she could safely escape Mamma's attention, Petronella wandered through the darkness to where the soldiers were on guard and listened to them talking. She tried to memorise certain phrases they used and then searched for the words in the dictionary. It did not tell her anything about what the future held, but she was beginning to learn a smattering of English.

A little more than a fortnight after the wagons had first left the British camp, they arrived at a place where metal tracks were embedded in the earth, and Petronella heard one of the women explain that they were railway lines. The wagons followed these lines for some distance, and on the horizon, to the right of the tracks, they saw that tents had been pitched in a square to form a large cordon. At first the women assumed this cordon was the 'place of safety' to which they had been told they were being taken, but as they drew nearer they could see that it held a heaving mass of sheep and cattle which milled around in their thousands. As the wagons drew level with the cordon it became clear that the tents were occupied by British soldiers who were obviously guarding the livestock, while patrols of cattle-guards rode around the cordon, driving back any straying animals.

Le Roux said with a pleasant smile, "Ladies, your livestock will be left here, under guard."

"You mean," Mamma exclaimed, enraged, "that you are stealing them in the name of the British Army! Just as those other animals have been stolen from farms, because they are all branded with different marks!"

"A receipt will be issued," le Roux said smoothly, "promising compensation as soon as your men have laid down their arms in obedience to Lord Roberts's proclamation."

"We are not leaving our animals here!" Mamma protested angrily.

"You have no choice, Mevrouw. They will not be able to accompany you to where you are going."

"And where *are* we going?"

"I have told you, to a place of safety."

It was as useless to fight against leaving the livestock there as it had been to refuse to join the British camp in the first place; as useless as all Petronella's efforts to join Marcus had been. The livestock were driven inside the cordon, and the wagons went on.

Now, they were finding that curious constructions had been put up alongside the railway line. They were square-shaped buildings of stone, each with a protruding look-out window from which an armed soldier kept watch. They were fortified and linked to one another by means of barbed-wire fences, and when Petronella's curiosity got the better of her contempt for le Roux, and she asked him what they were, he replied, "They are blockhouses, put up to stop your burghers from blowing up the railway lines."

Then the wagons came within sight of a wooden building which was clearly not a blockhouse, facing the railway lines and with a large, open space stretching to the sides and the back.

"*Dames*," le Roux announced, "you will leave your wagons and oxen here at the railway station. You may each take only a blanket and a change of clothing. Your journey from now on will be by train."

Uproar greeted his words. Many of the women, who had begun to sink into moods of hopelessness, regained their courage and refused to budge from their wagons. But the soldiers fired threatening shots above their heads and when even that had no effect they began to manhandle the women physically from their wagons.

Then almost all the women were struck dumb, the fight going out of them, as they heard a fearful sound approaching and watched an iron monster come speeding along the railway lines, emitting black smoke and white steam at the same time, its great wheels making a thundering, metallic noise. It shuddered to a halt outside the wooden building, and Petronella could see, through its windows, that there were people inside it already.

Knowing that they could not escape their fate, she hurried to the wagon which held her possessions and wrapped the dictionary with Pappa's writing box inside the blanket she had been told she would be allowed to take. She tried to hide the bulky shape by draping a skirt and a blouse and some underclothing over it.

She turned, and found Mwende coming towards her, shaking visibly, her eyes large and showing white with terror. "Nonnie – what that iron caterpillar?"

If I am frightened at the thought of having to travel on it, Petronella chided herself, then think how much worse it must be for poor Mwende. I, after all, have seen trams in Johannesburg, and even though this is much bigger and looks far more dangerous, at least I know what it is.

"It is a train, Mwende," she said. "Don't be afraid. I shall stay close to you. Go and fetch your blanket now, and some clothes – "

"No," she was interrupted by le Roux, who had obviously been listening to their conversation. "The servants are not going with you." He looked around him, and called out in Fanakalo, "All you black people, you stay behind."

There was a moment of silence. Then Mwende's mother asked diffidently, "Where we go, Baas?"

"You are free to go where you like, and do as you please. But you cannot go with your former masters."

As his words sank in, a long, keening sound of protest from the servants filled the air. The soldiers ignored it and chivvied the Boer women and children towards the train. After Dorothea, looking desperate and waxen, had climbed aboard with her baby in her arms, Petronella helped Mamma to squeeze her bulk through the narrow door, and then she looked back.

The servants were sitting on the ground, the aprons of the women covering their faces, weeping in a loud, continuous lament as they expressed their bewilderment and their fear and loss. The soldiers, Petronella thought bitterly, probably did not grasp that they had almost all been born on the farms of their masters, that they regarded themselves as part of their families, and that freedom to most of them would probably spell starvation. But le Roux was a Boer, and he could not fail to know it.

Then the sound of the weeping servants was drowned by a roaring of the train's wheels and a piercing whistle. Petronella almost lost her footing and collided with someone.

It was a woman she had not seen before, for she was not someone who would escape recognition once one had clapped eyes on her. Her face had the appearance of having been carved from weathered wood and she might have been any age between fifty and a hundred. On her head she wore a man's battered felt hat, and as well as the regulation blanket, she carried over her arm a white gown which looked incongruously like one intended for a young bride. For the first time Petronella realised that the train was so full that people were packed together in solid, upright ranks, and that she had become separated from Mamma and Dorothea.

Her glance fell again on the old woman with her strange burden. Since she had obviously boarded the train earlier, she might know more about their destination than any of those who had only just joined the other passengers.

"Excuse me, Mevrouw," Petronella said, "but you were already on the train when we climbed aboard, weren't you?"

"Yes, child. I am one of the Free Staters. They only gave me time to collect a blanket and my *doodsklere* before they burnt down my farm too, and forced me to join others on the train."

Petronella stared with horrified fascination at the bride-like white gown. She understood, now, what it was. This old woman had chosen, as her only spare clothing, the gown set aside to be worn as her shroud.

Unsteadily, Petronella said, "Mevrouw, you cannot think something so terrible will happen to us that you will need your *doodsklere* – "

"All I know," the old woman interrupted, "is that they are taking us to one of their *konsentrasie kampe*. I'm old, and I want to be buried respectably when my time comes."

9

Petronella had never heard of *konsentrasie kampe*, but as she tried to make her way through the packed, swaying train, squeezing past women and stepping over small children who clung, weeping, to their mothers' skirts she heard the term being used several times. A *konsentrasie kamp* must be the 'place of safety' which le Roux had been talking about.

"They say it's for our protection," she heard one woman exclaim bitterly. "We didn't need protection until they came and burnt down our house and set fire to our land and slaughtered our livestock!"

At last, Petronella succeeded in squeezing her way to where Mamma was standing beside Dorothea. The baby was crying with hunger, as were other infants, but even if Dorothea had been able to overcome her inhibitions it would have been impossible to feed him, for they were all too closely packed.

"Mamma," Petronella began, "farms here in the Free State have been deliberately set on fire and the livestock slaughtered. Do you think that on Jakkalsdrif – "

Mamma did not wait for Petronella to complete the question. "From what I've been hearing, the farms were burnt and the women's livelihood destroyed because the British accused them of feeding and sheltering burghers. Since there's no one left on Jakkalsdrif to feed and shelter burghers, the British will have neither reason nor excuse for destroying it."

"What do you suppose these camps are like, Mamma?"

"I don't know. I heard someone saying that we are to be taken to the Bloemfontein camp." Mamma smiled grimly. "Whatever the camp is like, reaching it will be a relief after this accursed journey." As the train juddered, slowed down and with an explosive escape of steam came to a halt, she added, "We shall soon see."

But in that she was proved wrong. As the women and children were disgorged from the crowded train, soldiers stepped forward and chivvied them along, gesturing to them to form lines. Beyond the tracks they could see the outskirts of a town which was obviously Bloemfontein. But it transpired that the camp for which they were heading was not inside the town itself, and that they were to walk to it.

It was a scorching afternoon, and apart from small children there were several old people among them. Their pace was painfully slow, and armed soldiers on horseback clip-clopped alongside them. Snatches of bitter accounts from the Free State women and old men reached Petronella.

"The soldiers dynamited our house, but first they forced us to watch them using the portraits of our families on the walls as target practice."

"They burnt our whole village. Most of our possessions were confiscated, and then we were put on open bullock-wagons and sent to the station . . . ."

And now, Petronella thought grimly as she listened, these people, like themselves, were being taken to 'a place of safety'.

They had come to a shallow stream in which brackish red water flowed over rocks, and the women hitched up their skirts to wade through it. Throwing modesty to the wind, and ignoring the soldiers, the nursing mothers began to suckle their hungrily crying babies as they stumbled on through the dust of the bare brown veld with the sun baking down on them, and after hesitating for a while Dorothea fed her own baby too.

Petronella longed to reach the *konsentrasie kamp*, because at least it would offer shelter. In the meantime, mindful of her need to learn English, she concentrated hard on the conversation of the British soldiers who were escorting them, trying to translate what they were saying and striving to imprint on her memory the words they used.

Everyone fell silent as their 'place of safety' came within sight. Petronella stared at it in numb disbelief. Dumped down on the southern slope of a kopje, with not a single tree anywhere in sight and no shade of any kind, stood a township made up almost entirely of bell tents. Far away in the distance beyond the tents, the sun glinted on a row of corrugated iron buildings, and the camp was surrounded on all sides by barbed wire, with soldiers armed with fixed bayonets on guard all around its perimeter.

Even though they had been forced to leave their wagons and board the train, it had not entered her mind that they were bound for a prison. She heard the soldiers who had accompanied them use the words 'concentration camp' and now she understood why the term had been unfamiliar to her before. The Free State Boers, learning of the existence of the camps, had simply pronounced their English name in their own way.

The newly arrived prisoners were ordered, by gestures, to wait outside the gate. "The tents are so closely packed together," Mamma broke the heavy silence, "that any fever would sweep like wildfire through the place. Thank heavens I smuggled my *bossiemiddels* from the wagon, and also the caustic soda in case we should need a weapon."

"It would have made more sense if you had taken some biltong," Dorothea said with a sharpness that could only have been caused by despair at what was facing them.

Mamma gave one of her grim smiles. "I am not as foolish as you think me. I always suspected that the British had their eyes on our provisions, and so I sewed long strips of biltong inside my spare pair of corsets during our journey in the wagons, and I put it on over my other corset when we were told that we had to leave all our belongings behind."

Petronella looked at Mamma with admiration and awe. Even in their natural state, her corsets were fearsome things, rigid with whale-bone. Mamma's bulk made walking difficult for her at the best of times, and yet she had not only worn her usual pair of confining corsets, but also another made rigid and heavy with the biltong with which she had replaced the whale-bone, and she had made that gruelling journey on foot from the station without fuss or complaint.

A man in the kind of uniform which made it clear that he was in a position of authority came to the gate of the camp, accompanied by two soldiers. The first man addressed the prisoners, speaking slowly in English, but his expression made it plain that he expected frustration and delay before his meaning was finally brought home to the Boers. But a girl of roughly Petronella's age stepped forward and addressed the man haltingly in English, and then translated that the prisoners were to enter the camp in batches of five, each accompanied by a soldier.

While they waited for their turn to enter the camp, Petronella studied the girl who could speak English, deciding to make use of her if she could. The girl was short and plump, with a fresh complexion and dark hair showing underneath her *kappie*. Petronella moved to her side, and introduced herself.

The girl smiled shyly. "I am Jakoba Steenkamp."

"Where did you learn to speak English?"

"I can really only speak a few words of it, but I understand quite a bit. My parents farmed in the British Cape Colony."

Petronella gave her a puzzled look. "But if you are a British subject from the Cape, why are they putting you into a concentration camp?"

Jakoba's lips trembled. "My mother is dead, and my father and I were visiting relatives in the Free State when the war broke out. Pa decided to fight for the Boers." She stared into the distance. "The British caught him, and I've daily been expecting to hear that he has been shot as a rebel. After my father was captured the British called at the farm of my relatives, where I was staying, and they drove us out and set fire to everything. For some reason I was split up from my aunt and uncle, and I don't know where they were sent." She stared inside at the rows upon rows of bell tents. "I hoped to find them here, but it looks so impossible, doesn't it?"

The near-impossibility of locating any prisoners one might know became even more apparent when it was their turn to enter the camp. Perhaps because the wind had been in a different direction earlier, they became aware for the first time of the overpowering, foul smell which hung over the camp. Each tent looked exactly the same as its neighbour, and at a rough estimate Petronella thought there must be a thousand of them altogether inside the barbed-wire enclosure. Only narrow strips of hard, red earth separated one row of tents from another, and no attempt had been made to give these strips names or numbers, so that it would be extremely easy to lose oneself in that bleak maze.

It soon became apparent why the prisoners had been ordered to enter the camp in batches of five adults. This was the minimum number allocated to each tent, and because Jakoba Steenkamp was still at Petronella's side she was ordered to share the van Zyl tent, but by some oversight there was no fifth adult.

As they entered the tent they stood together in silent, mutual despair. There were no furnishings of any kind; no mattresses or chairs or chests in which to store their few belongings. There was simply the hard, earth floor and the single, thin canvas of the tent through which the heat penetrated with suffocating intensity. The only item the tent contained was a bucket which was obviously intended for use as a slop-pail.

"Well," Mamma broke the silence in a blank voice, "perhaps it is as well that there is no furniture. We would not have been able to move around in here if there had been."

Dorothea was trying to silence her crying son. "How – how am I to care for poor Baby in these conditions?" she wept.

No one attempted to supply an answer. Mamma unwrapped her blanket and placed her boxful of *bossiemiddels* and her tub of caustic soda on the floor, and then she folded the blanket so that it resembled a square cushion, and sank down on to it. The others followed her example.

Mamma stared at the writing box and the dictionary which Petronella had had no choice but to reveal. "What on earth did you choose to bring those for, child? And who gave you permission to take Pappa's writing box with you in the first place?"

"I told you, Mamma," Petronella said quickly, "that I wished to learn English." She looked at Jakoba Steenkamp with an appeal in her eyes. "And I'm sure I shall be able to learn quickly, with Jakoba to help me – "

She was interrupted by the appearance at the door of the tent of a soldier accompanying a woman whose figure and bearing spoke of middle age, but whose face was criss-crossed with the wrinkles of an older person. She was smartly dressed and shod, and instead of the *kappie* worn by every other Boer female her hat was a confection composed of little more than curled feathers. The soldier said something to her and disappeared.

The woman stood in the opening of the tent, cradling an overweight lap-dog to her thin breast. "Oh no!" she breathed, tears brimming in her eyes. "Oh no! This is terrible . . ."

"Yes," Mamma agreed shortly. She heaved herself upright and held out her hand. "I am Mevrouw Lenie van Zyl, and this is my daughter-in-law Dorothea, my daughter Petronella, and Jakoba Steenkamp."

The woman rearranged the dog in her arms so that she could shake hands with Mamma. "Mevrouw Marie Naudé. How lucky you are to have a family," she added. "My late husband and I were never blessed, so this is my newest baby, Pikkie. Greet these nice people, Pikkie," she addressed the dog in an adoring voice, and beamed with pride when it uttered a yapping sound.

Petronella guessed that Mamma was thinking they were already overcrowded with five people and a baby sharing the tent, and could have done without a dog as well. But she kept her thoughts to herself, and commanded Petronella, "Let Mevrouw Naudé sit on your blanket, child. You may share Jakoba's."

The two girls had just made themselves as comfortable as they could on Jakoba's blanket when two soldiers entered the tent, one of them carrying a notebook and pencil. The other, older and obviously in command, addressed them in English.

Petronella was trying to pick out any familiar words, but Marie Naudé forestalled any attempt she or Jakoba could make at translating. "I am fluent in English," she told the others, and demonstrated her claim by entering into conversation with the soldier in charge.

"They wish to know," she interpreted, "how many of us have blood-kin among the burghers; their relationship to us and their names. I have already told them that *I* have no one on commando."

Petronella supposed the authorities wished to keep a record so that they could inform next-of-kin if any of their men were killed in battle. The soldier who had been doing the talking said something else after all the information had been noted down, and Marie Naudé answered him with what seemed to be a personal plea. The soldier shrugged and spread his hands, and the two of them left.

Marie Naudé sighed. "The officer said that rations will be dealt out to us tomorrow, and that all candles and lanterns must be extinguished by eight at night."

"Since we have neither candles nor a lantern," Mamma observed sourly, "it was a pointless instruction."

Jakoba stood up. "I think I'll go outside for a while. Would you like to come too, Petronella?"

The atmosphere inside the tent was stifling and it was difficult to make oneself comfortable, sharing a hard, folded-up blanket with Jakoba, and Petronella agreed readily.

Just outside the tent, placed in the only small spot of shade which the canvas cast, stood a wicker hamper. "It must belong to Mevrouw Naudé," Petronella said. "I suppose the dog sleeps inside it."

"Hmm . . . She was telling the soldiers that she shouldn't be here. Almost as if it's quite right and proper that the rest of us should."

Petronella did not comment. They were walking along the narrow strip of red earth separating the tents and the sun beat down on them, reflecting from the white canvas all around them, and the smell of open latrines was overpowering. She was about to suggest that they return to the tent when Jakoba exclaimed, "There are the soldiers who questioned us, just coming out of that tent. I wanted to ask them whether my aunt and uncle are here, but they left before I had put the sentence together in my mind. Let us catch up with them."

When they reached the two soldiers, Jakoba put her question haltingly. The officer took the notebook from his junior, leafed through it, and shook his head. Jakoba began to turn forlornly away, but Petronella spoke quickly. "Marcus Koen," she addressed the soldiers, making a question of the name. "Exile – " She turned to Jakoba. "What is the English for 'to which country has he been sent?' "

Jakoba groped for the correct words, and the officer said something. "He doesn't know," Jakoba reported. "I'm not certain, but I think he said that you would have to write letters to the Army headquarters if you want information about exiles."

Blank despair seized Petronella. It would be difficult enough to learn to speak English. How was she to learn to read and write the language?

The two girls had turned away when the young soldier came after them. He said something, his gaze resting on Petronella, and for a moment she forgot that he was an enemy because he looked so wistful and lonely and as if he wished himself a million miles away from this bleak, soulless camp which stank and baked in the sun.

"He says," Jakoba translated, blushing, "that he is free every afternoon from one o'clock to three, and that he would give us English lessons if we would like him to.".

"Oh!" Petronella smiled at the young man, her eyes shining. "Please thank him. Ask him where we should meet him."

"He'll call for us," Jakoba delivered the soldier's answer.

It was the first small chink of hope Petronella had yet been offered in her search for Marcus. Somehow, Mamma would have to be persuaded to give her permission, for the dictionary and Pappa's writing box would be vital to the lessons, and Petronella could not possibly smuggle them out of the tent without Mamma knowing.

As soon as the two girls returned to the tent Petronella put her plea to Mamma, who said flatly, "Certainly not! Mevrouw Naudé speaks English fluently, and she can translate for us whenever necessary."

"I should be glad to," the woman assured Mamma.

"What harm could it do?" Petronella argued passionately. "Jakoba and I would be together, and no one would talk if we took lessons – "

"You are not hobnobbing with English soldiers, Petronella, and that is an end to the matter! Mevrouw Naudé will do any translating on our behalf. And while I think of it – you and Jakoba will have to share a blanket tonight, so that Mevrouw Naudé may have yours." Without waiting for a response, Mamma added, "Now, if you will excuse me, I had better do something about supper, since we are not to receive rations until the morning."

Discreetly, Mamma turned her back and wriggled out of the extra corset while Marie Naudé, her dog still clasped to her thin bosom, looked on with horrified fascination. Her expression became more pronounced as Mamma began to rip open some of the stitching on the corset. As well as biltong, Mamma had also sewn into the garment a small, sharp knife wrapped in cloth. She sat down again and began to carve a length of biltong into slivers. With scrupulous fairness, she divided the biltong between all of them, adding an extra ration to Marie Naudé's share for the dog.

The woman thanked Mamma graciously, but she ate none of it herself. They watched, incredulously, as she fed her entire share to the dog. She looked up and explained defensively, "I am sorry, but I simply could not have eaten it." She did not make clear whether it was because of where the biltong had been hidden, or whether her digestion could not cope with it.

Mamma's expression was carefully blank, and Petronella knew that she was giving Marie Naudé the benefit of the doubt. She had obviously decided to ignore the matter of the biltong, for she asked the other woman, "You were saying, earlier, that your late husband was a doctor. I myself know a little about medicines – "

But Marie Naudé was not interested in Mamma's knowledge. Tears filled her eyes. "A most respected man in the community, and we counted many British people from the Cape as our friends, which makes it doubly unfair that I should find myself here. We lived in Bethulie, near the border. A dreadful mistake has been made and I am waiting for the authorities to sort it out. Simply because my late husband's two orphaned nephews are on commando, and we share the same name, the British think I am their mother, and I was taken from my beautiful house and brought here."

Mamma did not comment. She merely said, "I think we might as well prepare for bed."

They stretched their blankets out on the ground so that they could roll themselves up in them, for they knew the night would be bitterly cold. Petronella reflected that she and Jakoba, sharing one blanket between them, would be even colder and more uncomfortable than the others, and she wondered acidly why Mevrouw Naudé had not had the sense to bring a blanket of her own.

Almost in answer to that thought, the woman said, "I had the soldier leave my hamper outside the tent. Would you two girls please be good enough to carry it inside for me?"

They nodded and left the tent. If the hamper was, indeed, meant for the dog to sleep in it was certainly not empty, judging by its weight. A few minutes later they all watched, bemused, as Marie Naudé unpacked it. As well as spare clothing and other items, it held a plump eiderdown, and using Petronella's blanket as a groundsheet, Marie Naudé spread the eiderdown out on the floor. Then, with the dog under one arm, she picked up a large tin which obviously contained food of some kind, judging by the excitement of the slavering, sniffing dog as he tried to reach it.

"I am just going outside," Marie Naudé told them with a disarming smile, "to take my treasure for a walk."

"And to share with the creature whatever food is inside the tin," Mamma said under her breath as the woman left the tent.

Jakoba was staring in some awe at Marie Naudé's spare clothing lying on top of the eiderdown. "She must be quite rich. And that hat of hers is so elegant . . ."

Mamma snorted. "And see what good elegant hats have done her! She can't be more than forty, but her face is like a dried-up prune from the sun. Let that be a lesson to you, Petronella, never to go without your *kappie*." Mamma stooped, and with a vigorous gesture pulled out Petronella's blanket from underneath the eiderdown, handing it to her.

If Marie Naudé noticed its absence later, when she returned with the dog, she made no comment but prepared herself for bed and crawled beneath the eiderdown with her pet.

They all spent a wretched night, cold and uncomfortable with hardly any sleep. In the morning Mevrouw Naudé looked at Dorothea, who was nursing the baby, and asked wanly, "Does the little dear cry like that every night?"

Mamma gave Dorothea no chance to reply. "Only when he is woken up by a yapping dog!" she said tartly.

"My poor little love is homesick," Marie Naudé defended, stroking the dog.

A few minutes later soldiers arrived with rations, and now it was revealed why the camp authorities had wanted to know which of the prisoners had men on commando.

"Those who have husbands, sons, brothers or other blood-kin on commando," Mevrouw Naudé translated for them, "receive lower rations than others. They have decided to give me the benefit of the doubt while they try to find evidence that the two Naudé boys are not related to me by blood, and I have been allowed five and a quarter pounds of meat for the week, while the rest of you receive only two pounds each. And the seven pounds of flour are for me; you get none at all, but have to make do with three pounds each of mealie-meal a week."

Mamma stared grimly at the few pieces of wood which had been delivered so that they might build a fire. "I don't see how we are to prepare anything for cooking. To begin with, we have no water – "

"Oh, I forgot to tell you. The soldiers said a water-cart would be passing through the rows of tents soon, and we shall be able to collect our water ration from it."

"It's a good thing we have you to translate for us," Mamma said, and it was obvious that she had decided to let bygones be bygones, for she added diplomatically, "I couldn't help noticing last evening that you have a square tin among your belongings. It is the only thing we could use for collecting water and for cooking."

"Oh dear . . . It has sentimental value. My husband – "

"Do you have any better suggestions?" Mamma interrupted. "How do you intend cooking your rations?"

Mevrouw Naudé sighed. "You are right. I cannot cook at all; I have never needed to learn to do so, and I didn't think . . ." She brightened. "If you will do all the cooking, I shall share my rations with you. And you are right, of course; we shall have to use my tin."

Mamma looked at her with approval. "We'll use some of our ration of mealie-meal to make porridge for everyone's breakfast. I'll make more than we need, and then I'll mix the remainder with some of your flour and make it into flat cakes which we could bake on the lid of the tin, and have that later for our lunch. If you would give the tin to Petronella, Mevrouw Naudé, she could go and look for the water-cart."

The tin, now empty, smelled as if it had held cake, and Petronella took it and went in search of the water-cart. She had to wait her turn with other women and she noticed with misgiving that the water did not look very clean. She heard someone say that it had been brought from the Modder River, but it was all that was available, and when they had finished breakfast she would have to wipe the tin clean and go in search of the water-cart again to collect more for drinking purposes.

When she returned she found that Mamma had been out, visiting other tents, and someone had given her another tin, tall and circular in shape, which could be used for making coffee.

They breakfasted on mealie-porridge and drank the coffee, which tasted vile. "The soldiers told me," Marie Naudé volunteered, "that it is made of roasted acorns and roasted mealies."

"It is as well that we have you to ask questions on our behalf," Mamma said, "or we should never know what we are eating or drinking. Did they tell you what this terrible black sugar was?"

They had not, but Jakoba, who told them that she and her parents had once visited friends who owned a sugar plantation in Natal, added, "These are the black skimmings and the impurities left over in the sugar-boilers after the refining has been done."

"And the salt we have been given," Mamma put in, "is exactly the same coarse kind we used to put out for our cattle to lick. And it is not as if the British are able to plead poverty! When I think of all the supplies we were forced to leave behind on the wagons, and of the thousands of sheep and cattle the enemy commandeered – for which, by the way, we were never given the receipts we had been promised – "

She stopped, her expression taking on a look of outrage. Marie Naudé had picked up the tin which contained the remainder of the mealie-porridge Mamma had made and saved specially for the preparation of their lunch, and was offering it to her dog, which had already been fed. The woman saw her expression, and explained self-righteously, "My darling was still hungry, and after all, I am entitled to a larger share of the meals, because my rations are so much more than those of the rest of you."

Mamma was silent for a moment. Then, abruptly, she addressed Petronella. "You and Jakoba may go and learn English from that soldier after all."

Marie Naudé might not have realised it, but Mamma had just declared the opening of hostilities against her.

Petronella found it difficult to keep track of time as weeks merged into months, with very little to distinguish one day from another. She tried to blot out the many miseries of life in the camp by concentrating on the English lessons she attended daily with Jakoba. The young soldier, whose name was Rupert Brown, taught them inside the corrugated iron building which served him as an office, in which he wrote up information on the prisoners. At their first lesson he'd addressed himself to Jakoba, but his gaze had rested on Petronella as he spoke.

Instinct had warned her not to confide the more intimate details of her relationship with Marcus to Jakoba, and she knew that the other girl saw it as a fairy-tale romance. Now, she heard Jakoba advise, "I think it would be best, Petronella, if we made Corporal Brown believe Marcus is your cousin. He might, otherwise, stop our lessons."

"Why on earth should it make any difference to the Englishman who or what Marcus is to me?"

"Because of the way he looks at you," Jakoba said simply.

Petronella shrugged. She had no interest in Rupert Brown, or in how he felt about her. "Very well, let him think Marcus is my cousin."

And so the lessons continued, and Petronella made steady progress with the learning of English, so that even if she could not yet speak it with any fluency or write in it, she was able to understand most of what Rupert said to her.

"I would write to Army headquarters on your behalf," he told her, "but I don't believe they would give any information about your cousin, because I have no personal or official reason for needing to know where he is."

She thanked him, and persevered with her lessons. It had become a matter of pride that she should be able to write a letter to the British Army herself, a letter that would be understood and would not be sniggered over because of the mistakes it contained.

In the meantime, she tried to shut her mind to the grimness of life in the camp. No one could really have been said to be clean, because water was severely rationed and no soap of any kind was available. Once, when Petronella and Jakoba passed a couple of British officers talking together, Petronella forced herself to bite hard on her tongue as she heard them discussing what dirty people the Boers were.

"How," she exploded to Jakoba, "can we be anything but dirty when we have to try and wash in a cupful of water, and without soap?"

The issue of the lack of soap became a burning one among the prisoners. Hunger and overcrowding and hellish discomfort could be endured with a certain amount of dignity, but not being able to clean oneself because of the unavailability of soap was demeaning to the spirit.

One day a rumour spread through the prisoners that a group of women from the Cape, led by an English spinster called Miss Emily Hobhouse, were visiting the camp. The hostility directed towards these women was dispelled by Miss Hobhouse herself. A gentle-featured, middle-aged woman, she soon made it plain that the sympathies of herself and her companions were on the side of the prisoners.

"I shall speak to the camp superintendent about the provision of soap," she promised, "and also about the other privations you are being forced to endure."

But later, when she called at Mamma's tent for her news to be translated to the other prisoners, she reported with anger that the superintendent considered soap to be a luxury. Before they left she and her companions, whom she referred to as her Ladies' Committee, promised to raise funds by charitable means so that soap might be donated to the camp.

Mamma thanked her, but after a while she said thoughtfully, "In the meantime we shall make our own soap. I should have thought of it before."

Marie Naudé tittered. "And how, pray, would that be possible?"

Mamma gave her a long, direct look. "Yes, I don't imagine you have ever needed to make soap in your life. I daresay you think it can only be done in a factory. I have a supply of caustic soda, and I am going to visit the other tents to persuade people to save the fat from their meat ration and let me have it for the making of soap."

But the meat ration was shrinking as more and more people were being brought into the camp. The meat was from sheep so undernourished that the carcases resembled greyhounds; the beef was clearly from cattle which had died of disease, because Mamma identified the yellowish spots on the flesh. Such rations not only yielded very little fat, but often the meat was so maggoty that the women were driven to refuse it, and they were given bully-beef instead. Whatever horrors one might suspect *that* contained, the fat which helped to make up its bulk could not be extracted for the making of soap.

To Petronella, the plenty there had been on Jakkalsdrif now seemed like a dream. She tried to block from her mind the hunger and hardship and concentrate only on the matter of tracing Marcus's place of exile. But some things were impossible to shut out. Sanitary arrangements were crude and basic and had always added to their misery, but with the arrival of more and more prisoners matters became even worse. While new latrine trenches were being dug, slop-pails stood unemptied all over the camp and in the heat of the late autumn sun the stench became unbearable.

When the hoped-for rain came, the last before winter took over, it brought its own discomfort. The water streamed down through the canvas of the tents and came flooding in under the flap, soaking the blankets and their clothes. But at least they were able to catch rain-water for washing themselves and their clothes, and Mamma had at last been able to make a few bars of precious, rough soap.

The winter began to set in, with sharp, bitter frosts, and the camp authorities allowed the prisoners to leave the camp under guard so that they could forage for fuel with which to make fires to sit around for warmth. They picked up dry mule dung and dug up roots, but it was pitifully inadequate and many old people and babies died of the cold.

In the evenings when Petronella sat next to Jakoba, with the dictionary between them, working at the lessons set for them by Rupert Brown, her fingers were so numb and dead with cold that she could barely hold the pen. She knew she was using Jakoba and did not return the girl's unselfish devotion. The moments of guilt she suffered because of it were fleeting; Marcus was what mattered, and only Marcus. Jakoba was as much a means to the end of finding him as Rupert Brown was.

Almost as if she knew what Petronella was thinking and wished to reassure her, Jakoba said, "You are all I have now, Petronella. The Lord knows where my aunt and uncle are, or whether they are still alive, or indeed whether I have any kin left alive anywhere. You and I are best friends and I'll always do everything I can to help you." She put down her pen and rubbed her hands and then blew on her fingers in an effort to bring some warmth and life back to them.

Neither Mamma nor Dorothea displayed any interest in the conversation in English between the two girls. Petronella knew that her mother and sister-in-law were both concerned about baby Gabriel. Dorothea's milk had dried up because of their poor diet, and when there was no fuel to be found at all, she heated water in a spoon over a candle so that she could mix it with condensed milk for the baby. During those periods when there was no fuel at all, the prisoners had the added misery of being forced to eat their meat ration raw. Petronella shuddered, and declined hers, and watched as Marie Naudé seized it eagerly to feed to her dog, the only living thing in the camp on which the bones did not show through the skin.

As Petronella's knowledge of English grew, she discovered by eavesdropping on the conversation between the guards that the Transvaal and the Orange Free State had been officially annexed by the British Crown. She told Mamma and Dorothea and Marie Naudé, and the news spread through the camp, casting a pall of gloom over everyone. Previously, the camp had been starved altogether of news from the outside, whether good or bad, for censorship was strictly enforced.

At last the day came when Petronella felt that her knowledge of English had reached a standard which would enable her to write a letter to the Army headquarters. She submitted it to Rupert Brown when she had finished it, and when he had read it he said approvingly, "That is first-class, Miss van Zyl! I shall send it on for you, and you will soon have news of where your relative has been exiled to."

"Please don't bring the reply to our tent," she asked him. "I want to surprise my mother with news of where my cousin has been sent, and I also want to find out a little about the country where he is, so that I may perhaps set her mind at rest about the conditions under which he is living."

When the reply to her letter came at last, she could barely contain her total despair at yet another failure of her plans. The letter stated that it was not the Army's policy to give information as to the whereabouts of exiled prisoners.

For so many months now she had been sustained by the hope of finding out where Marcus was, and every path had led nowhere. "The fiends!" she burst out, tears welling into her eyes. "I hope they all rot in hell one day!"

Jakoba put an arm about her shoulder and said in Dutch, "Be careful. You are not behaving as if Marcus Koen is simply a relative."

"Oh, what does it matter? What does anything matter now? I don't care what the Englishman suspects! I have no further use for him." She switched to English, and addressed Rupert Brown. "There would be no point in taking further lessons."

She could see that her statement had brought him pain and utter dismay. "At the very least," he protested, "it would be a way of continuing to fill in time." *And I could go on seeing you,* his expression added.

Petronella shrugged her indifference to his suggestion and his feelings, and left with Jakoba. Her thoughts were bleak and bitter and filled with despair as the two of them walked through the rows of tents to their own. There was no hope left of any kind to which to cling.

An argument was raging inside their tent, because Marie Naudé's dog had found the opened tin of condensed milk upon which Dorothea's baby depended, and had upset it and licked up most of its contents before it could be stopped.

Oh God, Petronella thought, I can't bear it. Nothing but misery and constant quarrelling and hardship and always, whatever the season, the choking red dust that blows on the wind, and the stench from the latrine trenches. There is no comfort or hope anywhere, and I might as well forget Marcus, because he is lost to me. I shall have to learn to accept it.

That night she lay awake, wrapped up in her blanket, and made a determined, desperate effort to talk herself out of loving Marcus. Was it really love at all? It was not as if she had any past experiences by which to judge. Oh, there had been the night of Johannes's wedding, when the touch of Gerrit du Toit had stirred a painful longing in her loins. But when he'd kissed her she had felt nothing but revulsion, and as for that feeling in her loins – it was there often, usually when she first woke up in the morning, and even when she had not been dreaming about Marcus.

Perhaps, she reasoned, there was little connection between that feeling and love. Perhaps the feeling was as natural and part of life as – as, oh, as indigestion, say. For all she knew even Dorothea had that feeling when she thought about Johannes, or Mamma when she remembered Pappa.

A novel thought struck Petronella. Could it be that she responded so intensely to Marcus, not because she loved him, but because he was forbidden fruit? Could that be the reason why she'd felt nothing but revulsion when Gerrit kissed her and kneaded away at her breast? She had known Gerrit all her life; courtship, betrothal and marriage to him would have been encouraged and welcomed by Mamma and Pappa. Marcus, the *Uitlander* and the Jew, was someone Mamma had stated she would never accept, and if Mamma did not accept him, it was doubtful if Pappa would. So could all this pain and longing Petronella felt for him be based upon nothing more than the excitement of rebellion, the tempting lure of the outlawed?

Oh God, she prayed, since I am never to have Marcus, please show me a way of curing myself of him . . .

But God provided no ready solution, and after a while she fell into a tormented doze, from which she was woken by the joint sounds of the dog's yapping and the baby's cries. The day stretched ahead, with nothing but the hard, grim realities of camp life to fill it.

That afternoon Petronella addressed Jakoba abruptly. "It is time for our English lesson."

"But you said – "

Petronella gave her a warning look. "We had better not keep the Englishman waiting."

As they left the tent, she explained with a shrug, "If we stop the lessons, we would have to sit about like the others, with nothing whatever to do. At least the lessons are something with which to occupy our minds and kill time."

Rupert Brown did not hide his joy at seeing them when they entered his office. "After you left yesterday, I thought of a way of making the lessons more interesting, now that your English has become so good. I wanted to kick myself for thinking of it too late!"

Petronella was studying him dispassionately, taking in the vulnerable expression in his eyes as he gazed at her. "Anything even remotely interesting would be welcome."

It seemed to her that he had, uncannily, been party to her thoughts during the night, for he said, "Part of the excitement would come from the fact that what I'm suggesting is strictly against the rules. I receive newspapers from England from time to time, and we could read them together. Until now all the reading either of you has done has been of pieces of prose written down by me. The newspapers would help to improve your reading, and be more interesting than anything I could think up. No one ever comes to disturb us during the time I'm giving you lessons, so provided you said nothing about it, nobody need know that we are breaking the censorship rules."

He opened a drawer in his desk and brought out a newspaper, handing it to Petronella after he had folded it, contriving to touch her hand. "Miss van Zyl, you start reading the top left-hand column aloud."

Her tongue stumbling over some of the words, she began to read. He had exaggerated the interest which the newspaper would provide, she found, for its reports spoke of affairs in England, affairs which she could not comprehend or relate to, concerning a country for which she felt nothing but hatred as the country of the invading enemy. But reading a boring report from a forbidden newspaper was preferable to sitting inside the bell tent, listening to the warfare being waged between Mamma and Marie Naudé.

Petronella looked up from the newspaper to find Rupert's gaze fixed upon her face, his expression totally revealing. It held love and longing – and guilt. *Forbidden fruit*, she thought. She was to him what Marcus had always been to her.

The realisation caused her to give Rupert a wryly sympathetic smile. She watched the colour flowing into his face, saw the flame of hope in his eyes. And suddenly it came to her that for her, too, this Englishman, this enemy of her country, would be the ultimate in forbidden fruit.

When it was Jakoba's turn to read from the newspaper Petronella barely listened to her, so busy was she with her own thoughts. Could Rupert Brown be God's answer to her prayers for something to exorcise the utterly hopeless feeling she had for Marcus, whom she would never see again?

She studied Rupert from under her lashes, willing herself to feel something for him. But there was nothing. In despair, she chided herself for remaining unmoved by his good looks.

She became aware that Jakoba had stopped reading, and was

handing the newspaper back to Rupert. "Tomorrow we'll read the page on ladies' fashions," he said.

"Of what possible interest," Jakoba muttered as the two of them left the office, "can the fashions of ladies in England be to us? Especially to us, with no more than one threadbare change of clothing for the lucky ones? I shall choke if I have to read descriptions of rich Englishwomen's gowns."

Perhaps, Petronella thought, if she and Rupert were to be alone together he might take on the attraction of forbidden fruit, and dilute the longing for Marcus that was tearing her apart.

She touched Jakoba's arm. "It was not simply boredom that made me want to go on with our lessons; it was the hope that Rupert Brown might be persuaded to find out for me, in an unofficial way, where Marcus is. But I can see that it was selfish of me to expect you to carry on helping me."

"Oh Petronella, how can you say that? I would *always* do anything I could to help you!"

"Why should you have to endure such a waste of your time? So many new prisoners have been brought into the camp recently, Jakoba, that some of them might have news of your aunt and uncle. Instead of sitting inside Brown's office, reading boring English newspapers, you should be visiting their tents every day and seeing what you may discover."

"Yes," Jakoba admitted, "it has occurred to me that someone among the newcomers might have news of my family. But nothing would make me desert you, Petronella, and you know your Mamma would never allow you to carry on with the English lessons on your own."

"She needn't know about it," Petronella said carefully, "if we make sure that we always leave the tent together, and return together. I *insist* that you stop wasting your time on my behalf."

"Oh, you are so thoughtful and unselfish, Petronella!"

If you guessed, Jakoba, how selfish I really am, and what I have in mind, Petronella thought with guilt, even your blind loyalty would turn to disgust.

After that day the two of them kept up the illusion that they went together for English lessons; in reality Jakoba skirted the corrugated iron office of Rupert Brown and spent the following hours haunting the tents of newcomers to the camp. Petronella sat alone with Rupert, pretending to take an interest in the newspaper reports she read aloud to him, aware that he was pretending in turn to take a tutor's interest in the progress of his pupil. In reality she was desperately trying to feel *something* for Rupert, trying to respond to the naked yearning in his eyes.

But it was no use. She gave up, and asked a question about a point contained in the newspaper report she had been reading. He explained it to her and then went on to talk about his life in England. What he said held very little meaning for her, but she gained the impression that his parents were wealthy and there was both homesickness and resentment in his voice as he talked about his family.

"My father had influence enough with the Secretary of War to pull strings to keep me safe, which is the reason why I am acting as no more than a clerk here, instead of seeing active service with my regiment – "

"You mean," Petronella cut in, "instead of killing Boers." When he flushed with embarrassment, she added, "Don't worry, they would kill you if they had the chance."

He looked into her eyes. "It's difficult to remember that you and I are supposed to be enemies."

"I – suppose so," she said, a little breathlessly. The message in his eyes had been so very clear.

He went on in a husky voice, "According to the Bible, one should love one's enemy." He rose slowly, his gaze devouring her. "Petronella . . ."

She rose too, and forced herself to move towards him. Physical contact might achieve what everything else had failed to. His hands were unsteady as he drew her close and she felt the familiar ache stirring in her loins when he pressed himself against her. Oh, it was working. Praise the Lord, it was working . . .

He parted her lips with his own, and the ache sharpened momentarily, then withered and died. It was *not* working because he was not Marcus. She pushed at his chest and when he let her go she turned away, tears prickling behind her eyes.

Oh Marcus, she mourned silently. My love, my love. Even if I never see you again for the rest of my life, I'll know that what we had between us was real and rare and had nothing to do with forbidden fruit.

"I am sorry, Petronella," she heard Rupert say humbly and miserably. "I presumed – I thought – "

She turned to face him. "I shall not be coming for more lessons in English."

"Petronella! Please, I beg you – I love you and just seeing you means so much – "

"It would be pointless," she cut him short.

He spoke feverishly. "I shall not overstep the mark again, I promise you. And you enjoyed reading the articles, didn't you? Here – " He pulled open a drawer of his desk and brought out a newspaper. "I've only just received it and haven't read it yet. You may borrow it – only, be careful to hide it from view."

She understood his motive perfectly well. If she borrowed the newspaper she would have to return it. Her first instinct was to refuse it, and then she thought of the many uses to which a newspaper could be put inside their tent – as table-cloth, as floor-covering and ultimately as fuel.

She took the newspaper from him and stuffed it down the front of her bodice. She had no intention of returning it to him or seeing him again. With a nod, she turned away.

As she emerged from the office she saw Jakoba, as usual, making her way towards her. Jakoba prattled on about the people she had met and spoken to that afternoon, but Petronella was barely listening to her. Oh God, Marcus, she thought, I shall never be free of you. What am I going to do, how am I to live my life without you?

She now knew that the ache in her loins was something designed by nature, no·doubt with the continuation of the human race in mind. But only Marcus was capable of satisfying that ache, and the desolation of the future without him, the ache forever unsilenced, was so devastating that the grimness of camp life became as nothing by comparison.

She spoke only once before they reached the bell tent. "I shall not be returning for more English lessons. Corporal Brown is quite incapable of helping me to find Marcus."

"I am so very sorry, Petronella," Jakoba said sincerely.

After they had entered the bell tent Petronella unbuttoned the top of her blouse and brought out the newspaper. It would be a shame to use it for practical purposes before she had even read it, she decided, and turned its pages. Her desultory interest quickened when she discovered that the newspaper had devoted an entire section to the war in South Africa.

Then she read with a feeling of utter doom that contingents of soldiers from other countries such as Canada, Australia and India had been sent to join the British troops in South Africa, and that there were now more than 450,000 highly trained soldiers fighting against 18,000 guerilla farmers. She thought of Pappa and Johannes and Gideon, and wondered how they and the other burghers could possibly hold out for much longer against such a force. If, indeed, her father and brothers had not already been killed.

She decided to keep the news to herself, since there was no point in alarming the others. But in a separate column of the newspaper she came upon something about which she felt totally unable to remain silent, and she reached for the dictionary so that she could use it to translate the more obscure, difficult words.

"Listen to this!" she called out. "Just listen while I read to you what they've written about us in England!"

The others fell silent, and gave her their attention. " 'The people inside the South African refugee camps,' " she translated as she read the report, " 'have a sufficient allowance and are all comfortable and happy, and grateful to the British for the protection offered by the camps. The Secretary of War has assured the House of Commons that the people went voluntarily to the camps for their protection against the blacks.' "

Mamma uttered a mild oath, and then laughed savagely. "Does it say anything about the barbed wire around the camp, and the soldiers with their guns and their bayonets guarding it to see that none of these happy souls escape?"

"Listen to what else it says!" Petronella cried with anger. " 'The Boers are of a low, degenerate mentality who are far better off in camps than they had ever been in their own homes. The women in general are dirty, lazy and untruthful, creatures who neglect their children and have been known to poison them deliberately. In the camps, separated from their husbands who are little more than brutal brigands, marauding robbers and often murderers, they may well benefit from the civilising influence of the British.' "

All of them were united in their fury and outrage at such slanderous, contemptuous lies. A couple of women were passing the tent and Mamma called them inside so that Petronella could translate the newspaper report again for their benefit. Inevitably, the story spread through the camp, evoking such mutinous rage that a deputation of prisoners decided to march on the camp superintendent's office.

When she heard about it Petronella bitterly regretted that she had not kept the newspaper report to herself. The fact that she had an English newspaper in her possession would be investigated. Her only consolation lay in the fact that the people who had marched on the camp superintendent's office had heard about the report at third or fourth hand, and would hardly be likely to know who had translated it in the first place.

But only a short while later a senior officer entered their tent. His stern gaze went to Petronella and then to Jakoba. "Someone intent on mischief," he said, "has illegally come into possession of a British newspaper. You two young women receive lessons in English from Corporal Rupert Brown, and he has confirmed that a newspaper is missing from his office. He is unwilling to point a finger at either of you, and is determined to shoulder all the blame himself. But I have been asked to investigate the matter fully and ensure that all culprits are punished."

"There is only one so-called culprit – myself." Petronella took the newspaper from underneath her blanket where she had hidden it and stepped forward, her chin in the air, pretending a defiant courage she was far from feeling. The very last thing she wished for was an investigation, with Mamma discovering that she had been attending lessons unchaperoned and with everyone suspecting there was something between herself and Rupert.

"This is the newspaper containing the disgusting lies written about us," she told the officer. "I stole it. Corporal Brown had to leave his office for a moment, and I opened a drawer in his desk, and hid the newspaper inside my bodice." Her glance sought Jakoba's. "Miss Steenkamp was with me; she tried to reason with me but I ignored her."

The officer turned to Jakoba. "Is this true, Miss Steenkamp?"

"We – we stole it together." Jakoba bravely tried to share the blame, and at the same time cover up the fact that Petronella had been alone with Rupert Brown. But she was an unconvincing liar and the officer dismissed her claim to have been involved in the theft.

"I am afraid, Miss van Zyl," he told Petronella, "you will have to be punished for this. You have abused our tolerance and you have abused Corporal Brown's trust and his generosity in giving up his free time to teach you English. Please come with me."

As punishment, she was sent for a week to a small, wired enclosure on the outskirts of the camp, where she was forced to remain in the open during the day so that everyone would see her and know of her disgrace. There was a small tent in which she was allowed to shelter during the night, and the only ration she received was rice-water. Thankfully, Rupert had not been stupid enough to confess to what had really happened.

She paced the confines of the enclosure, cold, bitter, hungry and consumed with rage, glaring at the armed soldiers who were there to make sure that no one came to comfort her with words or with a share of their rations. She hated the British and the war which had torn Marcus from her forever and left only desolation in his place.

"And I hate the Almighty," she muttered, defying Him to strike her dead on the spot. She counted it as part of her punishment that He did not.

10

The end of Petronella's punishment also marked the beginning of the sickness that struck the camp. Dysentery and measles were rampant, and typhoid was rumoured, and almost ceaselessly ambulance wagons rumbled through the camp, ferrying patients to the corrugated iron hospital while buck-wagons carried out the dead.

And the survivors could not afford the luxury of being squeamish. When whole families died, the contents of their tents were picked over for utensils, for cooking pots or dishes or boxes which could be used as furniture.

Sometimes, Petronella wished she might catch one of the diseases which were felling so many prisoners, for with Marcus lost to her forever, she felt that she no longer had anything left to live for. But she remained, in spite of their privations, in spite of ever-dwindling food rations, remarkably robust. Mamma was perhaps wholly responsible for this.

She insisted that every drop of water they used should be boiled first, and that all meat should be thoroughly cooked. And she dosed her family relentlessly with her *bossiemiddels*.

Because hardly anyone who entered hospital came back alive, people stopped reporting illnesses, and cared for their sick themselves, with the help of others. Mamma was by no means the only *Ziekentrooster* in the camp; there were many older women who were wise in the preparation and use of herbal remedies, and the people turned to them for help instead.

As the deaths increased, official notices were circulated inside the camp, forbidding the prescription of what the authorities called 'native potions containing poisons', and claiming these were to blame for many of the fatalities.

Mamma dismissed the notices with scorn. "Do they think we are so stupid that we would have gone on using *bossiemiddels* for generations if they had contained poisons?"

Petronella watched the buck-wagons carrying dead bodies out of the camp and returning later with carcases of meat for the prisoners' rations. Why, she wondered bitterly, did the authorities appear to make no connection between this fact and the many deaths? And one needed no medical knowledge to realise that their water supply must be teeming with typhoid and other germs. Mamma forced them to go thirsty rather than drink it unboiled, but there was so little fuel available with which to boil water that others who did not possess Mamma's iron determination were drinking it in its filthy, polluted state.

Mamma ignored the new regulations and carried on dosing her family with preventative infusions, and supplied her *bossiemiddels* to anyone who turned to her for help. Marie Naudé looked on in disapproval as Mamma dosed a young child who had been brought to her. When it had left the tent with its mother, Marie Naudé said, "The child ought to be sent to the hospital, where they know what they are doing, and you know very well that you are breaking a strict rule!"

"How many people," Mamma rounded on her, "have you heard of who have left the hospital alive?"

"Even doctors cannot perform miracles. But speaking as a doctor's widow – "

"Listen!" Mamma exclaimed passionately. "I have been speaking to several people, and comparing notes. Your precious doctors are handing out precisely the same powders to people suffering from suspected typhoid as they give to those with broken legs!"

"You are ignorant of the properties of modern medicines, and cannot know what effect – " Marie Naudé began loftily.

Mamma made a rude sound. "When you catch the mange from that wretched mongrel of yours," she said, "don't bother coming to *me* for help!"

When an officer called, later that morning, to take Mamma before the camp superintendent to answer a charge of having prescribed illegal native potions, it was not too difficult to work out who had informed upon her. Marie Naudé had taken care to absent herself from the tent when he called, and Dorothea wept when Petronella translated to Mamma what the officer had said, while Mamma remained defiant and unmoved.

Petronella accompanied Mamma and the officer to the camp superintendent's office, so that she could translate what he said. She did not expect Mamma to receive more than a strong rebuke, and perhaps an order to hand over all her herbal remedies so that they might be destroyed. Instead, the superintendent began by demanding the names of all the people Mamma had recently been treating with her *bossiemiddels*, and the names were checked against a list.

To Petronella's horror, the superintendent announced, "One of the people, a man called van Wyk, died soon after being prescribed an illegal native potion by your mother. It is time for an example to be made to serve as a warning to others, and your mother will have to go to Bloemfontein, to appear before a magistrate, who will decide whether or not she is to stand trial on a charge of manslaughter."

Her lips trembling, Petronella translated to Mamma what had been said. Not by a flicker of an eyelid did Mamma betray any fear. Instead, she said with scorn, "Van Wyk was an old man, dying and already beyond hope when I gave him an infusion, and I only did so because his wife begged it of me, as a last resort. The British are in a panic, because they cannot control the sickness sweeping through the camp, and so they are looking for scapegoats. Tell the superintendent what I said, child."

But Petronella judged it prudent only to pass on to him the information that the dead man had been beyond saving in any case. The superintendent dismissed her claim, and said, "Tell your mother she will have to leave for Bloemfontein immediately. You will accompany her, Miss van Zyl, so that you may be able to act as interpreter. An armed escort will go with you."

When Mamma received the news, she demanded, "How am I to reach Bloemfontein?"

"You will walk there," the superintendent answered through Petronella.

Mamma drew herself up. If they wanted her to appear in a court in Bloemfontein, she said, they would have to convey her there, for she refused to walk at the behest of the British.

Impatiently at first, and then with an air of growing frustration, the superintendent insisted that there was no vehicle which could take her to Bloemfontein. All the ambulance wagons were working at full stretch inside the camp and the buck-wagons were packed either with dead bodies for burial or else with supplies for the camp.

"I don't care," Mamma returned inflexibly. "I won't walk. If they want me to go to Bloemfontein, they will have to get me there in some other way."

The superintendent went outside, and returned a while later. With the air of a man pulling a master-stroke, he said, "The only possible conveyance we have available is a wheelbarrow."

"That will do," Mamma nodded calmly. "Just as long as I don't have to walk a step to where I don't want to go in any case."

With a grim smile, the superintendent went outside to give instructions and a short while later Mamma, her dignity totally unruffled, gathered her skirts and clambered into the wheelbarrow where she sat, ramrod-straight, her bulk filling its space and her legs sedately arranged over the edge as if she were seated upon a throne, her pose a regal one, looking anything but the foolish figure the superintendent had clearly envisaged.

Puffing and panting, the soldiers took it in turns to push Mamma in the wheelbarrow, while Petronella walked alongside. When they reached the pebble-strewn, brackish stream which lay between the camp and Bloemfontein the soldiers pleaded in vain with Mamma, through Petronella, to get out of the wheelbarrow and wade across the stream.

In the end, two of them were forced to carry Mamma over the water in what they called a firemen's lift, while the other two carried the wheelbarrow. Mamma resumed her seat and the soldiers continued to push her to Bloemfontein.

They excited considerable ribald amusement in the streets of the town, but the amusement was directed at the soldiers. There was something about Mamma's attitude which defied anyone to laugh at her. Instead, other soldiers jeered at their hapless colleagues.

Petronella had been warned by the camp superintendent that Mamma would probably be held in custody for several days before her case was heard. But the soldiers, obviously thinking of the ridicule from their colleagues which they would have to endure while they remained in Bloemfontein, and of the undignified journeys they would have to make, pushing Mamma from place to place in the wheelbarrow, conferred together. Petronella heard them decide to search for a magistrate who would be prepared to listen to the charges against Mamma that same day. One of the soldiers disappeared, and when he returned he told Petronella that a provost-marshal had been found, a Captain Bamford, before whom Mamma would be able to appear immediately.

The magistrate's court was a surprisingly simple, austere room, furnished with benches and a table at which an elderly man was sitting, flanked by two clerks. Apart from Mamma and Petronella and the four soldiers, no one else was present.

Captain Bamford listened carefully as the senior of the soldiers listed the case against Mamma. Then he put questions of his own, which Petronella translated.

What, precisely, had she given the man who had died?

Buchu, mixed with a little brandy-wine, Mamma readily admitted. A dose of one tablespoonful.

Captain Bamford nodded. And what, he wanted to know, would she prescribe for, say, pneumonia?

A mixture of rue-water and haarlemmer oil, Mamma answered through Petronella, with a few drops of sweet oil added to it.

The Captain leant forward. "Would you ask your mother, Miss van Zyl, whether she has ever used stinging nettles as a treatment for rheumatism?"

The soldiers were beginning to look as bewildered as Petronella was feeling. "Stinging nettles, sir? Do you mean wait-a-minute thorns, or hook-and-stab, or sweet thorns? Or perhaps prickly pear stings?"

"No." He sighed. "I daresay stinging nettles do not grow in your part of the land. Indeed, I have not seen any since I arrived in South Africa, and my rheumatism has been plaguing me lately. In the past I have found an infusion of stinging nettles – " He stopped, as if suddenly remembering his position.

Mamma insisted on being told what he had said, and she ordered, "Tell him, child, to try treating the affected joints with a poultice made of grated carrots, *jalap*, some goat-fat and a little distilled tobacco water."

As Petronella began to translate, Captain Bamford reached for a sheet of paper and made a careful note of the ingredients, and she could not help noticing the stifled amusement of the two clerks by his side, and the discomfiture and dismay of the soldiers.

Captain Bamford straightened in his chair, and addressed the soldiers sternly. "A great deal of time has been wasted over a nonsensical matter! The defendant freely admits that she broke the camp regulations when she prescribed herbal remedies, but that was not why she was brought before me, and I shall refrain from placing on record my own opinion of that particular regulation. As for a possible charge of manslaughter – I have never heard anything so ridiculous. A tablespoonful of *buchu* and brandy-wine could not possibly kill anyone. I find that there is no case against the defendant, and I order that she be removed from this court with no stain upon her character."

Smiling broadly, Petronella translated his words to Mamma, who seemed never to have been in any doubt about the outcome. As Petronella escorted her outside, she realised that the soldiers had already left the court, and there was no sign of them when Mamma took up her seat in the wheelbarrow again.

Now that it was all over, and Mamma was not to face a charge of manslaughter after all, Petronella looked about her at the wide streets of Bloemfontein. The town did not compare in any way with Johannesburg, and the only people who seemed to be about were British soldiers. The British flag fluttered from many of the buildings, reminding them that what had been the Orange Free State was no longer free.

Mamma said composedly, "I have an idea, child, that our four soldiers have made themselves scarce, because they are hoping that we will take the opportunity to escape. I don't think they relish pushing me back to the camp, watched by their jeering colleagues."

Petronella thought briefly of the possibility of escaping. To reach Jakkalsdrif again, where she might find peace, and gradually perhaps cure herself of her grief and longing for Marcus . . . But it would be impossible. Apart from abandoning Dorothea and her baby, she and Mamma were without money or food and in a city which was in the hands of the enemy.

The soldiers returned, unable to hide their chagrin at finding their burden waiting patiently for them, seated in the wheelbarrow. Trying to ignore the ribald remarks of passing soldiers, they began to push Mamma the two and a half miles back to the camp.

A report of what had happened had obviously preceded them, for when Mamma and Petronella had been curtly dismissed by the camp superintendent, people turned out of their bell tents and raised a tremendous cheer for Mamma.

Dorothea, her baby in her arms, came running to embrace Mamma, her eyes reddened with the anxious tears she had been shedding. As Petronella entered their tent, Jakoba said with a broad smile, "You have just missed Marie Naudé. She packed up her hamper, took her dog and her rations and said she was going to ask the superintendent to find her other accommodation immediately."

"I'm glad," Petronella grinned. "If she hadn't removed herself, I think there was every chance that Mamma would have found herself faced with a *real* charge of manslaughter."

The story of Mamma's journey to Bloemfontein and back in a wheelbarrow was the only piece of light relief to cheer the prisoners in the camp. The warmer weather did nothing to stem the tide of sickness and disease spreading from tent to tent, and almost as if to compensate for the many deaths, more and more prisoners were brought in.

One batch of new prisoners brought news which laid a heaviness on the spirits of everyone. Miss Emily Hobhouse, the doughty Englishwoman who had made herself a thorn in the side of the authorities on behalf of the prisoners and had been responsible for several charitable donations of supplies to them, had been arrested and deported to England.

But her voice refused to be smothered. One day a small child called and handed Petronella a tightly folded sheet of newsprint. It could only have been sent by Rupert, and she wondered fleetingly whether he had been prompted by guilt, because she alone had borne the punishment of being in possession of an English newspaper. Then she forgot all about him as she began to read the piece of newsprint.

It appeared to be a report of a letter directed by Miss Hobhouse to the Parliament in England. Arrested and deported she might have been, but that indomitable lady had not given up the fight on behalf of the prisoners, for part of her letter read: "It is hollow and rotten to the heart's core, to have made all over the State large, uncomfortable communities of people whom you call refugees, and say you are protecting, but who call themselves prisoners-of-war, compulsorily detained, and detesting your protection."

Petronella glanced at other parts of the report. "Let the people go . . . this cruel system which falls with such crushing effect upon the old, the weak and the children . . . a whole nation carried captive . . ."

While Emily Hobhouse's passionate endeavours on their behalf cheered Petronella somewhat, there were no practical changes for the better inside the camp. Sometimes it seemed to her that it was the petty pinpricks, rather than the gruelling privations they suffered, which threatened to send one over the edge of sanity. Marie Naudé's dog Pikkie was one such intolerable pinprick.

She might have left the tent, but her dog obviously still regarded it as his territory, for he returned to it again and again and 'marked it' as his mistress put it, or fouled the earth floor before he could be chased out. On several occasions, too, he succeeded in stealing their pitiful rations. When they went to complain to Marie Naudé, in the room in one of the few newly constructed corrugated iron buildings which she now occupied, she always swore that Pikkie never left her side, and that in any case he had no need to steal food. This last statement was difficult to argue against, for indeed the dog continued to be as sleek and plump as he was crafty and greedy.

Mamma said darkly, "It's my belief Marie Naudé is being given extra rations, as a reward for carrying tales about other prisoners to the superintendent."

The first of the spring rain began to fall, resulting in a rapid growth of vegetation in the previously bare earth surrounding the camp. Petronella persuaded the superintendent to allow the prisoners to leave the camp and set crude, improvised traps in the hope of snaring small animals with which to supplement their rations.

They went regularly to inspect them, but apart from a field-mouse which someone found, they had no success. But even just being away from the camp for an hour or two was a treat, particularly as the soldiers who were meant to guard them did not pay them much attention but generally sat together, playing cards. They knew that however badly any of the prisoners might want to escape, there was nowhere to escape to; they had no food or money and would soon have been caught again if they had made the attempt.

The soldiers took no notice when Mamma, Petronella and Jakoba, after a routine inspection of their trap, rounded the kopje and disappeared from sight. "Look," Petronella cried with excitement, "that stuff growing over there – I'm sure it's *marog!*"

"What is *marog*?" Jakoba wanted to know.

"It's a wild plant which can be cooked as a vegetable. Don't you remember, Mamma, how Mwende was always being sent by her grandmother to search for and pick *marog*? Mwende said it tasted like spinach, and they preferred it above all the other vegetables we grew on Jakkalsdrif." Petronella's voice faltered as she thought of the past, and she went on, "I wonder what happened to her and her mother and the others. I wonder if we'll ever see any of them again . . ."

"Come," Mamma interrupted briskly, practically, "let us go and gather *marog*."

Petronella hurried back to dismantle their trap so that they could use the dish as a receptacle in which to carry the leaves, but when she returned to where she had left Mamma and Jakoba they were nowhere to be seen. Then voices reached her faintly and she called out to Mamma, receiving an answer, and she hurried in their direction. She stopped in astonishment.

Inside a narrow fissure or *donga*, at the foot of the other side of the kopje, and partially screened by rocks, Mamma and Jakoba were crouching and talking to two men. Only their beards, their felt hats with one brim tilted towards the crown and the bandoliers which they wore across their chests proclaimed them to be burghers. They were dressed in nothing but grain sacks, with holes cut in them to serve as sleeves. Instead of boots, they wore strips of sacking wrapped and tied about their feet with narrow hide thongs.

"Petronella," Mamma said, "come and meet Jan and Flip."

In spite of their sunken eyes and their gaunt faces, the two men grinned cheerfully as they shook hands with Petronella. "Best not to tell you our full names, *Nig* Petronella, just in case anyone should ask you questions in a way you would find impossible not to answer."

She stared at them, appalled at their appearance. "Where are you from? What has been happening?"

As they sat there in the *donga*, Jan and Flip painted a picture for the women of what their men had been going through. In spite of the desperate straits they were in, the men were determined to continue the guerilla warfare. The clothes of most of them had rotted, and like Jan and Flip, they were wearing grain sacks. Lord Kitchener had issued a proclamation to the effect that any Boer found wearing khaki was to be shot out of hand as a spy, so that they were unable even to clothe themselves in the breeches and shirts of their fallen enemies. As well as being ragged, the Boers were also starving, and they survived by foraging for sheep that had escaped the British bayonets, or by ambushing the enemy and stealing their food supplies.

"We have hardly any ammunition left, and the only way we can get hold of any is by trailing the British columns," Flip said. "They are careless with their ammunition, because they know there is plenty more to be had, so when they drop a round or two from their bandoliers they don't bother to get off their horses to pick it up." He laughed. "So we Boers glean the crumbs from the rich man's table."

Jan laughed too. "I wonder how many Englishmen have been shot by one of the bullets they themselves were careless enough to drop, and too lazy to pick up."

"How long," Mamma asked with a defeated sigh, "can you hope to last out?"

"We fight on to the bitter end," Flip said without hesitation, and Jan nodded agreement.

Mamma had already established that neither of them had any news of Pappa or Johannes or Gideon. She asked them what they were doing, hiding there in the *donga* so close to the camp, and after a moment's hesitation, Flip said, "It is also near Bloemfontein. Let us just say that our visit has something to do with the railway line. There won't be a moon tonight to help the look-outs in the blockhouses."

Petronella wanted to ask them how they hoped to get away afterwards, and where they had hidden their horses, but something in their expression warned her that it was best not to enquire too closely into their plans.

Mamma was studying the two men. "How long," she asked abruptly, "since you have eaten?"

Flip shrugged. "We had some rusks this morning. Was it this morning, Jan? Yes, I'm sure it must have been this morning."

Mamma stood up. "Since there will be no moon tonight, and you are not far from Bloemfontein, you need be in no great hurry to go there to do whatever has to be done. Come to the camp tonight as soon as it has grown dark, and you will be given a hot, cooked meal of meat and vegetables."

Mamma was behaving as if she were still on Jakkalsdrif, with a larder whose shelves were crowded with all manner of things to eat. She ordered Petronella and Jakoba to gather *marog*, and hurried to join the other women who were searching hopefully for birds' eggs in the grass or merely sitting down in the sun and enjoying a rare few minutes away from the stink of the camp.

Petronella soon learnt that Mamma had been busy organising a special feast for the two burghers. She had taken the other women into her confidence and most of them had promised to sacrifice something from their own rations so that Jan and Flip might be fed as they had not been fed for a long time.

They all returned to the camp, and before they separated to go to their own tents, Mamma warned, "Don't let Marie Naudé get wind of anything. I don't trust her."

Soon afterwards a steady trickle of women came to the van Zyl tent. One brought a small loaf of bread, another had been lucky enough to dig *uintjies*, an edible and prized bulb, from the slope of the kloof and she donated all of it towards the burghers' feast. Many more women brought scraps of meat which, when added together, would provide a meal the burghers would remember. Other women who had no spare food donated firewood instead for the cooking of the meal.

·A woman arrived with a last-minute donation of three precious potatoes, and Mamma thanked her, placing them with the rest of the vegetables. "I'll fetch my sharp knife to deal with these," she told Dorothea. "I want to peel them as thinly as possible."

She entered the tent and a moment later they heard her utter what was, for her, an obscenity, followed by a shout of *"Voertsek!"* Startled, Petronella turned away from the fire she had been laying, and saw Marie Naudé's dog running from their tent.

The others went inside to join Mamma, and in silence they viewed the disaster. The dog had eaten every scrap of meat contributed by the hard-pressed prisoners. He had started on the bread and then discarded it, dropping it on the ground where it had been soaked by urine as the dog cocked his leg against the wooden box afterwards. And two burghers, bent on heaven-only-knew what dangerous mission, who had been subsisting on nothing but dry rusks and had not tasted meat for a very long time, would be taking risks to visit the tent that evening for a meal, and they had nothing to offer them but a few vegetables and mealie-porridge.

Dorothea's easy tears had begun to flow, and Jakoba whispered, "Whatever shall we do?"

Mamma's face was arranged in lines of fierce concentration. "I have thought of something," she announced after a while. "I heard that someone at last managed to trap a hare today. She is a difficult, morose woman, but I hope to be able to persuade her to let us have it for the men. I have a small piece of biltong which I had been saving for a dire emergency, and I'll offer her that in return."

Mamma must have been forced to use a great deal of persuasion on the woman, for it was more than an hour before she returned with the skinned and cleaned carcass of the hare, and began to cut it up. Soon the meat was simmering in the pot on the fire, surrounded by *uintjies* and the potatoes. The *marog* was to be boiled separately, and Mamma also decided to cook some mealie-porridge.

"Remember," she said sternly, "those men have not had a square meal in weeks, perhaps months, and there's no knowing when they will eat again. The meat and the potatoes are for them alone. We shall have mealie-porridge and some of the *marog*, and we'll pretend that we had a large meal at lunch-time."

The two burghers arrived without mishap after darkness, and were quickly whisked inside the tent. Mamma filled great bowls with stew for them, and after their initial protest Jan and Flip accepted that the women had already eaten earlier and were merely keeping them company out of politeness by toying with mealie-porridge and *marog*.

There was not a great deal of conversation during the meal. Apart from the men's voracious hunger, which led them to accept second helpings, and kept them silent for long moments, there were not many topics which could have been discussed to the comfort of any of them. Harrowing details of what the burghers were going through as they harassed the enemy, blew up railway lines or rode swiftly and suicidally in open order among the British, firing from the saddle, petered out as the men realised the women were imagining their own menfolk sharing those experiences. And there was no point in describing conditions in the camp, because both Jan and Flip had wives and children imprisoned in Green Point camp.

The meal came to an end and the men stood up. "Thank you, ladies, that was quite magnificent. It was a meal we shall remember for the rest of our days."

Petronella said, "Lights have to be out by eight o'clock, and because few of us own a watch, we are never quite sure of the time. We wait until we see other lights going out, and then we blow out our candles, for otherwise we may expect a visit from one of the guards. I think I had better walk with you to the perimeter fence, because if the lights suddenly went out you might become confused and walk around in circles."

The men thanked her, and shook hands with the other women. When the three of them left to move swiftly among the tents towards the fence near the latrine trench, the men were still praising the meal they had just eaten in heartfelt whispers. Jan added, "When Piet Nortjé hears about it, he'll regret that he didn't come on this mission himself."

"Piet Nortjé!" Petronella echoed, stopping in her tracks. "*Field-Cornet* Piet Nortjé?"

"Why, yes, Cousin Petronella. Do you know him?"

She didn't answer the question. Tensely, she asked instead, "For how long have you served under him?"

"Since the beginning of the war," Flip said. "But what – "

She drew a long breath. "*Then you must have known Marcus Koen!*"

"Marcus Koen? Yes, certainly we knew him. At first we didn't know what to make of him, fighting for the Boers, but then – "

"Do you know to which country he has been exiled?" Petronella interrupted, and held her breath as she waited for an answer.

It came readily, without hesitation. "Why, yes. He was sent to a place called Bermuda."

She closed her eyes. *Thank you, God*, she acknowledged silently. "Where is Bermuda?" she wanted to know. "Is it in Europe?"

"Lord, *Nig* Petronella, we have no more idea where in the world it might be, than we know where Ceylon is, or St Helena, or any of the other foreign places to which the British send men in exile. Why?"

"It doesn't matter. I'll find out somehow where Bermuda is. Now, you had better hurry and get through the fence."

They shook hands with her, and melted away towards the boundary. She turned and began to walk back to the tent, feeling as if she were floating on air. *She knew where Marcus was.* At last, at last, she knew the name of the place where she would be joining him one day. He was not lost to her after all.

She arrived at their tent at almost the same moment as Marie Naudé did. The woman eyed Mamma uneasily. "You have claimed that my dog Pikkie has visited your tent once or twice."

"Rather more often than once or twice," Mamma answered grimly, and Petronella guessed at the frustration she must be feeling in not being able to report the dog's latest outrage without giving away the fact that rations had been donated for a special reason.

"He *was* here this afternoon," Mamma continued with feeling.

"Oh. And no doubt you shouted at him, so that the poor, frightened darling thinks himself to be in disgrace, and is hiding somewhere." Her glance fell upon the cooking pot in which the stew had been made, and which now held only bones. "If you have no use for those, would you mind if I had them? The scent of them would help to lure Pikkie out of hiding."

"By all means," Mamma shrugged, and wrapped the bones in a scrap of brown paper which had held their mealie-meal ration.

Petronella and Jakoba exchanged awed, incredulous glances. Dorothea seemed oblivious to any undercurrents. It had obviously not become clear to her, also, why she had been unable to find the sharp knife with which to peel the potatoes during the period while Mamma was away from the tent, before returning with the carcase of a 'hare'.

Late the next morning, the news percolated through the camp that a part of the railway line near Bloemfontein had been dynamited by Boer guerillas, who had succeeded in getting away in the confusion following the blast.

Absently, Petronella joined in the general rejoicing that Jan and Flip were safe, and that no more women and children would be coming to share their misery until the line had been repaired. Then she slipped away unnoticed and accosted the first guard she saw. "Can you tell me where Bermuda is, please?"

"Buggered if I knows, Miss. I think it's somewhere in Africa. One of them places your men gets exiled to." He gave her a look of compassion and of warning. "Any case, you know it's against the rules to give prisoners information about exiles."

She was forced to leave the matter there and contain her frustration. Then other events dulled even thoughts about Marcus.

Spring merged into summer, bringing flies and disease. The doctors could not cope with all the sick, and a blind eye was now being turned to the treatment of prisoners with herbal remedies by their own people. "Afterwards," Mamma predicted sourly, "they will be able to blame the sickness on the *bossiemiddels* of the Boers."

The camp was now a pitiful sight. Mothers in rags, or dressed in skirts made of khaki blankets, tried to care for children with emaciated bodies and so little flesh on their faces that their lips would not close over their teeth but were grotesquely drawn back as if in a macabre grin, and to add to the misery dust storms choked the camp.

Then something happened which Petronella guessed had been the worst fear tucked away in the back of Mamma's mind. Dorothea's baby, who had never thrived since they entered the camp, who had not crawled when he should have done so, and had only begun to crawl when he should have been walking for months, died in the night beside his sleeping mother. He had shown no signs of illness, for Mamma had been dosing all of them with preventative medicines. He had simply stopped struggling to survive in the heat and the dust, and on a diet of mealie-meal gruel mixed with condensed milk.

Dorothea's grief was terrible to behold, because it was so unreal and deviated from any normal pattern. At first she would not admit, even to herself, that the baby was dead. She clasped him to her, insisting that he was asleep. Her once-prominent eyes, which had reminded Petronella of those of a cow, were now sunk deep into their sockets and stared tearlessly, unblinkingly at Mamma as she begged Dorothea to give up the baby so that he could be laid out for burial. Mamma changed her tactics, and said, "Let me hold little Gabriel for a while so that you can get dressed."

Only then, reluctantly, did Dorothea hold out the small, still body to Mamma, who took it and whispered to Petronella, "Go and ask the superintendent for a coffin. Once she sees the baby inside a coffin Dorothea will have to accept that he is dead."

The camp superintendent looked tired, harassed and discouraged as he listened to Petronella's request. "There are no more coffins available, Miss van Zyl."

"Then one will have to be made, quickly."

"You don't understand. There is no wood left. Too many coffins have had to be made lately."

"Then how," she demanded, "are we to prepare my nephew for burial?"

The superintendent thrust his fingers through his hair. "You'll have to bury him in a sack."

"A sack? As if he was a dog?"

"God Almighty, it's not my fault!" he raged at her, losing control. "It's the fault of your men, damn them to hell! Why won't they give in? How dare they try to defy the might of the British Empire? Do you think I have been enjoying this job? Do you think I like being surrounded by dying people for whom no coffins can be made? And I'll tell you something else, Miss van Zyl – if you want your nephew buried today, he'll have to be buried in the same grave as one of the others who died yesterday or during the night, because my men cannot keep up with the demand for graves to be dug!"

Petronella said nothing. She returned to the tent, where Mamma had laid the baby's body down on a blanket and covered him with the other end of it. Dorothea seemed to have accepted, at last, that he was dead, for she sat limply, expressionlessly, beside it and stared into the distance as if she saw something which none of the rest of them could see. Dorothea, who had always before shed tears so easily, could find none for her dead baby.

Petronella drew Mamma aside, and told her what the superintendent had said. Grief had carved Mamma's face in harsh lines, but like Dorothea, she did not cry. She said in a fierce undertone, "My grandson will not share a stranger's grave. Stay with Dorothea, Petronella. Jakoba and I will go and ask for volunteers and we'll dig the grave ourselves."

Petronella sat down beside Dorothea. She thought of the day when Johannes had married her, and she remembered the night when she herself had helped to boil water for the birth of the baby. She tried to find words with which to comfort her sister-in-law, but she could find none, and she doubted whether Dorothea would even have heard her if she had spoken.

After several hours, Mamma returned with Jakoba, and both of them looked exhausted. Mamma was carrying an ordinary jute sack.

It was only when Dorothea understood that her baby was to be denied the dignity of a coffin, that he was to be buried in a sack, that her unreal silence left her and she broke into a long, continuous animal-like howl of protest and anger and grief.

Mamma held her, and forced her to swallow a herbal infusion, and spoke to her gently, telling her that it made no difference to the Almighty whether a soul's mortal remains were put into the ground in a casket or a sack. She said, "We shall carry him to his grave, Dorothea, as if he *were* in a casket, and we'll put his baby-bonnet on top of it, the pretty blue one you made for him before we left Jakkalsdrif, and it will be exactly as if we were carrying a coffin with a wreath on it."

Dorothea became calmer then, and by the time the baby had been placed inside the sack, she had sunk into apathy again. Mamma held out her hands; Petronella took one end of the sack and Jakoba the other, and they lifted it into Mamma's outstretched arms as if it were, indeed, a coffin. Then, with Dorothea stumbling after Mamma, and Petronella and Jakoba following her, they left the tent and walked slowly through the ranks of the tents. Those people who did not have funerals of their own to attend, or sickness among their families which required their constant attention, joined the procession. As they reached the gate of the camp the guards removed their hats and bowed their heads, and the mourners went to the place where the grave had been dug by Mamma and Jakoba and other volunteers.

Petronella was vaguely surprised to find that she was the only member of her family who wept at the funeral. Since there was no minister at the camp, Mamma conducted the simple service herself, her face grim with grief, her eyes dry. Dorothea stood like a sleep-walker and watched as the baby in its sack, with the blue bonnet on top of it, was lowered into the ground. Petronella wept brokenly, and she did not understand fully why she wept. Unlike most females, she was not drawn to children or to babies; she had never felt any affection for her nephew and had taken very little interest in him while he was alive. She was, she decided confusedly, not really weeping for little Gabriel van Zyl but for all the casualties of this dreadful, never-ending war.

Dorothea never recovered from the loss of her baby. They watched her fading before their eyes, and not even Mamma's bracing, angry reminders to her that she had to think of Johannes, and look after herself for his sake, could penetrate her numb, desolate grief. It was no surprise to any of them when she, too, died a few weeks later. They buried her with her baby. During the grim months which followed Mamma often said bitterly that at least Dorothea had been spared any more hardship and despair.

Early in 1902 a group of burghers arrived at the camp and, astonishingly, they were neither challenged nor hindered by the authorities. The clothes of the Boers were in tatters and some of them wore grain sacks or animal skins. Their cheeks were hollow beneath the beards, their bodies scarred with sores caused by lack of food. In the ferment of their arrival four words echoed and re-echoed in the camp.

"The war is over!"

One of the burghers turned out to be Dieter Steenkamp, Jakoba's cousin. He sat inside the van Zyl tent and spoke quietly, with muted emotion, of the surrender by the Boers.

"Some of the generals wanted to go on fighting to the bitter end, but there were no more than eleven thousand burghers left to carry on the fight, and a third of them were without horses. Then General de la Rey put our situation into perspective. He pointed out that our nation had been beggared, our dreams of freedom destroyed, and that all we had been clinging to was our pride. Without our being aware of it, he said, that bitter end to which we had been fighting had been reached."

All of them sat motionless, and listened as Dieter added quietly, "And one by one we realised that he had been speaking the truth. We stared the bitter end in the face and we knew we had to come to terms with our new masters."

11

Life inside the camp began to change dramatically. Rations became generous, because no more women and children would be coming to join the prisoners, and daily more and more of those already there were leaving. The Free State burghers who had families still alive in the camp borrowed mule wagons or donkey carts and came to collect them. The ones who arrived and found that their wives and children had all died knelt for a while beside their unmarked graves and then they left too, their faces gaunt and expressionless, their shoulders bowed as they rode away, and Petronella could only guess at the empty despair in their hearts as they contemplated what was left of their future.

Dieter Steenkamp borrowed a cart and horses from an acquaintance in Bloemfontein, and he and Jakoba left as well. When they parted she told Petronella, "Even if, by a miracle, my father was not shot as a rebel, our farm in the Cape will have been confiscated by the British. Write to me at Dieter's family's farm in the Free State, and I'll write to you at Jakkalsdrif. We must never lose touch with one another; we must always remain best friends."

She wept as Petronella embraced her and promised to write regularly. Petronella did not share her tears, and in her heart she knew that she would not be keeping her promise to write often. In future all her energies, the whole of her concentration, would be expended upon finding out where Bermuda was, how much it would cost to travel there, and where she was to find the money to do so. She was, she acknowledged to herself, like a blinkered horse, for she could see almost nothing but the one goal ahead – to join Marcus, at no matter what cost to herself or others.

In the meantime, many of the former regulations of the camp had been relaxed. The women and children were told that they would remain in the protection of the camp until they could return to their homes. The guards no longer patrolled the perimeter fence, and the women were free to wander outside and watch the horizon for signs of their menfolk approaching to collect them. But most of the burghers who arrived were Free Staters who had been fighting in the Cape Colony.

Petronella was also free, now, to question the British soldiers about Bermuda, but all of them were vague about it, and could volunteer little more than that it was part of the vast British Empire.

"Why don't you ask Corporal Brown, Miss?" one of them suggested. "He's got education, he has. He'll know."

Since their last meeting she'd had neither occasion nor the inclination to seek him out, but now she went immediately to his office. Rupert looked up from papers on his desk when she entered, and his voice was polite and stilted as he said, "Good day, Miss van Zyl. What may I do for you?"

He was clearly no longer in love with her. She did not care. "Could you tell me where Bermuda is?"

He looked surprised by her question. "I have never been there, but I know it is somewhere in the North Atlantic Ocean. It is a British Colony and is said to be one of our important naval stations. Why, Miss van Zyl?"

"Because Marcus Koen has been sent there."

"Marcus Koen? Oh yes, I remember now. The cousin of yours who had been sent into exile, and whom you were so anxious to trace."

"Do you have any newspapers from England which you no longer want?" she asked Rupert, thinking that a British newspaper might have published an informative article about one of their colonies, such as Bermuda.

He stood up and opened the cupboard, bringing out a stack of newspapers. As he handed them to her he said quietly, "Marcus Koen is not your cousin, is he?"

"No."

Rupert nodded ruefully. "No, I have long suspected that he was not. You would not have been so doggedly single-minded, or gone to such lengths to take English lessons, or been motivated into making such rapid strides in the learning of a foreign language for a mere cousin." He held out his hand. "Goodbye, Petronella, and good luck."

She had reached the door with the newspapers when something else occurred to her and she turned. "You know roughly where Bermuda is. How much do you suppose it would cost to go there?"

He thought for a moment. "You would have to travel to Cape Town by train and then take ship from there. I am not sure whether you would be able to sail directly to Bermuda, but I should imagine the very least you would need to cover all your expenses would be seventy-five pounds sterling."

She tried not to feel crushed by the thought of trying to raise such an impossibly large sum of money, and took the newspapers back to the bell tent which she now shared with Mamma alone, and read them meticulously. But Bermuda was not mentioned in any of them. She did learn, to her astonishment, that the British handling of the Boer War had been heavily criticised and condemned by many countries, and also by large numbers of people in Britain itself. How that knowledge would have cheered the inmates of the camp when life had been at its grimmest!

She watched Mamma's frustration growing as more and more Free State women left the camp with their menfolk. She could almost see Mamma's patience finally snap on the day when an elegant carriage arrived, drawn by a team of sleek horses and driven by friends of Marie Naudé, who had come to bear her home.

"I do not intend waiting another week!" Mamma fumed. "I want to shake from what are left of my shoes the miserable red dust of this stinking camp which killed Dorothea and my grandson. Petronella, come with me to the superintendent's office, and translate my demands."

The superintendent had not forgotten Mamma, and he regarded her with a wary expression as Petronella translated what she said. "Give us transport and provisions, and send us on our way, and then inform our men so that they may join us at a later stage of the journey."

The superintendent thrust a harassed hand through his hair. "Miss van Zyl, please explain to your mother the impossibility of granting her request. You don't know where your men are, so how do you expect us to know? If the Boers had behaved according to established convention; if they belonged to recognised regiments whose movements could be charted, who kept records and adhered to rules – "

"If they had been the kind of people who wasted time and energy on records and rules," Petronella retorted, "they would not have taken on the might of the British Empire in the first place, let alone forced them to carry on fighting for more than two years!" She turned to Mamma and translated what the superintendent had said.

"Nonsense!" Mamma responded vigorously. "If we are sent somewhere across the Vaal River, in large enough numbers, the men will get to hear by word of mouth where we are."

Petronella acknowledged the truth of this, and she put the matter to the superintendent. "After all," she added, "the burghers who have already called here to collect their women and children had been told where they were by others who had previously visited the camp."

"If your mother will only be patient," the superintendent pleaded, "you will all be sent home at the earliest possible opportunity. Here, read this, Miss van Zyl." He handed her the latest edition of a South African broadsheet. "This carries a report of the terms of the treaty signed by Lords Kitchener and Milner and by the Boer generals. Translate Clause Ten to your mother."

Petronella's glance flicked over the various clauses, one of which she noticed promised that the Dutch language would be taught in public schools of the Transvaal and of the Orange River Colony if the parents of the childen demanded it, and for a moment indignation swept over her at the thought that the issue should ever have been in dispute, that there should have been any question of children not being taught in their mother tongue. Then she dismissed the matter from her mind and concentrated on Clause Ten, which spoke of Commissions to be appointed to deal with the matter of returning people to their farms at some vague time in the future.

She knew, even before she translated it, what Mamma's reaction would be. "Tell him, Petronella," she said implacably, "that if he will not help us to cross into the Transvaal to join our men, I shall get the women to leave the camp and begin *walking* towards the border! He couldn't stop us, for we are no longer prisoners."

The superintendent's face took on a hunted expression as Petronella delivered Mamma's parting shot. He was obviously remembering the last time he had tangled with her, and recalling what a redoubtable opponent Mamma could be.

"Tell your mother," he said with a resigned sigh, "that I shall see what may be arranged."

Mamma had scented victory, and she was content to leave the office, certain that the superintendent would move heaven and earth to be rid of her. But Petronella lingered behind.

"Could you give me some information," she asked, "about Bermuda?"

He looked a little startled at the question, but then he nodded. "Ah, yes, I see. Someone of yours has been sent into exile there. Bermuda is the name of a group of small islands."

A *group* of islands, she thought with swamping despair. Not even one particular island or country. "How many islands?" she demanded, swallowing hard.

"I believe there are some three hundred altogether."

"*Oh God.*" The utter impossibility of finding Marcus on one of three hundred islands somewhere in the unknown world stared her implacably in the face. But then she heard the superintendent say, "I believe many of them are linked by bridges and causeways. Exiles would most likely have been sent to Main Island or to St George's."

She looked at him in gratitude for reducing the enormity of her task. "I have been told that Bermuda is in the North Atlantic Ocean but where, exactly, is that?"

He removed a volume from a shelf and leafed through it. "This is an atlas of the world, Miss van Zyl. These are the Bermudas."

She stared at the tiny speck, surrounded by blue. It was impossible to imagine that the speck was made up of three hundred islands and also impossible from the printed atlas to pinpoint where they were in relation to the Transvaal, for the continent of Africa did not even appear on the same page. She would need *Meester*'s spinning globe to put Bermuda into perspective for her.

She thanked the superintendent, and turned to leave. His voice stopped her, the anxious note in it apparent. "Miss van Zyl – try to discourage your mother from inciting the other women to walk out of the camp, won't you? She was right; I couldn't stop them, now that the war is over, and – well – " He shrugged, and she thought she understood the dilemma he would face if hundreds of emaciated women, many of them in poor health, should choose to take to the open country rather than remain any longer within a British camp. "I'll think of something," he added with feeling.

Only a few days later, the women were told that those who wished to leave the camp immediately would be transported by train to Johannesburg, where they would be given accommodation of some kind and from where their menfolk could collect them.

Many of the women had family members who were far too ill to face an immediate journey, but many others were only too glad to leave the camp with its desolate ghosts, to stand for the last time with bowed heads by the unmarked graves of their dead, and then clamber on to the wagons the superintendent had procured to drive them to the railway station at Bloemfontein.

The train which they boarded had previously been used for troops and supplies, and lacked any comforts, but the spent, demoralised women were too grateful to be on their way home at last to care about its shortcomings.

As their journey continued, the women were stricken to the heart by the devastation they saw everywhere. What had once obviously been prosperous farms were now nothing but barren, withered wastes, all fields destroyed and fruit trees pulled up by the roots and left where they had fallen, so that their bare, weathered branches etched against the black stubble of the scorched earth reminded Petronella of the bones of skeletons.

Near several of the stations where their train reduced speed preparatory to halting, Petronella had noticed that British Army camps had been set up, and outside the tent from which the British flag fluttered marking it out as being that of a commanding officer, she had seen lines of burghers waiting. She had been puzzled by this, but the reason did not become apparent until the train stopped a short distance away from one of these camps to take on water from a tank, and she had time to observe the burghers.

Without exception, they were little more than skin and bone. They wore the tattered remnants of their original moleskin clothes, or the now-familiar grain sacks, and some of them wore nothing but a blanket in the centre of which a hole had been cut for their heads. Seated at a table in front of the tent from which the British flag fluttered was an officer, while a small body of British troops stood close by. Each time, just before the line of burghers began to move slowly towards the tent, the one who was second in line fired his rifle into the air until all the bullets had been discharged. Then he smashed his rifle by banging it forcefully against the ground before tossing it away.

"What is going on there?" Mamma demanded, coming to stand beside Petronella. "My eyesight is not what it was."

"I believe the burghers must have been ordered to come and lay down their arms and sign an undertaking to accept the peace terms. The man who has just broken his rifle and tossed it away has moved up to the table, and is signing something, and the one behind him is cocking his rifle to discharge the bullets into the air."

The same ritual was repeated by each of the burghers in turn, to the obvious displeasure of the British officer and the troops, while the pile of useless, broken and discarded rifles was growing.

Mamma's eyes were narrowed in an austere expression. "The burghers made personal sacrifices to buy those rifles. No army supplied them at a rich government's expense. Why should the men not do with their own property as they please?"

Petronella made no answer. Even in defeat and surrender, she thought, the Boers were remaining defiant, and demonstrating their reluctance to bow to the inevitable.

All the passengers set up a cheer when the train finally crossed the bridge over the Vaal River near Vereeniging, and they knew themselves to be back in the Transvaal.

Not long afterwards, they reached Johannesburg. As they spilled out of the train they found that the platform was crowded with ragged and dishevelled burghers waiting to embark for what was once the Orange Free State, and which everyone now had to remind themselves they would have to learn to call the Orange River Colony.

The women from the camps and the burghers, although strangers to one another, stopped to exchange emotional greetings and such news as either side had of each other's kith and kin. But some of the burghers had no need to seek news; they had already learnt from others what lay ahead for them, and Petronella heard one of them sum up their situation with the grim and bitter joke, "One has to look on the bright side. My wife and my children died in a concentration camp; my home was burnt and my farm destroyed and my cattle driven away by the enemy. But I've heard that the British might give me a licence to buy a gun with which to shoot game to feed myself, so that's something to look forward to, isn't it?"

The burghers left to board their train, and the women and children from the camp found that, as promised by the superintendent, soldiers were waiting outside the station with wagons drawn by mules to take them to where they were to be accommodated while they awaited the arrival of their menfolk.

"My dear heaven!" Mamma breathed as they drove along the wide, busy streets of Johannesburg and she saw the high buildings, the many different kinds of vehicles and the trams running along rails. The other women were struck speechless by the sights and the sounds of the bustling city, which seemed to Petronella not to have been affected by the war at all. Or perhaps, she decided fair-mindedly, it was simply that the vital, thrusting community had lost no time in getting briskly back to normality. All the same, it was difficult to imagine that anyone there had suffered great hardship. Perhaps a little profit had been lost by the mine-owners because of the disruption of the war; perhaps the wealthy, such as Marcus's parents and their friends, had had to make do without some of the luxuries which they had been accustomed to having delivered to them from the Cape.

Petronella recognised the place to which they were taken as the Johannesburg Market. Tents had been pitched over a large section of it, but these were of stout canvas and not the thin, inferior kind of bell tents used in the concentration camp. Rations were issued to them which Petronella guessed came from the British Army's own supply, and they were lavish, even luxurious. With mixed feelings, the Boer women accepted from the officer in charge of this new encampment of tents bundles of clothing which had been donated to them by wealthy Englishwomen in Johannesburg.

Life inside the Market soon settled down to a comfortable but slightly unreal pattern. Apart from a few women and children who became ill, initially, because they could not resist the temptation to overeat now that they were offered such plenty, most of them were slowly regaining their strength. But all of them were aware of a sense of impermanence, for they were all marking time until their menfolk came for them. Petronella understood, but did not share their preoccupations, for she had plans of her own.

One morning she eluded Mamma and slipped away from the camp. She was wearing a brown worsted skirt donated by an unknown Englishwoman, teamed with a white blouse, its bodice decorated with pin-tucks. A tailored jacket which almost matched the skirt and formed a discreet bustle at the back kept her warm against the Johannesburg winter. She thought she looked smart and even sophisticated and not like someone who had spent all her life on a farm, let alone like a recent inmate of a concentration camp. She had deliberately set out to look as elegant and self-possessed as possible, for a scheme had been hatching in her mind ever since they had arrived in Johannesburg.

She was on her way to visit Marcus's parents, the only people in the world who she knew would be able to raise a large sum like seventy-five pounds sterling, to enable her to join Marcus in exile.

12

Now that she could speak and understand English, Petronella felt she was in a position to approach the Koen family on equal terms. A great deal had happened during the more than two years which had passed since their last meeting, and surely it was not impossible that the attitude of Marcus's family might have changed. Even they, with all their money, would not be able to have him brought back from exile. Was it too much to hope that they would be compassionate enough to want him to have some happiness on that strange island to which he had been banished?

She would explain to his parents that she and Marcus could not live without each other, and that she would rather starve, if necessary, in exile with him than live in comfort on her beloved Jakkalsdrif. Now that she was able to express herself she would make them understand the sacrifice she was prepared to make for Marcus, and ask only one from them – that they should make it possible for her to travel to Bermuda. She would undertake to repay every penny they lent her, even if it took her the rest of her life. She did not know how one might make a living on this unknown Bermuda, but she and Marcus would find a way.

Everything would depend upon the new impression she made upon the Koens, and upon her putting her case with dignity and conviction, commanding their respect. She felt sure she could do it.

She turned from the Market Square into Commissioner Street, and paused for a moment outside the arcade with its roof of leaded glass domes, remembering how Marcus had taken her to lunch in Moss's Grill Room inside it. A mental picture of him rose in her mind; the blue eyes, the clefts in his cheeks, the curve of his lips as he looked at her with love and desire, and a stab of hopeless longing pierced her, strengthening her resolve, so that she began to hasten her stride. It would take her a long time to walk to where Marcus's parents lived.

But outside Thorne and Stuttaford, she stopped to look at the goods displayed in the window. She caught sight of a girl watching her from inside the store; a girl with a pinched, pale face and shadowed eyes, whose lack-lustre hair had been scraped back into flaxen plaits which looked ridiculously incongruous, sticking out from underneath her hat of brown velour which must have been designed for a woman of mature years. Her clothes hung loosely on her thin frame and looked as though they had been made for someone else . . .

With a painful shock, Petronella realised that she had been staring at a reflection of herself in a mirror set into the side of the store's window. It had been more than a year since she had last seen herself in a mirror of any kind, and she had utterly failed for a moment to recognise the girl into whom she had been turned by time and circumstances.

All her confidence, all her hope, drained away and she turned from the mirror, devastated, diminished, and totally brought down to stark reality.

She looked no less incongruous and out-of-place than she must have done when the Koen family first clapped eyes upon her. She looked what she was – a beaten Boer girl fresh from a concentration camp, wearing the assorted cast-off clothes of several rich Johannesburg women which did not fit her and which made her appear pathetic. She looked like the humbled beggar she had been prepared to make of herself to the Koens, and not the dignified, commanding figure of her imagination.

Even then, she would have sunk her pride and been prepared to beg for the means of reaching Marcus, if she could have continued to make herself believe that it would work. But having seen herself in the mirror as she really was, she could also see, now, how she had been deluding herself.

It was hard to believe that she could ever have been stupid enough to imagine that Marcus's parents would help her to join him. Having burnt him out of their lives, why should they be prepared to resurrect him after he had thrown in his lot with the Boers, and had been caught spying for them? And all so that she, the cause of such a dreadful and dramatic event in their lives, might be reunited with him? Truly, she must have been mad.

She walked slowly back to the camp in the Market Square, her shoulders bowed. At its entrance she noticed that several wagons with spans of placid oxen yoked to their shafts had been drawn up. She tried to shake off her mood of despair and defeat by kindling an interest in the wagons. Burghers, she thought, had obviously been arriving during her absence to collect their women and children.

She went to join Mamma, to learn from her the names of the burghers. She found Mamma inside their sleeping tent, talking to one of them, an old man with only a few tufts of white hair showing on the crown and at the back of his otherwise bald, weather-beaten head. His eyes were deeply sunk into their sockets, making his nose appear prominent above a flowing silver beard. He must have been given a set of clothes to replace his moleskin rags or grain sack, but the slate-coloured coat and breeches he wore had obviously been meant for someone much larger, and gave him a diminished look.

Petronella waited politely for Mamma to introduce her to the stranger. And then a familiar voice spoke from his lips, a voice with a catch in it. "Petronella – my precious girl . . ."

"Pappa?" She stared blankly at him. In her mind her father had continued to look as he had when she'd last seen him, which she realised with a slight sense of shock was the night when he had discovered her in bed with Marcus. Pappa had been strong and vital; passionate in his anger and his grief. Someone in the prime of his life. How could this wasted, balding, silver-bearded old man with several of his teeth missing possibly be *Pappa*?

Then, fleetingly, she remembered her shock at recognising her own reflection, and simultaneously it came to her that Mamma had changed too, that although she was still a big woman and always would be, her bulk consisted of solid bone and muscle and that the skin hung loosely from her flesh. Without Petronella realising it, they had all changed.

The next moment, all thought suspended, she was wrapped in Pappa's thin arms, and they wept together. He let her go, and wiped his eyes with his hand. "Mamma was telling me, before you came in, about poor Dorothea and the little grandson I never even saw." Pappa hesitated, and went on quietly, "Now it is my sad burden to tell you that Johannes is also dead. He was killed in the fighting near Ermelo."

Tears again filled Petronella's eyes, but they were more because of her continuing shock at Pappa's appearance than because the news of Johannes's death had sunk in. But Mamma did not weep at all. She stared fiercely ahead of her and asked, "Did he receive a decent burial?"

"Yes, my wife, he was given a decent, Christian burial."

Mamma rounded on him. "In a coffin?"

Pappa made a helpless, trapped gesture. "A coffin, Lenie, when we scarcely had food, and we had been forced to steal the ammunition we were using?"

"Or picks or shovels," Mamma pointed out harshly. "How was he given this decent, Christian burial you spoke of, Hannes?"

Pappa went to her and touched her arm. "The British came with their ambulance wagons and picked up our dead and wounded, as well as their own. They dug a grave and a truce was called, and we came down from the krantz to stand with them and mourn our separate dead. Johannes was wrapped in his field-blanket and the British allowed us to drape the Republic's flag over the body of each fallen Boer before it was lowered into the common grave. They had an ordained minister with them who held a burial service." Pappa was silent for a moment. "Afterwards, the fighting went on again."

The only emotion Mamma displayed was in the slight tremor of her voice as she said, "So Johannes was buried in a common grave, together with British soldiers."

"Mamma," Petronella whispered through her tears, "I don't think Johannes would have minded that at all."

Mamma was silent for a long while. Then she asked in a frozen voice, "And what of Gideon? Is he lost to us too?"

"The last news I had of Gideon was that he had been taken prisoner by the British. He became very reckless, you know, as well as brave, and he was soon a thorn in the side of the British with his daring raids on their ammunition tents." Pappa sighed. "I have tried to discover news of where he has been held, but I think it must have been somewhere in the Cape. He will be released soon, if it has not been done already, and it will take him some time to reach Jakkalsdrif. I don't think we should wait for him. We must return immediately, for the winter ploughing must be done in time for the seed to be sown."

Pappa went on to explain that the same authorities who had donated the ill-fitting clothes he was wearing had also given him a wagon and a span of oxen, together with bags full of mealie-seed and a sum of money. "They said it was compensation," he added. "The burgher who translated for us did not know very much English, and he was not quite certain of his facts, but all of us who had laid down our arms and signed the peace treaty were asked a few questions and then were given compensation." Pappa frowned. "But for some reason several of the others received less in compensation."

"It would have been compensation for the livestock and the wagons the British took from us!" Petronella exclaimed. "Don't you remember, Mamma, the Cape Boer Hendrik le Roux said we would be compensated for everything after the war? And those Boers who received lower compensation must have had fewer losses than others."

They told Pappa how they had been forced to leave their wagons and oxen and surrender all their livestock before being taken to the concentration camp and Pappa nodded. "Yes, that must have been what the compensation was for. Although," he added bitterly, "it does not cover even half the true value of the livestock." Then he shrugged and sighed. "How soon can you be ready to leave for Jakkalsdrif?"

"Give us half an hour," Mamma said promptly.

The officer in command of the camp insisted that they should take the camp beds and blankets from their tents and load them on the wagon, for they would be sleeping out in the veld before they reached Jakkalsdrif. He also thrust on them an almost embarrassingly large supply of rations; far more than they would possibly need before they reached the farm.

"Conscience," Pappa said, briefly and bitterly.

"I don't think so," Mamma disagreed. "I think they are trying to show goodwill." She became practical. "The rations will come in useful. I don't know how long it will be before I can start making butter after we reach Jakkalsdrif, or whether Koos will have kept the cattle in such condition that a steer might be butchered immediately."

As Mamma had promised, within half an hour they were on their way, trundling through Johannesburg on the wagon. Petronella wept again for Johannes, but Mamma was doing her grieving for her first-born in her own way. She sat in silence on the wagon, her face harshly carved, staring into space. She spoke only once, and then it was to say, "Petronella, there is no need for Pappa to know that little Gabriel was put into his grave in a sack."

"No, Mamma."

Petronella remembered how her mother had reassured Dorothea that the Almighty did not care how one's remains were laid to rest in the earth. But *Mamma* cared deeply, and Petronella's awed admiration for her courage deepened as she recognised how Mamma had crushed her own feelings at the time for the sake of Dorothea.

They outspanned shortly after they had left Johannesburg, and while Pappa collected whatever fuel he could find to build a fire, and Mamma searched for something to serve as a grill on which to cook the meat they had been given by the officer at the camp, Petronella began to unwrap the meat from the sheet of newspaper which had been covering it.

It was from a British paper, and contained part of an account of a speech Lord Kitchener had made after returning to England. "Gold, iron and coal are very good assets, and when you add to them the development of agriculture and the introduction by assisted immigration of fresh blood into the country, I think you may assure yourselves that you have nothing less than the making of a new America in the South African hemisphere."

She screwed the sheet of newspaper up and put it on the fire. She remembered how Pappa had insisted, from the beginning, that gold had been the motive behind the war. He had been right, but he had not realised there were other assets the British coveted. But she decided to say nothing. The war was over, and it was best that Pappa and Mamma and all the other Boers should put aside their bitterness, and learn to live under their new rulers.

They made camp at nightfall, and continued the journey the next morning, hoping to be able to outspan at Doornboomstad in the evening and stay over with friends in the village.

But darkness had fallen by the time they reached it, and no lights showed anywhere, and Mamma and Pappa agreed that they would not wake anyone. They drove through the village's one wide street and carried on to the first outspan place outside Doornboomstad, a special clearing set aside for that purpose. They ate some of their rations without bothering with a camp-fire, and afterwards they settled down to sleep.

Petronella woke up first in the morning, and as she crawled out of Pappa's bed-roll she stiffened, numb with shock. For as far as the eye could see in that flat land, there was nothing but devastation. There had been a frost overnight and its white mantle provided a cruel contrast with the blackened stubble where once there had been fields of pasture land and cultivated acres for the growing of mealies. The thorn trees which had served as windbreaks had been burnt down and the few farmhouses that could be seen from here were all empty shells, with darkened sockets where windows used to be and no doors or stoeps and the corrugated iron roofs had been buckled into fantastic shapes by the heat of the fires.

"Poor souls," Mamma sighed with compassion when she, too, woke up and saw the desolation around them. "The British obviously burnt the farms to show the women that they had no alternative but to be driven into camps with their children. Let us praise the Lord that we gave them no reason for destroying Jakkalsdrif."

Pappa agreed, and they inspanned and went on. At mid-morning they came within sight of Jakkalsdrif. Mamma uttered a strangled cry and Pappa's voice shook as he called to the oxen to stop. Petronella stared, stricken to the heart, at what had been their home.

The shell of the house still stood, blackened by the fire which had devastated almost all of Jakkalsdrif. The wooden stoep had disappeared and there was nothing to show that a thriving orchard had once spread from the house.

In a dazed voice, Pappa urged the oxen on again. "They had no reason," Mamma said several times. "The British had no *reason*." Then she fell silent as they drew up beside what used to be the house. Where the front door had been was a gaping hole; the window-frames had burnt, and they could see through the empty sockets left behind into part of the interior of the house. Nothing but the walls were standing; every stick of furniture, every treasured family possession, would have been destroyed.

They heard a sound behind them, and Petronella recognised Koos, who was coming from the direction of the *stad* which was the only thing on Jakkalsdrif that appeared to have been left intact.

"Oubaas, Oubaas!" Koos cried, the sun glinting on tears upon his cheeks as he ran. "*Kwatheleka iviyo labelungu! Bashisa izwe! Kwasha izikhotna nezihlahla. Bathungela indlu ngomlilo yasha yaphela. Babulala nezinkomo. Basebephindela emuva. Ngakhala, ngakhala, ngakhala.*"

Pappa had heaved himself from the driver's seat of the wagon, and he had caught hold of the youth's shoulders. "Slowly, Koos," he said, "slowly, boy. You were talking in Zulu, and I understood only a few words. If you've forgotten your Dutch, try Fanakalo."

Koos wiped his eyes on his sleeve, and swallowed. Then he took a deep breath. "The many white soldiers came," he said in Fanakalo. "They burnt the grass and the trees, everything. They destroyed the house and then they killed the cattle before they all go back. Oh, I cried, Oubaas, I cried and cried."

Pappa nodded, and patted Koos on the shoulder, his eyes bleak, his voice bitter as he said, "I understand, Koos. There was nothing you could possibly have done."

Fragments of thoughts were splitting Petronella's mind in different directions. She remembered the insistent manner in which the officer in charge of the camp in Johannesburg had pressed upon them rations, blankets and beds. It was impossible not to believe that he had suspected the truth which would be awaiting them, and that he had been motivated by compassion, because he knew they would be needing the supplies.

She thought of all the other scenes of wanton devastation they had passed, and slowly everything began to make a kind of terrible sense. When the driving of their women and children into concentration camps had not persuaded the Boers to surrender, the British had decided on another tactic. By laying waste everywhere the homes and the farms of the Boers and slaughtering their livestock, they had hoped the message would reach the burghers – *You have nothing left worth fighting for. You might as well end the war*. But because the burghers had been scattered all over the country, the message had reached few of them, and in garbled versions which would have been dismissed largely as exaggerated rumours.

She remembered, suddenly, that day when she had driven in the pony and cart to see *Meester*, when she had been saying goodbye to Jakkalsdrif in her mind for she had not expected to see it again. It had, indeed, turned out to be a farewell of a kind, for that Jakkalsdrif was no more.

Perhaps, she thought, that burgher whose English was not very good and who had been employed to translate for Pappa and the other Boers, had been asked to explain to them about their farms, but he had been unable to pass it on because he had not understood it. The compensation which Pappa had been paid had been for the rape of Jakkalsdrif, but it could not pay to restore a fraction of what had been destroyed, and some of the losses could never be regained with money.

As Koos went on talking it became clear that he had, after all, been able to save something from the depredations of the British. With remarkably quick thinking, he had assured the soldiers that only the branded livestock belonged to the Boer family; those animals which had not been branded belonged to the people in the *stad*. He had also insisted that the chickens were their property, and because the chickens were scratching around near the native huts, the British had believed him.

"They not farmers, Oubaas," Koos said with derisive scorn. "They not think for themselves the chickens, they scratch by the *stad* because they know we feed them now. And the soldiers, they not think that animals with no brands, they young animals and must wait for Oubaas and Baas Johannes to come home. So they leave the chickens, and they let me take young heifers and steers to other side of river, through the drift, before they set the fires."

Petronella looked at the youth with gratitude and affection and also with admiration. After all this time of communicating mostly in Zulu with his grandmother and others in the *stad*, and in Fanakalo with people belonging to other tribes, his Dutch was a little rusty but it was returning. Remembering how hard it had been for her to learn English, she marvelled at the ability of an ignorant servant to express himself in three different tongues. It was something which she had always taken for granted before.

She congratulated him on his resourcefulness and his courage, and added, "And you so terrified of the *Tokoloshe* in the river too!"

Koos gave her a sheepish grin. "I shout at animals to cross river, Nonnie, and run like wind through the drift. The cattle they all fine and good, because the soldiers not burn grass other side of river, so I leave them there and I go through drift to feed them with cattle-cake the soldiers let me keep. One heifer," he added proudly, "she in calf already, and I think maybe one more other also."

Something else occurred to him. "Where my father, Oubaas, and my mother and sister Mwende? And where Baas Johannes and that *skelm*, Kleinbaas Gideon?"

Pappa broke the heavy silence that followed. "Your father and I became separated in the fighting, Koos. But he was alive and well, the last time I saw him, scattering with some other burghers after my own retreat had been cut off. I hope he'll make his way eventually to Jakkalsdrif, together with the other men from the *stad*. Johannes – " Pappa's voice faltered. "My first-born son is dead, Koos, and so are Nonnie Dorothea and their baby."

"Au, Oubaas . . ." A spasm of grief twisted Koos's face and he turned away for a while, staring in the direction of the river. "My mother and Mwende – they dead also?"

Petronella answered him, explaining how their servants had been prevented by Hendrik le Roux from accompanying them to the concentration camp. "I thought – I hoped – that Mwende and your mother might have found their way home by now. Don't worry, Koos, I'm sure they'll get back somehow."

Mamma climbed down from the wagon. She gazed with expressionless eyes at what had once been her home, and then spoke abruptly. "Come. The people in the *stad* will be waiting for us."

Petronella knew what she meant. It was only because Koos had been left in charge of Jakkalsdrif by Johannes that he had come to report on what had happened. The other servants had left them alone in the first of their grief, just as they would have left a mother alone with her dead child for a while. But now they would be waiting to greet them, to express their sorrow and to offer them the hospitality of the *stad*.

Smoke was rising in the air from the direction of the *stad*, but it was not the usual dense kind pouring from the doorway of each hut, and Koos explained the reason for this as he accompanied them. The fruit trees and some of the thorn trees had been killed by the fires, but their wood had not all been destroyed for it had been too green to burn. Koos and the women from the *stad* had chopped it up and waited for it to dry, and in the meantime they had used as fuel the store of cobs from mealies harvested in previous seasons, and which the British had allowed them to remove to the *stad* before setting fire to the outbuildings in which it had been kept. So now, in order to conserve their precious fuel, the people in the *stad* lit one communal fire each day in a clearing beside the huts, and used it to do their cooking.

Petronella realised that the British must have created fire-breaks to protect the *stad* before they destroyed the rest of Jakkalsdrif, for the area surrounding the huts was covered in winter-dry grass among which the chickens were scratching for insects. Beyond the huts, the fields which Pappa had set aside for the sole use of the servants had also been spared, and she could see orange-yellow pumpkins lying on the ground, still attached to their withered vines, and a couple of tethered goats were plucking at some reeds growing along the stream which had been diverted from the Vaal River for irrigation.

As they entered the *stad*, they found the servants waiting outside their huts to greet them. Pappa and Mamma and Petronella shook hands with everyone, and thanked them for their condolences as the people learnt of the deaths in the family. Afterwards, everyone moved to where the communal camp-fire had been lit, and on which cooking pots had been set.

Petronella had squatted on the ground by the fire, in the manner of the servants, and Pappa was taking Mamma's arm to help her do the same. But Koos stopped them with a grin, and called out something in Zulu. Several of the women disappeared inside their huts and emerged, beaming, carrying chairs. Mamma stared in disbelief as she recognised that one of them was her own favourite stinkwood chair which had been brought all the way from the Cape by her grandmother. The other two had been part of a set in the kitchen of the farmhouse.

The chairs were set out by the fire, but the servants retained an air of mystery. Women disappeared inside huts again and returned with other items salvaged from the house. Among them were family portraits, Pappa's leather-bound Bible, several pots and pans and – received with mixed feelings by Petronella – the embroidered sampler which had hung in her bedroom, with its dour message, 'Thy God Seest Thee'. Before setting fire to the house, it appeared, the British had invited the servants to take for themselves one or two items each, and they had all chosen what they had believed their employers would most wish to be saved. Now they were returning them to their rightful owners.

The crowning surprise was left until last. When the women began to serve the meal they had been cooking, Pappa and Mamma and Petronella received theirs on three prized Delft plates, which together with two others, a meat-platter and a sauce-boat, were all that remained of the family heirloom. As they sat with the plates on their laps, Petronella was struck by the irony of it all. These plates had always been considered far too precious to be used, and now she and Pappa and Mamma were eating from them with their fingers in the manner of their hosts, picking up doughy chunks of mealie-porridge and using them to scoop up some of the mashed pumpkin which accompanied it, washing it all down with *magouw* which was served to them in three crystal glasses, part of a set which had also been among the salvaged items.

The sour, fermented brew reminded Petronella of old Bolih, and when she asked after him she learnt that he had died. Mamma looked pensively at the huts which had been abandoned because their previous owners had also died, and said, "I know the Oubaas has been thinking about those huts which you no longer use. They have corrugated iron roofs and wooden beams. The Oubaas believes the material could be used for repairing part of the farmhouse."

Everyone nodded in agreement, and Pappa looked faintly surprised before he, too, expressed the opinion that if the disused huts were dismantled there should be a considerable supply of materials which could be used in making the farmhouse habitable again.

Pretending to voice Pappa's decisions became a familiar tactic of Mamma's from then onwards. She it was who pointed out that iron ploughs could not be destroyed by fire, making it seem as if Pappa had first drawn attention to the fact, and that the farm implements should be searched for among the rubble of the burnt outbuildings. The oxen which had drawn the wagon could be used for making a start on the ploughing. Later, when Gideon returned, she said, Pappa meant to send him to buy more oxen or perhaps even mules with which to plough the remainder of the fields.

And so, under Mamma's skilful and subtle direction, attempts were made to bring some kind of normality back to their lives. Pappa, with the help of several young boys from the *stad*, attended to the ploughing, and Petronella helped Koos and the women to dismantle the disused huts and salvage what materials they could. The farmhouse had been gutted, the corrugated iron roof so distorted that it would have to be removed and replaced by nailing together the roofing salvaged from the huts.

In the meantime, Pappa and Mamma and Petronella were camping out inside the wagon, living on the remainder of their rations, supplemented by gifts of mealie-meal which the servants pressed upon them, and which Mamma received with gratitude. She tried to repay the generosity of the servants by offering them some of their own rations, but they declined politely. If they could not have real meat to cook over their fire, they would prefer to do without, rather than eat unrecognisable substances which came out of tins. Occasionally, as a treat, Mamma sacrificed some of the older hens, making sure that the servants received an equal share of the meat.

She had discovered that the range in the destroyed kitchen of the farmhouse was still functional, and only needed cleaning, and they used it for doing their limited cooking. The servants were as generous in their offers of fuel as they were with their gifts of mealie-meal, but Mamma was reluctant to accept all they offered. Remembering their experience at the concentration camp, she told Petronella, "Take a couple of pails, and cross the river at the drift. Apart from the oxen after their work has been done, the young cattle which Koos saved from the British have been foraging there for many months, and there should be a good supply of dry dung which we could use for fuel."

The thorn trees lining the river had escaped the devastation of the fire, because, Koos had told them, the Vaal had flooded its banks only a few days before the arrival of the British, so that the trees had been surrounded by water when the fires raged.

As Petronella crossed the river boundary into what she knew she would always think of as the Free State, no matter what name the British might have bestowed on it, she would face the thick screen of trees and imagine that, on the other side, Jakkalsdrif looked as it once had. In her mind's eye she saw the waving fields of corn, the orchard, the *dik-dik* bucks streaking through the grass, the partridges rising from cover, the cattle and sheep and horses grazing sleekly in the lush meadows.

And then, her pails filled with dry dung which they had christened 'Free State coal', she would cross the drift again and the bitter, desolate reality would stare her in the face. Impotent rage would take hold of her and she would hate the British with a bitter malevolence. They had robbed her of Marcus, and they had not even left her the comfort of her remembered, beloved Jakkalsdrif in which to lick her wounds. They had destroyed everything with the purpose of bringing the Boers to their knees, and the amount of compensation they had paid was an insult in itself . . .

The thought led her to another, and her heart began to quicken with excitement. She hurried through the drift, crossed the charred stubble, and after abandoning the pailsful of 'Free State coal' at a spot from which they could be collected later, she ran to where Pappa was guiding the plough while two boys led the oxen.

"When the British offered you compensation," she asked, "did they give you some kind of document, Pappa?"

"Why, yes." He frowned at her. "Why do you ask?"

"You know that I have learnt English, Pappa. I should like to see what this document says. Where is it?"

Pappa shrugged. "I put it away inside my tobacco pouch. I don't know if it is still there."

She left him watching her with puzzled eyes, delivered the pails with their contents to Mamma inside the ruin of the kitchen, and hurried to look for Pappa's tobacco pouch among his belongings on the wagon. It had not held tobacco for a long time, since none had been obtainable. But the document was still there.

She frowned as she studied it. The compensation the British had paid Pappa had been for the estimated damage done to Jakkalsdrif, including an approximate number of livestock destroyed. If, however, other losses should come to light later, the authorities would be prepared to pay added compensation.

She thought of the sheep and the milk-cows and their wagons and oxen which Hendrik le Roux had taken from them. At first she considered discussing the matter of claiming compensation for the animals with Pappa and Mamma. But gradually a breathtaking idea took hold of her, and for several days she struggled with her conscience.

It would not really be stealing, she told herself, or cheating Pappa. Left to himself, it would never have occurred to him to claim compensation for the loss of their other livestock; indeed, he was not even aware that he would be able to do so. And if she claimed that the animals had been worth £250, the British would probably reduce the figure to £200. If she kept back £75, that would still leave Pappa with £125 which he would never have received at all if it had not been for her.

The more hopeless her chance of ever joining Marcus had become, the more her longing for him had grown. Here, at last, she had been offered the opportunity of reaching him, and Gideon would soon come home to help salvage what could possibly be resurrected from the ruins of Jakkalsdrif, and he would be more of a comfort to their parents than she could ever be.

She finally made up her mind when Mamma said in her now-accustomed diplomatic way, "I know it has been in Pappa's mind for some time, Petronella, that we ought to take the wagon and oxen and visit Doornboomstad. Apart from seeking news of our neighbours and friends, there might be a letter from Gideon waiting for us at the post office, explaining why he has not returned yet. And I know Pappa also feels that we ought to buy a pony and trap so that we would not continue to be quite so isolated on Jakkalsdrif." She looked across at Pappa. "You believe tomorrow would be a good time to go, don't you, Hannes?"

"Yes, certainly. We leave tomorrow morning, as you say. I'll tell Koos."

Later, when Mamma was occupied elsewhere, Petronella took out Pappa's writing box and composed a letter to the authorities at the address on the form which Pappa had been given.

She was, she explained, writing on behalf of her father, who had not yet recovered sufficiently from the privations suffered during the war to attend to his own affairs. Her elder brother was dead and her younger brother Gideon had not yet returned from the prisoner-of-war camp to which he had been sent. On behalf of her father she was claiming compensation of three hundred pounds, that being the estimated value of the livestock and supplies confiscated by Hendrik le Roux.

The letter was hidden inside the pocket of her skirt the next day when they set out for Doornboomstad in the wagon. As they took the dust road which stretched like a red ribbon through the blackened devastation on either side of it, they could see that some of their neighbours had returned, for they could make out wagons similar to their own drawn up outside the ruined farmhouses.

Doornboomstad they found to be almost a ghost-village, for many people had still not returned from concentration camps or would never return. The postmistress, a widowed lady named Moller with two young children, told them that no letter had arrived from Gideon. They took their leave of her so that they could visit the wagon-maker, but Petronella deliberately left her shawl behind so that she would have an excuse to return alone and hand in her letter to be posted.

After Pappa had bought a cart from the wagon-maker and a pony from the stable-owner, Petronella was allowed to drive the conveyance back to Jakkalsdrif while Mamma and Pappa returned with the wagon. She was *not* planning to cheat Pappa, Petronella continued telling herself, but in her heart she knew that she was, and that when it came to a choice between her conscience and Marcus, it would be Marcus who would win.

No more ploughing could be done, since with no sign of Gideon's imminent return and with many of the men from the *stad* still missing, the limited labour force would not be able to cope with sowing and harvesting more than a few fields of mealies, and so Pappa and Mamma and Petronella began to visit their neighbours in the pony and trap instead.

Their experiences had all been depressingly similar. Without exception, they had all lost some of their kin in the concentration camps, and all of them had been beggared. Several doubted whether their farms could ever be made productive again.

Petronella racked her brains for an excuse to take the pony and trap and drive to Doornboomstad, to find out whether there had been a reply to her letter, but she could think of nothing plausible. She had been out one morning gathering 'Free State coal', and when she returned Mamma said briskly, "Pappa has gone to Doornboomstad in the pony and trap. He decided we would have to buy nails from the blacksmith if we are ever to get started on a new roof for the house, and he also wants to ask the wagon-maker whether he has wood to spare which could be made into doors and window-frames."

Petronella turned away so that Mamma would not be able to see her expression. Why could Mamma not have mentioned earlier that Pappa had 'decided' to go to Doornboomstad, so that Petronella could have gone with him? There might well be a reply to her letter waiting at the post office, and Pappa had become so much a ghost of his former self that she could not rely on him to think of visiting the postmistress.

"I wish," she heard Mamma say with a sigh, "that Gideon would come home, or at least send a message."

"Don't worry," Petronella comforted her mechanically, "Andries Jooste was also taken prisoner by the British, and no news has been received of him either, and nothing at all has been heard of the entire du Toit family."

As she stacked the dry cow dung beside the range in the shell of the kitchen, Petronella reflected that in some ways life on Jakkalsdrif now was far worse than it had been in the concentration camp. No matter how terrible the conditions had been in the camp, no matter what hardships they suffered, they had all been helped by the knowledge that what they were living through was an abnormal state which could not endure forever, and that sooner or later those who survived would return to normality.

Her lips twisted with bitterness at the thought of their new 'normality'. It meant sleeping on the wagon at night; it meant foraging for dry cow dung with which to cook the mealie-meal and the pumpkins donated to them by the servants. It meant Pappa holding a travesty of his old Sunday services, perched on the driving seat of the wagon while Mamma and Petronella sat on their salvaged chairs and the servants squatted around them, with everyone pretending not to notice that Pappa was forever losing the thread of what he had been preaching about, and when he ended, as he always did, with the words, "Now let us give thanks to the Lord," she wondered bitterly what there was left for which to give thanks. The new 'normality' meant nothing but bleak discomfort and a struggle for survival which would go on and on, for in spite of Pappa's 'decisions' and his 'plans' as devised and prompted by Mamma, Petronella could not see a new Jakkalsdrif ever rising from the burnt wreckage of the old one.

She was still immersed in her gloomy thoughts when Pappa returned from Doornboomstad. "I managed to buy some nails," he reported, "and Wouter says he has ordered a consignment of timber for making new wagons, and he'll put aside any spare pieces and save them for us."

"I knew that if anyone could lay his hands on materials," Mamma praised him, "it would be you, Hannes."

For a moment a shadow of the old Pappa looked out of his sunken eyes, and he said, "I have had another good idea, wife. We shall need to replace with something the thorn hedges which the British burnt down, and I remembered that on the Free State side of the river, there is a place where prickly pears grow. Koos and I will take the ox-wagon and dig some up, and plant them where the old hedges used to be, to act as windbreaks and to separate the mealie-fields from the meadows."

"That is an excellent idea!" Mamma approved, and Petronella saw the rare shine of tears in her eyes because Pappa had shown a sign of returning to his old, decisive self again. "Everyone knows how quickly prickly pears grow."

Petronella was about to leave her parents alone on the wagon when Pappa said, "Oh, I almost forgot. I was about to leave Doornboomstad when the postmistress sent one of her children running after the trap to stop me. This came for you, Petronella."

He pulled the letter from his pocket and handed it to her, adding curiously, "Who could have been writing to you?"

She had had her answer ready for just such an eventuality as this.

Her heart beating like a drum in her chest, the inside of her mouth dry with suspense, she said, "I imagine it will be from Jakoba Steenkamp, who shared our tent in the camp, Pappa."

"But why would she address a letter to you in English?"

"Because we agreed to continue practising our English when we wrote to each other," Petronella lied, moving away from the wagon and turning her back as she broke the seal on the letter.

She read it swiftly before she refolded it and tucked it inside the front of her blouse. Then she began to walk away, towards the river, and instinct took her to the gap in the thorn-thicket which led to her secret place of long ago. She had deliberately not visited it before, recognising the futility of harrowing her own feelings by seeking out the spot where she had first met Marcus.

She sat down on the ground beneath the willow tree, winter-bare now and with its branches littered with the old, abandoned nests of weaver birds. She withdrew the letter and began to read it again.

After acknowledging her own correspondence, the letter went on, "Whilst checking our files upon your family, it was brought to my notice that your brother Gideon van Zyl attempted to escape from the prisoner-of-war camp in which he was being held, and was shot. Since your family were obviously not acquainted with this news, as evidenced by your letter, and your father's indisposition has made it necessary for you to assume certain of his responsibilities, I considered it to be my painful duty to inform you that your brother is dead."

A howl of grief and despair was torn from Petronella. She crushed the letter in the palm of her hand and threw herself face downwards on the cold, bare earth, and then she began to weep as she had never wept before, with a raw lament which startled the creatures of the riverside and put them to flight.

It shamed her deeply, and yet she could do nothing about it, to know that she was not weeping so much for poor, young, brave and reckless Gideon, or for the devastating pain the news of his death would bring to Pappa and Mamma when she told them about it.

Burnt into her brain were the concluding words of the letter. "I am also sorry to tell you that because the total amount allocated by the British Government for the payment of compensation is limited, no claims can be considered unless they are accompanied by receipts or other documentary evidence. Your claim on behalf of your father is therefore regretfully rejected."

What she was weeping over, more than anything else, was the fact that she would not be able to cheat Pappa after all, and steal from him the seventy-five pounds she needed to join Marcus in Bermuda.

13

Even the news of the death of her youngest child, the baby of her family, and always considered to be her unacknowledged favourite, did not cause Mamma to break down. Her face merely acquired a more granite-like expression and she would stare blankly in front of her, keeping her thoughts and feelings to herself. But Pappa had taken Gideon's death hard. He seemed to have grown even older, and less capable of coping with the many problems of their daily life, and often he would tell Petronella with tears in his sunken eyes, "You are all we have left now."

The reminder contributed to her burden of hopelessness. Sometimes she found herself wondering whether she could have been ruthless enough to leave Pappa and Mamma quite alone on Jakkalsdrif if the authorities had made it possible for her to cheat Pappa and go to Marcus. In her heart, she acknowledged that she probably would have been. Ever since the day when she had first met Marcus, he had come before everyone else. But she would never be required to abandon and betray Pappa and Mamma now, for she had finally admitted defeat.

Several of their servants had straggled home, so that work could have begun on restoring the house, but Petronella knew that the real problem lay in the lack of someone to take charge. Apart from the fact that Mamma knew nothing about the practical business of making and putting up a new roof, or replacing window-frames and windows, her loyalty to Pappa would not have allowed her to usurp his role so openly. And Pappa was becoming more and more unsure of himself, less able to take decisions.

"Now that we have enough labour," Mamma suggested to him instead, "why don't you get the other fields ploughed?"

"I don't know, wife . . . It's too late for sowing mealies. Better let the land lie fallow this season, and recover from the fire."

Mamma paced restlessly between the wagon and the shell of the house. "I think we should buy seed potatoes in Doornboomstad, and use some of the land for them. Those *weeskindertjies* may look pretty, but even the livestock won't eat them."

Petronella knew that she was referring to a strange new weed which had made its appearance among the burnt grass stubble and was fast hiding it underneath a colourful blanket. The plants had a delicate appearance, and produced flowers in pastel shades which resembled miniature snapdragons. Because of this resemblance, and because the origins of the plants which had produced the seeds were unknown, Mamma had christened them *weeskindertjies*, little orphans.

Another new weed had also appeared and was menacing the tender young mealie-plants which had thrust their way through the soil. There was nothing pretty about this weed, which had dark-green leaves and produced an evil smell when crushed between the fingers. Koos and the other men waged a daily battle against it in the mealie-fields.

While Pappa dithered about whether or not to grow potatoes as a crop, something he had never done in the past, the pretty *weeskindertjies* spread like a frivolous quilt over the untilled land, and the other foul-smelling weed continued to cause a problem among the mealie-fields and cropped up in many other places all over Jakkalsdrif.

When, eventually, Pappa agreed to Mamma's suggestion to go to Doornboomstad and buy potatoes for seed, and the two of them returned afterwards, they had a surprise passenger sitting on top of the bags of seed potatoes. It was Masadi, the mother of Mwende, and tears of shock and of joy filled her eyes as she stepped down on to Jakkalsdrif's land and was reunited with her husband and Koos and her old mother.

Mamma and Pappa had found her, it appeared, in a state of near-collapse from exhaustion, in the street in Doornboomstad. She had walked most of the way from Johannesburg, with the intention of reaching Jakkalsdrif.

Her story was simply related as Mamma fed her with coffee and bread and some of the precious tinned butter which they had been hoarding. Almost everyone from the *stad* gathered to listen to her account.

After Hendrik le Roux had ordered them to go where they wished and do as they liked, the black people had simply remained where they were, in total confusion and without purpose. Impatiently, le Roux had ordered them to help themselves to supplies from the Boer wagons and leave. They had armed themselves with such supplies as they were able to carry, but when they did leave the railway station they had done the only thing they could think of. They had tracked the departing British soldiers until they caught up with the main body of troops, and there they had stayed, unwanted camp-followers to the British, extra mouths to feed. At the end of the war the British had taken them to Johannesburg, given them supplies and a little money, and they had all set out to make their way as best they could towards the homes of their employers.

"Other women and children," Masadi said, "they home on Jakkalsdrif already, because they use money and buy cart and donkeys."

"No," Mamma contradicted, frowning. "They have not arrived."

Masadi shrugged. "Perhaps some donkeys get ill. They here soon."

"But why," Petronella wanted to know, "did you not travel with them, Masadi? Mwende, of course, must be with the other women. It will be good to see her again – "

She was stopped by the look of anger and pain in Masadi's eyes. "Mwende not come home, Nonnie Petronella. She bad, bad girl. She shame my eyes from my head by what she do, and she not listen to me at all."

"But what has she done?"

Harshly, Masadi said, "She find young man. Young *white* man. English soldier. She become his *mfazi* – his woman – and stay with him."

A long-drawn-out, hissing sound of shock and condemnation came from the servants at the news. Mwende's grandmother said something in Zulu in a fierce voice, and Petronella guessed that she was reminding everyone that no black man of any age would pay a single cow in *lobolo* for Mwende after this.

"I can scarcely believe it of her," Mamma said, shaking her head.

Of all of them, Petronella alone did not condemn Mwende. The girl had broken the same rule which Petronella herself had broken, the rule which said that like should choose like. Whatever happened to Mwende in the future, at least she had been spared a forced marriage to a 'wrinkled-up old man'.

Pappa changed the subject. "There was a letter at the post office for you, Petronella."

She recognised Jakoba Steenkamp's handwriting as she took it from him. "Dieter and I," Jakoba had written, "finally discovered that both his parents had died in Green Point concentration camp. My father is dead too, but I am glad to say that he was not shot as a rebel after all, for he cheated the British by succumbing to a heart seizure before the sentence could be carried out.

"Dieter and I have returned to the farm in what we are trying hard to think of now as the Orange River Colony. But oh, Petronella, if you could but see what has been done to it! Everything burnt and destroyed, and even though Dieter has been paid some compensation and has ploughed one field and put in mealies, we are struggling against a pestilent weed which threatens to take over the land. It has an awful smell when you crush it between your fingers or when the hot sun shines on it, and we have been told that the seeds were brought into the country among the forage which the British imported for their horses from Argentina. Because of this, farmers here are calling it 'khaki-bush' after the British soldiers. You may be thankful that it has not spread to your part of the world, since you told me that there was no reason why the British should visit Jakkalsdrif."

Petronella uttered a wry laugh and read the letter to Mamma and Pappa. "Jakoba doesn't mention *weeskindertjies*," she added. "Should we feel privileged because as well as 'khaki-bush' we also have a pretty new weed with flowers like snapdragons?"

"That reminds me," Pappa said with a sigh. "I must set the men to ploughing them into the ground – "

"No, Oubaas, no!" Masadi interrupted urgently. "They a devil plant! You plough them in, and their spirit poison the soil!"

"That's nonsense, Masadi – "

"I see them before, Oubaas, the plant like the mouth of a lion! I know they very, very bad things!" She went on to explain that the flowering weeds had been a common sight in the Free State, where the farms had been set on fire early in the war. While she was one of the British Army's unwelcome camp-followers, Masadi had met a Xhosa family who had decided to squat on one of those burnt-down farms. They had dug the *weeskindertjies* into the ground and put in mealie-seed.

"The mealie-plants come up, Oubaas, but they sick, sick, sick! I see them with my eyes. The spirit of the devil plant curse them. And when the sick mealies die the devil plant come up again and it is much, much more strong."

She had spoken with such passion and conviction that Pappa and Mamma exchanged uncertain glances. "It's true that we know nothing about these weeds," Pappa muttered.

"If they come up again after they have been dug into the soil, it means their roots remain alive," Mamma said thoughtfully. "It's probably coincidence that the Xhosa family's mealies failed but I think, Hannes, it would be best to forget about planting potatoes and instead try to kill those *weeskindertjies*, roots and all."

Pappa agreed, and it was decided to burn off the weeds. Because the spring rains had not made their expected appearance the *weeskindertjies* lacked sufficient moisture to withstand the flames when the servants fired them with the help of paraffin.

Afterwards, Petronella looked at the desolation all around her, and thought bleakly that it matched the desolation of her own life. She could imagine herself growing old, still camping on the wagon after Pappa and Mamma had died, living from hand to mouth on what fish could be caught in the Vaal River and on the few mealies Jakkalsdrif yielded, with the house remaining an empty, burnt-out shell because no one had the will or the resolution or the heart to begin the work of repairing it, least of all herself.

A few days later, the women and children Masadi had said were on their way to Jakkalsdrif arrived in the donkey-cart. They had been delayed by the illness of one of the children, and had been forced to take shelter in a *stad* on the way. They, too, were loud in their condemnation of Mwende, who had stayed behind in Johannesburg to be with her English soldier. Petronella thought of her old playmate, servant and friend, and wished her nothing but happiness. Of course what she was doing was wrong; the Bible said there should be no mingling of blood, which Pappa said meant that people of different colour and blood should not marry or consort with one another intimately. But the Bible also said many other things, such as honouring one's father and not stealing, and Petronella had been quite prepared to flout both commandments if only she had been given the chance.

It was not long before another conveyance was approaching Jakkalsdrif. This time it was a wagon, driven by Gerrit du Toit, with his sister Driena as his passenger. Petronella embraced Driena with conventional politeness, and shook hands with Gerrit, studying him. There was very little of the callow, pimply youth left. He had been honed by the hard school of a protracted guerilla war, and it showed in his hollow cheeks and his wary, bitter eyes.

Mamma offered the visitors chairs outside their own wagon. "We did not know that any of you had returned to Bulspruit," she said. "Are your – "

"They're dead," Gerrit interrupted baldly. "Pa in the war, Ma and my sister Nella of typhoid in Kroonstad camp; my sisters Marie and Ria of something else in Aliwal North camp. I ran Driena to earth in Heilbron camp, where our grandmother also died. I have been told," he added quickly, as if to forestall the convention of offering condolences, "that at the last count, more than twenty-four thousand people are known to have died in the concentration camps."

No one spoke for a moment, Petronella knew by the rock-hard expression on Mamma's face that she was thinking of Dorothea, and of the baby Gabriel in his sack with his blue bonnet taking the place of a wreath as he was lowered into the ground.

Mamma broke the silence. "Did you know what awaited you at Bulspruit?"

"I did not." Gerrit's eyes narrowed into slits. "The compensation I was given was so little that I thought only slight damage had been done to the farm. But there's nothing left, and I don't see how I am ever going to get back on my feet with what they have given me in compensation."

"Didn't they explain why it was so little?" Pappa demanded.

Gerrit shrugged. "I suppose they did, but there was no one to translate."

"You would think," Pappa burst out, "that if they are to be our new masters, a few of them would at least try to learn our language so that they could explain matters to us!"

Gerrit gave a hollow laugh. "I have news for you, Oom Hannes! There are rumours flying all around Johannesburg and outside it that Lord Milner, who is now running what used to be the free Republics, intends banning Dutch, and forcing everyone to learn English instead!"

"That can't be true," Petronella put in. "I read some of the clauses of the peace treaty signed by Lords Kitchener and Milner and the Boer generals, and it specifically mentioned that Dutch was to be taught in schools if the parents wished it."

Driena, who had said little so far, cleared her throat. "Womenfolk don't always understand these matters, Petronella," she offered diffidently.

In some ways, she reminded Petronella of Dorothea. She was a shy, quiet and self-effacing girl who clearly adored her brother and deferred to him in everything.

"*I* certainly understood," Petronella assured her. "I have learnt English, and I read the clause in an English newspaper. Gerrit, when you were given the compensation, were you asked to sign a document, as Pappa was?"

Gerrit nodded, fumbling in his pocket, and handed her a scrap of paper. "It says," Petronella translated, "that you have been awarded the agreed percentage of compensation for damage caused to land, property and livestock on the farm Bulspruit. Did you agree to receive only a percentage?"

"The only thing I knowingly agreed to was to sign the document, and that was only because I would still have been there now if I hadn't."

"I believe a mistake must have been made," Petronella mused.

"Why don't you," Pappa suggested to Gerrit, "let Petronella write to these people for you? She has become very clever, you know," he added with pride.

Petronella found that Gerrit was regarding her thoughtfully. "Would you be prepared to do so?"

"Certainly."

Mamma stood up. "I have to attend to the supper. You will stay for the meal, won't you?"

They accepted with gratitude, and Mamma disappeared into the kitchen of the ruined farmhouse. The arrival of spring and the appearance in the cultivated fields of green mealie-plants had been encouraging small animals such as *dassies* and rabbits to emerge from wherever they had been managing to survive, and the men from the *stad* had made and set snares for them. Although Mamma would be able to offer Gerrit and Driena, the first neighbours to visit them on Jakkalsdrif, a supper of stewed rabbit cooked with some of the potatoes which had been meant as seed, Petronella knew that it shamed her deeply that she would be unable to seat them at a table, no matter how crude, inside a house, and that they would have to eat from their laps instead, while sitting under the open sky.

She found that Gerrit was studying the shell of the farmhouse, and she saw him looking at the stack of materials, corrugated iron and lengths of timber obtained from the wagon-maker at Doornboomstad, which leant against one wall.

"You have been fortunate," he remarked. "It should take you no time at all to make the house habitable again now that you have managed to obtain materials."

Mamma had emerged from the kitchen in time to hear this. "Oom Hannes has just been waiting for the right moment to make a start on it," she said, as usual keeping up the fiction that Pappa remained his old, vital, decisive self.

Pappa nodded. "That's right. You can't rush these things."

Something in the atmosphere seemed to have warned Gerrit of the reality of the situation, for he offered, "I'll lend you a hand if you like. Even if I'd been given adequate compensation I couldn't have grown anything on Bulspruit this season, because the land is infested with a flowering weed. I heard, while I was in the Free State, that it ruins the soil for mealies; something to do with a parasite in the root of the weed."

"So Masadi was right!" Petronella exclaimed. "She warned Pappa not to plough them into the ground."

Gerrit nodded. "I've set the men in my *stad* to work on clearing the weeds. They can manage without me, so I'll be quite happy to drive over every day with Driena, and help to fix up the house."

Mamma, Petronella noticed, could not hide her relief. "Why drive over every day?" she suggested. "You and Driena are living in your wagon, in any case, just as we are in ours, so why not stay here? Your oxen could be driven across the river, where our livestock are grazing too, and Driena will be company for Petronella and me while you help Oom Hannes with the work on the house."

The arrangement was agreed between them. Gerrit returned briefly to his own farm the following morning, and when he arrived back on Jakkalsdrif he brought with him a shotgun and ammunition wrapped up in a piece of leather.

Pappa's eyes took on an envious glow when he saw the weapon. "It has become illegal to own a shotgun without a licence," he remarked. "How did you lay your hands on that?"

Gerrit grinned. "Driena remembered that they had hidden it inside a pail halfway down the well when they heard that the English soldiers were on their way. Poor old Ma, she was all for holding out against the soldiers, shooting as many of them as she could when they arrived, but the girls frustrated her by going behind her back and hiding the shotgun and the ammunition down the well. Illegal or not, the gun will enable me to make a contribution towards our food while Driena and I are here."

The gun proved to be an undisputed blessing, for whenever Gerrit was not working on the house he crossed the Vaal River and returned with gamebirds or small buck which formed a welcome addition to their dwindling stores. Mealie-meal was available for sale in the newly reopened general store in Doornboomstad, but both Pappa and Gerrit were husbanding the money which they had received in compensation, and they bought only small quantities at a time, enough to keep themselves and the people in the *stad* in rations.

Gerrit worked swiftly and efficiently on the repairs to the house, always taking care to defer to Pappa and to make it seem as if he was taking orders from the older man instead of working on his own initiative, and Petronella noticed that Pappa was gradually beginning to regain a little of his old authority.

She herself was largely indifferent to the presence on Jakkalsdrif of the du Toits, although she was grateful for the comfort which they brought to Pappa and Mamma. Petronella had as little in common with Driena as she had had with Dorothea, but the girl earned Mamma's approval with her willingness to help wherever she was needed, and Gerrit assumed almost godlike properties in her eyes because of the effect he was having on Pappa.

"It is almost," she once said to Petronella, in one of her rare references to the two sons she had lost, "as if Johannes or Gideon were still here."

Gerrit, with the help of Koos, had just finished nailing the roof together when Pappa returned from a trip in the pony-cart to Doornboomstad where he had gone to see whether it would be possible to acquire window-glass. Some might be available soon, he reported, and then he handed Petronella a reply to the letter which she had written to the authorities on Gerrit's behalf.

He listened with a grim expression as she explained the contents of the letter to him. "I am afraid there was no mistake, Gerrit. Bulspruit, together with the slaughtered livestock, belonged to your father, and not to you. Had your father survived, he would have received the same amount of compensation as that which Pappa has been paid, and so would his widow have done if she had survived. But according to Roman-Dutch law, the letter says, all of a dead man's property has to be divided equally among all of his offspring unless he leaves a will instructing otherwise. So, by applying that law, it means that after the death of your father and your mother, Bulspruit was deemed to have been split up between yourself and your four sisters. You and Driena automatically inherit the portions of your dead sisters, but you can't inherit the compensation which would have been payable to them. And that is why the amount you have jointly received amounts to two-fifths of the compensation which would otherwise have been payable. The letter goes on to say that, if your father had left a will, making you the outright heir of Bulspruit and all his other goods and chattels, they would review your case and consider paying further compensation."

"I see." Gerrit's voice was bitter. "How do they expect me to produce my father's testament when it had been placed inside the family Bible for safe-keeping, and was burnt with everything else when the soldiers set fire to the house? And any fool must surely realise that my father would have left the farm and everything on it to his only son, on condition that he continued to maintain any of his sisters who remained unmarried?"

Petronella shook her head. "They seem to have stuck to the letter of the law. Or perhaps they just don't understand our customs, and people in England do not keep their last will and testament inside the family Bible."

"Well," Gerrit said in a flat voice, "there is no possibility of my being able to make a living of any kind for Driena and myself on Bulspruit with what we have been given. I shall have to tell my black folk that they had best leave the *stad*, and try to find work elsewhere. As for Driena and me, we'll have to take the ox-wagon and wander through the country, looking for a farmer still prosperous enough to take in a *bywoner*, and – "

"No," Mamma interrupted him. "No, Oom Hannes has dropped a few hints to me recently, and I know he has decided that we should offer you and Driena a home here on Jakkalsdrif. If we put together the compensation you and Oom Hannes have received, then we could make Jakkalsdrif prosperous enough to support all of us." She turned to Pappa. "That is what you have been considering, isn't it?"

"Yes," Pappa agreed readily. "Oh yes."

"Thank you," Gerrit said after a while, "but I shall also have to consider the matter." He was looking thoughtfully at Petronella as he spoke, and she felt a lurch of dismay in the pit of her stomach as she perceived the trap that was yawning in front of her.

That night she had one of her most vivid dreams of Marcus. They walked together along a track through waving fields of corn such as had grown on Jakkalsdrif before it had been raped by the British, and Marcus was wearing his skull-cap and the embroidered Jewish shawl about his shoulders. The two of them reached Petronella's secret place by the river, and Marcus removed his cap and his shawl. For some reason he called out, *"Shalom Bayit!"* which she knew meant 'Peace and Love' and was used in greeting or farewell. He threw cap and shawl into the river and then he stood before her, totally naked with the magic only dreams could produce.

"For you, my Petronella," he said, "I renounce all, and I give my future into your hands."

And she, also magically naked, was pulled into his arms so that his flesh against hers scorched her and sent fires leaping inside her, and then he drew her down on the grass and his hands and his mouth were everywhere upon her body until she cried out with the ecstasy of it all.

The dream still clung to her mind, haunting her, when she set out the next morning to cross the river and collect 'Free State coal'. She had filled her pails when she saw that Gerrit was striding purposefully towards her. He stopped and faced her, his expression serious.

"The plan your mother proposed, Petronella," he said, "makes sense, but it would only make complete sense to me if I were to be sure of having a permanent stake in Jakkalsdrif."

Oh God, here was the trap she had recognised and which had temporarily been blotted from her mind by that dream about Marcus, who was so utterly lost to her.

"What do you mean?" she tried desperately to play for time.

"I think you know what I mean." Gerrit gave her a brief smile. "A great deal has happened to both of us since those long-ago days when we sat and tried to make conversation in your parlour with the *opsitkers*. I wanted to marry you then, but I could never have brought myself to form the words. I am asking you now, Petronella, to marry me."

It seemed entirely appropriate, she thought dismally, that she should be proposed to by a man she did not and could never love while she was holding pails full of dry cow dung in each hand.

When she did not answer, he went on, "All I have in the world – apart from a totally useless, unworkable farm – is a wagon, a span of oxen, some bags of mealie-seeds, a limited amount of money, and the labour of my two hands. I can either take those assets and leave, and use them in whatever way I can find to make a living for Driena and myself. Or I could invest the same assets in Jakkalsdrif. But I would only do so if I am to become your husband, so that when you inherit Jakkalsdrif from your father one day I would have a moral and legal share in it."

Thoughts were desperately churning in her brain. If Gerrit, with his vitality and his energy and his positive way of approaching problems, were to leave Jakkalsdrif, Pappa would soon slip back into his previous state of indecision and lethargy. Jakkalsdrif would not only remain a ruined place, but the little they had already achieved would soon deteriorate again and she and Pappa and Mamma would decay there with their land. And it was not as if she would ever see Marcus again, or find anyone else to take his place, or as if Gerrit had made any attempt to disguise the fact that he was making her what amounted to little more than a proposition of practical, mutual convenience, with no question of love involved . . .

But almost as if he had guessed what she was thinking, he went on, "I have always had a great regard for you, Petronella, even when – even in spite of – " He stopped, perhaps warned by something in her expression not to mention her relationship with Marcus.

A long silence stretched between them. Gerrit broke it. "I am waiting for your answer, Petronella."

She bowed her head. "Very well. I accept."

He did not attempt to kiss her. He merely said, "Let us go and tell your parents and Driena."

Before he fell into step beside her he took from her the two pails full of cow dung and carried them for her. A truly lover-like gesture, she thought with desolate humour, and closed her eyes briefly, saying a final goodbye to Marcus's ghost.

Pappa was overjoyed when he heard that Gerrit and Petronella were to marry. Mamma was pleased too, but extravagant displays of emotion were not her way, and she expressed her approval by loudly examining ways and means of somehow procuring something suitable for Petronella to wear for her wedding. Driena kissed her future sister-in-law and said, "I'm sure we shall get on very well. We have so much in common, for we both love Gerrit."

Petronella said nothing. She did not love Gerrit, any more than she had ever loved him. To her relief, as the weeks passed, he was far too busy to pay her the kind of attention which might have been expected from a betrothed. He was organising everyone and everything on Jakkalsdrif, orchestrating an orgy of improvements and laying the foundations for future plans.

"It is too late to put in more mealies," he told Pappa, "but there is no reason why we should not clear the khaki-bush from the fields which have not been affected by *weeskindertjies* and plough them and grow other crops. Think, Oom Hannes – what apart from mealies are going to be the most desperately needed crops for some time to come?" When Pappa did not respond immediately, Gerrit answered his own question. "Animal feed! We'll plant lucerne, and we'll grow sunflowers. While Koos and I concentrate on finishing work on the house, the other men from the *stad* must make a start on the ploughing. Tomorrow morning I'll call at Bulspruit and pick up my own farm implements which survived the fire, and some of the men from the *stad*. With two spans of oxen and two ploughs, the work will be done in no time at all – with you to supervise, of course," he added diplomatically.

He was a whirlwind of energy. In hardly any time at all, it seemed, the roof of the farmhouse had been replaced, the windows and doors fitted, and then he concentrated on the hurried planting of lucerne and sunflower seeds, while Mamma, Petronella, Driena and the women from the *stad* scrubbed the walls and the cement floors of the house from top to bottom to remove as much of the black soot as they could.

The money which Pappa and Gerrit had received in compensation had been pooled, and was being spent with judicious care, for it would have to be used to feed everyone on Jakkalsdrif and also the people on Bulspruit's *stad*, until the farm could provide for them again. One of the things which it had been agreed money should be spent upon was whitewash, and Gerrit took time off to drive to Doornboomstad. He returned with a supply of it and with brushes, and also with more pieces of wood begged from the wagon-maker. While Koos and some of the older youths from the *stad* whitewashed the interior walls of the house, Gerrit was busy fashioning the wood into a table, a bench and shelves for the kitchen.

Petronella admired what he did, and she was grateful. Jakkalsdrif had not been transformed to what it had been before; she doubted if it ever could be. But it was no longer the bleak, hopeless wasteland of the previous months; it had rained a few weeks ago and already the mealie-plants stood a little taller in their rows, and the lucerne and sunflowers had begun to show above the surface of the soil.

Soon, too, they would all be able to move into the house to live. If only, she thought, she could feel anything but a sense of trapped despair at the prospect of her marriage. Any hope she had had that it would be a businesslike arrangement only were dashed when Gerrit, on the few occasions when they were alone together, kissed her with hard, pursed lips and talked about creating a heritage for the son which they would one day have, the unborn son who was making all his labours worthwhile.

The day when Gerrit returned from a trip to Doornboomstad with a large brass bed lashed to the back of the wagon, which he had exchanged for two hare-carcases with a widow who no longer needed it, was the day when Petronella felt the trap beginning to close around her with inexorable inevitability. It came a little closer to snapping shut when Gerrit said briskly, "I spoke to *Dominee* Schalk, Petronella. We are to drive to Doornboomstad on Saturday, and stay overnight so that we may attend the service on Sunday morning, when our banns are to be called."

"Very well," she said matter-of-factly, and she knew that no one guessed at the devastation which was threatening to engulf her.

"I know we can't spare the money," Mamma exclaimed, "but you *must* have a new dress for the occasion! Now let me think . . ."

It did not take her long to come up with the answer. The hens had started laying again, and Mamma had been saving the eggs so that she could bake a cake for the wedding. But declaring a special dress to be more important than a cake, Mamma wrapped each egg individually in a piece of rag and said, "We'll take the pony-cart and leave for Doornboomstad immediately, Petronella. The hens are bound to produce a few more eggs before the wedding, and we'll just have to make do with sweet biscuits instead of a cake."

With numb resignation, Petronella accompanied Mamma to Doornboomstad, where she took the eggs to the general store and told the owner, "Many people will not have tasted eggs for a long while, and you'll get a good price for these. In return, I want a length of the best fabric you have in stock. Petronella, what colour would you prefer?" Her voice altering slightly, Mamma added, for Petronella's ears only, "Apart from white, of course."

Petronella shrugged indifferently, thinking that black crêpe would best have expressed her own feelings towards her coming marriage. Mamma had shrewdly calculated the transaction; if anyone had, before the war, tried to trade a dozen eggs for a dress-length of any kind of fabric they would have been laughed to scorn. But the store-owner had several rolls of left-over sateen in stock, for which he did not anticipate a market in these hard-pressed times, and he was happy to accept the eggs in exchange for the length of pearl-grey fabric which Mamma favoured, and upon which Petronella listlessly agreed. As soon as they returned home Mamma began work on making the gown.

Petronella and Mamma were alone in the house on the day when the gown was finally completed. There was less than a week to go before the wedding, and Gerrit and Driena had taken the pony-cart to Doornboomstad. Following the now-established system of barter, Gerrit had shot a young buck and he intended exchanging it for a shirt for himself, and a hat for Driena, who was to be Petronella's bridesmaid. Pappa was outside, engaged in his favourite pursuit of inspecting the fields on Jakkalsdrif, checking on the growth of the lucerne and the mealies and the sunflowers.

At Mamma's insistence, Petronella had put on her wedding gown so that it could be critically examined for any last-minute changes which required to be made. Mamma was just giving the pearl-grey sateen gown a final tug to make sure that it hung straight, when they heard the sound of cart-wheels outside.

"That's Gerrit back with Driena," Mamma said. "Quickly – change out of your wedding gown. Gerrit must not see you wearing it until the day. It's bad luck."

Petronella did not think anything existed which could possibly bring bad luck to a marriage which, as far as she was concerned, was already doomed to the very worst of luck.

But she began to move obediently from the sparsely furnished bedroom occupied by Mamma and Pappa, in which she had been modelling the gown, while Mamma stooped to pick up stray pieces of thread which had been shed by the garment.

As Petronella passed the open front door, which had once led out on to the stoep, she stopped, paralysed, telling herself that she had at last lost her grip on reality and was slipping into madness.

It couldn't be. It simply wasn't possible. Her growing despair at the thought of her coming wedding had resulted in crazy hallucinations. If she remained there, rooted to the spot, the spectre would vanish into thin air.

But he didn't. He came hurrying towards the house, as tall as she remembered him, but leaner, his dark hair longer and touched in a few places by strands of lighter colour as if bleached by the sun, the clefts beside his mouth not as deep as they used to be because his sun-browned face was thinner and his cheekbones more prominent. His shirt was not of silk this time, but appeared to have been made of white lawn, and he still looked as exotically different as ever from any other man, for he wore matching dark trousers and jacket, and a broad blue-and-white tie was knotted around his neck.

"*Marcus*," she whispered.

"Aai, my Petronella!"

She ran to meet him, dressed in the wedding gown meant for another man, and they came together in the doorway, clinging to one another as if they could never bear to let go again. He kissed her mouth, her eyes, her cheeks, while her hands moved over his body, making quite sure that he was real and not some phantom dredged up by her own crazed mind.

"Marcus," she breathed, reassured at last. "Oh, thank you, God! Marcus Koen, I never thought . . . Oh God, thank you, thank you, *thank you!*"

He drew her against him in a tight, fierce hold for a moment, and let her go. She turned, to see Mamma standing there and watching them with a stark, frozen expression.

"Mamma, it's Marcus!" Petronella cried. "It really is! I don't know how or why, but he has come back!"

"So I see," Mamma said, and the tone of her voice made it clear that it might as well have been Beelzebub himself who had walked into the house to lay a curse upon it.

14

Marcus stepped past Petronella, and held out a hand to Mamma, saying in less precise Dutch but still with a distinctive accent, "I hope you are well, Mevrouw van Zyl."

Mamma ignored his hand, and returned shortly, "Perfectly well, thank you." Her voice sharpened. "Petronella, go and change your clothes!"

"What? Oh . . ." Petronella dismissed the gown, and all it stood for, her eyes devouring Marcus. "You look – beautiful."

The clefts flickered beside his mouth and his eyes were both ardent and tenderly amused. "It is you who look beautiful, Petronella." Deliberately, he abandoned his acquired, more idiomatic Dutch and echoed the stilted phrase he had used so long ago at their first meeting. "The reflection which faces you from the mirror each day must reassure you of your beauty."

"Oh Marcus . . ." She uttered a sound which was partly laughter, partly an expression of pure joy.

"Petronella!" Mamma's voice crackled like a whiplash through their unspoken communication. *"Go and change out of that gown this minute!"*

It was not so much Mamma's command which moved her to back slowly away, her eyes continuing to drink in the wondrous sight of Marcus, as the fact that she did not want him to go on seeing her in a gown of nondescript pearl-grey which had been pressed upon her for the sole benefit of another man. For the very first time since Marcus had been wrenched from her, Petronella cared what she looked like.

In her bedroom, which held only Pappa's bed-roll in which Petronella had been sleeping, the sampler on the wall with its gloomy embroidered warning and a wooden chest for her belongings which Gerrit had made, she searched feverishly for something to wear for Marcus alone. The trouble was that the clothes donated to them by the Englishwoman in Johannesburg had been meant for cold weather, and it was now well into summer. The few light-weight blouses which Petronella had been given and which she had been teaming with the lighter of the skirts had been worn almost ragged.

At last, in spite of the fact that it would be much too warm for the time of year, she chose a dress made of light wool, in a pretty shade of rose, and she changed into it. There was a small, cheap mirror hanging in Mamma's bedroom but Petronella had seldom bothered to consult it, for she had become adept, while in the concentration camp, at plaiting her hair without the need of one. But now she hurried to Mamma's bedroom to study her face in the mirror. How silly and ridiculous it was, she thought, that at the age of twenty she should still be scraping her hair back tightly from her face and braiding it. Her glance fell upon the scissors which Mamma had used for making her wedding gown, and recklessly Petronella picked them up and cut each braid to just below her ear-lobes. She loosened her hair and brushed it. It reached, in rippling waves created by the tight braiding, to her shoulders. The result made her look daring and – she searched for the right word – *abandoned*. Mamma would be horrified but Marcus, she sensed, would like it. She did not care what anyone else thought. A miracle had restored Marcus to her, and he was the only one who counted.

She hurried into the parlour, where she knew Mamma would have taken him, in spite of the fact that the only furniture it contained was the bench Gerrit had made and the chairs which the servants in the *stad* had salvaged for them. But strangers, even unwelcome strangers, would always automatically be taken into the parlour. A stab of common sense broke through Petronella's feeling of euphoria and told her that Marcus would be unwelcome to everyone but herself.

She hurried into the parlour, and found Mamma seated there in her favourite stinkwood chair, while Marcus sat at the opposite end of the room on the bench. Mamma was regarding him with the kind of watchful suspicion she would have accorded a strange, unpredictable and possibly dangerous wild animal. She looked up when Petronella appeared, and said with angry disbelief, "What do you think you have done to your hair?"

"I've cut it." Petronella dismissed the subject, and hurried to sit beside Marcus, asking breathlessly, "How did you obtain a pardon? We were told you had been exiled for life. Oh Marcus, if you knew how much I learnt about the rest of the world while I tried to discover where you were! I had never even heard of Bermuda before, but now I know that it consists of about three hundred islands, and I also know where Ceylon and St Helena are – "

"Petronella," Mamma interrupted sharply, "go and make coffee for our guest." In spite of her commanding and abrasive tone, she had the shocked, stunned look of a parent who had believed her child to have survived an attack of a deadly disease, only to discover that the disease had merely been lying dormant and had suddenly broken out again after years during which everyone had been lulled into a sense of false security.

"Thank you, Mevrouw," Marcus declined politely, "I do not wish for coffee. Petronella has asked me how I came to be pardoned, and I wish to tell the story of my return to South Africa. The Church of the Reformed Evangelists paid for my passage and secured my release."

"I have never heard of such a church," Mamma stated flatly, with disbelief.

"Perhaps not, Mevrouw, but that it exists I can assure you." Petronella noticed that although Marcus now spoke in the simplified idiom of the Boers, instead of in pure, learned Dutch, some of his ways of expressing himself still owed more to Yiddish than they did to Dutch. And he would probably never lose the distinctive intonation which gave his speech such a piquant quality. He went on, "I am now ordained as a pastor of the Church of the Reformed Evangelists."

A stunned silence followed his words. Mamma was about to break it when she heard Koos calling to her. He came to the door, and nodded politely but indifferently to Marcus before informing Mamma, "Oubaas, he ask you to come quickly. He in sunflower field."

"Why?" Mamma demanded with some alarm. "Has something happened to him?"

Koos shrugged. "I don't know, Oumies. Oubaas sit on ground and call to me to fetch you."

Petronella could understand quite clearly the dilemma with which Mamma was struggling. She did not want to leave her daughter and Marcus alone together, and at the same time she dared not ignore Pappa's request for her to go to him, in case he should be in trouble of some kind. In the end, concern for her husband won, and she hurried from the room and from the house.

Petronella hoped fleetingly that Pappa was not having a heart seizure or something equally disastrous, and then dismissed him from her mind. She turned to Marcus, and kissed him in the way he had taught her so long ago, and felt herself to be really alive for the first time in years. His hands explored and caressed her face, and then he unfastened the bodice of her gown but he did no more than touch her, tentatively, gazing down at her naked flesh in the manner of a man who had been starving for years, and had suddenly been offered a feast, but was overwhelmed by the abundance staring him in the face. She twisted her hands through his hair, far more impatient than he, and drew his head down to her breasts. But he resisted, sitting up and rebuttoning her bodice, and then he moved away so that they were no longer touching.

"Petronella," he said, "we must talk, and it is not easy to do so while your family are present. First I must tell you how it was that I became a pastor."

"You really *are* a pastor?" she demanded incredulously. "I thought it was a lie, for Mamma's benefit, to make her change her opinion of you – "

"A lie? Well – perhaps deep down . . ." He took her hand, threading her fingers through his own. "When I was first caught by the British I wished to die in the name given to me by my family, Mordechai Cohen. But I was sent, instead, to exile in Bermuda with other burghers who called themselves *bittereinders* and refused to swear allegiance to King Edward of England when the end of the war came."

A shadow entered his eyes, as if there were many things he could have told her about his life in exile, but chose not to. "I was willing to swear allegiance, Petronella," he went on, "but I was told I would not be allowed to return to South Africa because I am a Jew, not born in this country, and I had been a spy for the Boers. Only to my own homeland would I be sent if I left Bermuda, and so I stayed with the *bittereinders*, but I tried to plan how to return to South Africa and to you. One day there arrived at the gaol where we were kept a missionary from the Church of the Reformed Evangelists, who preached to us and sought converts, and I began to consider how I might use this church to help me reach South Africa."

Petronella's fingers tightened about his. "Isn't it strange? All the time you were plotting and scheming to come back, I was doing the same thing in the hope of joining you in Bermuda!"

She told him about her many attempts, and revelled in his astonishment as she switched to fluent English. She described her long search to discover his country of exile, and confessed how she had planned to cheat Pappa and rob him of seventy-five pounds so that she would be able to travel to Bermuda.

"It is good that you failed, Petronella," Marcus smiled, "or we might have passed one another on the ocean. I joined the American Church of the Reformed Evangelists and told them I was Marcus Koen, a Boer born in the Cape. I attended all their meetings, studied their teachings and held services as a lay preacher. When some of the *bittereinders* at last agreed to sign the oath of allegiance I lied to the Church and said I had also signed. They believed me, and did not check with the military authorities, but sent me to America where I was ordained and despatched to South Africa to establish the Church of the Reformed Evangelists."

"Oh Marcus," Petronella breathed in awe. "I only tried to cheat Pappa. But you cheated *a church* to come back to me!"

"Perhaps I cheated, yes. But I shall use their money to make more.

And I shall also spread their teachings, because I owe them that as much as I owe them the money they gave me to establish their church here."

"But you do not believe in their teaching?" she asked.

His answer was evasive. "Some of it I understand and can feel sympathy with. It is not easy to be a Jew, Petronella, who has been divorced from his religion."

She decided not to pursue the matter, and sat in silence for a while, trying to take in fully everything he had told her. "You said you were sent into exile as Mordechai Cohen," she began.

"The name my parents gave me." His voice was flat. "Mordechai Cohen, exiled to Bermuda and refused permission to return to South Africa, has disappeared. Marcus Koen, ordained Pastor of the Church of the Reformed Evangelists, a Boer burgher, is alive. But if it is ever discovered that the two are one and the same man, it would not be difficult for the authorities here to find out the birthplace of Mordechai Cohen. And then, because I am an undesirable alien with false papers they will deport me – "

He stopped talking as Mamma hurried into the room, followed by Pappa. With an impatience she rarely displayed towards Pappa, Mamma exclaimed, "He only wanted to show me some plants which had come up among the sunflowers, and ask me whether I, too, thought they were sorghum! Hannes, you will," she added grimly, "remember Marcus Koen."

But Pappa was staring at Petronella. "What have you done to your beautiful hair, child?"

"I cut it," she explained again briefly. She guessed that Pappa was reluctant to acknowledge Marcus's presence because he was indeed remembering the last time they had met, when a violent struggle had been taking place between Marcus and Johannes, while Pappa and Gideon hurled their rage and their insults at the Jew who had dared to rob them of one of the things a Boer family prized most – the chastity of a daughter of their household. But Pappa was also remembering that Marcus had fought for the Boers and had spied for them and been sent into exile, for after a long moment he took the hand which Marcus had extended to him, and shook it.

The four of them sat down. "My wife has been telling me," Pappa addressed Marcus after an uncomfortable silence, "that you have joined some kind of foreign church while you were in exile in Bermuda."

"Foreign perhaps, Mijnheer van Zyl. But a Christian one all the same, the Church of the Reformed Evangelists, and I have not joined them only, but I have also been ordained by them as a pastor."

Mamma had obviously withheld this piece of information – which she had no doubt found impossible to believe – from Pappa, for he exclaimed, "You mean – you are a kind of *Dominee?*"

Marcus looked faintly amused. "That is right, Mijnheer van Zyl."

"Well! I knew you had converted to Christianity, of course. But a *Dominee . . .*"

"A pastor," Mamma corrected in a hard voice, "of a church which does not even exist in South Africa."

"It will, Mevrouw," Marcus assured her. "I have promised to make sure that it will."

Before Mamma could think of a retort to make to that, Gerrit returned with Driena, and came to join them. Marcus was not known to either of them by sight, but before Mamma could introduce him, Driena stared at Petronella and wailed, "Oh, what on earth possessed you, Petronella? Your hair is hardly long enough now to be arranged in a snood!"

"I believe," Mamma spoke in a hard, deliberate voice, "that Petronella had some misguided notion of making herself look more attractive for next Saturday." She turned to Marcus and said, "Allow me to introduce you to Petronella's fiancé Gerrit and his sister Driena du Toit. We do not have much to offer, Mijnheer Koen, but you are welcome to such hospitality as we can provide, because you must, of course, stay for the wedding on Saturday."

Petronella watched Marcus's eyes widen in an expression of shock and betrayal. She jumped to her feet. "There won't be a wedding now, Mamma! How could you possibly have imagined there would be? I couldn't marry Gerrit now that Marcus is back! Surely you must see that?"

"No, I don't! You made a commitment, and you must keep it!"

Petronella stared at Mamma as if she had lost her senses. "The only real commitment I have ever made was to Marcus! *You* know that! Nothing – nothing on this earth – could keep me from him, now that I have found him again!"

Gerrit moved across the room, and clasped Petronella's arm in a savage grip. "*You can't do this to me!*" he said harshly.

"I'm sorry, Gerrit."

"No, Petronella! Not after everything I have invested in Jakkalsdrif!"

"I didn't know Marcus would come back." She stated what must surely have been obvious to Gerrit. "I'm sure Pappa will repay from the harvest everything you have invested in Jakkalsdrif."

Gerrit dropped his arm and walked from the room, his face white, and with a little moaning sound Driena followed him. Mamma whirled about, and lashed at Marcus, "*Why did you have to come back?*"

He said quietly, "It was not to make trouble that I came back. It was to find Petronella, whom I love."

Petronella went to stand beside him, taking his arm. "Mamma, please try to understand. We belong together. I couldn't marry Gerrit now. I could barely stomach the thought of doing so while I thought Marcus was lost to me. Now – it would be totally impossible."

"You are under age," Mamma told her implacably. "Pappa has given his consent to your marrying Gerrit on Saturday. He would not consent to your marrying the Jew."

"He is a Christian, Mamma, who has earned the right to take his place as a Boer!"

"Whatever he is or is not," Mamma returned remorselessly, "you cannot marry him until you become of age, and in the meantime I shall make you see sense."

"No. I told you once, Mamma, that I would live in sin with Marcus if Pappa withheld his consent, and I meant it."

"Please, Mevrouw," Marcus began, but Mamma rounded on him.

"If you had an ounce of decency in you, you would go away and leave Petronella to marry the good, honest, hard-working man she is promised to!"

Marcus shook his head. "No. I have made too many sacrifices, and so has Petronella. You do not understand the sacrifices we have made to be together."

"I understand only too well the misery it will cause to so many if you do not disappear from her life! You say you are a pastor – behave like one!"

"A pastor is also a man, Mevrouw van Zyl," Marcus said quietly.

Mamma turned away from him, and said with the same granite-faced implacability with which she had always fought back at life, "Petronella, if you do not give this man up, if you do not keep your promise to marry Gerrit, then you must leave this house with him, and I shall no longer regard you as my daughter."

Petronella stared at her, appalled. Mamma had made that threat before, but then she had had Gideon and Johannes and Dorothea. Of their entire family, there were only Mamma and Pappa and Petronella left, and Mamma was prepared to cut her last remaining child out of her life too.

"You couldn't be so cruel," Petronella stammered. "Not – not just because Marcus was born a Jew – "

"Not just because he is a Jew. Because he has a destructive effect on your sense of morality – and I don't mean that in the way you probably think I do. Because of him you are ready to discard, reject and humiliate a decent man whom you had promised to marry in just five days' time. Marcus Koen comes back and suddenly all Gerrit's devotion and his hard work, all he has done for us here on Jakkalsdrif, count for nothing. You are prepared to rob Gerrit of the investment he has made in this place, not only in money but also in time and devotion and in his labour; you are prepared to rob him of his pride and his future. You have never had any sense of shame, of what is right or wrong, where the Jew is concerned, no regard for the feelings of others. And that is why I say to you, Petronella – choose him, and I will never again consider you to be my daughter. You will have no further part of my life."

"Lenie – " Pappa began in distress, but she silenced him.

"Keep out of this, Hannes. You have always been blind to her faults and ready to make excuses for her. Well, Petronella, make your choice!"

There were tears in Petronella's eyes as she turned to Marcus, and whispered, "Please – please wait for me outside. I do not have much to pack."

Mamma did not say goodbye to her. She stood in the doorway next to Pappa, who was weeping brokenly, the tears running down his sunken cheeks and disappearing into his beard.

"No matter what happens in the future, Petronella," Mamma said in a hard voice as she watched the two of them walk towards Marcus's mule-driven cart, "you will never set foot in this house again while I am alive."

Her words echoed and re-echoed in Petronella's ears. Mamma did not make idle threats. She was as strong and as unmovable as a rock.

Mamma, Mamma, Mamma, the child in Petronella cried soundlessly, piteously, and for a moment her footsteps faltered. Then she felt Marcus's hand on her arm, and the passionate, committed woman in her submitted as he helped her into the cart.

Part Two

15

Marcus had been sitting in silence as they drove away, and Petronella had supposed that he was self-absorbed, perhaps reflecting bitterly that after all the sacrifices he had made, all he had endured, Mamma still dismissed him contemptuously as 'the Jew'. But now he took the reins in one hand and turned to her, forcing her to face him.

"Perhaps you wish that I should take you back?" he asked quietly.

"No! Oh no! How could you imagine – " She swallowed, and wiped her wet cheeks with the backs of her hands.

He nodded, and said sombrely, "So we stand together, Petronella; you and I alone, each of us cast out by our families."

"That – that first time," she said unevenly, "I left Jakkalsdrif with you – of my own free will. Only now, banished by Mamma, do I *really* understand how you must have felt – that day in Johannesburg . . ."

"It may be more difficult than you perhaps imagine." He stared beyond her, into the distance. "While I was in Johannesburg, before coming on to Jakkalsdrif, I learnt that my father was dying. That was bad, Petronella – to know that I could not go to make my peace with him."

"I'm sorry," she said inadequately, and silence stretched between them.

"So," he broke it at last, "you still wish me to drive on?"

"Of course!"

But he did not pull on the reins. Instead, he turned and enclosed her in his arms, and then his mouth worked its old magic on her again, seducing her senses so that she forgot her grief and her anger and her pain and could think only of Marcus, her love and her obsession, for whom she would have walked through fire if she had to.

"I still have the ring you gave me," she said breathlessly, when he let her go. "The one with which we made Mevrouw Boshof believe that we were married. We'll drive to the farm of the van Tonders; none of them has set eyes on me since I was a child and they will believe that we are a married couple called Koen and give us a room for the night. We could also talk to them about becoming *bywoners* on their land – "

"No, Petronella," Marcus interrupted, "we do not go to these van Tonders, and we do not pretend to anyone that we are married."

She stared at him in bewildered disbelief. "But Marcus, it has been so many years, and it has been so lonely. Don't you want to – "

"More than anything, my Petronella," he answered her unfinished sentence, touching her mouth with the tip of his forefinger. The clefts appeared in his cheeks in a slightly sardonic smile. "But I am a pastor, remember. A pastor does not hide behind lies. He does not pretend the girl he sleeps with and pleasures is his wife."

She frowned. "This pastor business – you cannot be serious about it."

"I am very serious," he assured her, pulling at the reins again. "A pastor cannot command respect if he makes a scandal. It was scandal enough to take you from your home where you were awaiting marriage to another man. We shall do nothing to make things worse."

She had been listening to him with incredulous dismay. Now, she burst out passionately, "After all I have gone through, Marcus, after all the tears I have shed, and when I had at last given up all hope of ever seeing you again – you are now telling me that because you tricked a foreign church into making you a pastor, this – this false front of piety makes it impossible for us to be together? If you feel you have to repay these Reformed Evangelists, then let us become *bywoners* to the van Tonders, and use the money you have been given to buy stock and farm implements, and repay your debt when we can, and in the meantime – "

"Ah, Petronella." He rested one hand briefly on hers. "Always in the past you demanded everything *now*. And what did it all bring us, hmm? I have made plans for us. We shall not become *bywoners* to anyone, for I have made all the arrangements for a place of our own, and we have a good future – if only you will have a little patience, *mein tiere*."

In mutinous silence at first, and then with growing astonishment, she listened as he went on to explain, "Do you remember, Petronella, when you told me – so long ago now – of the piece of land between Jakkalsdrif and the farm of your neighbours, the van Tonders? You said it had become *uitvalgrond*, land without an owner, but which could not be claimed by your father or by van Tonder."

"I remember, yes. But what about it?"

"Before they sent me into exile, Petronella, I spoke to my Field-Cornet and friend, Piet Nortjé, about many things. He was – still is, if he survived – a lawyer. I questioned him about *uitvalgrond*, for never before had I heard of it. And he told me that under Roman-Dutch law the land may be claimed by an outsider as what is called an *Inkruipplaas*, a Creeping-in farm." Marcus laughed softly. "Such strange terms the Boers have. It calls to my mind a picture of someone creeping in at dead of night with his possessions, and building a farmhouse without the knowledge of anyone. But it is not like that at all; it is not secret or sly, as the name seems to imply, and when I reached Johannesburg, before I came for you, I made a legal claim for the land. The law has not been changed by the British and the land is registered in my name now, after payment of a very small token sum. After we are married we shall live there. We shall not be *bywoners* to anyone, but owners of property."

She stared at him, amazed at this clever, resourceful man who had not only succeeded in returning illegally to South Africa as an ordained pastor but had also ferreted out an obscure law and acquired land of his own for next to nothing.

She laughed helplessly. "Oh Marcus, I do love you . . ." Then something else he had said struck her, and frustration and hunger for him overwhelmed her again. "When we are *married*. We cannot marry for at least another year. And in the meantime, because you don't want any scandal, because you want to cling to your position as a pastor of a foreign church which is not even known in this country, we have to waste another year of our lives apart, without happiness or pleasuring – "

He turned his head slightly, his blue eyes glinting at her. "There will be such pleasuring, Petronella, as you have never even imagined yet, and long before a year has passed. I have told you, I have made plans. We are going to Doornboomstad now, and I shall speak to *Dominee* Schalk. I shall explain matters to him, and he will help us. It is important for me to gain his goodwill."

She did not think he was at all likely to gain anything but condemnation from *Dominee* Schalk, who was an old man, set in his ways, and who would be shocked and horrified when he learnt that, only five days before she was to have married Gerrit du Toit, Petronella had left home with what the minister would regard as a Jew and an *Uitlander*, just as Mamma did. She thought rebelliously that she did not want anyone's goodwill. She wanted to lie naked beside Marcus, their limbs entwined, satisfying the long starvation for him which had been gnawing at her for years. And she wanted it now, tonight, and not at some unspecified time in the future when they could be married. Even Marcus could not accomplish the impossible, and Mamma would see to it that Pappa withheld his consent to their marriage for as long as that consent would be legally required.

They entered Doornboomstad with its one long, wide thoroughfare bounded on both sides by brick-and-corrugated iron houses, with the general store in which everything from safety pins to saddles was sold occupying a prominent position beside the post office, which was no more than an ordinary dwelling-house whose front parlour was used for the sale of stamps and the receipt and delivery of letters. On the opposite side of the street, also jostled by dwelling-houses, was the smithy, and a little distance away the village school. On the outskirts could be seen the mills to which the farmers had always taken their mealies to be ground into meal, flanked by the warehouse owned by the wholesale firm which bought and redistributed local crops, and by the coal-yard. But the focal point of the village was the small church, with the cemetery on one side of it and the manse on the other, and the church hall standing a short distance away.

Their arrival in Doornboomstad attracted a good deal of curious attention, for Petronella was known to everyone there, and all of them were obviously wondering what she was doing in company with a man who was not only a stranger but whose clothes and bearing proclaimed him to be a foreigner, an *Uitlander* and therefore probably British. Hostility was sharply mixed with the curiosity which followed their progress along the street.

Marcus tied the reins to a hitching post outside the manse and climbed the steps of the stoep with Petronella. A servant opened the door to them, and showed them inside the parlour, and a few minutes later the minister joined them. He was a childless widower in his early sixties and the most powerful man in the district, because he not only acted as spiritual guide but also as adviser on any problems which beset his parishioners, whether they were domestic issues, the drafting of wills, or the composition of letters to authorities.

He looked surprised when he saw Petronella, but before she could think of any explanation to offer for being there, Marcus introduced himself.

"*Dominee* Schalk, I am Pastor Marcus Koen of the Church of the Reformed Evangelists."

Dominee Schalk shook hands with Marcus, and said, "I am glad to meet you, Pastor, even though I have to admit that the name of your church is not familiar to me."

"It was founded in America, and I became inspired by their Christian message while I was in Bermuda, where I was sent in exile by the British when they caught me spying for the Boers."

In one sentence, which he must have been rehearsing, Marcus had captured *Dominee* Schalk's interest, his curiosity and his sympathy. Petronella sat down, forgotten and ignored, as the two men discussed first the war and then theology and doctrine. She stirred restively, wondering when Marcus intended getting to the point of their visit, which had supposedly been to gain the *Dominee's* help in the matter of their marriage. As she listened to Marcus's passionate arguments about certain interpretations of the Gospel, she wondered how much of it he genuinely understood, let alone believed, and how much was repeated, parrot-fashion, and intended to impress *Dominee* Schalk.

That he was impressed was made clear when he exclaimed, "My word, young man, what a pity it is that you did not join the Dutch Reformed Church instead, so that you could have succeeded me here when I retire. Our loss is the opposition's gain."

Marcus merely smiled, and said, "We are not in competition like men of business, *Dominee*. I do not mean to oppose you, or try to lure any of your flock away from you – even if I had a church for the use of preaching. But the American church will send money to me for the spreading of their message, and if I can perhaps hire premises for an evening – " He spread his hands in a disarming gesture. "I hope you would not be angry if a few of your parishioners came to listen, because they are curious."

"Indeed not. I would be most interested to attend myself. And since we are broadly in agreement about fundamental doctrine, I do not see why you should not be able to use the church hall for an occasional service some time in the future."

They shook hands in perfect amity, and afterwards Marcus said in an altered voice, "I wish to speak to you now on a very personal matter. I know you have been wondering why Petronella has come here with me."

Slowly, movingly, Marcus began to speak of how they had first met, leaving out such details as would have scandalised *Dominee* Schalk, while freely admitting what common gossip would swiftly have told the minister of their relationship. He described how his own parents had burnt his possessions and declared him to be dead when he had made his choice between Petronella and the faith of his forefathers. He told of his desire to become a Boer instead, and of how he had been caught spying for them and exiled to Bermuda. He did not mention, however, that he had been sent there as Mordechai Cohen, or that his motive for embracing the Church of the Reformed Evangelists was so that he could use them in order to sneak back to South Africa as Marcus Koen. His voice with its distinctive accent clearly mesmerised *Dominee* Schalk as Marcus went on to give an edited version of Petronella's own efforts for them to be reunited, leaving out her plan to cheat and rob her father, and making much of his own haste to reach her as soon as he returned to South Africa.

"And I was almost too late. As you know, *Dominee*, she was to have married on Saturday Gerrit du Toit, a most decent, upright young man. But she does not love him; she has never loved him. I can understand very well the anger of her parents when she told them she could not marry him after all; I can understand why her mother disowned her and told her to leave at once – "

"Lenie van Zyl did that?" *Dominee* Schalk interrupted, horrified.

Marcus bowed his head. "Do not judge her. She did no more than my parents did also when they cast me off. But I am sure you can understand our dilemma, *Dominee* Schalk. It will be a full year before Petronella comes of age and could marry without the consent of her father. What is to become of her in the meantime? The money from the American Church of the Reformed Evangelists is partly to be used for me to live upon until I have gained followers enough to earn a modest tithe. But the money is limited, and for a few weeks only can I afford to pay for lodgings for Petronella in Doornboomstad. I have land of my own, you see, bordering on Jakkalsdrif, and I shall need money to spend on the building of a house, and the clearing of the land for crops. To live there in sin with Petronella until we can marry without her father's consent would not only be wrong, but – "

"Yes, yes, out of the question!" *Dominee* Schalk turned to Petronella, addressing her for the first time. "Could you not talk your parents round, child, when their first anger has cooled?"

"No." She thought of Mamma's implacable, granite-hard face, and tears filled her eyes again. "It would be impossible. Mamma has always been bitterly against Marcus. She ignores the fact that he has become a Christian and that he fought for the Boers, and she talks of him as 'the Jew'. And she had set her heart, years ago, on my marrying Gerrit. You do not know what Mamma is like, *Dominee* Schalk. She never gives in."

The minister was silent for a while, and then he spoke firmly. "I do know your father, however, and I am sure that I shall be able to make him see that it would be cruel and immoral to withhold his consent for you to marry Pastor Koen."

Marcus thanked him, and asked, "I wonder if you know of a place in Doornboomstad where Petronella can stay in respectable lodgings?"

"Willa Moller, the postmistress, has a spare bedroom which she lets out to strangers who happen to be stranded here. As for yourself, Pastor Koen, if you would not mind sharing my bachelor home – "

"Thank you, *Dominee*, but I must drive to Wolmaransstad to buy a Special Licence for our marriage, and there is also much work to be done on my piece of land. I shall be comfortable enough sleeping on my cart in the meantime."

They left the manse, with *Dominee* Schalk's assurances ringing in their ears. He would visit Jakkalsdrif the next day, and talk sense into Hannes van Zyl, and obtain his written consent for the marriage of his daughter and Pastor Koen. And he himself would be happy to marry them as soon as it became possible.

When they were out of earshot, and Marcus was helping Petronella into the cart, he said with a faint smile, "You see, my Petronella, how important it was for me to be Pastor Koen, and how it has brought over to our side a man who would otherwise have condemned us? To him, your parents will listen."

She gave a gurgling laugh. "I think the Almighty will very likely strike you dead, for sacrilegiously using the Gospel to twist *Dominee* Schalk around your little finger!"

Marcus's blue eyes stared into hers, no longer teasing or amused. "I used my knowledge of the Gospel, yes, to convince *Dominee* Schalk that I have learnt to become a Boer. I wished him to tell others, also, that my teachings are sound, that I am qualified to spread the Christian Gospel to those who wish to listen, that I am an ordained pastor, a man of God."

She gave him a puzzled look. "It is important to you, isn't it? Why?"

"Because I need to belong," he said simply. "And because I owe a debt to the Church of the Reformed Evangelists. Perhaps I will not find it possible to make converts for them, but I must try."

People stopped and stared at them as they drove to the postmistress's house, and Petronella stared defiantly back. Marcus nodded politely, but no one returned the gesture. Outside the post office, she turned to Marcus, uncaring about the onlookers. Once again they were to be parted, after such a short time together, and she put her hands to the sides of his head to bring his mouth down to her own. But he caught her hands in his, and said softly, "Patience, my Petronella. We shall now go to ask for lodgings for you."

Mevrouw Moller, the postmistress, knew as well as everyone else in the village that Petronella was supposed to be marrying Gerrit on Saturday, but she succeeded in suppressing her curiosity and astonishment when the smartly dressed young man with the startling good looks asked her to provide Petronella with lodgings. The woman would have refused, Petronella felt certain, if Marcus had not added that *Dominee* Schalk had directed them to her.

Marcus took his leave of Petronella by kissing her circumspectly on the forehead, and then she followed her new landlady to a bedroom at the back of the house, feeling lost and lonely and deprived. Whenever she had allowed herself to dream of being reunited with Marcus in the past, this was not how she had imagined their first evening would be spent, with herself a lodger in a stranger's house, with Marcus driving away again and not sure when he would be returning, and with a village full of curious, disapproving people to be faced whenever she put her head outside her lodgings.

The curiosity and disapproval turned into silent hostility and stares and whispered condemnation as news percolated through of what had happened on Jakkalsdrif. Apart from joining Mevrouw Moller and her two teenaged children for meals, Petronella kept to her room. Her only contact with anyone from the outside, during the days that followed, was with *Dominee* Schalk, who reported that while Pappa was wavering about giving his written consent to her marrying

Marcus, Mamma remained as immovable as a rock in her resolve not to allow him to weaken.

"I had not realised before what a stubborn woman your mother could be," he said, shaking his head.

"She is not just stubborn. She is – oh, *Dominee* Schalk, if you could have seen her at the concentration camp! No one could dent her courage or her spirit, let alone break them . . ."

Petronella was suddenly overcome by a storm of tears and she ran to her room, threw herself down on the bed and wept like an abandoned child because Mamma, with her incredible strength, her courage and her implacable will, had turned her face against her only daughter and her sole surviving child.

Marcus returned a few days later from Wolmaransstad with the Special Licence which would enable them to marry as soon as Pappa gave his consent. He had been shown into the back parlour while Willa Moller went to call Petronella. She left them alone afterwards, and Petronella ran to Marcus, flinging herself against him with passionate abandon. But although his face softened with desire and hungry response as she moved her body against his and kissed him in the way he had taught her so long ago, he soon put her aside and went to sit in an upright chair.

"Marcus," she cajoled, "Mevrouw Moller will be busy in the front parlour, sorting the mail which has just come in, and her children are at school. Come to my room – "

"No, Petronella," he said firmly. "We must wait."

She had always been the reckless one, and he the one who urged caution and restraint, and that was how it continued. Whenever he called to see her during his subsequent visits to Doornboomstad she tried her blandishments on him, to no avail.

"My Petronella, you must learn patience. We have much to gain, and also much to lose. To cause more scandal now will be bad for us."

"You don't know what it is like for me, Marcus, living here in lodgings and knowing that everyone condemns me! For how long are we to continue like this, with you calling only occasionally to see me, and then behaving towards me like a – like a monk?"

He laughed softly. "A monk, Petronella, would not have allowed you to kiss him as you kissed me." He became serious. "But I am a pastor, and as a pastor I must behave. And if I do not call as often as you wish, it is because I am engaged in work for our future."

"What kind of work?" she asked mutinously.

"I am building us a house on the land that belongs to me."

"Take me to see the house," she begged, telling herself that on their remote strip of land, in the privacy of the shell of the house he was building, she would be able to make him forget he was a pastor.

But he shook his head. "I wish the house to be a surprise for when you are my wife." The clefts flickered in his cheeks, and his eyes told her that he had recognised her scheming motive. "Also, it will cause people to talk if I take you there before we marry."

"They are talking in any case!" she argued desperately. "So why not ignore them, and let them talk?"

But Marcus refused to listen to her pleas and he left her feeling hungry and frustrated, with nothing to fill her time, and the hostility of the villagers to face. Most of them sympathised with Gerrit, but there were a few in Doornboomstad who were inclined to take the view that Gerrit had tried to feather his own nest by asking Petronella to marry him in the first place. Strangely enough, Marcus did not come in for as much of the general condemnation as Petronella did. He was an object of curiosity and suspicion, because he was a stranger, but he had also fought for the Boers and been sent into exile, and he was a pastor. These were points in his favour, and the villagers were suspending their judgement upon him without in any way ranging themselves on his side.

While Petronella waited there in the house of the postmistress for her immediate future to be decided upon, a letter arrived for her from Jakoba Steenkamp, which she seized upon eagerly as a welcome diversion in an otherwise empty existence. Coincidentally, Jakoba was also about to be married.

"Dieter and I decided," she had written, "that as we have no one left but each other, we would get married." Petronella looked up from the letter and thought how typical it was that Jakoba should have decided to get married for such a limp, negative reason, and she looked forward to writing an account of her own circumstances. She would say nothing about this present long period of boredom and uncertainty, but would make much of her dramatic, last-minute rescue from a marriage which she had been contemplating with dread.

But Jakoba's letter went on, "You will not be able to answer this, but will have to wait until I write again, for we have left the farm in the Orange River Colony and are now at Johannesburg. It was impossible for us to make a living on the farm, and we were forced to join so many others who had packed up their few belongings and taken to the road in search of a living elsewhere.

"Dieter and I decided to make for Johannesburg, where he hopes to find work in the goldmines. All along the outskirts of the city are encampments of Boers who have been impoverished by the war, and who are living in shacks made of boxwood, or built of mud and roofed with bits of tarpaulin, or simply camping in their wagons. Dieter and I, as you may have gathered, are also living on our wagon, but at least we have more hope than some of the others, because Dieter speaks English, and the new policy of Lord Milner, the British High Commissioner, is to turn all Boers into good British subjects by forcing them to speak only English.

"I shall write to you again as soon as Dieter and I are married, and settled, and have a permanent address. Please do not let us lose touch; you failed to answer my previous letter, but when I am able to receive one from you, please do write and tell me of the changes in your own life. I often think of the days in the camp, and of how your Mamma gave all of us the courage to carry on . . ."

Petronella dashed tears from her eyes. She felt sorry for Jakoba, of course; it must be truly dreadful to have been forced to drift, with others, to Johannesburg in the hope of finding work. Anger surged through her momentarily as she considered the news that the peace treaty was being broken by a blatant policy of trying to drive Dutch out of existence and forcing everyone to learn English if they wished to survive. But her tears had really been because of Mamma, because of that hard, courageous, inflexible woman who was carrying out her threat to wipe her only daughter out of her life.

Then anger hardened inside her. She put Jakoba's letter away and made one of her few appearances in the street of Doornboomstad as she walked to the manse. She found *Dominee* Schalk sitting on the stoep, leafing through a book of sermons.

"Have you been making any progress, *Dominee*, in persuading Mamma to allow Pappa to give his consent?" Petronella wanted to know.

The minister closed the book he had been reading. "I am afraid not, child. I cannot think of anything more to do or say, to persuade her."

"Please pay one more visit to Jakkalsdrif, *Dominee*. Tell Mamma – tell Mamma that since she has declared I am no longer a daughter of hers, she is not justified in behaving as if she still had the rights of a mother over me, and of deciding whom I should or should not marry. If she is no longer my mother, then I am no longer her daughter, but a stranger whose affairs should not concern her."

Dominee Schalk sighed, and considered what she had said. It was clear that he had never before had to adjudicate in a situation quite like this. Finally, he agreed. "Very well, child. I shall give her your message."

Petronella lingered. "Is she – are she and Pappa well?"

"I doubt if anything would weaken, let alone destroy, your mother," *Dominee* Schalk answered wryly. "Your father – " He shrugged. "Hannes has been hit hard by what happened."

Petronella clamped her lips together to stop them trembling, and told herself that Mamma was at least as much responsible for Pappa's misery as she was. "Are Gerrit and Driena still on Jakkalsdrif?"

"They are. Your mother is hoping they will make it their permanent home, but – " He shook his head. "Gerrit is bitter and he feels humiliated. I doubt if he will stay in the district after the harvest has been gathered."

Petronella was about to leave the manse and return to her lodgings when *Dominee* Schalk stopped her. "Will you be attending your young man's service tomorrow evening?"

She turned slowly, staring at him. "*Marcus*'s service? He called briefly yesterday, and said he was in Doornboomstad to buy a few sticks of furniture for the house, but he said nothing about any service! Where is it to be held?"

"In the church hall. I could see no harm in allowing him to preach there and a sermon by someone other than myself would be a diversion for the people. The Lord knows, they have had little of that recently. I imagine he didn't tell you about it because he was a little shy, or otherwise he meant it to come as a surprise to you."

Petronella walked thoughtfully back to her lodgings. Marcus was not shy about anything, and she did not think he meant to surprise her with a last-minute announcement of the service he would be holding. No, he had not wanted her to be present, and she could not imagine what his motive might possibly have been.

She felt angry, and shut out. For some reason she was reminded of that time she had spent in his family home in Johannesburg, where their religious rites and ceremonies had also made her feel excluded, and Marcus in his brimless cap and the silk shawl over his shoulders setting out for the synagogue had given her the disturbing feeling that he was a stranger. She loved him, he possessed her utterly, and she lived for the day when they could be married, and in the meantime his few brief visits to Doornboomstad were the only bright patches in a dull and painful life among a community who knew that Mamma had thrown her out. But she did not really know Marcus at all, she was beginning to sense.

The following evening she dressed in the rose-coloured gown of fine wool which was now almost unbearably warm for the time of year, but it was the best she had, and she decided she would have to endure its discomfort. She covered her shoulder-length hair in a shawl because she had long ago discarded that ugly brown velour hat, and then she left her room. In the corridor she almost collided with her landlady, who was also wearing what could easily be identified as her best formal clothes. The woman darted an uneasy, embarrassed glance at her.

"So you have decided to attend the service in the church hall also?"

"Yes." Petronella gave her a direct look. "Are you surprised? It is to be held by the man I am waiting to marry, after all."

"Well – it was just – he suggested it would be better if you were not told about it. He thought it would be embarrassing for you, with people staring at you."

Petronella's mouth curved in a relieved smile. So that had been the reason why Marcus had not wanted her to attend. "Let them stare," she said defiantly. "They do so in any case, whenever I put my head outside the door."

The two of them walked together to the church hall. It was an austere building of modest size, and before the war it had been used for various purposes, not all of them connected with the church, such as political meetings or the occasional auctioning of local land.

Collapsible wooden chairs had been brought out of store, and had been arranged in rows inside the hall. Only a few of them were occupied. Petronella took a seat right at the back, so that she would attract as little notice as possible, but it was beginning to seem as if there would hardly be anyone to notice her in any case, and her heart twisted with sympathy for Marcus as she thought of his arriving to take his place on the rostrum, and discovering that only a handful of people had decided to attend.

But then, singly at first and afterwards in whole, large family groups, villagers began to cram inside the hall, taking their places on the hard chairs and staring expectantly at the rostrum, in the centre of which stood a table holding a Bible. A hum of conversation filled the hall; people had come out of curiosity, she learnt, wanting to hear what kind of sermon would be preached by a man who, for all that he had fought on the side of the Boers and had been sent into exile, was a Jew and an *Uitlander*, and was known to have run off with a girl almost on the eve of her marriage to one of themselves. Marcus, Petronella realised with dread, would face a sea of judging faces, and would be pilloried by their determined lack of response. And how could he possibly preach a convincing sermon when the Church of the Reformed Evangelists had never been more than a means to an end for him?

The buzz of conversation died down as *Dominee* Schalk entered the hall by its main door and walked along the aisle between the rows of chairs towards the rostrum. A sound of mingled surprise and disappointment drifted through the hall. Had Marcus decided not to preach a sermon after all, Petronella wondered with the others?

But *Dominee* Schalk greeted the audience, and made a short, semi-humorous speech, saying that the people of Doornboomstad must be pretty bored with his own sermons by now, and asking them to welcome Pastor Marcus Koen of the Church of the Reformed Evangelists, who had accepted the *Dominee*'s invitation to come and conduct a service to the glory of God.

Marcus had obviously been waiting and listening outside the other door which led into the hall, for he entered and walked to the table.

Dominee Schalk stepped down from the rostrum and sat down on one of the chairs in the front of the hall.

Marcus looked, Petronella thought with a clutch at her heart, magnificent. It was not just that he was tall and good-looking and well dressed. He had presence, authority, and however unwillingly, the audience began to respond to that, sitting up straighter in their chairs and leaning forward. "I will take my text from the Book of Exodus." Marcus opened the Bible, and his voice rang through the hall as he read. "And the Lord said, I have surely seen the affliction of my people, and have heard their cry by reason of their taskmasters, for I know their sorrows."

Marcus looked up from the Bible. "God was addressing Moses, and speaking of the children of Israel in Egypt. But to you, my friends, to the Boers who suffered much and lost all, those words of God are also true!"

It was clear to Petronella that he had captured the imagination of the congregation. His distinctive accent and the slight eccentricity of his phrasing added something compelling to his voice as he continued drawing comparisons between the tribes of Israel and the congregation's ancestors, likening the Great Trek to the exodus from Egypt.

Marcus leant forward, seeming to speak individually to each member of the congregation as he went on, "In the Bible God says to Moses, 'I have seen the oppression wherewith the Egyptians oppress the children of Israel, and I am come to deliver them.' Do you doubt, my friends, that He sees *your* oppression?" Marcus spread his arms wide, and his eyes glowed with passion. "Believe, and God will restore to you your Canaan, your land flowing with milk and honey, to which he led your grandfathers as surely as He led the children of Israel through the wilderness!"

Marcus cast his eyes down to the Bible. "I shall read for you now, but I shall change the words a little so that you will understand how true they are also of you." His voice resounded in the hall, holding the congregation spellbound as he paraphrased from the Bible.

"I am the Lord, and I will bring you out from under the burdens of the British, and I will redeem you with a stretched-out arm and with great judgements, and ye shall know that I am the Lord your God."

A deep, concerted sigh echoed through the hall when he had finished, punctuated by a few fervent, muffled exclamations. He waited until everyone had grown silent before he went on, "I should like you to join me in the singing of a hymn. It will not be one known to any of you, and perhaps it will not sound to you at all like a hymn until you have learnt the words." He gave them a self-deprecating smile. "The reason for that is simple. I have written the words myself, but I am not so clever that I am able to compose music. I have, therefore, fitted my words to a tune I learnt in exile."

He lifted his head, and his voice soared with immense feeling in a clear, beautiful baritone through the hall.

> "Would Christ our Lord have brought us
> To our sweet promised land,
> Knowing it would beat us
> And beggared we would stand?
> Would He have thought to guide us
> To these far forbidden plains
> If shame and degradation
> Were to be our only gains?
> Hear us, Heavenly Father!
> Rid us of this hand –
> This foreign hand that rules us
> And robs us of this land – "

Marcus paused for the merest second and then, his voice filled with emotion, he delivered the final, soaring line of his hymn, " 'Our land pledged by you to our people!' "

Petronella had felt dazed as she listened to his sermon, and the hymn had affected her profoundly. The tune was compelling and insistent, almost martial and unlike the slow, solemn dirges of most hymns or psalms to which Boer congregations were accustomed. The painful, angry, bitter sentiments expressed by the words had struck a chord in the hearts of people who had lost the sovereignty of their land to a conquering enemy, of people who had once been proud and prosperous and were now struggling to survive.

Marcus began to repeat the verses and slowly, one by one, people joined in. They faltered over some of the words at first but their voices increased in passion as they became more confident of the lines Marcus was teaching them.

Over and over again they sang the hymn, putting their hearts into the emotion it expressed, allowing themselves to be swept up by it, so that when they came to repeat the verses for what must have been the dozenth time many were sobbing the words instead of singing them.

Petronella had found herself caught up almost as totally as the others in the fervour which moved the congregation. But one small part of her mind remained detached, and more than a little dismayed.

This was a side of Marcus which she had never dreamt existed, and she did not understand it, or the power which it gave him over others. And instinctively, she feared it.

16

When, at last, the singing came to an end, Marcus offered a short but emotive prayer, and people sat up afterwards, blowing their noses and wiping their eyes.

"Thank you, my friends," Marcus addressed them, "for listening to my simple message. Good night, and may God bless you all."

But no one moved from their chairs. Several voices said something about a collection, and after some hesitation *Dominee* Schalk rose and left by the same door through which Marcus had entered the hall, and which led to the church. He returned after a short while with the collection plate, and it seemed to be a matter of pride that everyone should contribute, no matter how small a sum.

Petronella remained in her seat until there was no one left inside the hall apart from herself and *Dominee* Schalk. He came to join her as they prepared to leave too, and she could see that he was deeply preoccupied.

Marcus looked astonished when he saw Petronella, and then embarrassed. "I did not know you were present," he said. "I told you nothing about the service because I feared that if you were there, I would be thinking of you and of what you would be thinking, and – " He stopped, shrugging as if he were not quite sure of the precise nature of his reservations.

"You feared you would be self-conscious?" Petronella suggested.

"Yes. That is correct." Then he smiled, and took her arm. "But it went well!"

I should be feeling nothing but pride, Petronella thought, instead of having this nagging fear at the back of my mind . . .

She heard *Dominee* Schalk clear his throat. "Would the two of you care to come to the manse for coffee? I'll have to find a container for the money donated to your church, Pastor Koen, and I also have something to say to both of you."

They followed him the short distance to the manse, guided only by the moonlight and by the glow of lamps inside some of the windows of the homes in the street. No one spoke, and it was only when they were seated inside the parlour of the manse, waiting for *Dominee*

Schalk's maid-servant to bring in coffee, that the minister said, "You have a rare gift for communicating with people, Pastor Koen, and reaching their hearts."

"Thank you, *Dominee*. Almost everyone wished to learn when my next service will be held. I was obliged to tell them that it depends on your great kindness over the matter of the hall."

"We shall have to see," *Dominee* Schalk returned evasively. He changed the subject. "I have some very good news for both of you. I repeated your message to your mother, Petronella, and she is nothing if not fair-minded. She agreed that you have a case."

"And what is this case?" Marcus interrupted with a puzzled frown.

"Petronella asked me to tell her mother," *Dominee* Schalk explained, "that if she is disowning her, then Lenie van Zyl no longer has the right of a mother over her. As I've said, she saw the justice of that argument, and I have obtained written consent for you to be married."

Marcus jumped up, his face alight. "Aai, my Petronella, at last, *at last!*" He turned, grabbing *Dominee* Schalk's hand. "Thank you, my friend! When is it possible for you to marry us? Tomorrow?'

"I don't see why not," *Dominee* Schalk smiled.

A feeling of dazed disbelief swept over Petronella. She had never expected Mamma to concede defeat. No, she amended, not defeat. Mamma would be incapable of that. She had merely acknowledged a flaw in her own stated position once it had been brought to her notice. And tomorrow, after all these years, after all both of them had been through, she and Marcus were to be married at last!

She felt as if she were not quite earthbound, but soaring above the ground when at last she and Marcus left the house and he was seeing her home to her lodgings. It had been arranged that Marcus would spend the night at the manse and that they were to be married at noon the following day.

Outside the postmistress's house, Marcus pulled her into his arms and cupped her face in his hands. "Aai, my Petronella, I had not believed it possible to be so happy! I shall remember tonight always."

She responded with her usual uninhibited passion when he kissed her, but as he released her she thought about the service he had conducted, and she could not help remembering her unformed, vague uneasiness.

"Marcus," she began tentatively, "that sermon which you preached this evening – did you believe in what you were saying?"

He did not answer immediately, and she sensed that it was a question he had not wished to be asked. Was that the real reason why Marcus had tried to prevent her from attending the service? Because she knew him better than anyone else, and she was the only one who would have doubts about his sincerity?

When he answered her question at last, he did so obliquely. "The people believed. Would all of them have believed if I had been telling them untruths?"

She stirred restively, wishing she could have left the matter there. But that same feeling of unease made her say, "That song you sang . : . You had written the words yourself. And you put so much feeling into it . . . as if . . . What I meant was, *you* have not lost land pioneered by your forefathers, for which they had given their toil and their blood, and yet – "

"You mean," Marcus interrupted quietly, with a note of bitter hurt in his voice, "that I am not a Boer, I do not belong, I have no place here and no right to speak for the Boers or express their feelings."

"No! Oh no!" She was instantly contrite, and she threw her arms about him and pressed her lips against his. When he did not respond she drew back, and said pleadingly, "All I meant was – you were so passionate, you moved them so deeply, that it was almost as if you knew exactly how they feel. I have never been to a service before, Marcus, where people were so united in their response. You are truly gifted."

He relented then, and cupped her breasts in his hands, kissing her mouth briefly but ardently. "Goodnight, Petronella, *mij beminde*. Tonight is the last one we shall ever spend apart."

She entered the house of the postmistress, hugging herself with happiness and trying not to allow anything to spoil the joy of knowing that, by this time tomorrow, she would be Marcus's wife. She would not think of Mamma and Pappa, who would be absent from her wedding, or of the disquieting power Marcus had to move a potentially hostile crowd of people to a pitch of emotional response, or to wonder why the matter of his preaching filled her with unformed fear.

Entirely because of the service which Marcus had conducted the evening before, everyone in the village attended their wedding. Petronella had no illusions at all as to who was responsible for the crowded church, or for the fact that people had hurriedly taken up a collection as soon as they heard of the imminent ceremony, and had bought for them the kind of things newly-weds would need; pots and pans and a few odd pieces of crockery which had been on sale at the general store at a reduced price, because none of them matched. In other circumstances, Petronella knew, she and Marcus would have had difficulty in persuading a mere two people to attend the ceremony as witnesses.

At last it was over. They were man and wife, and the gifts they had received were packed on the cart, together with Petronella's few belongings and some provisions which Marcus had bought earlier that morning, and she took her place beside him in the driving seat. To shouted messages of good luck, they drove out of the village.

Marcus held the reins in one hand, and pulled her against him with the other. Lustily, he began to sing a lively, tuneful song in a strange language, and when she asked him what it was, he said, "a Jewish wedding song." His mood changed completely; instead of his previous exuberance he looked pensive and sad and she remembered suddenly how he had sobbed in her arms that night in the bed which Mevrouw Boshof had prepared for them, only hours after his family had disowned him and burnt his possessions.

She groped for his hand, and after a moment his fingers tightened over hers, and he leant across and kissed her cheek. But he did not sing again, and neither of them spoke much as they continued towards their new home.

Petronella was astonished and bewildered, and then dismayed, to discover to which part of the previously disputed land he was driving. The land, which now belonged to Marcus, was shaped roughly like the letter 'L' and ran alongside two of Jakkalsdrif's unmarked borders. The original pioneers had simply paced out the land they were claiming for themselves and this was what had led to the dispute between Pappa and Zak van Tonder. But Marcus was heading for the branch of the 'L' which was closest to the house on Jakkalsdrif.

As they reached their new home, Petronella did not know which distressed her most – the house itself, or the fact that it had been built on slightly rising ground, from which she could look down and see her old home quite clearly. She turned her head away quickly when a figure appeared around the side of the house in which she had been born, and she knew it was Mamma because of the black dress the figure was wearing. It would have taken her no more than fifteen or twenty minutes to walk to Jakkalsdrif from here, crossing a shallow *spruit* which followed from one of the tributaries of the Vaal River.

"Why," she faltered, "did you choose this spot?"

Marcus touched her cheek tenderly. "Because I thought perhaps it would soften your Mamma's heart if she saw you living so near." He jumped from the cart and held out his hands to her. "Come, Petronella, look at the home I have built for us."

"What," she played for time, "have you called the farm?"

He did not answer for a moment. "I registered it in the name of Korah."

"Why? What does it mean?"

He smiled at her, but the smile did not seem to reach his eyes. "It is from the Bible. Korah was the name of a chief of one of the tribes of Israel led out of the land of Egypt by Moses." Marcus added somewhat defensively, "I had to think of a name when I registered the land, and Korah was what came into my mind."

She stared at a sheet of rusty corrugated iron which had been embedded in the earth on one side of a ditch some distance away. Clearly, the ditch was meant to be their lavatory. She heard Marcus ask anxiously, "You are not pleased with our house, Petronella?"

"I have not yet had a chance to look at it properly," she stalled, and straightened her shoulders, trying not to reveal her dismay as she approached, with Marcus's arm about her waist, the crudest *pondok* she had ever seen.

It was small and rectangular in shape, and had been built of wattle-and-daub, which meant that a framework of wooden poles had been set up, between which branches and saplings had been threaded and then the whole had been covered in thick layers of clay. It was roofed with corrugated iron, which was now for sale again in Doornboomstad, as were cement and other building materials. The wooden poles for the framework could have been bought in the village also, imported from other parts of South Africa, but how could Marcus have come by the necessary saplings and branches in a landscape almost totally denuded of trees by the fires the British had set? He could have taken the cart and driven across the Vaal River to search for and cut them, but what a formidable task that would have been, working single-handed.

There was nothing resembling a stoep at all, but a single step made of clay which had been built up in layers and moulded and allowed to dry in the sun led to the stable-type door. Apart from the fact that it was slightly larger and that it had a chimney, the *pondok* was not unlike the huts in the *stad* on Jakkalsdrif, which had been built with no thought of permanence. As Marcus pushed open the two parts of the door for her to enter, she saw that it did, at least, contain a small window set into the wall opposite the door. No attempt had been made to soften the interior of the clay walls with whitewash or other materials and the floor was of plain, bare earth.

The room was furnished with a small iron cooking range, a crudely fashioned table and two upright chairs, and a marble-topped, obviously second-hand wash-stand with two doors below it. When Petronella opened the doors she saw that the shelf inside, which would normally have been used for holding chamber-pots, was now to be used as storage space for their food, because it held a tin of condensed milk, sugar, salt, coffee and a bag containing mealie-meal.

A doorway without any door fitted to it at all led into another room. This was furnished with an iron bedstead and a small chest with a standing mirror on top, flanked by a wash-basin and matching jug.

The floor of this room was also of plain earth. Not the kind of hard-packed earth floors which were to be found inside the huts of the *stad*, and which needed only a daily sweeping to keep them free of dust. Here, the ground had simply been cleared of weeds and other growth and had been levelled off with a spade. Even as she walked from one room to the next Petronella found that red dust was rising from the ground in eddies.

She was aware that Marcus was anxiously awaiting her reaction. "It – it was very clever of you to build it," she said. "You have had no experience and no help."

"I did not build it alone, Petronella. As you say, what do I know about the building of houses? Two black men came, and informed me they were previously servants of Gerrit du Toit, and that they needed work. So they planned how the house should be built, and I made a few changes, and bought the materials they said we needed, and together we built it."

So that was why it resembled a hut from the *stad*, she thought. Gerrit's former servants had built the *pondok* in the only way known to them, adding at Marcus's insistence a chimney and two windows. And of course, the workmen had been unable to do anything more about the floors, because the war had put paid to the availability of ox-blood and ground-up antheaps which were normally used for creating a hard, durable surface. But the floors were not the only features inferior to the huts in the *stad*. The latter had ceilings made of animal hide, which gave protection against the heat of the sun beating down upon the corrugated iron roofs. The *pondok* had no ceiling of any kind.

I am luckier than Jakoba, Petronella tried to tell herself. Jakoba has to live on a wagon. And at least Marcus saw to it that we should have a chimney, and two windows. Then her thoughts took a rebellious turn and she wondered why he could not have spent some of that money given to him by the Reformed Evangelists on cement blocks for the structure instead of allowing the men to use wattle-and-daub.

"You do not like it," she heard him say quietly.

"Oh, Marcus!" She turned, instantly contrite, moving into his arms and clinging to him. "I would happily live in a hole in the ground, so long as it is with you!"

He did not take the lips she was offering him. Instead, holding her away from him, he clasped her hand and led her into the room which was to serve as their bedroom. Standing close to her, he began to unbutton the bodice of the rose-coloured woollen gown. Sheer desperation at the thought of having to wear it during the full heat of the day had prompted Petronella to put it on that morning without any undergarments at all, and as each button was slowly undone Marcus paused to kiss and tease with his lips and his tongue the area of exposed flesh. She shivered convulsively, and tried to hurry him by fumbling at the rest of the buttons herself, but he imprisoned her hands and said softly, "Slowly, my Petronella, slowly. If you desire work for your hands, then remove my shirt."

All thought of their surroundings wiped from her mind, she felt as if she were drowning in delicious anticipation, and as his mouth and his hands made their long, slow exploration and rediscovery of her body, waves of rapture swept over her. At last the gown was lying in a heap on the earth floor, and he knelt down, kissing and caressing her thighs, and she tangled her hands in his hair, begging him, "Now, Marcus, *now!*"

He rose, and picked her up in his arms. "Always," he said huskily, "with you it is *now*, Petronella. But did I not promise you pleasuring such as you had never imagined?"

He laid her down on the bed, and continued to torment her with exquisite, lingering caresses as if he were a musician seeking perfection by experimenting with different chords. He kissed and fondled and probed and teased and when, at last, she had been brought to such a towering pitch of frenzied excitement that she thought she would explode, he covered her body with his own and began to pleasure her, once again taking his time, tantalising her, putting off for as long as possible the climax of the consummation of their marriage. When, finally, they arched together, something which he had said to her at their very first meeting slipped into her mind.

"Marry soon, and then you will discover how good pleasuring can really be."

They lay quietly together afterwards, just stroking and touching as if seeking mutual reassurance that the other was real. Two disconnected thoughts suddenly entered Petronella's mind. One was that no other man, least of all Gerrit, would have been capable of taking her to such previously undreamt-of heights of rapture and fulfilment. The other, far less comforting thought was that Marcus could not have been performing his magic entirely by instinct, and for the very first time it struck her that she could not be the first woman in his life, that there had been others whom he had pleasured with similar skills, perhaps even some particular woman in Bermuda while she herself was aching and hungering for him . . .

She killed the thought as if it had been a dangerous reptile. Marcus helped in its demise by murmuring against her cheek, "It is a very poor house, Petronella, I know."

"No, it isn't! It's wonderful." And in that moment she truly believed it to be so.

"Both of us," he contradicted her, "are aware that it is the poorest house possible. But when you consider that only months ago I was in Bermuda as an exile, and told that I would never be permitted to return to South Africa and to you . . . And now we are here, together at last and married. When you reflect on all of that, my beautiful Petronella, the house is a miracle."

She slid her palm along his thigh. "Oh Marcus, you are right."

He caught her hand in his, and once again they sated themselves with love. Afterwards, as if there had been no gap in their conversation, he said, "You shall have a better house one day, that I promise you. Have I not already achieved the almost impossible, and become a Boer, who belongs, who has a place in the community, who is respected?"

Before she could form a response to that, she found that he had fallen into an exhausted sleep. She sat up, careful not to disturb him, and put on her gown, and then she went out to the cart to bring some of their possessions inside.

For the first time she looked around her. Marcus had done nothing at all yet to clear the land, apart from the small area close to the house. Khaki-bush and other weeds flourished everywhere. She frowned slightly. Before he had fallen asleep, she had meant to tell him that she understood why the minimum of money had been spent on the house. Most of what he had received from the Church of the Reformed Evangelists, and would continue to receive, would have to be reserved for livestock, for farm implements and seed for next season. No doubt, she thought, he had been waiting to ask her advice as to what ought to be done. Marcus was, after all, a city-dweller and would have to be taught how to become a farmer.

But something would have to be done about the khaki-bush soon, before it spread its seeds and contaminated the land even further. She would also have to think of a solution to the problem of the earth floor.

She put these practical matters behind her as she remembered the joy of their pleasuring, and smiled tenderly as she pushed open the stable-type door, her arms filled with some of their things she had collected from the cart. Marcus had been right; the *pondok*, for all its bleak poverty, *was* a miracle.

She placed her burden on the table. Among the things she had taken from the cart was the Bible from which Marcus had chosen his text last evening. She began to turn its pages, searching for a reference to Korah, after whom he had named their piece of land.

She found it at last, and reread the passage slowly. Korah had led a rebellion against Moses, who had then been ordered by God to isolate from the tribes of Israel Korah and his fellow-traitors: "And the earth opened her mouth, and swallowed them up, and their houses, and all the men that appertained unto Korah . . . and the earth closed upon them, and they perished from among the congregation."

Petronella closed the Bible, and discovered that her hand was trembling slightly. She thrust it through her disordered hair. Did Marcus truly believe himself to have been cursed and doomed, like Korah, so that he had named his land after that other Jew who had defied the law of Moses?

But if so, how could he speak of belonging to the Boers, of being one of them? How could he have preached that stirring, electrifying and convincing sermon last night as the pastor of a Christian sect?

She shook her head slowly. She loved Marcus with every atom of her passionate nature, but she was finding him harder and harder to understand.

17

For more than a week, reality or twinges of unease or doubt rarely encroached upon life in the *pondok*. Petronella and Marcus gorged themselves on love, and the practical matter of physical survival became almost an irrelevance; mere bothersome interludes with which they dealt only when it became vital to do so.

Their only water supply was from the nearby *spruit*. Daily, Petronella and Marcus would each take two pails and collect water. Some of it was poured into pans and set upon the cooking range to be boiled for drinking purposes, and while Marcus went to collect more water Petronella would make coffee and mealie-porridge which they ate with a teaspoonful of condensed milk stirred into it. Afterwards they would undress and, standing just inside the main room of the *pondok*, each would soap the other, slowly, lingeringly, and then take turns at pouring a pailful of water over each other. Gasping, laughing, soaking wet, they would move to the bedroom to possess one another once more, and Petronella spared scarcely a thought for the fact that the water had turned the floor of the *pondok*'s other room into a morass of mud. By the next morning the heat which baked down through the ceiling-less corrugated iron roof would have dried it again. Neither she nor Marcus noticed the stifling heat during those first few days. Apart from when they walked to the *spruit* to collect water, they wore no clothes, and during the chilly nights which invariably followed on this high plateau, they kept each other warm with their bodies.

But the day inevitably arrived when reality had to be faced. It came for Petronella as she prepared to make mealie-porridge, and noted that their supply of meal was getting low. A trip would have to be made to Doornboomstad to buy more. And, she thought with a frown, they could not go on living on nothing but mealie-porridge and coffee. She poured water into another pan to boil it for drinking purposes, and noticed that the water, taken from the *spruit* only a short while ago, already held a sprinkling of red dust on its surface, kicked up from the floor. Inside the bell tent in the concentration camp, the floor had also been of bare earth, but because there were so many people living in a confined space, the earth had become beaten down and had produced little dust. Something would have to be done about the floors of the *pondok*, however.

She set the pan on the range to boil, and checked whether more fuel would be needed. For the first time, she was struck by their extravagant folly in having used nothing but the expensive coal which Marcus had bought in the village and piled in a heap at the side of the house.

She went outside to assess the size of the heap. In spite of the fact that she had done very little cooking and no baking at all, the heap had dwindled noticeably. They could not carry on in this profligate way.

Her glance went to the surrounding land. The infestation of khaki-bush seemed to have become worse, but when she moved closer to examine the weeds she realised that the summer growth had merely made them uglier and denser in appearance than when they had first sprouted. The weed had produced strange, seed-like arrows which, as she moved through the growth of plants, detached themselves and stuck to her skirt. One of them pierced the material and entered the flesh of her calf, producing a burning sensation. She pulled it out gingerly, examining it with a frown. If these sharp little arrows were the seeds of the plant, then why did the weed also produce flowers? She picked some of the flowers, wincing at the smell. The flowers were small, olive-green in colour with a slight yellow tinge, and when she pulled open the petals she found that they enclosed tiny black seeds.

Whether or not the weed propagated itself by means of the stinging arrows or the seeds, or even both, it would have to be eradicated quickly.

But there were more urgent matters to be taken care of first. She returned to the *pondok*, and as she and Marcus sat down at the kitchen table to eat their mealie-porridge she said, "Today, my dearest, there will be no time for pleasuring."

"Never," he grinned, "did I think to hear such words from your lips! What is it today that is more important than pleasuring?"

"I want you to hitch the mules to the cart. Load on to it those two barrels which the workmen used for the mixing of the clay when they built the house, as well as a spade. I want you to drive me through the drift, into the Free State."

"For what purpose?"

She answered abstractedly, "I've remembered another way of treating earth floors. When Mwende and I were little, she and I used to fight over the privilege of dealing, each month, with the floor of an old aunt of hers. Her hut had been built in the year when *rinderpest* destroyed most of Jakkalsdrif's cattle, so that there was no ox-blood to be had."

"What," Marcus demanded with a puzzled frown, "is this you talk about, Petronella? Even you, my love, cannot be contemplating crossing the Vaal River, where the oxen of your parents and of Gerrit du Toit graze, and killing one for the benefit of its blood for your floors? And ox-blood for floors is something I do not understand at all, or even like to think about!"

She smiled. "If I really did steal and kill an ox, it would not be merely for its blood. I'm growing tired of eating nothing but mealie-porridge." She had decided not to tell him yet what she had in mind; remembering his beautiful family home in Johannesburg she thought his adjustment to the *pondok* – although he had never admitted it – must have been difficult enough without her facing him, sooner than she had to, with yet more crude realities of rural poverty.

"So, why do you wish to cross the river?" he persisted.

"I want us to collect 'Free State coal'."

He did not ask what that was. Perhaps, she thought, this city-bred husband of hers imagined there really was coal to be had for the picking up on the surface of the veld across the river. He went outside to hitch the mules to the cart and load the equipment she had said would be required, while Petronella changed into the most worn and expendable of her skirts and blouses.

As they drove along the track towards the drift, she began to speak to him seriously. "Marcus, if the two men who built our house are still in the district you must employ them to help us clear the land. The khaki-bush is getting ready to spread its seed, and if it does we'll never win the battle against it. We must drive to Doornboomstad, and you must buy a plough and a harrow and seed-mealies for storing until next spring, before the price rises – "

"No, Petronella," he interrupted quietly but firmly. "A farmer I cannot be. To buy all those things would be a waste of money."

She turned to him in total dismay. "But – but if we do not cultivate the land, Marcus, how are we to live? I thought the whole point of claiming the land in the first place was so that you might become a farmer!"

He inclined his head. "Yes, in the beginning, I argued that way also. But now I perceive that our land is too small, our money is too little, and of farming I am ignorant. For me, money must be made in other ways."

"Marcus, our land may be small, and I admit we'll never be rich, but it's possible for us to make a living there! When the land has recovered we could keep a few cattle and sheep, and grow enough mealies for our own use, and have enough left over to sell so that we may pay for things like clothes – "

"You forget," he reminded her, "that I have taken money from the Church of the Reformed Evangelists, given to me to spread their message and become their missionary. If I do not devote my life to this, then I must refund the money to them, and to do so I must make more money."

Oh, damn the Reformed Evangelists, she thought fiercely. *Damn them.*

"So," Marcus went on, "for me money must be made in other ways than trying to be a farmer on our small piece of land."

"What other way is there?" she asked sullenly.

"You ask that, Petronella," he explained, "because your people do not consider changing old habits, but always do things in the same way. It is the tradition that they grow their mealies and harvest them, and what they do not need for themselves, they take to the wholesaler in Doornboomstad. He pays them a small sum, and then he fills a wagon with the mealies, and he sends a servant to the market in Johannesburg with them where the load sells for many, many times the price the wholesaler pays to the farmers. It is a bad tradition, Petronella, and enriches only the wholesaler. I shall break that tradition, and buy a wagon and a strong team of mules and take the farmers' mealies to the market in Johannesburg. I shall sell them for a good price and pay myself a percentage. The farmers will receive far more for their harvest than when they sold it to the wholesaler, and I shall make a profit in addition."

Logic told her that there could be no argument against such a simple but brilliant plan. But instinct made her want to commit Marcus to the world of farming, of cultivating their own small piece of land and perhaps, in time, acquiring more land. With relief, she perceived a flaw in Marcus's plan.

"There is only one harvest each year, when you would be able to make money by taking the farmers' mealies to Johannesburg. How will we live during the other months of the year if we have no harvest of our own to depend upon?"

"I have thought of that also. I shall take the wagon to Johannesburg, and at the market I shall buy things at a good price – all manner of commodities the people need, like bales of cloth for the manufacturing of clothes, and furniture for replacing what was burnt by the British. Anything for which the price is low, and which could be sold at a profit to the store in Doornboomstad."

"And what am I suposed to be doing in the meantime, Marcus? Sitting alone at home, waiting for you, and seeing you only for a few days between your trips?"

He reached for her hand. "There will not be so many trips, Petronella. They will not last long, with a strong team of mules to pull the wagon." When she drew her hand angrily from his, he added placatingly, "You need not sit alone at home; you could come with me."

She became slightly reconciled to the idea, but only as a short-term plan. If she could persuade Marcus to develop an interest in farming, in between trips, he would settle down to working the land just as soon as he had paid his debt to the accursed Reformed Evangelists. But she would have to go about it in a subtle manner.

"What a clever man you are, my love," she said. "But we cannot allow our land to deteriorate altogether, Marcus. You may not be a farmer, but farming has been bred into my bones, and I want to grow mealies for our own use. And I also want a milk-cow – no, perhaps not a cow, because there is not enough grazing yet. A nanny-goat, on the other hand, would eat almost anything incuding – hopefully – the khaki-bush. So before you spend all the money you have on a wagon and mules, will you buy for me the things I shall need?"

He considered for a moment. "Very well, Petronella. We shall drive to Doornboomstad tomorrow for them." He hesitated. "We will lodge for a night or perhaps two with Mevrouw Moller, so that I may preach a sermon while there."

In spite of the fierce heat of the sun, she shivered. "You have paid your moral debt to the Reformed Evangelists. You have preached a sermon in their name."

"One sermon, Petronella, cannot be called spreading the word of their church!"

"You cannot take it for granted that *Dominee* Schalk will allow you to use the church hall again – " she began.

"No," he agreed, and went on quietly, "I am a good preacher, Petronella. I know it; you know it and *Dominee* Schalk knows it also. And it is because he knows it that he will never again let me use the church hall. So I will try to hire the schoolhouse for my sermon."

When she said nothing, he went on, "Not only have I to pay the debt to the Church of the Reformed Evangelists, but I will need more money than they send me for all the things we must buy. When people are moved by a sermon they wish, very much, to make generous donations. You have seen that for yourself."

She caught her breath. "Are you saying that the *real* reason why you wish to preach is to make money?"

He shrugged, and did not answer, but the gesture had clearly been an admission.

Petronella felt nothing but relief. She was not deeply religious and she had, in her short life, encountered sufficient instances of hypocrisy disguised as religion to allow herself not to be disturbed by it in Marcus, in whom she would have condoned far worse sins. On the occasion of one *Nachtmaal* gathering, she remembered, a visiting *Dominee* had been preaching a fire-and-brimstone sermon about the evils of drink, and when he had stumbled and fallen over several hours later, and people rushed to his aid, a half-empty bottle of brandy-wine had slipped out of his pocket. And then there had been the Church Elder who had collected money for widows and orphans in the district. The widows and orphans had not appeared to be much better off afterwards, but the Elder had suddenly acquired a magnificent new team of horses.

So, now that Marcus had admitted that he regarded his ability to preach as a talent with which to make money, she was neither shocked nor censorious but relieved. It was something she was able to understand, and not something to fear, as she had instinctively feared his power to move people with his sermons and his singing.

From now on, she thought, she would look upon his preaching as the performance which it was. It was a form of selling his talents, much the same as the traders she had listened to in Johannesburg Market selling their wares – with passionate conviction. In any case, his preaching was likely to be no more than a nine-days' wonder in Doornboomstad; it was inconceivable that staunch members of the Dutch Reformed Church would defect to some obscure American sect. Hopefully, Marcus would be able to draw people to his services for just long enough to enable him to pay the debt he owed to the Church of the Reformed Evangelists, and by then she would have awakened his interest in farming.

His voice broke through her thoughts. "We have crossed the drift, Petronella. Where, now, do we find this 'Free State coal'?"

Grinning, she jumped from the cart after she had told him to rein in, and dragged one of the barrels from the vehicle, taking the spade in the other hand.

" 'Free State coal', Marcus, is what we christened dry cattle dung. It makes excellent fuel, and it costs nothing. Take the other barrel and collect as much of it as you can."

He wore an expression of disbelief and distaste. "This is true?"

"Perfectly true. We would be beggared in no time if we continued to burn nothing but expensive coal, and the odd scrap of wood left over from building the house."

"But you have the only spade," he protested.

"You won't need a spade. Dry cattle dung is quite clean." She smiled grimly. "Unless you would prefer to change chores with me? I am going to fill my barrel with fresh dung."

He blanched. "For what, Petronella?"

"If you mix it with a little water, and spread it over an earth floor, it dries to a hard surface which only has to be renewed once a month. Don't look so disgusted, Marcus. It is far more hygienic than the red dust which settles on everything inside the house, including our food. And I promise you, it does not smell when it is dry."

But he continued to wear a look of disgust as he hunted through the veld for pats of dry cattle dung, lifting them gingerly and dropping them inside the barrel. His disgust deepened, later, when Petronella went down on her hands and knees inside the *pondok* and began to smear the unsavoury wet mixture over the floors with her hands. He beat a hasty retreat, and when she left the *pondok* afterwards to go and wash herself in the *spruit*, and give the floors a chance to dry, she saw that he was tackling the khaki-bush weeds.

She joined him afterwards, and they worked together, but it was clear that his heart was not in it. No one, she conceded, could become enthusiastic about pulling up noxious weeds; when he began to watch for the appearance of seeds he had planted, his interest would gradually be captured. But now, as soon as she assured him that the floors of the *pondok* would have dried, he disappeared, and when she went inside later she found that he was sitting by the table, writing.

"Notes for my sermon," he explained, and added with a grim smile, "It will take much preaching, as well as buying and selling, but as soon as it is possible we will have a house where the floors are not covered in the shit of cattle."

She laughed, and put her arms around his neck from behind. If he could adjust to life in the *pondok*, he would also adjust quite soon to dung floors. "You must admit, though, that I spoke the truth when I said that it does not smell when it is dry." She slid her hands down the front of his shirt and moved her palms over his chest. "We have done enough work, both of us, to deserve some pleasuring now."

But he removed her hands gently, and dropped a kiss upon each palm. "Perhaps later," he said. "Now, I must think what to say in my sermon."

She experienced a feeling which Mamma used to describe as 'a duck walking over my grave'. It was not a sense of rejection and neither was it her earlier unease evoked by Marcus's preaching. It was, she told herself, just silliness. Not a foreboding at all.

Her random thought about Mamma sent her outside again. She squatted on the ground, her knees pulled up to her chin, and gazed down at the house on Jakkalsdrif. Did Mamma ever stare at the *pondok* in a similar way, she wondered. Did it ever enter her uncompromising mind to spare a thought for how her only surviving child was faring in this bleak little dwelling-place? Very likely not, she decided forlornly, watching smoke curling from her parents' house.

In all probability, Mamma was treating Driena as a daughter now, just as she had treated Dorothea as a daughter during those long, bitter months when she had refused to speak to Petronella.

It struck her suddenly that she did not miss Pappa, who had always doted on her, nearly as much as she missed Mamma, who would never have considered coddling or spoiling any of her children.

For a few moments, Petronella considered asking Marcus for money, and walking to Jakkalsdrif to ask Mamma whether she would sell her some eggs and milk. Then she shook her head. Mamma would refuse to see her at all; she would merely tell Driena or one of the servants to give Petronella the things she needed, with the message that they did not sell their farm produce. But the message would also conceal another – that Mamma's love and forgiveness could not be bought either.

She sighed, and stood up, and went back inside the *pondok*. Marcus continued to work on his sermon and Petronella sat down too, with Pappa's writing box which she had taken with her when she left Jakkalsdrif, and began to write a long letter to Jakoba in Johannesburg, telling her all about the dramatic events in her life and describing her blissful happiness.

But that night, after Marcus had pleasured her, she clung to him and wept bitterly. She did not know why she was weeping, she told herself; she was being silly, because although she was dead to Mamma, just as Marcus was dead to his own family, the two of them had each other and that was the only thing in the world that really counted.

They set off, early the next morning, for Doornboomstad. Willa Moller was delighted to give them the use of her spare room and refused to accept any rent for it. Everywhere they went, they were besieged by villagers, who wished to speak to Marcus, and wanted to know when he would be holding a service again. In spite of the fact that she accepted Marcus needed to preach so that he could raise money, Petronella felt dismayed by all this enthusiasm on the part of the villagers.

"I am hopeful of gaining permission from the schoolmaster to use the schoolhouse, perhaps tonight or tomorrow," he told them.

He left Petronella at the general store, where she chose an inexpensive plough and other basic farm implements, as well as two readymade skirts and blouses for herself. She ordered the provisions they would need to keep them going until they could once again visit the village, and asked for everything to be put aside until they could collect it.

Afterwards, she returned to Willa Moller's house, and was treated to coffee and milk tart. Marcus had gone to see about the purchase of a nanny-goat in milk and also of some hens and a cockerel which Petronella had been determined to acquire. She could only hope that he would not be cheated over these purchases, for he knew nothing about farm stock of any kind. Even if he would not have felt slighted if she had insisted on going with him and giving the final decision before money changed hands, the farmers from whom he bought the stock would certainly have considered it an outrage to have to negotiate with a wife instead of with her husband.

When he returned with the animals in crates on top of the cart, she discovered that, far from having been cheated, he had been sold the goat and the chickens at very reasonable terms. The farmers from whom he had bought them had heard of him by word of mouth; they considered it an honour to do business with Pastor Koen and they and their families would certainly be attending the service in the schoolhouse that evening.

"So," Petronella said, surprised, "you have already had a chance to speak to the schoolmaster, and arrange everything?"

Marcus grinned. "It was not necessary. Others organised it for me. And not only that, Petronella, but it has been arranged for there to be music also. A young man with an accordion and another with a fiddle."

She stared at him in blank astonishment. The only music she had ever associated with a church service had been that provided by a harmonium. But he explained, "The Church of the Reformed Evangelists argues that there is no need for hymns to be mournful or sad. Or even if they are sad, why not express them with music that is alive and raises the spirit or wakes the emotions? So when I heard of two young men who own instruments I asked them to come and join us."

It all sounded quite alien to her, and she felt that the accompaniment of hymns by accordion and fiddle would so outrage the audience that they would walk out of the schoolhouse, and Marcus would be unable to inspire the fervour he had previously aroused, and he would lose the source of revenue upon which he had been banking. While she dreaded the thought of his humiliation, and knew that the sooner he raised enough money to cut himself free from the Church of the Reformed Evangelists the better, some deep instinct prompted relief at the thought that, after tonight, no one would wish to attend any more of his services.

That evening, the whole of Doornboomstad streamed to the school-house. They were followed by people arriving in carts or on wagons from outlying farms and there was clearly not going to be room for all of them inside the two interconnecting rooms of the schoolhouse. The late-comers were obliged to stand outside on the stoep, and

Petronella was embarrassed to discover that *Dominee* Schalk was among them.

"I decided, at the last moment," he said wryly, "to come and witness once more what I am up against."

She gave him an apologetic smile. "Marcus's services are a novelty, that is all."

"If I thought that, Petronella," he returned sombrely, "I would not have hesitated to offer your husband the use of the church hall again."

She had to leave *Dominee* Schalk then, and go to take her seat in the front of the schoolhouse. Marcus's sermon was, if anything, more stirring than it had been the last time. He swept the people up so that, spontaneously, they punctuated what he said with fervent cries of *"Halleluiah!"* and *"Praise the Lord!"*

Once again, Petronella found herself affected by it all in a way which she could not understand, or define. She knew that Marcus was simply putting on a performance for which he hoped to be adequately rewarded and yet, in spite of knowing it, she found herself at times *believing*, being moved just as others were being moved. And how could he speak with such passion and fire when he, himself, did not believe? She did not sit in judgement on him for playing the hypocrite so well; she merely felt afraid, and she did not know why.

All the doubts she had had about the use of an accordion and fiddle were proved unfounded when the singing began. The words of the hymns which Marcus introduced were all new to the people, and were simple, repetitive and easy to learn. The tunes were similarly quick for the ear to follow, and were so lively that they might, Petronella thought, almost have been dance-tunes.

To the accompaniment of the accordion and the fiddle, the congregation sang lustily,

> "The sun shines there, the sun shines there,
> Halleluiah, the sun shines there!
> Darkness never falls
> Across Heaven's halls!
> Halleluiah, the sun shines there!"

It took little time for the congregation to become familiar with the words and the tune, and they began to clap their hands spontaneously in time to the rhythm. The effect of it all was rousing, uplifting and emotional. But the true emotion, the real passion, was reserved for the hymn which Marcus had first taught the villagers, and once again they wept as they sang:

> "Would He have thought to guide us
> To these far forbidden plains
> If shame and degradation
> Were to be our only gains?"

At last the service was over, but Marcus found it difficult to get away. Apart from the money which had been placed on the collection plate, people had arrived with gifts, with eggs and butter from farms, biltong and joints of fresh meat, a pot of cream and freshly pulled bunches of carrots and turnips.

Petronella looked on with mixed feelings of pride and dismay as Marcus thanked the people for their donations, and exchanged a few words with everyone. But now that the service was over, she could push the memory of her instinctive fear to the back of her mind. What did it matter, she reminded herself, whether Marcus was sincere or not? He had given the people what they wanted; a feeling of unity, of hope and renewed patriotism. There was nothing dishonest about the way in which he had acquired the money and the gifts freely donated. But far more important than the money he was acquiring, she felt, was the feeling of acceptance, of belonging to a community, and that would last even after the interest in his preaching had faded.

She could not help noticing the way in which the young and unmarried women were looking at Marcus. They had clearly not only been stirred by him in a spiritual way, but had also fallen heavily under his physical spell. After an initial surge of jealousy, she reminded herself with possessive complacency: Let them make calves' eyes at him if they wish; he belongs to *me*.

That night, for the first time since their marriage, he did not want to pleasure her. She began to stroke his chest as they lay in bed, but he muttered that he was exhausted and turned on his side. She felt hurt and rejected, and kept to her own side of the bed, pretending not to care by breathing evenly, as if she had fallen asleep.

A while later, she felt him quietly rising from the bed. She heard the slight sounds he made as he pulled on shirt and trousers before tiptoeing to the door. At first she thought he had gone outside to check that the goat and the chickens they had bought were securely inside their crates. When he did not return she became concerned, thinking that he might have lost his way in the dark, unfamiliar house of their landlady. She rose too, and went quietly in search of him.

She could hear the low sound of his voice coming from the back parlour. She gave the swing-door which led into it a push, expecting to find him engaged in a late-night conversation with their landlady.

But he was alone, and he had not seen her. A lighted candle stood on a low chest behind him, shining down on him where he squatted on a cushion on the floor.

Petronella drew in her breath in a soundless gasp. Marcus's hands covered his eyes and he was chanting in what she guessed was Yiddish. It was not merely the grief and torment in his voice that struck her to the heart. On his bowed head he had draped one of the small, round crocheted doilies which adorned so many surfaces inside the house, and he had torn his shirt.

He was not simply praying. He was mourning. He was mourning in the Jewish manner, as if someone very close to him had died.

Very quietly and carefully Petronella withdrew. She knew intuitively that Marcus must not learn that she had seen and heard him, and that she must not refer to the matter at all in the future. Once again, in Mamma's words, she felt as if a duck had walked over her grave. She could not begin to comprehend the conflict inside Marcus, but mixed up with her own confusion and perplexity and concern for him was the same instinctive fear she had experienced before, and it was all connected with the Church of the Reformed Evangelists.

She pretended to be asleep when he returned to bed later. In the morning there was no sign of his torn shirt and she made no comment about its absence when she packed the few personal belongings they had brought with them.

Marcus seemed so normal and cheerful that it was hard for her to remember the full impact of what she had seen and heard. He thanked Willa Moller, and loaded up the cart with all the gifts they had received. Petronella lingered for a moment inside the back parlour. The crocheted doily which Marcus had worn as a Jewish skull-cap was neatly back in place beneath an arrangement of dry grasses. She shook her head, and made up her mind to forget the incident, and went to join him so that they could pick up the things she had ordered from the general store.

At the last moment, as they were about to leave the store, inspiration struck her. "If there is any room to spare on the cart, Marcus," she suggested, "let us buy some potatoes for seed. It is too late to plant anything else, but potatoes will not only thrive before the first frost kills the top-growth; they will also help to clear the soil of weeds afterwards when we dig them up."

He agreed cheerfully, and made a joke about having married such a practical farmer's daughter, and on the way home he sang lustily again. It was not a Jewish song he sang this time, however, but the rousing ditty which he had taught the congregation the evening before. " 'Halleluiah, the sun shines there!' " Petronella wished she could have found some comfort in his choice of song, but she could not.

*   *   *

The days and the weeks which followed were happy ones on what Petronella tried to make herself think of as Korah. Using the two mules, she taught Marcus how to plough a straight furrow, and together they put in seed potatoes. He worked if not with enthusiasm then at least with great application, and afterwards he helped her to clear as much of the khaki-bush weeds from the remainder of the land as possible. Not once did he mention the Reformed Evangelists or the planning of another sermon, and she told herself that she would make a farmer of him before too long.

They had barely finished burning the uprooted khaki-bush when it began to rain; what Mamma called 'ten-eight day rain', because it generally continued for more than a week in a mournful, grey drizzle without passion or fire but with great benefit to farmers. Petronella and Marcus dashed outside the *pondok* only to feed the hens and for Petronella to milk the goat, and much of the rest of the time they spent in bed, engaged in pleasuring which never grew stale but instead inspired new and rapturous deviations, all of which Petronella embraced eagerly, without inhibition.

When the rain began to diminish, and the occasional blue patch appeared in the sky, Marcus said, "Soon I must buy the team of mules, Petronella, and then we must travel to Johannesburg, to buy from the market. I shall pay one of the young boys who still live in the *stad* on Gerrit du Toit's farm to come each day and look after the goat and the hens."

With eager excitement, she began to plan for the trip to Johannesburg. She now knew Jakoba's address, which was in a suburb on the outskirts of Johannesburg called Newlands. Jakoba had written that the house was not much, and the rooms very small, but at least it cost them little in rent because it was owned by the bosses of the goldmines where Dieter had found work. Petronella meant to take great care not to be drawn into any description of her own home to Jakoba. She would be vague, and just say that it was what one would expect of a farmhouse.

But a week before they were to set off for Johannesburg, Petronella rose one morning and was immediately assailed by nausea. She had barely time to run outside before she was violently sick.

For the rest of the day she felt unwell and queasy, and could eat little. The same thing happened the next morning, and the next. It was Marcus who diagnosed the reason for her sudden attack of ill-health.

"A baby, Petronella! That is what is making you sick!"

"A baby . . ." she echoed in dismay. Somehow, babies had never entered into her plans for the future. Perhaps, if her marriage had had a normal start, with Mamma constantly asking the kind of probing questions with which Petronella remembered she used to bombard Dorothea, it would have been different. She would have regarded a baby as the inevitable outcome of marriage, and would have been prepared for it. As it was, she found the idea frightening, alien and totally unwelcome.

She pushed the fact of her pregnancy to the back of her mind, and said, "I shall feel better by the time we leave for Johannesburg." She would *force* herself to feel better.

"No, you will not, Petronella," Marcus contradicted. "You cannot come to Johannesburg with me."

"So I am to stay here," she demanded furiously, "having a baby and all on my own?"

He laughed, and kissed her. "It will be eight or nine months before the baby comes, and I shall be away for a few weeks only. The sickness, however, will go on for a while; a month, maybe more. The shaking wagon would make you feel worse, and we would have to travel very, very slowly. So – you cannot come with me, and be sick all the way."

"You don't care about me at all!" she cried, and burst into tears. "If you did, you wouldn't think of leaving me here alone – when I feel ill – and I'm to have a baby!"

He took her into his arms. "It is *because* you are to have a baby that I must go to Johannesburg, Petronella. Things will be needed for a baby – many things. A place to sleep, clothes . . . And everything will cost money. You will be safe here, and considerably more comfortable than if you were to *shlep* along with me."

Nauseous, wretched and resentful, she watched him set out, a few days later, with the wagon and mules. Already this baby which she did not want was beginning to spoil things. She decided to ignore its existence inside her as much as it was possible to do so, as if by pretending it was not there it would somehow go away.

But it did not go away, and as well as feeling sick and wretched she was intensely lonely. She missed Marcus almost more than she had during the years when they were separated, and she also longed for Mamma's forgiveness, her strength and her support. That first night alone in the *pondok*, she saw it as the stark, comfortless place it was, and she dissolved into tears of loneliness and misery.

A young black boy riding a donkey arrived at the *pondok* on the day after Marcus left, explaining his was one of the few families still on the du Toit farm, and that Marcus had sent him to help Petronella with the chores. But the chores of milking the goat and looking after the hens were all she would have to fill the empty days, and she was about to give the youth some mealie-meal and biltong and send him home, when an idea struck her.

Once Mamma knew that she was pregnant, everything would change! Why hadn't she thought of that before? She remembered Mamma's concern for Dorothea and how she had fussed over her, and how the baby had almost made Mamma seem sentimental and how, in spite of her grim show of stoicism, she had suffered when little Gabriel died. Yes, this pregnancy which had come as such an unwelcome surprise to Petronella would bring about a reconciliation between herself and Mamma.

"Go to the house on Jakkalsdrif," she told the boy. "Ask to see the Oumies. Tell her that I am sick every morning, and that I need her help."

She stood outside the *pondok* and watched him ride his donkey towards her parents' house, her heart filled with longing and with hope. It would not be long now before she saw Mamma's ample figure making its way towards the *pondok*, coming to lay down the law to her as she had to Dorothea, brusque and bullying and telling her what she ought and ought not to do, forcing her to swallow foul-tasting herbal infusions . . .

Instead, she saw the boy riding back towards the *pondok* on his donkey. Hope began to turn into a dead weight inside her heart, then flickered and burst into renewed life as the obvious answer struck her. Mamma would know that she was alone here; even if the boy had not told her, she would know it by the absence of Marcus's wagon drawn up beside the *pondok*. Mamma had ordered the boy to tell her to pack some things and come home at once until Marcus returned, so that she could be looked after properly until the sickness had left her.

She hurried eagerly towards the boy. "I tell Oumies what you say – " he began.

"Yes? Yes? And – "

He slid from the back of the donkey, and handed her a twist of paper. "She send you this."

Numbly, she took the twist of paper from him and blundered inside the *pondok*. She placed it on the table and opened it. As well as some powdered herbs, it contained a note from Mamma.

"Boil for five minutes in four cups of water and let stand to cool," it read. "Take two tablespoonsful of infusion on empty stomach."

That was all. Not one word of comfort or forgiveness or concern. Petronella sat down by the table and her tears blurred the words of Mamma's message into a meaningless smudge.

18

Petronella had meant to spurn Mamma's herbs just as Mamma had spurned her, but sheer misery at the continuing nausea prompted her to prepare and take the infusion, and she found that it worked. But nothing happened to raise her spirits, even though she tried to keep busy by hoeing between the potato rows which had responded to the rain with rapid growth, milking the goat and making sure that it did not stray into the potato fields, setting a broody hen upon a clutch of eggs and looking for the places where the other hens might have laid their eggs.

The weeks went by, and Marcus did not return. Now that she was no longer physically sick she might have forgotten about the coming baby, were it not for the fact that her waistline was thickening noticeably. One of the things Marcus had bought before he left for Johannesburg had been a hip-bath make of zinc, and Petronella had carried water in pails from the *spruit* and heated some of it, and she was taking a bath inside their bedroom when she heard the sound of Marcus returning at last. She jumped out of the bath and grabbed a towel, draping it around herself.

He came bounding into the *pondok*, and the angry, bitter reproaches she had been storing up because of his long absence died in her throat as she looked at him, so tall and handsome and sure of himself, and so happy to see her.

"Aai, my Petronella!" He caught her to him, and as she responded automatically by putting up her hands to receive him the towel slipped and fell to the ground. With his mouth fastened on hers, Marcus explored her body with his hands, and she stiffened as they encountered her thickened waist, hesitated and then swiftly went to her shoulder-blades instead.

She began to weep. "Yes, I know. I'm fat and ugly now!"

"No! Oh, no, no, Petronella!"

"*Then look at me!*" She stepped away from him and watched him narrowly through her tears as his gaze examined her body. He could not conceal the spasm which twisted his mouth as he stared at her thickened waist and her slightly rounded stomach.

She threw herself down on the bed, and sobbed hysterically, "I don't want a baby, I never did want one. And you hate it already, because it has made me fat and ugly and miserable, and that is why you stayed away . . ."

"Petronella." He sat down beside her on the bed, stroking her back, speaking with difficulty. "I do not hate the baby. Perhaps you *are* a little fat, but that is natural. You are not ugly, my darling Petronella, but more beautiful than I remember."

"I – I saw your face," she accused. "You could not bear to touch me, or even to look."

"Petronella." His voice was quiet, hesitant, searching for the right words. "Try to understand. For another man, it would be enough to know there is to be a baby, *his* baby. For me – Petronella, what is he or she, that baby? Is it a Jew or a *shiksa*, a *goy*? For years now I have wondered only – what am I? Where do *I* fit? And suddenly I have found that the question does not end there. It goes on with the baby."

It had never occurred to her to wonder, or to care, about the mixed blood the baby would have, but she could see that it mattered to Marcus, and she grew calmer. "Is it only that? It isn't that you find me repulsive now?"

"*Repulsive?* Aai, aai, aai . . ." He slid his hands underneath her and began to fondle and stroke her, and she forgot all about the baby and about her own distorted waistline as she began to help him remove his clothes. And when he pleasured her it was as it had always been, but with an added intensity born of their long separation.

"Where have you been all this time, Marcus?" she demanded afterwards, when she remembered her grievance. "How could you have left me alone here for so long?"

"I could not help it, Petronella. I tried to come home as soon as I could. I bought goods at the market and I set out for Doornboomstad, but in every small town I passed on the way there, the people came and asked me to stay, and to preach – "

"You left me here alone while you *preached*!" she cried with a note of hysteria in her voice. "How dare you, Marcus!"

"Petronella, what can I say to the people? They have heard of the Reformed Evangelists, and that I am its pastor. Do I say that I am too busy to spread the message? That it is not convenient? So – I have to stay, and my journey home takes longer and longer."

I hate the Reformed Evangelists, she thought. *They might bring comfort to others, but they bring only misery to me.*

As if he knew what she was thinking Marcus rose, shrugging himself into his clothes. By the time she had dressed too he entered the *pondok* from outside, carrying a large wooden box from which he brought out gifts from his various congregations; ground sorghum, several jars of chutneys and jams, biltong, two pumpkins and a water-melon, an earthenware crock full of butter and a cured ham.

"Still on the wagon, Petronella," he said, "there is also a bagful of mealie-meal, enough to last us for the coming winter. And there is *this*." He took from his pockets two bundles of banknotes. "The smaller amount is the profit I earned from buying goods in Johannesburg Market. The larger is what I exchanged with the store for the coins from the collection plates. Now I can begin to pay back my debt to the Church of the Reformed Evangelists."

In the days that followed she did her best to foster in him an interest in farming. She took him to see the broody hen sitting on her clutch of eggs, and pointed out their potato fields to him. "Is it not wonderful, Marcus, to see something you have planted yourself growing and thriving?"

He shrugged. "If you plant something, it grows. It is nature."

She refused to be discouraged. "In another few weeks, we can start lifting the potatoes, Marcus, and any surplus we have, you can take with you to Johannesburg when you drive the other farmers' mealies to the Market."

He merely nodded, and began to tell her about the changes he had found in Johannesburg, describing the goods he had bought there and the people he had met. She told him how the goat had finally been persuaded to eat khaki-bush weed by Petronella refusing to feed her anything else, but how the animal had got her revenge when the milk she yielded smelt of khaki-bush and presumably tasted like it too, for Petronella had been unable to drink it and had been forced to throw it away.

"We ought to keep some pigs," she said, without thinking. "They could be fed on such things as we aren't able to use."

"I think not," was all Marcus said, and went on to talk about something else. It struck her briefly that they talked about almost anything, apart from Marcus's feelings about preaching for the Reformed Evangelists while his Jewish roots still retained such a strong hold upon him. Another subject which neither of them discussed, and to which they made only passing references, was the baby.

As autumn set in, Marcus lifted the potatoes under Petronella's direction, and the two of them stored them in cartons and boxes. Then Marcus announced that it was time for him to take the wagon and mules and drive to the various farms whose owners had agreed that he should sell their bags of mealies at Johannesburg Market. Petronella had known that he would have to leave and had been expecting his announcement daily, but even so she felt desolate at the prospect of another long separation.

This time she did not have even a rough estimate of how long it would take him to return. He would have to drive from farm to farm, picking up mealies as they were harvested and separated from the husks and piled into bags, before he could set out for Johannesburg. He had promised to send someone to stay with her, and to help with the work, but no one arrived, and as well as loneliness she also had to cope with her own ungainly body which made her daily chores more and more arduous to perform.

It was winter now too, and nights inside the *pondok* were bitterly cold. By day, the sun sparkled upon a blanket of frost which seldom melted before noon and sometimes remained all through the day, glittering under a cold sun shining from a hard blue sky. Her hands and face were chapped and she felt miserable and tearful most of the time.

She tried to prepare for the baby, struggling to make garments from a length of flannelette Marcus had brought with him from Johannesburg after his last trip, but she had no pattern to guide her, no one to help or advise her, and very little enthusiasm for the task. If only Mamma would relent . . .

All her confused feelings and her loneliness began to crystallise into rage against Mamma. She cast about her for something which would hurt Mamma and make her regret her relentless, unforgiving attitude. Inspiration struck her. She would ask Mevrouw van Tonder to help her with the delivery of the baby. Mamma and Pappa regarded the van Tonders as enemies, and Mamma would be sorry when the whole neighbourhood learnt that Petronella had had to rely on Mevrouw van Tonder to deliver her baby. Just as soon as she felt physically able to undertake the walk to their farm, she would ask Mevrouw van Tonder to help with her confinement.

But one morning she was at the *spruit*, filling pails with water, when she heard a voice bellowing in Fanakalo, and as she straightened laboriously she saw Koos a short distance away, trying to force a straying cow back to Jakkalsdrif. He saw her too, and abandoned the animal and hurried towards her.

"Nonnie Petronella!" he exclaimed, and took the heavy pails from her. "I carry these."

"Thank you." Her mouth trembled. "Is everyone – are Mamma and Pappa well?"

He assured her that they were, and as they walked together to the *pondok* he told her the other news. Gerrit and Driena had taken their share of the proceeds of the harvest and had left with their wagon and oxen, for Johannesburg, where Gerrit hoped to find work so as to raise sufficient capital to start farming his land again. Nothing more had been heard of Mwende, and the van Tonders, Koos told her, had put their farm on the market and had left the district with all their servants. Koos had heard they had gone to live in the Cape.

The tears which she seemed unable to control these days filled Petronella's eyes at this news. So she was to be robbed even of her revenge against Mamma, and Marcus would have to go and fetch another *Ziekentrooster* to help with the baby's birth.

Koos touched her arm in an awkward gesture, and said, "I ask Oubaas if he let me come help you every day, Nonnie Petronella."

She was moved by his concern, but she did not think Mamma would allow Pappa to agree to this. But only a few hours after Koos had left the *pondok* he was back again, and to her astonishment he said, "Oubaas tell me to fetch you. He say you must come speak to him."

"Did he say what he wanted to speak to me about?"

"No, Nonnie. He just say you come."

"And Mamma?" Petronella asked with a stab of hope. "Did she also say I must visit them?"

Koos looked away. "No, Nonnie Petronella. Only Oubaas."

Hope died, but she set out to walk with Koos to Jakkalsdrif, mystified as to Pappa's reasons for wishing to speak to her but also looking forward to seeing him. He had been waiting for her outside the house, but as she approached with Koos he hurried to meet them. Koos melted away as Pappa embraced her.

"What kind of man, Petronella," he demanded angrily when he let her go, "have you married, that he leaves you alone in your condition, in that miserable *pondok* he has built for you?"

"Don't criticise Marcus, Pappa," she told him fiercely. "He went away because he had to. I'm quite sure you will have been told that he is earning money by taking the harvests of other farmers to Johannesburg Market for them!"

"And making more money with his hypocritical sermons!" Pappa said harshly.

Even though she knew them to be hypocritical, Petronella would not allow Pappa to say so. "If you have asked me to come here simply so that you may insult Marcus – " she began angrily.

"No. No, child. Why did you not let us know that you were expecting a baby?"

She stared at him. "But I did! I sent a boy to Mamma with a message months ago, telling her that I was sick every morning and that I needed her help." Bitterly, Petronella added, "She sent me some herbs."

"She did not understand, child! Neither of us did! From the way in which the boy delivered the message, we thought you were suffering from an upset stomach! We had no idea of your condition until Koos told us today."

"Oh . . ." Hope, raised and dashed so many times before, sparked into life again. Pappa would never have been allowed to send for her without Mamma's consent . . .

Petronella shivered against the cold, and looked at the house, but Pappa said regretfully, "I am sorry, Petronella. I tried very hard to persuade Mamma to see you. That was why I sent for you, instead of going to see you myself. I hoped, if she knew you had come all this way in your condition, she would relent and allow you to enter the house, and speak to you herself . . . But you know what Mamma is like. She was very angry with me when she heard that I had sent for you."

"Then – then why did you?" Petronella asked, feeling as if she had been slapped in the face.

"Mamma wanted me to give you a message. When your time comes, she will deliver your baby. In the meantime, Koos will go to your *pondok* every day, and when you need her, you must send him to let her know."

"I see," Petronella said bleakly. Obviously, Mamma would deliver the baby in her capacity as *Ziekentrooster*. There was nothing personal about the matter at all.

Pappa took her hands in his. "The baby will make a difference, Petronella. Mamma may not think so now, but she has feelings, like everyone else. Once she has seen your baby, once she has held it – her own grandchild – she will not be able to turn her back on either of you afterwards."

Petronella gripped his hands tightly. "Oh Pappa, do you really believe that?"

"I'm sure of it, my dear child. It will not be easy for her at first; she will make excuses to go and see how her 'patient' is recovering, but gradually things will come right between you again because of the baby."

She kissed Pappa and, with an unsteady smile, began to walk back to the *pondok*. How could she ever not have wanted this baby? Of course it would bring about a reconciliation between Mamma and herself.

As Pappa had promised, Koos came every day after that to attend to the tasks and to carry water from the *spruit* for Petronella. But grateful as she was for Koos's help, he was not much company, and with Marcus still away she felt desperately lonely. When Petronella felt the baby give a tremendous kick inside her, she thought of an excuse for visiting Jakkalsdrif again in the hope that Mamma might see her this time.

When Koos told her at mid-morning that all the chores had been taken care of, and that he was returning to Jakkalsdrif, she announced her intention of accompanying him.

He looked concerned and worried, but he matched his pace to her own slow, cumbersome one as they stepped over stones through the *spruit* and then continued on towards the farmhouse on Jakkalsdrif.

Pappa had seen her and he came to meet them, looking at Petronella in alarm. "Is anything the matter? You should not have walked such a long distance so near to your time! Why did you not send a message with Koos?"

She waited until Koos was out of earshot, and then she said, "It would have been too embarrassing, Pappa. I – I wanted to ask Mamma how I will know when I should send for her."

"I'll go and speak to her, Petronella. I wish – " He broke off and shook his head, and then he changed the subject. "Mwende is back."

"Is she! Koos said nothing to me about it!"

"He wouldn't. She has been cast off by everyone in the *stad*, and her family have been deeply shamed by her."

"Oh, poor Mwende! And I suppose her English soldier also cast her off . . ."

"It might have been better for her if he had," Pappa said grimly. "Instead, he brought her back himself yesterday, and not only her but their half-caste *basterkind* as well. The two of them were clinging together as bold as brass, in full view of everyone, as they said goodbye before he drove away. As far as I know, not a single soul has spoken a word to her, and that is probably how matters will remain. If she and the child had struggled home to Jakkalsdrif alone, defeated and in need, perhaps it might have been different." Pappa shrugged. "Wait here, Petronella, while I go and give Mamma your message."

She felt cold and tired and she wanted to sit down somewhere, but Mamma had forbidden her the house and she could not enter it unless invited to do so. "I'll go and see Mwende, Pappa," she said. "I'll come back here afterwards and you can tell me whether Mamma will see me or not."

Pappa sighed heavily. "Sometimes it has seemed to me that you and Mwende are two of a kind. Go on, then, and see her. I'll watch for your return from the *stad*."

As Petronella moved through the *stad*, a short while later, she was offered a warm welcome by the servants whom she passed, but their warmth faded when they learnt that she was looking for Mwende. That bad girl and her *basterkind*, they said, had taken shelter inside one of the abandoned huts, since no one else would offer them a home.

As Petronella appeared in the doorway of the abandoned hut she saw that Mwende was kneeling beside a baby lying on some straw on the floor. Mwende straightened and saw her, and looked warily at her. Obviously, she imagined that Petronella still lived at Jakkalsdrif and was married to Gerrit du Toit or some other Boer. She seemed to be waiting for words of condemnation.

She was even more beautiful than Petronella remembered her to be. Her smart bright-blue woollen coat and skirt seemed incongruous inside that bare hut. No one else would live there because it was where a death had taken place, and it could only harbour bad spirits and bring ill-luck.

"Oh, Mwende," Petronella said at last. "I thought – I feared – I would never see you again!"

Then Mwende moved, and they embraced, clumsily because of Petronella's size. Mwende brought out a lace handkerchief with which to wipe her eyes. "This my little girl Tina, Nonnie Petronella," she said, indicating the baby lying on the straw.

To Petronella, who had never been able to wax sentimental over babies, the only remarkable thing about the infant was her light complexion, so that the colour of her cheeks reminded one of honey in the comb.

"She looks very healthy," Petronella said awkwardly and inadequately. She would feel quite differently about her own baby, of course, for not only would Marcus be its father, but it would cause Mamma to forgive her, and in any case, every woman thought her own baby special. She had discovered that long ago.

She turned back to Mwende. "Why did you come home? From what Pappa told me your soldier seemed sad to be leaving you."

"Oh, he very sad, Nonnie," Mwende confirmed mournfully. "He want me and little Tina. But his boss very angry when he find out I am the *mfazi* of soldier Bobby, and Bobby think I will be better with Tina where my family live, and I cannot make him understand . . ." She broke off with a sigh, and after a moment changed the subject. "And you, Nonnie Petronella, you have baby too soon. What man you marry? Baas Gerrit?"

"No, I married my Marcus. I live – " She stopped, straightening her shoulders. Was she much better off in her *pondok* than Mwende was in her abandoned hut?

"Please Nonnie, let me come work for you! Remember how we always say I go work for you if something happen so I don't marry that wrinkled-up old man my grandmamma choose for me?"

Petronella sighed. "I live in a *pondok*, Mwende. There is no room for you and the baby. But you are welcome there at any time, and if you need anything – food, anything – "

"My Bobby," Mwende interrupted with quiet pride, "give me mealie-meal and biltong and plenty money. But I come work for you all the same."

"It is not the kind of place which needs work done to it, apart from renewing the dung floors every month."

"Then I come do that for you," Mwende promised, and Petronella thanked her, recognising the offer as a token of friendship and gratitude because she had not rejected her as others had done.

Petronella left the *stad*, and as she approached the house Pappa came out to meet her. He shook his head regretfully. "Mamma won't see you, Petronella. She said I was to tell you that you'll know for yourself when you should send for her." He put his arm around her as her shoulders slumped in defeat. "Mamma won't be able to hold out after she has delivered her own grandchild herself. You'll see."

And to that thought Petronella was forced to cling as she toiled all the way back to the lonely *pondok*, without having been allowed so much as a glimpse of Mamma.

But even though Marcus still did not return, the *pondok* was no longer quite so lonely after that. When Koos arrived the next day Mwende came too, her baby strapped to her back in a sling. Brother and sister did not speak, and Koos carried out his normal chores, ignoring Mwende, who could not hide her dismay as she glanced about her. "Where the baby sleep when it come, Nonnie Petronella?"

Oh God, Petronella thought helplessly. She had never even considered the question before. Aloud, she said, "Marcus will have to go to Doornboomstad and buy a cradle, and all the other things that will be needed."

It was obvious, from Mwende's expression, that she thought Marcus was not allowing himself much time to attend to all these practical details, and Petronella tried to hide her own growing anger at his long absence. She was grateful when Mwende changed the subject by saying, "I will make coffee."

As the two of them talked Petronella learnt that Mwende's soldier had been deeply in love with her and had installed her in an unoccupied house in Johannesburg which had formerly been commandeered by an Army officer. Tina had been born in their illegal love-nest, delivered by Bobby himself. Their association had been discovered when an unexpected visit was made to the house by soldiers who had come to inspect it before restoring it to its owner. From the few words of English she had learnt, Mwende understood that Bobby was to be sent home to England in disgrace, and dismissed by the Army.

Mwende called regularly at the *pondok* after that, to renew the dung floors for Petronella or bring her 'Free State coal' or merely to show her the coat she was knitting for Petronella's baby with wool which had been meant for little Tina. Petronella was grateful to be spared the chore of going down on her hands and knees to smear the floors with dung, and she welcomed the 'Free State coal' because it was now so bitterly cold that the cooking range had to be fuelled all day long.

The explosive rage against Marcus had been growing inside her. No matter how long he had had to wait for harvests to be completed at each of the farms where he had called, he should have been home many weeks ago. For all he knew she was quite alone and isolated in the *pondok*, heavily pregnant, unable to go and find fuel with which to keep herself warm in the fierce cold.

Neither Mwende nor Koos was at the *pondok* when Marcus returned at last, or Petronella might have restrained herself. As it was, she hurled herself at him, not in loving welcome but in hysterical rage, beating at his chest with her fists and screaming, "You bastard! You pious, hypocritical bastard! You've been preaching and praying again, haven't you, wallowing in being the centre of attention, in holding people in the hollow of your hand, watching them melt at the sound of your voice, while I've been here alone and helpless!"

"Petronella," he began, trying to grab her hands in his.

But she was beyond all reason. "Why should you have hurried home, after all, to a swollen, shapeless wife with raw, chapped skin from the bitter cold? Did you linger after your sermons for some whoring, Marcus? All those girls at your services making calves' eyes at you, more interested in your body than in salvation – I've seen them! Yes, that would have been it, Marcus Koen, whoring and preaching pastor of the God-cursed Reformed Evangelists!"

"You blaspheme, woman!" he bellowed at her. "And you fabricate poisonous lies! Such a homecoming – aai, *ver darf es*?"

The passion in his voice had diminished her own rage, and she burst into tears. He took her by the hand, and led her into the bedroom, forcing her to sit down on the bed. "You say you have been here alone," he began. "What happened to the woman I paid to come and stay with you until my return?"

"What woman?" Petronella demanded, drying her eyes.

"I went first to the *stad* on Gerrit du Toit's farm," he said, "and I found all the servants gone. So I went to the van Tonder farm, and a woman in the *stad* there agreed to come and stay with you. I gave her money and I left – "

"You paid her first! You fool, Marcus! The van Tonders had already arranged to move to the Cape, and to take their servants with them! The woman who took your money had no intention of coming here!"

He looked stricken. "I did not know that." He struck his forehead with his palm. "What a *klutz* I am! Forgive me, Petronella. I would not have stayed away so long if I had guessed that you were here all alone!"

She might have been appeased had it not been for something which she had faced and finally admitted to herself while she raged at him in her furious passion. She was as deeply resentful of his preaching as if it were another woman. Whether it was sincere or not, it took Marcus away from her. She was jealous of the passion which he stirred in others, jealous of the passion he himself poured into it.

"You stayed away so long," she said bitterly, "because you were stopping on the way to hold services. Even if that woman you paid *had* come to stay with me, do you think that would have made up for the months you have been away?"

He made no answer. Instead, he stood up from the bed and she heard him go outside. He returned, carrying a large hamper. "Petronella," he said quietly, "when I travelled to Johannesburg that first time, and I stopped on the way to hold services, I told people in conversation that my wife was to have a baby. So this time I found them waiting for me, and they brought me things they have made for the baby. It is all in the hamper – coats, nightgowns, napkins, dresses – everything the baby will require. On the wagon, too, is a cradle of wood someone made, with a mattress filled with duck-feathers. So, how could I refuse when they asked me to preach? When I knew that *you* would not have found it possible to make much for the baby, and I believed that you had a woman to help you and be with you? My plan had been to come home quickly, and stop in Doornboomstad to buy for the baby what it will require. So when those good people gave me instead all those things, and asked only that I hold a service for them, would you have had me refuse them?"

She could not put her own half-formed feelings into words. There was a spot in the Vaal River which held a whirlpool, and she had once watched a water-fowl being sucked helplessly into its depths. She felt that Marcus was being sucked into something very like it, and that she had the choice of either joining him and being sucked in as well, or else standing by, watching helplessly.

But she could put none of these feelings into words which would have made sense, and so she said instead, in a sullen voice, "You must have made enough money by now, Marcus, to be able to repay what you owe to the Church of the Reformed Evangelists. I want you to promise to give up preaching."

He answered without hesitation. "That I cannot do, Petronella."

Rage quickened inside her again. "Why not?" Once more, because she could not put her true fears into words, she jeered angrily, "Is it the thought of all those adoring girls, hanging on your every word – ?"

"Be quiet, Petronella! I have no interest in girls. For me, there is only one woman in the world . . . and that is you. Always you have known that." He leant over her and kissed her mouth, and even swollen with pregnancy as it was, she felt her body cry out for his, and she curled her arms tightly about him.

But part of her mind was registering the fact that his manner of speaking seemed subtly altered upon his return from trips to Johannesburg. Of course, Dutch itself had changed considerably during the short time since the war and had become even more simplified, both in speech and in writing. Petronella had noticed this herself while she was in Doornboomstad, and in her last letter Jakoba had mentioned that many people had stopped calling their language Dutch and were calling it Afrikaans instead. Marcus still used some of the formal terms and words in the High Dutch he had been taught, even though he had generally adopted the simplified speech of the Boers. And yet there was something – something quite apart from his distinctive accent – about his manner of speaking when he returned from a trip . . .

The answer came to her suddenly. During the periods when his thoughts were all he had for company, those thoughts were in Yiddish. He had not forgotten, let alone destroyed, his roots. Did he sometimes weep when he was alone, and cover his head, and rend his clothes in mourning? A shiver tore through her.

"You are cold, *mein tiere*," he said, misunderstanding. He went on seriously, reasoning with her, "I need to continue preaching for a while longer, Petronella. If the van Tonder farm is for sale, the price will be low, and I wish to buy it."

The van Tonder farm! All those strange fears and fancies of hers about whirlpools, she decided, must have been caused by her condition. Buying the van Tonder farm put a different complexion upon everything. Marcus would not wish to buy the farm unless he had given serious thought to the matter of becoming a farmer after all.

"The van Tonder farm," she repeated aloud. "Koos told me they had repaired their house before they decided to sell and move to the Cape." She giggled. "You'll have your wish, and live in a house in which the floors are not made of – " Her voice ended in a shriek of panic and anguish as pain, the like of which she had never experienced before, convulsed her body.

"Petronella, what is it?" Marcus cried anxiously.

"I – I think – the baby – too early . . ." she managed before another pain shot through her. "Get Mamma," she gasped.

He hurried from the *pondok*, and she waited in terror for another of those searing pains, but none came, and she began to think it had been a false alarm after all.

But just as Marcus returned to the *pondok* with Mamma, followed by Mwende, the worst pain of all racked Petronella, so that she began to scream.

"Stop that at once!" she heard Mamma say in a brisk voice, and automatically she obeyed, biting hard on her lip. "How long between the pains?" Mamma wanted to know.

"I – I – *oh!*" She gripped the edge of the bed as more pain assaulted her.

After that, everything seemed to hover between a dream and a nightmare. She heard Mamma ordering Marcus to boil water and fetch more from the *spruit*, and telling Mwende to help undress Petronella. Then Mamma's capable hands were examining her stomach, probing and squeezing lightly. "I don't think it's early," she told Mwende. "It seems like a full-term labour to me. And it will be some time before it's over."

Occasionally, between pains, Petronella was able to doze. Or she would lie there, looking at Mamma, hoping for a sign of weakness in her, a flicker of love. But Mamma was there as a *Ziekentrooster*, and Petronella was merely someone she had come to assist in the birth of her child. That was all.

When the pain was finally over, Petronella thought, when Mamma held the baby in her arms, everything would change. Pappa had said so . . .

In the meantime, Mamma addressed all her remarks to Mwende, and occasionally issued an order to Marcus. The only time she spoke to Petronella was when, after countless hours of agony, she commanded her sometimes to push down, and at other times to resist the contractions which tore through her.

It was not until past midnight that Petronella heard herself make the same animal sound which she remembered having come from Dorothea's bedroom so long ago. There was a final, excruciating explosion of pain and then, at last, nothing but a dull ache and a sense of overwhelming fatigue.

She heard a piercing scream from the baby, and then Mamma's voice telling Mwende, "Wash the child and dress him while I finish attending to his mother." With professional efficiency, she began to probe and prod at Petronella's stomach.

It required an enormous physical effort for Petronella to lift a hand and lay it over Mamma's. "The baby . . . A boy. Mamma, what do you think – ?"

"He is strong and healthy," Mamma's voice was totally neutral.

"Is he – like Gabriel, Mamma?"

The hands on Petronella's abdomen became still for a moment, and then continued what they had been doing. "Raise yourself slightly," Mamma said without expression.

Desperately, Petronella tried again. "Mamma – shouldn't you be seeing to the baby – examining him – or something?"

"He needs no further attention from me. Mwende is taking care of him."

Mamma called to Marcus to bring more water, and she washed Petronella with brisk, efficient movements. Petronella's tears were slowly seeping into the pillow. Oh Mamma, she grieved, you terrible, wonderful, unbelievable old woman. How hard you are, and I wish I could hate you. Oh Mamma, Mamma, Mamma . . .

She hovered somewhere between exhausted sleep and grieving wakefulness, aware that Mamma was changing the sheets and making her comfortable, and the last words Petronella heard her say were addressed to Marcus.

"No, I won't stay for coffee, thank you. You must send for me, of course, if the need arises. But it shouldn't. It was a perfectly normal, routine delivery."

Petronella must have fallen briefly asleep then, for the next thing of which she became aware was Marcus's voice, saying, "Petronella, I present to you your son – *our* son."

Mwende watched as he handed her the small bundle wrapped in a beautiful white knitted shawl which Petronella had not seen before. She looked at her son and a wild laugh escaped her and then turned into uncontrollable sobbing. She handed the baby back to Mwende and buried her face in the pillow.

She was still sobbing, deaf to anything Marcus or Mwende tried to say to her, when fatigue overcame her and she fell asleep, utterly exhausted and drained. She woke up, to find herself alone in the room and with no sight or sound of anyone else, and for an instant she thought she had dreamt everything. Then she turned on her side and a downward glance showed her the wooden cradle beside the bed, with her son asleep inside it.

She looked down at him, praying for maternal instinct to take over and fill her with tenderness for this small scrap of humanity. But nothing happened, and it was impossible for her even to believe that he could once have been part of her own body.

She had always, in the past, considered newly born babies to be ugly. But this son of hers was ugly in a totally different, alien way. His nose was enormous, and out of all proportion to the rest of his face, and his plentiful dark hair stood away from his head, like the bristles of a brush. A bitter smile twisted her lips as she remembered how she had asked Mamma whether he looked like Gabriel. Fate, or Nature, or perhaps the Almighty Himself, had played a mocking trick on her by making her believe that Mamma would only need to clap eyes on *this* baby and take him to her heart, and forgive Petronella.

He did not remotely resemble any Boer baby. But he did not resemble Marcus either. The baby opened his eyes, slate-coloured and flat beneath heavy lids, and she realised, suddenly, whom it was he did resemble.

If one could have added a beard to that small face, and a brimless cap, it would have been a miniature version of Marcus's father lying in the cradle. Even the expression in his eyes as he stared back at her seemed, to her fancy, to be like the accusing one of Marcus's father.

19

Almost simultaneously, two things happened. An unfamiliar, dismaying heaviness surged into her breasts, and she found to her horrified distaste that milk was flowing from them and staining the front of her nightgown. And the baby began to scream, reminding her of a predator which had sensed the presence of food.

Marcus rushed inside the room and picked up the baby. "I think you should feed him now, Petronella. Mwende said your milk would arrive this morning, and she has gone home."

Petronella stifled a burst of hysterical laughter. Marcus had made it sound as if her milk were to be delivered in churns, instead of leaking so disgustingly from her breasts. With trembling hands she received her son from Marcus and laid him down on her lap, her hands going to the buttons of her nightgown. "Please," she whispered to Marcus, "don't watch."

He frowned. "But why not, Petronella? It is part of nature. And for a man to watch his wife feed his son – "

"Please," she repeated desperately, "I don't want you to watch." She was afraid of experiencing revulsion when she put this alien-looking baby to her breast, and afraid of being unable to conceal her feelings from Marcus.

Sighing, he turned and went out. She unbuttoned her bodice and picked up the baby. Perhaps, she prayed, a miracle would happen. Perhaps, as she began to feed him, she would feel compassion and tenderness for the baby, who could not help looking so alien and ugly, after all.

His mouth groped for her nipple and she began to feel – *something*, she could not be sure what – as he started to suck noisily and greedily. But after a moment or two he rejected her breast and began to scream angrily, as if what she had to offer had not come up to his expectations. She put him to her other breast, but he rejected this, too, after only a few moments.

His screams, and Petronella's weeping, brought Marcus to the room. "He – he won't drink my milk," she sobbed. "He doesn't like it."

"That is not possible, Petronella!"

"It is! It is! You wanted to watch – *so watch!*" She put the screaming baby to her breast again, and after tugging and sucking for an instant he removed his mouth and began to scream again. It was, she thought with wretched despair, like going out of one's way to prepare a meal for a self-invited guest only to have him say he did not care for that particular dish and push it aside.

She laughed hysterically. "I think it's because – because it isn't *kosher!*"

"What nonsense is this, Petronella?" Marcus frowned. "Perhaps the baby is hurting somewhere. Perhaps the pin on his napkin has become loose."

She tried to impose calmness on herself, and checked the baby's napkin. Then she tried again to feed him, but he continued to spurn what she had to offer.

"I don't know what to do," she wept. "Fetch – fetch Mamma, Marcus."

She sat there on the bed, with the screaming baby across her lap, flailing his fists in the air as if he were trying to reach her and assault her physically, and prayed Mamma would come, and take over, and forgive her, and accept that it was not her fault that the baby bore no resemblance at all to a van Zyl but looked like Marcus's father.

But it was not Mamma who came back with Marcus, but Mwende. "Petronella," he reported, "your Mamma says it is possible your milk will not be enough yet for the baby. Perhaps later today – " He shrugged. "For now, Mwende says she will feed our baby."

Petronella looked at Mwende, whose own baby was strapped to her back. "*Could* you feed both babies, Mwende?"

"I have plenty milk, Nonnie."

Marcus left the room, and Mwende sat down on the bed, and when she had unbuttoned her blouse she picked up the baby and suckled him at her breast. Petronella watched her son's rapacious little mouth pulling at Mwende's nipple, and saw the dribble of milk seeping from one corner to run in a little rivulet to his neck. She felt as if she had been personally rejected by the child, and she could not believe that her own milk was insufficient for his needs. If it were, then why was it continuing to stain the front of her nightgown?

When the baby had finished feeding, and had given a loud burp, Mwende put him back in his cradle. Marcus appeared in the doorway, in time to hear her ask, "What you call your son, Nonnie Petronella?"

So many other matters had been filling her mind that it had not even occurred to her to think of a name for the child. But before she could say anything, Marcus announced, "He must be named Joshua, for my father – "

"No!" The protest had been torn from Petronella.

Marcus gave her a puzzled look. "It is tradition, Petronella. When a man's father is dead, his first-born son should be named for the father."

He already looks like Marcus's father, she thought wildly. If he is named after the man as well, how could I ever learn to love him? And oh, I must, I must love my son, mine and Marcus's . . .

"Your father burnt you from his life," she reminded him.

"He is dead now, Petronella, and one should forgive the dead."

"I don't want him to be named Joshua," she said implacably.

After a few moments, Marcus asked, "Would you make any objection if we named him for my grandfather, who was called Abel?"

"No," she agreed readily. "Abel Koen sounds fine."

Mwende announced that she would stay until the baby's next feed was due, in four hours, and would busy herself with domestic tasks in the meantime, and Petronella went back to sleep.

She woke up when Abel began to scream hungrily again. Her own breasts felt as tight as drums and must surely be filled with milk. She received the baby from Mwende and offered him a breast, looking at his poor, ugly little face and praying that he would not reject her again, so that she could begin to love him.

But after tugging a few times at her nipple he began to scream. Mwende held out her arms to take the baby, but Petronella shook her head, tears rolling down her cheeks, and put him to her other breast, begging brokenly, "Please, Abel, please. I'm trying, so why can't you? Just – just suck a little harder . . ."

Her voice was drowned by the baby's screams. Mwende reached over the bed and took him, telling Petronella, "Your milk, she is not enough yet, Nonnie. Perhaps, this evening."

Petronella lay back, weeping, and watched her son accepting Mwende's breast eagerly when he had spurned her own, and felt her milk seeping away uselessly into the bodice of her nightgown. When he had drunk his fill of what Mwende had to offer, Petronella stopped weeping and asked for the baby to be placed beside her in the bed, instead of being returned to his cradle. If she cradled him, now that he was no longer crying angrily, the miracle of mother-love would invade her and he would grow accustomed to her also, so that he would accept her breast this evening.

But this son of hers did not wish to be cradled by her. He screamed furiously in her arms and did not stop until Mwende had taken him from her and placed him inside the wooden cradle, where he fell asleep immediately.

Perhaps I held him too tightly, Petronella thought. Perhaps I was trying too hard. Oh God, let me love my son. Let him love me. Make things come right.

But when Abel woke up again, and screamed his hunger, nothing had changed. Petronella's tears mingled with his screams as she tried desperately to make him feed and he beat his small fists against her breast instead. She continued trying while Marcus hurried to the *stad* to fetch Mwende, and prayed for compassion and love to flood her for this small, uncooperative son of hers, but all she felt was misery and failure and exhaustion.

The moment Mwende arrived and took him from her, and even before she had offered him her own breast, he became quiet. It was as if he were deliberately setting out to make his rejection of her public.

"Nonnie," Mwende said, "I ask your Mamma, and she say it possible your milk is not enough for perhaps a week – "

"Then why does it *feel* as if it were more than enough?" Petronella interrupted with frustration. "My breasts are painful and tight as drums when my milk comes in, and it leaks and soaks my clothing. So how could it not be enough?"

"I ask your Mamma this also, and she say it happen sometimes. Your body act like you have plenty milk, but there is very little; not enough for hungry baby. Almost all the milk you got has leaked out by time your baby start to suck and then he scream. But you rest and drink plenty water and goat's milk, Nonnie, and perhaps in a week you have enough milk. Your Mamma say the best thing we do is if I stay here with you, and feed your Abel and my Tina until your milk come properly."

She placed the sated Abel in his cradle and Marcus, who had been discreetly waiting in the other room, appeared in the doorway. Mwende had obviously already discussed Mamma's suggestion with him, for he said, "We must take the advice of your Mamma, Petronella."

"But how – " She looked helplessly at him. "There is no room. And the baby will need feeding during the night also." Something else occurred to her. "Dorothea used to feed her baby condensed milk mixed with water when we were in the concentration camp. Why can't I feed Abel with that also, using a bottle?"

It was Mwende who answered her question. "That no good for very young baby, Nonnie Petronella. It make him ill. In three months, perhaps – but now he need breast milk. If he cannot get from you, then I must give him what he need."

"But where will you sleep, Mwende? And Tina? We have no room."

Marcus cleared his throat. "The solution, Petronella, would be for me to go to Doornboomstad, and lodge with Willa Moller. The mattress on my wagon which I use for sleeping on when I am in the veld can be spread on the floor of the other room, with blankets also, and Mwende and Tina could sleep there."

She began to weep bitterly again. "You – you only came home yesterday, and now – now you want to leave me so soon . . ."

"It is not what I want, Petronella. It is what is necessary. Only until your milk is sufficient for the baby."

Through her tears, Petronella looked at her baby, who stared unblinkingly back at her. In that moment he seemed almost to be the ghost of Marcus's father, reborn and come to haunt and punish her. After all the misery he had already brought her, he was now to be the cause of yet another indefinite separation between Marcus and herself.

But that was unfair. She must not allow herself to think such things. The baby could not help looking like Marcus's father, and she must – please God, she *must* – learn to love him.

A vicious circle had set in. As Mwende had predicted, because the infant was not suckling at his mother's breasts, what milk she did have was drying up. If Petronella had ever thought about such a state of affairs, she would have imagined that her breasts would simply return to normal, and that would be that. But instead, she suffered excruciating pain, and she began to loathe the smell of her own stale milk which still oozed into her bodice and bedclothes during the night. Mwende simply did not have the time or the facilities to change and wash her things regularly.

Marcus returned from Doornboomstad at the end of the week. He kissed Petronella and then picked up his son who stared at him curiously and did not cry in the way he usually did when Petronella picked him up.

"You feed him yourself now, Petronella?" Marcus wanted to know.

"He has decided that my milk is not at all to his taste," she said with a harsh laugh.

Marcus gave her a defeated look and returned the baby to his cradle. "So, I shall have to return to Doornboomstad."

He did not, she thought resentfully, appear to be heartbroken at the news. He had brought with him from the village a supply of coal for the range, and also the kind of provisions which she knew he would not have been able to buy from the general store. He had been spending his time preaching again, and the provisions were gifts from spiritually uplifted congregations.

She said sharply, "I know you want to buy the van Tonder farm, Marcus, and that is why we have agreed that you should go on preaching. But do you think it's fair to *Dominee* Schalk to lure away his own parishioners?"

"I do not preach in Doornboomstad alone, Petronella. I visit other small towns and farms in addition. The people feel the need to have their spirits raised. They have had so little to give them hope since the war ended." He hesitated. "And *Dominee* Schalk is no longer able to hold services. He has suffered a stroke, which has impaired his speech."

She couldn't help wondering about the possible connection between *Dominee* Schalk's stroke and Marcus's seduction of the old minister's parishioners away from his church.

"I must leave again now, Petronella," he said, bending over the bed to kiss her.

She turned her head away. "Yes, Marcus," she said bitterly, "hurry back to your preaching and praying. You must thank God that you have the perfect excuse not to be cooped up inside the *pondok* instead, doing all the things for me which Mwende is doing."

"Aai, Petronella, that is not fair! It is for the feeding of the baby that Mwende needs to be here. How could I help with that?" When she did not answer he sighed. "On Saturday I shall return."

Tears oozed between her closed eyelids. During all those years when she had yearned for Marcus, and learnt English, and plotted and planned for them to be together, she had not visualised that she would end by sharing a *pondok* instead with Mwende and two crying babies, while Marcus swept people up in religious fervour with his sermons which had always made her feel uneasy and which she was regarding more and more as a threat to their relationship.

Abel was screaming again, and above the sound Petronella heard Mwende say, "Perhaps you try one last time, Nonnie, to see if he will take milk from you."

"It won't do any good." She laughed harshly. "He hates my milk, and he hates me."

Mwende clicked her tongue. "That nonsense, Nonnie Petronella! No young baby hate his mother."

Perhaps hate was too strong a word, Petronella thought. But he certainly disliked her, as she disliked him . . . Guilt tore through her. That wasn't true. No mother could dislike her own child; it wasn't natural. This was just a temporary difficulty she was going through, and as soon as Abel was a little older and began to respond to her she would also be able to respond to him as mothers the world over responded to their children. Then she thought of Mamma and she laughed again, a cracked, brittle, uncontrolled sound. Mamma no longer had any love or tenderness or compassion for her own daughter, and she had rejected her only grandchild at sight. Were they, after all, so unlike – she and Mamma?

Then Petronella looked at Abel in Mwende's arms, and renewed guilt swamped her because she had not yet learnt to love her child. "Give him to me," she said. "I'll try again."

But the attempt was useless. Abel screamed more angrily than ever and would not even try to suckle, and Petronella was forced to hand him back to Mwende to be fed.

Gradually, as one bleak day blurred into another, Petronella found her strength returning, and her breasts no longer ached all the time and only occasionally leaked, staining her bodice. She was able to get up, and to help Mwende with the many chores. There was scarcely a moment of the day when the tin hip-bath was not being used for the washing of babies or of napkins or clothes or bedding which were then spread outside, safely out of reach of the goat, to be dried in the sun. It was no longer quite so bitterly cold and Petronella knew that spring must be approaching, although there were few visible signs of it now that hardly a tree remained on Jakkalsdrif or on Korah.

She often stared in the direction of the house on Jakkalsdrif. Would Mamma have melted towards Abel if he had not looked so aggressively alien, she wondered. And if she had accepted him as her grandson, and helped Petronella with the problem of feeding him, would that maternal instinct which she had fully expected to come surging over her with his birth have materialised? She couldn't tell; all she knew was that she was consumed by guilt because she did not feel as she ought to for this baby who was increasingly responding to Mwende and invariably cried when Petronella picked him up, as if he regarded her as a suspect stranger.

Regularly each week, Marcus called to enquire whether the baby was sleeping through the night yet, so that their living room would no longer have to serve as a bedroom for Mwende and Tina, and he could come home. But Abel was continuing to demand night-time feeds, so that Marcus had to return to Doornboomstad again.

The old longing and hunger for Marcus gnawed away at Petronella, but instead of welcoming him with joy and love when he called she vented her frustration on him, goading him with insinuations about the love-struck young girls and unmarried women who attended his services, so that the two of them invariably parted in anger.

It was Mwende who suggested a temporary solution and saved Petronella from being driven crazy with bitterness, jealousy and unfulfilled desire for the man who still possessed her, and frustration that the child who appeared to have no need of her and who rejected her was keeping them apart.

"Why," Mwende suggested, when Marcus arrived for his weekly

visit and before Petronella could assault him with her festering grievances, "why, Nonnie Petronella, you not go to Doornboomstad with Baas Marcus? I stay here, and look after everything. Then, next week, you come back and you feel better."

"Oh Mwende, would you? *Could* you?"

"For a week I could, Nonnie. I save up much dirty washing for when you come back."

Hastily, Petronella changed into her best skirt and blouse, and packed a few things. She took her place beside Marcus on the wagon and it struck her that they seemed like strangers now, with nothing to say to each other.

She made a determined attack on the silence between them. "When do you think, Marcus, you will have earned enough money to buy the van Tonder farm?"

"I do not know, Petronella." His voice was sombre. "The harvest last year was not good for anyone. The people are becoming poorer and poorer, and I have told them that I do not wish them to put money on collection plates."

"You are doing it now for *nothing*?" she cried, outraged.

"Not precisely for nothing. I have thought of a new way of raising capital, and also a new way of holding services. I am now taking the church to the people. I visit farms, and all the neighbours come to share in my services."

The enthusiasm in his voice dismayed her. It was not the enthusiasm one would expect of a man eager to buy the van Tonder farm and devote himself to tilling the land.

"How," she asked, "does all this earn you money?"

"I have asked my congregation in Doornboomstad to donate, each according to his means, articles such as pots, pans, plough-shares, fabric for the manufacturing of clothes – all manner of things farmers cannot produce for themselves. I then take them on my wagon to the farms where I preach, and sell them to the farmers. Because they, in turn, wish to make donations I accept from them a chicken here, some animal skins for tanning there, or a *muid* of mealies – and these I sell to the store-owner in Doornboomstad. That is how I make money."

Petronella was silenced by this totally alien concept of a travelling man who combined salesmanship with preaching, and Marcus seemed more of a stranger than ever to her.

Even when they arrived at his lodgings she could not shake off this feeling. They were to share the same bedroom which they had had before, but this, too, had been altered subtly. It had become Marcus's room. A small table had been added to serve as a desk and on it was stacked a pile of books, some in English and a few in languages unknown to her. "Where did you get these?" Petronella asked.

Marcus's answer was defensive. "They did not cost much. I purchased them from a Roman Catholic priest in Johannesburg, while I was visiting the city before the birth of the baby."

She stared at the books with enmity. When Marcus had not been travelling the countryside, preaching and selling, he had obviously been immersed in these learned books. Had it mattered to him at all that she was dragging out a miserable existence without him in the *pondok?*

Her thoughts were interrupted by a knock on the door. It was Willa Moller who informed them brightly that she and her two children were about to set out on a visit to relatives and would be away until late that evening. It was an unsubtle way of making it known to them that Marcus and Petronella would have the house entirely to themselves.

Petronella went to stand by the window, and listened as the front door banged shut behind the departing Mollers. She would never have believed that she would feel awkward and self-conscious alone with Marcus. She was striving for some mundane remark with which to break the silence between them when she felt his hand against the nape of her neck in a tentative touch. And that was all that had been needed. She whirled around, and fell into his arms, her body responding immediately with all the fire and passion he had always been able to command with his touch.

As Marcus pleasured her in all the many ways which had sometimes seemed to her like a half-forgotten dream during their long period of celibacy, Petronella forgot all her bitterness and her rage and resentment.

"Oh Marcus," she pleaded as they lay in each other's arms afterwards, "never leave me alone for such a long time again. I can't bear it. At times I found myself beginning to hate you. I could never just be indifferent to you. I love you so much, Marcus, but if I stopped loving you, I would hate you instead."

"You must not say such things, my Petronella. Always between us there can only be love." He kissed her mouth, and then her throat, and drew her against him once more, to engulf her with the magic of his pleasuring.

In the morning he woke her up with a kiss, and said, "It is Sunday, my love. I must prepare for the service."

"Oh." The new foundations which they had built up during the previous evening received a slight jolt. "I had forgotten. Must I – " She saw the hurt in his eyes, and went on quickly, "I'll get ready."

If Petronella had been disturbed by the first two of Marcus's services which she had attended, she was totally dismayed by this one. It was no longer a matter of a simple, emotional sermon preached by Marcus, followed by rousing hymns and a short but passionate prayer.

The difference struck her with a shock when the time came for the prayer. It had changed from the former style when Marcus had prayed and the congregation had made an occasional heart-felt response. While some of them sobbed loudly, unrestrainedly, others contributed prayers of their own, so that Marcus's voice could hardly be heard.

Even when the prayers came to an end, it did not mean that the service was over. There followed what Marcus announced as 'Attesting'. It was a curious and, to Petronella, intensely embarrassing public baring of breasts. People competed with one another to come forward to the platform on which Marcus was standing, and to share with him and with the congregation admissions to sins to which they had been tempted by the Devil. The sins were all so petty that Petronella considered their solemn confessions almost laughable, and she looked at Marcus, wondering how he succeeded in keeping a straight face.

Galvanising shock tore through her as she saw his expression when he touched the head of the latest 'attester' and murmured a short prayer.

Dear God, she thought, *he believes*. He is no longer doing this to make money. He believes in this grotesque, hysterical show of religious fervour and public breast-beating.

At last it was over. The collection plate was filled with promissory notes for goods which Marcus would sell at outlying farms, and feeling cold with fear and foreboding Petronella returned with him to his lodgings.

"All that 'attesting'," she broke the silence between them. "Did you get the idea from the Roman Catholic priest in Johannesburg?"

"No, Petronella. The people themselves began to come forward to confess to what lay heavily upon their hearts."

She said nothing. Perhaps the hysteria, too, had begun spontaneously, aroused by Marcus's fervour, so that it had become a force of its own. But he could have stopped it, and he had not. She did not believe that what she had seen and heard today bore much relation to the teachings of the Church of the Reformed Evangelists. No, Marcus had been forced to abandon his own Jewish faith, and he had created another of his own to put in its place.

Once more, after lunch, Willa Moller and her children left the house to visit relatives, and as soon as she was in Marcus's arms again Petronella succeeded in blotting out the memory of the service. The Marcus who pleasured her with such uninhibited passion seemed to bear no resemblance at all to the man who had prayed for forgiveness for lustful thoughts in others. She did not understand this, but she could only conclude, confusedly, that he was able to divorce Marcus the man from Marcus the preacher.

On the night before he was due to take her back to the *pondok*, she lay in his arms and said fiercely, "Marcus, Mwende says the baby should have been sleeping through until the morning long before now. During this coming week he must be weaned of his night-feeds, and next Saturday you must come home for good."

He moved his hand caressingly over her thigh. "Very well, my Petronella. Do you think I do not wish for that also?"

She stopped his hand before he could seduce her into uncaring, mindless rapture. "When you do come home, Marcus, will you – do you intend carrying on with the business of preaching and selling during the day?"

"But of course, Petronella. I must. How else am I to earn money for all we need?"

"You mean, for buying the van Tonder farm?"

He leant over to kiss her. "Naturally."

She sighed, and abandoned herself to him. Please God, she thought, let it not be too long before he can buy the van Tonder farm, and give his thoughts and his energies to working the land.

He drove her back to the *pondok* the next morning. In spite of not having succeeded in forcing herself to miss Abel while she had been away, at the back of her mind there had lingered the hope that he might have changed during the week; that he might have developed a sunny disposition and be less aggressively demanding of both the food and the attention which he sought from Mwende, and respond to his mother, so that she in turn could respond to him with tenderness and affection.

But she found that Mwende, left alone with the two babies, had been forced to tie both of them to her back inside a sling, and Abel either slept contentedly with his face pressed against Tina's or else he crooned with delight as the two babies jogged up and down with Mwende's movements, and he bellowed with rage when Petronella tried to lift him out of the sling.

Defeated, Petronella turned to Marcus. She kissed him goodbye and said, "Don't forget – one week, and then you return home."

Poor Mwende, she noticed after Marcus had gone, looked exhausted and Petronella made her remove both babies from her back and lay them down on a blanket on the bedroom floor. Then she ordered Mwende to sit down while she brewed coffee for the two of them, and afterwards she changed her clothes and began to tackle the washing which Mwende had been forced to put to one side.

"Tonight," Petronella said, "you must refuse Abel when he cries for a feed. He must learn to sleep through until the morning. Marcus is coming home at the end of the week, where he belongs, and – "

"I understand, Nonnie. After that I come in the morning to feed your baby, and I stay with you until his feed for the evening."

Petronella looked at her with tears in her eyes. "Mwende, I don't know how I could have borne these past weeks without you!"

"You help me also," Mwende said quietly. "The people in the *stad* – my people – my mamma, my pappa, my grandmamma and Koos even – they never speak with me again." She sighed. "Remember how your Mamma always say you and me bad girls together, who end in trouble one day?"

Petronella remembered. *I* am not in trouble, she told herself. I have the only man I have ever wanted, and before long he will be a farmer, and we shall live happily together on what used to be the van Tonder farm.

Belatedly, she added to herself, And we have Abel, our son who has already changed since he was first born and is no longer so ugly, and who will change in other ways also, and become easy to love.

But she would have defied anyone to feel much love for Abel that night. He kept them awake with his screaming demands for food, and Tina joined him in his protest, but Mwende agreed with Petronella that it was past time for him to do without night-feeds.

Both women were exhausted the next morning, but Petronella was determined to try to establish an emotional bond with her son. "He likes being strapped in a sling to your back," she told Mwende. "Take a sheet and tie him to *my* back instead so that I may carry him as I work."

But perhaps because carrying a baby in a sling did not come naturally to her, as it did to Mwende, and her movements were clumsy, the experiment was a failure and Abel screamed until Mwende removed him from the sling, cuddled him for a few minutes and then laid him on a blanket on the bedroom floor with Tina.

Depressed and tired, Petronella helped Mwende to tackle the tasks of the day. Petronella was at the cooking range, making porridge, while Mwende milked the goat, when she heard heavy footsteps outside, and she turned.

Gerrit du Toit stood framed in the doorway of the *pondok*. But he was a Gerrit she had not seen before. His appearance was unkempt, his eyes red-rimmed and his clothes soiled. He entered the room, and as he came close she recognised the smell of brandy-wine on his breath.

"Where," he demanded, "is that Jewish bastard you married?"

She shrank away from him. "What do you want? How did you get here?"

"Why should you care, bitch? If you must know, I walked most of the way from Johannesburg. Got one or two rides . . ." He bared his teeth and put out a hand, grabbing her shoulder. "Alone here, are you?" he jeered. "Damned if I won't – take some of what I've been cheated of . . ." He began to pull her towards him, and she kicked out at him, terrified by the violence she sensed inside him.

"Baas Gerrit!" With relief, she heard Mwende's voice, and saw that she had entered and was grabbing Gerrit by the arm. "You leave Nonnie Petronella alone – "

"Out of my way, *fokken kaffermeid*!" he bellowed, sending Mwende sprawling with a jerk of his elbow.

Petronella's fear had left her and she was consumed now by nothing but fury. "How dare you!" she raged at Gerrit as Mwende picked herself up and scuttled into the bedroom to attend to the two babies who had begun to scream. "How dare you insult Mwende like that, or talk to her in that way? Insult *me* if you like, but whatever you have sunk to, Gerrit du Toit, in *my* house you will treat Mwende with the respect which her people and ours have always had for one another, in spite of the fact that they are black and servants – "

"*Respect!*" Gerrit laughed with a dull, bitter sound and sank down into a chair, resting his elbows on the table and taking his head in his hands. After a while he began to speak with searing passion.

"You live in the forgotten past, Petronella. You are protected from reality here on your bit of land far away from the cities. The kind of respect you are talking about has been destroyed. Go to Johannesburg and discover what 'respect' will be shown to you as a Boer. Address anyone in Afrikaans and even if he can understand you perfectly well he'll tell you to 'talk white' and call you a Dutch bastard to your face. Line up with other Boers and with blacks at the Labour Bureau for hours, hoping to be given menial work in a factory or in roadmaking or even in sweeping the streets. And then sit there as some superior Englishman tells you you don't qualify for the job because you can't 'speak white', you can't speak English, and watch him smile and offer the same job to the black man behind you who cannot speak English either, but often cannot speak anything but his own tribal tongue and Fanakalo. So don't talk to me about 'respect', Petronella. There is none left in this country for Boers; the British have never forgiven us for forcing them to continue a war which disgraced them in the eyes of the world, and they are taking their revenge by reducing us to rubbish and by encouraging the blacks, whom they themselves despise and openly call ignorant Kaffirs, to treat us with contempt. So why the hell should I be expected to have respect for anyone when I am denied even the self-respect of being able to earn a miserable living for Driena and myself?"

Petronella did not know what to say, because she only half-understood the conditions he had been describing. "Where is Driena?" she asked after a while.

Gerrit looked up. "Living on our wagon in a poor-white settlement outside Johannesburg. She ekes out an existence for the two of us by making embroidered pillow-shams and taking them from door to door, trying to sell them to rich English bitches, who more often than not insult her by giving her hand-outs of money or food instead of allowing her a little dignity by buying what she has to sell. That is what I have been reduced to, Petronella – living on what my sister can earn or be given as charity. I have no respect left for myself, so why should I give it to others?" He reached in his pocket and brought out a bottle, waving it at her and showing his teeth in a travesty of a grin. "And if you are wondering where I got the money for the brandy-wine, the answer is that I stole it from the pocket of the last man who gave me a lift on my way here. *That* is how completely my self-respect has been destroyed."

"I'll get you some breakfast," was all Petronella could think of to say, and she was relieved when he put away the brandy-wine. He was obviously on his way to Jakkalsdrif, and it would grieve and shock Mamma and Pappa if he arrived there drunk. But as she dished mealie-porridge on to a plate and poured out coffee, she remembered that he had asked her where Marcus was, and it began to seem that Jakkalsdrif had not been his destination after all.

"Why did you come here, Gerrit?" she asked.

"I tried for a job in the mines. I'd heard about a Boer called Dieter Steenkamp who had managed to find such a job, and I went to see him, hoping he could put in a word for me. He wasn't able to help me." Impotent rage blazed in Gerrit's eyes. "Immigrants had been brought in from England; people who'd had nothing and *were* nothing in their own country, Dieter says. Now they live in luxury in Johannesburg and the wives offer Driena charity and each husband is a 'baas' in the mines or elsewhere, looking down upon Boers who can't 'speak white', and hiring only what they call Kaffirs and treat like dirt."

Gerrit took a swallow at his coffee as if trying to swallow his own anger. "Dieter Steenkamp knows you, Petronella," he went on, "and his wife has been corresponding with you, and he told me you had written to his wife Jakoba that your husband is planning to buy the van Tonder farm. I came to ask him – " Gerrit broke off, banging his fist on the table. "God Almighty, that I should have been forced to come and ask a favour of *him*! But I came to beg him to consider buying my farm, Bulspruit, instead."

Petronella looked helplessly at him. "Marcus is away at the moment, Gerrit, but he will be home at the end of the week. I shall speak to him about the matter. And – I am sorry to hear how things have been for you and Driena."

"Are you?" He stared at her, and she knew what he was thinking. If she had not broken her promise to marry him, life would have been different for himself and his sister.

When he had finished his breakfast she offered him water in which to wash, and he did not look quite so disreputable as he set off to walk to Jakkalsdrif. He would not be able to wait for Marcus's decision at the end of the week, but would have to begin making his way back to Driena as soon as possible. Petronella promised to write to Jakoba, giving her Marcus's answer to pass on to Gerrit.

But when Marcus did return to the *pondok*, and Mwende and Tina left to sleep in their own hut in the *stad*, and Petronella put the matter to him, he was non-committal and would only say, "We shall see." She put the misery of Gerrit behind her, for to dwell on it only brought her feelings of helplessness and guilt.

For the previous three nights, Abel had been sleeping through until the morning, and even when colic had woken Tina up the night before, so that she began to cry, he had slept through the noise.

But that night, just as Marcus had kissed and fondled Petronella into her usual pitch of frenzied desire before he began to pleasure her, the child woke up and started to scream. Marcus moved away from her and said, "You had better see why he is crying, Petronella."

She got out of bed and lit a candle so that she could investigate whether Abel needed changing, or whether he was suffering from wind. But he was dry and clean, and his screams did not seem to indicate pain of any kind. This was confirmed when she replaced him in his cradle and he grew quiet as Marcus leant out of bed to rock the cradle. By the time the baby had fallen asleep both Marcus and Petronella were too tired to do anything but fall asleep also.

And so it continued on almost every following night. Petronella tried to contain her irritation, fatigue and frustration and told herself that Abel cried at night because he sensed that Mwende, to whom he had become attached as he was not attached to his mother, no longer slept in the *pondok*, but had removed herself from his presence.

But the inevitable result of the baby's nightly crying was that Marcus became reluctant to initiate any love-making and when he did, and Abel began screaming so that Petronella would have to rock his cradle to quieten him, Marcus would often get out of bed and go and sit in the kitchen to read his learned books by candle-light, and very often he became so engrossed in them that he did not return to bed at all.

Because Mwende still had to arrive at the *pondok* at dawn each morning to feed Abel, and stay until his evening feed, Petronella could not complain about Marcus taking his wagon and mules out each day to preach and sell wares on outlying farms. There simply was not enough room in the cramped *pondok* to accommodate Marcus as well as two women and two babies, with one of them needing privacy for breast-feeding. So, even though Marcus was now spending the nights at the *pondok*, Petronella did not feel that she was any better off than when he was lodging with Willa Moller.

But at last the day came when Mwende announced it was time both Abel and Tina were weaned. She would suckle each baby for a few minutes and then sit down to feed Tina pumpkin mashed with gravy, leaving Petronella to do the same with Abel. But whereas Tina accepted semi-solid food placidly, Abel regarded it as an affront and he screamed almost continuously, and such food as Petronella succeeded in shovelling into his mouth he promptly spat out. One day her spirit cracked and she lowered Abel to the floor, cradled her arms about her head and sobbed hysterically.

"You try too hard, Nonnie," she heard Mwende's voice when she became quieter. "You too nervous, and you make him nervous also. I think it easier if I take Abel to *stad*, and wean him there with Tina for a while. You need good rest, and when you feel better, you send for him."

With gratitude and relief, Petronella grabbed at the offer. She watched Mwende carrying both babies away from the *pondok*, strapped to the sling about her waist, and carrying supplies of mealie-meal and condensed milk for them, and felt as if a huge and increasingly intolerable weight had been lifted from her shoulders.

Now that Abel was being cared for by Mwende in the *stad*, Petronella insisted that Marcus stay at home during the day, and whenever the guilty thought entered her mind that it was time for her to send for Abel to come home, she would tell herself: Tomorrow I'll do it, or perhaps the next day.

In the meantime she and Marcus behaved again as they used to when they were first married, and absorbed only in each other. At these times it was possible for Petronella to forget altogether Marcus the preacher, and she told herself that she had imagined that look she had thought she had seen in his eyes in Doornboomstad, that look that had seemed to say he was believing in what he preached. She dismissed it altogether when she suggested that they ought really to start ploughing their piece of land and get ready to sow mealies, and he responded, "It would be a waste of time and trouble, Petronella. When I purchase the van Tonder farm or that of Gerrit du Toit, all our seed and all our energy will have to be used in working that land."

She was about to ask him whether he had reached a decision as to which of the two farms he meant to buy when they were interrupted by the arrival at the *pondok* of Koos. His face looked gaunt with grief and he had been weeping.

"Nonnie Petronella," he gasped. "You must come! Your – your – "

"Pappa!" she cried in anguish. "Pappa has been taken ill – ?"

"No, Nonnie. No. Your Mamma – the Oumies – she fall down dead."

As Petronella stared at him in dumb shock, the stupid thought came into her head – Mamma would not have *fallen* down dead. She would have had to be dragged down by force, fighting every inch of the way.

20

It became more and more impossible to think of Mamma as being dead. That defiant, indomitable old woman – no, she would not have allowed herself to succumb to what sounded, from Koos's description, like a heart seizure. Feeling frozen, her teeth chattering, Petronella allowed Marcus to support her with his arm about her waist as they walked to the house of Jakkalsdrif, with Koos flanking them and weeping again.

All the servants from the *stad* were lined up outside the house, the heads of the men bowed, the women's aprons covering their faces in the traditional gesture of grief.

Petronella hesitated outside the door of the house. Mamma had said she would never be allowed to set foot inside it again while she was alive. A spasm tore through Petronella. But Mamma was no longer alive, they said. No, there had to have been a mistake. It must have been Pappa – poor, frail, sickly Pappa – who had died of a heart seizure.

Even when she heard Pappa's weeping coming from the parlour Petronella could not fully believe that it was Mamma who had died. She shook her head when Marcus tried to guide her inside the parlour, and left him to go and speak to Pappa while she made her own way to the kitchen.

Masadi was there, Mwende's mother. She was weeping as she stirred a foul-smelling mixture on the cooking range. "What happened?" Petronella asked through numb lips.

Still weeping, Masadi explained that Mamma had simply collapsed. One moment she had been alive, and the next she was dead. She had not complained of pain or of feeling unwell beforehand.

No, Mamma would not have complained. If she had had a pain, she would have kept it to herself, and taken a dose of her own *bossiemiddels*. How furious she must be, wherever she now was, to have been robbed of the chance to get at her *bossiemiddels* . . .

"What had she been doing before she – collapsed?" Petronella asked.

"Making soap, Nonnie Petronella." Masadi indicated the cauldron of evil-smelling mixture on the stove.

A picture rose in Petronella's mind of Mamma going from tent to tent in the concentration camp, ordering everyone to save the fat from their meat ration, because she had some caustic soda and would use it to make soap so that they would all be able to wash themselves at last. Caustic soda which she had smuggled into the camp in case she needed to use it as a weapon . . .

Something cracked inside Petronella, like ice breaking after a long winter. "Where – where is she?" she whispered.

"Come. I take you."

With Masadi's hand on her arm, Petronella moved to the bedroom which Mamma had shared with Pappa. She had been laid on the bed, a sheet covering her. Masadi removed the sheet from Mamma's face and Petronella stood looking down at her.

Death had not diminished her, or made her seem vulnerable. She did not look dead at all, but merely as if she were taking a well-earned rest before tackling another daunting task, and it was not until Masadi pulled the sheet away completely and Petronella saw that Mamma was dressed in her *doodsklere*, the dress of black bombazine for her burial which she had insisted on making as soon as they had settled into Jakkalsdrif again after the war, that Petronella at last accepted reality.

But at first, grief took the form of illogical fury. "You've left off her corset!" she rounded on Masadi. "Mamma would never have gone anywhere without her corset, let alone to her – "

Her voice caught, and she sank to her knees beside the bed, covering her mother's cold, calloused hand with her own and sobbing, "Mamma, Mamma, how could you have died without forgiving me? Oh Mamma, how could you have been so cruel?"

She continued to sit there, saying Mamma's name over and over again, promising not to allow her to be buried without her corset, when Marcus came and drew her gently away from the room, and took her to see poor Pappa who was dazed with shock and grief.

At last, when Pappa had sufficient control over himself again, he said, "Marcus has agreed to hold the funeral service."

"*No!*" Petronella almost shouted, with revulsion in her voice. "Pappa, how could you? Marcus, of all people? It would be – it would be *indecent*. She would never accept Marcus in life. I know she was hard and unforgiving, but – " Petronella began to weep wildly again. "Oh no, Mamma, I won't allow Marcus to bury you! *I won't.*'

"Petronella." Marcus's hand groped for hers. "There is no one else. *Dominee* Schalk cannot do it, and the day after tomorrow your Mamma must be laid to rest. It is too far for a Dutch Reformed minister to come in time. I am all there is available to do it."

"*No!* It would be an insult to Mamma! I am sure she would far sooner be buried without any service at all than – "

"Petronella," Pappa interrupted in an unsteady voice, but with an authority which could not be denied. "She was your mother, but she was first and foremost my wife, and – and I wish her to have a Christian burial. Marcus is not the preacher she would have chosen, but he is all we have, and – and he will conduct the service, and there is an end to the matter."

Petronella ran from the room, and in what had been her bedroom since she was a little girl she flung herself down on the bed and wept. Marcus came to sit beside her, but he did not speak until she had grown calmer.

"I am sorry, Petronella," he said quietly. "About your Mamma, and about having to hold the service for her burial. I think, where she is now, she will be laughing just a little at the irony of it all."

Petronella swallowed. It was indeed possible to imagine Mamma laughing grimly at the knowledge that there was no one to bury her but 'the Jew'. But Mamma would not laugh at all at the kind of service which it was likely to be unless Petronella prevented it, and she said in a hard voice, "Marcus, many of the people in Doornboomstad, your followers, knew Mamma and they will wish to attend the funeral. Understand this – I will not have an accordion or a fiddle or a trumpet played at Mamma's funeral. I will not have people drowning your voice with their own personal prayers. You'll keep the service simple and dignified. Just a short sermon, then the burial service, a prayer and the singing of one simple hymn – 'Safe in the arms of Jesus'. Is that clear?"

"It will be as you say," Marcus agreed. "She did not like me; she would not have approved of the Reformed Evangelists, and I will not insult the memory of your Mamma by making her burial a service for my followers. Trust me, Petronella."

And indeed, she found during the harrowing period which preceded Mamma's burial that Marcus was a rock upon which both she and poor, devastated Pappa were leaning, for he took all the arrangements upon his own shoulders.

He it was who drove to Doornboomstad and returned with a coffin. No fresh flowers of any kind were procurable, and he bought, instead, several glass domes containing arrangements of artificial flowers. Petronella thought Mamma would have considered them a senseless and tasteless waste of money, but she herself conceded that Marcus was doing his best under very difficult circumstances.

The servants from the *stad* dug Mamma's grave in the family burial plot some distance from the house. As Petronella had predicted, people from Doornboomstad arrived in droves for the funeral, and so did neighbours from outlying farms. This large turn-out said much for the respect in which Mamma had been held, for times were hard, farms were remote and transport slow and cumbersome, and coming to pay their last respects meant a real sacrifice on the part of those present.

Welcoming them as they arrived and offering them refreshment diverted Petronella's mind temporarily from her grief. The women all asked to see Abel, to whom they referred without exception as Baby, and perhaps because of the occasion, it struck her for the first time why it was the custom not to refer to and often not to think of an infant or young child by its given name. Who knew whether or not that child would survive? And if it did not survive then its Christian name, by tradition a family name, would have to be bestowed upon the next-born child of the same sex. Far better, she supposed, to grieve for anonymous Baby, rather than have one's feelings harrowed over and over again later by remembering him through his namesake . . . Oh, the Boers were a practical people who armed themselves in advance against sentiment. But one lost Baby could be replaced by another Baby, while a Mamma lost, an estranged, unforgiving Mamma . . .

Petronella swallowed hard and blinked the tears from her eyes and busied herself with pouring more coffee, and wished the ordeal of the funeral were over.

A bright spring sun was shining as the long procession of people finally set out to walk slowly to the burial ground. There were four coffin-bearers; two of them sons of old friends and neighbours, and the other two were Mwende's father and Koos, representing the people from the *stad*. Behind the coffin walked Petronella, supporting Pappa, with Marcus on the outside. They walked very slowly and solemnly, followed by the long cortège of other mourners.

True to his word, Marcus kept his address short and simple. He spoke of Mamma's reputation, and of the stories he had heard about her courage and her fortitude while in the concentration camp. He also admitted frankly that she had never accepted him as a son-in-law and he expressed the hope that she would forgive the fact that circumstances had decreed that he should be the one to conduct her burial service.

Petronella wept quietly as she listened to him repeating the familiar words while Mamma's body was being lowered into her grave. "'. . . for dust thou art, and unto dust shalt thou return . . .' "

After he had come to an end, Marcus bowed his head and offered a short prayer for Mamma's soul. Then he led the mourners in the singing of a slow, solemn hymn.

As the last strains of the hymn died away, Petronella turned from the grave, tears blurring her vision. Some of the mourners had begun to move away when a lone voice suddenly began to sing another hymn, one quite unfamiliar to her. She stiffened with shock and utter dismay. The words and the rousing beat and rhythm of the hymn marked it clearly as one of those Marcus had taught to his followers. Others took up the words of the hymn and then the air echoed to the sound of it issuing from dozens of throats.

"I shall live for that tomorrow,
For that near or distant morrow,
So be sure to come and meet me; I'll be there – Halleluiah!
You may expect me on that morrow,
There'll be no more pain or sorrow
As we meet again, eternal love to share!
So be sure to come and meet me,
I shall wait for you to greet me,
At the golden gate of glory I'll be there – Halleluiah!"

Petronella closed her eyes, and tried to close her ears also to the sound of the hymn. A sob escaped her, but it also held a note of hysterical laughter. She could imagine Mamma looking down on them grimly from some other plane, and saying in her implacable way, "*You* may all wait for me at the golden gate of glory, wherever that may be, but don't bother to expect *me* to be there!"

It was not the singing of the hymn with its insistent rhythm and its foot-tapping beat which had shocked and horrified Petronella the most. It was the fact that the lone voice which had started the singing of it, before it was taken up by the others, had belonged *to Pappa*.

And that meant that while on visits to Doornboomstad without Mamma, he must have attended Marcus's services. Pappa, with his stern, solemn, conventional beliefs which he had been instilling into his family and into the people in the *stad* ever since Petronella could remember, and who had once called Marcus a hypocrite.

The creed of the Church of the Reformed Evangelists, as reshaped and interpreted by Marcus, was clearly sweeping through the country district as rapidly and as inexorably as the khaki-bush weed which had also been introduced to it in the aftermath of the war, and the seeds of which had also been carried there from a foreign land.

Because Pappa was clearly in no fit state to be left alone now that Mamma, his sheet-anchor, was dead, Petronella and Marcus accepted his plea that they should leave the *pondok* and move into the farm-house.

Petronella had very mixed emotions about this. On the one hand, she could not help feeling that by moving into the house which Mamma had forbidden her she was somehow taking unfair and dishonest advantage now that Mamma was dead. Returning to the house also sharpened her grief, for there were reminders of Mamma everywhere, and they in turn reminded her that Mamma had died without forgiving her.

On the other hand, it was a blessed relief to leave the *pondok*, with its dung floors and its wattle-and-daub walls in which all kinds of insect pests had begun to breed. It was a wonderful experience to have more than two small, basic rooms in which to live, and to be able to share Johannes's old room with Marcus. Best of all, she told herself, was the opportunity to remove Abel from the *stad* and instal him in what used to be Petronella's bedroom where he slept soundly through the night, but only if Mwende put him to bed in his cradle. At last Petronella could encourage Marcus to pleasure her without him being inhibited by the fear of waking up the child.

Abel would still not accept food from Petronella, and so she arranged for Mwende and Tina to occupy what used to be called the *stoepkamer* in the days when there had been a stoep, before the British had burnt it. The room which had led off the stoep had been used as a domestic store-room, but now it was furnished as a bedroom so that Mwende could be at hand to care for Abel as well as for Tina.

But surely, Petronella told herself, now that they were not all cooped up together in the austere two rooms of the *pondok*, or with Mwende weaning Abel in the *stad*, she and her child would begin to respond normally and naturally to each other. It was only a question of being patient. When Abel had been totally weaned, Petronella assured herself, she would take over the care of him from Mwende.

It was only gradually that she realised returning to Jakkalsdrif had also meant the end of her dream of turning Marcus into a farmer. There could be no question now of their buying either the van Tonder farm or Gerrit's, for Pappa could not be left alone on Jakkalsdrif, and it was inconceivable that he would agree to leave the farm where he and his father had been born and where Mamma lay buried, and go to live elsewhere with Petronella and Marcus.

The obvious answer occurred to her one night as she lay in bed with Marcus, and she said with all the diplomacy she could muster, "Pappa is becoming old and frail, Marcus. He ought to be sitting back and resting while a younger man takes charge of the farm – "

Marcus had obviously understood what was in her mind, for he interrupted with a sound of derision. "You believe your Pappa would agree that *I* become the master at Jakkalsdrif? He has Koos and the other men to do the hard work, and he has his own ways of deciding matters. He knows that I am not a farmer. Do you think he would be willing to sit in the sun in his chair, and allow me to make decisions of which he would almost of a certainty not approve?"

"So," she asked in angry defeat, "you are proposing that we should carry on as we did before, with you preaching and selling while we live under Pappa's roof, with never a hope of owning a home of our own?"

Marcus caressed her cheek with his fingertips. "I have it very much in my mind that we should one day own a home – *Jakkalsdrif*. Out of respect for your Mamma, how could your Pappa feel morally justified in allowing you to inherit the farm when his end comes? A wife's property is also that of her husband, and would your Mamma have wished *me* to inherit a share of Jakkalsdrif? Your Pappa and I are agreed on the matter, Petronella. He will continue to make decisions as before, and see that work is done in a proper manner by the men of the *stad*. I shall buy the farm from your Pappa over the years."

"I see," she said bleakly. "And of course, you will earn the money with which to pay Pappa by continuing with your selling and your preaching?"

"That is correct. It is sensible, and it is what both your Pappa and I feel will be for the best."

Petronella tried very hard to come to terms with the frustration of her failure to wean Marcus away from his church and turn him into a farmer instead. There were no plausible objections she could make to any of his arguments, and she knew it must be a secret relief to Pappa not to face the dilemma of leaving Jakkalsdrif to her in his testament, knowing Mamma would have objected, or of disinheriting his only remaining child.

In the end Petronella decided to accept matters instead of pointlessly trying to change them. It was not impossible that Marcus would, over the years, develop an interest in farming and in the meantime she would try to tolerate his church and attend occasional services, instead of regarding the Reformed Evangelists as a sinister threat.

After all, the love between herself and Marcus was as strong as ever, their pleasuring as passionate and intense as it had always been, and his religion could not take that away from her.

She was helped in her decision to bow to fate by the fact that life was so much more tolerable now that they had left the miserable *pondok*. Moving to Jakkalsdrif, Petronella told herself, had benefited Mwende as well. It had removed her and her almost-white child from the silently condemning eyes of the other servants, and caring for the two children had given a point to her life.

Instead of their previous emptiness, Petronella's own days were now full while Marcus was away, preaching and selling. There was the house to run, servants to oversee, Mamma's garden to tend. And most of all, there were clothes to be made for Abel. Petronella had given Marcus a list of the materials she wanted, and while he was away from home she spent every free moment in fashioning new garments for her son, often staying up until midnight to work by lamplight. The jackets and baby-dresses she made for him had their tops exquisitely smocked, and the little bonnets were trimmed with embroidery. She often thought what a pity it was that the war had put an end to the former habit of leisurely visits between neighbours, and that everyone was far too busy trying to scrape a living from their farms to pay calls, because she would have enjoyed having other women admire the beautiful clothes she spent so much time in making for her son. Sewing, embroidering, smocking, knitting and crocheting for him gave her a sense of fulfilment, and she felt more content and at peace than she had for months.

It was doubly hurtful, therefore, when Pappa remarked one day, when he saw Mwende going outside to feed the hens with Abel toddling next to her and holding on to one side of her skirt while Tina was gripping the other, "You neglect that child of yours, Petronella."

"How can you say that?" she demanded with passion and disbelief. "Does he look neglected? Have you ever seen anything more beautiful than that smock he's wearing? I almost ruined my eyesight, doing the fine embroidery on its front!"

Pappa looked uncertain of his ground now. "It's just – Well, it seems to me that Baby believes Mwende is his mother, Petronella."

"What nonsense, Pappa! It isn't Mwende he follows about, but his little playmate! Do you want me to banish Tina from the house, and have him moping and crying, with no one at all to play with?"

"No, of course not." Pappa gave her an uneasy glance. "But *you* never play with him . . ."

She threw up her hands. "When am I supposed to find time to play with him? I have my hands full with the house and the kitchen garden, not to mention making clothes for him almost non-stop! And do you imagine he would prefer me to Tina as a playmate even if I had the time?"

"That isn't what I meant," Pappa persisted stubbornly. "Marcus plays with him when he is at home."

"He unsettles him, you mean!" Petronella contradicted her father vigorously. "Marcus over-excites the child. Whenever he has 'played' with Baby as you put it, it takes Mwende ages to calm him down again and make him go to sleep. That isn't the kind of play Baby needs – being bounced into the air, or tickled, or carried about shoulder-high. So please, Pappa, don't criticise me over matters that you don't understand." He looked so crestfallen that her voice softened and she patted his arm. "When Baby grows a little older, you can start taking him around the farm with you."

Pappa's face cleared. "I could teach him about crops, and make a farmer of him."

Petronella nodded, and the subject was closed. No one else suggested that she neglected Abel, for how could they, when he was so obviously happy and healthy and looked so smart in all the little outfits she made for him and insisted Mwende change the moment he dirtied them. She would have defied anyone to find a better cared-for child of his age in the district.

One night, after Marcus had pleasured her, he was stroking Petronella's body with his usual loving tenderness, and he murmured teasingly, "You are getting fat, *mein tiere*."

"I am not!" she cried indignantly.

But the next day, when she shut herself in their room to have a bath, she explored her body with her hands, and looked down at herself. She *was* putting on weight. She had not noticed it before, because she had become so thin after Abel's birth that her blouses and skirts had hung loosely on her. She shrugged. It was no doubt because life was so much more relaxed than in the *pondok* that she had put on a little weight.

But she continued to grow noticeably plumper, particularly around the middle, and her breasts also became fuller. The cows which Koos had saved from the British while they had still been heifers had just calved for the second time, and Petronella decided that she would stop taking so much cream with her porridge and in her coffee.

Marcus arrived home from a visit to Doornboomstad one day, with a letter for her from Jakoba. "I have not written to you for some time, Petronella," the letter began, "because I have been rather busy. I have just given birth to our first child, a beautiful little girl! Dieter and I could not decide what to call her, for he wanted her named after his own mother, Susannah, while I wanted her called after mine, Sarah. So we have compromised and put the two names together and we are calling her Susarah. I had almost despaired of ever having children at all, and I did not even know for several months that I was pregnant, for I had none of the usual early symptoms – "

Petronella allowed the letter to fall into her lap, and stared into space, her mouth dry with shock. Her monthly flow, which Mamma had called Eve's curse, had been erratic ever since Abel's birth, and so she had not been alarmed when, after it had disappeared and reappeared unexpectedly several times, she had not been visited by it at all for the past months. And because she had suffered none of the sickness which had made her so wretched while she was expecting Abel, it had never entered her head that her increased girth could possibly have anything to do with another pregnancy.

The thought of a second baby gripped her with panic and wild rebellion. She said nothing to anyone, hoping against hope that she might still be wrong, that her monthly flow would appear at any time. But then, with a sense of doom, she felt the baby quickening inside her.

Marcus had taken her increasing size so much for granted that it did not occur to him, either, that she was not merely putting on weight. "Your Mamma was a big woman, Petronella," he teased, fondling her belly, "and your figure is maturing to be like hers."

She pushed his hand away and dissolved into tears, burying her face in the pillow. "Aai, Petronella," she heard Marcus protest, "I did not intend any criticism. I love you – big, small, any way at all. You are the wife of my heart, and that cannot be changed by anything – "

"I'm – I'm having another baby!" she wailed.

He was still for a moment, and then he forced her to turn and face him. "When?"

"I don't know," she admitted miserably. "There were no early symptoms to warn me. It could be in as little as two months' time."

"Another child would be good, Petronella." He hesitated for a moment. "For you, for me, for our son. Especially for him. We did not do right by Baby, Petronella. Life was hard for us when he was born, and so – you allowed him to become more a child of Mwende than of your own."

"How dare you say that?" she cried angrily. "Does Mwende stitch her fingers to the bone, making clothes for him? Baby likes to be where Tina is, and since Tina is always with her mother – "

"It will be better for him to be with a brother or sister of his own," Marcus interrupted. "Another baby will be better for all of us."

No, it won't, she thought inconsolably. I'll have all that misery again; trying to feed him or her and being rejected, the constant screaming and sleepless nights, the heavy burden of guilt . . .

She caught herself up on that last thought. She had no reason at all now for feeling guilty about Abel, who was healthy and happy, and for whom she had just finished making an extremely ambitious coat for next winter.

She turned her attention to practical problems. "Marcus, I don't know when this new child will arrive. And there is no one now to help me. We are miles away from the nearest *Ziekentrooster*, and you may not even be at home when I go into labour."

"Tomorrow, my Petronella," Marcus soothed, "we shall drive to Wolmaransstad, you and I. I shall take you to a doctor there, and he will examine you and discover when the baby is to be expected, so that we may be prepared."

It was no more than a slight consolation to Petronella. They set out early the next morning, with Marcus taking care to avoid the holes and bumps in the road so that Petronella would not be unduly jolted in her seat. They arrived in Wolmaransstad by late afternoon. The town had changed little. The same furrows still ran along either side of the wide main street to carry away waste household water and to act as storm-drains during the increasingly rare times of torrential rain.

The doctor was a young man with a superior air, and even though he was a Boer called de Bruin he insisted on addressing them in English.

It had been a long time since Petronella had had occasion to speak English, and she stumbled over her words as she started to explain to him her dilemma. She stopped suddenly, and asked in Dutch, "Why must we speak English? You were probably born in this town, and can speak Dutch as well as I can!"

"My dear Mrs Koen," he replied in English, "you are right when you say I was born in this town. But I do not intend remaining here. I have hopes of practising in Johannesburg. And the truth is that no one in this country has a future unless he can speak English fluently. Indeed, Dutch – or Afrikaans as some call it – will soon have disappeared in all but the most backward areas, for Lord Milner is expected to bring in legislation which will force all children to be taught in English. So my wife and I have been speaking nothing but English for some time, in order to encourage our children to forget the Dutch language altogether."

"Is that so?" Petronella retorted furiously, in Dutch. "I am glad you told me, Doctor de Bruin. From now on I shall not allow one single English word to pass my own lips! Dutch to be stamped out, is it? After the pledges written into the Peace Treaty – "

The doctor interrupted briskly. "You are not here to discuss politics, presumably. Mr Koen, if you will wait in the office outside, I shall examine your wife."

Petronella's anger and indignation were swamped by depression at the reminder of her new, unwanted pregnancy. She lay down on a leather couch and tried to think of mundane things while this doctor, whom she already disliked, examined her for a reason of which the outcome could not possibly bring her any cheer.

His news was worse than she had expected. Not only was the baby due in six or eight weeks' time, but it was lying in the wrong position, and there was also a possibility of premature labour. She would need a qualified midwife on hand from now on until the birth, and he could recommend one who would no doubt be prepared to accompany them to Jakkalsdrif and stay until after the confinement. He did not, he added delicately, recommend relations between Petronella and her husband in the meantime.

She wept miserably as she went to join Marcus, and told him what the doctor had said, and handed him the address of a midwife, but she did not mention the matter of a ceasing of 'relations'.

Marcus kept a comforting arm about her as he took her to a small, unpretentious hotel where he asked for a room for them for the night. He left Petronella there while he went to visit the recommended midwife, to enquire whether she would be prepared to return to Jakkalsdrif with them.

When Marcus joined Petronella at the hotel later, he said the midwife, a childless widow, was quite prepared to return to Jakkalsdrif with them and that they had come to an agreement about her fee. She would be ready to leave in the morning after she had consulted Doctor de Bruin about Petronella's case. Knowing that the midwife, who called herself *Mrs* van Vuuren, would also be told that there were to be no 'relations' before the birth, Petronella used every feminine wile, every seductive trick she possessed that night, and Marcus pleasured her in a way which she knew would be the last for a long time, and on the memory of which she would have to survive for more than three hungry months.

Mrs van Vuuren was another Boer who had decided to obey the new masters and 'talk white' only. She was a large, bossy woman, and Petronella wished wistfully that Mamma had still been alive, for she would have annihilated this superior, know-it-all woman who persisted in speaking only English as she laid down the law to Petronella even before they had left Wolmaransstad. Petronella refused steadfastly to respond in anything but Dutch, and Marcus supported her by doing the same.

But after they had arrived at Jakkalsdrif, and they had explained the situation to a bewildered Pappa, Marcus took Petronella aside and said, "My love, since English only is to be taught in schools from now on, then you and I must also make the decision to speak nothing else in front of our children."

"No! I would have been perfectly happy to speak English if a law was not to be passed forcing me to do so! I shall not speak a word of English to anyone until I can do so by choice."

He did not pursue the subject, and she settled down miserably to await the birth of a second child who would throw her newly ordered life into chaos, and who was also adding to her troubles by inflicting

Mrs van Vuuren on her, a thorn in Petronella's side from the very first. Not only did she repeat the doctor's edict against 'relations' but she made sure it was enforced by insisting on Marcus leaving the marital bed and asking for a spare bed to be brought into the room for herself so that, she explained smoothly, she would be on hand to attend her patient night and day.

Petronella's only faint pleasure, in the weeks that followed, lay in manoeuvring the midwife into situations in which she was forced to address herself to Mwende or one of the other servants in the Dutch which had been her mother-tongue and which she now wished to deny.

Even in advanced pregnancy, celibacy came hard to Petronella, and as before she took her frustrations out on Marcus. She felt particularly affronted because it did not seem to matter nearly as much to him, and he was quite content to sit and pore over his learned books when he came home after preaching and selling.

When he tackled her again about the wisdom of speaking English in the presence of their children in future, stressing that he wished them to receive all the benefits of education, she rounded on him.

"You mean, so that they may be able to understand all those clever books of yours which I am too stupid to make head or tail of?"

"No," he answered quietly. "To have a son who makes something of himself – a doctor, perhaps, or a lawyer – that is what I want. And if English alone is to be taught in schools – "

"When they change their minds about English only being taught," she retorted relentlessly, "I'll start speaking English."

As Doctor de Bruin had predicted, Petronella did go into early labour, but it was not a difficult birth and the baby assumed the right position at the last moment. It was another boy, and in spite of being born a few weeks early he weighed almost seven pounds, and he was quite healthy. The great tidal wave of adoration Petronella had expected to sweep over her did not materialise, and she was forced to accept that she possessed no strong maternal instincts, but with this baby at least she felt a sense of contentment.

Mrs van Vuuren proved her worth after all, for she helped Petronella from the start to feed the baby, and there were no problems as there had been with Abel. Petronella would feed him and lay him down in the wooden cradle which had been passed on from Abel, and he would usually sleep until it was time for his next feed.

Three days after his birth Mrs van Vuuren was ready to return to Wolmaransstad. Because Marcus did not want to leave Petronella and his new son so soon, it had been arranged that Koos would drive the midwife home, and while Marcus was outside, giving him last-minute instructions on the handling of the mules, Mrs van Vuuren entered the bedroom to say goodbye and to deliver a few parting comments to Petronella.

"Have you decided," she asked, straightening up after a critical inspection of the baby, "what you are to call him?"

Marcus had, once again, wanted the name to be Joshua after his father, and once again Petronella had refused to consider it. In the circumstances, she did not think it would be fair if she insisted on calling the baby after her own father, and so they had compromised on the name of Pappa's father, which had been Dirk. But before Petronella could tell Mrs van Vuuren what they intended calling the baby, she added, "If you'll take my advice you'll give him an English Christian name. Koen could be pronounced as Colne, and it would stand him in good stead later on."

Petronella was about to announce, on the spot, that they had decided to call the baby Karools, which could by no stretch of the imagination sound English, when the woman went on, "If you'll tell me the names you've chosen for Baby, I could register his birth for you and save you the trouble of doing so by post."

"Register the birth?" Petronella echoed blankly.

The midwife gave her a taunting smile. "The Dutch equivalent of the word is not so different from the English that you can play your favourite game of pretending not to have understood!" She shrugged. "However, please yourself. It would have been quite easy and convenient for me to register the birth in Wolmaransstad, but if you want to go to all the trouble of sending away for the forms, filling them in and then posting them again – "

"No, please," Petronella interrupted, making her voice as conciliating as she could. "We'd be grateful if you would do it for us." Registering a birth was obviously some complex new regulation which had recently been introduced.

Mrs van Vuuren nodded briskly and sat down, fumbling inside her capacious hold-all for a pencil and writing paper. As she wrote she muttered aloud, "Place of birth . . . date of birth . . . father's name . . . mother's name . . . infant's sex . . . infant's name – " She stopped, looking questioningly at Petronella.

"Dirk."

Mrs van Vuuren continued writing and when she had finished she put her notes away and stood up. "I had better leave you now. The driver will be waiting for me. Remember, drink plenty of liquids and avoid eating strongly flavoured food. What you eat and drink will affect the baby's feeds."

"I'll remember," Petronella said, glad to be seeing the last of the woman.

At the door, Mrs van Vuuren paused suddenly. "I forgot to note down the father's occupation. Does your husband describe himself as a pastor, or as a travelling salesman? What did he put down the last time?"

"The last time?" Petronella echoed blankly.

"After your first child was born," Mrs van Vuuren said, enunciating her words with a sarcastic slowness which implied that if Petronella wished to pretend to be stupid, she would be treated accordingly. "When, by law, you sent details of the baby's sex, name, date of birth, and so on, to the Registrar of Births and Deaths within a month after he was born."

Petronella was about to blurt out the fact that she and Marcus had been unaware that this law was in existence at the time, but she stopped herself. Mrs van Vuuren was not a woman to whom it would be wise to confess a misdemeanour committed in ignorance.

"Marcus described himself as a farmer," Petronella lied instead, "because that is what he eventually intends to be."

Mrs van Vuuren nodded and left the room, and a few minutes later Petronella heard the sound of the mule-cart driving her away from Jakkalsdrif. Soon afterwards, Marcus came to join Petronella.

"So," he remarked with satisfaction, "we are rid of the woman – "

"Marcus, listen. She told me something I hadn't known about before. There is a law that says we should have registered Abel's birth within a month after he was born. She is going to register Dirk's birth for us, but we shall obviously have to do something about Abel – "

"*Oy a broch!*" Marcus interrupted with a terror she had never known him to betray before. "What a calamity! Such a disaster, and so unexpected . . ."

"Calamity?" she echoed, frowning. "A disaster? Surely not – "

"This means trouble, Petronella, and of the worst kind! We have violated the law. No, *I* have violated the law, for I am the husband and it is my duty to take responsibility for such matters."

"But you didn't know about this law, any more than I did!"

"Petronella, it matters not at all that I acted in ignorance! For me even a small transgression means that records will be scrutinised to discover if I have previously violated a law!"

"Well, you haven't!" she said impatiently. "You're making a big fuss over what is surely a minor matter. You will have to go and see someone – a *landdrost*, I imagine – "

"They are called magistrates now," Marcus put in abstractedly.

"Very well, then, a magistrate. Explain that we didn't know Abel's birth should have been registered. The worst that could happen would be that you'd have to pay a fine."

"You do not understand at all, Petronella! It is *not* the worst that could happen! And it does not help at all that Marcus Koen has not previously violated the law – *because Marcus Koen has no previous existence!*" He made a gesture of despair. "Marcus Koen was born during the war, and it is known that he was a Jew who fought for the Boers. The authorities here will have no difficulty in discovering that Marcus Koen, who claims he was born in Holland, is also Mordechai Cohen who was sentenced to death as a spy, but then exiled for life. Here there will not be the same problems as in Bermuda to discover to which country I belong – "

"Which country is it, Marcus? You've always been vague about it." If she could change the subject slightly, Petronella was thinking, he might begin to see the matter of failing to register Abel's birth in its true perspective.

Marcus gave her a blank, unseeing look. "I was vague because the matter of *der heim* – my homeland – is itself vague. My birth took place in Germany, but does that make me German? I do not know. My father's country was Poland and my mother's Lithuania. They were forced to remain in Germany and await my birth before they could continue the long journey to South Africa. But Petronella, wherever the authorities decide *der heim* to be, they will send me there when they discover that Marcus Koen is also Mordechai Cohen!"

"You're talking nonsense! The very idea is ridiculous! Good Lord, one would think you'd murdered someone, instead of failing to register a baby's birth!"

"My crime, Petronella, does not matter! If they investigate my past they will discover that I am an undesirable alien! Have you forgotten what I told you of matters in Bermuda? Of how they refused to allow me to take the oath of allegiance to the British Crown because I had spied for the Boers, and had been sentenced to death before it was changed to exile for life?"

"But that's in the past! Besides, how could they possibly connect you with Mordechai Cohen? Why should they even *want* to dig into your past over such a trifling matter?"

"I dare not risk it! I must not give them cause to investigate me!" He slapped his palm against his forehead and began to pace the floor, his features cast in lines of strain and acute anxiety. "If only the midwife were not already on her way, and with the intention of registering Dirk's birth! We could otherwise have registered both children together ourselves, and recorded them as being twins . . ." He shook his head in despair at such a lost opportunity.

He made an abrupt movement towards the door. "I shall go outside, and walk for a while, and consider what should be done about this very dangerous situation."

A long walk, Petronella thought, would restore his sanity, and force him to acknowledge that he had been seeing danger where none lurked. She fed the new baby and replaced him in his cradle, and she had just settled herself against the pillows again when Marcus returned to the room.

"I have decided what must be done," he announced with resolution.

"Go and see a magistrate, and explain – "

"No, Petronella. Dirk will be registered by Mrs van Vuuren and will appear to be our first-born son. That is a fact we cannot, we must not, change. In the meantime we shall do nothing about Abel. Then, when a year has gone by, we will register him as our second-born son."

Petronella stared at him in disbelief. "Pretend Abel was born almost two years after his actual birth?"

Marcus stooped and clasped her hands in his. "It is the only way, Petronella. The only safe way for me – for us!"

"It would never work!"

"It would," he insisted in a way that said he would make it work.

"Marcus, people know that we already have two children, and that Abel was born first!"

"And do you imagine anyone remembers the given name of our first-born son? By Boer custom, we and others have spoken of him only as Baby, and other than Mrs van Vuuren, who is not of this neighbourhood and does not count, only your Pappa knows that our second son is to have the name Dirk. But your father does not leave Jakkalsdrif these days to visit Doornboomstad. And who comes here to visit, Petronella, and to remember in the years to come which brother is the elder? So many of the neighbourhood farms are deserted and derelict since the war, and on others people have to work too hard for a living to make calls here, even to see a new baby."

Petronella stared at him in silence. No, people would not call to see the new baby, any more than they had called to see Abel. Like so many other social customs, that one had been killed, or at least suspended, by the war. Life was too hard, the struggle to survive too time-consuming for such niceties. Only for a funeral would they make time.

"When the two boys have reached the age for the blessing ceremony of the Church of the Reformed Evangelists," she heard Marcus go on, "people will think no more than that Abel is large and advanced for a child of three. In the years between, Petronella, we will make sure, you and I, that we avoid people from outside Jakkalsdrif seeing the children together."

She bestirred herself to repeat helplessly, "It would never work!"

"It would, and it must! Only you and I know of the matter of the registering, so what cause would people have to be suspicious if we handle things correctly? From now on, when I speak of my sons to others, I shall speak of Dirk and of Baby. That, also, would be following custom. With the years that pass, Petronella, if we always treat Dirk as our first-born son, who will there be to inform the authorities that it is not so? Who will know that it is not so?"

"Pappa will know – " she began.

"Your Pappa is old and frail, and more and more now he forgets things and becomes confused. Also – forgive me for speaking the truth – he cannot have many years left to him. In the meantime we shall not trouble his mind by telling him anything. His age, and his inclination since your Mamma died, makes him wish to live a solitary life here on Jakkalsdrif, and he will present no danger."

"What about the servants?" Petronella demanded. "What about Mwende?"

"Mwende will honour any promise you ask of her. As to the other servants – they do not have sufficient curiosity about our babies to remember, in the years to come, who was born first."

Petronella was unable to think of anything more to say for a moment. Were it not for the iron-hard resolve with which he had been speaking, she wouldn't have believed that Marcus was serious about the fantastic deception he was proposing. And all over such a trivial matter! He was well enough known in the district as Marcus Koen, a Dutch-born Jew who had fought with the Boers and was now the revered founder of the Church of the Reformed Evangelists. Why should anyone wish to dig into his past?

"Marcus," she pointed out at last, "if we did this crazy thing, we could land in worse trouble! Say I were to have a third baby in the meantime? Or even a few months after Abel had been registered? The entire deception would become known!"

"There will not be a third baby to cause such dangers for us. That we cannot risk." Marcus's voice and his expression were implacable. "We shall sleep apart, Petronella, with no pleasuring at all until the birth of Abel has been registered." He stooped, and kissed her forehead. "You look exhausted, and I shall leave you now to rest."

It was not exhaustion from which she was suffering, but a bruising disbelief. She lay there after Marcus had left her, unable to take in at first the full meaning of what he had said.

It was only slowly that she began to face what it would mean. Her physical appetite for Marcus had not diminished with the years; instead, it had sharpened. The most she could hope for would be to persuade him that Abel should be registered after ten months, instead of a year. That still left an average of three hundred nights of bleak celibacy staring her in the face. *He* would be able to endure it; he would fill the emptiness by writing his sermons and reading his learned books. *She* would have nothing but growing frustration. She could not even comfort herself with the thought that she would be able to seduce him into abandoning such self-imposed restraint. Misplaced but totally sincere terror of being unmasked as Mordechai Cohen, an illegal, undesirable alien, would render him quite impervious to any blandishments on her part.

But what haunted her most, and shattered her completely when she forced herself to face up to it, was the knowledge that their marriage would never again return to normal afterwards. As she grew more and more frustrated and resentful and shrewish, he would take refuge in his preaching and make it far more important to him than she had ever been. At last she understood the instinct that had always made her fear Marcus's preaching. By the time Abel's birth had been registered, she would have lost Marcus to the Church of the Reformed Evangelists.

At that moment Abel came toddling into the room, staring at her with wide eyes which had lightened now to grey. She couldn't remember him ever before willingly leaving Mwende and Tina and seeking her out. Why had he chosen this moment to attract her attention?

"Get out of my sight!" She hadn't meant, consciously, to scream at him and she listened with surprise and shock to the echoes of her own wild, uncontrolled voice hanging in the air. The new baby had woken up and had begun to cry. Abel continued to stare at her and she evaded his eyes by reaching for the baby.

Mwende ran into the room. "I hear you shouting, Nonnie – "

"Take Abel out of here. He disturbs the baby."

"Nonnie," Mwende said bluntly, "you treat this child of yours like he is a stray dog!"

"That's a lie! How dare you say such a thing?"

"Because it true. You think because you make for him more clothes than any small child can wear you a good mother to him. But you not. You throw Abel away, and you try to hide what you do by making for him more and more clothes."

Petronella opened her mouth in furious denial, but the words stuck in her throat. Oh God, it was true. She could no longer bury her real feelings about Abel, stifle them and cover them over with excuses and hide them behind exquisitely stitched garments. When had she stopped trying to love this child of hers who had never given the slightest sign of wanting love from her?

She looked at him, and tried desperately to dredge up from somewhere warmth and affection for him. Instead, she found herself remembering how he had come between her and Marcus ever since his conception. Because of the sickness he had caused her, she had been prevented from going to Johannesburg with Marcus. It was during that first long separation that preaching had begun to claim its hold over Marcus. And with each subsequent separation, also caused by Abel, that hold had strengthened until he had grown to believe his own sermons. Now, during the long months ahead, she would lose Marcus entirely to his religion.

"Take – take Abel away," she commanded Mwende, and turned her head into the pillow and began to weep with bitter despair.

Mwende shook her head, and carried Abel out of the room, and took him to where Tina was playing in the sand outside the house. The little girl rose unsteadily to her feet and toddled towards them, and as Mwende put Abel down the two children hurried to meet and to link hands.

Mwende sighed. It was lucky, perhaps, that the little outcasts had each other for company and mutual comfort. The unloved, thrown-away son of Nonnie Petronella, and her own light-skinned daughter who was spurned by the others in the *stad* and always would be.

A tingle of fear, of foreboding, passed down her spine. They would grow up together, these two little outcasts, but the instincts of her own ancestors who used to 'smell out' witches warned Mwende that witches lay in wait for Abel and Tina in the future.

Part Three

21

Abel squatted on the floor in a corner of the stoep, mending a harness. His bare legs stuck out below his faded, outgrown short trousers, and when a spasm of cramp shot through one of them he shifted position and then let out a yell. The summer sun had been baking down, not only on him but also on the cement floor of the stoep, and moving to another spot had been like sitting down on the kitchen range just as Mwende was getting a good fire going in it.

He thought fleetingly of taking himself and his materials around the corner to the shady part of the stoep at the front of the house, where the wrought-iron table and chairs and benches were, and then dismissed it. Nothing would be more likely to bring him to the notice and arouse the fury of *die Vrou* – the Woman.

Although she was his mother, if he had ever thought of her as Ma, let alone called her that in the way his brothers did, he could not remember it. In the same way, he thought of his father as *die Man*. In spite of the fact that they were as much his parents as they were the parents of his brothers Dirk and Simon, there seemed to Abel to be an unbreachable barrier between them and himself, a barrier that would not allow him to think of them as Ma and Pa. So in his mind they were simply *he* and *she*, or more often the Man and the Woman. Since he only ever spoke to them when it was unavoidable – to answer a question put to him, say – they had probably never noticed that he did not address them by any title. There had been a time, when he was younger, when Abel had sometimes thought that if only the Man did not go away and stay away from Jakkalsdrif so often, he might have begun to think of him as Pa, and so gradually also of *her* as Ma. But by now it was too late.

Mending the harness in the shade of the front stoep would make a mess, he decided, and there would not be time to clean it up before they returned from Doornboomstad with his elder brother Dirk and his younger brother Simon. The reason given to anyone who asked why Abel did not go with them on Sundays was that he was needed to keep an eye on the farm. The real reason, he had worked out for himself a long time ago, was that the Man and the Woman did not want him, had never wanted him, and were afraid people would realise this if they all appeared together as a family.

The four others had left early this morning, as they always did on Sundays when the Man was at home, so that he could preach to the villagers from the pulpit of the Tabernacle of the Reformed Evangelists. Once they reached home, lunch would be served on the front stoep with its highly polished red surface of which the Woman was so proud.

The building of the smart new cement stoep to replace the wooden one which the British had burnt, Abel knew, had been bound up with the building of the Tabernacle in Doornboomstad –

His thoughts were interrupted by Tina, who had appeared around the corner of the stoep with a white damask cloth in her hands. "I lay the table now," she said. "Soon your Ma and Pa and brothers come home, so you should go wash, Basie Abel."

He stared at her without responding. He had always accepted the fact that something about him set him apart and made him different, inferior, so that he had to work on the farm from morning till night while Dirk and Simon went to the farm school a mile away and spent their afternoons as they wished. The thing that made him different must also have had to do with the fact that Tina had been his playmate when they were small, until Mwende had suddenly put a stop to it by moving out of the *stoepkamer* and going to live in the *stad* with her daughter, and she had chased Abel away when he went looking for his playmate.

When Tina had emerged from the *stad* a few years later and started helping her mother with the lighter household chores, she had called him 'Basie' and there had been a shy awkwardness between them. He had tried to make a playmate of Dirk instead, but every time the two of them fought over something the Woman always took Dirk's part and slapped Abel, and gradually Dirk had become aware of his own favoured status so that *he* instigated every game, *he* made the rules and always declared himself the winner. The two of them had never been equals as playmates in the way Abel and Tina had been equals.

Tina was certainly different too, with her almost-white skin and her long, curly dark-brown hair, and her uncle Koos had told Abel with deep disapproval in his voice that it was because she was a *basterkind*. For a time he had believed that he, too, must be a *basterkind*, but Mwende had been shocked when he'd asked her and had told him it was not so. That was all she would tell him. He had stopped questioning the matter of what it was that set him apart and made him an outcast, because there was no one who could or would give him answers.

When hair started growing in his armpits and on his chest and around his private parts, while none appeared on the bodies of Dirk and Simon, Abel had decided with sick certainty that this was the visible evidence of what made him different from others. He could remember the self-disgust which had added to his acceptance of his own general lack of worth.

But then, about two years ago when Dirk was thirteen and Abel twelve, Dirk had started strutting about naked in the evenings when the Man was away and the Woman safely in bed, showing off his newly sprouting body hair to his brothers, and talking about the girls at school and bragging that Nella Venter had said his thing was the biggest she had seen yet, and that she had allowed him to put his hand up her knickers and feel between her legs. Simon had turned pink and said he was going to tell Ma, and in the next breath he'd wanted to know what it felt like inside Nella's knickers, but Abel had been concerned only with the fact that Dirk also had hair in secret places, and far from hiding it in shame he was bragging about it. Dirk, of course, had friends and went about with other boys at school, so he knew what was normal and what wasn't.

Abel had just been coming to terms with the knowledge that the difference in himself must lie elsewhere, in some deeply shameful thing that he had done without being aware of it, when Oupa died.

Memories of Oupa threaded through Abel's mind as he continued working on the harness. Something had happened to the old man; Abel was not sure what it had been exactly, or when it had taken place. But almost for as far back as his memory stretched, his grandfather had seemed to him to be three-quarters dead, and for years the quarter that remained alive had been lifted from his bed each morning, and propped up in a chair where he sat with spittle running from a corner of his mouth, his eyes empty and the colour of watered milk, his head shaking like the reeds by the river when the August winds blew. If Oupa had been a horse or a dog, Abel thought dispassionately, he would have been given a bullet between the eyes years before and put out of his misery.

When that last quarter of Oupa had died and been buried with the long-ago-dead remainder of him, well . . .

Abel lifted his head from his work and stared with hard eyes into the distance, remembering the day of Oupa's funeral a year ago and the quarrel that had followed it – a quarrel that had begun to colour Abel's long acceptance that he had somehow deserved his fate and must bear it uncomplainingly, and added to it a burning, unexpressed resentment.

Everyone at the funeral had cried for Oupa; everyone but Abel. He could remember crying only once in his life, and that had been when he was very little. Mwende had been cradling Tina on her lap and Abel had tried, jealously, to pull himself up on to it as well. At first Mwende had seemed content to allow it, as she usually did, but then she had suddenly pushed him away and said, "I not your Mamma, Abel! You go sit on your own Mamma's lap!" Weeping, confused, he had gone to look for the Woman, seeking confirmation that she *was* his Mamma.

"Don't call me that!" she had screamed at him. "There was only one Mamma, and she is dead!" Then the Woman, too, had begun to weep and Abel's sobs had mingled with hers for it seemed then that he had no Mamma of his own and the only one who had ever existed was dead, and he was somehow to blame for it.

So he hadn't wept for Oupa, and when one of the mourners from Doornboomstad discovered that he was one of the Koen boys he'd said reproachfully, "I can see that you're the eldest, but one is never too old to weep for the loss of someone he has loved." Abel had stared blankly at the man. Love was a word in the Bible, like faith and hope, and none of them had anything at all to do with him. So he had merely explained that he wasn't the eldest but just the tallest and strongest.

The Woman had cried more than anyone else at the funeral, but Abel had noticed that she'd spent less time at Oupa's grave than she had at the one beside his. But the next day her grief had turned to rage when Oupa's testament had been taken from inside his Bible.

Abel had been sitting against the side of the barn, sorting mealie-seeds, when the Woman and the Man had entered it for their quarrel. He supposed they had failed to see him there, even though there had been many other occasions when he might have been invisible as far as they were concerned. The Man usually avoided looking at him or speaking to him, as if he were a shameful secret one would sooner pretend did not exist. The Woman also ignored him when the Man was at home; it was during his long absences that Abel had to watch out for himself, because she seemed to blame him for everything that went wrong, almost as if it were his fault that the Man had gone away.

Abel couldn't understand why she hated the Man's absences so much, because when he was at home they quarrelled most of the time, usually at night when they were in bed, and their low, angry voices would reach him incomprehensibly. Occasionally, the next morning, her face would wear a glow and she would look quite beautiful and would touch the Man in ways in which she never touched even Dirk or Simon; running her finger along his cheek, smoothing his hair, resting her hand on the back of his neck.

Abel had overheard every word of their quarrel inside the barn.

"You lying, hypocritical bastard!" the Woman had screamed at the Man. "Making me believe you were buying Jakkalsdrif from Pappa! You must have thanked that God of yours, Marcus, the one who gives you so many excuses to stay away from home, when poor Pappa lost the power to speak and you knew your lies were safe!"

"Aai, Petronella," the Man had tried to defend himself, "above all else I desired to buy Jakkalsdrif for you. But in the beginning I could not discuss the matter with your Pappa. Your Mamma had just died; your Mamma who hated me and would not even have wished me to have a home on Jakkalsdrif. I needed time for your Pappa to finish grieving before I placed before him my proposition. But then he became ill and no longer capable of understanding business matters or signing an agreement. So what could I do? Who else, I argued with myself, is there to inherit Jakkalsdrif when he dies? Who but his only living child – you, Petronella?"

"But you were wrong, weren't you?" the Woman had raged. "I didn't get it! What I did get was a slap in the face!"

Abel, listening to them, had wondered what was to happen now that Oupa had apparently left Jakkalsdrif to someone outside the family. Presumably the Man would buy another farm somewhere, but Abel did not expect life for himself to be any different to the way it had always been. He neither understood nor shared the Woman's love for this farm on which he toiled day in and day out, and he would not care if they were to leave it.

But as the quarrel continued, he had learnt of the contents of Oupa's testament, because the Woman had read it aloud, spitting out the words. If Oupa died before his beloved wife, Helena Siena van Zyl, everything he owned was to pass to her. If he outlived her, then his beloved daughter Petronella Koen was to inherit the farmhouse and outbuildings and that part of the land which contained them, including the kitchen garden and the parcel of land where the orchard used to be. Everything else was to pass to his first-born grandson.

The Woman had kept repeating the words. "His first-born grandson. *His first-born grandson!*"

"That testament, Petronella," the Man had said, as if it would somehow soothe her, "was written when you and I were first married, and your Pappa never altered or rewrote it. It was written when we had no children at all. By law, the ownership of Jakkalsdrif now passes to Dirk."

Strangely, it *had* soothed the Woman, but only for a moment or two. "What did you do with the money, Marcus?" she had begun to rage again. "All that money you made when you were away for months, pretending to be scraping it together to buy Jakkalsdrif from Pappa?"

"I did give money to your Pappa, Petronella. Money for the support of my family, and also as a contribution towards buying many things needed on Jakkalsdrif which your Pappa could not afford."

"But the rest of it, Marcus? The money you were supposed to be banking in Pappa's name, in payment for Jakkalsdrif? Where did that money go? On all those other women who mark your holy trail of preaching and praying and whoring while you are away?"

Abel could still remember the force of the Man's voice as he roared, "Petronella, you blaspheme and you shame yourself when you say such things! I have told you again and again, there *are* no other women! The money – well, I have been saving that for the building of a Tabernacle for the Reformed Evangelists in Doornboomstad."

That had merely fanned the flames of the Woman's fury and she had been placated only when the Man pointed out that, with a Tabernacle in Doornboomstad, he would need to spend more time at home, so that he could hold services at the Tabernacle. He had also promised to use some of the money on the farm and on the house, including the building of the new stoep which the Woman had wanted for a long time. He had agreed to pigs being kept at Jakkalsdrif; they had added one more chore to Abel's daily grind and the new stoep had been built. But the Man had since sold the pigs and also broken his promise about spending more time at home.

Another reason Abel had for remembering Oupa's funeral was the fact that he had never before seen so many people together in one place. And those who were not telling one another what a wonderful man Oupa had been, were discussing Abel and his brothers as if all three of them were deaf or couldn't understand what was being said.

"I remember, Dirk was a baby when his grandmother died. Not a pretty child at all, nor a sweet-natured one."

That remark hadn't pleased Dirk at all. Then someone else had switched the attention to Abel. "Who would have thought he would grow to be so big and strong? Dirk is quite weedy by comparison. When one remembers what a sickly baby Abel was . . ."

Dirk, Abel remembered, had liked even less being described as weedy. He frowned as he recalled how the speaker had gone on, "He was so prone to infection of every kind that poor Petronella was virtually a prisoner on Jakkalsdrif during the first years of his life, when he spent more time in his sick-bed than he did out of it."

Abel had no recollection at all of being sickly, or of spending time in bed. He recalled following Mwende about and begging to be allowed to play with Tina, so how could he have been sickly? He shrugged. The speaker must have confused him with Simon, who had continued to be called Baby until he was five years old and who was always whining about some pain or other and going about with a running nose.

"Basie Abel!" he heard Tina calling again. *"Kona manje!"*

Her use of Fanakalo had emphasised the need for him to hurry and get ready for lunch. He remembered suddenly how Mwende had taught both of them Fanakalo, and it struck him for the first time that Tina had not been considered, even by her own mother, to be worthy of being taught Zulu. Fanakalo, it seemed, was good enough for a *basterkind*.

He shrugged the thought of Tina aside and stared at the horizon, which was streaked with the red dust of an approaching conveyance. He left the harness, cursing under his breath, because he had hoped to finish mending it this morning. There was a missing ewe for which he had to search this afternoon.

Dirk's ewe, he thought bitterly, on *Dirk's* farm – even if the place was dying on its feet. The only small comfort for Abel lay in the fact that Dirk did not know the farm belonged to him. The Woman must have persuaded the Man not to tell him, and as true as God Abel did not intend telling him either. Locked in this strange, secret conspiracy with the Woman, Abel guessed that she could not bear to admit the fact that Jakkalsdrif, for which she had such an irrational love, had not been passed on to her.

He washed under the pump and went into his bedroom to change. He put on a clean shirt and his best pair of trousers, and thought how ridiculous he looked, at least six feet tall and still wearing short trousers. Fifteen-year-old Dirk, over whom he towered, looked equally ridiculous in the smart long flannel trousers which had been bought for him at the store in Doornboomstad. Not that *Dirk* thought he looked anything but grown up and elegant and a fine, swaggering figure, of course.

Envy and resentment rose like bile in Abel's throat. As if it were not enough that he had to work his guts out on Dirk's farm, he had to do so in the knowledge that his elder brother was never going to soil *his* hands with that kind of labour. Dirk had announced, just before Oupa's death, that farming was not for him, that he had no intention of burying himself on Jakkalsdrif for the rest of his life, and that he was going to be a businessman in Johannesburg when he left school. Perhaps that was what had comforted the Woman about the farm belonging to Dirk. If he became a businessman, he would not want to interfere with the decisions she had always made about Jakkalsdrif. She could have no fears that Dirk might one day decide to sell the farm, for she owned the house and outbuildings and the land immediately surrounding them, and who would want to buy a worn-out farm of which the very heart belonged to someone else?

The Man had been delighted by Dirk's decision. "If you wish to be a businessman then you must learn better English than the master teaches you in school, because it is not possible to do business in Johannesburg speaking only Afrikaans. So I shall teach you good English."

Simon, the little arse-crawler, had said piously, "I want to be a preacher like you, Pa."

"Yes, yes! My son the businessman, and my son the preacher!" The Man had not mentioned at all his son the nothing, his son the never-will-be-anything but an unpaid farm labourer.

Abel pulled a comb through his curly dark hair and stared at his face in the mirror for a moment. Mwende had told him that when he was a baby his nose had appeared to be enormous. It was still prominent, but not unduly so and seemed in harmony with his high cheekbones and firm chin. But his features did not interest him particularly; what had caught his attention was the suspicion of a moustache on his upper lip. He must be a more hairy person than Dirk, who had no such dark shadow on his face.

Abel left the room and hovered in the doorway leading to the stoep, watching as the cart stopped outside the house. The Man got out and helped the Woman to the ground, and Abel saw her leaning her body against his for a moment. But Koos appeared from the stables and the Man put her aside, and called to Koos to come and take care of the horses. Simon jumped from the cart, his Bible clutched to his chest, and went to sit on the stoep, ostentatiously opening the Bible and pretending to immerse himself in it. But Abel saw the surreptitious glances he threw to discover whether the Man had noticed. Dirk also alighted from the cart, picking imaginary pieces of fluff from his long flannels, walking in his usual strutting manner. God, Abel thought, when he learns that he owns Jakkalsdrif he'll be unbearable.

Abel waited until they were all seated on the stoep before he took his own place. He did not so much join his family as hover on the fringe of it. He remembered a stray mongrel dog that had once appeared on Jakkalsdrif. No one had wanted it there and the dog had known this, but it had learnt that if it crawled slowly and unobtrusively on its belly and remained very still, no one would kick it and somebody might even throw it a scrap or two. He was like that dog, Abel thought.

Mwende and Tina carried lunch out to the stoep. There was roast lamb with potatoes and pumpkin, and as Tina placed the bowl of gravy on the table Abel studied her with a frown.

She was roughly the same age as he was, fourteen. He knew this to be so, for he could remember the two of them competing for Mwende's attention as small children. And yet Tina had acquired the body of a woman, for he was noticing consciously for the first time the swell of firm breasts and slim thighs beneath her plain blouse and skirt. It puzzled him, just as the shadow of a moustache on his upper lip had puzzled him.

The Man was talking about the service he had held in Doornboomstad that morning. He would be repeating that service here at home this evening, for the benefit of Abel and Mwende and Tina and Koos and the few other black people who had not yet left the *stad* to find other work in the towns, and those who were too old to do so. The Woman interrupted to read from a letter she had collected in Doornboomstad, and which had been written by a friend of hers whom none of them had ever met.

"So Jakoba has another son," the Woman said. "I've lost count of how many that makes in all, besides that daughter of hers with the fanciful name – Sannamara, something like that." She gave a strange, brittle laugh. "Poor Jakoba, I feel sorry for her with her dull husband who obviously doesn't have the brains even to read a book, who spends every night of his life with her and doesn't care how many children he fathers. But then, she always was happy with very little, and no doubt she wouldn't envy me my brilliant, handsome husband who inspires people with his sermons and gives them so much of his time."

Abel had recognised the sting in her remark. But the Man pretended not to have noticed the barbed grievance about his many absences from home, and was opening letters of his own which had been collected in Doornboomstad that morning.

He threw some of them on the table, and said with triumph in his voice, "So, the matter has been agreed! Petronella, Jakkalsdrif is to become a post office!"

"*What?*"

Deep grooves of delight appeared in his cheeks. "I considered the matter, but I decided to say nothing to you until it had been approved. Licensing Jakkalsdrif as a post office will bring us some revenue from the government, but what is more important, it means that we shall be supplied with a telephone! Consider, Petronella! When I am absent from home, you and I will be able to speak to one another!"

"So I am to be content with *speaking* to you, Marcus, through some machine? Thank you, no!"

"The matter will be to the advantage of all of us, my wife! Dirk is fifteen, and soon his schooling will be completed. He will be able to learn about business by keeping account of the sale of stamps and of telegrams sent. For myself, a telephone will mean that I shall be able to learn from my connections in Johannesburg what commodities are best to buy, and when. A telephone would also enable me to discover someone who would be willing to take Dirk for training."

"And when he does leave Jakkalsdrif," the Woman demanded angrily, "will I be expected to spend my days selling stamps, sending telegrams, keeping accounts?"

The Man laughed. "Aai, Petronella, the government – like most governments – is a donkey! They do not have the sense to realise for themselves that people will wish to continue using the post office in Doornboomstad, because they have to go there in any case to shop and to have their mealies milled. Perhaps two neighbours, maybe three, will come here each week to buy a stamp or post a letter. But what do farm people know about sending telegrams, and who is there they would wish to speak to on the telephone? Doctor Lourens in Doornboomstad perhaps, but how sick must a person be before money can be spared to call a doctor? No, the post office will mean a convenience for ourselves, as well as a small profit, and when Dirk has gone I shall keep the accounts."

"When you are at home!" the Woman snapped.

"I'll keep the accounts when Pa is away," Simon said with excitement. "I would be able to speak to Frans Lourens on the telephone." He caught the Man's eye and added earnestly, "We always enjoy discussing the text of your last sermon, Pa."

Dirk also welcomed the news. "I would look a fool, trying to go into business in Johannesburg without knowing how to use a telephone."

"You will look a bigger fool," the Man reminded him, "if your English is not of a good standard. So fetch my English Bible, Dirk, and read for me the Twenty-third Psalm."

Since the official status of Jakkalsdrif as a post office was not likely to affect his own life in any way, Abel dismissed the matter from his mind but he listened intently later when his brother began to read, and he matched the English words to his own knowledge of the Psalm in Afrikaans, squirrelling them away in his mind with other knowledge he had gleaned. By picking up crumbs dropped by his brothers, by furtively studying their school books whenever he could, he had taught himself simple arithmetic; he could read simple sentences and write his own name.

It was only after he learnt that Jakkalsdrif now belonged to Dirk that he had begun to consider the matter of his own neglected education, to recall things only half-understood at the time but which had contributed to it, and to try to do something about it.

In protest against the practice that pupils should be taught only in English, parents had ignored the farm school and kept their children at home. Then the Reformed Evangelists had opened a school of their own in Doornboomstad, and found a qualified teacher to educate the children in their own tongue. But parents had to pay for this service, and the Man could not afford to send both his elder sons there, so only Dirk had attended the school.

When Abel was nine the government acknowledged defeat and agreed to fund the farm school under an Afrikaans master, Meneer Els, and it had been reopened. Already bigger and taller than any other child of his age, Abel had suffered the daily humiliation of having to sit with the seven-year-olds in Grade One, where he had been the target of everyone's ridicule. To this day he could remember the torment.

"He's all muscle and bone," Dirk had jeered, "even where his brains should have been."

When news came that a government inspector was to visit the school and test each pupil's progress, the thought of being singled out again as an oddity had been too much for Abel, and he had flatly refused to continue going to school.

Instead of being furious, as he had expected, the Man and the Woman had accepted his stand. They would, they'd said, arrange with Meneer Els to tell the inspector that Abel was ill. And afterwards – well, Meneer Els understood the problems of farmers, and he knew that Abel was not the only strong, capable son whose help was needed on the farm and who could learn more by working the soil than struggling with lessons that were beyond him.

It had been his own choice not to return to the farm school, Abel knew. But he also knew, now, that he had been too young to make such a choice at the time, and he should have been prevented from making it. He had been allowed to have his own way because he was strong and capable when it came to farm work – and because he did not matter to the Man or to the Woman. But because he had received no education he was now doomed to be a farm labourer to Dirk for the rest of his life. Until Oupa's death last year Abel had assumed that he would one day inherit Jakkalsdrif jointly with his two brothers, and that whatever work he put into the farm would ultimately benefit himself.

He watched as the lunch dishes were removed by Mwende and Tina. Simon stood up, the Bible ostentatiously clutched to his chest, and said he was going to his room to read the Gospel of St Luke. Dirk rose too, and announced that he meant to improve his English by studying the Bible in that language which the Man had lent him, but Abel thought it was more likely that both of them were going to look for the dirty bits in it which Dirk said the Bible contained. Even if Abel could read he would have had no more interest in the dirty bits than he had in the bragging tales Dirk liked to tell his younger brothers about himself and Nella Venter.

Without having spoken, without a word having been addressed to him, Abel moved away too, to the other side of the stoep to continue working on the harness. He could hear the Man and the Woman talking in low voices and he knew they were quarrelling. It seemed the Man had decided to go on his travels again, and Abel heard the Woman say, her voice rising bitterly, "Even when you are here, you spend most of your time with your nose stuck in one of your learned books, and I might just as well not exist!"

He heard a chair being scraped across the cement, and a little later he saw the Man's tall figure walking away from the house. He often did this, Abel knew, to get away from the Woman's angry tongue.

When the harness had finally been mended Abel picked it up to take it to the stables. The Woman was still sitting on the front stoep, her hands clenched together in her lap. As he approached she turned her head and looked at him. He stopped, chilled by what he saw in her eyes. It was as if *he* were entirely to blame for the Man's decision to go on his travels again. Could it be true? Did the Man go away so often because he was ashamed of Abel? What could have been the terrible thing I did, Abel wondered, the thing I don't remember?

The Woman addressed him sharply. "If you've nothing useful to do, you can come and help me to pull up khaki-bush weed."

"There's a ewe missing," he told her. "I have to search for it."

When he emerged from the stables a while later he could see her slim, energetic, erect figure walking towards the fields. He had to give her her due; she never ceased struggling for the survival of her beloved Jakkalsdrif – or rather, Dirk's Jakkalsdrif. She worked just as hard as she made Abel work in fighting the khaki-bush invasion and in trying to coax crops from the increasingly grudging soil.

It was a futile battle, slowly being lost. From the stories Koos had told him, Abel knew that this had once been fertile land, but nothing had been the same since the British burnt the grass to its roots and destroyed all the trees. It no longer rained regularly, as it used to, and when it did rain the topsoil was washed away to colour the Vaal River like blood. Planting prickly pears as hedges had been a mistake, for they took whatever goodness there remained in the soil, and each year the mealie harvest was a little more meagre than the last had been. If it had not been for what the Man earned by preaching and buying and selling they would have been forced, like many of their neighbours, to grow only subsistence crops, and they could not have supported their livestock without buying extra feed for them.

The sun scorched down on Abel as he searched for the ewe, first along the thorn trees that grew by the river and then in every other likely spot he could think of. A *meerkat* sat bolt upright on its haunches, its front paws dangling loosely in front of it, its large eyes ringed with black fur watching Abel inquisitively, and in his frustration he picked up a large pebble and threw it at the animal, which made an undignified escape.

Moodily, his shoulders hunched, Abel considered where to look next. A hot breeze was blowing, sending some of last year's dry tumble-weed scudding across the veld. Cursing the ewe, he stood still, gazing around him, and suddenly he remembered the *pondok* which stood on a hillock overlooking the house on Jakkalsdrif. It was built of wattle-and-daub, and did not look unlike the huts of the people in the *stad*, and it contained some old, crude pieces of furniture. He had never been particularly interested in it, and assumed it had once housed *bywoners* in the days when Jakkalsdrif was prosperous enough to support them. The last time he had passed the place the stable-type door had been secured, but it was possible that the wind had damaged it since then, and the ewe might have found her way inside. He began to stride away in the direction of the *pondok*. If the ewe was not there, then to the devil with her. He would tell the Woman that a jackal or one of the stray dogs in the district that had turned wild must have eaten the animal.

He was out of breath by the time he reached the *pondok*, and he stopped to lean against its wall while he cooled off a little. Movement through the grimy window caught his eye, and he went to peer through it. What he saw caused the blood to thunder in his veins and brought a dryness to the inside of his mouth. He ducked his head, so that he could look inside without being easily seen.

The Man was sitting on an old *katel* with one of his thick books open on his lap, and the Woman stood before him. Slowly, as Abel watched in hypnotised fascination, she was taking off her clothes. Her blouse lay on the earth floor and now she was removing a boned undergarment and he could see her firm, rounded breasts faintly marked with a network of blue veins etched across the whiteness of her skin.

"Do you remember, Marcus?" she was asking. "Remember the old days?"

The Man said nothing, but his hands tightened upon the book. Sweat trickled down Abel's temples as he watched the Woman slip out of her skirt, and then out of another skirt of pink silky material. Finally she was standing there naked, and for the first time in his life Abel discovered what the female form looked like in its natural state. She pulled the pins from her hair and it cascaded like a pale-gold river to her shoulders.

"Jesus," Abel whispered soundlessly. "She's beautiful. She's – " He could not supply the word he was searching for.

She was holding out her arms to the Man, enticing him, inviting him, pleading with him. "Marcus? Like in the old days?"

The Man closed the book and put it on the floor. Slowly, he got to his feet and went to her. He thrust his hands into her hair and held it up, and her fingers began to undo the buttons of his shirt. He just stood there, and allowed her to undress him, touching him and stroking him as she did so. When both of them were naked the Man picked the Woman up in his arms and carried her to the *katel*.

Abel knew that he ought to move away from the window, that if they saw him his punishment would be terrible, but a tumultuous, throbbing excitement totally unfamiliar to him kept him rooted to the spot, watching.

The Man was kissing her. Not the way in which Abel had seen him kiss her before, swiftly on the mouth. Oh no. He knelt by her side and kissed the inside of her leg, slowly, working his way upwards to her thighs, to where a triangle of short golden curls seemed sculpted to her otherwise hairless, smooth body. Abel heard her moan as the Man parted the curls with both hands and kissed her there. She locked her fingers in his hair but after a moment he lifted his head and continued to kiss her all over; her belly, her breasts, and finally her mouth. And then he moved and sat astride her and he let her stroke and caress his huge, swollen thing for a while before he allowed her to coax it deep down inside her.

Throughout all this Abel had been consumed by a thundering sensation which engulfed him in waves, and he had to force himself to bite off a cry of mingled ecstasy and panic. Jesus Christ, his own thing had exploded!

He put trembling hands to his crutch and felt wetness on his legs below the hems of his short trousers. He stifled a shout of relief. His thing was quite intact, and he had noticed sticky wetness like that before, occasionally when he had woken up in the morning with the remnants of some exciting dream still hovering on the edge of his mind. But there were always too many chores waiting for him to have wondered more than fleetingly about it.

The Man and the Woman were lying side by side now, panting. After a moment she sat up, and Abel saw that she was crying. "You can pleasure me like that, Marcus Koen, when the occasional mood takes you, or when I sink my pride and I beg you, and you expect me to believe that your sermons and your hymns and your books are passion enough for you? You expect me to believe that you never go near other women when you are away from me?"

"Aai, Petronella," the Man protested. "I do not know what it is you want. When I pleasure you, you always accuse me of false things, and when I do not pleasure you at all you also accuse and insult me." His voice softened. "Do not cry, my Petronella." He began to kiss her again and this time Abel knew that he must not, dare not, stay to watch any longer.

He hurried quietly away. But after a while he found it impossible to hurry, because of the inflamed, engorged instrument his thing had once again become. Oh God, why did *he* not know a Nella Venter who allowed boys to feel between her legs? He would do more than feel. He knew exactly what he would do . . .

A picture entered his mind, of Tina bending over the table as she set down the bowl of gravy. Because it was Sunday she would not have returned to the *stad*. She would be helping Mwende to prepare a cold supper for the household, and to sort the laundry which had to be washed in the morning.

Abel went directly into the kitchen, positioning his hands so that neither Mwende nor Tina would see the grossly extended bulge between his legs. He made his voice as matter-of-fact as he could.

"Tina, I've found some eggs in the barn. I think other hens have been laying there too. Bring a basket, will you, and come and help me to look."

Obediently, totally unaware of his excitement, she picked up a basket and followed him from the house. Once they had entered the barn he closed the door behind them.

"Basie Abel," she protested, "we do not see the eggs with the door shut."

He took the basket from her, and blurted out, "Tina – I – I want to pleasure with you. Please, Tina!"

"P-pleasure, Abel?" In her consternation she had forgotten to call him Basie.

"Yes, Tina," he whispered hoarsely. "Please – take off your clothes."

"Au! No, no . . ."

"I won't hurt you. I promise. I really, truly promise. It doesn't hurt. It's – " He swallowed, and wiped away the sweat beading his forehead. "Pleasure, Tina." He searched for more powerful words of supplication, and realising for the first time why he had never allowed himself to become excited by Dirk's dirty talk, he cut through instead to the grim truth. "You're the only girl I know, Tina. The only girl I'm likely to know. And who is there for you in the *stad*? There's no one. All the young men have gone away, and even if they hadn't, they wouldn't want you because of your white father. Please, Tina. First of all, you have to take off your clothes."

She shrank away from him. "No, Abel . . ."

He moved close to her. He could see that the waistband of her skirt fitted her too loosely, and with trembling hands he pulled up her blouse, hoping to encourage her to take it off as the Woman had done. *She* wore no boned garment underneath, and her honey-coloured breasts were immediately exposed, their dark-pink nipples erect. Unable now, in his eagerness, to copy the Man's actions in precise sequence, he took each nipple between his lips in turn, and felt her shudder, but not with fear or revulsion, and he knew he had no further need for persuasion or pleading.

He told her the order in which she had to undress, and instructed her to undress him in turn. When they were both naked he carried her to a bed of straw and this time he followed the Man's example precisely, doing all the things he had seen through the grimy window of the *pondok*. He controlled his own eagerness and bursting excitement, and Tina was now as awakened and aroused as he was himself. But after he had coaxed her to slip his rampant thing inside her, as the Woman had done, and he had penetrated the delicious soft, moist warmth of her, she suddenly cried out. When at last he experienced his own thrumming joyous ecstasy inside her, she began to weep.

He didn't know or care why she was weeping. The Woman had wept too, but in anger. He supposed weeping was a common female reaction. He was sure he had given Tina as much pleasure as he had experienced himself, but he was sure of this only because of the Woman's obvious pleasure. He did not really care about Tina's feelings, physical or emotional. What he did care desperately about was that he should be allowed to repeat the experience as soon as possible, and for that reason he held her and kissed her while she wept. He knew no endearments, so he offered her none. He did not speak of love, because he did not know what love was and all he wanted was for her to stop crying so that she would cooperate and he could experience that wonderful fulfilment yet again.

The two of them froze as the door opened. "Tina! Basie Abel!" Mwende called out. "The Oubaas is ready for holding his service – "

Her voice died as she saw them, and she stared at them in petrified horror and fear. After a moment she began to weep. "Tina . . . Abel . . . Au, Abel, *ya limaza, ya bulala* Tina *ka mina!*"

He was pulling on his trousers. "No, Mwende, no! I didn't hurt her – I didn't damage her – "

Mwende was not listening. She squatted on the floor, rocking backwards and forwards, her apron flung over her face. "Always, always in my heart – I fear this thing," she keened. "I try to warn Nonnie Petronella, but she not listen, she not care . . . To throw away her first-born son, treat him like a dog . . . That not right. Oh no, no, that not right."

Abel had finished dressing, and he went to her, touching her shoulder. "Mwende, I'm sorry, but I – " He stopped, frowning as he thought of something she had said. "Mwende, what did you mean about the first-born son thrown away and treated like a dog? Dirk is the first-born, and no one could say that he – "

"You already one year old when Dirk is born, Abel." Her voice was weary, as if she had been carrying the truth like a heavy load inside her for too long.

He stared at her, unable to believe what she had said. "You must be mixing things up, Mwende. I'm a year younger than Dirk, not older."

Mwende sighed heavily. "I cut the summers of Tina's life in a stick. They number sixteen now. She born two months before you, Abel."

"*Sixteen!* You're saying I'm sixteen, and not fourteen?"

Mwende did not reply. She stood up, and with her shoulders bowed she moved to Tina's side, and began to help her to dress.

"Tell me what happened, Mwende," Abel pleaded, still half-dazed with shock and disbelief. "Tell me why."

"I say no more. Nonnie Petronella do wrong, but – she *my* Nonnie Petronella, and I promise her I say nothing." Mwende had been speaking in a dead voice, but now she looked up and there was an implacable expression in her eyes. "If you tell her what I say to you, Abel, I tell what you do to my Tina. I tell everybody."

His heart thudded at the threat. Tina was a symbol of shame to black and white alike, and if what had happened became known he would be even more of an outcast than before –

An outcast. Everything else was suddenly driven from his mind as he took in the enormity of what Mwende had told him, and matters began to slot into place.

The Man and the Woman had been only too happy for him to stop attending the farm school, because he'd been attracting too much attention. It didn't matter with people who knew them, or with Meneer Els who would not have questioned the word of a pastor. But government inspectors were outsiders and posed a threat, and would poke their noses into people's secrets. And when Abel emerged visibly into manhood while Dirk remained a boy, the Man and the Woman had been afraid people might begin to search their memories if both brothers attended services in the Tabernacle on Sundays.

"The bastards!" he shouted. "The bloody bastards!" Then he began to run towards the house through the dusk, sprinting up the stairs of the stoep where his family were assembled, waiting for the people of the *stad* to come and listen to the Man's sermon.

He stood with his legs aggressively apart in front of the Man and the Woman, and again he shouted, "You bloody bastards! You've been robbing me all my life! You meant to rob me of Jakkalsdrif! *Why did you pretend that Dirk was born first?*"

The Man muttered something in a language Abel did not understand, and covered his face with his hands. The Woman was on her feet, and then she dealt Abel a stinging blow across the cheek. He caught her hand in his and said with menace, "Don't ever do that to me again, you bitch!"

Simon squealed that the Good Lord would surely strike Abel down, and Dirk jumped to his feet, crying, "Abel, have you gone off your head? Swearing and cursing and talking nonsense! Of course I was born first. Pa, if you won't give him a good hiding for what he has just called Ma, then I shall – "

"Try it!" Abel shouted. He raised his head, and his voice echoed through the darkening air, a violent blend of rage and bitterness and desire for revenge. "I'll beat you to a pulp, because I not only look sixteen and feel sixteen, but I *am* sixteen! And I want my stolen years back! I want what is mine!"

22

Grimly, mechanically, Petronella applied herself to the harvesting of the mealies. Reach up, twist off the dry cob, throw it as close as possible to the pile of other cobs lying on the ground, search through the khaki-dry leaves of the stalk for more cobs until it has been plucked bare, and then go on to the next plant, the next row. In other parts of the field Koos and Abel were harvesting too, and so was Tina.

The hot sun baked down on Petronella as she stopped for a moment to wipe her forearm across her brow. A chameleon, hitherto invisible where it clung to a mealie-stalk, darted out its tongue at an unwary fly and then slithered away, at one with its surroundings. Near the end of the row of mealie-stalks, she could see a secretary bird killing a mamba. Its dignity remained unruffled throughout, the feathers on its head reminding one for all the world of a clerk with his pen tucked behind his ear. If the bird had not killed the mamba, thought Petronella, the snake would probably have eaten the chameleon. It was a pity that the same harsh laws of nature could not be made to apply to human beings. If she had had the right to destroy Abel –

An old guilt, buried or smothered with varying degrees of success over the years, raised its head and forbade her to continue that line of thinking. All the same, who could deny that Abel was now destroying *her*?

Her throat tightening, she continued with her work. She knew that she had no need to help with the harvesting. The yield was so small this year that Abel and Koos and the women could easily have coped with it by themselves. But she needed the release which hard physical work brought because, God knew, she had no other means of release available to her for the chaos of anger and bitterness and hatred and frustrated passion which churned inside her.

Marcus had gone away again, and she knew he would stay away for as long as he possibly could once more, and as always it was because of Abel. This new Abel, who would not be silenced, but went on and on and on, accusing, questioning, probing, insulting, no longer wary and cowed but afraid of no one.

She remembered the bitter quarrel between herself and Marcus that night, two years ago, after Abel had hurled the truth in their faces. Marcus had paced the floor of their bedroom, muttering, "We have denied everything, but instinct warns me that Abel will not allow the matter to rest. Today he learnt a part of the truth and he will continue to dig and to question until he has learnt everything and has found proof."

"He will not!" There had been an edge of angry despair in her voice. The new start she had hoped for after their pleasuring in the *pondok* that afternoon was being destroyed, ripped to pieces by Abel and his accusations. She had tried to continue more calmly, "All that happened, as he told us himself, was that he asked Mwende how old Tina was. Because she said Tina was sixteen, and he remembers playing with the girl when they were both little, he seized on that as evidence that he is older than Dirk."

"And it *is* evidence, Petronella!"

"Nonsense! Mwende can count, but she can't do arithmetic, and almanacs mean nothing to her. She doesn't even know her own age, so why should anyone believe that she knows her daughter's age?"

"Abel will search for more evidence." Marcus's voice was sombre. "He will ask questions, and he will learn the truth."

"Who could he ask, Marcus? Who is there left who could swear to the truth? Pappa is dead, and I'm positive Koos knows nothing. He was only a boy himself when Abel was born, and he took no more interest in him than he did later in Dirk. Koos hasn't spoken to Mwende since she returned to Jakkalsdrif with Tina, so Mwende couldn't have broken her promise to me and confided in her brother."

"You and I, Petronella," Marcus said quietly, "*we* know the truth. And it is at us that he will continue to direct his questions."

"He'll learn nothing from me – " she began, and stopped, arrested by something in his expression. "Marcus, are you trying to say that you would allow him to worm the truth out of you?"

"I fear my own weakness," he admitted. "I am not like you, Petronella. You have tried to pretend, but I have always known that you have felt no love for the boy since the day of his birth. But for myself – I have the feelings of a father for my son, and I am filled with pity for him and shame for what we have done to him, while *your* heart remains cold and hard towards him – "

"Damn you, you sanctimonious bastard!" she screamed at him, enraged. "*You* were the one who insisted he should be registered after Dirk! *You* were the one who made my life a cold, lonely hell by not touching me for almost a year so that Abel could be registered as our second son! And you have the gall, now, to sit in judgement on me!"

He thrust his hand through his hair. "We are both equally guilty – "

"Like hell we are! *I* never wanted to go through with the deception! *You* were the coward who had such a senseless fear of the law that you had Dirk registered first, and kept yourself away from me! Or *was* it cowardice, Marcus? Weren't you just looking for another excuse to go off on long preaching trips? Promising men salvation in the after-life and offering women rather more earthly pleasures – "

"*Gottenyu!*" he exploded, slapping his forehead. "Always the same lies and insults!"

· "Lies, Marcus? *You* lied to *me* when you pretended you were considering buying the van Tonder farm! You lied for years about buying Jakkalsdrif from Pappa! You are an expert at lying!"

"If I lied to you in the past, it was because you drove me to it! I tried to explain that I could never be a farmer, but you would not accept it! It became easier to lie than always to argue with you, and to listen to the poison of your tongue!"

"And it is easier to lie too, is it not, about those other women? You tell me that you stay with members of your church when you are away from home. How many of those members are eager young widows, Marcus? How many have even more eager young daughters who slip into your room at night – "

He cut through her sentence with a bellow. "A wise woman, Petronella, it is written, buildeth her house, but the foolish plucketh it down with her hands!"

"Don't you dare use your sermons on me!" she cried, but he wasn't listening, for he was storming from the room to walk about outside. Much later, when he joined her in bed, he turned away from her, just as he had done so often over the years that it had sometimes seemed to her as if an invisible barrier existed in the centre of the bed which she had to storm with bitter words and venomous accusations, followed by abject advances in order to reach him.

But that night nothing could have reached him, and she lay miserably on her own side of the barrier. Very occasionally, as then, she admitted in some usually sealed-off part of her mind that she did not really believe in the existence of another woman. But somehow it was less humiliating, more acceptable, to pretend that other women were her rivals, and not a religion and learned books. She also admitted to herself that Marcus was right, and that instead of building up their relationship she was plucking it down, not with her hands but with her words.

She resolved yet again that night to control her tongue in future, and stifle at birth the angry, bitter and hurtful taunts and accusations which were forever driving a wedge between them.

When she woke up early in the morning and put her arm around him it had seemed like a hopeful sign that he did not shrink from her touch, or grow rigid under it, but held her hand in his and listened as she said, "Last night Abel was not himself. Rage gave him courage, but as I pointed out to him, we have birth certificates stating clearly and legally that Dirk was born a year before him. Abel will have as little as usual to say for himself this morning."

"Over the years we have not encouraged him to speak to us," Marcus said heavily, swinging his legs out of bed. "So perhaps you are right."

Certain that she was right, she vowed to herself. Tonight Marcus and I will make a new start. We have wasted too many years.

But only a matter of hours later that Devil's spawn, Abel, ruined everything yet again with his venom, his total fearlessness and contempt for his parents as he hurled his accusing questions at them.

Marcus stood up, his face white.

"Hypocrite!" Abel hurled after him. "You holy fraud – *who was born first?*"

When Petronella joined Marcus in their bedroom she found him packing a suitcase. "The poison of your tongue, Petronella," he said, "is already almost more than a man can endure for long. To be forced to listen also to the insults of my son – and to know *they* are deserved – no, that is too much. Perhaps, the next time I return home, Abel will allow the matter to rest."

But Abel had continued like a terrier worrying a rat, and again and again Marcus had been driven away from home after staying only long enough to hold a few services in the Tabernacle in Doornboomstad. And each time Petronella had been abandoned once again to loneliness and frustration and despair . . .

She had finished one row of mealies and was about to start on another, when she found herself face-to-face with this son of hers whom she now loathed with an intensity which frightened her at times. The question came relentlessly, and even though expected she still dreaded its never-ending repetition. "Who was born first?"

Today her control snapped. "I wish to God *you* had *never* been born!"

"You've always made that more than clear," he said, unmoved, watching her through narrowed eyes.

God, how she hated him! And – yes, feared him. It was ridiculous. He might be tall and muscular and strong, but he was only sixteen. No, she amended, remembering, he was eighteen. But even so no one could fear their own son.

She turned her back on him, and began to work on another row of mealies.

Abel stared after her with hard eyes. He no longer thought of her as the Woman, but as the Bitch, just as the Man had become the

Preacher in his mind, mentally giving the title a note of bitter scorn. The Bitch was strong, and was the one least likely to crack. The Preacher would be an easier target, but he was seldom at home, damn him, especially now that Jakkalsdrif was officially a post office and he could maintain contact by telephone.

Abel looked about him. He would not allow Jakkalsdrif to die as other farms in the district were dying, not now that he knew it belonged to him. A few times, Dirk had started boasting about the fact that Oupa had left the farm to *him*, but the menace in Abel's eyes had soon shut him up. In any case, Dirk neither loved nor valued Jakkalsdrif but was living for the day when he could leave it and go to Johannesburg to become a businessman. Abel did not believe that what he himself now felt for Jakkalsdrif was love. It was a sense of possession. Jakkalsdrif was his *right*, and he would work until he dropped to protect it and to claim it.

Grimly, he noticed a new *donga* which had appeared in the next field, where the soil had eroded away to form a shallow crater. As soon as the harvesting was done he and Koos would dig out mud and gravel from the river bed and fill it in. He didn't know whether it would work, but it was worth trying.

He turned his head and caught sight of Tina, and stared dispassionately at her. He felt nothing for her, and often he didn't bother with any preliminaries such as kisses but simply took her quickly and urgently. He knew that discovery of their relationship would lead to a tremendous scandal, that he would be ostracised by the entire district if it ever came out, and he resented more and more the fact that because of the way he had grown up in isolation he knew no other girls and came into contact with none. For a while he'd found himself obsessed with the idea of taking Nella Venter away from Dirk, mostly because she belonged to Dirk but also because a relationship with a Boer girl, no matter how lowly her status, would not bring the odium which that with half-black Tina would if it became public knowledge. And Nella Venter's status *was* lowly, for Abel had discovered that her family were among the earliest poor-white squatters on one of the farms in the district. He had called at their *pondok* with the excuse that he was looking for some broody hens to borrow. Nella Venter had turned out to be a fat, slovenly girl with lank, unwashed hair who stank of stale sweat, and from the way she had eyed him it had been clear that she did not 'belong' to Dirk but to anyone who chanced to come along. It was also clear that she was pregnant, and Dirk would have no trouble at all in disclaiming responsibility.

So Abel had returned to Tina, who was available, and obviously and thankfully barren, and who fulfilled his needs even though she irritated him by always weeping after they had finished what he no longer thought of as pleasuring, but as fucking. While Tina did well enough for the present, he continued to feel deeply resentful of the fact that he had no contact with the kind of girl whom he might one day choose to marry. He would be spending his life on Jakkalsdrif, which belonged to him – as he meant to prove – but he would need a wife. And where was he to find one, when neither the Preacher nor the Bitch had ever done a thing to help him meet any girls – not even a Halleluiah-girl who, if he had befriended her two years ago, he could have seduced away from the Reformed Evangelists. Now it was too late, for nothing would induce him to set foot inside the Tabernacle.

So in the meantime he was forced to content himself with the illicit affair with Tina. When his worst fears were realised and Mwende found out about it, he'd faced her with a defiance he was far from feeling. "If you tell about us, I'll have you and Tina sent away from here! Oupa left Jakkalsdrif to his eldest grandson, and *I'm* his eldest grandson, as both of us know!"

He had seen, immediately, that his threat had filled her with fear. "Please, Abel," she'd begged, "leave my Tina alone."

"Tell me about Dirk's birth, and I will!" he'd countered swiftly. "Why did they claim I was born two years later than I really was? And who else knows about it?"

But she pretended she could not answer any of his questions, and so Mwende was included in his hatred of those who were conspiring to keep his birthright from him.

He remembered again, suddenly, the comments that had been made on the day of Oupa's funeral; comments about himself having been sickly as a baby and during the first years of his life. So *that* was how the Bitch and the Preacher had fooled people! The story had given the Bitch and the Preacher the excuse to keep their two sons isolated on the farm so that others wouldn't realise the 'baby' was some two years older than his supposed age.

He could imagine what must have happened. If the Bitch's second child had turned out to be a girl, the deception would not only have been impossible; it would never even have occurred to her or to the Preacher. But when Dirk was born a year after Abel – Dirk, the wanted one, the loved one – they must have said to each other, "If only *he* had been our first-born". And from that 'if only' had grown the entire deception. While the Bitch remained in isolation on Jakkalsdrif with her two sons, the Preacher must have begun to refer to his eldest son as Dirk, so that even those who had previously been told the first-born had been named Abel would have become confused and decided they must have been mistaken. Who, after all, would disbelieve a man of God, a pastor? By the time people were allowed to see his first two sons the difference in their ages would not have been so obvious.

Abel's jaw set. He would find out the truth; the whole truth. His best hope was to break down the Preacher. He, Abel sensed, felt deeply guilty about the matter, a feeling the Bitch did not share. But the Preacher never stayed at Jakkalsdrif for long enough nowadays to give Abel time to wear away at that guilt, and his long telephone calls had given no hint as to when he would be coming back this time.

Almost as if Fate were on his side, Abel saw the cloud of dust on the horizon. From the speed with which it was travelling it could only be a motorised vehicle, and it was too early in the day to be the mailvan. It was therefore the Preacher, returning in the truck which he now used for his buying and selling and his wandering preaching. No one else in the district was able to afford more than a cart and horses or mules.

Slowly, with mounting excitement, Abel saw a way in which to break down not only the Preacher, but also the Bitch, and in a short space of time at that. Why in the name of hell had he not thought of it before? It was so damned obvious!

He hurried to where she was standing, a look of yearning and hope on her face, as she too watched the dust cloud travelling towards Jakkalsdrif.

"The Man of God is coming home," Abel said.

She made no answer, and tried to pass him, but he stepped into her path. "His congregation in Doornboomstad will be expecting him to stay for long enough to preach a few sermons. Every time I take mealies to Doornboomstad to be milled, people ask when he'll be back. They don't think much of the lay-preacher he left in his place."

"Since you announced that you no longer regard yourself as a member of the Church of the Reformed Evangelists," she returned coldly, "I don't see why the subject should interest you."

"Oh, but it does. I have been thinking for some time of attending a service in the Tabernacle in Doornboomstad."

He enjoyed the wary, nervous look she was giving him. "Why?"

"Why not?" he shrugged. "*You* attend the services when you have to, pretending to be a good pastor's wife, but you don't believe in any of that stuff that goes on in the Tabernacle."

He saw her flush. "What is brewing in that evil mind of yours, Abel? I'll make sure that you aren't allowed inside the Tabernacle!"

"The services are free, to be attended by anyone, and it doesn't take long to reach the Tabernacle by mule-cart. Why are you so afraid?" he mocked her. "Now that Dirk has grown that stupid moustache which he thinks makes him look so grown up and dapper, people aren't likely to compare the two of us and decide that I must be the first-born."

She moistened her lips. "If it's not to spread that wild story of yours, then why do you want to attend a service in the Tabernacle?"

"It's the Attesting they do at the end of the service that interests me. The bit where everyone confesses to some silly little sin or other. I have been waiting for some time now to confess to a sin of my own which is not in the least silly and will be remembered forever hereabouts."

"Con-confess?" the Bitch echoed in bewilderment and obvious dread.

God, it was a good feeling, playing with her in the way a cat plays with a mouse! "Yes," he said. "First of all, I want to bare my soul and explain why I have not attended a service in the Tabernacle for so many years. Oh, don't worry; I won't say anything about the fact that *I* was growing a moustache at a time when Dirk's face was still as smooth as a girl's, so that you dared not take me with you for the two of us to be compared. No, I'll explain about the past two years, and the matter which preyed so much on my mind that I decided I could gain peace only by attending a service and confessing what I did."

The Bitch's tension had visibly increased. "The last two years . . . If you imagine that, by confessing how you have made our lives a misery with your accusations for two years, you'll be offered evidence of some kind – "

"Oh no, nothing like that! I want to confess to the congregation how I watched through the window of the *pondok* as you took off all your clothes, and begged and pleaded with the Man of God to – I believe the Bible calls it fornicating, so that is the word I'll use. I want to describe every single thing I saw the two of you doing, and ask to have my mind put at rest that what I saw were normal and natural acts between married people."

He watched her reaction with triumph and elation, and went on, "My problem, you see, is that I have only Dirk's stories to judge by. As the so-called eldest, he thinks he's an expert on the subject, and he's always talking about it to Simon and me. But I've never heard him talk of any of the things the two of you were doing that day in the *pondok*."

Petronella felt as if all the blood was seeping from every vein in her body, and for an instant the field spun around her. With a strenuous effort, she gathered some semblance of control, and held herself ramrod straight as she walked past him. *"Tell the truth about who was born first!"* he called after her, and she knew this time it was a threat and a condition, and not a demand.

Her very soul shrivelled at the thought of him standing by the *pondok* window and watching her and Marcus. She had reason to remember with vivid clarity almost everything that had occurred between them, because it was the last time anything remotely like it had happened. What pleasuring there had been since then had been grudgingly performed only to stop her bitter tongue, like scraps thrown at a yapping dog to gain a few minutes' peace, and had been almost mechanical on Marcus's part. To have had *anyone* witness what had become a treasured memory, an intimate scene like that, would have been debasement enough. For that someone to be Abel . . .

The new, unafraid, malevolent, relentless Abel would carry out his threat. He *would* stand up before a congregation and confess to having watched his parents; he *would* describe in detail what they had done. But the confessed sin of having spied on his parents would be totally lost in the congregation's horror and revulsion as he described the details of what he had seen.

The ways in which Marcus pleasured her when it was not a grudgingly performed act to buy peace had, from the very beginning, bound her to him with strong, almost unbearable bonds. But they were not Boer ways; they were alien ways contradicting everything the Bible said about denying the temptations of the flesh and corrupt acts. She had no doubt whatsoever that the congregation would regard everything Abel described as perversions, just as he had hinted they would. And what would be considered the grossest perversion of all, she knew, was the fact that she and Marcus had behaved in such a way in broad daylight, not in the privacy of their bedroom but inside a *pondok* where they could be watched by their own son.

Everything in her life was disintegrating. For a moment, watching Marcus's truck approaching, hope had been kindled in her heart, and she had told herself that this time she would not greet him with angry accusations and bitter reproaches. This time she would seduce him carefully, subtly, so that he would brush aside Abel's accusations and taunts as mere irritations, and he would stay on Jakkalsdrif. Now what hope she had been clinging to had been swept into an abyss by this son whom she had never wanted and who had set out to wreck her life ever since his conception.

Marcus would never be able to bear the disgrace that would follow upon Abel's 'confession'. His life would lie in ruins. He would not consider retiring quietly to Jakkalsdrif, working the land and facing the scandal with her. It was not because of selfishness or cowardice, but apart from the fact that he was not and never would be a farmer, she knew from long and bitter experience how necessary his religion had become to him.

He had woven into it strands of Judaism, such as the ban on eating pork which he had introduced some years ago, and even the modest churches which had sprung up everywhere in the Transvaal to which the word of the Reformed Evangelists had spread, were given the Hebrew name of Tabernacles. Marcus could never go back to being a Jew, but the Reformed Evangelists were the substitute for the Jewish roots he had been forced to destroy, and preaching its gospel was as necessary to him as breathing.

So, Petronella knew with a terrible certainty, Marcus would leave Jakkalsdrif for good this time, and lose himself somewhere far away where scandal could not follow him and where he could start again, establishing his Church of the Reformed Evangelists and making converts. It would be impossible for him to take his family with him, for Jakkalsdrif could not be sold, since it legally belonged to Dirk, and Dirk was a minor. Besides, even if it could be sold it would fetch little, too little to support all of them for long. No, she would have to stay here, with Abel who would go on doing everything to make her life an unbearable hell, and with Dirk and Simon, all of them existing on the proceeds of what the farm produced, the money which the post office brought in, and such sums as Marcus could afford to send from time to time. Total devastation was staring her in the face, the irrevocable loss of Marcus.

Gradually, common sense began to assert itself as she realised that Abel had nothing to gain but revenge if he were to make his 'confession' with reckless disregard for its timing. Abel might be out for revenge, but what he wanted most was to be acknowledged as the first-born and the heir of Jakkalsdrif. He was no fool, and he would not throw away such a powerful hold over his parents by telling his story to the Tabernacle's congregation in their absence. He must know that without the reaction of shame and guilt on the faces of Marcus and herself to confirm the truth of his confession, no one would believe it. So all Marcus had to do was avoid holding another service in the Tabernacle in Doornboomstad, or anywhere else within easy reach of Abel.

The knowledge brought scant comfort, for she recognised it would mean that Marcus would be going even further afield from now on. He would continue to buy from one farmer and sell to another, preaching as he carried on his business, sending money home and telephoning her, but their separations would last longer and longer, and they would be strangers when they did meet; she hostile and he guarded and wary and already planning how soon he could leave again.

Even now the line within her between love and hatred was often blurred where Marcus was concerned. It was his fault that they were in this dreadful situation, with Abel possessed of such power to use against them. If it had not been for Marcus's exaggerated, illogical terror of breaking an insignificant law, they would not have broken a bigger one and falsely registered Abel as their second child. And now, instead of staying and helping her to cope with the situation, Marcus would be withdrawing once again to find release and fulfilment in preaching and praying. *And other women?* An angry inner voice prodded at an old and self-inflicted wound. For her, there would be no release or fulfilment anywhere.

Without consciously having set out for it, she found herself at the family graveyard, and she knelt beside Mamma's grave, her arms resting on the headstone, her head sunk on to them.

"Oh Mamma, Mamma, my life has gone so wrong, and you would say, *I told you so*, wouldn't you, Mamma? I don't know what to do, and I'm afraid of the future, Mamma. Oh Mamma, help me . . ."

Her voice died in a wretched little sound halfway between laughter and a sob. Mamma had died without forgiving her and hadn't acknowledged her as a daughter during the last years of her life. Why should Petronella expect that hard woman to reach out to her from beyond the grave and offer her comfort and possible answers?

She stood up, and began to walk towards the house where she could see Marcus standing beside his truck. Abel was watching her from the edge of the mealie-fields, his arms folded across his chest, knowing that he had won. As she approached Marcus she felt the hopeless anger knotting her muscles, her bitter, corrosive greeting already trembling on her tongue and beyond her control.

But this time she was given no opportunity to voice the words. Instead of the wary tension with which he usually faced her after one of his long absences, the grooves danced in Marcus's cheeks and his eyes sparkled as he swept her into his arms, cutting off what she had intended to hurl at him with a kiss. Not one of his meaningless, public kisses, either, but one which held an eager desire she had almost forgotten in him. It threw her totally off balance and drove everything but physical awareness of him from her mind.

He released her, and said, "It is necessary for us to talk, Petronella, so come with me to our bedroom. I have a great deal to say to you, but first I must tell you that I have met again in Johannesburg a cousin of mine. He is the son of my late father's brother, and I have stayed with him and with his family for many weeks."

His cousin. His *Jewish* cousin. Oh, thank you God, she thought light-headedly. Marcus is to become a Jew once more. They have forgiven him. No more Reformed Evangelists, no more fear of Abel's threats. I shall take instruction, as Marcus once wished me to, and

I'll light candles, and learn to make that funny plaited bread, and all the other things . . .

Marcus sat down on the edge of the bed and drew her down beside him. "My cousin Reuben and I held long, intimate discussions, and he revealed to me how I should put matters right with you. I confided fully in him, and he persuaded me to accept that it is my fault that you and I always fight more than we love."

He took her hand in his. "Petronella, our difficulties began after the birth of Dirk, when I slept in a separate room and you and I became like hostile strangers. For me, the easy way was to go away, to buy and sell and preach. But for you there *was* no easy way, and I failed to appreciate this. Then, after we registered Abel as our second child, something else happened, Petronella. *Guilt.* You did not experience it, I know, but for me it was always present, and it still is. Each time I look at Abel I am filled with shame. So more and more I have been going away, because I could not bear to look at the son in whom I should feel pride, but whom I cheated instead – of everything, including an education. All this, Petronella, was what I felt even before Abel discovered that he is our first-born and began to ask the same question over and over again, until I felt he would drive me insane if I did not leave Jakkalsdrif quickly once more."

Abel, she thought. Always it had been Abel who had taken Marcus away from her. Even at times when she had not remotely suspected him to be the direct cause.

"So a pattern was created, Petronella," Marcus went on. "I would go away, and each time I returned you raged at me, insulted me, accused me. Between you and Abel I could think only of leaving yet again. I understood why the situation existed, but I did not know how to change it – until my cousin Reuben showed me the way."

She waited breathlessly for Cousin Reuben's magic wand to be waved and for Marcus to be restored to her.

"What I have to do first of all, Petronella, is to make compensation to Abel and present him with a future, so that he will no longer care who was born first and he will leave Jakkalsdrif – "

"Oh God, thank you! What is this compensation that will take him away, Marcus?"

"I shall tell you about that later. Most importantly, I must stop travelling. One of Cousin Reuben's many businesses is a sale-room for motor cars. He is willing to teach Dirk, and afterwards allow him to manage the business, so that Dirk will also have a good future – "

"Marcus," Petronella interrupted, "how will you explain to Dirk that you have a first cousin named Cohen? Surely it would be dangerous to admit the relationship? It is not in Dirk's nature to be discreet – "

"Cousin Reuben and I discussed that also. My parents, I shall say, before coming on to South Africa settled in Holland, where they changed their name to Koen. It is something that happens commonly with Jews, for convenience."

"I see."

"So," Marcus continued, "with the departure of Abel and Dirk from Jakkalsdrif, I shall remain here from now on. I shall take over the management of the post office, and consider what additional commodities to sell to those who come to buy stamps or post letters. On Sundays I shall preach in the Tabernacle in Doornboomstad. We shall have less money than before, but we shall never starve because there will always be donations from the congregation to add to what the post office and Jakkalsdrif earn for us. Simon must learn to help Koos, and even if I can never hope to be a farmer I shall learn from you what tasks I should perform. So – we shall be happy again, you and I, together again – "

He broke off to kiss away the tears of happiness which had risen to her eyes. "I shall continue teaching Simon so that he may become a pastor one day, and thus all three of our sons will have secure futures. Now," Marcus went on, "I shall explain to you about Abel's future, and the compensation I am making to him. Cousin Reuben agreed with me that we can never restore him to his rightful place as our first-born, because of the terrible danger that would hold for me. But in my discussions with my cousin I realised what I should do. So, while I was in Johannesburg, Petronella, I went to look for Gerrit du Toit – "

"Gerrit?" she interrupted, surprised. "Nothing has been heard of him or of Driena for years! How did you know where to look for him, Marcus?"

"I did not like to tell you of this before," Marcus said quietly, "but one day when I was preaching in a Tabernacle in Johannesburg, Driena was among the congregation and she began to shout at me with great bitterness. She did not come to attend the service, but merely to accuse me. Because of me, she said, she and her brother lost everything. She has work in a factory, but he could find no work at first and now – now it is too late. He lives only for buying and drinking cheap wine, and when she tries to help him by taking him into the room where she lives, he steals from her to buy more wine."

"Oh, dear God," Petronella said with pity, remembering the many different changes there had been in Gerrit over the years. But this change must surely be the last, hopeless one, while for herself life was about to take a turn towards happiness at last.

"So I searched for Gerrit du Toit," she heard Marcus go on, "and I found him in the park inside the city where all the lost souls who share, or fight over, their cheap wine live and sleep. I do not know if I helped him, or simply caused his end to come sooner, but I have bought his farm Bulspruit from him, and this I shall present to Abel in compensation for Jakkalsdrif – "

He stopped as Petronella began to weep. He could not know they were tears of utter misery because the dream he had been holding out to her with such eagerness and sincerity, and in which she had believed so completely, had had all the substance of a soap bubble.

"Oh Marcus," Petronella cried through her tears, a note of hysterical laughter in her voice at the bitter irony of it all. "You still know nothing about farms or farming, do you? Whatever you paid for Bulspruit, it would have been too much. It is worthless. It has not been cultivated since the Boer War, and the land has been taken over by khaki-bush and prickly pear and thorn-scrub. Abel would laugh in your face if you were to offer it to him, and what is more, he would know it is a bribe, an admission of guilt. And oh God, Marcus, he has thought of a terrible threat to use against us."

She watched horror etching its lines on Marcus's face as she pricked his own bubble of hope and told him what Abel had in mind. "He'd do it, Marcus. The very first time you held a service in Doornboomstad he'd be there, grabbing the chance to expose us and ruin us if we do not give him the proof he wants."

"*Gevalt!*" Marcus stood up and paced the floor. "Petronella, this has changed everything! You understand that? I cannot stay. I can never again stay for long while Abel threatens to do this. I must leave again – today."

"*Today?*" she echoed with desperation in her voice. "Why so soon?"

He went to her and held her tightly. "It is Friday, Petronella. When I drove through Doornboomstad people saw me and waved to me. They will expect me to take the service in the Tabernacle on Sunday, just as I always do when I come home. Abel will know this too, and he will be there, waiting to execute his threat. I must, therefore, leave here as soon as possible with Dirk, and stop in Doornboomstad to explain to people that I have hurried home this time only to fetch Dirk because I have found employment for him in Johannesburg." He made a hopeless sound. "From now on I shall be forced to take extreme care not to be trapped into holding a service in Doornboomstad, and that means I shall have to be apart from you even more. To others, I shall have to pretend that I am travelling greater distances to spread the word of the Reformed Evangelists."

"I see," she said in a flat, dead voice. "Abel has once again driven us apart, and our marriage might just as well no longer exist."

"I cannot see any other alternative, Petronella. Simon will have to help you with the post office work when he comes home from school each day."

Sudden hope flared inside Petronella. "Marcus, there is no reason why Simon should not leave school immediately, and take over the post office full-time! It's not as if he's a brilliant scholar, and if he really wants to become a pastor one day, your Church does not require school certificates. I could leave with you, and share your travels. Jakkalsdrif does not need me, and while Abel believes it will one day be his, he'll work hard and not neglect anything – "

"Petronella," Marcus dashed that hope, "no matter how hard Abel might work, there is less and less money from farming Jakkalsdrif each year. We need the regular funds the post office brings in, but the licence would be taken away from us if no adult person were in charge. We have many extra mouths to feed, *mein tiere*; those of Mwende and Tina and Koos and the old men in the *stad* and the women whose husbands have gone away and cannot, or will not, send money to them."

"Yes," she said dully, and rose from the bed. "I'll go and tell Dirk to get ready."

"I have bought a suit for him to wear to Johannesburg. My plan was to drive him to the railway station on Monday. Now – " Marcus spread his hands, and sighed heavily. "Tell Dirk to pack, Petronella, and I shall fetch the suit from the truck."

Abel had continued with the harvesting of the mealies, deliberately giving the Bitch more than enough time to tell the Preacher that he held them in the hollow of his hands, and for the two of them to discuss the matter. Now he was sauntering towards the house, confident that at last they would confess what they had done and take whatever steps were needed to put Jakkalsdrif in his name. His first intimation that something was wrong, that he had been baulked yet again, came when he saw Dirk emerging from the house, his hair slicked down and wearing a smart suit of matching trousers and waistcoat and jacket, a tie knotted at his throat. He carried one of the Preacher's leather suitcases in one hand.

When he saw Abel he put the suitcase down and thrust his hands into his pockets with a swaggering air. "Like the city clothes?"

"What's going on?" Abel demanded tensely.

"I'm off to Johannesburg to manage a business of my own."

"What? You mean – straight away?"

"That's right. Pa didn't come back to stay this time, but only to collect me." Dirk removed his hands from his pockets and smoothed the lapels of his jacket with a self-important air. "Pa's cousin Reuben can't wait for me to come and run his motor-car business for him. The next time you see me, I'll be driving a car of my own."

Abel had stopped listening to his boasts. "The bastards!" he ground out. They had got the better of him. He did not believe for a moment that the Preacher had meant to come back only to leave again immediately with Dirk. He was leaving because he, Abel, had been stupid enough to give them time to plan. He should have kept quiet, and joined them for the service in Doornboomstad on Sunday, and made his threat just before they all entered the Tabernacle.

What made his defeat all the more bitter was to see Dirk standing there in his smart suit, waiting to go off to Johannesburg. Dirk, who had always had everything, who was being given more, and would also keep Jakkalsdrif unless Abel could find a way of proving that *he* was the first-born son mentioned in Oupa's will.

The Preacher and the Bitch came outside as well. Her face held none of the usual anger when the Preacher was about to go away again; it was desolate, and she had been crying. Neither of them looked at Abel; they clung together for a long moment as they kissed and then the Preacher got into the driving seat and Dirk climbed in beside him, and the engine sparked into life. Dirk leant out of the window and called mockingly to Abel, "Mind you look after Jakkalsdrif well for me!"

Rage grew inside Abel, so violent that he felt he would explode and that pieces of him would be scattered all over Jakkalsdrif. He made a growling sound in his throat, and the Bitch turned slowly, staring at him.

"I'll make you pay," she said, such chilly menace in her voice that Abel's rage was temporarily banked down. "One day I'll make you pay in full." She began to walk away, in the direction of the river.

"*You'll* make *me* pay, bitch?" he shouted after her, fury rising anew inside him. "When you were the one who stole and lied and cheated?" But she did not turn to give any sign that his words had reached her or penetrated her mind, not even when he bellowed, "I'll show you! I'll show all of you yet!"

He hurled himself inside the house. He wanted to smash something – anything. Something belonging to her. He crashed open the door of the bedroom where she slept alone so often and would be sleeping alone for even longer periods, he knew, because she had warned the Preacher not to be trapped into holding a service in Doornboomstad. He searched the room with a wild gaze, looking for something precious to her so that he could destroy it. He went to the dressing table and pulled out a drawer, intending to scatter its contents on the floor and then smash the drawer to pieces, and then another drawer, and another.

But the sight of bundles of letters stopped him, and he stared at them for a moment. Somewhere in one of them might be a clue, some kind of evidence that he had been born before Dirk.

He scooped up the letters, and went into the parlour where Simon was celebrating his new status as part-time postmaster by speaking on the telephone to his friend Frans Lourens in Doornboomstad.

"Put that down," Abel commanded tersely. "I need you."

Everyone had grown afraid of Abel, and Simon did as he had been told. He stared at the letters which Abel threw on the desk in front of him.

"Read them to me," Abel ordered.

"They're Ma's letters, and private – " Simon began primly.

"Shut up, crawler, and read them!" Abel snarled.

Simon began to read. The letters were all from Jakoba, the Bitch's friend whom none of them had ever met. They recorded the births of her own many sons, and infuriatingly, the earlier ones never mentioned the Bitch's sons by name, but inquired instead, "And how is Baby? You never seem to mention him when you write."

The letters contained none of the information for which Abel had been hoping, but merely boring, everyday details of a hard struggle to survive in Johannesburg, where her husband worked in the mines. Abel uttered a harsh, bitter laugh when one of the letters mentioned that Jakoba and her husband Dieter had left the Dutch Reformed Church and become converts of the Church of the Reformed Evangelists, "founded by that great and good man you married, Petronella."

"Read on," Abel ordered Simon.

"There's only one letter left," Simon returned sulkily. "They are all full of boring stuff, and we shouldn't be reading them at all, because they are Ma's personal property."

"Read the last letter," Abel commanded, but without much hope.

As he had feared, it held nothing to help him. It announced the death of Jakoba's husband, from a disease which Simon could not pronounce, and the birth to Jakoba of another son a few months after the funeral.

" 'If it were not for my dear Susarah,' " Simon read, " 'I do not know that I would have had the strength to carry on. I could not tell her so, of course, but she is my greatest treasure on earth. She is quite beautiful, but thank goodness, she does not realise this and is totally unaware of the way in which the young men in the Tabernacle stare at her on Sundays. Needless to say, I do nothing to encourage vanity in her, and I force myself to be quite harsh with her, and suppress her rebellious spirit. There are dangers here in Johannesburg for a beautiful young girl, dangers altogether different from the ones we faced in the concentration camp at the same age.' " Simon broke off.

"Do you want me to go on reading? It's all about this wonderful Susarah of hers."

"Finish the letter," Abel instructed. None of the letters had helped him in any way, but his rage had diminished, and there was something about the very sound of the name Susarah that intrigued him.

" 'I have to keep my feelings for her to myself,' " Simon went on, " 'because I must not appear to favour her above her brothers. She works so hard and uncomplainingly, helping me with them and with all my other tasks, that I wish I could send her away for a short rest and a change of scene as a reward. Do you know that my Susarah, the daughter and granddaughter of farmers, has never in her life set foot on a farm? She is forever asking me what it is like to live on a farm.' "

As Simon continued to read the letter Abel tried to conjure up an image of Susarah in his mind. He had never heard such a name before, and he was quite sure she must be as different from other girls as was her name. It was obvious that her mother had been hinting Susarah should be invited to stay at Jakkalsdrif, but the Bitch had ignored the hints for the letter was dated months ago.

Rage quickened inside Abel again as he took the letters from Simon and returned them to the Bitch's drawer. This girl, Susarah, could have been sent to stay at Jakkalsdrif and he could have taught her all about farming and farm life while Dirk sat in the parlour being postmaster and Simon was at school. She was interested in farms and so she would have been interested in him. There had been a chance for him to meet her, and even that had been denied him by the Bitch.

"Susarah, Susarah, Susarah," he repeated the name. It sounded like music.

Her mother had said she was beautiful and had a rebellious spirit. It did not sound at all as if she were a Halleluiah-girl, even though she attended the Tabernacle on Sundays. She was probably made to go, whether she wished to or not. She sounded as if she was exactly the kind of girl he would one day like to marry.

His mouth set grimly. The first thing he would do when Jakkalsdrif was finally acknowledged to be his property, would be to invite Susarah to come to stay as *his* guest.

And in the meantime, when he was with Tina he would try to block out the knowledge that she was the only one available to him, and he the only one available to her, and pretend that she was a beautiful, rebellious girl called Susarah instead, and that she had picked him out from among everyone else.

The lines of his mouth softened as he tried to picture Susarah in that home of hers in Johannesburg, and to imagine the colour of her hair and her eyes, and he tried to decide whether he would prefer her to be small and slender or softly curved, without being fat, of course. A girl called Susarah could never be fat.

Susarah, Susarah, Susarah, he said to himself again and he knew – he just *knew* – that one day they would meet and she would indeed choose him above everyone else.

23

Simon was getting ready to drive to Doornboomstad for the Sunday morning service, and for once Abel appeared to be in no hurry to leave the breakfast table and attend to his tasks. Petronella sensed that he was about to break the silence between them, and she gave all her concentration to the slice of bread she was buttering.

Instead of asking the remorseless, nerve-racking question she had been expecting and dreading, he demanded abruptly, "What did I do to make you hate me?"

Her head jerked up. "God in heaven, what have you been doing *not* to make me hate you?"

"I meant, in the beginning. Why did you hate me so much that for the first two years of my life you pretended I didn't exist?"

She looked at him, jolted by the question, staring down the years. There had been so many reasons. Inconsequentially, it struck her that he no longer resembled Marcus's father in any way. A certain vulnerability, a hint of pleading, almost, seen in his eyes disconcerted her, and she looked away, blurting out childishly, "You hated me first."

Recovering quickly, she amended, "You're talking nonsense. There was no question of trying to pretend for two years that you didn't exist. Yes, I hate you now, but it's because of the way you have wrecked my life and your father's."

And dear God, she thought, watching him rise and walk out of the room, how thoroughly he had wrecked her life. Because of Abel, she was worse off than a widow, for she had none of a widow's feelings of finality, loving memories or freedom. She could not mourn the loss of her husband and then set out to create a new life for herself, or even resign herself to a solitary future.

In vain, Petronella had pleaded with Marcus the last time he had come home. "Many years have passed since you slipped back into South Africa illegally. Another war, a world war, has taken place. An Act of Union has been passed. Who will care now, Marcus, that you were once exiled and returned under a false name?"

"What is it you are suggesting, Petronella?"

"I am saying that we should put an end to Abel's power over us. We should tell the truth to the authorities – that in the isolation of the *pondok*, with no one to guide and advise us, we did not know we ought to register Abel's birth, and that it was an honest mistake. We were young and stupid and we acted in a panic."

Marcus had shaken his head at her. "You still understand nothing, Petronella, do you? *I have broken the law.* Not only once, but several times. First I did not register Abel's birth, then I registered it fraudulently, and thirdly I sent Dirk's name as our first-born son and the legitimate heir of your Pappa to the Courts."

"No, I don't understand your irrational terror of the law! And please don't repeat that nonsense about being exiled to your father's country, or to Germany where you were born but which you don't remember at all! The only thing likely to happen would be that you would have to pay a fine, and life would at last be normal for us, Marcus – "

"*Normal!* To confess that I broke the law so many times would mean that for me nothing would ever be normal again!"

"Marcus, you are accepted by everyone as a Boer! Is it likely that a Boer would be sent to live out the rest of his life in some unknown country overseas? Hugo Slabbert in Wolmaransstad is a magistrate and one of your followers. Go to him, and explain the mistake we made when we were young and ignorant. He would understand, because it happened at a time when we had new masters ruling the country and no one trusted them, and he would sympathise with you *as another Boer* for being too afraid to confess our mistake – "

"No, Petronella! You know so little of reality! You ask me to go to Hugo Slabbert, but if I confessed to him he would be forced to forget that he is one of my followers. He would remember only that he is a magistrate. It would be his duty to take action, and that action would be to report the matter to the police. And Petronella, *it is not possible to choose the magistrate who judges one's case.* I have made enemies, my wife, not only in Wolmaransstad, but in many other places."

"*Enemies!*"

"Do you think it has pleased the Dutch Reformed Church, the Apostolic Church, the Dopper Church and all the other churches concerned that so many of their congregations have left and joined the Reformed Evangelists instead?" His eyes had darkened. "If I were to appear before a magistrate who is an enemy, and who has discovered that Marcus Koen was formerly Mordechai Cohen, so that my case would be referred to a higher court . . . No, I will not risk that. I have told you many times before what would happen. The authorities would send me away to a European country where I would be a stranger and where I would not be wanted but where I would have to remain."

She could not believe that anything so dreadful could possibly happen. Except in wartime, people simply were not sent into exile against their will. But she had been unable, as usual, to sway him with her arguments.

Petronella and Abel were left united, in their completely separate ways, in rage and frustration and their bitter hatred of each other. Sometimes Petronella's feelings merged and fused, so that she could not be certain whom she hated most, Abel for keeping Marcus from her or Marcus himself for using her as a sacrifice to his unreasonable, obsessive fear of the law.

Sighing heavily, she stood up with the intention of washing the breakfast dishes, but on an impulse decided to write to Jakoba instead. Poor Jakoba, she thought, with her huge brood of orphans. From what Petronella knew of her, she would be getting herself and her many children ready at this very moment to set out for the Tabernacle. Jakoba prided herself on never missing a Sunday morning service. How shocked she would be if she knew that Petronella, wife of the Founder of the Reformed Evangelists, had not been to church for almost as long as she could remember. How shocked Jakoba would be if she knew about so many areas of Petronella's life . . .

Straightening up after removing writing materials from a drawer in the bedroom, she caught sight of her reflection and smiled wryly. What irony it was that she could boast to Jakoba of so many things that weren't true, while modesty forbade her to mention that because she had followed Mamma's advice through the years and always wore a *kappie* against the sun, and regularly patted buttermilk into her skin, she had retained the complexion of a girl.

She sat down instead and prepared to write lies to Jakoba, as she had been doing throughout the years at times when her life was at its most bleak and wretched. She did not refer to Jakoba's latest letter; she never reread any of them and scarcely knew why she bothered to keep them at all. Jakoba might think of the exchange of letters between the two of them as correspondence but to Petronella, writing to her girlhood friend fulfilled only one function – it enabled her to portray her life as she would have wished it to be.

"Simon," she wrote, "has left to attend the service in the Tabernacle while Abel has ridden out to the distant acres of Jakkalsdrif to check on our stock. I am afraid the demands of a prosperous farm take little account of the Sabbath.

"I am sitting on the stoep as I write this. The mealies are green and lush in their fields and in the meadows our cattle and horses and sheep are sleek and fat. It should also be a good year for fruit, and when I consider the bottling and preserving and drying that lie ahead for me and the servants, I find myself wishing that Nature might be a little less bountiful.

"I am forced to end my letter here, my dear Jakoba, because I have just noticed the dust on the horizon which means that Marcus is hurrying home, far sooner than I had expected him, and must have driven throughout the night in his eagerness for our reunion. I have to go and change into my prettiest dress and arrange my hair in the way he likes best."

During the writing of the letter, as she willed herself to live in her fantasies, Petronella had been able to believe her own lies.

But now she looked up from the letter and stared at the blank, empty horizon with equally blank, empty eyes.

Moments later, Petronella saw there was, indeed, a cloud of dust on the horizon, and she could think of no one it might possibly be other than Marcus. He really *had* driven through the night to return home.

The thought was cut off in her mind by the emerging lines of the vehicle now visible through its accompanying dust-cloud. It was not Marcus's truck, but the kind of smart motor car she had never seen and had only had described to her by Dirk over the telephone. It stopped outside the house and a complete stranger got out and approached her.

"Mrs Koen?" he asked in English, and it was the kind of English that reminded her of Rupert Brown in the concentration camp.

"Yes." She studied him with a frown, judging him to be roughly the same age as herself. He seemed totally out of place on Jakkalsdrif with his smart city clothes and his quiet good looks and well-cut fair hair, and she could not imagine what could possibly have brought him here.

"My name is Robert Washburn, Mrs Koen." His light-grey eyes studied her for a moment, almost as if he were waiting to see whether the name meant anything to her. "Is your husband at home?" he asked after a moment.

"No, Mr Washburn." Her English had become rusty and hesitant after long disuse. "Why do you wish to see him?" Surely the man must know that if Marcus were not away on his travels, he would be conducting the service in Doornboomstad's Tabernacle this morning? Could this visit possibly have something to do with the false registration of Abel's birth? She felt torn between fear and relief at the thought of the whole problem being brought out into the open.

But Robert Washburn said, "I wish to discuss a business matter with him. I understand he buys and sells all manner of commodities."

The business matter was presumably of importance, since it had brought him here on a Sunday morning. "He does," Petronella answered, "but I do not know where he is at present, and I don't know when he will be returning home."

Robert Washburn looked about him, and she tried to see their surroundings through his eyes. With the help of Koos, she and Abel fought a daily, almost fanatical battle against the insidious illnesses which were killing so many of the neighbouring farms, but even so, large areas of land lay like raw, naked wounds among the cultivated fields and the meadows, their surfaces scarred by cracks because the topsoil had been washed away, and the wind was scooping up useless earth from inside the cracks and performing a crazy dance with it. Dry tumble-weed lay piled up against barbed-wire fences or rolled about in the wind on an aimless journey to nowhere.

There had been no rain for months, so that the mealies stood wilting and undersized in the fields, and in the meantime the grass had been scorched to a drab khaki. The cattle were waiting by the barbed-wire fence which separated one of the meadows from the mealie-fields, plaintively calling to be fed with the expensive cattle-cake which had to be bought to supplement their meagre grazing. In this merciless heat, it only needed the sun to shine on a piece of carelessly tossed-away bottle glass for a fire to start and rage out of control, fanned by the hot wind, so Koos and Abel were busy in one of the meadows, burning strips of grass to create fire-breaks. The acrid smell of burning and the smoke added to and intensified the effect of Jakkalsdrif's desolation.

Robert Washburn's gaze returned to Petronella's. "It has been a long and dusty drive, Mrs Koen. I wondered whether I might beg a glass of water before I leave?"

Common courtesy compelled her to invite him inside for coffee and rusks instead and she took him straight into the kitchen, where the sudden appearance of a total stranger startled Mwende so much that she almost dropped the plate she had been drying.

"Mr Washburn," Petronella said, "this is Mwende and her daughter Tina. I am afraid neither of them speaks or understands English." She switched to Afrikaans. "Mwende, would you put some coffee on the stove, please?"

Mwende nodded and turned to the stove, and Washburn engaged Petronella in polite conversation. If he was surprised or curious at the sight of Mwende's almost-white daughter he was too delicate to pry into the matter, and he talked instead of the drought and questioned Petronella on the long-term effect it was likely to have on Jakkalsdrif.

When he had finished his coffee and rusks, he thanked her for her hospitality and said he would leave a written message for Marcus regarding the business he wished to conduct with him. Petronella went to find writing materials, and when she returned he decided it would suffice if he just left his name and a telephone number in Johannesburg where Marcus would be able to reach him. He wrote it down and then stood up, smiled at Mwende and Tina and held out his hand to Petronella.

"Thank you for your hospitality, Mrs Koen. I shall not impose on you any longer."

She stood on the stoep and watched him climb into the driving seat of his smart car. But something was evidently wrong, for the engine made a sluggish sound and died. He tried several times more before he left the vehicle and walked back to the stoep.

"I am so sorry, Mrs Koen, but I fear I have to inconvenience you further. I noticed that your farm is also a post office, so you obviously have a telephone. May I use it to contact the petrol station and garage which I noticed in the village on my way here? Even though it is Sunday, I hope to persuade them to send someone to put right whatever is wrong with my car, and I trust it will not take too long."

It took far longer than either of them had anticipated. His motor car required a spare part which the garage in Doornboomstad did not have in stock and would have to send away for. In the meantime there was no alternative but for Petronella to invite him to stay at Jakkalsdrif, and Mwende prepared Dirk's room for him.

Robert Washburn was an undemanding, self-effacing guest, obviously embarrassed at having to impose upon their hospitality, even though Petronella assured him repeatedly that he was welcome. Abel had picked up a few English phrases, she couldn't imagine from where, and Simon's knowledge of the language was limited to what he had learnt at school, so that they did little more than exchange polite greetings with the man. They were, in any case, more interested in his motor car than in him. During the day Washburn sat on the stoep, reading one of Marcus's collection of books, and in the evenings, when the air had cooled down, he usually set out for a walk.

Even though he went out of his way not to intrude upon their lives, Petronella could not but be aware of the man's presence. For one thing, it forced her to pay attention to her own appearance, which she had increasingly neglected because of Marcus's long absences. Now, for the sake of her own pride, she was obliged to take an interest in what she wore, and spend time on dressing her hair.

More and more, as she did so, she was made conscious of the fact that she was still a very attractive woman. Her figure was still slender, her breasts firm, and apart from a few lines at the corners of her eyes her complexion was smooth and flawless. Petronella brushed her pale-gold hair and coiled it into an attractive knot on top of her head, instead of just bundling it into a bun at her neck. If there was any grey in it, it blended perfectly with the natural colour of her hair. Yes, the years had dealt kindly with her where looks were concerned . . .

And all of it was being dissipated by neglect, allowed to go to waste. She was, she thought with a sudden surge of bitterness, like a flower blooming in a desert, unseen, uncared for and unappreciated. When at last she withered, like that flower, no one would even notice. She did not know where Marcus was; he had not contacted her of late and she had no idea when he would be back. Even when he did come home their brief time together would be poisoned by his implacable refusal to take the only step which would end the present unbearable state of affairs.

All of her simmering anger and resentment and frustration began to boil up into a reckless tide of mutiny. How dared Marcus take it for granted that she would be content to remain here forever in the background on Jakkalsdrif, faithful and celibate? She refused to believe his protestations that *he* was faithful and celibate during all those long absences. He was a handsome, passionate man, with a strong attraction for women, and he had every opportunity to take advantage of their willing offers. Why should she deny herself a similar opportunity?

More and more, she began to leave the farm work to Abel and Koos and make excuses to join Robert Washburn on the stoep. All she wanted, she told herself, was a little attention, reassurance that she was still desirable, some small comfort, however transitory. She also wanted to pay Marcus back, even if he was not likely to find out about it –

The thought remained suspended in mid-air. For Marcus to find out was exactly the spur she needed! It would bring him to his senses and make him realise, as none of her angry words ever could, that the truth should be told so that their lives could at last assume normality. Particularly if Abel were the one to tell him what had happened, particularly if Abel were to add *that* threat of public disclosure to the one he already held over their heads.

So she chatted to Washburn, and invited him to call her Petronella, and called him Robert in return, and smiled more often than she had smiled in years. His English reserve made his response to her difficult to gauge, and she also sensed that he would be reluctant to take advantage of Marcus's absence.

This morning someone had at last come from Doornboomstad to fit a spare part to his car, and she knew tonight would be the last he would be spending on Jakkalsdrif. In the evening, as he emerged from the house for his usual walk, she was waiting on the stoep.

She said softly, "Won't you keep me company for a while, Robert?

Simon went off with the garage mechanic to Doornboomstad; he'll be staying the night with his friend Frans Lourens so that he may attend the service in the Tabernacle in the morning, and then he plans to borrow a horse from Frans's father to bring him home. As for Abel – " She searched her mind for a convincing lie. "He's attending to a sick cow, and will probably have to stay up with her all night. Not, of course, that two grown sons are interested in keeping their mother company when they *are* here."

Robert hesitated, and then came to sit down beside her. "I haven't been able to avoid noticing that you are not close to your sons."

"Abel and I have never got on, and Simon irritates me with his piety." She changed the subject. "I know you are not married, for if you were you would have used the telephone to explain your absence, but isn't there anyone – "

"I *am* married, Petronella," he interrupted.

"Oh . . ." So that was the real reason for his lack of response. He had always been reticent about his own private affairs and would steer the conversation to another topic if she tried to probe beyond the mere facts that he was born in England and still owned property there, even though he was in business in Johannesburg.

Bleakly, she commented, "If you travel as often as Marcus does, and communicate just as seldom with your wife, she must be a very lonely woman and she has all my sympathy."

"I am legally separated from my wife. There is someone else in her life, so loneliness is not a problem for her."

"I see." Petronella sat very quietly, unable to think of anything more to say. All at once she felt unutterably humiliated. Here she was, a woman in her prime, not separated, not married in any meaningful sense of the word, lonely and neglected and trying to screw up her courage to entice into her bed a man she would never see again after tomorrow.

She started to rise. "I shall not keep you any longer from your walk."

He stood up too, and reached for her hand, his fingers stroking hers gently. "We both know why you asked me to keep you company. Shall we go inside, Petronella?"

She swallowed, and nodded. The house was very quiet. It was true that Abel was out somewhere, probably seeing to the animals, but he was sure to return soon, and he would certainly not ignore sounds coming from the bedroom of the English stranger.

Only her anger against Marcus sustained Petronella during what followed. It was not that Robert Washburn was an insensitive or selfish lover. In many ways he was quite as skilled as Marcus, but he was not Marcus, and she was forced to pretend a response that was totally false. But what was far, far worse was something she sensed in his – no, she could not call it pleasuring.

It was a polite guest's farewell gift to a hostess who had put herself out to make him welcome; the gift he knew she most wanted and would appreciate. There was no more to it than that. He was thanking her for her hospitality, punctiliously sparing no pains in performing a well-mannered duty. It was the most debasing experience of her life, and it was also totally pointless, for the house was still silent when she left his bed and went to the one which she shared so occasionally with Marcus. Abel had not yet come in.

Petronella cried herself to sleep that night, and in the distant darkness a hyena seemed to mock her shame with its manic laughter.

In the morning she had to force herself to face Robert Washburn. But his manner was as correct as if nothing whatever had taken place between them as he said goodbye to her in the presence of Abel and Mwende and Tina, and then climbed behind the wheel of his motor and drove away. Abel went to help Koos with the milking, while Tina started on her usual morning round of bed-making and Petronella and Mwende returned to the kitchen to wash up the breakfast dishes.

Mwende must have been weeping for some time before Petronella became aware of it, so silent was her grief. Immediately, Petronella threw aside the dish towel and held her close. "Oh Mwende, whatever is the matter? Have the women in the *stad* been cruel to Tina again?"

Mwende shook her head. "Nonnie Petronella – he not come to say goodbye. Soldier Bobby not come to say goodbye, like he promise."

"Soldier Bobby?" Petronella echoed slowly, with growing horror.

Then, between her tears, Mwende's story spilled out. Robert Washburn was on a visit from England, and had made sure Marcus would be out of the way so that he could use him as an excuse to call at Jakkalsdrif. All Robert had wanted was to see Mwende again, and make sure that she and Tina were well and not in need. While Petronella was out of the kitchen that morning of his arrival, finding writing materials, he and Mwende had communicated with each other by their old means of mime. He had given her some money, and that would have been the end of it if his motor car had not refused to start, making it impossible for him to leave again immediately.

"Last night I wait for him in our meeting-place, Nonnie Petronella," Mwende wept, "but he not come."

"Oh God, Mwende," Petronella said, her voice blurred with guilt and self-disgust. "I'm sorry. So very sorry."

"It not your fault, Nonnie." Mwende pulled away, and wiped her eyes on her apron. "It just – just the way things is."

It *is* my fault, Petronella told herself. Poor Mwende, she has had so little, far less even than I, and I robbed her of her last scrap of happiness.

But that night, as she lay in bed unable to sleep, Petronella decided bleakly that Mwende had been right after all. Both of them had made an alien choice where love was concerned, and both of them had suffered the consequences.

It *is* the way things are, Petronella acknowledged to herself. What is the point in continuing to fight them?

A mirthless laugh escaped her as she remembered how she had fought to be with Marcus, fought to find him and to marry him. And it had all come to this – the way things were and would remain.

24

"I'm going to tell Ma," Simon protested feebly.

"Do so," Abel returned, "if you fancy a broken arm."

Simon paled, but he persisted, "Reading Ma's private letters is wrong. And I can't see why you want me to read them, because they're always boring, and almost always about the wonderful Susarah – "

"Read it!" Abel cut him short, cupping his chin in his hand as he leant forward in his chair, filled with eager anticipation. The Bitch had gone for a walk – though God knew why she should wish to do so on a hot and dusty day – and he had taken advantage of her absence to remove from the drawer in her bedroom the latest letter she had received from her friend Jakoba, and closet himself with Simon inside the post office room. It was precisely because the letter would be full of news about Susarah that he was waiting impatiently for Simon to begin reading it to him.

He was not to be disappointed. " 'Only to you, my dear Petronella,' " Simon read, " 'can I confide my feelings about my poor, dear, brave Susarah. As you may remember from my previous letters, after Dieter's untimely death I was awarded a widow's pension and an allowance for each orphan until that child's sixteenth birthday. Susarah, of course, being twenty has long since lost *her* allowance, but a few months ago my eldest boy, Barend, turned sixteen and that meant that eight of us have had to manage on benefits paid only for six. Barend has been unable to find work; here in Newlands there are, apart from the mines, only the market-gardens on the outskirts but they are owned by the Portuguese community who prefer to employ members of their own families. It is very hard indeed for a young Boer to find work hereabouts, and so life has been a struggle for us.

" 'You may imagine my surprise, therefore, when Susarah returned home late one day, after doing the shopping, beaming all over her face and announcing, "Ma, I've got a job, serving in a café by the tram terminus! I'm to be a waitress, and as well as earning a pound a month I shall be able to bring home perishables that won't last until the next day!" It turned out that she had simply walked into the café and asked whether they had a job for Barend; they hadn't, but there was an opening for a waitress and they already had several applicants whom they were considering, but they decided on the spot to offer the job to Susarah instead.

" 'Oh, Petronella, how my heart aches for my poor, dear daughter! I was forced to forbid her to take the job. I had to produce every excuse I could think of. I told her the uniform she would be obliged to wear was improper; I said her father would turn in his grave at the thought of his daughter going out to work. In short, I had to portray myself as the kind of stupid old woman who refuses to move with the times as I dashed my daughter's spirits. How could I tell her the truth? Barend's self-esteem is low enough as it is. If his sister were to become the family breadwinner while he fails to find work, it would destroy him.' "

Simon looked up. "That's all, apart from the usual bit about Ma's letters being an inspiration to her. Go and put it back now before Ma comes home."

"No," Abel said. "I want you to read it to me again. But not yet." He leant back in his chair and pictured her, the unknown, beautiful Susarah of his dreams setting out to find work for her brother. He couldn't begin to imagine what a tram terminus might be, but from the sound of it a café was a place where food was sold. And Susarah had been chosen out of many other girls who had applied for the job, which proved that she must be very beautiful, very special indeed.

In fairness, he could not blame her mother for refusing to allow her to take the job. He could understand how her brother Barend would have felt if she had been bringing money into the house while he was unable to do so.

Abel's mouth set in hard lines. *His* Susarah should not have been in need of a job in the first place, nor should she have to live in poverty and hardship in that place called Newlands which was – confusingly to him – a part of Johannesburg and yet not the city, from the sound of the letters. Susarah could have been living right here, as his wife, if only the Bitch had invited her to Jakkalsdrif two years ago.

"Now read the letter to me again," he commanded Simon.

But he had read only a few lines when two things happened, almost simultaneously. The Bitch came in unexpectedly, so that Simon hurriedly pushed the letter out of sight, and before any questions could be asked about what had been going on, the telephone rang in the sequence that denoted a call for Jakkalsdrif.

The Bitch herself removed the instrument from its hook and answered the call. Her expression remained neutral and she uttered only an occasional "Yes" or "No" or "I see," before she replaced the telephone on its hook.

"That was your father," she said. "Dirk has married a girl called Hester and the three of them are coming to Jakkalsdrif tomorrow."

Dirk married! Rage built up inside Abel as he stared at her retreating back. Bloody Dirk, who'd already had everything else, now also had a wife at the age of twenty while he, Abel, at twenty-one had not yet even met his Susarah! Nor was he likely to while the Bitch continued to ignore her friend's hints that Susarah should be invited to Jakkalsdrif . . .

Something else entirely seeped through to Abel's mind. Ignoring Simon, who was babbling on about Dirk getting married without telling his family or trying to arrange for them to be present, Abel concentrated on his own devastating thoughts.

From her monosyllabic responses and her total lack of any emotion, the Bitch might have been talking to the postmistress in Doornboomstad when she answered the telephone. And this was something totally new. The sight of the Preacher, the sound of his voice, had always made her come alive before, even if only with resentment and rage. The nameless something between the two of them, underlying even the most bitter of their quarrels, had always been the only really effective weapon Abel possessed to use against them.

His threat to expose them to the congregation in Doornboomstad had long since ceased to be a means to an end, but had become an end in itself. By forcing long separations on them, slowly destroying their marriage, he had hoped to bring them to their knees so that they would confess to the wrong they had done him and put it right.

He shook his head in shock and disbelief as he thought of the way the Bitch had responded to the Preacher over the telephone. Instead of hurling passionate abuse at him, instead of raging that she'd had the right to be told of Dirk's wedding plans, instead of some snide, bitter remark about his homecoming tomorrow, she had simply said "Yes" and "No" and "I see" with her voice and her expression totally wooden.

Had he, Abel, succeeded so well in destroying their marriage that she no longer cared whether or not the Preacher ever came home to her again? If that was so, Abel thought with despair, then he had nothing left with which to fight them, and no hope for the future.

This time Petronella did not watch the horizon for the cloud of dust that would tell her Marcus was arriving with Dirk and their new, unknown daughter-in-law, Hester. This time no shrewish, wounding words were forming in her mind either, to be unleashed on Marcus when he arrived. It was not simply because appearances would have to be kept up in front of Hester. The bitter sense of shame and guilt that had swamped her after Robert Washburn's visit was still with her, blunting other emotions.

Of course, what had happened had been bound up with Marcus, and as always it had ultimately been bound up with Abel.

Because of Abel, she thought, there was no normality in her life, nor would there ever be again.

Normality would have meant an official announcement of Dirk's forthcoming marriage, and his family travelling to Johannesburg to attend the ceremony. Petronella had known nothing about it until Marcus's telephone call. He had claimed that he'd tried to contact her before but without success, and that the exchange had said there was a fault on the telephone line. In any case, Marcus had added, since the wedding had been a very quiet affair, arranged at short notice, and Dirk wanted to bring his new wife to Jakkalsdrif for a visit afterwards, and since the post office could not be left unmanned, it would have been both pointless and impossible for Dirk's family to attend the wedding.

If there really had been a fault on the telephone line, it was news to Petronella. No, Marcus had manipulated matters in such a way that news of Dirk's wedding did not reach Jakkalsdrif until after the event, and his motive, of course, had been to avoid a large gathering in a Tabernacle from which it would have been impossible to exclude Abel. Abel, who had stopped hinting and was openly threatening to cause a scandal if he were given the opportunity to attend a service held by Marcus.

With no normality left in her life, it was difficult to know how to prepare for the arrival of a new daughter-in-law who was a stranger, or how to greet her husband who had become almost as much of a stranger.

Abel did watch the horizon, for he was trying to think of a way in which Dirk's new wife might possibly prove to be a weapon in his fight for Jakkalsdrif if he really had lost his power over the Bitch and the Preacher.

He had no personal curiosity about this new sister-in-law of his. Under Simon's persistent questioning, the Bitch had revealed what little the Preacher had told her over the telephone about Hester. Dirk had met her at a Tabernacle in Johannesburg. That item of news had cheered Abel considerably and removed some of his envy of Dirk. She was just another Halleluiah-girl, prim and pious except when being swept up by the fervour of the services. He had seen her sort all over Doornboomstad, secretly eyeing him, casting down their lashes when they realised he was looking at them. On Sundays they probably mounted the platform inside the Tabernacle and confessed to immodest thoughts.

He removed his gaze from the horizon and glanced around him, his hands forming into fists. This land was his. It might not be much, *but it was his.* But how could he ever hope to claim it if he had lost his only weapon against the Preacher and the Bitch?

He bitterly regretted, now, that he had gone so far in his threats to expose them in front of the Tabernacle's congregation. But surely they should have been able to work out for themselves that, as time had gone by, the threat had become more and more empty? Even if people believed him – which they were hardly likely to do after all the years that had passed – he himself would be condemned and despised for making such matters public about his own parents. And that was the very last thing he wanted.

He desperately needed people to think well of him, because when he had proved that Jakkalsdrif was his, he needed to be respected, to be *someone* in the community. For that reason, whenever he took mealies to be milled in Doornboomstad, he put himself out to be friendly and considerate towards everyone he met. But all that effort would be wasted if he did not find a way of proving that Jakkalsdrif was his, and that Dirk, who did not even want it, had no right to it.

Bitterly, Abel acknowledged that even the customs of the Reformed Evangelists had helped the Preacher and the Bitch in their deception. Instead of young babies being christened, as in the Dutch Reformed Church, they were 'blessed' by full immersion at the age of three, and who would have thought to doubt the pastor's word when he said that his son Abel was three years old, and not almost five?

His expression hardened. The Bitch's mother, he had learnt, had been dead when her second son was born, and someone else must have helped her with the delivery. He would concentrate on finding out who it had been.

He dismissed the subject for the moment, and found himself thinking how strange it was that, hating each other as they did, he and the Bitch alone were united in their dedication to Jakkalsdrif. Sometimes he tried to imagine what it would have been like if they had not hated each other, but it was impossible, for he had no yardstick to go by.

He was not sure, either, whether he was succeeding in making people like him. Should he be less eager to call on farms when he drove to Doornboomstad, offering to take farmers' mealies to the mill for them, or buy on their behalf anything they might need? Or should he offer more? Should he be as fulsome as he was in praising the small cakes and the rusks offered to him in refreshment by their wives? He had not experienced love or liking in the past, and so he did not know. But it was important that he should be liked, so that the same liking would extend to include Susarah when he invited her to *his* Jakkalsdrif, when he courted her, when he married her . . .

His thoughts snapped off as he saw the dust appearing on the horizon. But surely it was shifting too fast to be the Preacher's truck? Puzzled, he watched the vehicle's progress, sunlight glinting on something bright on its exterior.

It was not until it had stopped near the house and the dust had settled that he saw the dashing, elegant lines of the most flamboyant car he had ever set eyes upon. He could make out two figures inside it, but he was too fascinated by the car to pay them attention. The driver blew imperiously on the horn, and Abel shook off the spell which the vehicle had cast over him and moved towards it.

The driver's door opened, and Dirk's voice drawled, "Get our luggage out of the back, will you, and carry it into the house."

Abel was too bemused still at the sight of the car, and now the sight of Dirk, standing there in his smart city suit with a trilby hat perched at a rakish angle on his head, to react immediately to the arrogant command. Then he flushed and said, "Get your bloody luggage out yourself!"

Dirk looked him up and down. "The years haven't improved you, I see," he said, still in that exaggerated, put-on drawl. He looked beyond Abel, at Koos who was staring in wonderment at the car, and clicked his fingers together. "Koos, *tshetsha!* Take in our bags."

Abel felt so enraged that he wanted to knock Dirk down. There had never been any love lost between the brothers and it was no surprise that Dirk had tried to make him look small in the presence of his Halleluiah-girl bride, but the way he had treated and spoken to Koos was a different matter entirely. Not even to offer him a greeting, and then to click his fingers as if he were summoning a dog!

"Johannesburg certainly hasn't improved *you*," Abel told his brother with contempt.

Dirk shrugged off the criticism. "What do you think of the car?" he asked smugly. "It's the latest Oldsmobile on the market."

Abel wanted that car with an almost physical lust. But he said dismissively, "It wouldn't last a month on the corrugated roads out here."

"I don't intend staying for a month, thank God. I suppose I'd better introduce you to my wife, and let her get over the shock of what she has married into." Dirk swaggered towards the passenger side of the car, and only continued fascination with the car itself moved Abel to follow him.

Over the years, Abel had taught himself to drive the Preacher's truck. He considered, but only briefly, the thought of humbling himself by asking Dirk if he could take the car for a short run, and then also dismissed the idea of getting up in the night and sneaking a spell behind the steering wheel. Dirk was bound to find out about it.

Then the car, and the urge to drive it, were wiped from Abel's mind as a girl jumped lightly from the running-board, released Dirk's hands and turned to Abel, smiling.

Jesus, he thought, gulping and staring at her, this was no Halleluiah-girl! How small she was, how dainty. Her clothes were like nothing he had ever seen before in his life. A dress of some kind of soft material floated from her shoulders in a series of panels, skimming her knees so that he could see her shapely legs. She wore fine stockings which gleamed in the sunlight, and dainty little shoes. An elegant small hat covered one side of her head only, ending in a narrow upswept brim, and he could see that her hair was a rich, shining brown and cut short so that it curled in her neck. Her face was round and pretty, her pale-blue eyes gentle.

"You must be Abel," she said, holding out a slim, gloved hand. "I am Hester, and so very glad to meet you."

Abel could think of nothing to say. He was afraid of squeezing her hand in case he hurt her, for it reminded him of a bird as it lay in his calloused one. He heard Dirk's jeering drawl. "I'm afraid, Hester dear, he has the manners of an oaf. But then, he has never been further than Doornboomstad, and I don't suppose he has ever even spoken to a girl before, let alone shaken hands with one."

Abel allowed his fingers to close over the gloved ones, and immediately regretted it when he saw the grubby stains it left on the fabric and heard Dirk's derisive laughter. He felt the blood throbbing in his temples, and he wanted to go to Dirk and throttle the life out of him for being the possessor of such a car and such a bride and for making him feel like a clumsy yokel.

But then the Bitch appeared with Simon, who had decided to stay away from school that day so that he could meet his sister-in-law, and Hester whispered to Abel, "It doesn't matter about my glove. It will wash."

He nodded dumbly, gratefully, and tried not to listen as Dirk bragged and boasted about the price he had paid for the car, the speeds it was capable of, the surprise and envy of other motorists along the way as he passed them, and the cleverness of his forethought in placing a card at the rear of the car giving the name and address of his showroom in Johannesburg where the same model might be purchased.

Dirk, of course, had not come to Jakkalsdrif so that his new bride could meet his family. He had come to show off his success and his wife and his car. And dear God, Abel thought with bitter envy, what a wife . . .

The Bitch interrupted Dirk. "Where is your father? I took it for granted the three of you would be arriving together in the truck."

"God, Ma, you didn't imagine I would travel in a rattling old truck, or expect Hester to do so? Pa couldn't keep up with us in the truck and will be along later."

They all went to sit in the shade of the stoep, and Mwende brought out coffee and rusks. The Bitch wanted to know where the couple were living now they were married and Hester began to explain that they rented a flat, but Dirk took over in his boasting way.

A flat, it appeared, was a particularly smart kind of place in which to live, vastly superior to a house. Abel tried not to make it obvious that he could barely take his eyes off Hester, and only half-listened as Dirk went on talking, telling them all about the wonders of Johannesburg, in a way which suggested that his family would naturally consider them to be wonders, while to someone like himself they were nothing out of the ordinary; conveying the impression that the most truly wonderful thing in Johannesburg was himself and his motor car showroom and the success he was making of his life.

"I was under the impression," the Bitch said drily, "that the business belonged to Reuben Cohen, and you are only managing it."

"Oh Ma, how behind the times you are," Dirk drawled languidly. "Reuben is a sleeping partner, sure. He's a figurehead, really, but he comes in useful at times like this, when I have to be away, and he can pop in and make sure the Kaffirs are doing their jobs properly – "

"Since when," the Bitch interrupted in a sharp voice, "have they been Kaffirs to you, Dirk?"

"Everyone calls them that in Johannesburg." Dirk waved the subject aside. "Poor old Reuben is past it, I'm afraid, so Hester and I will have to leave again tomorrow. We only came so that you could meet her."

"And to have the snap taken," Hester reminded him.

"Snap?" the Bitch echoed, frowning.

"I've bought a camera," Dirk explained, adding unnecessarily, "the latest and most expensive model. Hester insisted that because you could not come to the wedding, we should bring our wedding clothes and dress up in them so that Pa can take a snap for you to keep."

Abel saw, by the haze of dust on the horizon, that the Preacher was finally arriving, and he slipped quietly away. He would not be able to bait, taunt and goad the Preacher and the Bitch about the matter of his birth this time; not with Hester there. He felt his throat tightening. God, why did Dirk have to have *everything*? The chance of success in Johannesburg, fine clothes, that miracle of a motor car, and now Hester with the soft voice and the sweet, gentle face.

He'll not have Jakkalsdrif too, Abel thought savagely. He'll bloody well not.

It was no longer merely a question of proving that Jakkalsdrif was *his*. Equally fierce had become his determination that its deeds and title should not go on belonging *to Dirk*.

His mind went to more immediate problems. Springhares had been at the wilting mealies again and perhaps it was time he and Koos went out at night with lanterns and shotguns and hunted the bastards. He could have done with more help on the farm, more money spent on it.

He heard voices approaching, and when he turned he saw that Dirk and Hester were strolling arm-in-arm towards him. Both of them had changed their clothing; Dirk was now wearing well-cut casual trousers and an open-necked shirt, and Hester had put on a blue dress with a floating kind of belt tied about her hips, and her shoes, although still dainty, were more serviceable than the ones in which she had arrived. A wider-brimmed hat shaded her face against the sun.

"Well, Abel," Dirk said bombastically, with heavy censure, "I'm not at all happy, I might tell you, with the way you've been running things here on Jakkalsdrif."

"No?" I want to kill him, Abel thought. Since when has he cared how things were run on Jakkalsdrif? What does he *know* about running things on Jakkalsdrif?

"Look at these mealies, man! What a pathetic sight! They should have been twice their size by now – "

Abel moved, towering over Dirk, grabbing hold of his shirt collar. "It has not," he ground out between his teeth, "rained for three bloody months! And Jakkalsdrif is not your affair! It belongs to me!"

"Oh God, not that old fantasy again!" Dirk blustered, but his face had grown red and there was fear in his eyes.

Hester's voice reached Abel, trembling slightly and obviously anxious to avert an ugly scene between the two brothers. "What – what are those birds doing on the backs of the cattle?"

Abel released Dirk, turning his back to him. "They are *renostervoëls*," he said. "Those red bills of theirs are searching out ticks on the hides of the cattle."

"They eat the ticks?" she asked, her eyes wide.

"Yes."

He saw her shudder, and in anyone else he would have despised such squeamishness, but in her it merely added to her feminine appeal and her desirability. "Each bird 'adopts' a particular animal," he told her, "and never deserts it for another."

"Really? How amazing! And how clever of you to have noticed it!" Abel's heart responded dizzily to the admiration in her eyes. But then Dirk took her arm again and turned to go back to the house. When he had reached what he obviously considered to be a safe distance, he called over his shoulder to Abel, "If you buck up your ideas, you'll have a job here for life. But if you continue to let Jakkalsdrif go to rack and ruin, I shall have to think seriously about putting someone else in your place to manage it for me."

You bastard, Abel thought with stony hatred. I'll show you. One day I'll show you. Jakkalsdrif is mine.

But he had no way of proving it, and what made it all the more galling was the fact that Dirk had no real interest in Jakkalsdrif. He was merely showing off to Hester, using his supposed ownership to add to his swaggering and bragging. For the life of him, Abel could not understand why she did not see through Dirk, but gazed at him with adoration in those wide, lovely eyes of hers.

That night, when Abel took Tina in the barn, it was not the unknown fantasy figure of Susarah he put in her place, but Hester. He was particularly tender and considerate, because Hester was so small and frail. And for the first time since he had discovered how he'd been cheated of his birthright, he copied the Preacher, and thought of it as pleasuring as he delighted and enraptured Tina-Hester, because he knew for a fact that Dirk was ignorant of these little tricks, and Abel did not imagine he would have learnt any of them in Johannesburg. Oh yes, tonight Hester was discovering which one of them was the oaf.

Tina again cried quietly. Instinct was strong in her, and she knew precisely for whom all those sensuous caresses had been meant. But that was not why she wept. She was crying because no matter whether Abel was rough and inconsiderate with her, or passionate and sensitive because he was pretending she was someone else, it would all come to the same thing in the end.

Primitive foreknowledge inherited from her Zulu ancestors told her that just as her whole life had been a disaster for herself and her mother, Abel had been created for the purpose of sweeping her towards another disaster.

She could not obey her mother and keep away from Abel, because quite apart from the feelings she had for him, she was put on this earth so that he could enact his role in the destiny that awaited her; a destiny she could not name but which she dreaded even as she accepted it.

The next morning, after breakfast, Dirk and Hester dressed up in their wedding finery so that the Preacher could snap them with the expensive box-camera Dirk had brought with him. Abel scarcely glanced at Dirk, but he could not take his eyes off Hester.

She was the most beautiful sight he had ever seen, in her filmy white dress and her veil and the band of artificial blossom which she wore about her forehead. Dirk had gone to stand beside her and the Preacher was pointing the camera at them, ready to take the snap, when she made a little sound of dismay. "It won't look right without a bouquet of some kind! Wild flowers would do."

But there were no wild flowers on Jakkalsdrif; no flowers of any kind. Then Abel remembered the pumpkins he was growing for the winter, and their yellow flowers of which the females would later turn into pumpkins. "I'll fetch you flowers," he told Hester, and loped off to the pumpkin patch. But this morning the flowers had either not yet opened or they were dying off, and he did the best he could, picking the least wilted of them and adding some pumpkin leaves to make a bouquet.

Hester laughed when he presented it to her, but it was gentle, amused laughter, and she accepted it with thanks and posed for the camera, holding her absurd bouquet as if it were the most costly arrangement in the world.

"We'll send you the snap when we've had it developed," Dirk told the Bitch. "It would have been too expensive to order extra copies of the wedding pictures taken by a real photographer."

Simon left for school, and Dirk and Hester went to change out of their wedding clothes. They were to leave Jakkalsdrif immediately afterwards.

This time Abel clasped Hester's hand tightly in his in farewell, and he tried to think of something to say to her, anything to delay the moment when she would have to take her place beside Dirk, who was tooting the car-horn with impatience.

Abel cleared his throat. "That snap of you and Dirk – would it cost too much to have an extra copy made?"

"I don't think so. Why?"

"I – I'd like one for myself. To remind me of the pumpkin-leaf bouquet," he added, managing a grin to make it seem as if he regarded the matter as a joke.

"I'll send you one, Abel," she said in that gentle voice of hers. "Goodbye. I hope we shall meet again soon."

He nodded dumbly, and let go of her hand, and a few minutes later he watched the flamboyant, expensive car roaring away from Jakkalsdrif in a storm of dust.

Bearing away his brother's wife. His lucky, unfairly blessed brother, damn him to hell.

"Hester, Hester, Hester," Abel said to himself, just as he had once said, "Susarah, Susarah, Susarah," and now – as then – he thought it sounded like music.

Uncannily, he heard the Preacher mention Susarah's name only minutes later. He and the Bitch were on the front stoep and were not aware of him standing just around the corner, watching Dirk's car until not even the dust it left behind could be seen colouring the air.

"I have a letter for you from your friend Jakoba," the Preacher was telling the Bitch in a formal, stilted voice.

"Oh? I suppose it came with the mailvan last evening." Her voice was equally formal, and in the past Abel would have said that behind it lurked bitterness and rage, and that in another moment she would be hurling a stream of wounding abuse and accusations at the Preacher's head. Now it seemed that Abel had lost his only remaining savage triumph: the knowledge that he was responsible for the trouble between them, that he was keeping them apart and warring when they were briefly together.

"No," he heard the Preacher reply. "I brought it with me from Johannesburg. Your friend Jakoba had, by chance, just completed writing it when I called at her home a few days ago, and for me to deliver it to you saved her the cost of a stamp."

"Indeed!" Now there was anger in her voice, but an anger that puzzled Abel. "How dared you go round there behind my back? Am I to be left nothing of my own – not even an old friendship? If I'd wanted you to visit Jakoba I would have asked it of you long ago!" Her anger seemed to be touched with wariness now. "What did the two of you talk about, Marcus? Compare notes about my shortcomings?"

"How can you suspect that of me or of her, Petronella? She speaks nothing but well of you. Besides, I was there for a very short while only, and I had more conversation with her daughter than with Jakoba." His voice altered and softened. "She reminded me of you, Petronella, when you were her age. She possesses beauty and spirit, and Wessel du Plessis is a fortunate man indeed."

"Wessel du Plessis? Who is he?"

"The newly married husband of Susarah. I suspect your friend Jakoba's letter will tell you of the marriage. He is a good man, if somewhat older than Susarah; a thrifty, thoughtful man who is a great support to Jakoba, and also a man of talent, for he plays the accordion in the Tabernacle in Newlands on Sundays. He deliberately arranged for them to live next door to Jakoba so that Susarah can continue to be of help to her mother."

If Abel had needed anything more than the reality of Hester to supplant the fantasy of Susarah in his mind, it was the news that she had chosen to marry such a pious, dull-sounding man.

"Well, Marcus, I hope Susarah's beauty and spirit will bring her greater rewards in her marriage than mine ever brought me." There was bitterness now in the Bitch's voice, and Abel's spirits rose. It was not dead after all, that strange, strong force between them, and she must have been keeping an iron control upon her feelings because she hadn't wanted Hester to know about their troubled marriage.

"Please, Petronella," the Preacher's voice begged her for a respite. He changed the subject quickly. "I judge Wessel du Plessis to have passed the age of thirty, but I do not know how old Susarah is."

The Bitch seemed to be responding to the appeal, for she said, "She is the same age as Dirk. I remember, it was Jakoba's letter, telling me that Susarah's birth had been a bombshell to them, that first made me realise I was pregnant again. I'd had none of the usual symptoms I'd had with Abel."

It was a moment before the significance of what she had said struck Abel with full force. He raced around the corner of the stoep, and confronted them.

"You've admitted it!" he shouted in triumph. "By God, you've admitted it at last! I *was* born first!"

They stared at him for a moment in total, stunned silence. Then the Bitch spoke in a hard voice. "I don't know what you are talking about."

"Yes, you do! You admitted that Dirk was born after me, and I heard you!"

Just for a moment he thought she meant to give in and acknowledge the truth. He had the oddest feeling that it would be a relief to her to do so. Then she glanced at the Preacher, whose face had a greyish tinge to it, and the – *something* – that was definitely still between them in spite of all the quarrels and the bitter, wounding words, showed in her eyes. "Did anyone else hear this non-existent admission?" she asked in a cold voice.

God Almighty, they had won again. There were no witnesses. It would be their word against his, with birth certificates to back them up, and as always he would be the loser.

"Since this friend of yours wrote to tell you about the birth of her daughter Susarah," he told the Bitch, clutching at straws, "it follows that you would have written to her about the births of each of *your* children. I'll find your friend Jakoba, and I'll get the truth out of her."

It had been no more than a defiant shot in the dark, but as he recognised the look in the Bitch's eyes and the sick fear on the Preacher's face, he knew that it had found its target.

But the Bitch was a fighter; he had to hand her that. "And how," she mocked coldly, "would you go about finding her? Even if you managed, somehow, to reach Johannesburg – which is a very large city, I assure you – how would you search for her? All you know is

that her name is Jakoba and that she has a daughter called Susarah."
Mockery turned to acid in her voice. "What will you do, Abel? Stop
passers-by and ask them if they know a woman called Jakoba who
has a daughter by the name of Susarah? In *Johannesburg*, where tens
of thousands of people live?'

Damn you, bitch, he thought. But aloud he said tauntingly, "I
know rather more than you think! I know she lives in a place called
Newlands, and I need only find the Tabernacle, and the pastor would
tell me where she lives."

He turned away, filled with savage satisfaction at the renewed fear
in their eyes, and punched the air with his fist.

But it was an empty gesture, meant only for their benefit. How
was he to reach Johannesburg when he had no money and no fancy
motor car like Dirk – no vehicle at all, in fact?

Then he squared his shoulders. Somehow he would find a way,
now that he knew where to obtain the proof that Jakkalsdrif was his.

25

Just as Abel was passing the door of the post office room, he heard
the telephone ringing. He shrugged and began to walk on, but it
rang again, four short rings followed by a long one, the signal for
Jakkalsdrif. The post office was no concern of his and he had farm
chores to attend to, so if both the Bitch and Simon chose to absent
themselves why should he care? All the same, when Jakkalsdrif's
signal shrilled yet again some impulse moved him to enter the post
office and lift the instrument from its hook.

"I'm connecting you," he heard the voice of the exchange operator.
"Go ahead, caller."

"Thank you." It was a male voice, precise and somewhat ponder-
ous. "May I have the honour of speaking to Pastor Marcus Koen?"

"He is away from home," Abel said. *He has been away for so long
now that the Bitch wanders about like a sleepwalker. I am having to
content myself with the knowledge that she suffers and that I am the
cause. One day, when she has suffered so much that she's beyond
caring, she'll break down and make me a present of the proof I need* . . .

"Oh," the voice said over the line, with a note of deep disappointment in it. "To whom am I speaking, please?"

"I'm Abel Koen."

"One of the pastor's sons! Allow me to introduce myself. It is
possible that you may have heard of me. My name is Wessel du
Plessis."

Abel had heard the name before, but he couldn't remember in what
connection. Then the voice continued, "I am the husband of the
former Susarah Steenkamp."

"Oh!" Interest stirred inside Abel. "I'm sorry my father isn't at
home, Wessel, but if there is anything I can do – "

"Yes, perhaps there is. You see, I am planning a holiday for Susarah
and myself, and we wish to spend it in Doornboomstad."

Jesus, Abel thought, of all the places there must be to choose from
in which to spend a holiday! Even as he thought it Wessel began to
explain earnestly, "Holiday is, perhaps, the wrong word. I look upon
it as a *pilgrimage*. Doornboomstad is the town in which the very first

Tabernacle of the Reformed Evangelists was established, and Susarah and I have a great desire to attend a service there. I wondered, Abel, whether you could recommend a hostel or boarding-house in which Susarah and I could stay for a few days?"

"Doornboomstad is not a town. It is – " Abel stopped, excitement shooting like a flame through his blood. "You obviously have transport, Wessel. Why don't you and Susarah come and stay here with us, as our guests?"

"Well – !" Wessel's voice suggested that they had been offered a glimpse of heaven. "That would be – Are you quite sure?"

"You and Susarah would be very welcome. You'll be travelling by car?"

"No. We intend taking the train. But I could send my motorcycle combination to Doornboomstad by freight in advance, and use it to come on to Jakkalsdrif."

"Yes, do that," Abel said. "When should we expect you?"

"Susarah and I will catch the night-train to Doornboomstad on the last Saturday of the month, and then after attending the morning service in the Tabernacle we could travel to your farm in the motorcycle combination."

"Fine!" Abel made his voice as warmly welcoming as he could. "My mother would be especially pleased to meet the daughter and son-in-law of her oldest friend." Just before ending the conversation he added, on an apparent afterthought, "Oh, by the way, there's something quite important you could do for me. My mother has been intending to write to Susarah's mother about it for some time now, but we've been kept so busy . . . The thing is, Wessel, that my birth certificate has been destroyed. It was among several other papers and letters that were eaten by mice. We want to send away for a copy, but my mother is not sure if I was born in June or July. We tend not to bother much with almanacs on a farm – "

"Oh, I understand completely! My late parents were farmers, before the Boer War ruined them. If one asked them when something happened, they'd say, 'in the year of the great drought' or 'the year when the locusts wiped out the harvest'."

"That's right! Anyway, my mother is certain that she wrote to Susarah's mother a few days after I was born, and that she would have a record of the date. Could you ask Mevrou Steenkamp about it? My mother feels certain she would have kept all the old correspondence so if you could bring with you the particular letter, recording the exact date of my birth, it would be a great help."

"I'll certainly do so," Wessel promised.

Abel danced a jig towards the door after he had replaced the telephone. He'd got the Bitch! By God, he'd got her at last! He could hardly wait until the Sunday when Wessel du Plessis and his Halleluiah-wife Susarah would be arriving at Jakkalsdrif. Their totally unexpected arrival would be shock enough for the Bitch, but just wait until they handed over the letter recording the date of his birth!

He went outside, intending to join Koos in the fields. But suddenly Mwende was blocking his path. With an authority she had not used towards him since he had been small, she said, "Abel, you come with me. We speak together where no one hears."

He frowned. "What is it, Mwende? I'm busy – "

"You not going to be too busy to hear what I must say to you! You come now, to the barn."

Mystified, he followed her into the barn. Tina was inside, sitting on some straw, and she had been crying. Mwende went to her, hauling her to her feet and holding her arm in a gesture that was at the same time protective and punishing.

"Abel," Mwende said bluntly, "you make baby with my Tina."

"*What?*" He stared at both of them.

"You know what you do, you and Tina! You think you can go on doing it, and never make a baby? Huh!"

Tina was weeping again, and Mwende gave her a slight shake. "Too late for crying, girl! Time for crying was *before* you start doing bad things with Abel!"

"It isn't mine!" Abel almost shouted. "It can't be! Not after all these years – "

"Who else, then?" Mwende demanded. "You tell me."

There was no one else, and all three of them knew it. Christ, Abel thought, is nothing in my life ever going to be fair? To receive news like this, when he least expected it, at a time when he had victory within his grasp . . . What good would it do him to be acknowledged the rightful master of Jakkalsdrif if it were known to everyone that he had fathered a half-caste *basterkind*?

"I don't believe you!" he bellowed. "It's a lie! Tina is barren – "

"You think I *want* this thing to be so?" Mwende demanded, and her own voice cracked with emotion for the first time. "You think I *want* my daughter to do like her Mamma do?"

"When?" Abel asked dully, after a moment.

Mwende shrugged. "Not for long time. Eight months, perhaps."

He stared at her. "Then how the hell can you be sure? It's nothing but a false alarm – "

"No, Abel. I see the truth in Tina's eyes, and then I throw the *dolosse*, like my old uncle Bolih teach me long ago. The bones, they never lie. The *dolosse* speak of a baby coming."

Abel could not dismiss the message of the *dolosse*. He had seen the predictions, interpreted from the way in which the bones fell, come true too many times to shrug it off as superstition.

"You tell anyone that the child is mine," he raged, "and I'll kill you! I'll burn down your hut while you sleep! Let people think it was some young buck from another *stad*, someone not fussy about Tina's white blood! Do you hear me? Keep my name out of it or you're both dead!"

He flung himself out of the barn and strode out into the fields. He had seen the fear in their eyes and he knew they would not dare involve him in this pregnancy of Tina's. There was no reason why anyone should ever know that the child was his.

But gradually, as the days passed, Abel began to face the hideous truth that his responsibility in the matter could not possibly fail to become common knowledge. The chances of Tina's baby being more negroid than white in appearance were slim, since both its grandfather and its father had been white. Given his luck, he thought bitterly, it would be far too much to hope for that the baby might be a throwback to Tina's Zulu blood.

Panic began to overwhelm him. Of course everyone would know immediately who the father was! Who else was there on or near Jakkalsdrif who had to make do with the comfort Mwende's *basterkind* could offer him, because he knew no other girls and even if he did he couldn't hope to form a relationship while he had nothing to offer but a position as wife to an unpaid farm labourer? What made the affair doubly bitter was the fact that, at long last, his status was about to change. Wessel du Plessis would bring with him the letter proving that Abel had been born first.

Once Tina's child was born, shouting aloud the truth about its parentage, Abel would be ruined, doomed, ostracised for the rest of his life, just as Mwende and Tina had been ostracised by their own black folk. Tina would not suffer, for already she had nothing to lose, whereas he . . . Every dream he had ever had of taking his rightful place as the owner of Jakkalsdrif and living there with a wife like Hester who had chosen him above everyone else, commanding the respect of their neighbours, being *someone*, would disappear like dew before the sun.

Unless he could get away from Jakkalsdrif immediately and stay away until after Tina's child had been born, so that no one would connect him with the event . . . But *how*?

As he laboured with Koos and the Bitch to plough the hard earth, to rake over the soil and painstakingly gather up hardy weeds so that they would not strike root again, Abel's mind was equally busy, picking at the dilemma facing him.

As if to reward them for their hard work a shower of spring rain fell, while the ploughed earth was still porous enough to retain the moisture, and the seeds swiftly germinated. It didn't seem to matter that one blazing, cloudless day followed another after that, for the young plants pushed their heads to the surface and unfurled their leaves, full of promise of a good harvest for once if only the rain didn't stay away again this year.

Mocking that promise and that hope, it suddenly began to rain with a ferocity and a destructive violence Abel had never known before. In the space of a few short hours the mealie-seedlings had been sluiced out of the ground; the river had risen, bursting its banks and swelling its tributaries and streams, and all of Jakkalsdrif and the surrounding districts became flooded. The river rose at one stage to the level of the stoep, so that they had to wade, knee-deep, to get the cattle and horses and sheep safely into the barn and the corral. The small stock, however, fared badly, and drowned chickens and young lambs bobbed on the red-brown water surrounding the house and outbuildings, promising a feast for the hovering vultures.

Between the desperate tasks of saving as many as possible of the stock, and worrying about the need to avoid being connected with Tina's pregnancy, Abel had almost forgotten about the forthcoming visit to Jakkalsdrif of Wessel du Plessis and Susarah.

When he did remember it, he began to perceive it as the answer to a prayer. Whatever a motorcycle combination was, it was clearly a vehicle with a combustion engine. So why should he not offer to drive it back to Johannesburg for Wessel, instead of having it sent by freight?

He looked at the devastation surrounding them and smiled grimly. He had even been offered a believable motive for leaving Jakkalsdrif; his departure would be connected with the flooding and not with Tina's pregnancy. To this end he began to complain bitterly and often, particularly when neighbours arrived to use the post office service, that if Dirk did not invest money in Jakkalsdrif the farm would never recover from the ravages of the flood. When Abel left, people would assume he had given up the thankless task of working the farm for Dirk and gone to see him, to ask him for money. The Bitch, of course, would think it was the business of getting Jakkalsdrif legally transferred to his own name that was keeping Abel away.

When he did return it would be in triumph as the rightful master of Jakkalsdrif, and no one would have the slightest cause to connect him with Tina's illegitimate *basterkind*.

All he had to do now was to wait for Wessel and Susarah du Plessis to arrive on the motorcycle combination which was to be his passport out of Jakkalsdrif and trouble.

*　*　*

Petronella had at first been totally and cruelly fooled by the distant sound of an approaching motor. Forgetting that it was a Saturday, when the mailvan always arrived in the morning instead of in the afternoon, she had immediately thought: *Marcus!*

Marcus is coming home, her mind and her senses had exulted. Marcus, of whom nothing had been heard or seen since the day of the last and most devastating quarrel in what had always been a stormy marriage. As usual Abel and his threats had been at the root of it, and in a temper she had taunted Marcus with the reminder that all he had a right to on Jakkalsdrif was his miserable strip of waste-land, his Korah named for a doomed leader of a tribe of Israelites.

So now Petronella, with hope lifting her heart and making her step light, hurried to the stoep to await Marcus's arrival, only to recognise the approaching mailvan instead. She turned away, painful disillusionment like a rank taste in her mouth, facing the knowledge that before her stretched yet more untold, empty and tortured days and nights without Marcus.

There was a brief, slight easing of pain and despair when she sat down to breakfast in the kitchen with Abel and Simon a little later, and her youngest son said, "There's a letter for you from your friend in Johannesburg, Ma."

As she stretched out her hand for the letter, she thought: Jakoba is the only constancy left in my life, my only enduring comfort. This time I'll answer her letter by return. I'll tell her how well things are going here on Jakkalsdrif and how happy Marcus and I are together, how much he hates our separations and always hurries home whenever he can. And as I write it I'll be able to make myself believe it for a short while.

"Well, let me have the letter!" she commanded impatiently, because Simon had withdrawn it and was studying the envelope with a frown.

"It isn't for you after all, Ma," He announced. "It's your friend's handwriting, but the letter is addressed to Abel."

"*Abel!*" she echoed blankly. "It can't be. Let me see – "

But Abel's hand shot out as Simon was about to pass the letter to her, and he wrested it from his brother's grasp. There was no sign now of his recent preoccupation; his eyes were bright with triumph and malice. "It's addressed to me, right? You have the word of Simon the crawler, Simon the little holy shit, so the letter is most definitely mine!"

Petronella passed her tongue over her lower lip, and said weakly, "There must be some mistake. Jakoba would only write to you if you had written to her first, and you can't write. You don't even know her address – "

Abel merely grinned at her, the malice sharpening in his eyes.

Desperation entered her voice. "There is bound to be a note inside, addressed to me – "

"Why should there be? If she wanted to write to you, she would have done so in the usual way."

This was so patently true that Petronella was momentarily silenced. At last she cleared her throat. "You – you won't be able to read what Jakoba has written. Let Simon – "

Abel made a scornful sound. "You must take me for a fool! Do you think I'd trust that arse-creeper any more than I'd trust you to read to me what the letter really says?" He thrust the unopened envelope into his pocket, and then he leant his elbows on the table, sitting with his chin resting on his fists and smiling at her with fiendish triumph. "Besides, I don't need to have the letter read to me. I know what your friend Jakoba has written. And you know it too, don't you?" He rose, pushing his chair back at the same time, and walked out of the room whistling.

As soon as he was a safe distance away from the house, and therefore out of earshot of the Bitch, Abel stopped whistling and his hand touched the letter in his pocket. Christ, it was humiliating that he was unable to read for himself a letter addressed to him, but had to trot to the schoolhouse like a small boy and ask Meneer Els to read it aloud to him.

He frowned as he strode away in the direction of the schoolhouse. He had been just as astonished as the Bitch to receive a letter from her friend. Why should Jakoba have written to him, when her Bible-thumping son-in-law Wessel du Plessis and his Halleluiah-wife Susarah were due to arrive at Jakkalsdrif tomorrow, as if out of the blue?

The puzzle of the letter pushed to the back of his mind for a moment, Abel stood still and stared blankly about him. God, the sight was enough to take the heart out of anyone.

Because the soil had been so hard and dry after last year's drought, the water had not been able to soak into it to any appreciable level and had instead been sucked back gradually into the Vaal River as its own level subsided, taking with it yet more of the valuable topsoil. As well as the corpses of chickens and lambs, the ground had been strewn with carp and barbel washed from the river, all adding to the stink of putrefaction, and luring the circling vultures. Whole areas of Jakkalsdrif now looked like an enormous dry water-course, with the earth surface cracking in the sun, and the dry grass and reeds caught up untidily on the tops of thorn bushes showed where the water level had briefly reached. The cultivated fields themselves were still a morass and it would be days, perhaps weeks, before they had dried sufficiently to be reharrowed and reseeded, and by then it would be too late to put in mealies and he would have to think of some other crop to grow.

He remembered, suddenly, that this particular responsibility would not rest on his shoulders, and he only hoped the Bitch and Koos would not put the land under something that would impoverish it further.

Shrugging, he hurried on his way to the schoolhouse. Normally, on a Saturday morning Simon would be holding a Bible class there, but today no children would be coming. All the farms in the district had been similarly affected by that vicious cloudburst and some low-lying ones along the Vaal River had come off even worse, so that families were still marooned inside their houses. But everywhere, the older children would be needed to clear away the debris and dead stock left by the flood and no one could be spared to take the little ones for Bible lessons.

Set back a short distance from the two-roomed schoolhouse was the home of Meneer Els, flanked on one side by what would normally have been a small patch of mealies grown for the use of the school-master and his wife and children. On the other side was a large kitchen garden, but mealie-patch and kitchen garden alike had been devastated by the flood.

Abel did not trouble to walk on to the schoolmaster's house, because he guessed that Meneer Els would have found some excuse to go to the school now that there was no garden or mealie-patch in which he could legitimately seek his usual Saturday morning refuge. His wife was always nagging at her husband because he did not do more to bring himself to the notice of the authorities so that he would be offered advancement. Meneer Els would have wanted to remove himself from his wife's nagging tongue, and the schoolhouse was his only possible sanctuary today.

Abel found the schoolmaster inside one of the classrooms, engrossed in a book. Withdrawing the letter from his pocket, Abel said, "I'd like you to read this for me, please."

Meneer Els's eyebrows rose. "It could be personal. Why didn't you ask Simon or your mother to read it for you?"

Abel had his answer ready. "I think I know what it's about. I've arranged for old friends of my mother's to pay a visit to Jakkalsdrif tomorrow, and I don't want to spoil the surprise by having her or Simon read it."

Meneer Els did not comment, but took the letter, slit the envelope and began to read aloud:

" 'I am writing on Susarah's behalf, because she is too overcome by grief to do it herself, and as you must know from your conversation with Wessel, she is expecting a baby. I have to tell you that Wessel was killed two days ago when a motor car struck him. I am sorry that you were never fated to meet one another, but if you should ever find yourself in Johannesburg do not hesitate to call on us. We would make you as welcome as you were prepared to make poor, dear Wessel and my grieving daughter. I cannot describe to you what your invitation to Jakkalsdrif meant to Wessel, and how greatly he and Susarah had looked forward to their visit. With best wishes, Jakoba Steenkamp.' "

Abel had been listening in a daze of shock and disbelief. Afterwards, he scarcely heard the schoolmaster's expressions of sympathy and his probing attempts to establish precisely who the people involved were, and how the sudden death of Wessel du Plessis was likely to affect the Koen family.

Abel thought he must have reacted in a way that seemed normal, for he was aware of Meneer Els gripping him by the hand and saying, "I know you'll break the news gently to your mother. Please convey my condolences to her, will you."

Abel nodded, stuffed the letter back inside his pocket and blundered from the schoolhouse. Jesus God, was nothing *ever* going to go right for him? He had counted – totally relied – upon that visit tomorrow and now he had been left high and dry.

The letter hadn't even given him the answer to the question he had asked Wessel du Plessis to put to Jakoba. The damned, worthless letter was just a piece of paper leaving him with no way out of his troubles at all.

He cared nothing for Jakoba's loss, and viewed Wessel's death as no more than a personal catastrophe for himself, the ruination of his plans. As for Susarah, the pregnant widow . . . He gave a sour, despairing crack of laughter. He had another pregnant girl to lose sleep over.

Abel sat down on a giant termite-hill and swore savagely, hopelessly. He'd had it all worked out so neatly. He would have got away from Jakkalsdrif in time to avoid being connected with the birth of Tina's child and with a perfect alibi for leaving and staying away. He would have had the evidence that he was born before Dirk and he would have had the added, vengeful bonus of leaving the Bitch alone and helpless on the farm, full of terror as she waited for the world to learn how she and the Preacher had cheated him.

And it had all been ruined by Wessel's death. Once again fate had dealt Abel a sideways swipe and left him with no weapon with which to fight, let alone defend himself. He would have to stay here on Jakkalsdrif, dealing with all the added problems and hard work the flood had left in its wake, knowing the full force of condemnation would be turned upon him when Tina's child was born.

His sour, jaundiced gaze fell upon a part of the fence that had been trampled down by their cattle before the flood. For what it was worth, while they were waiting for the cultivated fields to dry out, he and Koos might as well set about repairing it . . .

Unbidden, a memory flashed into his mind, the recollection of an incident connected with their cattle breaching the fence and getting into Meneer Els's kitchen garden. It had seemed too trivial to be given a second thought but now he recognised how it might well be turned into the very weapon he needed.

He began to smile slowly, with dawning hope, and jumped up from the termite hill, his strides lengthening in his urgency to return home and put into practice his simple but ruthless plan.

There was no sign of the Bitch when he reached the house. Fretting and worrying about that letter from her friend Jakoba, she had probably gone for a walk to gather her thoughts. Abel dismissed her from his mind, and went to the post office room. Simon was talking on the telephone and from the pious pitch of his voice Abel guessed that he was in conversation with the pastor in Doornboomstad.

Closing the door behind him, Abel said, "Finish your conversation. I want to talk to you."

At first it seemed that Simon meant to ignore the command, but something in Abel's expression must have moved him to think again, for he said, "I'll see you at the service tomorrow, Pastor," and replaced the telephone on its hook. "What do you want?" he asked warily, watching Abel.

"Ten pounds," Abel said.

Simon's mouth fell open. "What do you mean – ten pounds?"

"I mean it the way it sounds."

Simon gave a disbelieving titter. "You must be out of your mind! Even if I possessed a sum like ten pounds, why should I lend it to you? I suppose it has something to do with that letter from Ma's friend – "

"It has. And I'm not asking you to lend it to me," Abel cut him short. "I'm telling you to give it to me."

Simon jumped up. "You *are* off your head! In the first place, I don't have ten pounds, and if I did I certainly wouldn't give it to you!"

"Oh, you would!" Abel contradicted, watching him. "You most certainly would. It's going to cost ten pounds to keep you out of trouble of a rather nasty kind."

He watched Simon's tongue darting out and moistening his lips. "I know you're bigger and stronger than I am, but – "

"Oh, I shan't lay a finger on you. Instead, I'd tell everyone what I saw at the schoolhouse last Saturday after your Bible class. I'd been on my way to talk to Meneer Els about some of our cattle that had got into his kitchen garden when I happened to look through the window into the classroom, and I saw you with Rieta Els."

"She was helping me to tidy up after the children!" Simon cried shrilly.

"*I* could say that something quite different was going on. Think about it. Rieta is sixteen, and quite pretty in a washed-out sort of way. She's the apple of her father's eye and her mother thinks she's far too good for anyone around here. You wouldn't be allowed to use the school for any more Bible lessons, but that would only be the start – "

"No one would believe you! Meneer Els knows that I feel strongly about purity – "

Abel interrupted him with a cynical sound. "He also knows that there's many a creeping Jesus who preaches purity and secretly pinches the cat in the dark! You'd be finished, little brother! No more Bible classes, no more hopes of becoming a sainted pastor! From what I've seen of Rieta Els it wouldn't surprise me in the least if she went along with the story I'd tell. She'd love all the drama and the attention. It wouldn't surprise me if Meneer Els brought criminal charges against you."

Simon's legs seemed to buckle under him and he fell into the chair. He didn't say anything; he merely stared at Abel with wide, horror-filled eyes.

"So," Abel went on briskly, "I think you'll agree that my silence is worth at least ten pounds."

Simon made several attempts at speech before his voice came out coherently, high-pitched and trembling. "I – I don't have ten pounds. You must – must know that . . ."

"Of course I know it." Abel glanced pointedly at the locked steel box in which the post office funds were kept. "It's almost the end of the month. There'll be far more in there than ten pounds."

Simon looked as if he were about to burst into tears. "It w-would be s-stealing," he stuttered. "I w-would be held responsible. H-how would I account for the m-money – "

"That's your *indaba*," Abel cut in, and then relented. "You could say that you'd left the post office unattended for a few minutes and the cash-box unlocked, and that I stole the money. But I want it, and I want it *now*."

Simon did begin to weep then, tears of hopelessness and despair as he fumbled in a drawer for the key to the cash-box and unlocked it, counting ten pounds from its contents with trembling hands.

Abel stuffed ten-shilling notes and silver and copper into his pockets. Then he hurried from the room without wasting another word or glance on Simon, and in his own room he threw his clothes into a rucksack normally used for hand-sowing mealies. He added the only two items of personal value he possessed – the letter from Jakoba, bearing her address, and a well-thumbed envelope containing a note from Hester and the snapshot of her in her wedding dress, and then he left the house.

The Bitch had still not returned home when he set out with Koos in the cart, supposedly to buy seed potatoes in Doornboomstad. As soon as they reached the village Abel intended sending Koos home. If he himself caught the eleven o'clock train he should reach Johannesburg by late afternoon.

Grinning to himself, he patted his pockets containing the ten pounds, his passport to escape from the blame and disgrace of having fathered Tina's child, and also the means of obtaining from Jakoba the proof that he had been born before Dirk.

Somehow he would find a way of surviving in Johannesburg, and when he returned within the space of a year it would be as the respected master of Jakkalsdrif. No one would hold it against him that he had 'borrowed' ten pounds from the post office once they knew why he had needed it.

26

Marcus had deliberately timed his journey so that he would pass through Doornboomstad after darkness had fallen. For him to be seen travelling along the village street on a Saturday would have meant being hailed by members of his flock and he would have been forced to stop and try to find excuses why he could not hold a service there the following day. Even after all this time, he dared not risk giving Abel an opportunity of attending a service held by him, and exposing his parents to scandal and disgrace before the congregation.

Marcus sighed and watched the truck's headlights glinting on water-filled *dongas* after Doornboomstad had been left behind. He knew all about the flood; he had kept in contact by telephone with the pastor in the village, without giving away the fact that he was not in similar contact with his wife on Jakkalsdrif. The flood, Marcus acknowledged to himself, had been the excuse he had subconsciously been seeking to take him back to Jakkalsdrif and Petronella. Aai, but he had been missing her, longing for her, wanting her in spite of everything.

Had it all been worth it, he had asked himself many times while he was away from her. Often, his countless sacrifices to love had seemed to him to have been a thoughtless squandering of the future, the folly of youth blind to everything but what seemed desirable at the time. This feeling was strongest when he stayed with Cousin Reuben, knowing himself to be a close relative and yet an outsider, excluded from the rites and rituals of Judaism. On Friday evenings in particular he felt like a wistful child looking through a window at a scene in which he would never again be allowed to participate because of misbehaviour in the past.

It was then that he thought of his stormy marriage, and of his three sons who should have compensated for so much he had given up but who did not. Dirk – Marcus shook his head sadly. Such a good business brain his second son had, but with the flaw of ostentation and arrogance that would yet be his downfall. Dirk would take no advice from his father these days and the way he treated poor, sweet-natured Hester was a scandal.

And Simon . . . Marcus shifted uneasily in the driving seat. Why could he not take pride in Simon, who wished only to follow in his father's footsteps? Perhaps it was because he tried too hard, or because he showed no initiative of his own but could only copy.

Then there was Abel, for whom such a crippling guilt was felt that Marcus could barely look him in the eye. Perhaps if Abel had not been cheated of his birth-right *he* would have been the one to fill his father with pride, the son Marcus had dreamt of.

He remembered how he had felt when Petronella was carrying their first child. A son it would be for certain, Marcus had told himself; a son named Joshua who would make something of himself, be clever, become a lawyer or a doctor. A son in whom to delight, as Cousin Reuben delighted in *his* first-born David, named for Reuben's dead father according to tradition and on his way to becoming an architect.

Marcus sighed deeply and tried to exclude thoughts about his sons, and concentrate instead on the coming reunion with Petronella. It was late, and she would be asleep, but no doubt the sound of the truck would wake her up. Perhaps he should switch off the engine before he reached home and allow the truck to coast the rest of the way. Perhaps the surprise of seeing him in the morning would silence Petronella for long enough to make her listen as he tried to explain to her once again what the consequences would be if he fell foul of the law. He had discussed the subject many times with Cousin Reuben and his Jewish friends, and none of them had any doubt that he would be deported, unless he left voluntarily for some country outside the British Empire, like America.

The Church of the Reformed Evangelists in America, which might once have helped him to settle there with Petronella and those of his sons who wished to join them, would no longer do so. Marcus had kept it to himself, but there had been growing dismay and disapproval in the United States about the way in which he had reshaped the dogma of the Church of the Reformed Evangelists, and the mother church had finally disowned him and their South African branch. To pay his own passage to a country of his choosing outside the British Empire, let alone one for Petronella and any of their sons, was quite out of the question. Apart from a modest amount to help support his family, all the money Marcus made with his buying and selling had always gone into Church funds.

So, with no money for voluntary exile, that would leave deportation. If Germany, poverty-stricken after the war, would not take him the British authorities had sufficient influence to force Poland, the homeland of his father, to accept him.

Der heim, his father had called it. It was a term used by both his parents and all their friends when they spoke about the various countries of their birth. The term had a nostalgic ring to it and it always puzzled him that they could think of it in that way when all their talk was of bitter poverty and fear, of being herded into ghettos and despised, of people disappearing mysteriously and of young girls being raped with impunity simply because they were Jewish, and their violators knew they need fear no official retribution, that authority would turn a blind eye. *Der heim*, from which his father's generation had fled to start again with nothing in the new countries of their adoption.

But South Africa, Marcus's country of adoption, had thrown him out, and he would try again to make Petronella understand that if the authorities realised he, who had been declared an undesirable alien, had slunk back like a thief, they would most certainly send him to *der heim*. Even if one discounted the fear of persecution, of being herded into a ghetto, and if one disregarded the rumours among the Jewish community about a worsening of conditions for Jews in that part of Europe – even if one ignored all that, what would there be for him in that so-called *heim* of his? A country he did not know, and where he had no close family or friends, where he would have no means of earning his living and where he would be classified as a Jew but despised by the Jewish community for having converted to Christianity?

He would explain all this to Petronella and maybe, please God, this time she *would* understand and she would cease her demands that he should go and confess everything to the authorities.

As Marcus switched off the engine and cruised silently down the gentle slope of the track towards the house, he could see by the headlights some of the devastation wreaked by the flood. No farmer himself, he could still recognise the seriousness of what had happened. But even so he could not help feeling glad that the flood had forced him to make a choice, and that in making that choice he had allowed his heart to rule his head.

The house was silent as he let himself in by the front door. Feeling his way, he tiptoed to the kitchen and groped for the candle which he knew would be standing in its stick on the edge of the dresser, a box of matches beside it. Then, with the flickering candle lighting his way, he moved quietly to the bedroom he had not shared with Petronella for such a long time.

He set the candle down and looked at her. She lay on her side, part of her long pale-gold hair fanned out on the pillow, the rest brushing her cheek and spilling over her shoulder. The night was warm and she had tossed aside the bedclothes, and his mouth softened with tenderness and desire as he took in the fact that she was wearing an old shirt of his instead of a nightgown. Had she chosen to wear it because she felt cooler in it than in a nightgown, or because of her longing for him? Whatever the reason had been, she looked both endearingly vulnerable and sensual in it, with the top buttons undone and the shirt-tail barely covering her thighs.

He kept his eyes riveted upon her as he undressed. Dear God, she looked so *young*, barely older than she had that first time he had seen her by the river. Even that shirt of his which she was wearing recalled their first meeting, and set him remembering how he had given her his silk shirt to wear when she'd been too embarrassed to put on her clothes in front of him.

He snuffed out the candle and slid into bed beside her. He had had every intention of keeping to his own side of the large bed so that he would not disturb her sleep, but the memory of how she had looked in his shirt, both innocent and abandoned, stirred an overwhelming longing for her inside him, and he moved closer, touching her shoulder. She turned over, flinging her arm above her head. He drew her against him, thinking how rightly and naturally her body seemed to fit the contours of his own, even after all these years and so many separations.

"Aai, my Petronella, my love, *mein tiere*," he muttered huskily and sought her mouth while his hand caressed the seemingly ageless curves of her breasts and thighs, and he knew by her instant response that she had woken up.

Petronella's hand slid from his bare shoulder to his waist. This was a dream about Marcus that often recurred, but ah, so real this time, so sweet and haunting and yet so wild as she felt herself being swept up by all the old magic of his pleasuring and they moved together in a rhythm that for all its familiarity was at the same time as fresh and unique as Marcus always succeeded in making it.

"Petronella, I love you and I could not stay away from you . . ."

"Thank God. Oh, thank God, Marcus . . ."

Their exchange, too, was part of the recurring dream, and so was the way he held her afterwards, with her head tucked against his chest and his fingers stroking her hair. She slid back into the darker depths of sleep, hugging the beautiful dream to her.

When she woke up in the morning, shreds of it were still clinging to her mind. She felt the pain of reality washing over her for it had, as always, been only a dream. And then reality became starker and she sat up in bed, her knees drawn up to her chin, her mind still slightly dulled by the herbal infusion, one of Mamma's recipes, which she had made for herself last night to ensure that sleep would temporarily blot out the most cataclysmic situation with which she had ever been faced.

She knew herself to be alone in the house. Because it was Sunday, Mwende and Tina would not be along until later in the morning and Simon had saddled a horse yesterday afternoon and ridden to Doornboomstad so that he would be able to attend the service in the Tabernacle there. And Abel . . .

Dear Christ, Petronella thought in terror. Dear Christ, *what am I going to do?*

The blood was pounding so loudly in her ears that she did not hear footsteps approaching, and she looked up in total disbelief as Marcus appeared in the doorway, carrying a cup and saucer.

"I have made coffee for you, *liefling*," he said, smiling at her so that the grooves danced in his cheeks.

Her first instinctive response was one of overwhelming joy. But even as she hurled herself out of bed to run to him things were slotting into place, and the joy turned into hysterical rage.

"You bastard!" she screamed at him. "You bloody bastard! You dared to come back, to – to sneak into my bed while I slept – *I thought it was a dream!*"

He set the coffee cup down and frowned, moving towards her. "Petronella, you woke up and you spoke to me – "

"*I was asleep!*" Even as she spat the words at him an inner voice told her that she must have surfaced to a certain level of wakefulness, blurred by the herbal infusion she had taken at bedtime. She had already closed her mind to that inner voice when Marcus asked in horrified disbelief, "You imagine that I would – that I would pleasure you while you slept? That I would not care how you felt or whether you were willing – ?"

Harsh, bitter laughter spewed from her. "Pleasure? You *raped* me, you despicable bastard! As if it wasn't enough that you had already betrayed me!"

"Betrayed?" he echoed, his voice stiff and distant now.

"Don't pretend that you don't know what I'm talking about, you hypocritical shit!" She knew that she was hurtling towards an abyss but she could not force herself to stop. "You went to see Jakoba and confessed everything to her hoping she would be on our side and keep the truth from Abel! Instead she wrote to him, and no more than half an hour after he received the letter he left Jakkalsdrif!"

Marcus shook his head and said with distaste, the stiffness more pronounced in his voice, "It is yet one more game Abel has thought to play. I did not go to Jakoba, and how can it be possible that she should write to Abel?"

"She did write to him, and if nothing else the letter made things easier for him by giving him her address, and he left as soon – "

"You saw this letter yourself, Petronella?" Marcus cut in. "You studied it closely and you assured yourself that it was written by the hand of Jakoba?"

"No, but Simon did! And stop trying to take attention away from your own treachery! You – "

"This letter," Marcus interrupted, "the one you did not even see – it was clearly part of Abel's game. You have told me that you destroyed all the letters received from Jakoba so that Abel would not obtain her address, but it appears obvious that an envelope was overlooked, and that Abel found it. He gave it to one of his friends, one of the neighbours, and asked for her writing to be copied, saying it was meant to be a joke. You know how clever Abel can be when he plays his games of fear with us – "

"Then what about the ten pounds? Yes, Marcus, ten pounds stolen by him from the post office funds while Simon was out of the room! Ten pounds for which *I* am responsible because you transferred the post office licence to my name! And the day after tomorrow the man will be coming to check the accounts and collect the month's money! So what do I tell him, Marcus? That my lying, treacherous husband, masquerading as the great and good Pastor Koen, says it is only a game, *a joke?*"

Her voice had risen as she spoke, and then it was spinning out of control, raging at him, uttering unforgivable insults about rape and about other women and anything else that came into her mind, and she could see the abyss yawning at her feet but she was totally incapable of drawing back from it.

"Petronella!" It was a tone of voice Marcus had never before used to her, and it brought an abrupt end to her tirade. She saw him tossing banknotes on to the foot of the bed. "There are well in excess of ten pounds there. It was intended for the purchase of goods from the market, but I am giving it to you even though I know that Abel will soon be back, laughing at the success of this game he has been playing with you."

"He won't! This time – "

Marcus went on as if she had not interrupted. "Always in the past, Petronella, you have accused me of having an interest in other women, and I have always told you your accusations were false. Now, they are no longer quite so far from the truth. I came home to you because I knew that I had to make a choice, because now there *is* a woman, a widow who, like myself, was not born in this country. And the things you have been saying to me this morning have shown me where my choice must lie."

She was falling into the abyss and there was nothing for her to grab hold of to save herself. She could not even find the voice to cry out in terror or beg for help.

Marcus's voice followed her relentlessly into the abyss. "She is not like you, Petronella, this woman of whom I have told you. She is not all fire and passion and rage. She is not beautiful like you either. But she offers me peace and she gives me comfort. When I am not travelling I stay with her – very discreetly, in a way that will not give rise to scandal. I do not love her as I love you, but with her I can live. She does not demand anything of me."

From the bottom of the abyss, Petronella whispered through frozen lips, "Do you – sleep with her, Marcus?"

"Once only have I shared her bed, but from today I shall share it all the time when I am not travelling. It is not pleasuring as you and I have known it, Petronella. It is a giving and receiving of comfort. So I shall make my life with her from now on. You have been responsible for showing me how to choose."

She watched, crouching in the abyss as he opened drawers and removed what still remained of his belongings and made parcels of everything that might ever have reminded her that he had once shared her life, however intermittently. He went on speaking in a passionless, practical tone that told her, more than anything else could have done, that this time he really was leaving her for good, and leaving her for another woman.

"Every month I shall send you money and I will also continue to settle all accounts in Doornboomstad. If you should find yourself in financial difficulties, telephone Dirk and ask him to put you in contact with my cousin Reuben. My cousin alone will know where I may be found."

"Marcus," Petronella whispered, "believe me, this time Abel – "

He silenced her with a cold, remote look. "If between you you choose to cause trouble for me, you and Abel – either by making public the fact that I have decided to live in adultery, or that I have no right to be in this country – I shall hear of it through my cousin Reuben, who will have gained the news through Dirk. If this should happen, Petronella, we will leave at once, this woman and I, and we shall go and live in the land of her birth, and there I will re-establish the Church of the Reformed Evangelists."

He filled his arms with the parcels he had been making of his possessions and went out to his truck, and she followed him closely, her arms hugged about her breasts, uncaring of the fact that all she was wearing was an old shirt of Marcus's.

That shirt was all she had left of him, she thought as she stood there, watching him turn the truck around and drive away. She was too numb to feel anything but later, she knew, feelings would rush in to torment her and turn her life into an unbearable hell.

Some lines of poetry she had once read in one of Marcus's books slipped into her mind. She had not understood the poem in its entirety and she had thought she'd forgotten those particular lines. But perhaps she had merely forced herself to try to forget them, for now they returned to her with haunting clarity.

> Warped by his hate and anger,
> Neglecting what love had sown,
> Reaping his bitter harvest –
> A starveling, forever alone.

It had seemed to her like a prophecy when she'd first read those lines, and now it was indeed about to come true.

27

Johannesburg bewildered, frightened and excited Abel. The train journey itself had been an unnerving experience of noise and smoke and steam, of being hurtled across the countryside, catching brief glimpses of small villages and larger towns. Just as he had begun to adjust to it all a huge, sprawling settlement had come into view, rimmed by what seemed like small, flat-topped whitish mountains. From the way in which the other passengers had gathered together their belongings, Abel had guessed that they were about to arrive in Johannesburg.

Standing outside the station building, he watched the many different kinds of vehicles passing and listened to the noise. What looked like miniature trains were clanking along on tracks in the middle of the street, carrying passengers and ringing bells. As he tried to gather his courage to cross the busy street Abel strained his ears to listen to passers-by talking, but none of them spoke anything but English, and so he couldn't ask them for advice on what to do next.

A little desperately, he told himself that he could not continue standing there indefinitely. Somehow he would have to find his way to Newlands and ask for directions to the house of Jakoba Steenkamp. In the note Meneer Els had read to him she had said he would be welcome there at any time.

But surely, a voice of common sense urged, she had not meant a few days after the death of her son-in-law Wessel? Distaste touched him too as he thought of walking into an atmosphere of gloom, with an open coffin no doubt standing in the front parlour, and of having to sit around with a long face and speak in a hushed voice as if he cared about the death of Wessel du Plessis.

He removed from his rucksack the envelope containing Hester's note, which he knew read: 'To Abel with fond regards', and the snapshot she had sent him, and his heart melted as he stared at her lovely, smiling face. By an unfortunate coincidence the snapshot also showed the privy with its door ajar, as well as the iron cauldron in which soap was made on an outdoor fire, but he concentrated only on Hester. More than anything, he wanted to see *her*. She would insist that Dirk invite him to stay with them for a while, Abel felt certain, and the visit to Jakoba could wait. After all, there were many months which would have to be spent in Johannesburg before he dared return to Jakkalsdrif.

Having made up his mind as to his immediate destination, there still remained the problem of how to reach it. Everyone passing appeared to be in a desperate hurry and they seemed to speak nothing but English, so he could not ask them to direct him to Dirk's address.

Then he saw a middle-aged black man strolling along at a leisurely pace, and with sudden inspiration Abel approached him. "*Molo nkosi,*" he greeted the man respectfully, with due deference to his age. "*Wena siza mina?*" He held out the note Hester had written to him, and pointed at what he knew must be the address. "*Upi kaya ka yena?*"

The man had looked startled at first at being asked for help in Fanakalo, and Abel had feared that in Johannesburg the dialect was unknown. It also struck him that the man might be no more able to read Hester's script than he was himself.

But then a smile spread across the black man's face, showing gleaming teeth, as he looked from the note to Abel. "Ah, basie," he said in Afrikaans. "You from a farm, I think. Here, only white peoples speaking Fanakalo is in mines. Sure, I help you find the house of your friend. You come with me, basie."

As Abel fell into step beside the man he only half-listened to his talk of how he, too, had lived on a farm when he was younger but had been forced to come to Johannesburg to find work. But Abel paid closer attention when the man, who said his name was Isaac, explained that the miniature trains were called trams, and that one paid to ride in them, but it was not necessary to take a tram to Dirk's address because it was not so very far away and was, in fact, one of the flats above some shops in Market Street.

Threading his way through the crowds with Isaac, Abel reflected bitterly on the gross unfairness of life. Dirk had not had to flee to Johannesburg as a bewildered stranger, unable to read the street names, unable to converse with the people who seemed to know only English, nor had he had to rely on Fanakalo to get a kindly black man to help him find his way. Oh no, Dirk had been introduced to Johannesburg by the Preacher and had been handed, by a Jewish second cousin, a business of his own to run. Dirk had been eased gently into the maelstrom that was Johannesburg.

A sour laugh escaped Abel as he remembered that Dirk, too, had been responsible for a pregnancy outside marriage. The reason why Hester had not accompanied him on his brief visits to Jakkalsdrif had emerged when she gave birth to a son only seven months after their wedding. Oh, there had been a clicking of tongues among their neighbours at Jakkalsdrif but that had soon blown over. Dirk had done the right thing by the girl, after all, and had married her, so that was all right, the matter forgiven and forgotten. It would have been a vastly different bucket of shit if it had become known that Abel had also fathered a child, but one that would have to remain illegitimate and was a *basterkind* into the bargain.

Never mind, Abel told himself. Soon he would have in his possession the proof that Jakkalsdrif belonged to him. It might not be much, but all the work he did on it in future years would be for his own benefit, and it was more than likely that, while he stayed in Johannesburg, he would meet a girl whom he wished to marry and take home to his farm. And when Dirk came on one of his periodic showing-off visits Abel would bloody well rub in the fact of his ownership in every way he could.

Isaac came to a stop outside a shop that sold strange-looking plaited bread with black seeds on top and sticky cakes and half-moon-shaped buns. He pointed to a flight of stairs leading from a doorway to the left of the shop and said, "Up there, basie."

Abel fished in his pocket and brought out a silver tickey, handing it to Isaac who accepted the coin with grace and gratitude. Then, thanking him, Abel turned away and began to climb the stairs, marvelling at people living so high above the ground. He also noticed the flaking paint on the walls and the worn linoleum that covered the stairs. For all his big talk, Dirk's flat could not be so very grand after all.

At the top of the stairs was a small area of floor-space and to the right of it a door. As Abel knocked on it he could hear the fretful sound of a baby crying. His mouth was dry with excited anticipation now, and he pictured Hester coming to the door, wearing her dress of soft, floating panels that showed her knees and with her short, rich-brown hair curling in her neck. He swallowed. Why did Hester have to be married to Dirk, the mother of his baby? It seemed impossible that he, Abel, would find another such as she to marry, even in Johannesburg . . .

The door opened, and he stared stupidly at the faded, defeated-looking young woman whom he barely recognised as Hester. She wore a print house-dress that hung dispiritedly about her too-thin body and her legs were not encased in the bright, shiny silk stockings he remembered but were bare and showing unsightly knotted blue veins, and she wore ugly lace-up brown shoes. Her hair was covered in a scarf-thing so that he couldn't tell whether or not it was still shining or curling in her neck. Her face, once round and pretty, looked as if it had not been exposed to fresh air for a long while and had acquired a pasty colour and her blue eyes were surrounded by dark circles so that they appeared to have faded almost to the colour of skimmed milk. On one bony hip she was balancing her crying baby.

"Abel," she said flatly, with little surprise and even less interest.

"How are you, Hester?" he asked, feeling deflated now that his first shock had worn off. How could she have changed so much in little more than a year?

She shifted the crying baby to her other hip and said wanly, "I'm fine, thanks. What brings you here, Abel?"

What had brought him to the flat specifically had been the desire to see her again. But he couldn't tell her that, especially now that he *had* seen her again and it had not been worth the effort. But it came to him suddenly that Dirk owed him something, and should be made to help him find his feet in this noisy, bewildering city.

"I've left the farm," he said, "and I wanted to see Dirk. Is he at home?"

Hester shook her head. "Come inside. I'm expecting him back quite soon."

He entered the flat and looked around him as he followed Hester. For all his boasting, Dirk's flat was not grand after all, for the linoleum in the passage was only slightly less worn than that on the stairs. Abel saw that several doors led from the passage; some were shut but those that stood ajar showed the rooms beyond to be furnished with obviously cheap unmatching pieces that looked as if they had been bought second-hand, and the whole place was long overdue for repainting. But at least, Abel told himself, there were sufficient rooms in the flat for Dirk to be unable to pretend that they could not let him stay for a while because of lack of space.

Hester entered one of the rooms and he followed her. It was the kitchen, and along the left-hand wall a built-in enamel basin held unwashed dishes. Flanking it were cupboards, with shelves above holding plates and cups, and on the other side stood a cooking-stove, although he could see no sign of any fuel for stoking it. Flat-irons were heating on round steel surfaces on top of it, and in the centre of the room the kitchen table had been covered with an ironing blanket marked with flat-iron-shaped scorch marks. It was clear that Hester had been pressing one of Dirk's smart suits when Abel knocked on the door.

"This is little Marcus," Hester said belatedly, lifting the crying baby from her hip and laying him down inside a wicker cradle resting on two chairs. He continued to cry until she dipped a dummy into a bowl of sugar and put it in his mouth.

"Oh," was all Abel said. What did he care about Dirk's brat, named after the Preacher? He looked away from the baby and stared about him. God, his brother was a lying braggart! Making out that it was so smart to live in a flat, without mentioning that the walls which must once have been painted cream had turned into a drab khaki and that the furniture looked as if it had been scavenged from a public rubbish dump. And yet Dirk did make money; it showed in the clothes he wore and the cars he drove.

"Sit down, Abel," Hester invited him in a lack-lustre voice. "As soon as I've finished pressing Dirk's suit I'll make some coffee."

Coffee, Abel thought, aware of hunger-pangs and knowing that it could not be long before sundown. Surely Dirk would be expecting a cooked meal when he returned from work? Abel himself had eaten nothing since breakfast this morning. How long ago that seemed now . . .

Such light as filtered through the mean little window into the room was fast fading and Hester stopped what she was doing, replacing the flat-iron on the stove to heat it up again, and flicked a switch set into the wall. Instantly, the room was flooded with a light brighter than Abel had ever seen. He knew it must be the electricity he had heard about but he had not expected it to be so bright, showing even more cruelly the shabbiness of the flat and accentuating Hester's washed-out look.

The baby began to cry again just as Hester resumed her meticulous pressing of Dirk's suit and with a defeated sigh she replaced the iron on the stove and mixed some white powder with sugar and water from a kettle, poured it into a tittie-bottle and sat down on one of the chairs to feed the baby.

The bottle was just being emptied by the greedily gulping baby when the sound of a key in the front door reached them and a moment later Dirk walked into the kitchen. The contrast between his appearance and that of Hester could not have been greater. He looked smart in his blue suit, wearing his usual air of swaggering arrogance, and his hair had been slicked down with scented oil that Abel guessed had been expensive. He also looked as if he was in a hurry, with something so urgent on his mind that after his first astonishment at seeing Abel he merely rapped, "What the hell are *you* doing here?" He didn't wait for an answer but after a hard glance at his suit-jacket lying on the table he left the room, without even having bothered to greet Hester or pay attention to the baby.

Looking distressed and guilty, she rose and followed Dirk from the room, patting the baby's back as she did so. Left to himself, Abel tiptoed to the door and stood just inside it, listening to their voices coming from what must be their bedroom.

"I *told* you I wanted my grey suit ready pressed when I got in!" Dirk was snapping at Hester.

"I'm sorry. Baby has hardly stopped crying all day and I've had to keep picking him up. And then Abel arrived. I'll finish your suit off in a minute – "

"God Almighty, woman!" Dirk exploded. "There's a button missing on this shirt! Can't you get up off that skinny arse of yours occasionally and do some of the jobs you're supposed to do? And don't drag up the baby as an excuse! You're not the only woman ever to have had a baby!"

Hester's voice answered him defeatedly. "I didn't know a button was missing. I didn't notice one was loose when I was ironing the shirt. Do you have to wear that particular shirt, Dirk? You have several clean white ones – "

"It just so happens," Dirk said sarcastically, "that I wished to wear the striped one tonight. Well, it doesn't look as if I'm going to have any choice in the matter, does it? Go and finish off my suit. I haven't got all evening."

Abel quickly went to sit down again, and Hester returned to the kitchen, lifting the flat-iron from the stove. She seemed to remember Abel's presence only after she had spent some minutes on Dirk's suit. She looked up at him and said, "As soon as Dirk has gone out I'll fry some dough or something."

It had already been made clear that Dirk had come home only to go out again as soon as he could. Why, Abel wondered, did Hester not stand up for herself?

"Fried dough would be fine," he lied, saying goodbye to any hope of a proper cooked supper.

But before Hester had even started preparing to mix dough for frying, Dirk came into the kitchen, wearing the suit Hester had freshly pressed for him, and said, "Come with me, Abel, and you can tell me while I'm driving what the devil you thought you were doing, leaving the work you should be attending to on Jakkalsdrif. After all the years you've been living off *my* land I've a right to expect some sense of responsibility from you!"

The familiar rage bubbled inside Abel, threatening to choke him. But he controlled it, and he also controlled the urge to tell Dirk that he had no wish to go anywhere with him in his car. The promise of fried dough for supper was not alluring enough to offset the embarrassment he knew he would feel at being alone with Hester, who would very likely break down and cry and tell him what a bastard Dirk was. Of course he *was* a bastard-and-a-half, but the Hester about whom Abel had been thinking yearning thoughts for so long would never have allowed herself to be treated in such a way, and instead of sympathy he felt only mild pity and contempt for her. There was also the future to be considered. The money he had left over would not last forever and he needed to find work and somewhere to live, and Dirk represented the only chance of help he could hope for.

So Abel merely said, "Can I use the privy before we leave? Where is it – downstairs at the back?"

Dirk uttered a crack of derisive laughter. "The *water-closet* is the second door along the passage, on the right. And it's not for washing your feet in, as I expect you'll imagine. Pull the chain after you've finished."

Forcing iron control upon himself, Abel left the room. He had never heard of a water-closet before and he was far too furious to be impressed by it when he found it. Deliberately, he pulled the chain as hard as he could after he had relieved himself, so that it broke off in his hand.

Arranging an apologetic smile on his face, he returned to the kitchen and held out the chain. "Sorry. I'm not used to anything but a wooden seat over a hole in the ground."

Naturally, Dirk took the remark at face value and merely said shortly, "Leave the chain on a chair and let's get going."

So that Hester would not think he was taking it for granted that he could come and install himself as their guest, Abel said goodbye to her and picked up his rucksack before he left the kitchen in Dirk's wake. Perhaps because he realised, belatedly, that the appearance of the flat did not square with all his previous big talk, Dirk said with a dismissive look about him, "The furniture came with the flat and doesn't belong to me. I've been keeping an eye open for a suitable house to buy, somewhere to which I could invite friends and business contacts, but then Hester – " He stopped and shrugged, making clear Hester's inadequacies as a housewife and possible hostess.

Abel said nothing, but bitter envy rose like bile inside him a moment later when he followed Dirk into the sitting room, and his brother removed a small suitcase from a cupboard with bottles of liquor standing on its top, and he placed the suitcase on the sofa before opening it. It was filled to the brim with banknotes, a considerable number of which Dirk transferred to his wallet. All that money at his disposal while he, Abel, had had to use all his wits and guile to get his hands on a miserable ten pounds!

Dirk gave him a sidelong glance to see if he was suitably impressed, and Abel thought sourly that his brother could easily have filled his wallet while he himself had been in the water-closet. No, Dirk had deliberately delayed so that Abel would see the suitcase full of money, and now he was returning it to the cupboard, saying, "No sense in paying the government more taxes than I absolutely have to," obviously pretending to have forgotten that Abel knew nothing at all about the payment of taxes.

It was difficult to believe, when the two of them finally stepped out of the building, that the sun had set almost an hour ago and that Jakkalsdrif would be in darkness and the Bitch would have lit candles and oil lamps. Everything here was so brightly lit, and there was as much traffic, as many pedestrians, as there had been while it was still daylight.

Abel was not in the least surprised to find Dirk leading the way to where yet another new car, more obviously expensive and flamboyant than the last, was parked underneath an overhead street-lamp.

"Do you have to work at night?" Abel asked curiously as he took his place in the passenger seat beside Dirk. "On a Saturday night at that?"

Dirk laughed scornfully. "Idiot! I'm spending the evening with a lady, of course."

"A lady?" Abel echoed, confused. "What kind of lady?"

"A very smart, beautiful lady, actually," Dirk said smugly. "A girl whose parents were born in England. A girl any man would be proud to be seen with."

Abel's immediate, uppermost reaction was one of fury that *everything* should always be within Dirk's easy grasp. Then he exclaimed, outraged, "But you're married!"

Again Dirk laughed, but in an extremely irritating way this time, making it clear that Abel was a *japie* from the farm with cow dung between his toes and didn't understand the ways of sophisticated city men.

"Does Hester know about this girl?" Abel persisted, damping down his anger.

Dirk shrugged. "She'd have to be very stupid not to have guessed there's someone, and that I don't leave the flat in the evenings to go hymn-singing. Not that I intend handing her any evidence she could use against me in a divorce court. We were married in Community of Property and I'm damned if I'm going to let her walk away with half of everything I own."

Abel said nothing. He had never heard of divorce courts or Community of Property and he sensed that Dirk was trying to impress him with his worldliness more than anything else. He kept his expression resolutely unimpressed, and Dirk changed the subject.

"Now tell me what you're doing in Johannesburg. You obviously scrounged a lift from someone in Doornboomstad."

Abel could see no advantage to himself in contradicting Dirk and telling him about the ten pounds from the post office funds, and so he merely said, "I've left the farm. I've slaved for your benefit for long enough, Dirk, and the flood we've just suffered was the last straw." Abel waited for his brother to enquire about the flood, but Dirk was not sufficiently interested to question him, and so he went on, "The very least you owe me is to help me find work."

"You?" Dirk queried with amused contempt. "What use would you be to anyone in Johannesburg? You can't read or write or speak English! And what do you know about anything except farm work?"

Abel's fists itched with the overwhelming desire to beat Dirk to a bloody pulp, and only the fact that they were weaving through heavy traffic and Dirk's hands were those in control of the car helped him to fight the desire.

Dirk lapsed into silence, but suddenly he said in that patronising way of his, "Very well, little brother, I'll help you." He pulled the car up outside a building and switched off the engine. "I'll do the one and only thing I can to get you a job you're fitted for. Wait here."

Since he could not read, Abel could not tell from the frontage of the building inside which Dirk had disappeared what kind of trade or business was being carried out there, but he felt quite certain it was some demeaning kind of job Dirk had gone to enquire about on his behalf. Well, no matter. Everyone had to start somewhere, and any kind of job, no matter how demeaning, would give him a toe-hold in Johannesburg until something better turned up.

Dirk came back and opened the passenger door. Abel got out of the car because whoever was considering giving him a job would naturally wish to see and speak to him. Everything in Johannesburg was so strange that he did not find it difficult to accept that one could be hired for a job on a Saturday evening.

Dirk held out a small piece of cardboard to him and automatically Abel took it. "What is it?" he asked.

"Your train ticket back to Doornboomstad. Working Jakkalsdrif for me is all you're good for, so get going or you'll miss the last train." The street-light showed the gleam of Dirk's teeth as he grinned. "Didn't you even recognise the station building, you poor bloody sheep?"

Abel hadn't recognised it, and the fact that he had been fooled into sitting there outside the station, believing Dirk was actually trying to get a job for him, brought his already simmering rage to boiling point. Before Dirk could take evasive action Abel did what he had been wanting to do for years. He swung his right fist, catching his brother straight on the jaw, and at the same time his left fist slammed into Dirk's midriff. Christ, he had never felt as good as this in his life before! Another swift right to the jaw and Dirk slumped, unconscious, across the bonnet of his expensive car.

Abel experienced a tremendous feeling of release and euphoria, tinged with regret that it had taken so little to knock Dirk out. He would have liked to go on hitting him for a while longer. One or two people had stopped to watch what was happening but the majority had merely glanced at the scene and walked on.

Abel turned his back on his unconscious brother and hurried inside the station building. Fuck them, he thought with the assurance and self-esteem that had come from using his fists on Dirk. If they can't understand Afrikaans, let them send for someone who can.

A man was sitting behind a counter and Abel marched up to him. "I want the money back on this," he said, pushing the train ticket across the counter.

The man did not pretend not to understand Afrikaans, and neither did he argue. He counted out several silver coins and pushed them across to Abel, who pocketed them and went outside. Dirk was still unconscious but a couple of men were trying to revive him.

With his rucksack slung across his shoulder, Abel strode away from the scene. After he had walked for a while he noticed through the window of one place that people were sitting at tables and eating plates of food. He went inside, prepared to use the same belligerent approach as he had with the man at the railway station. A pretty girl wearing a white frilly apron and jaunty cap spoke to him in English and he responded flatly in Afrikaans.

"I want some food."

She smiled, giving him a look of interest. "Food is what we sell," she said, also in Afrikaans. "Please sit down, and I'll take your order."

He asked for a mixed grill after the girl had explained to him of what it consisted, and as he ate he noticed that she kept looking at him whenever she wasn't serving anyone else, but they were not the kind of looks that said, Here is a *japie* from the farm who is not used to anything, not fit for anything but ploughing fields and dipping livestock. Her eyes did not laugh at him because he was dressed in khaki shirt and cotton twill trousers but seemed almost to be admiring him, although the reason for such admiration was a complete mystery to him. It was not even as if she had witnessed him knocking out Dirk, or knew about it.

He dismissed the girl from his mind and considered what he ought to do next. He could return to Dirk's flat and take Hester to bed. But apart from the fact that after a little initial resistance she would probably oblige him in much the same limp way as she had been prepared to fry dough for him, he no longer wanted her, and it was only partly because Dirk no longer wanted her either.

He should have felt sorry for her, he supposed, but he didn't. The Hester of his dreams and imagination would never have pressed

Dirk's suit, guessing full well that he wanted it so that he could spend the evening with another woman. The truth was that the Hester he had yearned for had never really existed, except in his own mind.

I was a fool to have wasted all those feelings on her, Abel thought, and rooted in his rucksack for the envelope containing the snapshot she had sent him. He was about to tear the snapshot into small pieces and leave them inside the ash tray on the table, but then a slow smile spread over his face.

No, he would preserve the snapshot carefully. What a marvellous weapon it might yet turn out to be one day, a weapon to use against Dirk. To anyone not knowing the circumstances the snapshot would give the impression that Dirk had married Hester on the farm, with her carrying a bunch of pumpkin leaves as a bouquet, and that the 'wedding feast' had been cooked in the three-legged cauldron out in the open, close to the crude privy. Oh, how that snapshot would embarrass Dirk with his flashy cars and his big talk about entertaining 'business contacts'!

Abel had just put the envelope containing the snapshot back into the rucksack when the girl with the frilly apron and cap approached him, smiling. "Can I get anything else for you? More coffee?"

"No, thank you." He saw her take a small notepad from the pocket of her apron and begin to write something on it, and he added quickly, "Just tell me what I owe."

She did so and he counted out the coins carefully. "I haven't seen you in here before," she said as she took the money from him.

"I haven't been here before." ·

"Oh. I just thought – I only work here during the day and I would have gone off duty by now if the girl who takes over from me in the evenings hadn't been late. I thought you usually came in later, perhaps."

The instinct that told him when to turn something to his own advantage made him say frankly, "I've only just arrived in Johannesburg. I'm from a farm and I don't know anything about cities. I don't know my way about at all."

"Oh, shame," she said with sympathy, but not the kind of sympathy that went with pity. "Where do you want to get to?"

"A place called Newlands. Perhaps you could give me directions?"

"Better still," she said, "I could walk with you to the tram terminus, and see you safely on a Newlands tram. The girl who takes over from me has arrived, so I'll be ready to leave as soon as I've got rid of my cap and apron."

A while later they left the eating-house and she was holding on to his arm, supposedly guiding him but he sensed that she was enjoying this bodily contact. Her name was Maria and she was pretty enough, and she made it quite clear that she was interested in him, but he did not mean any of his warm assurances that he would return to the café where she worked each day. Apart from the fact that he was hardly likely to find it again, he had no intention of wasting any more silly feelings, such as he had wasted on Hester, on another girl. From now on he would look out for someone who would make him a suitable wife, and pretty Maria with her slight body and soft hands would never adapt to life on Jakkalsdrif.

She showed him the tram he had to take, told him what the fare would be and assured him that he would not need to worry about missing his stop, because Newlands was at the end of the line and everyone would be getting off there.

Reluctantly, and only after she had wrung another false promise from him that he would return to the café, she left him and he climbed the stairs to the top of the tram, marvelling at the many varied experiences he had crammed into one single day.

The tram remained stationary for some time. Before it eventually began to clank along the rails, many more people got on and one of them, a plump, dark-haired girl with the suspicion of a moustache on her upper lip, sat down next to Abel and darted glances at him. When the tram began to move she was somehow thrown against him, even though there had been no violent jarring over the tracks. Abel steadied her and she thanked him and apologised in the same breath, and he stored away in his mind the fact that the English word 'Sorry' had exactly the same sound in Fanakalo.

The girl was not pretty but her smile was warm and something in her eyes made him suspect that it had not been an accident that had caused her to fall against him. He made a remark in Afrikaans and she answered him in the same language, and soon they were deep in conversation.

Her name was Juana and she, too, was travelling all the way to Newlands, where she lived. She had been to visit her married sister who lived in a suburb south of the city. No, she didn't know anyone called Jakoba Steenkamp in Newlands, but then it was quite a large suburb. If Abel would tell her the address, she would direct him to it.

He placed the rucksack on his lap to search for Jakoba's letter, and Juana asked, "Is she a relation you are visiting? Will you be staying with her for long?"

"I don't know." Abel hesitated, and then instinct again made him go on frankly, "To be honest, I don't want to stay with her at all. She's an old friend of my mother's, whom I've never met, and she isn't expecting me. Also, there has been a recent death in the family so I'm not even sure if I'll be welcome."

Juana's dark eyes shone. "But if she is not expecting you, and you don't want to go there, why don't you come home with me instead? My mother takes in lodgers occasionally and we have a spare room at the moment."

Abel thought about the offer for a few minutes, and then said, "I'd like to accept, but the trouble is that I don't know for how long I could afford to pay for lodgings. I've only just arrived in Johannesburg and I must try to find a job."

Juana beamed at him. "Well, come home with me for the night, and worry about a job tomorrow. You couldn't start looking for one until Monday, in any case."

Recklessly, he decided to accept. Lodgings for two nights would not make desperately serious inroads into the money he had left, and by Monday night Wessel's funeral would surely be over, so that he could apply to Jakoba Steenkamp for hospitality without being caught up too much in gloomy family mourning.

When the tram terminated in Newlands Abel walked with Juana to the home of her family. They were Portuguese, and their surname was Mendoza, and being pitched into their household was an experience as strange and new as everything that had befallen him during the past twelve hours.

The family was large and friendly and noisy, and everyone seemed to talk at the same time, either in Afrikaans or English or what he supposed was Portuguese. But it didn't seem to matter into which language they slipped; Abel understood himself to be welcome, and he accepted the coffee and sugary cakes which Mevrou Mendoza insisted on setting before him, even though he assured her he had already eaten. Juana looked at him with the proud expression of a mother whose child was being fussed over by an appreciative audience.

As the evening wore on friends of the family, also Portuguese, kept dropping in and Abel was introduced to them, the story he had offered his landlady repeated for their benefit.

The family farm, Abel had said, could no longer support himself and his younger brothers, and so he had decided to seek work in Johannesburg and relieve his parents of at least one financial burden and hopefully send money home.

The Portuguese men and women clucked sympathetically and nodded their heads. They knew all about the uncertainties of farming, for without exception they were involved in the market garden business, and even though some of them never so much as touched the soil but ran shops or wholesale outlets supplying vegetables, fruit and flowers to hotels and restaurants, they were all dependent upon what was grown in the gardens.

Wine was brought out and offered around. Abel did not care much for its unfamiliar sharp, dry taste and sipped slowly at his own glass, but even such a small amount made him feel warm and happy among all his new friends. Even before he had properly realised it, he found himself being offered a job, accompanied by a great deal of back-slapping and hand-shaking. He was to work as a van-driver for one of the Mendozas' friends, and his job would be to pick up vegetables at the gardens and deliver them to the network of Portuguese retail shops in Newlands.

It was late when he retired to the bedroom which he had briefly inspected after his arrival and where he had left his rucksack. He flicked on the electric light-switch as if he had been doing it for years, closed the door and looked around him. The wooden cross hanging on the wall above the bed reminded him of the embroidered picture in his bedroom at Jakkalsdrif, which he knew from Dirk and Simon bore the words, 'Thy God Seest Thee'.

He sat down on the bed and smiled with satisfaction as he took stock of events. One of the most important things he had discovered today was the fact that he was attractive to women. Maria from the café, Juana and her mother, all their female Portuguese friends . . . One by one they had succumbed to whatever it was they found appealing about him. Looking back, he realised now that he had even been offered the job as a van-driver because his new boss's wife had suggested it to her husband and all the other females had immediately backed her up.

Another important thing he had grasped today was the fact that he possessed an instinct which told him when people or situations could be turned to his own advantage. No, it was more than that; it was like a sixth sense that warned him in advance how it would be in his own best interests to proceed.

He stretched luxuriously. Jakkalsdrif and his troubles seemed millions of miles away, and tomorrow he would ask Juana to make a list for him, in printed capitals, of the street names in which he would have to deliver vegetables. In the light of the street-lamps as they'd walked together from the terminus earlier he had noticed that the streets ran in criss-cross lines, forming blocks, so that it should not be difficult to find his way about.

He would pretend to Juana that he was anxious to make no mistakes in his job by misreading her handwriting. That instinct which had been serving him so well told him that while there were some who would react sympathetically to his illiteracy, the Mendozas and their friends would never be able to understand that a grown man who could not read or write was not necessarily a simpleton. So he would have to be careful to pretend with them, and once Juana had made a list he would spend most of tomorrow in tramping the streets of Newlands, matching the names printed on the sign-plates positioned on each street corner with the names on Juana's list, until he had familiarised himself with his delivery round.

Jakoba, he thought, could wait. There was plenty of time for him to go and collect the proof that would make Jakkalsdrif legally his. In the meantime, life in Johannesburg promised to be a very pleasant change from the hard work on the farm, an interlude to look back upon with pleasure once he was master of Jakkalsdrif.

His mind dwelled briefly on Susarah, mourning the death of her husband, and he shook his head at himself as he remembered how he had once built up foolish fantasies about her, just because her name had seemed so unusual and exotic.

As well as being a Halleluiah-girl, he thought dispassionately, she was probably as meek and spineless as Hester, about whom he had also once built up foolish fantasies. From everything he had learnt about her, Susarah's life obviously revolved around the Tabernacle of the Reformed Evangelists.

He did not have the slightest desire ever to meet her.

28

Susarah straightened up from the kitchen table to ease her aching back. She was busy mincing meat for an enormous dish of *bobotie* which was to serve as Sunday lunch for herself and Ma and the boys, but every now and again the hand-mincer seemed to take on a rebellious life of its own and dig in its heels as if deciding, No, I've had enough now; my blade hurts and my holes are clogged up and I want a rest.

She unscrewed the front of the mincer, removed bits of gristle with which the temperamental machine should have been perfectly able to cope, and put the parts together again. All this tedious, frustrating work could have been avoided, of course, by buying minced meat from Mr Karyppi, the butcher. But unlike most other everyday activities Ma did not condemn mincing meat on a Sunday as a sin, and she said butchers' mince was rubbish; she knew for a fact that everything went into it, from chicken entrails to the top of the butcher-boy's thumb when he accidentally sliced it off. Susarah considered this to be a gross insult to Mr Karyppi, who prided himself on the quality of the meat he sold, but there was no arguing with Ma.

Susarah stared thoughtfully at the mincer, realising consciously for the first time that she was *still* taking orders from Ma. She was providing and cooking the Sunday lunch in her own home but she had to do it Ma's way. She had, however briefly, been a married woman and now she was a widow with a baby and she had merely switched from obeying Ma to obeying Wessel and back to obeying Ma again.

Still, she thought with only a touch of bitterness, what did it really matter? None of the issues was ever important enough to justify the fuss and the upheaval of defying Ma. At least, what had once seemed important no longer did so. She remembered the passion with which, until marriage and widowhood crushed it, she used to long for smart, modern clothes and face powder and hair cut fashionably short. She thought of her one bold attempt at independence when she had applied for and been offered a job as a waitress in a café, only to find herself facing Ma's relentless opposition. Between them Ma and Wessel had laboured to stifle what they saw as Susarah's sinful frivolity, and now Wessel was dead and Ma no longer had legal jurisdiction over her.

Still, no woman could be independent once she had a baby to care for, and while Ma could not stop her, now, from having her hair cut short and buying face powder and using it, what would she gain by it? She might not care that Ma would be scandalised by such behaviour, but she did care about the fact that Ma would be truly hurt at such a show of disrespect for Wessel's memory. Ma was mourning him far more deeply than Susarah honestly could.

So, she still looked much as she had before, except that she now wore dated dresses in drab mourning black, instead of dated dresses in sombre prints. Even without a mirror handy to show her reflection, Susarah knew what kind of appearance she presented. Her figure had not suffered through childbirth and she was once again small-waisted and deep-bosomed in a way that was not at all fashionable, but it scarcely mattered what her figure was like, since it was hidden behind the shapeless black house-dress which skimmed her ankles in dreary defiance of the current mode. Her reddish-brown hair was pulled back and secured in a coil in the nape of her neck but she knew – no longer with bitterness but with resignation and even a touch of indifference – that she was capable of looking a great deal more attractive than she did.

She turned her head to look at her baby sleeping inside the battered wooden cradle that had served for most of Ma's infant sons and had been taken out of store again when Susarah went into labour, and her entire being softened with love and tenderness. Only because she realised how much it meant to Ma, she had agreed to the baby being called Corabella, when Susarah herself would have liked something prettier and more romantic like Laetitia or Rosa.

"I had a twin sister called Corabella who died when we were both nine years old," Ma had confided for the very first time. "It was because I wanted to call my second daughter after her that your Pa and I named you after both his mother and my own, Susarah." Ma had stared into space and then shrugged. "But I never had a second daughter, of course."

A beloved twin sister who had died, Susarah thought, went a long way to explaining all that wasted devotion Ma had been lavishing for years on the wretched Petronella Koen, who had never made the slightest effort to bring about a reunion with Ma, who wrote only when she felt like it and hadn't even taken the trouble to send a letter of condolence when she learnt of Wessel's death.

"I'll call the baby Corabella, Ma," Susarah had said gently, and touched her mother's shoulder, and forced herself to stop thinking of her daughter as Laetitia or Rosa.

"Corabella," she muttered softly, so that the baby wouldn't wake up. "What a responsible-sounding name for someone so small and helpless. Will you grow up to be Corabella, I wonder? There ought to be special names for babies, which get changed completely when they're older and one can see what kind of adults they are going to become. How can *any* baby possibly be a Corabella? Still, there are many different ways of saying the name, aren't there, my treasure? I say it so that all the other sounds are blurred and only the 'bell' is emphasised, but your grandma stresses every single syllable. She thinks I don't know about the pride and the love she hides behind the grim way she says your name. And it could have been worse, you know. If your father had been alive when you were born he might have insisted on having you named Mollie, after his mother, and what a limp sort of name that is, without any backbone to it. No one could say that about Corabella – it is almost nothing *but* backbone."

Susarah shook her head with a mixture of sadness and guilt as she thought of Wessel. He had been dead for over six months, and while she did miss him she knew that she missed him only for reasons that would shock others if they knew about them. She missed him not being there to bring in coal from outside; she missed the occasional outings on the motorcycle combination which now stood, draped in tarpaulin, on the vacant plot next to that useless old car . . .

Susarah was glad to have been reminded of the car, for it gave her cause to still her conscience by dwelling on one of Wessel's many good qualities. While small acts of wastefulness on her part used to earn her his stern reprimands, he could be astonishingly generous towards others less fortunate than himself. That old car, which must have come out of the Ark, had been offered to him as surety against a loan of five pounds he had made to an acquaintance of his. The car was clearly worthless, as Wessel must have known full well, and its owner had not come forward to repay the loan and reclaim the car. But somehow Susarah could not bring herself to have it taken away as scrap, or allow her younger brothers to take it apart. Wessel, she felt, would have wanted the original owner to be given the benefit of the doubt for as long as was reasonably possible.

She listened to the silence, and thought that one of the things she missed about Wessel was the company of another adult human being in the house, especially in the evenings, even though he and she had rarely talked to each other and he'd usually been reading the Bible or writing a hymn while she'd been sewing. It was lonely in the house with only the baby, once they had left Ma and the boys in the house next door. Most of all, Susarah missed the coherence, the *pattern* Wessel had given to her days. No longer was there anyone to cook breakfast or supper for, and Susarah had slipped back into her girlhood routine of sharing meals next door with Ma and the boys, because Ma said it was wasteful and senseless to cook for one person, and of course she was quite right. Corabella was such an undemanding baby that Susarah found herself doing more or less what she had always done during the days before her marriage – helping Ma with the housework and with the boys and doing the shopping – before going home to an empty, quiet house with Corabella.

It had been a surprise to find out how much she missed the creativity of cooking, but of course Ma would never allow her to take over that particular chore. Preparing Sunday lunch while Ma and the boys attended the service in the Tabernacle was the only concession granted to Susarah. She and Ma pooled their resources, which were now considerable compared to the bad old days when there would certainly not have been something like *bobotie* for Sunday lunch, because apart from the two older boys being in work and earning, Susarah received a widow's pension from the Johannesburg Municipality.

It was indirectly in the matter of this pension that Susarah missed Wessel most and regretted his untimely death. The Municipality was not, strictly speaking, obliged to pay her a pension at all because Wessel had not been working for them sufficiently long, but they had stretched a point and were providing her with an income that would cease a year after his death.

"Why a year?" Susarah had asked, bewildered and disturbed, when a letter arrived from the Municipality explaining their decision.

"Because," Ma had placed her own interpretation on official thinking, "they would naturally expect you to marry again, a girl of your age, and the year takes care of the period of mourning and gives you time to look around for a suitable second husband."

The thought of marrying again was totally unwelcome. To have to learn someone else's little ways, to have to adjust to them, to endure his 'loving' at night . . . Oh no, she had finished with that. "I'll take in lodgers when the pension comes to an end," she had told Ma flatly.

"Indeed?" Ma's grim tone had warned her in advance that some scandalous flaw had been perceived in the idea of taking in lodgers. "And what kind of woman, young or old, can you think of who would possibly need lodgings? Young women, whether they go out to work or not, would naturally live at home with their parents, and older women would either have homes of their own or else relatives with whom to live. No, Susarah, the only people who ever seek lodgings are young men come to work in Johannesburg, whose own families live on far-away farms. And can you imagine the talk there would be if you, a young widow, were to have male lodgers living under your roof?"

Feeling trapped, Susarah had said, "In that case I'll sell this house and the vacant plot and Wessel's motorcycle combination and put the money in the bank, and Corabella and I will go and live with you – "

"No, Susarah. We are already overcrowded and will become more so as the boys grow up and need more space. Besides, I rent the house from the Phthisis Board and there is never any security in a rented house. What if something were to happen to me? You would find yourself homeless. You must keep the house Wessel bought for the two of you because, apart from anything else, it will improve your chances of finding another husband."

"Oh God, Ma," Susarah had exploded, "where am I supposed to find him, this new husband you want me to take?"

"At a meeting in the Tabernacle, of course. Where else?"

Where else indeed, Susarah had thought drearily, seeing before her another future dominated by the Reformed Evangelists' God; that joyless, humourless God who deemed almost everything vaguely pleasurable to be a sin and demanded hours spent on one's knees in prayer.

She shrugged and returned to the task of feeding chunks of meat into the mincer and turning the handle. The mincer had stopped sulking and soon afterwards the meat was being mixed with breadcrumbs and chopped onions, with curry powder and other spices, a few seeded raisins and lemon juice, and then transferred to an oven dish and covered with eggs beaten in milk, the surface dotted with crushed almonds and the dish placed in the oven to bake.

At present Ma was not making too much fuss about Susarah missing the Sunday Meetings in the Tabernacle but the pressure on her to join Ma and the boys would be increasing before long, Susarah knew. Already, it was becoming difficult to claim that a baby as young as Corabella would disturb the congregation. _Nothing_ could disturb the congregation, which caused quite enough disturbances itself with all the chorused 'Amens' and 'Halleluiahs' and 'Praise the Lords' that punctuated the sermons, and the noisy personal laments that accompanied the prayers. Corabella was such a strangely self-contained baby that it was difficult to imagine her either disturbing anyone or being disturbed herself. Her conception had caused so little fuss that Susarah had miscalculated the duration of her pregnancy; her birth had been trouble-free to the point almost of polite consideration and she had been displaying the same kind of good manners ever since. On the rare occasions when she cried she did so with something akin to reserve, as if she were saying, "Excuse me, I wet my nappy some time ago and if you'll change it I'll go back to minding my own business while you mind yours."

She was minding her own business now, Susarah thought as she bent over the cradle. The baby was awake and lay there, looking up at her with serious eyes that had been blue at birth and were turning a clear, strangely wise grey. It was as if she had been thinking private, solemn thoughts of her own but was now politely putting them aside and giving her attention to her mother.

"My funny little Cora-*bell*-a," Susarah said with a vast, melting tenderness, and picked up the cradle to carry it to the stoep. With the *bobotie* in the oven and the rice not due to be cooked until about the time the service in the Tabernacle would be coming to an end, Susarah meant to sit on the stoep in the shade while she topped and tailed the string beans for lunch.

Mercifully, it had rained recently so that loose sand was not likely to be blown from the surrounding mine-dumps and to swirl in 'dust fiends' through the streets of Newlands. Apart from the vacant plot on one side of the house, which Wessel had bought as an investment, the houses on both sides of the street stretched in unbroken, symmetrical lines, all built to the same design with wrought-iron railings surrounding each stoep, very little space between the houses and back-yards hidden discreetly from sight. Beyond the back-yards ran narrow alleys, used only by the dustbin-men and the nightcart men who called after dark and lifted up a flap at the rear of each privy, emptying the contents on to their cart and replacing the receptacle after it had been sluiced and liberally Lysoled.

Susarah had just put the cradle down in a spot from which the sun had already moved when she noticed that a young man was standing on the stoep of Ma's house and knocking on the front door. Susarah frowned, because Ma did not know anyone who would not, at this moment, be attending the service in the Tabernacle. And since it was Sunday, the visitor could not possibly be from the Phthisis Board, which paid Ma's pension and the younger boys' allowance, because Pa had died of the disease.

Susarah cleared her throat, and called out, "Excuse me, can I help you?"

He turned towards her and walked to the railing a few feet away from that of Susarah's own stoep. He was tall; quite as tall as Wessel had been, but muscular in a way that suggested he was accustomed to hard physical labour. He wore flannel trousers of the kind she knew were called 'bags' and a dark blazer and grey trilby hat, but he wore them as if they were brand-new and he was not accustomed to them and felt uncomfortable, and as if he worried that he might look a fool in them. Without knowing who he was or anything about him at all, she felt her heart softening towards him.

He removed his hat, and now she saw that his hair was dark and curled rather untidily, suggesting that he'd felt he had made quite enough concessions in wearing the clothes he had on and wasn't prepared to go as far as slicking his hair back with citified scented oil. He was not Johannesburg-born and bred, something about him clearly proclaimed. His face was clean-shaven, as if he couldn't be bothered with the fiddly business of the fashionable pencil-moustache most men were currently wearing. A firm jaw, high cheekbones, a somewhat prominent nose and green-flecked grey eyes combined to give the impression of toughness, even hardness bordering on ruthlessness, and at the same time there was something irresistibly vulnerable about him. He was the most interesting-looking man she had clapped eyes upon since – oh, since Marcus Koen had paid them a surprise visit.

She was studying him so intently that she didn't take in, at first, the meaning of his reply to her question. "I don't suppose so, thank you. I wanted to see Mevrou Jakoba Steenkamp, but there's no one at home. I'll have to come back some other time."

Susarah gave herself a brisk mental shake. "They've gone to the Meeting at the Tabernacle – "

"Oh God, yes!" he interrupted with sudden enlightenment. "Of course! How could I have forgotten that they're part of the Praise-the-Lord-Halleluiah flock of sheep!"

"Halleluiah – " Susarah echoed, and then began to laugh. "I don't know what you want to see Ma about, but you'd better not let *her* hear you talking about the Reformed Evangelists like that!"

It was his turn to stare and to echo, "*Ma!* Mevrou Steenkamp is your mother?"

"That's right. I'm Susarah du Plessis, formerly Steenkamp."

"Good lord!" He sprinted over the railing of Ma's stoep and then swung his long legs over that of Susarah's. He studied her without any attempt at hiding his surprise and curiosity and at the same time offered her his hand. "I'm Abel Koen."

"No!" she cried idiotically.

"What do you mean?" He looked at his own outstretched hand as if it might have something to do with her reaction. "Would you like me to leave? Is that it?"

She shook her head, accepting his hand which part of her mind noted was hard and calloused, and she winced slightly as he gripped hers in a firm hold. "It – it's just. . ." she stammered. "Oh dear, how am I going to put this? We thought – Ma and I – we thought there must be something wrong with you – not physically . . . Oh, I'm making this worse. Your father once paid us a brief visit, and when we asked about his sons he said something about you only being able to do farmwork, but it was the way he said it that made us believe . . ."

She saw the passion that had leapt into his eyes as she spoke and she tried wildly to justify herself and Ma for thinking that he was mentally retarded. "And then, when you didn't respond to Ma's letter, telling you of Wessel's death, we thought someone else must have been playing a stupid joke on us – someone who answered the telephone on your farm and pretended to be you, inviting the two of us to Jakkalsdrif, and that you were, after all, not quite – " She stopped, floundering.

"I can't write," he said simply. "That's why I didn't answer your mother's letter."

"Oh." For some ridiculous reason she wanted to put her arms around him and tell him that it didn't matter, that being able to write was not that important. At the same time she burnt to ask him how it came about that the son of Marcus Koen, that obviously learned and clever and charming founder of the Church of the Reformed Evangelists, could not write. Instead, she said, "It was kind of you to invite us to Jakkalsdrif, even though Wessel's death prevented us from going. It meant a great deal to him that you *had* invited us." She hesitated. "I was surprised that your mother permitted you to do so, when she didn't even know us – "

"She didn't. She didn't know about the invitation."

Susarah stared at him in perplexity. Then she said, "In a way I'm glad to hear that. Ma has never mentioned the matter, but I know she was very hurt at the thought that *we* had been invited, while your mother never once invited *her* to Jakkalsdrif – " She stopped, disconcerted, as he gave a crack of laughter.

He did not explain the cause of his cynical amusement. Instead, he studied her. "Did you really want to spend a holiday in Doornboomstad?"

"Oh lord, no! When Wessel said we were to have a holiday I thought he meant some such place as they write about in the newspapers, where one can see the ocean, not a pilgrimage . . ." She broke off, blushing both at her own disloyalty to Wessel's memory and at the implied disparagement of the Church Abel's father had founded. Changing the subject quickly she went on, "Ma and my brothers won't be home for another hour at least. Would you like to wait here for them? There's coffee on the stove and it won't take me a moment – "

"I'd like to wait, thank you, but don't bother about the coffee. May I sit down?"

"Of course." She gestured towards the chairs on the stoep and added, "If you'll excuse me, I'll just fetch the string beans. I have to prepare them for lunch."

When she returned to the stoep he was staring into the cradle. "That's my baby, Corabella," she said, trying not to sound too boringly like a proud mother because she knew, from her own older brothers, that males could see little to get excited about in babies.

"I don't know what I'm meant to say," he confessed. "I could lie and tell you that she's pretty, but she isn't, is she? She doesn't have any hair. I could also say that I'm sorry about your husband being dead, but I didn't know him, so that would be a lie as well."

Susarah looked at him, a little helplessly. "You're a strange man, Meneer Koen. You don't act in the way other people do."

"My name is Abel. No one has ever called me Meneer Koen. Yes, I suppose I am strange, but then I was never taught how to behave in polite company." He changed the subject unexpectedly. "You're not a Halleluiah-girl after all."

Her mouth dropped open. "A *what*? If you mean I don't belong to the Church of the Reformed Evangelists, you're wrong —"

"Oh, I know you must belong to it, just as I'm supposed to belong to it." His lips twisted cynically. "They have you dunked in the water and 'blessed' when you're small, whether you like it or not. But if you don't know what a Halleluiah-girl is, I can't explain it to you."

Strangely enough, she did know what he meant. She smiled at him. "So I'm not a Halleluiah-girl, and there's nothing wrong with you apart from the fact that you — " She broke off, fearing to embarrass him.

"That I can't write, or read," he finished for her. "It doesn't mean that I'm stupid, you know. It only means that my parents didn't send me to school but kept me at home so that I could do the farm work. I was born first, but my parents cheated me out of my inheritance by claiming my brother Dirk was the eldest. My grandfather left the farm in his will to his first-born grandson, but unless I can prove that I was the one who was born first it will go on belonging to Dirk."

Susarah had dropped the knife with which she was working and it fell with a clatter on the cement floor of the stoep. "You — you're making this up?" she suggested helplessly.

"Oh no. Why should I?"

"Dear God . . ." He really was telling the truth, Susarah thought, telling it quite matter-of-factly and not making out of it the big drama it almost certainly was.

"One day," he continued, "when I thought I was fourteen, my former wetnurse Mwende let slip the fact that I was really sixteen and had been born first. She said my mother had thrown me away like an unwanted dog." He glanced at the baby in the cradle. "I don't know why my mother threw me away. Can you think of a reason, Susarah?"

"No," she said, her voice choked by emotion and resisting the urge to go to him and offer him the comfort of her arms. "No, I can't. If — if you'd like to tell me more, then perhaps — " She left the sentence in the air because she could not imagine *anything* being capable of explaining, let alone justifying, what had been done to Abel by his parents.

He went on readily to tell her about his childhood. He spoke without self-pity but just occasionally rage would blur his voice. The rage was quite understandable, she thought as she listened to him, appalled and filled with compassion and tenderness for the boy who had grown up without ever receiving an atom of love. The only certain conclusion she had come to when he finished was that Ma must never be told this terrible story.

Ever since Susarah could remember, Ma had spoken of Petronella Koen as her best friend and had looked up to her. Even when Marcus Koen called on them briefly and let drop, in all innocence, snippets of information that made it clear Petronella had not always told the truth in her letters to Ma, the latter had chosen to dismiss the lies as 'slight exaggerations' or 'misunderstandings'. She would not be able to dismiss the woman's cold, cruel treachery towards her first-born. It would make a mockery of Ma's years of devotion and loyalty to someone who deserved neither.

"And that is why I need to speak to your mother," she heard Abel conclude. "She alone has the proof I need that I was born first."

"Oh no!" Susarah exclaimed. "I cannot – please, you must never tell Ma what you've just told me! It would hurt her too much. I can't think why you imagine she might have proof – "

"I don't imagine it. I know it. Your mother and mine have been writing to each other for years, and if your mother has kept the letters then there will be one among them mentioning the birth of her friend's first son. *Did* she keep the letters?" Abel added with obvious tension and anxiety.

Susarah nodded. She had often seen the letters lying in Ma's drawer in the bureau which they used to share. Ma would no more have thought of destroying a letter from Petronella Koen than she would have thought of blaspheming.

"Surely your grandparents would – " Susarah began.

"Both of them died years ago. The letters are my only hope."

For the first time, she remembered the tale Abel had told Wessel over the telephone about a lost birth certificate, and that he had asked for Ma to be questioned about the exact date of his birth. Still trying to protect Ma, Susarah pointed out, "If your mother hated you at birth, it's not very likely that she would have written about your birth."

"She *did* write about it. My mother all but admitted that she'd done so, and her one fear has been that I might come and see your mother." A hard note entered his voice. "I'm sorry, Susarah, about your mother's feelings, but you must understand how important it is for me to ask her about the letters, and get the proof I need."

Susarah caught her lower lip between her teeth. Of course he was more than justified in insisting on speaking to Ma. What was at stake for him was his inheritance. And yet poor Ma had so little in her life that to be disillusioned about her dreadful 'best friend' would diminish her completely.

"Wait here," Susarah said, making up her mind and rising. "Don't worry about the baby; she hardly ever cries. I won't be a moment."

She hurried next door and went straight to the bureau of the bedroom which Ma shared with four-year-old Willem, and removed the small pile of letters from the drawer. Ma would consider what she was doing to be unforgivable, but it would be far more unforgivable, Susarah judged, to allow Ma to hear the stark truth from Abel. Armed with the letter he needed, he would have no cause ever to mention the subject to Ma, and if she should discover that one of the letters was missing it would just remain one of life's small insoluble puzzles.

Susarah returned to the stoep of her own house, and said breathlessly, "I'll read all the letters to you. We can be thankful that your mother didn't write as often as mine did."

The letters were in no particular order; Ma must have taken one from the pile at random from time to time to reread it. Abel uttered bitter, astonished exclamations as he learnt of the lies his mother had written over the years.

"Jakkalsdrif a prosperous farm! I only wish it were! And all those stories about bottling fruit and a telephone specially installed . . . There isn't a single fruit tree on the farm, and the only reason there's a telephone is because Jakkalsdrif has been licensed as a post office. We couldn't have survived without the money the post office brings in!"

To Susarah, one thing shone with truth through the welter of lies. Petronella not only loved her Marcus; she was besotted with him, possessed, obsessed by him. This came across so strongly that Susarah could understand her having little love to spare for her children, but there was nothing to explain her hatred of her first-born, and Petronella had given no clues. Indeed, she'd seldom mentioned her children in her letters to Ma, except when she'd used them to help with the fabrication of the picture of an ideal marriage and a prosperous, enviable family life.

"Ah!" Susarah exclaimed suddenly as she reached for yet another letter. "Here's something at last! 'A few days ago,' " she read from the letter, " 'I gave birth to our second son. It was an easy birth, and not remotely like that of the first. Baby is very good and healthy and I feel perfectly well, although Marcus insists on fussing over me and he has even gone to the expense of having a trained midwife attend the birth. Between him and Mrs van Vuuren I feel like a spoilt child . . .' " Susarah's glance flicked over the rest of the letter. "She just goes on to say how happy Marcus is with his fine sons, and describes the presents he has showered on her, and things like that."

"What is the date of the letter?" Abel asked tensely. "If it matches Dirk's birthday, the letter is proof that *he* was the second son."

Susarah looked at it again, and frowned. "She didn't date it. It must have slipped her mind."

But as she paid more particular attention to Petronella's letters it became clear that forgetting to date them was a recurring foible of hers. Susarah remembered that Wessel had said something to her about almanacs meaning little to people on farms.

She could have wept for Abel when at last she found the letter that recorded his birth. " 'Well, Jakoba,' " the letter read, " 'so I have at last experienced the joys of motherhood. Marcus is beside himself with happiness because it is a boy, and even though the birth was a long and difficult one it was well worth it just to see the expression on his face as he looks at our son. I am the luckiest woman alive because not only do I have Marcus and Baby, but my dear Mwende has returned to Jakkalsdrif in time to help me with the nursing. She has a baby of her own, half-white which I know will shock you, but I cannot condemn her for I know what it is to love the forbidden. In any event it means that she will be able to wetnurse Baby for me, until such time as my milk is sufficient for him. Mamma and Pappa, I need hardly tell you, are overjoyed at having a grandson.' "

Susarah looked up from the letter, and said gently, "It *was* your birth she was writing about, Abel, because of the mention of Mwende as your wetnurse. But – I'm afraid she did not date that letter either."

His face like a frozen mask, he stood up and went to stand by the rail, staring into the distance. Desperate to find *something* that would help him, Susarah read the remaining letters swiftly but carefully. When Petronella began to mention her sons by name, she found Dirk was always referred to as the eldest. Another fact struck Susarah. Petronella had not written to her 'best friend' about the deaths of her parents; she had merely stopped mentioning them. Was it because writing about their passing had been too painful, or because she had wanted to obscure the order of events to avoid anything which could be used, later, to help pinpoint which of her sons had been born first?

Susarah laid the letters aside and cleared her throat. "If Mwende would be prepared to swear on oath that she acted as wetnurse to you and not to either of your brothers," she said, "I think the letter might be evidence after all. You could show it to a lawyer – "

"It wouldn't help," Abel interrupted in an expressionless voice, without turning his head. "Mwende would refuse to swear to anything that would cause trouble for my mother."

Susarah longed to make him aware of her deep compassion, and because she could think of nothing else to say she commented, "If only people of our parents' generation hadn't made a habit of always talking about Baby instead of using their names. It made them seem so anonymous, like objects instead of tiny human beings, or as if they might die within the first two years of their lives and so it wasn't worth getting used to their names. That is why I refused to let anyone call my daughter Baby, and I insisted from the start that she should be referred to as Corabella."

He said nothing, and she wondered if he had even listened to her inadequate little speech. She saw him look down at the trilby in his hands as if he couldn't quite remember how it came to be there; then he jammed it on his head so that when he turned to her its brim cast his face into shadow and she couldn't read his expression.

"Thank you – for your trouble," he said in a blurred, jerky voice, holding out his hand to her in farewell.

Even as she took it she wanted to say, "Don't go. Stay and let me comfort you and try to soften your hurt and your bitter disappointment."

Instead, she heard her own voice saying, "If you would like me to, Abel, I'll teach you to read and write. You could call on Sunday mornings, when I'm here alone."

He didn't respond to the offer, but turned and hurried away with long strides. She wished she had bitten off her tongue before saying something so crass, adding to what he must already be feeling the humiliating reminder of his illiteracy.

I'll never see him again, she thought, and was alarmed and astonished at the feeling of loss she experienced at the knowledge.

Abel clenched and unclenched his fists as he walked away from the house. *Jesus Christ Almighty, it was a conspiracy.* Fate, or Satan, or whoever had control of these things had tied matters up in ways that he could never unravel, however hard he tried.

He had staked everything on those letters the Bitch had written to her friend Jakoba. He uttered something that should have come out as a bitter laugh but sounded like a muted howl of rage instead, so that a man passing by stopped and stared at him. Abel ignored the man and went on thinking his searing, corrosive thoughts.

With what careless confidence he had been telling himself that he had plenty of time, that those letters wouldn't run away! In the meantime he had been saving whatever he could from his modest earnings as a delivery-man so that he could buy decent clothes for himself. He had expected to see Jakoba, and not her daughter Susarah, and he had sensed instinctively that it would only antagonise the Bitch's friend if he were to tell her the unvarnished truth. No, he'd had his story ready; a slightly different version of the story he had told Wessel du Plessis during their telephone conversation. He was in Johannesburg, he'd meant to tell Jakoba, to take up a temporary job because the year's harvest on Jakkalsdrif had been destroyed by floods and they needed whatever money he could earn. But now, suddenly, his boss was demanding to see his birth certificate – something to do with the company pension – and the certificate had been mislaid or destroyed years ago. He would lose his job if he didn't do something about the matter quickly, and as there had always been confusion about the exact day on which he'd been born, his mother had suggested, when he telephoned her, that he should approach Jakoba, to whom she had written at the time of his birth. Then he'd meant to ask Jakoba if he could borrow the letter for long enough to enable him to get a copy of his birth certificate.

He'd had to look as if he had the kind of job that offered a company pension, and that had partly been the reason for his new clothes. But he would also have needed them for when he took the Bitch's letter, given to him by Jakoba, to a lawyer. A clever lawyer wouldn't have taken seriously someone who called dressed in khaki shirt and twill trousers.

And these stupid bloody expensive clothes had been totally wasted. No one had seen them except Susarah, and he'd sensed from the outset that it wouldn't have mattered to her how he was dressed. His instinct had urged him to tell *her* the truth, and it had worked like a charm. Who could have guessed that the Bitch would win again, simply because she seldom bothered to date her letters?

There was no point in carrying on fighting. He had no weapons left. He would have to stay here in Johannesburg, earning a pittance as a van-driver, and from now on he would have to live with the bitter knowledge that it was no longer merely the means to an end, but the end itself.

It isn't fucking fair! the raw, explosive protest raged inside him. Jakkalsdrif was his, and now he could never hope to claim it. As the legal owner of Jakkalsdrif, his status known to everyone, there would have been pride in being poor. Battling against the elements and soil erosion and pernicious weeds to scrape even a bare living from the farm would have been its own challenging reward. But being poor in Johannesburg, owning nothing apart from his few pieces of clothing, would eat away at his pride. What future was there for him as a van-driver? None at all. The most he could ever hope for was to get a job that offered a newer model of van to drive and a few shillings more in wages. While Dirk –

A red mist swam before his eyes as he thought of Dirk, who would own Jakkalsdrif for the rest of his life and whose son Marcus would inherit it one day. Dirk, who had always been handed everything denied to Abel himself, and then decided he didn't want it. Dirk, who had never wanted Jakkalsdrif at all, but who had gained possession of it by the most monstrous injustice done to Abel himself.

He shook his head to try to clear it of thoughts of Dirk, and as he turned the corner into the street where the Mendozas lived he attempted to bank down his rage. To the Mendozas he was a model lodger, a good worker and a prompt payer, someone who laughed at their jokes and could be relied upon in turn to tell anecdotes about the farming methods used by the poor-white *bywoners* in the Jakkalsdrif district. He would have to school himself to slip into that uncomplicated role before he entered the house.

But today he found it impossible. The family had returned from Mass in high spirits which, he thought sourly, were presumably caused by the fact that their sins of the week had been lifted from their shoulders by the simple means of confessing them to their priest. Today their heartiness was too much for his black mood, and after he had eaten his lunch he excused himself, saying that he had to go and see a friend.

They were too polite not to pretend to believe him, but they knew perfectly well that he had no friends other than themselves and their own circle, most of whom would be dropping in during the course of the afternoon for a visit. Van-drivers did not make friends; they picked up produce and delivered it to shops with the minimum of chat, day in and day out, from Mondays to Saturday afternoons.

Abel was wandering aimlessly along the Sunday-quiet street, again clenching and unclenching his fists, when a sudden decision formed in his mind. He would go and see Dirk. The very least Dirk owed him in exchange for Jakkalsdrif was help in getting a better job, and he would choke it out of his brother if he had to.

Abel had become quite familiar with the city. Sometimes on his free Saturday afternoons or on Sunday mornings while the Mendozas were at Mass, he took the tram and wandered along the city streets, looking through the windows of the large stores. It was almost his only diversion and cost him no more than his tram fare, and on one memorable Saturday afternoon the man in fancy uniform who stood outside one of the city's grand hotels had been too busy to notice Abel, who had slipped past him and gone inside. He had stared in wonder at the opulent settees, the potted palms and the glittering centre-light made up of hundreds of tiny pieces of glass, and luxuriated in the feel of the soft carpet under his feet. To his astonishment he had been approached by a young woman with a startling amount of powder and paint on her face and blood-red lips that matched the colour of her dress. She had switched to Afrikaans when she realised he didn't understand what she was saying in English, and almost before he realised what was happening he was in bed with her in her flat nearby. It had come as a nasty shock, afterwards, when he discovered that she expected him to pay her, but suddenly she had laughed and said, "Never mind, I hadn't enjoyed myself so much in years, so you can have that one on me. Do come again, but make sure you have money with you next time." He hadn't been near that hotel since but he had gone home with a few other girls met casually on Saturday afternoons, and although none of them had expected payment they'd all wanted to see him again too. But not one among them would have done as a wife to take home to Jakkalsdrif, and so he had put them out of his thoughts.

Shattering waves of anger and bitterness washed over him once more as he thought about the loss of Jakkalsdrif, and he tried to put it from his mind. At the city terminus he alighted from the tram and this time there was no need for him to ask the way to Dirk's address, because he knew how to reach Market Street.

Even though it was Sunday there were a fair number of people about; mostly black men who were on their way to or from Sophiatown where their families and friends lived. The white people who frequented the city on Sundays, he had learnt, were mainly wealthy businessmen who visited their clubs where they lunched and drank, or ordinary people who crossed the city, changing trams on their way to pay calls on friends.

With his shoulders hunched and his head down, Abel strode along Market Street towards Dirk's flat. He had not seen his brother since the evening when he'd knocked him out, and he had felt no need or desire to visit Dirk or Hester. But, Abel thought with rage again knotting his stomach, that had been because he'd still been under the delusion that establishing his ownership of Jakkalsdrif was only a matter of time.

He climbed the stairs and knocked on the door of the flat. It was opened to him by Hester, who looked even more faded and defeated than the last time he'd seen her. Her baby had grown and was crawling towards her along the passage but he was still crying.

"Oh, hullo Abel," Hester said limply, as if he called at the flat every day.

"Is Dirk at home?" Abel asked. He would damned well wait for him if he wasn't.

But Dirk was at home, rubbing his eyes as he stumbled to his feet from the sofa in the sitting room, where he had obviously fallen asleep. Pages of a newspaper lay scattered on the floor.

Abel was conscious of a drumming sound in his ears. *Say something insulting,* he begged wordlessly. *Make a cheap joke about my new clothes. Come on, little brother, give me the excuse to beat the shit out of you again . . .*

But Dirk was running his tongue nervously over his lips, and he almost stammered as he said, "Oh, Abel. I knew you were still in Johannesburg . . ."

"Did you now? How?"

"Ma telephones me either here or at the office at least once a week. Pa seems to be spending even less time than usual on Jakkalsdrif." Nervousness seemed to be making Dirk talkative, and he added with false heartiness, "Sit down, Abel. Have a drink. Brandy? Gin? A sherry or a liqueur?" And then, Dirk being bloody Dirk even when he was almost pissing his pants with fear, he added, "Or I could mix a cocktail for you. I'll bet you've never tasted a cocktail before."

"All I want from you," Abel said in a clipped, menacing voice, "is some help in getting a decent job. I've been working as a delivery-man but there's no future in that."

Dirk gave him a pleading look. "Honest, I'd help you if I could. I'd give you a job myself if only you could read and write and speak English. But as true as God, Abel, there's nothing I could do as things stand. Not in Johannesburg." He gave a sickly smile. "You've done very well, getting yourself a job as a delivery-man. I admire you, I really do."

"Is that so?" Abel sat down, staring at him in frustration. Miserable damned coward! Why couldn't he be a man, and square up to the brother who had left him lying out cold across the bonnet of his flashy car?

"Yes, and I don't blame you for leaving Jakkalsdrif. I'd sell the place if I could but Ma would never agree to sell her share of it, and without that it's totally worthless. She says that even though she and Koos do all they can, the place is little more than a wilderness since you left. She – she sounds worried about you."

Abel bared his teeth. "I'll just bet she does! Well, you can give her a message from me, next time you speak to her. Tell her I mean to contact her friend Jakoba Steenkamp soon, just as soon as I feel like getting round to it." That, Abel thought savagely, should give the Bitch reason for more sleepless nights, even though it would not do one single damned thing to help him.

Dirk looked bewildered, but he nodded and said, "I'll tell her." The false heartiness entered his voice again. "If you don't want a drink, let Hester get you some tea and cakes – "

"No." Abel stood up. Dirk was obviously not going to give him the satisfaction of an excuse for hitting him, and he could do nothing to help where a better job was concerned. It was a waste of time staying any longer.

At the door, Abel turned. "Any other news from Jakkalsdrif?"

"Let me see . . . Yes, there were a few bits and pieces. Bible-punching Simon is now lay-preacher in Doornboomstad. The pastor had a heart attack and he won't be fit to take services again for a long time, if ever, so Simon goes to Doornboomstad on Friday afternoons and stays in lodgings until Sundays. He has also turned the *stoepkamer* on Jakkalsdrif into a small shop where he sells groceries and stuff to neighbours who use the post office. It all helps to bring in a bit more money. What else? Oh – Koos had a slight accident when the mules took fright at something and overturned the cart, but he's fine again now."

Abel said nothing. He nodded goodbye to Hester, ignored Dirk and the wailing baby and let himself out of the flat. Tina, the stupid cow, hadn't been pregnant after all, because if she were Dirk would certainly have learnt about her condition and he would have passed on the news. Still, the false alarm had served a useful purpose, for it had given him, Abel, the spur to get away from Jakkalsdrif and from wasting his life in slaving for Dirk's benefit.

Jakkalsdrif is mine! The thought throbbed in Abel's mind and even the sound of his footfalls on the pavement seemed to echo the words. *Mine, mine, mine.*

He looked up, thrusting his balled fists into the pockets of his trousers. Mechanically, he noticed that a tall, well-built man in a smart suit, his tie awry and his hat tilted at a peculiar angle on his head, was weaving unsteadily along the pavement. He had obviously been spending most of the day in drinking at his club, one of the few places in Johannesburg where liquor was obtainable on a Sunday, and he was equally obviously trying to force his fuddled mind to locate the spot in which he had left his car. Coming from the opposite direction was a black man in his Sunday-best clothes, and even though he swerved several times to avoid a collision with the drunken white man, the latter staggered against him.

The drunk reeled off a string of oaths and insults, and Abel had picked up sufficient English to understand that he was calling the cowering, apologetic man black rubbish whose place it was to walk in the gutter. He took no notice of the black man's apologies but began to throw punches at him. A small crowd was gathering but no one was doing anything about the gross injustice of the attack, and the black man was obviously too scared to retaliate by hitting a white, and merely tried to fend off the blows aimed at him.

Abel uttered a roar, and then he was pushing the black man out of the way and landing a blow with his fist on the jaw of the drunk. The latter was in a state of intoxication that made him dangerous, because there was no self-control behind his punches and drink had anaesthetised him against pain. But Abel ducked and parried most of his blows, and each time his own fist connected with the man's face and body he was thinking, *This* one is for the poor innocent black bugger; *this* one is owed to Dirk, *this* one for the Bitch, the Preacher, and *this* one is for the loss of Jakkalsdrif . . .

The man gave a grunt and collapsed in the gutter, unconscious and with blood trickling from a cut on his lip. Abel looked around him. The black victim and black onlookers had melted away and all that were left were a few white people.

"You shouldn't have done that," one of the men reproved Abel.

"Say what you want to say in Afrikaans," Abel commanded, even though he had understood well enough.

"You shouldn't have interfered, man. He was only giving the Kaffir what he deserved."

"Oh yes?" Abel grinned ferociously. "Would you like to make something of it?"

The man shrugged and hurried away, and the few remaining onlookers tried to pretend a total lack of interest in what had happened. Abel stepped over the unconscious drunk as he crossed the street to catch a tram, aware of a wonderful feeling of release and satisfaction. By avenging the attack on the blameless black man he had cooled his own boiling rage, even if only for a while. He was whistling a tune as he climbed aboard a tram.

It came to him suddenly what he ought to do with the rest of his Sunday afternoon. He would go to see Susarah du Plessis and apologise for his rudeness in leaving so abruptly this morning. Even though she was not the Halleluiah-girl he had imagined her to be and was even rather pretty, in spite of her heavy mourning and old-fashioned appearance, he had no particular interest in her but her company would make a welcome change from that of the Mendozas. She had been gratifyingly sympathetic towards him this morning, and now that he felt a degree or two less raw and violent about the loss of Jakkalsdrif some more of her sympathy would be soothing. Besides, with luck he might be invited to supper. He was growing a little tired of Portuguese food.

It came as an unpleasant surprise to find that she was not alone at home with her baby, but that the stoep seemed to be splitting apart at the seams with boys of different ages and that her mother was there as well. Remembering Susarah's insistence that her mother must not learn the truth about the Bitch, he sensed that she would have said nothing about his earlier visit and so he pretended this was the first time he had called. Susarah's look of gratitude confirmed that he had guessed right.

"Since I'm lodging in Newlands," he said, "I decided to come and call on my mother's old friend and her family."

He had resigned himself to eager questions about the Bitch, and to having to listen to her praises being sung, but strangely enough Jakoba Steenkamp made no more than a polite enquiry after her and the rest of the family, and then persisted in talking to him about her late son-in-law, Wessel du Plessis. Since he hadn't known the man Abel felt puzzled, and he saw that Susarah was looking uncomfortable. He remembered suddenly that he had invited Wessel and Susarah to Jakkalsdrif and that Jakoba had formed the impression that he had struck up a friendship with the man over the telephone. Abel changed the subject by talking about the Mendozas, but this proved a mistake because as soon as she realised that he had been living in Newlands for months without troubling to look them up, Jakoba Steenkamp grew noticeably cooler towards him and she also made some very pointed remarks about not having seen him at the Tabernacle on Sundays.

Abel wondered why he did not excuse himself and leave, now that the atmosphere had grown so strained. There was nothing to stay for, so why did he continue to sit there while Jakoba looked at him with disapproval and her many sons fidgeted as they sensed the undercurrents and Susarah tried desperately to keep the conversation going?

It was, he recognised suddenly, because of that rare instinct of his; the instinct that warned him there was something here which could be turned to his own advantage. But what could it possibly be, he wondered in puzzlement. Not Susarah herself, obviously. Even if she had been far prettier than she was, she was encumbered with a baby and he guessed that she lived on a widow's pension. Then he remembered her offer to teach him to read and write. Yes, that must be it! Once he had mastered those skills he would be able to break out of the trap of earning a meagre living as a van-driver.

Silence fell as Susarah ran out of stilted remarks with which to keep some kind of conversation flowing. He sensed the desperation that made her break it by saying, "I wonder, Abel, if you could advise me on something. My late husband owned a motorcycle combination and I know I ought to sell it because it is just standing uselessly on the vacant plot next door, but I've no idea how to go about it or what it ought to fetch."

"I'll take a look at it," he agreed, relieved to escape from Jakoba's chilly presence. The motorcycle combination, he thought, had almost certainly been deteriorating, standing for more than six months in the open on waste ground where neighbourhood children had no doubt been playing with it and removing anything that was not welded on to it.

But when they had left the stoep together, with the boys streaming after them, and Susarah led the way to the vacant plot of land, Abel saw that pieces of tarpaulin had been draped over two objects. When he had removed the tarpaulin from the one Susarah indicated, he was surprised to discover that the motorcycle combination seemed in very good condition, in spite of having stood there unused for so long. Even so, she ought to sell it soon because if it remained there through another winter it would almost certainly start rusting.

"I could make enquiries for you about selling it," he said, wishing he could afford to buy it for himself. His glance went to the other, larger shape covered in tarpaulin. "What is that, Susarah?"

"Oh, it's a worthless piece of rubbish," she answered ruefully. "A worn-out old car Wessel took as security for five pounds he lent someone at his work. The man hasn't repaid the loan so it looks as if I'm stuck with it. I can't imagine why anyone ever wanted it in the first place, because it must be goodness-knows how old."

"May I see it?" Abel asked, still wondering how he could possibly raise the money to buy the motorcycle combination for himself. Then he realised, with bitterness, that even if he could have afforded it he would hardly ever have the time to enjoy driving it. He was as much a slave to his delivery-round of fruit and vegetables as he had been to Jakkalsdrif.

He helped Susarah to spread the tarpaulin over the motorcycle combination again, and her brothers showed their lack of interest in the old motor car by wandering away before it had been uncovered. Abel felt a prickling of his scalp as he stared at the exposed vehicle. He had never seen anything like it before.

Its bodywork was in good condition, as if someone had spent a great deal of time and trouble on preserving and refurbishing it, but it was something that belonged to another age. Common sense insisted that it *was* a worthless piece of well-kept but worn-out rubbish, looking more as if it should be drawn by horses than as if it had ever run on petrol, and if it could be made to work again at all it would probably be incapable of going faster than five miles an hour. Its engine was unbelievable; simply unbelievable in this day and age. The car wasn't anything that anyone in his right mind would possibly wish to have rusting away in his back-yard, so why did Abel's instinct scream at him that here was a rare find, something to be turned to his own advantage?

"This fancy lettering on it," he spoke at last. "What does it say?"

"Benz Voiturette," Susarah answered. "I'm not sure if I'm pronouncing it right. Why?"

He shrugged. "If spare parts are still to be found for it, and it could be put into working order, you might just be able to recover the five pounds your husband lost on it." Privately, in defiance of that instinct of his, Abel could not imagine anyone wanting to be seen driving an old freak like that, but he went on, "Write down the name for me, and I'll ask around at the same time as I'm making enquiries about the motorcycle combination for you."

"You're very kind," she said, touching his arm briefly. She went on with obvious embarrassment, "We're having supper soon, and of course you're welcome to stay, but I'm afraid Ma – "

"Yes," he cut her short. Jakoba Steenkamp would continue to freeze the atmosphere with her disapproval of him. The same instinct that told him the Benz Voiturette was important now urged him that it was important, also, to make his peace with Susarah's mother.

He grinned. "In your mother's eyes, I'm a sinner. Of all the many sins the Reformed Evangelists think up, there's none worse than not attending the Tabernacle regularly."

She gave him an answering rueful smile. "I've often wondered why things that sound as if they might be fun, like going to the bioscope or close-dancing – whatever *that* is – should be sins while nothing that's boring or disagreeable is. Why couldn't God have made washing-up a sin, for instance?"

Abel's eyes gleamed at her in approval. "You're definitely not a Halleluiah-girl!" He linked his arm through hers. "Come; I'll go and make peace with your mother."

When the two of them returned to the stoep he went straight to Jakoba, who was alone with the baby now, and said frankly, "I know you're hurt because I took so long to look you up, and you disapprove of the fact that I haven't been attending services at the Tabernacle, and I expect you are also thinking that common courtesy ought to have made me answer your note, telling me of Wessel's death. The truth is, Mevrou Steenkamp, that I've deliberately hidden myself away in my lodgings until now because I didn't want to bring shame on my parents."

"Shame on your parents?" she echoed, and he could tell that she was wondering what other dreadful sins he had been committing that were worse than not attending services at the Tabernacle. Another part of his mind was registering the fact that although she must be roughly the same age as the Bitch, she looked a great deal older. Unwillingly, he thought of the Bitch, lithe and slim and smooth-complexioned, and compared her with Jakoba who was squat and overweight and heavily wrinkled.

"I can't read or write," he answered her unspoken question. "I don't suppose my mother ever told you this in any of her letters."

"No," Jakoba admitted, staring blankly at him.

Abel nodded. "She has always been ashamed of the fact. It was nobody's fault but my own. I was young and stupid and I decided that working on the farm was more important than going to school."

"I – I see," Jakoba said uncertainly. "And how old were you when you reached this decision?"

He made his voice guileless. "I was nine years old, Mevrou." He didn't suggest by tone or expression that no child of that age ought to have been allowed to make such a decision, but went on ruefully, "I wouldn't listen to reason, and of course I couldn't foresee that the time would come when I would have to leave the farm because it could no longer provide a living for all of us, and that I would be handicapped by not being able to read and write. So – well, I couldn't answer your note, telling me of Wessel's death – which someone else read to me – and I didn't want to embarrass my parents by having it come out that their son was illiterate, as it would have come out if I had started attending services at the Tabernacle here in Newlands and made friends. I'm relying on you not to tell people the shaming truth, that Pastor Marcus Koen's son can't read or write, and the reason why I plucked up the courage to come and see you this afternoon was because I've made a start on learning those skills. I spoke to Susarah just now when she was showing me the motorcycle combination and she very kindly promised to help me with extra lessons on Sunday mornings."

He had glanced at Susarah as he spoke, his gaze both conspiratorial and questioning, and he recognised the approval and the admiration in her eyes. He had struck just the right note. He had placed himself in a sympathetic light by taking all the blame for his illiteracy, and Jakoba Steenkamp could go on deluding herself about the virtues of her old friend if she wished to do so. Somehow he did not think she would.

He gave her a limpid look. "When you write to my mother, Mevrou, perhaps you would tell her that I'm learning to read and write? I know how much that would please her." Sudden inspiration prompted him to add, "Oh, and you might also mention to her that I've made contact with an old friend of hers and my father's, a Mrs van Vuuren. She'll be pleased about that as well."

Jakoba nodded, her eyes cast down so that he couldn't tell what she was thinking. But after a moment she looked up and said warmly, "I'd take it as a compliment if you would call me Tant' Jakoba instead of Mevrou, Abel. And of course Susarah must help you, for as long as it's necessary, to learn to read and write." She stood up. "Now, I'm sure you must be hungry, so I'll go and do something about supper. I hope you like cinnamon pancakes, Abel."

As she left the stoep to hurry to her own house Susarah looked at Abel with a smile, and again he was struck by how pretty she was, or could be if she didn't wear such old-fashioned black clothes and dress her hair in the style of a true Halleluiah-girl. "You should feel honoured," she said. "Ma doesn't put herself out to make cinnamon pancakes for just anyone."

The bitter blow of having lost Jakkalsdrif had been softened considerably, even if only temporarily, by the time Abel left to return to his own lodgings. The Mendozas were attending evening Mass as he had known they would be, but at first he was unpleasantly surprised to find Juana had not gone with them and had obviously been lying in wait for him. Even though her parents were tolerant and easy-going and they liked Abel, she must be perfectly well aware that they would never countenance any kind of relationship between the two of them, and yet it did not stop her from making less than subtle approaches to him and gazing at him in unspoken invitation. It was an invitation he was not in the least tempted to accept, but on the other hand he didn't want to antagonise her, because if she turned on him she could make things so unpleasant that he would be forced out of his congenial and reasonably priced lodgings and perhaps even lose his job with her father's friend.

So tonight he resigned himself to the fact that he would have to sit and keep her company and pretend to be blind to the messages her dark eyes flashed at him, when what he really wanted to do was go to his room and think about that Benz Voiturette and puzzle out why his instinct screamed at him that it was important. The infuriating thing was that Dirk, who knew all about cars, could have told him what he needed to know, but he would not be able to go and see Dirk until next Sunday afternoon, after his lesson in reading and writing with Susarah, and even then he had no guarantee that Dirk would be at home.

It came to him suddenly that being alone with Juana might be turned into an advantage rather than a liability. He leant towards her and said, "I was just wondering . . . You know where your father keeps the keys to his shop?"

"Yes. Why, Abel?" She smiled in a way that made him wince inwardly. "Is there something you fancy in the shop that you can't get in the house?"

"There's a telephone in your father's shop," he answered, a little shortly.

"I see. And you want to use the telephone. Well, I'll go with you and let you in, and my father needn't know about it. He doesn't like anyone going into the shop when he isn't there."

Abel rose eagerly and then sat down again with a muffled oath. "I want to telephone my brother, but I don't know his number."

"Do you know his address?" When Abel nodded, Juana said briskly, "Then that's all right. I'll ask the operator to connect you."

The Mendozas lived just around the corner from their fruit and vegetable shop, and it was not long before Juana had Dirk on the line for Abel. She was obviously not going to leave him to speak in private, but he shrugged mentally as he took the instrument from her. His conversation would mean little or nothing to her.

Abel cleared his throat, trying to decide how to begin, and then he heard Dirk saying in an excruciatingly put-on accent, "Dirk Cone here."

"Cone?" Abel exploded. "What the hell is all this *Cone* nonsense?"

"Oh, it's you." Dirk's voice returned to normal and he slipped into Afrikaans. Safely out of physical reach of Abel, he resumed his usual arrogance. "It's how I prefer to pronounce Koen. You stick to being Abel Koen from the farm; it doesn't matter how *you* pronounce our name because you're never going to get anywhere in life whatever you call yourself."

Abel filed the insult away in his mind, to be avenged later, and asked with curiosity, "If Koen is too Afrikaans for you, why don't you call yourself Cohen, which would have been our real family name if the Man of God's parents hadn't gone to Holland and changed it to Koen?"

"Cousin Reuben doesn't think it would be a good idea," Dirk said shortly. "In any case, I haven't changed my name; I merely pronounce it differently. Look, you haven't telephoned to talk about surnames, have you? What do you want?"

"I want to ask you something. Would there be any market for a Benz Voiturette motor car?"

"A Benz – Voiturette?" Dirk echoed, a catch of astonishment, of disbelief, in his voice. After a pause he went on sharply, "What the devil do *you* know about a Benz Voiturette?"

"Oh, nothing," Abel said casually, but he felt as if the blood was whizzing around in his veins in sheer excitement, because he knew now that his instinct had not played him false. He went on, "A friend has one and is thinking of selling it, and I promised to try and find out what it's worth."

"I see." Again Dirk paused, and when he went on his tone was matter-of-fact, too matter-of-fact, and highlighted rather than hid his excitement. "To be honest, it's worth very little."

To be honest, Abel thought scathingly but at the same time exultantly. You lying bastard, do you think I can't tell that you're almost wetting yourself in your eagerness to get your hands on it? Aloud, he said, "Oh well, that's that then. I'll tell this friend of mine to have it carted away as scrap."

"No, wait!" Dirk could not hide the note of near-panic in his voice. He pretended to be seized by a brief coughing fit, and then continued with would-be casualness, "I didn't say it was worth *nothing*. In fact, I might be able to offer a few pounds for it if you'll give me your friend's name and address."

"I'm afraid I can't do that," Abel said, grinning to himself. "I can't imagine why, but my friend doesn't trust motor car salesmen. In any case, if all it's worth is a few pounds, then it might as well be used for my friend's children to play with. You know," Abel added cruelly, "take bits of it apart and see if they can put them together again."

"That – wouldn't be a very good idea." Dirk was sounding tortured now. "A Benz Voiturette would be very old, practically out of the Ark. What I was thinking was that it might have curiosity value – you know, make people stop and look if they see it displayed outside my showroom. As a *motor car* it's worthless, of course, far too old and slow, that's if it still works at all. No, as I say, I quite like the idea of having it for display purposes if it's in a reasonable state."

"How much?" Abel asked bluntly, and added, "It's in beautiful condition."

"Well . . . I would be prepared to go as high as twenty-five pounds."

"I'll tell my friend what you said," Abel returned as matter-of-factly as he could. "I have to go now – "

"Wait." There was anxiety mixed with greed in Dirk's voice. "If you could get your friend to let me view the car, and if it isn't just a pile of rust after all, I'll pay you ten per cent commission on the purchase."

"I'll hold you to that," Abel said, and replaced the telephone on its hook. He gave Juana a smile that made her eyes light up with false hope.

Her parents had returned from Mass by the time they reached the house, and while Juana slipped away to return the shop's keys to the place where they were kept, Abel said goodnight to her parents and went to his room.

He punched the air ecstatically with his fist. If Dirk was prepared to pay twenty-five pounds for the Benz Voiturette, then it must be worth at least five times as much. And Susarah had no inkling of its value. She would be more than glad to sell it to Abel for the five pounds her husband had loaned the car's original owner.

With a nest-egg like that, Abel thought, I could start saving for a business of my own. I could bloody well outstrip Dirk *Cone* in no time . . .

Then he remembered that he had finally and irrevocably lost Jakkalsdrif, and he sat down on the edge of the bed, staring into space. Would anything he achieved in his life ever compensate him for having been cheated out of what was his right?

He thought of the farm, *his* farm, going to rack and ruin because Dirk who owned it by fraud did not want it, and the Preacher was not interested in it, and the Bitch and Koos could not run it without his help. He smiled grimly to himself. In a way the Bitch was being punished for what she and the Preacher had done to him, for *she* loved Jakkalsdrif and she would be sitting there on the farm, helplessly watching it slowly being destroyed before her eyes.

His smile became grimmer as he remembered something else. Jakoba Steenkamp would most certainly be writing to the Bitch, telling her that Abel had been to visit them. The fact that he had asked her no questions about any letters containing information about his birth would have been enough in itself to puzzle and worry the Bitch. She would be wondering what was going on, and the news that he was learning to read and write would suggest that he had some concrete, long-term plan for her destruction. What would increase her anxiety a hundredfold would be the information that he had made contact with Mrs van Vuuren, the woman who had helped her at Dirk's birth and would remember that there had already been one older son named Abel toddling about the place.

As he undressed for bed Abel wished that he might have been there on Jakkalsdrif when the Bitch opened the letter from Jakoba Steenkamp. Then he began to plan how he would use the small fortune he would get for the Benz Voiturette.

29

Petronella was in the kitchen when the mailvan called at Jakkalsdrif. She had left it to Simon, as usual, to attend to the driver even though it was Friday afternoon, and Simon was in a hurry to leave for Doornboomstad where he would be spending the weekend in lodgings so that he could write and deliver his sermon in the Tabernacle on Sunday.

It had become second nature to her to avoid contact with outsiders, because she could no longer endure their probing questions which always followed the same predictable pattern.

"Any hope of Pastor Koen coming home soon, Mevrou?" they would ask.

Hope? I've forgotten what it is to hope. He will not be coming home soon, or late, or ever. Aloud, fixing a rueful smile on her face, she used to answer, "I've learnt to expect Marcus when I see him."

"Oh, but surely he lets you know about his movements?"

His movements are no longer considered my business. If anyone knows his movements it will be the whore he has put in my place. "Oh yes," she'd always lied brightly. "He telephones me often. But you know what Marcus is. People ask him to stay on a while longer to take a particular service, and he can never say no."

"And where is he at the moment, Mevrou?"

If he's not on the road, preaching and selling, he'll be with his unknown, nameless foreign whore – God curse them both . . . Straining to keep her bitter thoughts from showing, she would pluck from her mind another far-away district in which Marcus was supposedly preaching the gospel of the Church of the Reformed Evangelists.

But one morning she had decided she'd had enough, and since then she had done her lying and her keeping up of appearances through Simon. Now, while he was talking to the mailvan driver, she was supposedly too busy to leave the kitchen, but all she was really doing was sitting by the table, battling with the endless circle of grief, pain, rage, bitterness, hatred, desolation and loss.

She tried to clear the destructive thoughts from her mind by fixing her attention on a preserving jar filled with cream which stood on the kitchen dresser. The old butter-churn had finally fallen to pieces, and not only were they unable to afford a replacement but the milk yield on Jakkalsdrif was now so small that its purchase would not have been justified. Instead, the skimmed-off cream inside the preserving jar would have to be shaken laboriously and rhythmically from side to side by hand until the butter began to form.

I'll do it later, Petronella decided, and then thought bleakly, Does it really matter whether or not I make butter? What does anything really matter?

But pointless as day-to-day occupations seemed now that she had lost Marcus, the chores had to be done by someone and if Petronella ignored them Mwende would take them all upon her own shoulders. And Mwende seemed to have aged prematurely within the past months – almost as if she, too, were dwelling in some private hell.

Perhaps she was. Perhaps she was reliving the past and measuring it against an empty, futile present and future, for she had suddenly said to Petronella last week, "I wonder if Soldier Bobby ever think of me and of his daughter Tina."

Petronella had glanced at Tina, who had no hope of ever finding a husband of her own and had allowed herself to go to seed, looking unkempt and old before her time in a dreadful, shapeless dress bought from the Indian pedlar.

He was a mystery figure who had, for years, been visiting neighbourhood farms at intervals. No one knew where he came from or by what means he travelled across country, for he only ever appeared on farms on foot, bowed down by a huge bundle containing merchandise of all kinds, from chamber-pots to what he called church-hats.

Several months ago the Indian's familiar figure, hunched beneath his enormous bundle, had been seen on the horizon and Petronella had found Mwende signalling to him with a mirror, and she had explained that she wanted to buy dresses from him for herself and Tina.

"But why, Mwende? He only sells those awful, bunchy print dresses which I'm sure a relative of his must run up for him, and which look like sacks. You can make much better dresses yourself."

Mwende had shrugged. "Too much work, Nonnie Petronella, and the dresses from the bundle-coolie is cheap."

Even as she'd been mentally criticising Tina for allowing herself to go to seed, Petronella had been pulled up short by the reminder that she, too, no longer cared about her appearance. Somehow she could raise neither the interest nor the enthusiasm to make new clothes for herself and in the end she had asked Simon to bring home for her on approval from the store in Doornboomstad half a dozen of the overall dresses known, for some reason she couldn't fathom, as Mother

Hubbards. They were cool and easily laundered and they covered her respectably, and that was all she'd cared about, so she had bought them.

But how could she criticise Tina and Mwende for buying the Indian's dresses which were designed to fit anyone and flatter no one, when her own Mother Hubbards were wholly functional and lacked any style or beauty? Somehow the ugly, shapeless garments worn by Petronella, Mwende and Tina symbolised the fate they shared in common.

The three of us, Petronella had thought, trapped here on Jakkalsdrif, with no future and no hope and powerless to fight against our own dreary destinies. But Tina is so clumsy and slow these days that I wonder if she doesn't try to forget her own hopeless state by secretly brewing and drinking *skokiaan*. How could I blame her if she does?

Aloud, Petronella had belatedly answered Mwende's question. "I'm sure Tina's father often thinks of both of you."

And Mwende, recognising it as the empty lie it was, had sighed deeply and responded, "Your Mamma tell us, when we small, that you and me bad girls, Nonnie, who end in trouble one day."

Oh Mamma, Petronella thought now, if you could have foreseen the terrible nature of my trouble it would have softened even your flinty heart . . .

Simon broke into her thoughts by entering the kitchen with his suitcase in his hand. "I'm off now, Ma."

"Very well," she nodded indifferently.

He hesitated, and when he spoke again there was criticism in his voice. "Don't you think, Ma, just this once you might attend the service on Sunday? I'll take Koos with me, and then he can come back for you early on Sunday morning to drive you to Doornboomstad."

"Sunday is Koos's day off," she said firmly. "He works hard enough as it is, and sees precious little of Suki and his children. I'm not prepared to ask him to sacrifice his free time."

"Well," Simon said with a baulked look, "people are talking, you know! You haven't been to a single one of my services since I became lay-preacher. You hardly ever went to the Tabernacle before that, but people expect you at least to come and listen to your own son preach. I'm forever being asked why you haven't been seen and whether there's something wrong with you. It's bad enough being pestered with questions about when Pa will be coming home. Have you any idea when that will be?"

"He telephoned again yesterday morning, when you were delivering that telegram to the Therons," Petronella lied. "He's in the Free State, holding services and making converts, and there's talk of building a

Tabernacle as soon as enough money has been raised, so he can't tell when he'll be able to leave."

"It's time," Simon said pointedly, "that he remembered his *old* converts, not to mention his family. It must be six months since he was last home, the longest time he has ever stayed away."

It's seven months, three weeks and two days, Petronella corrected mentally. Two hundred and thirty-five empty, desolate days; two thousand, eight hundred and twenty hours of bitter, lonely hell. God help me when I start working out the minutes, the seconds . . .

"People are beginning to talk," Simon repeated. "It doesn't make things easy for me in my position."

She cared nothing for his position. What she did care about, with blind desperation, was that no one should know Marcus had left her for good, let alone that he had left her for another woman. All she had left was her pride, and it would not allow her to make herself known as an abandoned wife, an object of pity. In addition and against all logic, she clung to the desperate, irrational hope that if no one ever found out the truth, Marcus might yet return to her one day.

But the lies and the inventions were an increasingly precarious balancing act to maintain. She could tell that even Simon, accustomed as he was to Marcus's long absences from home, was beginning to wonder about all those supposed telephone calls from his father which always came when he was absent from the post office room. And if Simon stopped believing the lies, he would not be able to repeat them convincingly to others.

Rashly, Petronella said, "Your father mentioned that he might be able to make a quick visit home this weekend, crossing by the drift in the river. He couldn't promise anything and that's why I haven't mentioned it before. So you can see, the last thing I'd wish to do is to go to Doornboomstad and miss spending time with him."

Simon swallowed the lie, for his eyes shone and he said, "Make him attend the service in Doornboomstad on Sunday, Ma! He has never heard me preach either!"

"Yes, yes, if he comes, I'll ask him . . ." Could a 'visit' be plausibly invented? she wondered. Yes, perhaps – with Mwende's cooperation. It would mean confiding in her, but if there was one person in the world in whom Petronella could bear to confide at all it was Mwende, her childhood playmate and loyal servant and friend. *She* would help to compound the lie that Marcus had come home for twenty-four hours. The people still living in the *stad* were all so old, some of them in their dotage, that they hardly ever left their huts at all, and none of them would be able to nail the lie. Tina, whether or not *skokiaan* was the cause, lived in a world of her own these days and scarcely seemed to notice what was going on around her, and with Mwende's help she would be easy to fool. But Koos could not be fooled at all . . .

With no clear idea in her mind as to how she meant to deceive Simon – and through him everyone in the district – into believing that Marcus had paid a swift visit home to see his wife, but knowing it would be quite impossible if Koos were on Jakkalsdrif, Petronella went on, "Whether or not your father does manage to come home, I think Koos deserves a short holiday and we can easily spare him for a few days. So take him with you and drop him off at the farm of Suki's people, and you can collect him again on your way home."

Simon nodded, but said disapprovingly, "It's high time Koos and Suki got married, *lobolo* or no *lobolo*. If Pa does come home I'll ask him to talk to Koos about it, because he takes no notice of me when I tell him he's living in sin."

Petronella stifled a burst of wild, hysterical laughter at the thought of *Marcus* preaching to Koos about the evils of living in sin, and watched with relief as Simon finally left with his suitcase to prepare for the drive to Doornboomstad.

After he and Koos had gone she took the preserving jar of cream out to the stoep and sat down, her mind busy as she shook the jar to and fro with even, horizontal movements. She tried to plot a plausible illusion that Marcus had paid a fleeting visit home, but other thoughts kept on getting in the way, not least of all the despairing one that, at some stage or other in the future, she would have to stop lying simply because the time would come when the lies would no longer be believable. The most she could hope for, then, was that no one would learn another woman was involved.

Her gaze swept bleakly over Jakkalsdrif. They were approaching the end of what had been a mild winter and the air had the hard, bright quality of rainless Highveld winters, a quality that somehow emphasised the poverty of the land.

If it had not been for her own efforts and those of Koos, the farm would all but have stopped producing anything by now. Simon lent a hand when he was ordered to do so but he had no interest in the land. Jakkalsdrif needed the almost fanatical devotion Abel had given it . . .

Staring hard at the cream inside the jar to see whether the small blobs of yellow butter were about to form, Petronella thought, Abel has given up his fight for Jakkalsdrif. His attempts have cost me Marcus, and I hope he rots in Johannesburg where I need never lay eyes on him again.

There was no sign at all yet of the cream turning, and her arms and shoulders were aching from the relentless shaking of the jar. The trouble was that if she stopped now, the cream would thin again as it merged with what would become the buttermilk, and the whole tedious and tiring business would have to be started once more from the beginning.

Mwende had gone to feed the chickens and to collect the eggs, but Petronella could hear Tina lumbering about with slow, heavy footsteps somewhere inside the house, and she called to her.

"Take over from me for a while, will you, Tina?" she asked, still shaking the jar as she rose to her feet.

· Tina sat down heavily in the chair Petronella had vacated and held out her hands to receive the jar. But as Petronella transferred it to her Tina uttered a stifled sound and simultaneously the jar slid from between her palms, shattering on the cement floor of the stoep in a mess of cream and milk and broken glass.

Petronella looked sharply at Tina. "You've been drinking *skokiaan*, haven't you?"

"No, Nonnie," Tina mumbled.

Petronella turned away to fetch a cloth to clean up the mess. "Go home, Tina," she said resignedly. "You're of no use to me like this. Stop by the barn on your way and tell your mother I want to see her."

Mwende was crouching inside the barn, searching for any previously missed eggs concealed in the straw. Her back was turned upon the half-open door when she heard Tina say, "Nonnie Petronella want you, Mamma."

Mwende stiffened, alerted by something in her daughter's voice, and hurriedly transferred the eggs she had just collected to the basket containing the others. She straightened and almost ran to the door, calling out urgently, "Tina, *buya fika!*"

Tina turned, and stumbled obediently back towards the barn. Mwende could see that sweat was beading on her temples, and trying to deny her own fear she called softly, "*Ayikona saba*, Tina."

But it was not fear that gazed from Tina's eyes. It was numb, animal misery, and as she blundered inside the barn she began to shake with sobs. Mwende folded her in her arms, muttering, "*Ayikona kala. Tula, tula, Tina ka mina.*"

Convulsive shudders passed through the girl's body. "Mamma, Mamma, Mamma," she keened, but Mwende recognised all the emotions jumbling in her mind that were being left unexpressed. She eased her daughter down on to the straw and began to question her.

"*Au, siza Nkosi Jesus!*" Mwende appealed hopelessly for divine help as she rose to her feet again. Deciding to take advantage of Koos's absence from Jakkalsdrif, she had given Tina the medicine, but it had worked too soon and now all of her carefully prepared plans would have to be abandoned. Most importantly, Nonnie Petronella must not be allowed to suspect anything.

Mwende commanded Tina to remain where she was and hurried from the barn with the basketful of eggs. She thought of the shelter built in secret on the bank of the river, its floor covered in clean straw, of the twigs and branches of thorn-scrub carefully arranged nearby, needing only a match to set water to boil in the three-legged cauldron left inside the shelter. All of it useless, for Tina could not walk the distance to the river now that her waters had broken.

Dear gentle Jesus, Mwende wondered in despair, how will I manage the business now? It will have to be done right there inside the barn, and what if Nonnie Petronella comes to it for some reason? Help me, Jesus, to do the thing the *dolosse* tell me to do. Keep Nonnie Petronella away from the barn because she will stop me doing what is necessary.

Mwende straightened her back and narrowed her eyes in desperate thought. She would have to build on the advantages she possessed, such as the fact that Koos was away from Jakkalsdrif. She would insist on doing the milking alone, both to keep Nonnie Petronella away from the barn and also to enable herself to carry pails of hot water and old towels from the house without raising questions. Nonnie Petronella might think she was being over-fussy about washing the cows' udders, but she would suspect nothing more. Then afterwards, when it was all over, Mwende would tell Nonnie Petronella that her bad daughter Tina had drunk so much *skokiaan* that she couldn't stand on her feet, but had to remain in bed inside their hut.

Gentle-Jesus-meek-and-mild, Mwende prayed, let it all be over tonight so that I can help Tina back to our hut before morning, before the old people in the *stad* are stirring, before Nonnie Petronella wakes up.

Petronella was staring at the letter in her hand. The sight of Jakoba's handwriting as she went to sort the mail had brought a stab of warmth and pleasure to her heart, and no sense of foreboding at all. And then, as she opened the envelope, the extreme brevity of Jakoba's letter had struck the first chill in her heart. The chill had become a deathly coldness as she read the curt note.

"I am writing to you," Jakoba had started baldly, "at the request of your son Abel, who spent last Saturday afternoon and evening with us. As you will probably guess, it was a very enlightening visit. Abel has asked me to pass on to you the news that he has begun to learn how to read and write, and also that he has made contact with an old friend of yours, a Mrs van Vuuren." The letter ended with what seemed to Petronella to be mocking menace, "With best wishes, Jakoba."

The letter could not have been more terrifying in its enigmatic ambiguity. " 'Enlightening visit'," Petronella muttered through numb lips. Enlightening for Jakoba, who had been told everything by Abel? For Abel himself, because he had been handed the proof he needed that he had been born before Dirk? Both, it would seem.

The letter made no direct threat, and yet it constituted nothing but a threat. Jakoba would not have written to Petronella at all if Abel had not asked her to do so, and the message he had sent was this: I have made contact with your friend to whom you wrote at the time of my birth; I have run to earth the woman who helped you with Dirk's birth, and I am learning to read and write.

The essence of the threat must lie in the fact that Abel was learning to read and write. Whatever hideous, Abel-like punishment he was planning for his parents must make it necessary for him to express himself on paper . . .

Petronella's attention was dragged away from the haunted circle of her fear by Mwende's voice. "I feed the animals, Nonnie, and I milk the cows also."

"Did Tina tell you that I'd sent her home? I'm sure she had been drinking *skokiaan*, Mwende."

"Yes, Nonnie Petronella." There was such weariness and despair in Mwende's voice that Petronella leant forward and touched her arm.

"We'll keep the yeast locked up from now on."

"Yes, Nonnie," Mwende said again, and reiterated, "I go milk the cows now."

"If you can't manage alone, Mwende, call me."

Vaguely aware that Mwende was stoking the range in the kitchen and setting receptacles of water to boil on it in preparation for doing the milking, Petronella retreated to the post office room and sat, staring at the telephone.

The yearning to speak to Marcus – about *anything* – just to hear his distinctive voice again was almost overpowering. But if she told him about Jakoba's letter she knew what he would do. He would take his whore and leave the country.

Time and again Petronella stretched out a hand to remove the telephone from its hook, and then withdrew it again. Once Marcus had left the country with his whore it would mean the end of any faint glimmer of hope for Petronella herself.

Inside the barn, Mwende had lit a storm lantern but she had first closed the door firmly so that Nonnie Petronella would not be able to see its light from the house.

Tina began to say something, but her words were cut off by a low bellow of pain. Mwende knelt beside her where she lay stretched out on the straw, pulling up her shapeless, loose-fitting dress, and slid her palm over Tina's swollen stomach. "Be brave, my Tina. I will help you, and when the time comes I will be quick and merciful."

Tina grabbed at her hands and beseeched weakly but with desperation, "Mamma, Mamma, please – *don't kill my poor baby!*"

"I must, my child." Mwende's voice, for all the sadness it held, was also implacable. "You know that I must. The *dolosse* say it has to be done, and you and I also know it is the only way."

Tina began to weep with great wrenching sobs, and Mwende tried to comfort her. If only her plans had not gone so wrong. It would have been a simple matter to take the child before it had drawn its first breath and drown it in the river, allowing the current to sweep away all evidence that it had ever existed. But now she would have to smother it at birth and she would not be able to prevent Tina from seeing and hearing it being done, and her daughter would also have to watch the small body being taken out of the barn to be thrown into the river.

"Mamma, Mamma, I want my baby!" Tina cried before another contraction caused her to arch her body and brought a scream to her lips.

Mwende swiftly placed a muffling hand over her daughter's mouth, and when the contraction had passed she spoke gently to Tina, reminding her of her own lifelong isolation inside the *stad*, asking her if she wanted to wish that fate upon her own child too. She talked of their success in hiding Tina's pregnancy from everyone, so that not a shred of suspicion had ever been aroused.

"And wasn't it lucky, my Tina, that your belly did not start swelling until only a few months back, when everyone had long grown used to seeing you in the ugly dresses sold by the bundle-coolie? You looked no more or less pregnant in those dresses than I did. It will not be long now – "

"*Mamma, don't kill my baby!*"

"There is no other way, Tina. And the baby will not suffer. It will die very quickly and then I will carry the body to the river and nobody will ever know."

But in between the contractions Tina continued to plead with desperate sobs for her baby's life, promising to take it and go far away and somehow find a way of caring for it.

Mwende pointed out to her, over and over again, the impossibility of such wild plans, and reminded her they had no other course but to destroy the newborn child and pretend it had never existed. But as she talked she was thinking with searing bitterness, Where are you now, Soldier Bobby? Do you ever think of your poor daughter Tina who fits nowhere? Would you care if you knew that I had to murder my grandchild and yours, so that it would not have to suffer as Tina has suffered? Was it all worth it for you, Soldier Bobby? Do you even remember those moons we shared together when we made Tina, you and I?

"Oh Mamma, Mamma," Tina's voice shattered her thoughts, "please don't kill my baby! *Please!*"

Mwende wiped her eyes and nose on her sleeve, and as she bent closer to probe Tina's stomach with her hands the girl's body arched and she uttered a scream of such animal pain that even Mwende's hand, swiftly clamped over her mouth, could not stifle it.

Mwende sat back on her haunches, filled with a sense of her own impotence. The recipe for the medicine to induce birth had been handed down to her by family lore, but she knew almost nothing about midwifery. The only birth at which she had ever been present before had been that of Nonnie Petronella's thrown-away son Abel. But the Oumies had been in charge and Mwende merely an onlooker and passer of bowls of hot water and of towels. Were matters proceeding normally? In years gone by, black women had given birth in their huts in the *stad*, but Mwende could not remember them bellowing with pain as Tina was doing. Of course, her daughter's white blood had always made her more physically fragile than if she had been a full Zulu woman, and it also seemed to her that Tina's waters had broken far too early for a normal labour. Desperately, Mwende wished that they did indeed have *skokiaan* available so that she could give some to Tina to blur her pain.

The barn door opened, and above the noise Tina was making Mwende heard Nonnie Petronella's voice. *"Dear God, what – ?"*

Then she was kneeling beside Tina, examining her and saying urgently, "Help me to get her inside the house, Mwende. She's having a dry labour."

Mwende gazed at her in despair. Everything had gone wrong, and Nonnie Petronella would never allow her to do what had to be done. And then Mwende remembered what the *dolosse* had said. There had been no ifs or buts about the way the bones had fallen when she shook them to foretell events. They had spoken of death being the solution to the problem. With or without Mwende's agency, the baby would die. The *dolosse* had said so.

Half-carrying, half-supporting Tina, Mwende and Nonnie Petronella succeeded in getting her inside the house, the wavering light from a single storm lantern dangling from the Nonnie's wrist showing them the way. Listening to the uncontrollable screams of agony coming from her daughter, Mwende gave thanks for the fact that Koos was away from Jakkalsdrif with Kleinbaas Simon, and that the people in the *stad* were too old and deaf to hear her from this distance.

"We'll put her in my bed," Nonnie Petronella said when they entered the house.

"Better we put her in Baas Abel's room," Mwende protested, "with old sheets we can burn later – "

"There isn't time to waste in finding old sheets! Besides, my bed is a good, large one and will give the doctor more space in which to work – "

"*No doctor, Nonnie!*" Mwende cried urgently.

Nonnie Petronella stared at her. "Mwende, your daughter needs help! Neither you nor I have any experience of delivering babies, and so I *must* telephone the doctor in Doornboomstad."

"Please, no doctor! Nobody else, Nonnie. Only me and you."

They had helped Tina on to the bed as they spoke and she lay there, her body arching convulsively from time to time and inhuman, bellowing roars tearing from her as pain racked her.

Nonnie Petronella frowned at Tina and then at Mwende. "Why the secrecy? Why no doctor? You couldn't keep the baby a secret – "

"The baby will not live," Mwende interrupted quietly.

Her words had penetrated the pain enveloping Tina, and she gasped desperately, "Nonnie Petronella – stop Mamma . . . Please – don't let her kill my baby!"

"Dear, sweet Jesus," Nonnie Petronella breathed faintly, and she stared at Mwende. "You – you planned . . . Out there in the barn, if I hadn't heard Tina screaming . . ." She broke off and knelt by Tina's side. "I won't allow your baby to die. I'm going to telephone the doctor in Doornboomstad – "

"What you tell him, Nonnie?" Mwende put in tonelessly. "What you say to him? That Mwende's *basterkind* Tina is having a baby? Whose baby you tell him it is, Nonnie? Whose baby *you* think it is?"

"Oh Christ, I hadn't even thought – " Mwende watched her Nonnie's eyes darken with shocked understanding. "Simon, the pious little hypocrite!"

Mwende opened her mouth, and closed it again. Instinct told her that it would be best to keep Abel, the hated thrown-away son, out of the matter.

Nonnie Petronella had clapped her hand to her forehead. "Dear God, *this* scandal on top of . . . No one would come near the place again to buy from the shop, or post their letters, and the licence for the post office would be taken away – "

"And we all starve," Mwende finished for her. Yes, far better that Nonnie Petronella believed the baby was that of Kleinbaas Simon, the preacher, if it would stop her from sending for the doctor.

Nonnie Petronella bent over Tina, and then looked up, frowning with anxiety. "She has begun to bleed quite heavily. Is it normal for there to be bleeding before the birth?"

"Perhaps the blood help the baby to be born more quickly," Mwende hazarded.

Nonnie Petronella straightened and moved to the door, rolling up her sleeves as she went. "I'm going to get hot water from the stove, and some old towels. And we'll give Tina a mugful of *buchu*-brandy to help deaden the pain."

The *buchu*-brandy took effect after several minutes and Tina's bellowing roars became inward rumbling groans instead. Between them, Mwende and Nonnie Petronella washed away the worst of the blood but as fast as they washed more flowed from inside Tina.

"Can this be normal, Mwende?" Nonnie Petronella asked in a worried voice.

Mwende pondered, and nodded. "When Tina born, and Soldier Bobby help me, he covered all over with blood."

"When Tina has recovered from the birth," Nonnie Petronella changed the subject, "we'll find a place to which to send her and the baby, and Simon must send money to keep them. Koos can be relied upon not to talk, and no one else will ever know."

Mwende nodded agreement, but she knew there would be no need for Koos or Simon to be told anything about tonight's business, because the baby was already dead. The *dolosse* never lied, and it was clear that the reason Tina had been in so much pain, and was bleeding so much, was because the baby had died inside her.

The *buchu*-brandy had had greater effect on Tina than Mwende would have imagined, because she seemed half-asleep now, even though her body was still arching spasmodically with contractions and she moaned with pain. After a while the clock in the room that was now a post office struck twelve times.

"Mwende," Nonnie Petronella said, "the contractions seem to have stopped. I think the first stage of labour is over and we must wait for the second, and that means the baby isn't going to be born for some time yet. Go and make coffee for us while I sit with Tina."

Mwende left the bedroom and went into the kitchen, where water was being kept on the boil. She measured ground coffee into the pot and filled it with boiling water and while she waited for it to brew on the side of the range she found mugs and set them out. Several different sounds, each following swiftly upon the other, caused a mug to slip from Mwende's suddenly useless, numb fingers. First had come a high-pitched scream which ended in a strange, rattling sound, and almost simultaneously the air was filled with the noise of a baby crying. Above it came a frantic call from Nonnie Petronella for Mwende to come quickly.

The baby should have been born dead. The words drummed in

Mwende's head as she moved with difficulty, like an old and stricken woman, from the kitchen to Nonnie Petronella's bedroom. *The baby should have been dead.*

She stood stock-still in the doorway of the bedroom. Nonnie Petronella was wrapping the baby, still attached to Tina by its cord, in a piece of torn sheeting. It was a boy and it was still crying lustily and Nonnie Petronella had wiped away enough of the blood and slime from his body for Mwende to see that he was completely white. She did not need to look at the still body of her daughter on the bed to know that she was dead.

Mwende sank to her knees, and flung her apron over her head. "The *dolosse* tell me one must die," she cried on a terrible note of grief, "and all the time I think it the wrong one will die."

She wrapped her apron around her head and began to sway from side to side. "*Au Tina, Tina ka mina,*" she mourned brokenly. "*Tina, Mamma ka wena sori . . .*"

With fingers clumsy and trembling through shock, Petronella had succeeded in tying and cutting the umbilical cord attaching the baby to its dead mother. Everything had happened so suddenly that she could not be certain of the exact sequence of events. She remembered Tina's body heaving in an unexpected, tremendous convulsion and the next moment the baby's head had appeared. One thing only Petronella knew quite clearly. The baby had cried before it had been fully born, and at the very moment that its mother had breathed her last.

Poor Tina, Petronella thought, her mind numb with shocked confusion and sadness and physical fatigue. Poor, poor little Tina. What had been the point of her existence? What happiness had she ever known? She could not even have had the brief joy of a relationship with Simon, who was a cold, unctuous creature with no great interest in girls. No, the hypocritical little swine had probably raped her in a rare moment of impious lust. Poor, lost little Tina . . .

Petronella laid the baby, still screaming, beside its dead mother who had even been denied a brief glimpse of her son. Then Petronella went to Mwende, enclosing her in her arms. "I should have called the doctor," she reproached herself in a shaking voice, but even as she spoke she knew that the doctor could not have arrived from Doornboomstad in time to save Tina. And hadn't Mwende said the *dolosse* had predicted a death? Petronella had learnt, over the years, not to mock the native faith in the omens revealed by the *dolosse*.

The baby was demanding attention and Mwende seemed unable or unwilling to give it, so Petronella rose with a heavy sigh and hurried into the kitchen, fetching a kettle of hot water from the stove.

Back in the bedroom she mixed it with cold water from the porcelain pitcher on her wash-stand, pouring it into the matching basin. Then, unwrapping the baby from the sheets in which she had first swaddled him, she began to sponge him clean.

He was a big baby, and in spite of the terrible drama which had catapulted him into the world he seemed extremely healthy. He was also totally white, with no negroid characteristics whatever. He had an abundance of straight, dark hair and when he ceased screaming for long enough to show the colour of his eyes Petronella could see that they were blue.

She was still examining him bemusedly, this totally white grandson of Mwende's, when she realised that Mwende herself had risen and after pulling a blanket over Tina's body she was staring at the baby, tears pouring down her cheeks.

"Nonnie," Mwende begged hoarsely when she could speak at all, "help me. Let me press pillows on his face."

"Mwende! Your own grandson and – good God, mine as well! I agree, it would have been better for everyone if he'd never been born, but now that he has, how can you think of such a terrible thing?"

"Nonnie, look at him!" Mwende cried passionately. "See how white he is!"

"Yes. Do you hate him because he is white, Mwende? Or because he reminds you of what was done to poor Tina?"

"Au, Nonnie! How to think I can hate my Tina's child? But I too old, Nonnie, too tired, for a white grandchild. *Help me to kill him, please!*"

Petronella hesitated, and then she said gently, "You're not yourself, Mwende, or you would not be asking such a terrible thing of me."

"You speak of terrible things," Mwende said in a voice shaking with raw passion. "You not think the life of my Tina was a terrible thing? What she ever had, Nonnie Petronella? All her life – *nothing*. Always she pushed aside because she a *basterkind*." She stared at the baby. "And now this one, Nonnie. How I tell him when he grow up, looking just like white basies, how it come that I his black grandmamma? How I explain, Nonnie? How I say to him: You a white Zulu, child. How, Nonnie Petronella?" She stopped to wipe her eyes on her apron.

"I – yes, I see," Petronella muttered, and shook her head. "But to want to kill him . . ."

"Better he dead," Mwende said with stark grief. "Much kinder he dead. For him and for me, Nonnie. You think I not suffer enough after I bring home my Tina? Now it all start again, with a white grandson who I must watch suffer more than my Tina suffer." Her voice thickened with desperate, anguished tears.

While his black grandmother wept her little white grandson had stopped crying and he was staring up at Petronella, almost as if he had been able to follow the conversation and knew that his fate rested in her hands. And suddenly Petronella knew with an instinctive, terrible conviction that it did, literally. If she did not find some way out, and she handed this child over to Mwende, he would not live more than a day at most. And even knowing full well what must have happened, how could Petronella ever call the police to Jakkalsdrif and accuse Mwende of murdering the baby?

"There's an orphanage in Wolmaransstad," Petronella began, "founded by the Church of the Reformed Evangelists – "

"They take white babies with black grandmammas, Nonnie Petronella?" Mwende asked bleakly.

Petronella bit on her lip. No, they would not knowingly take in such a child. Besides, even if she could hide the fact that Mwende was its grandmother, how could the baby be sent to the orphanage without it coming to light that it had been born on Jakkalsdrif? People would think it was her unwanted baby, hers and Marcus's, and that she had abandoned it –

The thought led her to the only logical solution there was. "We'll pretend to the world that the baby is mine," Petronella said abruptly.

"Nonnie?" Mwende looked at her in stupefaction.

"It's the only answer to the problem, Mwende. No one guessed for a moment that Tina was pregnant. So why should we not say that *I* had been pregnant, without even guessing it? It happened to me before, with Dirk, and now I am of an age to make such a thing even more possible." And, she thought with raw and bitter humour, such a story would even fit in with Marcus's last known visit to Jakkalsdrif, the last night he had ever slept with her and pleasured her.

"But – " Mwende began.

"It would work! I'd have to start taking an interest in the way I look, lose some weight, stop wearing shapeless Mother Hubbards. And you would be able to love your grandson, look after him, see him every day without the world guessing the truth. Both of you would be saved from all those future troubles you've described to me." Petronella became brisk. "But we'll have to work quickly, Mwende, before people in the *stad* begin to wake up."

She explained carefully and patiently to the grief-dazed Mwende what they ought to do. Tina's death must not be connected in any way with the birth of a baby on Jakkalsdrif, and so an illusion must be created that she was ill inside their hut, with her mother caring for her. With Koos away this would not be difficult, for the other inhabitants of the *stad* were old and even if they hadn't been concerned with their own aches and pains, shunning both Mwende and Tina had been their habit for so many years that no one would think of going near their hut, and they certainly wouldn't show interest in Tina's 'illness'.

Poor Tina, Petronella thought again, no one but Mwende had cared about her when she was alive and no one would care that she had died, or question the circumstances of her death. And officialdom did not concern itself too much with the births and deaths of black people, and so she would be buried without a doctor having to examine the body and issue a death certificate.

A drawer was removed from the bureau in the bedroom, a pillow placed inside it and the baby laid down upon it while Mwende and Petronella together carried Tina's body, wrapped in a blanket, from the house to the hut in the *stad*, their way lit by the full moon which reflected an eerie white glow from the frost crunching underfoot.

Petronella returned alone to the house afterwards, leaving Mwende to hold mourning vigil over Tina's body. The baby was crying again and Petronella went to the *stoepkamer* which had been turned into a shop, and took from its store a feeding bottle, some teats and a tin of powdered baby-milk formula. If such things had been available to her at the time of Abel's birth, she wondered involuntarily, would her life have turned out differently?

The thought of Abel reminded her that he was hatching some fiendish plot for the destruction of his parents, and that she ought to contact Marcus and warn him. But the baby's needs were too immediate and urgent for her mind to do more than pick at the looming disintegration of her life, and she hurried to wash the feeding bottle and fill it with warm, sweetened water with which to comfort him until his digestive system would be ready to receive his first feed.

It came to her suddenly that she, who had never liked babies and had been irritated by their constant crying and demands for attention, should have resented all she was being forced to do for this child of Simon's and poor Tina's. But she didn't, perhaps because it was only a temporary necessity and because the real, behind-the-scenes responsibility for him would belong to Mwende.

The baby fell asleep after he had drunk the sweetened water and Petronella put him back inside the improvised bed of a bureau drawer and covered him with a blanket. Several practical matters had to be seen to, because when the mailvan called in the morning its driver must find her in bed, apparently recovering from her surprise delivery of a son during the night. He would naturally spread the news throughout the district, and it was far too much to hope for that neighbouring women would not come flocking to Jakkalsdrif to see her and the new baby. They had been condemning her for her continued non-appearance at Tabernacle services but they would almost certainly now blame it on her 'condition' and show their forgiveness and goodwill by calling on her. She would therefore have to suffer being imprisoned in bed for at least ten days.

Petronella went into the post office room to make sure that there was nothing requiring urgent attention. But the only question of any importance or urgency was the one concerning Abel's plans, and whether or not she should make contact with Marcus.

She sat down by the table that served as a desk and dropped her head in her hands. The ache for Marcus was not lessening with age, and when she couldn't sleep at night for hungering for him, she was able to weave a fantasy in which he left his whore and returned to her. Once he had fled from South Africa, she would be robbed of even that fantasy – a flimsy, futile comfort though it was.

To put off the moment when she would have to decide, she went through a drawer in search of the official forms needed for registering a baby's birth by post. One must be on hand to be filled in when the mailvan arrived so that it could be sent off by the driver.

Joshua, she thought with a bleak, twisted smile. That's what I'll call the baby. Marcus begged for each of his sons in turn to be named Joshua after his father, and now this baby, this illegitimate *basterkind* who is Marcus's grandchild, can bear his Jewish father's name. Even though Marcus will never know it, and even though it will be fact only on an official piece of paper, Marcus will have his longed-for son Joshua Koen after all.

She looked at the clock on the wall. It was five in the morning, still too early to telephone Dirk and invent some reason why she needed to be put in contact with Marcus's cousin Reuben. As she had the thought, she realised that she had unwittingly made the decision that would send Marcus away from South Africa and out of her reach forever.

Her shoulders bowed, she stumbled wearily out of the post office room and went to the kitchen to mix a feed for the baby, who had again begun to cry. The outer door into the kitchen opened and Mwende stepped inside.

"I can manage," Petronella said gently. "Go home and be with Tina."

Mwende shook her head, and spoke hoarsely. "Nonnie Petronella, the baby – what you do for me and for him – "

"Is being done for my own sake as much as for yours and his." Petronella's tone turned grim. "What Simon did would spell disaster for all of us if it came out. But you needn't think that he won't be made to pay – for poor Tina, for the baby – "

"No Nonnie," Mwende interrupted quietly. "I come to tell you – Baas Abel is baby's Pappa, not Kleinbaas Simon."

"*Abel!*" Petronella stared at her in disbelief. It was almost eight months since Abel had left Jakkalsdrif. It was not possible that he could have known of Tina's pregnancy. She herself would probably not have known of it at the time. Besides, he had left because of that letter from Jakoba which had supplied him with her address. "Are you sure it was Abel, Mwende?"

"Quite sure, Nonnie. Never anybody else touch my Tina; only Abel." Her body slackened in an attitude of weariness, defeat and resignation. "At first I scared to tell you. But it not right for Simon to get the blame. Now – now you won't want to pretend you the baby's Mamma."

Abel's child, Petronella thought with fury and outrage. As if he hadn't caused enough trouble already throughout his misbegotten life . . .

The thought petered out in her mind. This baby was the weapon she'd needed against Abel!

She filled the feeding bottle with the milky liquid she had been mixing, and fitted a teat to it as she spoke. "I haven't changed my mind, Mwende. The baby will be registered as Joshua Koen, my son and Marcus's. But *no one* must know it isn't true; no one at all, not even Abel – *especially* not Abel. Is that understood?"

Mwende wiped her hand across her eyes as she nodded.

"It will be your secret and mine only." Petronella handed the feeding bottle to Mwende. "Your grandson is hungry; go and feed him. There is something I have to attend to."

She patted Mwende's shoulder in passing, and hurried into the post office room. Seating herself at the table, she drew a blank sheet of paper towards her and picked up a pen, dipping it into the inkwell, and began to write:

'I, Mwende Mngadi, swear on the Bible and on the souls of my ancestors that the baby boy born on Jakkalsdrif on the – " Petronella paused to consult the almanac on the wall, and continued writing, "morning of the 28th of July, 1926, and registered as Joshua Koen, is the natural son of my daughter, Tina Mngadi, who died in giving birth to him, and that his father is Abel Koen."

Petronella smiled grimly to herself. Mwende would readily put her mark to the document when it was explained to her that it was a statement that she had assisted in the birth to Petronella herself of a son during the night, and required for official reasons.

But the document would be locked away and guarded as if it were more valuable than all the money in the world. With that document, she had the perfect weapon to use against Abel in whatever plot he was hatching.

Knowing Abel, he would not spring his plans on her when he was ready to put them into operation. Oh no, he would be contacting her beforehand, dropping sly, tormenting hints, wanting to drag out his revenge for as long as possible so that he could savour it to the full.

Well, she would let him. And when her right moment came, she would drop her bombshell – that he had fathered a son by Tina, and that Petronella had sworn, written proof of the fact.

"You want possession of Jakkalsdrif," she would say to him. "Of what value will it be to you to be its owner when the whole district will know you for the father of a *basterkind*?"

Second only to wanting Jakkalsdrif, Abel cared for the good opinion of the neighbours. He would realise that gaining the farm would also gain him a lifetime of contempt and lonely isolation. He would have no alternative but to admit defeat.

Marcus would never know any of this, and would continue to live in South Africa with his foreign whore, and Petronella would retain her pitiful, impossible fantasy with which to feed her hunger for him. It was very little, but it was better than nothing at all. And there would be no public scandal to face because they had cheated Abel of his inheritance.

Hatch your schemes and plot your revenge, Abel, Petronella thought as she picked up the document so that Mwende could put her mark on it. I shall be more than ready for you when the time comes.

30

Susarah settled Corabella into her cradle and then sat down on the stoep to wait for Abel. All over Newlands church bells were still pealing and a few stragglers were hurrying by to obey their summons, waving to Susarah as they passed. Their smiles were sympathetic and said that, of course, they understood she was being denied the solace of the Sunday morning service because her baby was still too young to be taken to a place of worship. They could not, fortunately, guess at the excitement bubbling inside her.

She was ashamed of the excitement and yet she could do nothing to kill it. She tried to tell herself that it was because she enjoyed Abel's company, and because it made a welcome change from the dull weekly routine of seeing no one but Ma and the boys, unless one counted Mr Perreira and Mr Karyppi and Mr Sundarjee when she shopped for the two households.

Yes, she liked Abel, she assured herself firmly. How could one help but like him when he was so childlike in his eagerness to learn to read and write, when he accepted without self-pity and only an occasional flash of rage the fact that he had been cheated of his inheritance and could never hope to claim it? When he had made such a clumsy and endearing attempt to compensate Susarah for giving him lessons?

"I'd like to buy that old car of yours," he had told her weeks ago, and had started emptying his pockets of silver and coppers. "I have five pounds here; the sum your husband lent on it – "

"No, Abel," she had stopped him. "Put your money away."

He had stared at her, looking like a child denied a treat to which he had been looking forward. "Why not? *I* want it; *you* don't. The car legally belongs to you now, and there's nothing to stop you selling it to me."

"You don't fool me," Susarah had said softly. "I know perfectly well what you're up to, Abel."

He had actually blushed, that tall, rough-hewn young man, again as if he had been a child but this time looking like one who had been caught stealing jam. "What do you mean?"

Susarah had smiled at him. "You can't possibly want the car.

You're trying to help me by taking it off my hands. Thank you, Abel, but I'm not going to accept your generous, well-meant offer."

"There's nothing generous about it!" he'd protested. "If I could get it to work I'd be able to use it as a runabout . . ."

"At a speed of – what? Five miles an hour, I seem to remember Wessel estimating. You'd have all the children in the street keeping pace with you and jeering at you! I wasn't born yesterday, Abel! All you'd really do with it is have it carried away as scrap."

He had blushed again and left the matter there, but it was only one small incident that showed the kind of man he was and made her like him. There was also the way he never put on false airs and pretended to make a fuss of Corabella, but admitted frankly that he didn't understand babies and had never had anything to do with one.

Susarah saw his tall figure turn the corner and come striding towards the house, and her excitement mounted, her heart thumping in her chest. It was no use trying to fool herself. It was not just liking she felt; she was beginning to experience lustful thoughts about Abel Koen.

With Wessel, she had known from the start that lustful thoughts would be quite impossible. She'd known, vaguely, that they fitted in somewhere in the business of producing babies, and went with kissing on the mouth, and since children were all she could perceive that would make their marriage bearable she had decided to play her part in the mouth-kissing but to leave the lustful thoughts to him. The reality had come as a dreadful shock but obviously he'd had his share of lustful thoughts because she had become pregnant soon after their wedding.

And now she herself was beginning to think lustful thoughts about Abel Koen . . . No, not *beginning* to, she corrected herself. Since she was being honest she might as well admit that those thoughts about him had been stirring inside her almost from the moment she'd first met him, and the thoughts were becoming stronger all the time. And because of them she was very careful not to touch him in any way, other than shaking him by the hand when he took his leave.

Had she been younger and still ignorant, Susarah knew, she would have been fooled by her lustful thoughts and fallen into the trap they were trying to set for her. But she had been married, and she knew the end result of lustful thoughts – for women, at any rate – was the anti-climax of uncomfortable, often physically painful and always thoroughly distasteful 'loving'. In any case 'loving' went with marriage, which at least justified it, and it was only too patently obvious that marriage to her had never even crossed Abel's mind. When she came to think of it, if he in turn harboured lustful thoughts about her, he managed to hide them very well.

Another reason why Susarah was determined to keep Abel physically at arm's length was because it had already occurred to Ma that he might make a suitable second husband for her. It was humiliating and debasing, Susarah thought resentfully, that almost the only way for a respectable female to keep herself and those who depended upon her from starving, lay in marriage. It had been bad enough to be forced to marry Wessel, because Barend had been unable to find work and Cornelius was soon to turn sixteen and lose his allowance from the Phthisis Board and the younger boys were stealing food because they were hungry. But Ma's practical plotting and scheming to get Abel as a second husband for Susarah was even worse.

"Of course, he doesn't earn very much as a delivery-van driver for the Portuguese," Ma had mused, obviously following her own private train of thought. "But once he can read and write he might well find a better job, perhaps with the Municipality like Barend and Cornelius. In the meantime, he wouldn't have to worry about paying rent, and the vacant plot would provide an income if it were sold and the money invested – "

"Ma!" Susarah had burst out, flushing. "If you're talking about what I think you are, then stop!"

"It won't be long, Susarah, before your pension comes to an end and then you'll have no income at all! What harm would there be in making it clear to Abel that you own your house and the plot beside it? I'm sure he believes you're living in rented property – "

"You're not to tell him!" Susarah had interrupted fiercely. "Not one single hint, Ma! Do you think I want *any* man to marry me for the sake of a house and a piece of building land?"

"Susarah, listen to me – "

"No, Ma, I won't listen! Abel comes here to be given lessons by me, and that is all! He's not the kind of man who would marry someone because she owns a bit of property, and he might be illiterate but he's very shrewd and intelligent. If you drag into the conversation the fact that I own this house and the land next door, he would know what you're hinting at and he would go miles out of his way to avoid visiting us again! Worse, you'd have made a complete fool of me! Good lord, you might as well put a 'For Sale' notice around my neck."

"You're being very silly," Ma had muttered, but she hadn't pursued the subject since and she had promised not to let Abel know that Susarah possessed anything that could be termed a dowry.

Abel had reached the house by now and was climbing the steps to the stoep. He smiled at Susarah, and to her annoyance and discomfort she felt the blood rising to her cheeks. To divert attention from it she said briskly, "Hullo, Abel. I've borrowed my brother Piet's

Grade Two *Reader* for you to copy from, so don't let us waste any time."

Obediently, he sat down by the small table with which the stoep was furnished and she watched with a dismaying stab of tenderness the frowning concentration with which he copied out, laboriously, simple sentences from Piet's *English Reader.*

Since she and Abel had agreed that it was also necessary for him to learn English, it had seemed to make sense that he should kill two birds with one stone by learning to read and write in English.

"You've already taught yourself to read and to print a few simple words in Afrikaans," Susarah had said. "By teaching you to read and write in English, I could explain to you what the words mean, and later on we could concentrate on teaching you to translate sentences into Afrikaans."

Now, he looked up from the exercise book in which he had laboriously copied down a sentence from the *Reader*, and enunciated slowly, "THE CAT SAT ON THE MAT."

"That's very good!" Susarah applauded. "You're a fast learner, Abel!"

He grinned at her. "Cats on mats won't get me very far when it comes to trying for a better job. Stupid sentence, isn't it? Have you ever seen a cat sitting on a mat? He'd be more likely to sharpen his claws on one."

Susarah couldn't help laughing when she realised that he was serious. Unlike a child, for whom the *Reader* had been meant, he didn't treat the sentence with passive acceptance but questioned its logic.

"Perhaps," she suggested, "mats in England aren't made of coir, but are comfortable. Even when I was in Grade Two, I remember, the cat in the *English Reader* always sat on a mat."

"Cats in England must have it easy," Abel commented. "On Jakkalsdrif, the cat was too busy catching mice in the barn to sit anywhere." A note of suppressed rage and frustration had entered his voice as he spoke of Jakkalsdrif, and Susarah knew that he was thinking of the inheritance he would never be able to claim. She dared not touch him in a gesture of comfort, and so she stretched out a hand instead and turned the page of the *Reader.* The new one carried a picture of a boy in a silly shirt with a fancy square collar trimmed with braid and embellished with what looked like a length of knotted rope, and holding a piece of wood in his hand.

"This one reads 'TOM HAS A BAT'," Susarah said. "I never thought about it when I was a child, but simply copied down the words and learnt them. But the sentence is even more stupid than 'THE CAT SAT ON THE MAT'. Bat is the English word for *vlermuis*, so why doesn't the picture show one? And what does Tom want with a *vlermuis*, presumably hanging upside down from his bedroom ceiling during the day and flying about at night?"

"Perhaps he doesn't want it, and the piece of wood in his hand is for whacking it," Abel suggested, and they laughed together.

A glow spread through Susarah. There had not been much laughter in her life before, and the way Abel could make her laugh about silly things was one of the reasons why she loved him . . .

Confused and dismayed, she cut the thought off in her mind and turned away abruptly, moving towards the cradle and pretending to minister to Corabella, who was lying there perfectly contentedly and minding her own business. But by bending over the cradle she could perhaps hide from Abel the flush in her cheeks and the expression in her eyes that gave evidence of the fact that she had just admitted to herself that she loved him.

Abel was studying her from under his half-veiled lashes. He understood perfectly well the reason for the delicate colour that washed into her face whenever he looked at her and the softening of her eyes, because he had seen those same signs in other girls and it meant that they wanted to end up in bed with him. What he didn't understand at all was the inconsistency of Susarah, for unlike other girls she did not seek excuses to touch him, or pretend to brush against him in passing. This puzzled him, because it did not follow a pattern he recognised. She was not a Halleluiah-girl, and she had been married, so that she was not a confused innocent, ignorant of the meaning of her physical urges. She must surely be hungering to be kindled by now, so why did she do nothing at all to invite it?

Kindling was how Abel had decided to think of his sexual adventures. Although he used tricks copied from the Preacher, he did not want to associate himself with the man by using *his* word – pleasuring. Fucking was what Dirk had done with Nella Venter and what Abel himself had done with Tina, and the word did not describe, either, the technique of his own which Abel had perfected, a kind of earthy, thrusting virility that followed upon a preliminary and leisurely, erotically sensual arousal which left women lusting for more. The Portuguese men, when they talked together about the sexual act, used expressions like 'jig-a-jig' but this was always applied to their adventures outside marriage. Although they did not talk about their relationships with their wives, Abel had formed the impression that they regarded those as a duty they owed to their wives and especially to their Church, which seemed to demand a never-ending cycle of newborn babies, and duty had nothing at all to do with the pleasures of what the husbands called 'jig-a-jig'. *Kindling* seemed, to Abel, to sum up perfectly the slow setting on fire of the senses, rising to a crescendo of leaping, consuming tongues of flame – and afterwards settling down into pleasant, glowing embers which could be rekindled if the mood took him or else could be allowed to go out.

Even before they had experienced his style of kindling, girls invariably invited it, the way Juana Mendoza did so relentlessly and irritatingly. But not Susarah. And that was a pity, because if she had been susceptible to kindling he knew he would be able to get her to part with the Benz Voiturette. And they could so easily go to bed on Sunday mornings before her mother and brood of brothers returned from the Tabernacle.

Since first setting eyes on the Benz Voiturette, Abel had been asking questions about it of everyone in the motor trade with whom he came into contact. An older, honest mechanic with an interest in old vehicles had told him, "If you have an original model of a Benz Voiturette in good condition I'd say you're sitting on a small fortune. In 1897 a fellow called Hess imported the first car into Johannesburg. It was a Benz Voiturette, and he sold it to a coffee merchant who drummed up business by handing out tickets to his customers to come and view the new mechanical marvel. If your Benz Voiturette is not actually the first car ever to have arrived in Johannesburg, it would still have been among the first in the country and its value at auction could be as high as two or three hundred pounds, and it might even make four hundred."

Abel's mind had reeled at the thought of such a fortune. No wonder Dirk, the bastard, had wormed out of him the address of his lodgings and had taken to calling there on Saturday or Sunday afternoons, not actually lowering himself to come inside, of course, but sitting in his car outside the house and hooting his car-horn until someone summoned Abel. And then, pretending to have come to see Abel out of brotherly interest, he would steer the conversation around to the subject of the Benz Voiturette which he was hoping to buy for twenty-five miserable pounds, with a commission to Abel of two pounds bloody ten shillings! He'd see Dirk in hell before he let him get his hands on *his* Benz Voiturette . . .

Hiding his frustration, Abel turned the page of the *Reader* and copied down the fact that stupid Tom in England had a stupid bat. The Benz Voiturette wasn't *his*, as he had to keep reminding himself. He had been so certain that Susarah would sell it to him for the five pounds her husband had lent on it that her refusal had come as a stunning blow.

He'd had to leave the matter for the time being, because to have pressed her further would have aroused her suspicions. But it was an increasing agony, calling at the house each Sunday morning and passing the piece of wasteland beside it, seeing the shape of the Benz Voiturette underneath the tarpaulin next to that of the motorcycle combination.

An idea struck him, and he looked up from the page on which he had been copying the English sentences. "About that old motor car, Susarah – "

"Yes?"

"I almost forgot to tell you. I met someone during the week, a man whose hobby it is to collect old vehicles of all kinds. I told him about the Benz Voiturette, and he said he'd be willing to give ten pounds for it."

"Oh." She frowned thoughtfully, and glanced to where the vehicle stood shrouded in tarpaulin. Then she shook her head slowly. "If it's worth ten pounds to him, Abel, then to the car's original owner it must be well worth the five pounds which he borrowed against it."

Mentally, Abel cursed himself for a fool. It had been a gross tactical error to offer her twice the amount her husband had lent on the car. It wasn't even as if he possessed ten pounds; he'd have had to borrow it from Meneer Mendoza, so why had he been so damned stupid?

He tried to keep the frustration from his voice as he pointed out, "The man has defaulted on the loan and no longer has any right of ownership."

"I know. But it has just struck me that he might have been unable to repay the debt through no fault of his own. Wessel never told me his name, only that he was one of the Municipality drivers. For all I know, this man may have been doing everything he could think of to discover my address so that he could repay the loan and get back his car."

"It's much more likely," Abel said desperately, "that he's congratulating himself because he got rid of a piece of worthless junk for five pounds!"

"It can't be worthless junk," Susarah pointed out thoughtfully, "to people who collect old vehicles as a hobby."

"Ten pounds," Abel pointed out, almost through clenched teeth, "is a lot of money to let slip through your fingers."

"I know," she agreed, and seemed to realise that her attitude had offended him in some way, for she added in a conciliating voice, "No doubt the time will come when I'll have to sell the car if this man you've met still wants it. But in the meantime, while I'm still receiving a widow's pension, I'm not yet in desperate need of ten pounds, Abel, and the car is doing no harm, standing there on the vacant plot. I feel that Wessel would have wanted me to give its original owner every chance of reclaiming it, rather than make a quick profit by selling it."

Inwardly cursing Bible-punching Wessel *and* Susarah for appointing herself his conscience, Abel managed to make some remark that hid his rage and frustration, but after he had finished copying the sentences she had set as his lesson for the morning he pushed the exercise book towards her and stood up abruptly, saying, "I won't stay for lunch today if you don't mind, Susarah."

It was perfectly obvious from her expression that she did mind, quite desperately. Sell me the bloody car and I'll stay until kingdom come, he thought savagely. Outwardly calm, pleasant and smiling, he held out his hand and she took it in her small, work-hardened one. "Give my regards to your mother and brothers, and thank you for the lesson, Susarah."

"You *will* be coming back next Sunday?" she asked, unable to hide her anxiety and her bewilderment at this sudden change in what had become the established weekly routine.

Not unless you sell me the car! he wanted to shout. Instead, he said warmly, "Of course," and embroidered, "The reason why I have to leave early today is because I'm seeing a man who I've heard is looking for a motorcycle combination, and if I could sell that for you, at least it would be some kind of repayment for the lessons you've been giving me."

"I don't want repayment," she said softly. "But – thank you for being so thoughtful."

As he looked at her he thought again what a pity it was that she did not invite, by word or gesture or insinuation, even a touch of kindling – and it was not only because of the Benz Voiturette. She really was very pretty and sweet, and she also had a kind of strength which he had not come across in other girls before. She could not really care, personally, about that old car and ten pounds would obviously be extremely useful to her in her situation, but because she felt her late husband would have wanted it of her, she was refusing to part with it yet. She might flush and melt each time she saw Abel, and care very much that he should continue to call upon her, but she would not allow him to press her into doing what she didn't wish to do. He couldn't help admiring her for that.

But as he walked back to his lodgings his mind was preoccupied solely with the thought of that valuable car standing on a piece of wasteland, protected by nothing but a piece of tarpaulin. God, what he could do with the two or three hundred pounds it would fetch!

Ever since he'd been told the car's probable worth, he had been exploring the best way the money could be used to build himself a future. Listening to the Portuguese market-gardeners talking shop, he had been made aware of a gap in the local fruit-and-vegetable business. Sub-tropical fruit such as pawpaws, mangoes, avocado pears, lychees and pineapples expensively pre-cooled and then freighted by train to Johannesburg, where it was sold by market middle-men, had to be priced too highly in the suburban shops for a profit to be made. There had been one or two attempts to fill this gap in the market and it was not because people didn't want to buy exotic fruits that the Portuguese shop-owners had been left with it rotting on their hands; it was simply that their customers in Newlands couldn't afford the prices that had to be fixed if the vendors were to break even, never mind make a modest profit.

But if an enterprising, hard-working operator, Abel had thought to himself, with two large lorries and a hired driver to help him, were to make regular trips to the Natal coastal region, buy such fruit directly from the small growers at low prices and return to Newlands with full loads, a steady and expanding business could be built up. Abel had all the contacts he needed with the Portuguese retailers. He had the driving experience, the will and the guts to make such a business flourish. All he needed was the capital, and if he did not get his hands on that Benz Voiturette he would go on needing the capital until he was ready to drop through old age.

As he entered one end of the street in which the Mendozas lived, a flashily expensive car entered from the other end and drew up outside Abel's lodgings. He cursed under his breath. He was in no mood for Dirk today. Obviously, he had called again to try to prise out of Abel the name and address of the owner of the Benz Voiturette, because he was growing impatient with the lack of progress in buying it through Abel's agency. But if Dirk had called this early on a Sunday before, when Abel would normally still have been waiting with Susarah for her mother and brothers to return from the Tabernacle so that they could sit down to lunch, the Mendozas had neglected to mention the fact.

Dirk had begun to toot his horn imperiously by the time Abel sauntered up to the car. "What do you want?" he asked curtly.

Dirk answered the question with one of his own as he studied Abel in the only good clothes he possessed. "Where have you been?" he asked, and Abel could almost see him trying to make a connection between a Sunday morning social visit and the Benz Voiturette.

"To the Tabernacle, of course," Abel said sardonically, and repeated, "What do you want?"

Dirk leant across and opened the door on the passenger side of the car. "Get in," he invited. "I thought you would like a change from greasy Portuguese food, so I've come to pick you up and take you home to have lunch with us."

"Portuguese food isn't greasy," Abel returned, and remained on the pavement where he was. At the same time it struck him that Mevrou Mendoza had become so used to his taking Sunday lunch with anonymous friends that she would not have catered for him.

"Hester is roasting a leg of lamb," Dirk tempted him.

Abel thought of leg of lamb roasted with a hint of garlic and served with glazed sweet-potatoes, buttered cabbage and yellow rice and rich brown gravy. He couldn't remember when he had last eaten a meal like that. Susarah and her mother couldn't afford to buy leg of lamb, and Mevrou Mendoza seldom did a roast and never on a Sunday, when some kind of stew was usually left to simmer on the side of the range while the family were attending church.

"If you like," Abel accepted ungraciously, fully aware that the real reason for the invitation was the Benz Voiturette.

But as he drove through Newlands and then Sophiatown and other suburbs towards the city, Dirk confined his observations to Dirk-like bragging about how well he was doing with the business and how he was planning to buy a house in the stuck-up suburb of Auckland Park.

He was nosing the car into Market Street when he suddenly broke off and exclaimed, "Hell, I almost forgot to tell you the main reason why I wanted to see you! You're not going to believe this, but I had a telephone call from Simon last Sunday night, telling me that Ma has had a baby!"

Abel stared at him. "She's too old – "

"No, she's not. But because of her age she never had any of the usual symptoms, or if she did she ignored them, and she simply thought she was putting on weight. She was caught as much by surprise as everyone else. She had the child early on Saturday morning of last week, when only Mwende and Tina were on hand to help her. It's a boy, and Ma has called him Joshua."

"Good God!" Abel said, thinking that at the time he had been fooled by Tina and her mother into believing that Tina was pregnant, it was the Bitch who had been pregnant instead. Mwende had said the *dolosse* had predicted the birth of a baby, but Mwende had obviously misinterpreted that particular prediction.

"I know," Dirk agreed, misconstruing Abel's exclamation. "Disgusting, isn't it? You'd think, at their age, Ma and Pa would have finished with that sort of thing."

Not the Bitch, Abel thought, remembering as if it were yesterday how he had watched her and the Preacher through the window of the *pondok*. He didn't believe *she* would ever want to finish with that sort of thing. But he did not want to dwell upon the memory of the Bitch's sensuality, and so he said shortly, "It's their business what they do, and I don't know why you thought I'd be interested."

"Oh well," Dirk said huffily as he drew the car up outside the building that housed his flat. He turned to Abel. "Perhaps you'd be interested in something else Simon told me. It's beginning to look very much as if Pa has left Ma. In fact, Simon is certain of it."

Yes, that did interest Abel. It gave him a great deal of satisfaction, thinking of the Bitch sitting alone and abandoned at Jakkalsdrif. "What makes Simon so certain of it?" he asked.

"Pa has not set foot at home for more than six months, and even though Ma maintains he has been telephoning her regularly, Simon is sure she's lying. He doesn't believe Ma even knows where Pa is, because if she did she would obviously want to get in touch with him to tell him that he has a new son. But she refuses to 'distract him from his church work', as she puts it. And you know how she and Pa were forever quarrelling about God-knows-what."

Yes, Abel knew, and he also knew the cause of their quarrels. *My present to you, Bitch, for robbing me of Jakkalsdrif.*

"Simon," he heard Dirk go on, "argues, quite rightly, that Ma can't expect people to go on believing her lies now that there's a new baby who any husband would naturally want to hurry home to see. So, without telling Ma, he plans to put out a more believable story, if only to play for time. He'll tell people that Pa was suddenly summoned to America, to the headquarters of the Church of the Reformed Evangelists, and that he knows nothing about the new baby yet and can't be reached."

"Why are you telling me all this?" Abel asked indifferently.

"Well – I thought you would show a family interest." There was a sulky note in Dirk's voice now.

Abel laughed shortly and sourly. "Since when was I ever treated, or regarded, as part of the family?"

Dirk hesitated, and then clapped a hand on Abel's shoulder. "Of course you're part of the family!" he said with false warmth. "Why else would I want you to have Sunday lunch with us?"

So that you can try and get your hands on that Benz Voiturette, Abel thought, but he said nothing as he climbed out of the car and followed Dirk up the stairs to the flat.

If possible, Hester looked even more beaten, faded and lack-lustre than before. The baby was now toddling but he was still crying almost incessantly as he clung to her skirts, following her about while she worked to put the lunch on the table.

The meal came as a great disappointment to Abel. There was no hint of garlic in the roast lamb, and it was served with greyish boiled potatoes fraying at the edges and green beans which had been sliced lengthwise and simply boiled up soggily instead of being chopped and cooked with a little potato and onion and then mashed with butter and a sprinkling of nutmeg. The gravy was thin and khaki-coloured, and Abel had just poured some of it over his food, hardly believing that Hester could be such a terrible cook, when she passed him another sauce-boat holding a watery green liquid.

"What is this?" Abel asked, trying to sound politely interested instead of incredulous.

It was Dirk who answered – smugly, with his I-know-you're-quite-ignorant-of-such-sophisticated-refinements expression. "It's mint sauce. You're meant to pour some over the meat."

"*Mint!*" Abel echoed with disbelief. "You mean the stuff that cats chew when they want to make themselves vomit up balls of fur?"

"Trust you to be crude," Dirk said stiffly.

"Well, it is the same stuff, isn't it? The leaves people pour boiling water over to drink when they have indigestion." Abel studied the liquid, swirling it about in its container. "How can it be called sauce? It isn't a sauce. A sauce is something that's thick, and hot, and cooked. This is just – "

"It's chopped mint," Hester explained, "mixed with vinegar and a little sugar."

"Do you *like* it?" Abel demanded.

"No," she said honestly. "Dirk wanted it, and he told me how to make it."

In a furious voice, Dirk exclaimed, "It just shows what simple *japies* you both are! Mint sauce is always, by tradition, served with roast lamb in England."

"They must be bloody mad," Abel said, and thought with contempt, But not as mad as you, to want to ape them for the sake of it, and just because your fancy English girlfriend has told you about it. This whole meal has been cooked the English way, because you think it's smart.

"You don't have to try the mint sauce," Dirk said through clenched teeth.

"Don't worry, I won't," Abel assured him, and winked at Hester to show that he understood she was not a lousy cook by nature, but had been forced by Dirk to produce this unappetising spread. If the gesture comforted her she gave no sign of it but took her baby on her lap and began to feed him mashed-up potatoes mixed with the thin khaki gravy.

"If we could leave the subject of mint sauce," Dirk went on tersely, "I wanted to ask you about that old Benz Voiturette."

"Yes, I thought you did," Abel said serenely.

"If the owner won't come to a decision about selling it soon, I'm afraid I'll have to withdraw my offer."

"Just as well perhaps," Abel nodded. "The owner thinks it might be worth a bit more than twenty-five pounds, and is considering putting it up for auction."

He could tell what an unpleasant jolt *that* was to Dirk, who pretended to consider the matter before saying with would-be casualness, "An auction is always a gamble."

Abel said nothing, and after drumming his fingers on the table for a while Dirk spoke again, abruptly. "I'll tell you what, Abel. Help me to buy the car and I'll pay you twenty-five pounds."

"Twenty-five pounds," Abel echoed, pursing his lips. "That means you intend auctioning the car yourself, and the price you expect it to fetch is two hundred and fifty pounds."

Dirk decided not to deny it, but said, "Twenty-five pounds, cash in hand, is not to be sniffed at. I'm sure you could use such a sum."

"I'll see what I can arrange with the owner," Abel lied maliciously, and pushed aside his barely touched plate. "Now, if you'll excuse me, I think I'd better take a tram home – "

"No need to do that," Dirk interrupted. "Have some coffee, and I'll run you home afterwards. I have to go out in any case."

Apart from the coffee, and the home-made cake with which he satisfied his hunger, the afternoon had been a total waste of time as far as Abel was concerned. He tried to make conversation with Hester while Dirk changed his clothes before going out, but she was withdrawn, preoccupied with her own obvious unhappiness, and barely seemed to hear him. She spoke only once, and then it was to say unexpectedly, at a tangent, and with hopelessness in her voice, "He's going to spend the afternoon and evening with *her*, of course."

Abel could think of no response to make to that, and he felt relieved when Dirk finally emerged, dressed in a smart suit and smelling of expensive scented hair-oil, and they could leave the flat.

Once in the car, Abel burst out, "You really are a bastard, aren't you? I'd like to knock you out cold again, and only the fact that you're in control of the car is stopping me!"

"What are you talking about?" Dirk protested, giving him a sidelong look of fear. "What have I done?"

"You know damned well! *Mint sauce.* It's not enough for you to cheat on Hester, knowing that she knows about it, but you have to force her to cook meals according to the tastes of your fancy English whore. What do you do, Dirk? Get her to write out recipes and hand them to Hester?"

"Now look, man," Dirk spluttered, "it's not like that. When we've moved to the house in Auckland Park I'll have to invite business connections and their wives to dinner, and they'll expect something more than plain Boer food. With Maureen's help I'm trying to educate Hester."

"*Maureen!*" Abel echoed witheringly. "Why the hell don't you leave Hester in the flat and move into the house in Auckland Park with

Maureen, so that she can impress your 'connections' with her fancy, tasteless English cooking?"

"Are you crazy? If I did that Hester's father would push her into divorcing me, and I'd not only lose Marcus, but Hester and I were married in Community of Property!"

"What does that mean?"

"It means that everything I own belongs jointly to Hester, and if there was a divorce I'd have to split everything down the middle with her."

"I see," Abel nodded thoughtfully. "This Community of Property business – is that the way most people get married?"

"Yes, because if they don't it means they have to hire a lawyer to draw up an Antenuptial Contract and that's expensive." He added with feeling, "But not half as expensive as when you want to get out of a Community of Property marriage!"

"And does it also mean," Abel probed, "that because you're married in Community of Property you are entitled to half of everything *Hester* owns?"

Dirk gave a bitter laugh. "She doesn't own a thing! Her father has a small-holding near Kliptown where he keeps chickens and goats. I met her after she'd come to work in a clothes shop in Johannesburg because there wasn't enough money at home to support her as well as her younger brothers and sisters." Dirk cursed softly. "If I hadn't been lonely in Johannesburg and gone to the nearest Tabernacle one Sunday I'd never have met her . . . But she was pretty then, and she looked smart and modern, and I was a young fool who got her pregnant."

Abel said nothing. *Community of Property*, he was thinking triumphantly. If he married Susarah, he would automatically be entitled to half the value of the Benz Voiturette. But he wouldn't have to settle for half, because there was no need for her ever to know the true value of the old car. And there'd be no nonsense about holding on to it in case the original owner decided he wanted it back. Once they were married she would accept Abel taking over her affairs. She was a strange girl; strong and stubborn to the point of immovability when she felt a principle was at stake, but prepared to defer to her husband and carry out his wishes, even after he had died . . .

The thought brought him up short. Susarah would marry him, that unerring instinct of his told him. But she would not be prepared to marry him until after her late husband Wessel had been accorded the full year of mourning demanded by convention. Not because she truly did still mourn him, but because she loved and respected her mother and she knew her mother would be deeply hurt if she flouted convention and shocked people by walking up the Tabernacle's aisle so soon after Wessel's death. And it would *have* to be the Tabernacle's aisle, Abel thought bitterly. Tant' Jakoba would make sure of that.

It would mean a delay of more than four months before they could be married, and a further delay before he could sell the Benz Voiturette, because he could hardly be brazen enough to marry Susarah one day and sell the car the next. Six months, say, before he would be able to sell it, and during that time, who knew what might happen to it? Its original owner could turn up to reclaim it; children could wander off the street and wreck it or someone else might discover its worth and steal it. Abel knew he could not face the tension and uncertainty of such a long wait, not when so much was at stake. What was ultimately at stake was Jakkalsdrif, because since he could not claim what was rightfully his he would have to buy it from Dirk. But he could never even start out on that road without the Benz Voiturette.

Dirk's voice interrupted Abel's thoughts. "I won't be home next weekend, by the way; I'm planning a little jaunt with Maureen to Kruger's Waterfall, but officially I'll be away on business. Try to get a definite decision about the car during the next fortnight."

Abel shrugged non-committally, and asked, "Is there a way of getting married quickly and without too many people knowing about it?"

Dirk gave him a curious look. "You're very interested in marriage, suddenly! Do you have plans in that direction?"

"Don't be ridiculous! This friend of mine – the one who owns the Benz Voiturette," Abel embroidered, "wants to marry a girl whose parents don't approve of him. That's why he needs to raise as much money as he can."

"He could get married in the Magistrate's Court, by Special Licence," Dirk said.

Obviously thinking it might help him to get hold of the Benz Voiturette, Dirk went on to describe what would be involved but Abel was telling himself despairingly, I'd never manage to get Susarah to agree to such a furtive hole-in-the-corner affair. She'd want her mother to be present, as well as her whole damned brood of brothers, and I can't see her swallowing any story I might dream up. She would think it all sordid, and quite unnecessary when we could get married openly in five months' time.

After Dirk had dropped him outside his lodgings, Abel walked the streets for a while, thinking. At last, as the sun was nudging the horizon, he decided to go to see Susarah. Marrying her in four or five months' time and selling the Benz Voiturette six months from now would be better than saying goodbye to it altogether, so he might as well get his proposal out of the way and then just sweat it out and hope nothing happened to remove the car totally from his reach in the meantime. If something did happen, he would have to find some excuse not to marry Susarah after all.

As he had hoped, she was alone at her house, having just put her baby to bed. Her first surprise at seeing him had given way to the familiar, delicate blush.

He decided not to waste time on conventional pleasantries. "I've called to ask you to marry me, Susarah. Will you?"

"Oh . . ." She looked totally stunned, and groped for the door-jamb by which to steady herself.

He took her by the arm and led her inside the house, forcing her gently on to the settee in the parlour and sitting down beside her. He took possession of her hand, and continued, "I tried to ask you this morning, but my nerve failed me. That's why I left so suddenly. Please say you'll marry me, Susarah."

She blinked, and he noticed the shine of tears on her lashes. "You – you would be taking on another man's baby – "

"I know."

"Oh Abel – " She stopped, her lips trembling, and he knew she could not go on.

He leant towards her and kissed her mouth. Her lips were soft and yielding against his – but only for an instant, and then she put up invisible barriers to ward off further intimacies. She whispered, "Thank you, Abel. I – accept," and he knew then the barriers were there out of respect still for Wessel, because she went on, "I couldn't marry you until I'm out of mourning for my late husband."

"I know. I've accepted that."

"You see, Ma – " She hesitated, twisting her dead husband's wedding ring around on her finger. "Ma thought the world of Wessel, and in a sense he almost courted me through her. She took his death far harder than I did, and she would be dreadfully hurt if I didn't show proper public respect for his memory."

Abel stared at her. "You sound as if you didn't particularly want to marry him."

"I didn't," she admitted readily. "It was necessary, because Ma could no longer manage with a houseful of orphans growing up and unable to find work and – well, Wessel was very kind and generous, and one of the first things he did after we got married was to use his influence with the Municipality and find jobs for Barend and Cornelius."

Abel thought, cynically, that Wessel could presumably have used his influence before the wedding to find work for Susarah's brothers, but he decided not to voice the comment. Instead, he said carefully, "From the one conversation I had with Wessel over the telephone, he sounded – rather serious and religious . . . and you're no Halleluiah-girl. But I imagined you'd been married for such a short while that the excitement had never had time to wear off."

Susarah smiled wryly. "There never *was* any excitement."

"But surely there must have been excitement in the wedding day itself, the ceremony in the Tabernacle, knowing everyone was admiring the way you looked – ?"

"*Admiring* me?" She shuddered. "Wessel had saved his late mother's wedding gown – he had a habit of saving almost everything – and it was a perfectly hideous garment. Even though Ma remodelled it for me it still looked more like a shroud than a bridal gown. As if it wasn't bad enough that I looked such a fright I had to walk to the Tabernacle because we couldn't afford to hire a car, with my brothers following me, and people came out on to their stoeps to grin at the sight. The boys hated it and wanted to dart down side streets because they said they couldn't see why they should be made to look fools. I had to threaten them into following me slowly and making it look as if we had chosen to walk to the Tabernacle."

"Where was your mother?" Abel asked.

"She'd made an excuse to follow us later on." Bitterness entered Susarah's voice. "What she was really doing was emptying my box of face powder into the privy. The only thing I'd had to cheer myself up with was the face powder I'd secretly bought, but during the wedding ceremony Wessel took his handkerchief out of his pocket and wiped it from my face. It's one of the Reformed Evangelists' sins, of course, to cover one's God-given skin with powder or potions."

Abel squeezed her hand. He felt unexpectedly moved by the bleak account of her wedding day, but far more than that, he was filled with a growing excitement. "So you've no great sentimental yearning to get married in the Tabernacle for the second time," he said.

"No." She gave him a puzzled look. "But we'll have to. Ma would be terribly shocked and upset if we didn't."

"I know," he acknowledged. "Tell me more about your first wedding." He added, as if jokingly, "So that I won't make things as awful for you as they were before."

"Oh, you couldn't possibly!" She checked herself guiltily. "I'm being horribly disloyal to Wessel's memory. It wasn't his fault that we couldn't afford to hire a car – "

"*I* couldn't afford to hire a car either, but now that I know you had to walk to your wedding before, I'd certainly make sure of getting the use of one somehow. What else went wrong, Susarah?"

"It wasn't so much a question of things going wrong. It was just – for instance, after the ceremony there was the matter of my flowers." Susarah's voice took on a note of remembered bleakness. "Wessel had given me a pound to buy food for the meal which Ma was arranging to celebrate the wedding, and he told me I might buy myself some flowers. But when Mr Perreira heard I was getting married he insisted on making me a present of a beautiful bouquet of flowers grown in his family's market gardens, and I used the money I'd saved to buy the face powder. After I learnt that Ma had thrown *that* into the privy, I thought: Well, I still have my flowers. I'd planned to arrange them in jam jars and put them all over the house to cheer myself up."

"Go on," Abel urged, wondering if she was aware of how much she was revealing by talking about needing to be cheered up on her wedding day.

"First, Wessel lectured me about the flowers. He said they must have cost a great deal of money and that it showed I had an extravagant nature. Of course, I couldn't tell him that the flowers had been a present from Mr Perreira, because if I had I would have been obliged to confess that I'd bought face powder with the money instead, and I knew both Ma and Wessel would have considered that to be stealing. Then Wessel said that since I'd squandered the money anyway the flowers could be used as a mark of remembrance and respect."

Abel watched her wide grey eyes darken with a fierce resentment and smarting injury which the months between had obviously not diminished. "In the newspapers they write about the bride and bridegroom 'going away' after the wedding. I've never been able to make out where they go, but I'd bet no other bride ever 'went away' as I did on my wedding day! Wessel made me catch a tram with him to Brixton Cemetery and he forced me to put my flowers – *my* lovely flowers which I'd so much wanted to keep – on the graves of *his* parents." She was silent for a moment, and then she gave him an unsteady smile. "I expect you think it stupid of me to have minded so much about the flowers."

"No, I understand exactly how you must have felt." Abel stood up and pulled her to her feet, embracing her – but once again she would only allow herself a small measure of response before she became stiff and unyielding in his arms.

He was not discouraged. He lifted a hand and cupped it about her chin. "I promise you, Susarah," he said softly, "that you'll have a second wedding day whose memory you'll be able to treasure for the rest of your life."

He now knew exactly what to do to seduce her into marrying him quickly so that he could get his hands on that Benz Voiturette.

The only trouble was that he would need money to make his plans work.

31

The following Saturday Abel finished his delivery round as early as he could, and handed the keys of the van to his boss before he hurried to his lodgings where he washed and changed into his good flannels and dark blazer. Then he went to catch a tram to the city.

He thrust his way through the crowds in Market Street, towards Dirk's flat. Its door was opened to him by Hester, as he had known it would be, and the inevitably wailing toddler was clinging to her skirt.

"I've called to see Dirk," Abel lied.

"He isn't home – "

"Oh hell!" Abel exclaimed. "I needed to speak to him urgently."

She picked up the toddler and straddled him across one hip, wiping the hair out of her eyes with her free hand in a weary, depressed gesture. "I'm sorry you've come all this way for nothing, Abel."

"May I come inside for a moment?" he asked, knitting his brow as if in troubled thought.

She moved aside so that he could enter, and he followed her into the kitchen, where she had been washing clothes in a zinc hip-bath placed on the table. "I'll carry on with this if you don't mind," she told him, rubbing a pair of baby rompers against a wash-board. "Dirk will be away all weekend, on business." Her mouth twisted wretchedly. "No, what point is there in lying to you? You know as well as I do that it isn't *business* that's taken Dirk away for the weekend."

Impulsively, Abel asked, "Why the devil do you stand for it, Hester?"

"What else could I do?" she returned wearily.

"You could stop working yourself into the ground to suit Dirk's convenience, and go home to your parents," he suggested.

She gave him a ghost of a smile. "You wouldn't say that if you knew my parents or what home is like."

"Dirk is a bastard," Abel said with heat, and wanted to shake Hester when she protested, "It isn't his fault entirely. If I didn't feel so tired all the time and I made more effort, I'd be the kind of wife he wants, and then – "

Abel cut her short, deciding to come to the point of his visit. "Do you remember last Sunday, Hester, when Dirk and I were talking about an old car he wants to buy, a Benz Voiturette?"

She looked up, frowning. "I wasn't paying too much attention, but I do remember you mentioning a foreign-sounding car."

He had gambled on the fact that she hadn't been paying too much attention. "You'll also remember," he urged, "that we talked about the possibility that the car might be auctioned, and that Dirk was anxious to prevent that happening?"

"Yes, I think I do remember that," Hester nodded.

Abel affected an anxious frown. "Dirk couldn't have chosen a worse weekend to go away. The thing is, Hester, the friend of mine who owns the car Dirk is so eager to buy has decided to put it up for auction after all, and has already had it taken away by a firm of auctioneers. They wouldn't commit themselves as to its possible value, but you'll remember Dirk saying that it would fetch perhaps two hundred and fifty pounds at auction?"

"Not really. As I told you, I wasn't paying much attention."

"Well, although the auctioneers wouldn't name the price they expected the car to fetch, they've knocked on the head any hope Dirk had of getting it for a few pounds."

Hester shrugged helplessly. "I'm sorry, but I don't really understand Dirk's business affairs."

"The thing is, Hester, that my friend desperately needs money *now*, today. And auctioning takes time. We're not talking here about an ordinary second-hand car but of something rich people collect as a hobby, and an auctioneer would want as many interested people as possible, from all over the country, to know about the sale before fixing the date of the auction."

Hester gave him a perplexed, worried look as she straightened up from her washing. "There's nothing I could do about whatever it is, Abel. If Dirk had been here – "

"I know. I'm telling you the position so that you can tell him when he comes home. My friend was talking about going to a money-lender this morning, but it suddenly struck me that if *Dirk* were to lend him money instead he could use it as a means of getting the car he wants."

"In what way?" Hester's tone made it clear that she was trying hard to understand the situation.

"It's like this," Abel explained. "A money-lender would demand a high rate of interest, as I pointed out to my friend. I asked him to wait until I had spoken to my brother about a possible loan. You see, Hester, if Dirk had been here he would have agreed to lend my friend the money at a low rate of interest but for a fixed period of, say, three weeks. If the money wasn't repaid in time – and I can't imagine my friend being in a position to repay it by then – Dirk could have threatened court action, and my friend would have had no option but to withdraw the car from auction and sell it to Dirk for the rock-bottom price of a hundred pounds."

Abel stood up and paced the floor. "Dirk is really going to kick himself when he hears how he has missed out on buying the car for a fraction of its real worth. He's going to be angry enough to catch snakes when he learns of this opportunity which wasn't grabbed when it came up."

Hester locked her water-wrinkled hands together and nodded. Now she did understand what was involved and she was looking as if she knew Dirk would blame *her* for causing him to miss this opportunity. "Dirk keeps money in the flat," she said, "but I'm not supposed to touch it, and I wouldn't like to take the responsibility – "

"I wouldn't want you to take the responsibility," Abel assured her. "What really makes me want to spit teeth is this: Last Sunday Dirk wanted to give me twenty-five pounds to help him get that car, and I refused. My friend urgently needs thirty pounds, and if only I'd taken the money when Dirk offered it to me, *I* could have made up the extra five pounds myself, and stopped my friend from going to money-lenders – "

"That's right!" Hester remembered, as he had been gambling she would. "Dirk *did* offer you twenty-five pounds! I distinctly heard him doing so!" Her brow cleared and she looked as close to being happy as Abel supposed she was capable of these days. "I'll give you the twenty-five pounds Dirk offered you."

"Well, I don't know . . . He might be angry with you for touching his money."

"He'd be far angrier with me for *not* giving you the money in the circumstances!" She wiped her wet hands on her apron, and added with a sigh, "In any case, he usually finds some reason for being angry with me, so it won't really matter either way, and he might even feel grateful to me when he finally gets the car he wants so much."

Abel followed her, impeded by the baby who had increased the volume of his wails and was determined to reach and hang on to his mother's skirt, and they entered the room in which Dirk kept the small suitcase stacked to the brim with banknotes. Before Hester could remove it from the cupboard the telephone rang and Abel stiffened as she moved to answer it. If the caller was Dirk, Hester would naturally want Abel to speak to him and Dirk would not swallow for a moment the story he had told Hester. For one thing, Dirk knew that Abel was fully aware he had been planning to spend this weekend away from home. Abel was still trying to decide how to brazen things out if it was Dirk on the other end of the telephone line when he heard Hester say, "Oh, hullo Simon. I'm afraid Dirk is away for the weekend, on business." She looked at Abel, and mouthed, "Do you want to talk to him?"

Abel shook his head vehemently, and waited while she made monosyllabic responses to whatever Simon was telling her. It seemed to Abel, who still had a great many things to do this afternoon, that Hester was kept listening to Simon forever. But at last she returned the telephone to its hook, and began to search in a drawer for the key to the cupboard where the money was kept.

"Simon says," she remarked, "that your mother and the new baby are doing very well."

Abel did not have the slightest interest in the Bitch's welfare or in that of her new brat, but he experienced a spasm of almost physical pain in his sudden longing for Jakkalsdrif, *his* Jakkalsdrif. "I suppose the farm is going to rack and ruin," he said.

"It sounds like it," Hester agreed. "Simon mentioned that he won't be able to hold services in Doornboomstad until your mother has left her bed again, because one of your servants has died suddenly and Simon has to help with the farm work as well as attending to the post office and the shop."

"One of the servants died?" Abel echoed sharply, for they merited his concern whereas the Bitch and Simon did not. "Who? Not Koos, surely – ?"

"No, someone called Tina. Simon said she'd been ill with a fever for a few days before she died."

Abel stared at Hester in disbelief and shock. Poor Tina, his playmate and his first lover; his only source of comfort anywhere on Jakkalsdrif. He found it almost impossible to accept that she was dead.

"You're sure Simon didn't say it was *Mwende* who'd died?"

"No, it was definitely Tina." Hester looked at him curiously.

"She was so young," Abel muttered inadequately.

Hester brought out the suitcase stuffed with banknotes, and he was forced to focus his attention on the matter in hand. What a greedy bastard Dirk was, he thought with contempt. All that money hidden away and added to from time to time, not to mention what he kept in the bank, and still he tried to buy a valuable Benz Voiturette for a miserable twenty-five pounds. If ever anyone deserved to be cheated, it was Dirk.

But when Hester had counted out the banknotes and Abel held them in his hands they ceased to be the miserable, petty sum they were when measured against Dirk's wealth. To Abel, they were a fortune, more money than he had ever had in his possession before at one time, and as much as he could earn in three months. As he pocketed the notes Abel thought, *The first instalment of what you owe me for Jakkalsdrif, Dirk.*

He said goodbye to Hester and hurried from the flat. Dirk would realise immediately that he had been cheated out of the twenty-five pounds, but there wouldn't be a thing he would be able to do about it. He could not use physical force to make Abel hand the money back because Dirk was afraid of him and knew himself to be no match for Abel. And there was nothing he could do legally either, because Abel had not demanded or even asked for the money; Hester had insisted on giving it to him. Dirk had only his own greed to blame.

After leaving the flat, Abel had several other matters to attend to, and intermittent thoughts of poor Tina preoccupied him as he did so. He wished his last words to her hadn't been a threat. Such an unnecessary threat, too, since her supposed pregnancy had been nothing of the sort. He sighed, and pushed her to the back of his mind.

The next part of his plan proved unexpectedly difficult and nerve-racking. As Abel walked up to, hesitated before and then passed the frivolously be-tasselled awning above the entrance to the smart hotel, he wondered what the devil it was that was stopping him from entering it. He had had no qualms when he'd entered it before, and then he had been dressed in khaki shirt and twill trousers, and he'd had no business to go inside at all. Today, however, wearing his best clothes and with a legitimate reason for entering, he walked past the doorway two or three times before he finally plucked up the courage to go inside.

The carpet was as deep and soft as he remembered it, the armchairs as richly upholstered, the crystal chandeliers as impressive. But there were fewer people about than on the previous occasion and several of them were standing close to the highly polished counter behind which a young man in a smart suit and with delicate good looks was lounging, watching Abel with raised eyebrows and the kind of expression that said, Ah, *he* looks as if he might be good for a bit of fun and a few cheap laughs for the benefit of the bystanders.

Abel had not noticed the young man behind the counter the last time he had entered the hotel, and he had been counting on there being a young woman he could approach, who would respond to him so that he would be able to speak to her in Afrikaans with total self-confidence.

But if he went up to that young man instead, Abel had a feeling that it would end with him hauling the cocky little bastard over the counter and punching him in his pretty face.

He would, Abel decided, wait until the nancy-boy behind the counter no longer had an audience to play to, and he went to sit down in one of the armchairs. It seemed to wrap itself around him in soft, luxurious comfort. He didn't know what the hotel people called the place in which he was sitting but he thought of it as a grand kind of parlour, through the doorway of which he could watch the desk. There were several other people about, sitting together with drinks on tables in front of them, and engrossed in conversation.

" . . . drink, sir?" he heard a male voice enquire, and realised that the question had been addressed to him by a man who looked to be only a few years older than he was, and wearing a stiffly starched white shirt with a black bow-tie and black trousers and jacket.

Oh Christ, Abel thought, one obviously can't sit here without ordering a drink. What's the name of that wine the Mendozas are always drinking? Even if I could remember I wouldn't be able to pronounce it because it's something foreign. What other kind of drink is there?

"A – a cocktail," he managed at last, remembering how Dirk had once offered him one, but without having the slightest idea of what it was.

He heard the waiter rattle off a string of English words, and even though Abel could not understand them he realised that he was being asked to make a choice from several different kinds of cocktails. In desperation, he pointed to a greenish-coloured liquid in a glass which a woman in the corner was just raising to her lips.

"Listen, man," the elegant waiter suddenly said in Afrikaans, "why don't you go into the bar next door and buy yourself a beer? You don't really want to drink coloured piss at fancy prices, do you?"

Abel grinned at him in relief. "No. I don't want to spend money on a drink at all. I just wanted to sit here – "

The waiter winked at him. "Hoping to pick up a woman? I warn you, they're all high-class whores who prowl these expensive hotels and they'll rob you naked. Better try one of the commercial hotels if you're feeling lonely and far from the farm."

There was something about this waiter that robbed his words of any offence. Abel toyed with the thought of telling him that he had already had one of the high-class whores, and far from her robbing him naked he'd had her for nothing. But on reflection he decided it would be wiser to keep quiet about it, so he merely began, "It's a while since I left the farm."

"What happened? The farm got worked out, and your old man kicked you out to go and make your own living in the city?"

"No. I left the farm to try and find proof that it legally belongs to me. I'm the eldest son, but I was registered as having been born a year later than my younger brother, and so I was cheated out of my inheritance – "

The waiter's eyes had narrowed in an appreciative grin. "Man, it's a damned good story you've got there! But you need to milk it of more drama; make it tear at the heart – "

"Are you calling me a liar?" Abel growled, half-rising from his chair.

"Steady," the waiter advised, unperturbed. "Remember, *I'm* in a position to turf *you* out. If you want to rest your legs you're supposed to go and sit on a public bench, not park your arse in the lounge of an expensive hotel without so much as buying a drink." His manner changed as another, older waiter passed by with a silver tray laden with glasses and gave him a meaningful look, and when he addressed Abel again it was to say something in English, accompanied by a secret, conspiratorial wink. He moved away, towards another group of chairs to take orders from the people sitting there, who seemed to be looking pointedly at him as if they had been trying to catch his attention for some time.

Abel glanced at the desk, but there were still several people standing close to it. He thought of trying one of the other Johannesburg hotels but decided he would probably encounter similar problems there. Besides, the Afrikaans-speaking waiter's wink had said he would come back to resume their conversation, and when he did Abel would ask his advice.

When the waiter returned with his silver tray laden with glasses it bore not only the orders of the group of people nearby, but a fancy-looking drink which he placed on the table beside Abel's chair.

"A White Lady," the waiter said. "Remember the name, next time you want to order a cocktail."

"I told you, I didn't – "

"Don't throw a fit, man. I put it on the bill of that lot over there." He gestured with his head towards the group he had just served.

Abel was torn between amusement and wariness. "What a *skelme bliksem* you are! What if they check their bill?"

"They won't. They're out to impress one another, and the men will be fighting for the privilege of paying the bill, and won't want to lose face by querying it. You get to know about people in this game. My name is Manie Marais, by the way. What's yours?"

"Abel Koen. What part of the world are you from, Manie?"

"Oh, from here and there," was the vague reply. "Let's talk about you. You're a well-set-up young buck, and likely to appeal to women. Is that your game? Are you hoping to catch the eye of some rich, lonely old boiler? I could give you some tips there, but not speaking English might be a disadvantage. Still, some things need no language, do they? *Is* that your game?"

Abel had taken a gulp of his drink and it had spread a warm, happy glow through him. "You might know about people," he told Manie with a grin, "but you wouldn't even be able to guess my game. You could help me, though. I want to know the kind of prices these people charge, but that toffed-up nancy behind the desk looks as if he'd like nothing better than to get a laugh out of someone who can't speak English, and if he did I'd punch that pretty dimple right out of his chin."

"Hmm . . . So you want to know about our prices, even though you can't afford to order a drink in the lounge. There's plenty of cheaper places you could use for whatever it is you have in mind."

"I know that. But I need a special place for a special girl."

Manie smiled broadly. "I think I understand." He took a pencil and notepad from his pocket and wrote down a list of figures.

Abel studied the list in dismay. "As much as that . . ."

Manie glanced about him, and dropped his voice. "If some of my mates and I are on duty, it could be arranged for the cost to be – er – spread around, so that you needn't put your hand too deep in your pocket. When would you be wanting the bedroom?"

"Next Saturday night."

"Saturday night," Manie echoed thoughtfully, but before he could go on a man across the room clicked his fingers at him and he moved away with a muttered curse. He disappeared from view after he had taken the man's order.

When he returned, there was another White Lady on his tray for Abel. "This one is on some drunk in the cocktail bar."

Abel stared at him with suspicion. "What are you up to? You don't know me, so what are you hoping to get out of it all?"

"One never can tell, mate," Manie answered enigmatically, and then some sixth sense seemed to alert him to the fact that his services were required elsewhere, and he excused himself and hurried away.

When he returned a minute or two later, Abel tried to take up the conversation where they had left off but his tongue had acquired a strange perversity and refused to form the sentences his brain was dictating. "Hell, man," he heard Manie say, "you're supposed to sip the stuff, not gulp it down like water! I'd better get you out of here. Stand up, and I'll pretend to show you the gentlemen's lavatory and take you to my room."

"Don't want to," Abel managed to mutter.

"Come now," he heard Manie say briskly. "It's a lousy bloody job, but I don't want to lose it – *yet*. And I would if you made a nuisance of yourself, and it came out that I've been supplying you with drink at other customers' expense."

An innate sense of justice forced Abel to concede that he had a case, and obediently he rose and allowed Manie to steer him around the chairs with a "This way, sir," and a "Mind the ruck in the carpet, sir," the sense and purpose of which he understood, even though the words were beyond his grasp.

After climbing a short flight of shabbily carpeted back stairs Manie showed him into a small, dark room and said, "I'm off duty in half an hour. Make yourself comfortable and we'll talk later."

Abel sat down on the edge of the lumpy bed and debated fuzzily with himself whether or not he ought to try to leave the hotel by the rear exit. His mind was clear enough for him to acknowledge that he was not sure he could trust Manie Marais. The man was dishonest and he'd made no bones about the fact. A laugh escaped Abel as he remembered how he had cheated Dirk of twenty-five pounds, and how he intended cheating Susarah of a good deal more than that. Who was he to condemn Manie for dishonesty? Besides, the man was easily the most interesting acquaintance he had yet made in Johannesburg.

Abel's mind was almost completely clear by the time Manie returned to the room, and now his tongue only stumbled over the occasional word. "Why should you want to go out of your way to help me?" he demanded.

"Because you're a real bloke, not out to impress like most of the types I have to put up with." Manie considered him, his head on one side. "And then – like yourself I'm from the farm – except that I ran away from it when I was thirteen." He grinned. "I wish *I'd* thought up the bit about having been cheated of my inheritance – "

"It's true," Abel said, but without heat or rancour this time. "I don't give a damn whether you believe it or not. But since you've said I'm not out to impress, I don't see why you should imagine I invented it."

"Oh, there's a difference between bullshitting and living by your wits. If you're planning to live by your wits, the story of a stolen inheritance is a dream."

Abel studied him with interest. Manie Marais had probably spent a good many years living by his wits. "What made you run away from the farm?" Abel asked.

"Silly little things, like wanting to eat," Manie replied lightly.

"How did you come to be a waiter in a grand, expensive hotel like this?"

"By a long road, mate, by a long road. But I've just about had enough of it all – the finger-clicking, the 'Hey you!', the false, polite face behind which I have to hide all the time . . . But never mind about me. Tell me about that special girl you mentioned, and why you want to spend money on her."

Abel began to explain, and Manie made several constructive suggestions and pointed out obstacles which had never even occurred to

Abel, promising to take care of them himself. Abel started to thank him, and stopped abruptly.

"What is *your* game? What are *you* hoping to get out of all this?" he demanded.

"I don't know yet." Manie's voice was thoughtful. "But I'll get *something* out of it, sooner or later. I feel it in my bones."

The strange thing was that Abel, too, could suddenly feel it – the conviction that Fate had flung himself and Manie together for a purpose, and that their future paths were intertwined.

He held out his hand, and they shook on a wordless bargain between them.

32

Susarah sat on the tram next to Abel, her hand firmly clasped in his. He had taken Saturday morning off especially to introduce her to his brother's wife Hester, and Ma had said that of course Susarah must go and help the poor young woman prepare her anniversary dinner because after all they would soon be related, and Susarah ought to feel flattered that she had been appealed to for help.

Susarah was not at all sure that she had cause to feel flattered. From what Abel had told her of his brother Dirk, he was a swaggering braggart who thought himself better than others and it was difficult to imagine that he hadn't married a girl who was very like himself. The fact that Dirk's wife was useless at cooking supported the mental picture Susarah had of her. No, it was much more likely that Hester had said to Dirk, "We'll have to invite Abel, so why don't we also invite that little widow he's going to marry and make use of her? From what he has told us she's used to hard work, and she could cook and clean up afterwards and with luck people will think she's hired help."

Susarah glanced at the carpet-bag at her feet which held her overnight things and her overall. She was already wearing her only good dress of black art silk, and that would have to do for the dinner party tonight. She was not looking forward to the weekend at all, and she couldn't really understand why Abel had accepted the invitation for both of them, considering the way he felt about his brother Dirk. But perhaps blood was thicker than water after all, and each was the only family the other had in Johannesburg.

He turned his head to look at her at that moment, and joy and excitement gripped her heart. This was the first time they had been alone together since he'd asked her to marry him, because her two youngest brothers, Stoffel and Willem, had had violent stomach upsets last Sunday, due to something unknown and probably illicit they had eaten, and Susarah had been far too busy ministering to them in between preparing the lunch to spend time with Abel, so he had sat alone on the stoep, copying out sentences from Piet's *English Reader*. Unfortunately there had been no chance for Abel to tell her about the invitation to Dirk's anniversary dinner until after Ma had returned from the Tabernacle with the other boys, or Susarah would have told him about her reservations.

His greenish-grey eyes were studying her intently, and the pressure of his hand on hers increased. "Susarah – "

"Yes, Abel?"

He hesitated. "I lied to you and to Tant' Jakoba."

"Oh? About what?"

"About Hester needing you to help her with preparing tonight's dinner."

She stared at him in bewilderment. "But why?"

"Well – this is difficult." He turned her hand palm upwards in his and traced a line along it with a finger of his other hand. "Why do you suppose Dirk invited us to his anniversary dinner?"

"Why – because you're his brother, of course, and he knows you and I are planning to marry – "

"No. I've told you what Dirk is like. There's nothing he enjoys more than to make people compare the two of us. You know what I mean." Abel affected a bragging voice. " 'Look at me; see how successful I am, how clever, how rich, how well dressed. And look at poor stupid Abel, who drives a delivery-van around Newlands and can't even read or write.' That sort of thing. Only this time he wanted to score a few extra points. He knows, because of the letters your mother and mine have written to one another, that your late husband was just as strict a follower of the Reformed Evangelists as Tant' Jakoba. *I* know that you're not a Halleluiah-girl, Susarah, but you look like one, and Dirk knows that you can't look anything else. You were invited to tonight's dinner, along with me, so that Dirk's manner could say to people, 'Look at the girl poor stupid bloody Abel is going to marry, about twenty years behind the times, and look how smart and modern *my* wife is.' "

"Oh!" Susarah gasped in a strangled, furious voice. "Since you knew all this, why didn't you turn down the invitation? Why – ?"

"Because I wouldn't give him that satisfaction," Abel interrupted. "If I had, he'd simply have told people it was because you don't know how to behave in company. And also because I wanted to turn the tables on him." Susarah felt her hand enclosed in both of his, and tried to free herself but his grasp became tighter. "You're far, far prettier than Hester could ever be, Susarah! *I* don't mind the way you dress, or wear your hair, but I *do* mind very much the thought of anyone making fun of you – particularly Dirk. And even if I'd turned down his invitation, you would have had to meet him and Hester sooner or later anyway. So – the reason why I've taken the morning off work, Susarah, and why we're going to the city, is because

I want you to choose some modern clothes for tonight and have your hair cut. Will you?"

She looked at him, conflicting emotions clashing inside her. There was anger at the knowledge of why she had been invited to the dinner, and a humiliating suspicion that Abel was, perhaps, secretly ashamed of the way she looked, even though he pretended he wasn't. She wanted to get off at the next stop, take her carpet-bag and go home, and yet he was watching her with such an anxious, pleading look in his eyes that she hesitated to do something so drastic. "Why didn't you tell me all this before?" she asked tersely.

"Because, apart from the fact that I've hardly had a moment alone with you, I was afraid you would refuse to come with me," he admitted. "And also because if your mother had known what I wanted you to do she would have forbidden it, and you always do as your mother says, even when you don't agree with it."

The implication that she didn't have a mind of her own, but allowed Ma to dictate to her in everything, caught Susarah on the raw. "I *don't* obey my mother blindly because I don't have the courage to stand up to her. As a matter of fact, I had already decided some time ago to have my hair cut short, but I could see no point in doing so while I'm still in mourning for Wessel. And I wear mourning for him, not because I'm obeying my mother like a good little girl, but because it would hurt her if I didn't!"

"I know. I understand." He lifted a hand and touched her shoulder. "I like you just as you are – with your long hair pulled back, mourning clothes and everything. But when Dirk asked me to bring you tonight and I knew he was mocking me, challenging me, I thought: Right, you bas – you swine, I'll show you!" Abel's voice took on a chastened note. "I suppose you'll think it petty of me, Susarah, but I did so much want to walk into his flat tonight with you looking the way I know you could look, with your hair short and curling in your neck and wearing a pretty dress, outshining all the other women there, and to see the expression on Dirk's face."

His own expression was so vulnerable, so much like that of a wistful small boy that Susarah melted. "Oh Abel . . . I understand why you feel as you do, but have you any idea how much it would cost to buy the kind of pretty clothes you're talking about, let alone have my hair cut short? I can't see it coming to much less than five pounds! I simply couldn't afford it, even if I'd brought any money with me."

"*I* can afford it, Susarah!" he assured her eagerly, and withdrew a roll of banknotes from his pocket.

She stared at the money, biting her lip. "Abel, I couldn't let you . . . It wouldn't be proper . . ."

"Why not? I've been saving the money for *you*, working in the

evenings and on Saturday afternoons to earn it, ever since I decided
to ask you to marry me. I was going to buy you a fancy ring with a
stone, Susarah, but now I'd far sooner spend the money in this way."

The thought of him working long hours to earn and save money
for her, money to be spent on something frivolous like a ring, disarmed
Susarah completely. Even the wedding ring Wessel had slipped on
her finger had previously belonged to his grandmother. In all her life,
no one had ever spent money on her in a way that was not necessary
or useful or practical.

She blinked away unexpected tears. Yes, she thought, why not?
Let us turn the tables on Dirk! Invited me, did he, so that his other
guests could snigger behind their hands at me, and pity poor illiterate
Abel because of the drab, old-fashioned girl he was planning to marry?
We'll show him!

This time it was she who reached for Abel's hand. "Very well, I
agree. Thank you, Abel. But we'll have to keep it a secret from Ma
– not because I'm afraid of her, but because she would be shocked
and hurt, and there's no reason why she should be. She'll kick up a
fuss about my hair, of course, but she would have done so in any case
when I had it cut later as I'd meant to."

He grinned and put his arm about her shoulder, but only for a brief
moment as he sensed her involuntary stiffening. "I have the money
to pay for what's needed, Susarah, but I've no idea at all where you
would have to go to have your hair cut, or to buy new clothes."

"I have," she said happily. "John Orr's Department Store." Excitement was beginning to pound through her. She had learnt about John
Orr's from newspaper advertisements and had dreamt impossible
dreams of shopping there one day. She glanced at Abel from under
her lashes, a great surge of warmth and tenderness flowing through
her. *He* was making that dream come true, and she would repay him
by outshining all the other females at the dinner tonight. She would
be gay and amusing and witty and share with Abel the delicious
satisfaction of overturning all Dirk's spiteful plans.

When the tram reached the terminus she allowed Abel to hook his
arm in hers as they walked together through the Saturday morning
crowds. She had never even seen the outside of John Orr's, but Abel
knew where it was as soon as she told him the name of the street.

Inside the store, envy stabbed her as she watched the smart,
self-assured salesladies behind their counters. How wonderful it must
be to have a job and earn one's own living.

Then she thought of her baby, and she looked at Abel by her side.
She might not have a job but she had her beloved Corabella, and she
also had a future which included Abel. And wasn't she right now
experiencing the most exciting adventure life had held so far?

They took the lift, and got out when the girl operator in her neat, jaunty uniform announced, "Ladies' beauty and hair saloon!"

Abel hung back when he saw the overwhelming femininity of the hair and beauty saloon and he pushed a ten-shilling note into Susarah's palm with the air of a man who hoped to seek hasty refuge elsewhere. She, in turn, tried to overcome her awe and nervousness of the elegant women, employees as well as customers, who filled the place, and she forced herself to approach a kindly-looking woman of about thirty who was wearing the store's colours and seemed to be in charge.

"I want to have my hair cut in the latest style," Susarah said shyly. "But my – my fiancé – "

"Ah yes," the woman broke in with instant understanding, and smiled at Abel. "Perhaps sir would like to go and have a coffee in our restaurant while madam is being attended to?"

Susarah returned to his side and whispered a translation of what had been said. With relief, he nodded and escaped back to the lifts.

The older woman herself cut Susarah's hair and she kept up a flow of light, friendly remarks as she worked, so that Susarah gradually relaxed. She watched the pile of hair falling to the floor, and looked up to gasp at the slowly emerging transformation of her appearance. Who would have imagined that her hair *curled*? Not riotously, but sufficiently to soften the shortness of the style, and to respond dutifully when the hairdresser coaxed crescent-shaped ringlets to lie flatly against her cheeks and on her forehead.

Oh, Susarah thought, it was going to be worth every moment of Ma's shock and disapproval to look like this!

"You have lovely hair," the stylist said. "It's a real pleasure to work on hair that hasn't been cut before."

"It wouldn't have been cut today," Susarah confided, "if it hadn't been for the fact that my – my fiancé and I are attending a special dinner this evening. I'm going to choose a new dress when you've finished with me."

The woman smiled at her in the mirror, a smile of warmth, as if she understood perfectly the excitement pulsing through Susarah. "As it's for a special occasion," she suggested, "why don't you let one of the girls show you how to make up your face? A little rouge and powder and lipsyl would do wonders."

Susarah drew in her breath. Face powder was daring enough, but rouge and lipsyl? Ma would have a fit . . .

But Ma wouldn't know, she reminded herself. "How – how much would it cost?" she asked.

"Oh, there'd be no charge for a demonstration."

Since it was free, Susarah decided to accept this daring challenge but she rejected utterly the suggestion that she should have her eyebrows plucked into thin, symmetrical lines. She watched in the mirror as her face took on added definition when a hint of rouge was applied, emphasising her high cheekbones, while the powder neutralised the natural colour in her cheeks and the cherry-pink lipsyl highlighted the fact that her mouth was full and generously curved and possessed a natural cupid's bow. If Abel doesn't like me painted and powdered, she told herself, I'll wipe it all off with my handkerchief.

To her guilt and dismay, she found afterwards that while the demonstration had been free she had somehow allowed herself to be persuaded to buy a box of face powder, and lipsyl and rouge. With only a few coppers in change from the ten-shilling note Abel had given her, and her reckless purchases inside a paper bag clasped in her hand, she went to look for him, feeling guilty and miserable so that even the unexpected sight of her transformed hair and face meeting her in the many mirrors placed inside the store failed to cheer her up.

Abel stared at her when she entered the restaurant where he was sitting with an empty coffee cup in front of him, and he rose slowly as she approached. "Susarah – " he began in a dazed voice, and stopped.

"I'm sorry," she said wretchedly. "I've wasted your money. I let them paint and powder my face, and before I knew it I had let them talk me into buying the stuff . . ."

"But you look – " He shook his head. "You're beautiful!" A smile spread across his face and his eyes were alight. "Come on, let us go and get you out of that ugly black dress!"

She felt herself glowing, not only because of the genuine admiration in his expression but also because he had removed the guilt she'd felt. It was a totally unfamiliar experience, actually being encouraged in the spending of money on frivolous, self-indulgent luxuries.

The ladies' fashion department was more accustomed than the hair and beauty saloon to males escorting female customers, and Abel was offered a chair while Susarah disappeared inside a cubicle with a saleslady and a selection of dresses. With Abel's enthusiastic approval she chose one in apricot chiffon which seemed to float about her with each movement and ended just above her knees. He had struck up a conversation with the saleslady in Afrikaans, and between them they bullied Susarah into also having bought for her a pair of white, shiny silk stockings, white gloves and a pair of white shoes in the latest style. Someone from the millinery department had been summoned with a selection of hats, and a white straw cloche decorated with a single silk flower in the same shade of apricot as her dress was finally decided upon.

"Oh Abel," she protested when they finally left the department store, and he was carrying her carpet-bag which now also contained the clothes in which she had arrived. "You've spent a fortune – "

"Not a fraction of what I'd saved up for that ring," he assured her. "Now, we're going to have lunch at a hotel so that I can show you off, Susarah."

She hung back. "Lunch at a hotel! This is madness, Abel! No, I won't let you – "

"Oh." He looked totally crestfallen. "You would sooner have had a ring, wouldn't you? I don't have enough left to buy a decent ring, Susarah, and so I thought – "

"Oh Abel, you fool!" she cried, amused, exasperated and deeply touched all at the same time. "I don't want a ring! I never wanted a ring! I just don't want you to go on squandering your money like this!"

"But it would give me pleasure, and – well, I also want to watch the effect you have on other people, Susarah, so that I'll be able to imagine Dirk's face when he sees you tonight. I'd been looking forward to that . . ."

She slipped her arm inside his. "Very well. I – I have to confess that I'm feeling so excited, so – *frivolous* – that I just want to go on and on doing all the things that would have shocked poor Wessel out of his skin. Oh Abel, how can I thank you enough for these lovely clothes? For making me feel so young and carefree? I don't feel like a widow and a mother – good lord, I haven't even given poor little Corabella a thought for hours!"

His arm tightened inside hers so that their bodies touched. "I want you to think only of me today," he said hoarsely.

That, Susarah thought wryly, was not difficult at all. As they walked together through Johannesburg's streets she realised that she was turning heads, which was an intoxicating and totally unfamiliar sensation, but Abel was turning just as many female heads, and he had not just had a small fortune spent on him. She hoped he was as proud of being seen with her as she was of being the one whose arm he was holding tightly and possessively.

Her new-found self-confidence was more than slightly dented when she saw the imposing hotel towards which he was steering her, and she hung back. She couldn't set foot inside such a smart, expensive place, and what was far more important, Abel couldn't. They would sneer at him in there for not being able to speak English, and – oh God, didn't they have fancy menus in hotels? Abel couldn't read, and how was she to translate the menu discreetly to him in the sneering presence of superior hotel staff? All her protective instincts rose at the thought of Abel being humiliated.

"Let's go somewhere else," she begged.

"No. This is where I want to show you off, Susarah." His voice was firm, brooking no argument, and the next moment he was drawing her through the entrance of the hotel and she blinked at the splendour of the interior.

She glanced at Abel, but it was obviously a matter of pride to him not to show that he felt daunted, for he swept her across the deep-carpeted floor and the next moment a tall young man in black trousers and jacket and wearing a bow-tie came towards them.

"We'd like a table for two, please," Abel said in Afrikaans, and Susarah felt herself cringing as she anticipated the man's scornful pretence that he understood only English. Instead, to her astonishment, he answered Abel in a deferential voice.

"Very well, Meneer. If you would please follow me. But perhaps the lady would like to visit the powder-room first?"

Susarah swallowed. She could not imagine that her face required repowdering yet but she *was* in somewhat urgent need of visiting the privy. They must, surely, have a privy somewhere in the yard of the hotel. She blushed furiously as she contemplated asking Abel to question the man about the matter, but Abel seemed to have understood her dilemma, because he whispered in her ear, "There'll be a water-closet inside the ladies' powder-room. You have to pull the chain after you've used it." To the waiter, he said, "I'll wait here while you show the lady the way to the powder-room."

Imagine Abel knowing about such things as powder-rooms having water-closets, Susarah thought bemusedly as she followed the waiter's directions. And – and behaving with such an air . . .

She had never seen anything as luxurious as the powder-room with its built-in basins and its many mirrors, which reflected her new image from all different sides and made her stare at herself in renewed wonder. She was a little unnerved by her first encounter with a water-closet, and jumped hastily back after she had pulled the chain and water rushed in to fill the bowl, but it did not spill over as she had feared it would.

She washed her hands, took a final bemused look at herself in the mirrors and went to rejoin Abel. He was engaged in what seemed to be totally relaxed conversation with the grand-looking waiter, who immediately made Susarah a small bow and said, "I've asked for your table to be prepared, so if you'll permit I'll lead the way."

Their arrival inside the opulent dining room with its wealth of white damask, its shining silver cutlery and sparkling crystal glasses created a small stir, and Susarah was neither vain nor foolish enough to imagine that it was entirely on her account. No, it had a good deal to do with Abel. Something about his presence was causing the waiters to vie with one another to serve them, and to Susarah's astonishment it appeared that Abel had already discussed the menu with the waiter while she herself had been inside the powder-room and had decided on the choice for both of them.

One delicious course followed upon another; expensive, delicate, unfamiliar dishes, while waiters hovered to anticipate their every whim, and the one who had led them into the dining room arrived with a small silver bucket containing ice and a bottle. He opened the bottle with a loud 'plop' and then he was saying to Susarah, "Champagne, *dame?*" and filling her glass without waiting for her reply.

Champagne, she thought dazedly. She had read about it in the newspaper columns. It was something rich people drank. Never, in her most extravagant fantasies, had she ever imagined herself sitting in a smart Johannesburg hotel, with her hair cut fashionably short and wearing a beautiful, modern dress and silk stockings and rouge and lipsyl and *drinking champagne*. Imagine Abel even knowing about champagne, let alone being determined to squander money on buying it!

She sipped at her glass, and found the champagne to be delicious, slightly sweet, chilled and full of bubbles. It was, she thought, like drinking morning dew with the sun shining on it, and then laughed at herself for the silliness of the thought. Abel laughed too, as if he had been able to read her mind and was amused, and the hovering waiters smiled at them as if they were genuinely pleased to see two young people enjoying themselves, while the waiter who had brought the champagne filled Susarah's glass again. Looking at him, she thought how handsome he was, but slightly flawed-looking. He reminded her of those expensive, imported tins of a fish called salmon which Mr Sundarjee sometimes reduced in price because the tins had become dented or battered, and again she laughed aloud at the thought, and again Abel laughed with her and touched her knee briefly underneath the table. Oh, but she was happy; far happier than she had ever imagined she would be in her life.

She couldn't quite remember the meal coming to an end, but somehow she was leaving the dining room with Abel, feeling as if she were floating, while the waiters bowed and expressed the hope that they had enjoyed their lunch. She had no recollection even of Abel paying the bill, but of course he must have done so.

I'm drunk, Susarah thought with surprise, and giggled. I have partaken of Strong Drink. Strong Drink is raging, the pastor says. But I don't feel in the least like raging. I feel . . .

Before she could decide *what* she felt, the waiter with the flawed-handsome face was bowing herself and Abel from the hotel. "One moment, *seur* and *dame*," he said, leaving them underneath the decorative canopy at the front entrance and turning to speak to a man who wore a very gaudy and colourful uniform.

"He's nice," Susarah murmured dreamily after the waiter had returned inside the hotel, "even if he is a little dented. They were all nice. Oh Abel, it was wonderful – not just the meal, but – everything. I felt so special . . ."

"I'm glad." He squeezed her arm. "And you are special."

He began to steer her across the pavement and she saw that the man in the fancy uniform had halted a taxi and was talking to the driver, and to her amazement Abel made it clear that the taxi was meant for them.

"But – but – " she began helplessly as Abel forced her gently into the back seat. He sat down beside her and the driver started the engine.

It was the first time Susarah had ever been inside a motor car. The comfort of its upholstery, the quietness of its engine compared to that of the motorcycle combination, seemed to add to her dreamlike sense of unreality.

Then reality intruded briefly as she remembered something. "My carpet-bag!" she exclaimed with dismay. "I've left it in the hotel!"

"Never mind," Abel reassured her. "They'll keep it safely, and I'll go back for it later."

But she continued to fret about her own stupidity in forgetting the carpet-bag, adding aloud, "And I shouldn't have let you go to the expense of a taxi, no matter how far it is to walk to your brother's flat. Now it would mean that – "

She stopped in confusion. The taxi was drawing up outside an impressive-looking building with columns on either side of a wide flight of steps. "*Abel!*" Susarah protested. "That was – *lunacy!* No more than a block or two – "

But he merely smiled, and helped her out, and paid the driver. Then he was guiding her towards the building and she decided it would be churlish to go on making a fuss about the taxi, even though it had been madness; simply throwing money away. But it had been done now, and she, Susarah, had actually been driven *in a taxi*. It was one more novel experience to cherish in a day that had already held so much.

On the pavement on both sides of the wide flight of steps stalls had been set up, and black women were selling flowers. Abel forced her to halt at one of the stalls and pointed to a beautiful bouquet tied with white satin ribbon. A moment later he was giving Susarah the flowers to hold while he paid for them. She was about to protest at such further, wanton extravagance when she realised that this time it had been justified.

"A wedding anniversary present for Hester," she said.

Abel merely nodded. She noticed that he wore a worried look now, and she could only assume he still feared that something about her behaviour might cause Dirk and his friends to ridicule his fiancée and therefore, by association, him too. She shifted the bouquet of flowers into the crook of her arm so that she could touch his hand that was guiding her to the top of the steps.

"I can see that your brother must earn an awful lot of money to live in such a grand building, Abel. But you needn't worry that I might – "

His hand on her arm forced her to a halt. "Susarah," he said in a low, slightly uneven voice, "this is not where Dirk and Hester live."

"Oh! Where are we, then? Why are we here, Abel?"

"This is the Magistrate's Court, Susarah. I have a Special Licence, and all the other documents we'll need, and in five minutes' time we have an appointment to be married."

She stared at him, and shook her head to try to clear it. "You . . . This is a joke. We have to get married in the Tabernacle after my year's mourning for Wessel – "

"I know. And we'll have that ceremony in the Tabernacle when the time comes, with your mother and brothers present. But I wanted this one just for *us*, Susarah."

"No! It would be wrong – "

"Why? Who would we be hurting? You said yourself that a Tabernacle ceremony had little meaning for you. This will be our secret, yours and mine, and we would only have to keep it for a few months, Susarah. We'd carry on as before afterwards, with me living in lodgings and calling on Sundays to see you. Only you and I will know that we're already man and wife."

"But *why*, Abel? I don't understand."

He put his hands on her shoulders, and smiled down at her in a way that made her heart bump in her breast. "Do you remember, Susarah, how I promised you a wedding day whose memory you'd be able to treasure for the rest of your life? How could I give you that in Newlands, in the Tabernacle? When we left the hotel you said you felt special. That's how I wanted you to feel on our wedding day."

She thought of all the delights he had secretly planned for her, but it was the memory of the taxi that brought a lump to her throat and the sting of tears to her eyes. He had not forgotten how she'd told him about having walked to her wedding to Wessel, and he had been determined that she should not have to walk this time, even though it would only have involved a few blocks.

She looked at him, and said unsteadily, "You – you have indeed made me feel very special. And never, in a million years, would Ma have allowed *champagne* to be drunk on our wedding day."

"No," he grinned. "Nor would she have allowed the world to see your knees. Well, Susarah?"

"I used to imagine shocking the congregation by showing my knees in the Tabernacle," she said dreamily, and then gave herself a mental shake. "Those five minutes must be almost up, Abel. We don't want to be late for our wedding, do we?"

He laughed with exuberance, delight and relief, and kissed her briefly on the lips. "My God, Susarah, if you knew how I've been secretly sweating! I was terrified that you might throw your bouquet at me and storm back home, and leave me looking and feeling a complete fool!"

"After all the trouble you'd gone to, all the money you'd spent on me? After *hiring a taxi*? Come, let us go and be married."

The ceremony was brief and seemed slightly unreal to Susarah. Two strangers, relations of another couple waiting to be married, agreed to act as witnesses, and within minutes Susarah and Abel left the office of the Registrar as man and wife. Her new wedding ring might only be gold-plated, as Abel was at pains to point out, but at least it had been specially bought for her and she would wear it pinned inside her bodice after today, until it could be officially placed on her finger again during the ceremony inside the Tabernacle.

As they emerged into the late afternoon sunshine she smiled and asked, "Where to now? Your brother's flat?"

"That was another lie," Abel admitted. "We have a room booked for tonight at the hotel."

"Abel!" she exclaimed helplessly at such further profligacy. "It would cost a fortune!"

"The room has already been paid for. I told you, I'd been saving up to buy you a fancy ring with a stone. What kind of cheap ring did you imagine I'd think of buying you?"

She turned her brand-new wedding ring around on her finger. She did love Abel; she loved him even more now than she had before, because of the care and the thought he had put into making today so wonderful and special for her. She even had lustful thoughts about him, but she was dreading the moment of his 'loving' and she dreaded it all the more because she did love him and would have to keep from him, somehow, the fact that she loathed that side of marriage. If they went back to the hotel now and sat in one of its elegant rooms while they waited for bedtime he would be able to tell by her expression how much she was dreading it, and then she would never be able to act the part that would be required of her tonight.

"Perhaps," she said unevenly, "perhaps we could go for a walk – or something – instead of going straight to the hotel."

He smiled, and warmth and gratitude filled her when he did not insist on returning to the hotel immediately, but said, "I already have 'something' planned for this afternoon."

He would say nothing more, but took her arm and steered her along the pavement. She still carried her bouquet of flowers and instead of minding that people stared and smiled as they passed she smiled proudly back.

Abel indicated that they were to join a line of people waiting outside a building who were slowly moving forward towards the entrance where a man in a uniform was collecting tickets and then allowing people to enter in pairs or groups.

"*A bioscope!*" Susarah breathed, when they had moved up close enough to the entrance for her to realise what kind of building it was. "Oh Abel, I've never been to a bioscope before!"

"Neither have I," he admitted with a grin. "It will be a first experience for both of us."

Susarah sat in the dark, her hand in Abel's, her wedding bouquet on her lap, and watched the moving figures of real people flickering on the large screen, heard the dramatic notes of the music coming from an organ in a kind of pit below the screen. The people in the moving picture were enacting a story which caught her up completely in its magic and its romance and it did not really require the words which appeared at the bottom of the screen for one to follow the plot. She forgot reality as she drank in the drama unfolding on the screen. Her hand tightened on Abel's as she suffered with the beautiful heroine, and she buried her face against his shoulder when dreadful danger from the villain threatened the girl, and she cheered as loudly as the rest of the audience when the handsome hero saved the heroine from death in the nick of time.

Susarah did not return to reality until she found herself outside the bioscope with Abel again, and she discovered that it was now dark and that the street-lights had been lit. "I have," she told Abel unsteadily, "done all the things today, seen everything, I had ever dreamt of doing and seeing – and far, far more besides. Thank you – oh, *thank you*, Abel."

"It isn't over yet," he told her softly, taking her hand. Her other hand tightened about the bouquet of flowers and her entire being grew tense, for she knew to what he must be referring. She had returned to earth with a jolt. She said nothing as they walked to the hotel.

A middle-aged man stood behind a desk inside the hotel, and greeted them respectfully in Afrikaans as if he knew all about them, even though Susarah was certain she had not seen him before. He handed a key to Abel and said, "I hope you will find everything to your satisfaction in your room. Goodnight, Meneer Koen – Mevrou Koen."

Mevrou Koen, Susarah thought wretchedly, mindful of the wifely duty she would soon have to endure. Her mouth was dry as she climbed the stairs with Abel to their room on the first floor; all the magic of the day had been pushed to the back of her mind and only panic-stricken anticipation was left in its place. The wonder of the day was to be spoilt by 'loving'. It had only just become bearable to her before Wessel announced that it must cease with Susarah's pregnancy, and during the long interval since she had forgotten the conscious trick of making herself go limp so that she would experience the minimum discomfort. She was so afraid that she would cry out and spoil everything for Abel when he had gone to so much trouble and expense to make sure that today would be one she would treasure for the rest of her life.

He unlocked the door to their room and switched on the light, saying, "I ordered a light meal to be sent up to us, Susarah. Are you hungry?"

"N-not really." She swallowed hard, and then she forgot everything else for the moment in breathless wonder at the luxury of the room. There were already flowers in a vase on the dressing table but Susarah removed them. A copy of today's newspaper had thoughtfully been left on a table beside the bed and she took out some of the pages, wrapping the hotel's flowers in them and placing them on the window-sill where they would keep perfectly well overnight. In a corner stood a wash-basin with two taps and she refilled the vase with fresh cold water, arranging her wedding bouquet inside it. In the morning she would wrap her flowers in what remained of the newspaper and take them home, telling Ma they had been a present from Dirk and his wife, and before the flowers faded she would press some of the choicest blooms between the pages of a book so that she could keep them forever.

There was a knock on the door and when Abel opened it a waiter wheeled inside what looked like a large, mobile double tray covered with a white damask cloth. Abel removed the cloth after the waiter had gone and said, "They have sent us sandwiches, cold chicken, fresh fruit and pastries, and there is a bottle of wine cooling on ice. Don't you want anything, Susarah?"

"Not – not at the moment, thank you."

Abel looked at her through half-closed eyes, and smiled. "I think I'll also wait – until afterwards."

Her heart hammered and her blood seemed to be draining into her feet. She muttered something about visiting the privy and fled from the room. She was walking along the corridor towards the head of the stairs, with the intention of finding the same powder-room she had used earlier that day, but then she noticed that the door almost opposite their bedroom had a sign on it, reading 'BATHROOM AND W.C.' The initials must stand for water-closet, she decided, and pushed open the door, groping for the light-switch.

It was the first bathroom she had ever seen in her life. She gazed in awe at the massive bath, long enough for one to lie down in, and thought how wonderful it must be not to have to heat water on a range and fill a hip-bath with it and banish everyone from the kitchen while washing oneself, bent double inside the hip-bath, as quickly as possible before the water grew cold. She picked up a tablet of ivory-coloured soap and sniffed its scent appreciatively, and then she fingered the soft, thick towels hanging from a rail.

She hurried back to the bedroom, excited at the thought of using the bathroom and even more grateful for the reprieve it would give her. She picked up her carpet-bag and told Abel, "I'm going to have a bath."

He nodded. "I'll make do with the basin in here."

In the bathroom, Susarah stepped carefully out of her lovely new clothes, folded them and packed them inside the carpet-bag. It would be months before she would be able to wear them again. She ran hot and cold water into the bath and washed herself with the delicious scented soap, and afterwards she reclined there, running the hot tap every now and again, putting off for as long as she could the moment when she would have to join Abel in their room.

At last, with a sickly pounding heart, she stepped out of the bath, dried herself and put on her enveloping nightgown. After checking that no one else was in the corridor she picked up the carpet-bag and went to the door of their room.

Abel had left it unlocked for her, she found. That must mean that he had already gone to bed. Was it too much to hope that he might have fallen asleep after such an eventful day as they had shared? Yes, probably . . .

The most she had allowed herself to hope was that the room would be in darkness, so that he would not be able to see her expression. But the light was on, and Abel was sitting up in bed, leaning back against the pillows and the upper part of his body, at least, was totally naked. Even though her many brothers had accustomed her fully to the male form there was something very disturbing about Abel's muscular shoulders and upper arms and his chest with its mat of dark hair. It struck her suddenly that she had never seen Wessel even partially naked.

Abel grinned at her. "I was beginning to think you had drowned in the bath."

"No." She made a small ceremony of placing the carpet-bag beside the wardrobe, and then straightened slowly. "I – I'll turn off the light," she began.

"Why? If you have some secret deformity," Abel added, gently teasing, "I'd better know the worst right away. Take off your nightdress, Susarah."

"Take it – off?" she repeated, clutching the gown around her as if it had been a shield. Even Wessel had never seen her naked body.

"It's ugly, and it's unnecessary." Abel studied her, his eyes narrowing. "What's wrong, Susarah? You're playing for time. Why?"

"I'm – not." Desperately, she attempted a joke. "I suppose – I was automatically waiting for the prayer . . ."

"*The prayer?*" he echoed, his brows drawing together. "What do you mean?"

"Wessel used to make me pray with him – beforehand – for forgiveness. For – for yielding to the temptations of the flesh . . ."

"Good God!" Abel leant out of bed and took her arm. "Come here. Never mind the nightdress for the moment. I'll bet," he went on grimly, "Wessel wore his pyjamas throughout."

"Yes, of course . . ."

"Jesus! I wasn't being serious! You mean – Oh, poor Susarah! No wonder you never invited kindling!"

"*Kindling?*" she repeated, puzzled and trying to conquer the sudden shivering that had attacked her.

"The slow, slow lighting of a roaring fire." He pulled her on to the bed and gently forced her to lie on top of the bedclothes beside him. He was still partially covered by them. "Like this, Susarah," he said.

She lay tensely as he leant over her and then she felt his lips on her closed eyelids, moving along the side of her jaw while his hands stroked her body gently through the cheap material of her nightgown. Gradually the tension began to leave her, and she gasped as he caught her lower lip teasingly between his own. The next moment his mouth covered hers, but not tightly pursed as Wessel's had been. Abel's mouth was open so that his warm breath mingled with her own, and the tip of his tongue probed hers, producing a sensation she would never have imagined.

Without realising at first what she was doing, she put out her hands and touched his chest. "Good girl," he approved, moving his mouth from hers and unbuttoning the top of her nightgown so that he could kiss the hollow of her throat, and all the time his hand moved lightly, exploringly, over her body in the voluminous gown, his finger tracing the curves of her breasts, tantalising her until a cry escaped her and she sat up and pulled the gown over her head.

"Good girl, Susarah," Abel purred, just as she was beginning to feel appalled at her own unthinking, unreasoning action. "Beautiful Susarah." He thrust the bedclothes aside and measured his length against her own so that, for the first time in her life, she experienced the feel of a man's bare flesh against hers, his skin touching hers. She thought she was ready, then, for 'loving' which would not be so painful that she would disgrace herself and wound Abel by crying out.

But he showed no intention of mounting her as Wessel had done with the promise that it would soon be over. Instead, his mouth and his hands were everywhere, building up inside her a mounting excitement and eagerness, and without any urging from him she began to caress him in return and this, she found, merely added to her own growing, demanding urgency.

"I think," Abel murmured when soft moans were coming from her throat, "that you have been sufficiently kindled for the fire to take hold."

Only then did he enter her, kissing her as he did so, stroking her and sending wave after wave of delight coursing through her. He took his time, carrying her with him upon a mounting tide of rapture which astounded her with its intensity, and then all coherent thought became suspended as she found herself surrendering to a crescendo of unbelievable, enchanted ecstasy.

God, Susarah thought as they lay still together in each other's arms afterwards, you *did* have a plan, a point, a purpose for me after all. But what, then, had been your plan and your purpose for Wessel?

Poor Wessel, who had been so ashamed of what he'd called loving that he had made her shrink from it, never suspecting for a moment that there was anything more beyond the narrow boundaries he had taught her to accept.

Her wonderful day had not been marred after all. Instead, it had been crowned and enriched by an enlightenment previously beyond her imagination.

She tried to express aloud something of what she felt. "Abel, I never dreamt it could be like that. Thank you for teaching me . . . I'm glad it was you who taught me, because you're the only man I've ever loved. And I do love you so very, very much."

His head was cradled against her shoulder, and she expected him to make some response, ardent or teasing, or perhaps even a little embarrassed and sheepish. Instead, to her consternation and dismay she felt his hot tears upon her skin and she realised that his entire body had begun to shake with uncontrollable sobs.

She flung her arms about him, murmuring soothing endearments, comforting him in the way she used to comfort the boys when they had been hurt by something or someone and they didn't want Ma to know about it.

"Tell me, Abel, what's wrong. Tell me, my love, and I'll make it better. My dear one, my only love, tell me what the matter is. Is it something *I've* done or haven't done?"

"No," his voice came hoarsely as he clutched her tightly to him. "No, it was . . ." He stopped as if what had caused his grief went too deep to be expressed in words, and she moved her head and kissed him, not with the passion of a lover this time but with the tender comfort of a mother, murmuring soft endearments between kisses and stroking his hair, and gradually she felt him grow calmer.

No one, Abel wanted to say to her but couldn't, no one has ever before spoken to me of love. No one has ever loved me before. Not ever, in all my life. And it never even entered my head that I would –

Would *what*? he asked himself, trying to define his own unexpected reaction, the totally unforeseen twist that had been given to a day which had otherwise been so carefully plotted and planned to the minutest detail.

Pleasure he had expected, of course; triumph and elation, an assortment of physical feelings. Never this – this gratitude and humility, this sense of deep inner comfort, and a wholly unfamiliar tenderness for another human being. Nor had he expected to experience a sense of dependence on this girl whom he had seduced into a secret marriage for mercenary reasons. Was that how love felt, all those mixed-up feelings churning inside him? How could he tell? Love had never had any place in his life.

Confused and deeply shamed by the weakness of his tears, he drew away from Susarah and swung his legs from the bed. He heard her ask anxiously, "What is the matter now, Abel? Where are you going?"

"I won't be long." His voice was muffled and hoarse from the tears he had shed. "I'm – going to the bathroom to wash my face."

He pulled on his shirt and his trousers and groped for his shoes. He was grateful that she did not point out the obvious fact that he could have washed his face in the basin inside the room. He needed to – he didn't know what. To think, perhaps. But above all, he needed to be alone in his shame and bewilderment.

In the bathroom, he splashed cold water on his face and dried it with one of the thick, luxurious towels, lashing himself with scorn as he did so. *Weeping*, at his age! Crying snot-and-tears like some nancy-boy. Disgracing himself. He couldn't remember ever crying before . . .

Yes, he could. He had cried that long-ago day when the Bitch screamed at him, "There was only one Mamma, and she is dead!" At the memory, he felt his lips begin to tremble again like those of a four-year-old, and furious with himself, he muttered a curse. He could not return to Susarah in this stupid, weak, pathetic state. One word of tenderness or concern from her and he would break down again. She would think she had married a fool and a cry-baby. But someone was trying the bathroom door and he could not go on staying here either.

He straightened his shoulders and unlocked the door, muttering something to the man who had been waiting to use the bathroom. Where could he go, since he could not return to Susarah yet?

Manie Marais, he thought, remembering the small, ill-lit room on an upper floor of the hotel. He would tell Manie about the business he meant to start when he had sold the Benz Voiturette, and that he had decided to offer him a partnership. *That* should soon banish this shaming weakness that was emasculating him.

He moved along the corridor towards the door behind which he knew was the flight of shabbily carpeted back stairs, and a short while later he had reached Manie's room. The belated thought struck him that on his night off, a Saturday night at that, Manie would be out with some girl or even entertaining her in his room. But he had been wrong, for Manie was alone and half-sprawling on his bed, drinking brandy and reading a newspaper. He abandoned the newspaper when he saw Abel.

"I wanted to thank you for everything," Abel began, "and also for getting copies of all those certificates I needed."

Manie grinned. "My instincts urged me to cast my bread upon the water."

"I *do* have a proposition to put to you," Abel began and stopped. For some reason he felt disinclined to discuss the matter of a partnership now. "I'll talk to you about it later. Right now I want to make a telephone trunk call." Now what had made him say that? God, he was going crazy.

"No problem." Manie got to his feet. "I'll have a word with Wouter behind the desk and he'll take you into his little office." As they left the room together he asked, "Have my mates looked after you all right?"

"Thank you, yes. I hope no one will get into trouble – "

"Don't worry," Manie assured him cheerfully. "We're old hands at 'redistributing' costs among our less favourite guests."

Abel did not respond. He was wondering helplessly what was the matter with himself and what he thought he was doing.

Presumably because it was Saturday night the lounge downstairs was packed with people sitting at the tables and drinking. But while the waiters were kept busy, taking and supplying orders, Wouter stood idle behind his desk. He was a friend of Manie's and he had been party to the conspiracy of Abel's wedding-day arrangements, and he brightened when he saw the two men, obviously glad of any diversion. Manie spoke to him, and Abel was shown into a small office and left alone. He lifted the telephone from its hook and after he had contacted the exchange, he said, "Jakkalsdrif Post Office, please."

As he waited to be connected he asked himself in bewilderment: *What the hell do you think you're doing? What could you possibly have to say to the Bitch?*

Something to put the fear of God into her, he answered himself, glad to be making sense at last of his own chaotic behaviour. Something with which to punish her – for so much. For Jakkalsdrif, for making me cry, for making me feel – I don't know – the way I feel about Susarah.

Several minutes were going by. The Bitch would have gone to bed, of course. Perhaps she would not even hear the telephone ringing in the post office room. There was still time for him to put the telephone back and return to Susarah. Susarah, with her unexpected, radiant beauty, her tenderness and her love. Susarah, who had given such an unforeseen twist to his carefully forged plans.

"Jakkalsdrif Post Office," his mother's voice said in Abel's ear.

"Oh." For some reason he could think of no threat, no taunt, no veiled insinuation with which to torment her. "It's me," he went on at last, lamely.

"Abel." There was instant wary wakefulness in her previously sleepy voice. "What do you want?"

"I suppose – well, I suppose I wanted to say – I wanted to ask you – are you all right? I mean, alone there with only the baby and Mwende." God Almighty, what was the matter with him? He hadn't intended any such thing!

Her voice was justifiably suspicious and sharp as she responded. "This is another of your cruel, warped games, isn't it? Well, let me warn you, Abel – "

"No. I – I wanted to ask you – *Why did you hate me?* In the beginning, I mean." As soon as the words were out he realised that the question had subconsciously driven him from Susarah's side, had been behind his visit to Manie's room, had been the motive for asking to make a telephone call.

"Abel, it's very late! If you've got me out of bed because of one of your devilish tricks – "

"I only wanted to know what I did to make you hate me." His voice sounded pleading to his own ears.

The silence at the other end of the line stretched for so long that Abel thought she had replaced the telephone on its hook. Then, with a sense of disbelief, he heard her say, "I made you a winter coat once – in blue wool, with a sateen lining in a lighter colour. It was a very difficult, complicated pattern, but I got it right in the end."

His hand gripped the telephone angrily. He had asked her a serious question, and instead of answering it she was dragging up some old coat! Was she trying to mock him, make an even bigger fool of him than he'd made of himself by telephoning her? Or was the point about the coat that he'd ruined it, or looked ridiculous in it, making all her efforts worthless? Could she be trying to fob him off with such a petty reason for having hated him?

"Those who saw it said it looked as if it had been professionally tailored – " she was going on.

"Listen," he snarled, "what I really wanted to say to you was this – if I'm to lose Jakkalsdrif I'll drag you down, destroy you." He banged the telephone back on its hook without giving her a chance to respond.

Outside the small office, he evaded Manie and Wouter and made his way upstairs. When he reached the bedroom he stopped, lifting his hand several times to turn the door-knob and letting it fall again. What in the name of the devil was he to say to Susarah; how could he explain away his tears and his long absence? He didn't understand his own shaming behaviour or the stupid, stupid motive that had driven him to telephone the Bitch, so how could he even begin to make sense of it to Susarah?

I'll lie, he decided at last, desperately. I'll say I burst into tears because I hadn't wanted her to marry a miserable van-driver; I'd wanted to be able to offer her Jakkalsdrif.

He opened the door and saw that she was sitting up in bed. But instead of asking questions, demanding explanations, she merely held out her arms to him in mute comfort. He wanted to go to her, kneel by her side and rest his head in her lap, but something was stopping him. The lie he had meant to tell her fled from his mind and instead he heard himself say, his voice raw, "If you're wondering why I burst into tears like a baby, the answer is that I don't know – any more than I know why I left you to go and telephone my mother."

Another girl, he thought, would have murmured meaningless words of comfort, or felt embarrassed and changed the subject, or tried to draw him out about his conversation with his mother. Susarah simply sat there in silence, looking at him with tender patience in her eyes as if she knew that he would go on telling her what had happened, without any probing from her.

"I asked her what I had done to make her hate me from the start,"

Abel blurted out, and gave a crack of savage laughter. "I don't know what I expected. What I got was some tale about a damned coat she says she once went to great trouble to make for me."

"Come here, Abel," Susarah spoke at last. Her voice was gentle but it also compelled him to obey. He had heard her speak to her young brothers like that on occasion, when she'd wanted to comfort them and at the same time scold them or explain something.

He went to her, and this time he did bury his face in her lap and felt her hand moving in a tender caress along the nape of his neck. "Abel, can't you see that your mother was trying to explain that in her own way she did love you, even if she couldn't show it? It's a woman's instinct to want to make things for those she loves."

He raised his head, giving a hard laugh. "If she made me a coat it wasn't because she loved me! It was because she wanted to fool outsiders into believing she did." He stood up, shrugging to indicate a total dismissal of the subject, and undressed. He slid into bed and pulled Susarah into his arms, but she had no intention of dismissing the subject, it appeared.

She put up her hands and cupped his face, looking into his eyes as she said, "Go and see your mother, Abel. Speak to her face to face. Ask her what she meant about the coat."

"I don't care about the stupid coat!" Why couldn't she drop the subject? He wanted to forget all about it, and about how he had made a fool of himself.

"I feel it's important. If it weren't, you wouldn't have – " She stopped, but her uncompleted sentence hung in the air between them: *You wouldn't have cried like a baby and left me to telephone your mother.*

With relief, he seized the obvious and undeniable argument with which to put an end to the whole matter. "Going to Jakkalsdrif is out of the question, Susarah. I don't have the money for the rail fare and I can't take more time off from work. My boss wasn't very pleased when I asked to have this morning off."

"You wouldn't need to take time off. When Wessel was planning for us to go to Doornboomstad he asked about the times of trains. There are some that leave Johannesburg on Saturday afternoon and call at Doornboomstad and there's even a night-train, I remember, that gets in at dawn, but you'd better take an afternoon train. You would be able to get transport to Jakkalsdrif, wouldn't you?"

"Yes, but I don't want to!" he said, exasperated, and tried to kiss her into silence but she resisted.

"You can take a train back the next day, Abel, and go to work as usual on Monday morning."

He cursed inwardly. Didn't she ever give up? Then he remembered about the money and he said with finality, "I couldn't afford the fare."

"I've thought about that, Abel. You could sell the motorcycle combination for me and take the money out of that."

He was about to lie and claim there was no market for a motorcycle combination at this time of year, when he suddenly realised that she had offered him a possible way out of something that had been troubling him more and more.

Even when he had been planning his whole campaign in cold blood, Abel had wondered how long he would decently have to wait before he insisted on selling that old Benz Voiturette. Now that he had discovered his confused feelings about Susarah, the issue had become even more difficult and was weighing on his conscience in a wholly unexpected and uncomfortable way.

"I wouldn't take a penny of the money the motorcyle combination fetches," he said. "That's to be your nest-egg. Now if it had been the sale of that old car, a question of the few pounds you could expect to get for it – "

"Then sell the car!" she interrupted, as he had hoped and expected she would. "Go to Jakkalsdrif as soon as possible and talk to your mother."

He made a gesture signalling reluctant capitulation. He didn't want to return to Jakkalsdrif while it still belonged to Dirk, and he certainly had no wish to see the Bitch, had nothing at all to say to her. But by giving in to Susarah's tenacious demands he would soon have in his possession the hundreds of pounds the Benz Voiturette would fetch at auction.

One day he would tell her what the car had really been worth, how much it had meant. But not yet. He could not risk her finding out at this early stage of their relationship how cold-bloodedly he had set out to marry her, only to find –

His mind shied away from completing the thought, and he allowed her to draw his head down to hers. She did not wait for him to kiss her this time but took the initiative herself, and he felt both moved and humbled by the combination of tenderness and passion with which she was offering herself.

That old car for which he had married her was important; of course it was. It would give him the start he needed not only to buy back the inheritance of which he had been cheated, but also to make improvements on Jakkalsdrif once he had bought Dirk out, and to build another farmhouse on the land where he and Susarah could raise their children one day.

Yes, the Benz Voiturette was important, Abel told himself. But by far the most important thing about it was the fact that, but for that old car, it would never even have entered his head to marry Susarah, whom he –

No, he still couldn't form the words yet, not even to himself. Instead, he moved his lips from hers and said, "I'll go to Jakkalsdrif next Saturday."

It hadn't been what he'd wanted to say at all. As he covered her body with his own he wished he could have spoken, instead, the words hovering on the edge of his mind and which something intangible was preventing him from formulating or uttering:

"I love you, Susarah."

33

A vicious wind was blowing over Jakkalsdrif, screeching around the sides of the house, moaning like a lost soul as it entered through the gap beneath the front door which had been closed in an attempt at keeping the sand from blowing inside. It was Saturday afternoon and Simon was in Doornboomstad as usual, and Mwende was helping Koos to round up the cows and drive them into the corral for milking. At long last, after all these years, Koos was talking to his sister Mwende again. The death of Tina, her *basterkind*, her symbol of shame, had accomplished that at least.

The wind blowing inside the house rattled the beads Mwende had threaded on to a length of string and suspended above the wooden cradle which Koos had made for the baby, and Petronella heard him crooning with delight at the sound. It was time to bath and feed him, she decided, and went to the kitchen to fill a large bowl with warm water.

When she bent over him to lift the baby from his cradle he gave her a toothless smile of welcome, and she smiled in response, taking him in her arms and sitting down to undress him for his bath.

Not for the first time, she marvelled at the fact that this baby whom the world believed to be her own, who was Mwende's grandchild and the son of Abel, her scourge and her tormentor, should come so much closer to awakening maternal feelings in her than any of her own children had succeeded in doing.

She had told Mwende to accept Koos's invitation to visit overnight the *stad* where Suki, the woman for whom he was still trying to raise the full bride-price so that they could marry, lived with their children.

"I can manage alone," Petronella had told Mwende, "and it's high time you got to know your nephews and nieces. I'll take care of Joshua."

"Nonnie Petronella," Mwende had said with emotion, "never, if they know who Joshua's mamma really is, will they want to talk with me."

"They won't know, remember? It's our secret, yours and mine."

Mwende had nodded fervently, her face clearing as she obviously remembered how the entire neighbourhood had unquestioningly accepted Joshua as the afterthought baby of Petronella and Marcus.

"I wonder how you'll turn out one day, little Joshua," Petronella said aloud as she removed the last of the baby's garments. He gazed solemnly at her, as if such a question deserved serious consideration by him, and she marvelled again at the blueness of his eyes. No one would ever guess for a moment that his grandmother was a Zulu. Physically, he had inherited nothing at all from Mwende.

Only occasionally, Petronella remembered with a slight shock that she, too, was the baby's grandmother. In the same way as she had had little or no maternal feelings for her own children, she could not think of herself as anyone's grandmother. She had not yet even seen her official grandson, the child of Hester and Dirk, and when Dirk kept on making excuses for not bringing the baby to Jakkalsdrif Petronella felt no compulsion to press him into doing so.

"I don't *look* like a grandmother," she spoke her thoughts aloud, and smiled with bitterness. If ever ageless good looks, a smooth, unlined complexion and a slim, supple body had been wasted on a woman it was on herself. Who was there to see her, to care?

Petronella's thoughts were bleak as she began to soap the baby. Marcus was commonly supposed to be in America. How or where that story had started, she didn't know. But women calling to see the baby would say, "Won't Pastor Koen be astonished and thrilled when he comes back from America and discovers he has a brand-new son?"

Petronella could not ask questions about Marcus's visit to America without revealing the fact that he had left her, and for all she knew he might well be in that country. But when he returned to South Africa it would be to his foreign whore and not to her.

Petronella heard the sound of an outer door opening against the resistance of the wind, felt the rush of air and heard the door slamming shut as if the wind had forced it out of human hands. A few minutes later Mwende entered the bedroom, the turban on her head slightly askew, her eyes watering from the stinging, sand-laden wind.

"The milking is finish," Mwende announced, her gaze resting tenderly on Joshua as Petronella rinsed his soapy body and he splashed at the water with his tiny fist. "The milk is in the big bowl, Nonnie Petronella, for skimming tomorrow."

"Fine, Mwende. Go with Koos, then, to visit Suki and her children."

"You all right here by yourself, Nonnie Petronella?"

"What you really mean," Petronella said drily, "is will Joshua be all right here with me."

Mwende shook her head. "You look good after him, Nonnie, like he your own. *Better* than he your own," she added meaningfully, and then sighed. "What I really mean is – I scared to go with Koos. My heart say, perhaps if Nonnie Petronella need me I can tell Koos I must stay."

"Why are you scared to go with Koos?"

Mwende shrugged helplessly. "It a long time, Nonnie, since peoples speak with me."

"Too long, Mwende. The sooner you break the ice, the easier it will be from now on. So go with Koos and get it over with."

With a last, lingering look at the baby Mwende nodded and left the house to get ready to walk to the farm on whose *stad* Suki and her children would belong until Koos could marry her.

The house was quiet, apart from the howling sound of the wind as it tore at the roof and whined through every small crack or crevice. Petronella found herself hoping that the wind would wake Joshua up frequently during the night. He was her salvation in the lonely hours of the nights when she couldn't sleep for thinking of Marcus and hungering for him. Having to get up and make feeds or just change the baby helped to fill the desolate void, and more often than not she would take him into her bed afterwards because the human warmth of his small body saved her from feeling quite so alone.

She lifted him from the bath and wrapped him inside the large towel she had spread upon her lap. "You'll keep me company tonight, won't you, Joshua," she said to him. "I hate the wind; it is such a sad, lonely sound. Don't sleep too soundly, will you."

He crooned, almost as if he had understood her and wished to cheer her up by saying, Don't be sad and lonely. I'll be here.

She left him lying on her bed, wrapped in the towel, while she emptied the bath-water and took from the *stoepkamer* shop a fresh tin of talcum powder. Joshua had kicked the towel away and lay with his legs and arms flailing the air, and he watched them with fascination, as if they did not belong to him but were some strange diversion especially provided for his amusement.

She powdered him and put him into a clean napkin. Then she lifted him on to her lap and pulled a vest over his head before she reached for his nightgown.

"Be a good boy while I fetch your supper," she told him, placing him inside his cradle before going into the kitchen to mix his feed. Abel, she found herself thinking involuntarily, would have been screaming with furious, demanding impatience if *he'd* been this baby, whereas Joshua would be comforting himself by sucking his thumb while he waited for his bottle to be prepared.

In the bedroom, she picked him up and guided the rubber teat of the bottle into his mouth, and watched his lips closing over it as he began to suck hungrily. Her thoughts strayed to Abel again. If he had been more like this baby, would the entire course of her life have been different?

Thinking about Abel led her to recall that strange telephone conversation with him a week ago. What was it he had said? Oh yes, something about dragging her down, destroying her if he lost Jakkalsdrif.

She gave a sour laugh. As if she had not already been dragged down as low as she possibly could be; as if everything in her life had not already been destroyed. The only small comfort left to her now was this baby, and also the knowledge that Joshua's existence had robbed Abel's threats of any power –

The thought spinned away into nothingness in her mind. *How could she have been so stupid?*

She laid Joshua down on her bed and propped up his feeding bottle on a pillow beside him and then she almost ran to the front door, battling with the wind as she wrenched it open. She was in time to see Mwende and Koos emerge from the *stad*, wearing their best clothes and bending their heads to protect their eyes against the dust swirling in the air.

"Mwende," Petronella called urgently, cupping her hands about her mouth. "Mwende, come back here!"

Her voice had reached Mwende and Koos in spite of the wind and they stopped. Koos waited, his hand shading his eyes, as Mwende made her way hastily back to the house.

"You want for me to stay home, Nonnie?" she asked eagerly, hopefully.

"No." Petronella swallowed against a dryness in her throat that had very little to do with the wind-tossed dust and sand skirling about. "Mwende, tell me – and I want the truth – *did Abel know that Tina was expecting his baby?*"

Guilt crept into Mwende's expression, and she cast her eyes down. "I tell him the *dolosse* say there will be a child, Nonnie," she admitted.

"I see." Petronella's voice was heavy.

"I scared to tell you before," Mwende muttered.

Petronella said tonelessly, "It's all right, Mwende. Go with Koos to visit Suki."

Abel knew the baby was his; he had always known it. In some way she did not yet perceive she had played into his hands by passing Joshua off as her son and Marcus's. That had been the message behind his telephone call.

I no longer care, Petronella thought with weary despair. It has all gone on for too long and too much has happened to me. I am tired of fighting, tired of fearing the future. There *is* no future worth caring about, so let Abel do his worst.

She saw that Joshua's eyelids were drooping. In a moment he would be asleep and she would be left to face the remaining empty hours of the afternoon and the evening, and then of the night, alone.

She went into the kitchen and stoked the range with dry mealie-cobs. She supposed she ought to eat something, but it was too much trouble to prepare a proper meal for herself alone. Reaching for a mixing bowl, she scooped some flour into it, adding baking powder and an egg to make fried dough. Mamma had taught her that the best way to mix dough for frying was by hand, otherwise one never got the consistency quite right. Her lips twisted. Can you see me, Mamma, she wondered, wherever you are? Are you telling yourself that you always knew this would happen, that you tried to warn me and talk sense into me but I wouldn't listen and it's all my own fault? Petronella shook her head to clear the mistiness from her eyes.

She had one hand stickily imprisoned in the dough when she heard a vehicle stop outside. The sound of its approach had been drowned by the wind. It was the mailvan of course, arriving at the most inconvenient moment. She heard the battle for the front door being fought with the wind, and called out, "I'm busy, Petrus! Just leave the mail inside the post office room; there are no letters to go to Doornboomstad."

If the driver of the mailvan had heard her, he made no reply. Her hand suddenly stiffened in the act of mixing the dough. How could she have forgotten that it was Saturday afternoon, and that the mailvan had called this morning?

There was no danger in being alone on Jakkalsdrif with an unexpected visitor in the house, she tried to tell herself, but even so her heart had begun to beat unevenly. There was always cash on the premises and if someone knew that Simon was in Doornboomstad, and Mwende and Koos away from home –

The thought froze in her mind. The kitchen door, left ajar, had swung open and Marcus stood there, framed in the opening.

She looked at him, unable to speak. Had the best part of twenty-seven years really passed since she had first laid eyes upon him on the bank of the Vaal River? He seemed hardly to have changed at all. His eyes were as brilliantly blue, his hair as dark and abundant even though faintly streaked with silver at the temples. The grooves were still carved in cheeks that had not acquired a suggestion of fleshiness, but today they spoke not of amusement or tenderness but of explosive emotions, and to her bewilderment she recognised that rage was one of them.

"Well, Petronella," he ground out. "I wait for your bitter words, for your insults! Purge yourself of them so that *I* may begin."

She shook her head. There were no bitter words hovering on her tongue, no insults crowding into her mind, and it was not only because she was too tired to go on fighting life and Fate. Marcus's arrival was not a homecoming, awaited but overdue after an absence that had been a breeding-ground for resentment and grievance and frustrated passion. This was no more than a visit on his part. What had brought him here, and in a rage at that?

The baby! Thoughts came flashing with lightning speed through her mind. Marcus must have learnt about Joshua's birth, and had come to demand how she had dared to name him as the father. He could not possibly know that Tina was the baby's mother because apart from herself and Mwende only Abel knew that. He probably believed the child was Simon's illegitimate son, born to one of the neighbourhood girls and that Petronella was protecting the reputation of everyone concerned by passing the baby off as her own child by Marcus.

"The baby," Marcus began with force, confirming her thoughts. "You have called him by the name I have always desired a son of mine to bear, but how dared you – "

She flung up her head. "*I'll* take full responsibility for him, Marcus, in every way! You will not be asked to make the slightest sacrifice – "

"Many wicked, unforgivable things, Petronella," he cut in, his voice harsh, "you have been guilty of in the past. But of all of them this is the worst!" He moved towards her, grabbing her shoulder. She lifted her right hand to push him away and remembered that it was sticky with dough. The sight of the dough clinging to her fingers seemed to check his anger, as if he recognised the incongruity of venting his passion on her in such circumstances. He released her and watched as she dipped her hand into a scoop of flour and rubbed both hands together to free it of dough.

"You are preparing a cake?" he asked in an altered, formal tone, as if politely making conversation with a stranger, and she sensed that he was waiting until she had cleaned her hands before resuming his attack.

"A cake!" She laughed, a little wildly. "You think I make cake for myself on Saturday nights when I'm here alone? I was going to fry dough for my supper and save some to have cold for my breakfast tomorrow."

"Cold fried dough . . ." Marcus shuddered. "I recall that we sometimes ate it during the war, while on commando. You have a partiality for it?"

She shrugged. "It's convenient."

He said nothing for a moment. Then he touched her shoulder again, but without anger this time. "Do you remember, Petronella, how your

Mamma fried dough for supper on that occasion when I paid my first visit to the house on Jakkalsdrif?"

The question, his total change of mood from the rage which had brought him here and then the period of armed neutrality, startled her. She looked back down those long years to a half-forgotten memory. "And Pappa thought you were a spy for the British," she recalled, "and Gideon complained because Mamma had fried the dough in dripping because she couldn't use lard, knowing you were Jewish . . ."

"And the result of that visit was that you and I each sacrificed everything for the other," Marcus said quietly.

"Yes." Her mouth had begun to shake and she discovered that tears were running down her cheeks. She tried to hide them by turning her head, but Marcus had seen them and he drew her against him.

"Aai, my Petronella," he said softly, "how badly I have missed you."

She must have misheard him. He had come here to rage at her and hold her to account for passing another's child off as his own, not to tell her he had missed her. But then, unmistakably, he went on, "Every hour I have missed you, every day." He framed her face within his hands. "You remain beautiful as always, *mein tiere*." Marcus drew her closer and she responded to him with all the dammed-up passion of the long hungry months, a passion she had thought would desert her along with the will to go on fighting.

He lifted his mouth from hers. He took her hand, absently rubbing at the crumbly remnants of dough clinging to her fingers. Abruptly, he said, "Dough fried in lard is something I still cannot eat. It is forbidden by the Church of the Reformed Evangelists."

No, it isn't, she thought, reality laying its blight upon the miracle of Marcus's return. It is forbidden by *you*. You can't eat lard because at heart you are still a Jew. You are like that lost, doomed, wandering Jew in the Bible, and you will go away again and again, searching for what you've lost by making converts for the Church you've created in its place.

"Bread and coffee," Marcus cut prosaically through her thoughts, "we shall both eat – later." Then, not prosaically at all, he lifted her in his arms as if she were still a girl of barely seventeen and he a young man not yet twenty, and carried her to the bedroom. For an instant he stopped by the cradle in which Joshua slept, and then walked on. He laid her down on the bed, but did not let her go, and as he kissed and caressed her she thrust aside the thought that he might have come back, but that he would go away again as he had always done before.

He lifted his mouth from hers, and murmured, "Better the rage and the bitterness and the pleasuring, I discovered, Petronella – and, yes, the fear of the law – than nothing but peace and quietness. Peace and quietness – they wait inside the grave."

As Marcus began to caress her body in all the old familiar ways everything else was wiped from her mind, and their coming together was as fresh and as rapturous as if they were still two newly-met young strangers on the river bank on a hot Sunday afternoon.

Marcus lifted his head and looked into her eyes, and she saw the shine of tears in his own. "Never did I think to hope for a miracle! Aai, *liefling*, it was cruel – *cruel* – to keep from me the wonderful news of the gift of my son Joshua."

"Marcus . . ." Dismay and disbelief made her voice almost inaudible. This was the one possibility it had not even occurred to her to take into account. It was true that Joshua had been born just over eight months after the last night she and Marcus had spent together, but surely he must *know* that if the child had been his she would not have hesitated for a moment to send him a message and force him to return to her? Good Lord, how could he imagine that she would not have seized such a perfect weapon to fight for what she had lost and desperately wanted back?

She looked at his face, and she knew that he had no doubt whatever that Joshua was their son. She had to tell him the truth; she had to give him a full account of the story, for it had never remotely been her intention that *he* should be fooled.

She was still searching for the words with which to tell him whose son Joshua really was when he rose from the bed and went to the cradle, staring down at the baby as if he were indeed beholding a miracle. "From the bottom of my heart, Petronella," he said, his voice blurred with emotion, "I thank you for my Joshua, for the son named for my father. When I heard that you had bestowed on him the name I have always longed for a son of mine to bear, I knew that I had not only the excuse I needed and wanted for coming back, but I also understood that your heart had not changed towards me. You felt bitterness towards my father and did not wish him to be remembered, but for my sake you *have* remembered him."

"Marcus, listen," she began.

"No, my Petronella, *you* must listen. I have some understanding of why you did not send me news of my son's birth. It was because you believe nothing will change. But you are wrong. *Everything* will now change. For this son of mine, there will not be a father who comes home for only a few days and stays away for weeks or months. I shall stay here on Jakkalsdrif with you and him from now on."

A burst of wild laughter escaped her and Marcus naturally misinterpreted its cause, for he reiterated, "I mean it, Petronella. A *klutz* I have been not to see, long ago, that Abel has lost the power to cause trouble for us by creating a scandal in the Tabernacle. He lives in Johannesburg now, but even if he came back, who would believe a grown man telling such a story against his parents? So, I shall stay here from now on. A farmer I shall never be, but you will advise me what must be done and I shall carry out the tasks. I shall also stock more commodities to sell in the shop. The time has come for Simon to be ordained as a pastor, and he will go to Wolmaransstad to preach in the Tabernacle there. On Sundays I shall go to Doornboomstad to preach, and it shall be the three of us alone on Jakkalsdrif from now on – you, my Petronella, and me, and our Joshua, our precious gift."

Oh God, she thought in despair. It was like – like being a starving beggar, who had been mistaken for someone else and was being offered a fortune, and knew he would have to correct the mistake and go on starving.

"Come," Marcus cut through the desperate thoughts going on in her head, "let us eat bread and drink coffee, *my liefste vrou*, and afterwards – " His blue eyes sent her smouldering messages and the grooves danced in his cheeks, and she could no more have told him the truth then than she found it possible to do so during the 'afterwards' he had promised.

The wind ceased to blow, and Joshua did not wake up that night. Petronella alone lay awake in Marcus's arms, her thoughts following a circular pattern which always ended with the same bleak, uncompromising conclusion.

She had to tell Marcus the truth. Perhaps he might stay even when he knew that Joshua was not his son, but he would no longer feel himself bound by those promises he had made her. He would stay for a while only and then go away again, and their lives would resume their old pattern of separations followed by bitter quarrels. And oh dear Jesus, she would also have to tell him that the baby was an added weapon Abel meant to use against them. How would Marcus react to *that*?

On the other hand, if she did not tell him the truth he would learn it from Abel sooner or later. And then he would never forgive her for having cheated and used him and allowed him to dwell in a fool's paradise. He would almost certainly leave her again, and this time it would truly be forever.

Tomorrow I must tell Marcus the truth, Petronella thought. I must find the courage somehow. But when would be the right moment to tell him?

She should have told him before he went to sleep. She should have told him just after he had disclosed to her his happy plans for the next morning: they were to rise early, do the milking and other farm chores, and drive to Doornboomstad with Joshua, who would have been kept awake deliberately after his morning feed so that he would sleep through the journey. In Doornboomstad they were to attend the service at the Tabernacle and Marcus was to announce to the congregation that he had firmly established the Church of the Reformed Evangelists in all four provinces of the Union, and now it was time for him to stay at Jakkalsdrif and be their local pastor again.

I'll tell him just before we reach the Tabernacle, Petronella decided at last. He will then have to make up his mind very quickly as to whether he wishes to turn back and leave me again, or go on to the Tabernacle to tell the congregation – *what*? The truth about Joshua's birth? Or, to save me from public disgrace, that Joshua *is* his son? If he did that, people might not be so ready to believe Abel when he starts spreading his own story. Yes, facing Marcus with the truth just before they reached the Tabernacle might be the right moment.

But right moment or not, things would inevitably change between them. No man would relish having to pretend that another's child was his own, and the pretence would also add more guilt to Marcus's feelings of disillusionment and betrayal. To escape it, he would go away again and again as he had in the past. Besides, that wonderful picture of the future which he had held out to her had been for the sake of *his* Joshua, *his* son. Oh yes, whatever happened she would lose him again in some way. Tears slid down her cheeks and soaked into the pillow.

At least I shall have had tonight, she tried vainly to comfort herself. I might have stolen it, but no one could ever take it back.

Abel reined in the horse he had borrowed from the station master's son in Doornboomstad. The sun was just rising, but even the rosy glow with which it painted the horizon could do nothing to soften the bleak, harsh reality of Jakkalsdrif.

He looked around him in shock and disbelief. There were more *dongas*, more patches of bare, cracked earth where the topsoil had been washed away, more dense infestations of khaki-bush than he remembered, and even the prickly pears seemed to encroach more menacingly than before on such arable fields and grazing land as remained. How could the place have deteriorated so dramatically during the months he had been away?

Or – *had* it deteriorated to any great extent? Was it not simply that he was seeing everything with a fresh eye, recognising truths he had failed to face in the past?

Involuntarily, he found himself thinking, Can this – this *wasteland* – really be worth going on fighting for?

He dismounted and knee-haltered the horse. There was little point in setting it free to graze; he did not intend staying long and didn't wish to waste time in rounding the animal up. He would fulfil his promise to Susarah and return as soon as possible to Doornboomstad to catch a train. As it was, he had deliberately taken the night-train from Johannesburg so that he would not have to spend a moment longer than necessary in the company of the Bitch.

He noted the air of desertion about the farm. Sunday was Koos's day off, but Abel would have expected Mwende to be at work milking the cows at this time of the morning. But the cows were not inside the corral so it looked as if they had all dried up. He shook his head. If none of the cows was giving milk the grazing must have become poorer than it looked.

I don't want to be here, he suddenly thought, and this time it was not just because of his reluctance to see the Bitch. He wanted, quite passionately, to be back in Newlands. At this very moment he could have been getting ready to visit Susarah, looking forward to going to bed with her while Tant' Jakoba and the boys were at the Tabernacle. He experienced a curious feeling, as if his insides were melting, when he thought of Susarah.

The Benz Voiturette was safely awaiting auction, and Abel had borrowed ten pounds from Meneer Mendoza, buying his return rail ticket to Doornboomstad and giving the balance to Susarah. He had felt bad about lying to her and pretending it was the money realised by selling the old car.

I'll go and see her tonight, he vowed to himself, and tell her part of the truth. I can't tell her yet that I married her because of the car, but I'll pretend that I discovered at the last moment that it might be worth more than ten pounds, and I didn't want to tell her at first because I didn't want her to be disappointed if it turned out not to be true. I'll also tell her about the haulage business I've always wanted to start, and I *know* she'll suggest, herself, that the money should be invested in it.

Excitement churned inside him, partly because of Susarah, partly because of the challenge the haulage business would present, the rewards it would bring. And when he had made enough money he would –

Would what? an inner voice unexpectedly intruded. Use it to buy back this? Throw it away just because you were cheated of this miserable inheritance, and can't bear it belonging to Dirk – who doesn't want it because he knows how worthless it is, but would charge you through the nose for it?

He shook his head in confusion and uncertainty, and then squared his shoulders. There was no point in putting off any longer the coming meeting with the Bitch. He mounted the steps to the stoep and opened the front door.

No one had heard him. They hadn't heard him, he realised with stunned surprise, because the Preacher was at home. He was singing in what was presumably Yiddish, and Abel recognised what it was he was singing because it had been translated into Afrikaans and Susarah had told him that it was a very famous German lullaby.

As the Preacher crooned the last words of the hauntingly beautiful song, Abel heard a baby gurgling with delight. If it was true that he had left the Bitch, Abel thought, news of the surprise birth of another baby, a new son, had sent him back to her. Abel was amazed to find that he did not care. Once, the knowledge that they were together again and obviously happy would have driven him to a pitch of impotent rage.

Well, Abel decided with a shrug, he would have to think of an excuse for having called and then leave again. He was clearly not going to find the opportunity to speak to the Bitch about some damned coat she was once supposed to have made for him, not with the Preacher present. It had been a stupid reason for coming in any case, and he would never have agreed to it if it hadn't represented a chance of getting possession of the Benz Voiturette without arousing Susarah's suspicions.

He moved along the corridor towards the kitchen, from where the Preacher's voice and the baby's crooning and laughter were coming. For a moment he stood unnoticed in the doorway. The Bitch, still looking more like a young girl than a woman of middle age, was busy at the stove and the Preacher was bouncing the baby on his knee as he sang. The Bitch saw Abel first and froze, her face turning chalk-white as she dropped the lid of a pan with a clatter on the floor. The Preacher stopped singing and the next moment he was on his feet, putting the baby inside a cradle and holding out his hand.

"Abel, my son! *Vos iz mid dir*? And what a fine man you have become!"

The surprise and pleasure in his voice had sounded genuine, and Abel was so disarmed that he automatically accepted the hand held out to him. Then he realised how different he must be looking now in his city clothes, and that was all that had been meant, but even so he did not withdraw his hand and after a moment's hesitation the Preacher raised his other hand diffidently and laid it on Abel's shoulder.

Unexpectedly at a loss and feeling almost embarrassed, Abel dropped the Preacher's hand and moved away, staring down at the baby in the cradle while he tried to gather his thoughts and find an excuse for having come. Because nothing occurred to him, he played for time by bending down and offering the baby his finger. It was seized in a chubby hand. "Would you like to hold your brother?" he heard the Preacher ask.

Abel straightened, regretting the idiotic impulse to pay attention to the baby, the more so when he noticed the frozen expression that had settled on the face of the Bitch. All right, he wanted to snarl at her, you needn't look like that! I've no wish to defile your doted-upon brat by touching him.

He had half-turned away from the cradle and was about to speak his thoughts aloud when the Preacher lifted up the baby and held him out to Abel. The baby's questing hands grabbed Abel's lapels and after that it seemed impossible not to take him from the Preacher. Holding him awkwardly, Abel said the first thing that came into his head. "He looks like you."

"Ach no!" the Preacher protested. "Such beauty I have never possessed!"

The baby gurgled, as if he had understood the remark and found it funny, and the sound sparked off laughter in the adults too, but it was strained, uneasy laughter. It also seemed to Abel that there was a hint of hysteria in that of the Bitch. She had still not said a single word since his arrival in the room.

He looked down at the baby in his arms, and then he looked directly at her. "Perhaps, if *I* had been pretty as a baby . . ." he suggested in a hard voice. "But Mwende used to tell me that my nose was enormous."

A tense silence followed what he had hinted at but not spelt out. It was broken by the Preacher with a determined change of subject. "I received news from Dirk that you had found employment in Johannesburg, Abel. But it is poor work, I understand, driving a van, and so you have returned home – "

"No," Abel interrupted, and put the baby back in his cradle. "I may be only a van-driver now, but I have plans." Excitement blazed in his voice. "I can spot a business opportunity far better than Dirk can! I'm going to start working for myself just as soon as I've raised the necessary capital."

The Preacher could not quite hide his relief. "So you have not come back to Jakkalsdrif to stay . . ." He stopped, and gave Abel a look of sudden understanding, of shame, wistfulness, and regret all jumbled together. "I wish, very much, that it was possible for me to provide money for your business. But I have a new son, and such limited capital as I possess – " He spread his hands in a helpless gesture.

Abel heard the Bitch making a strangled, desperate sound. Obviously concerned, he thought with bitterness, that this new, favoured son should not have to go short of anything. He looked at her and said in a hard voice, "I haven't come to demand money. I know very well that what there is to spare will have to go on this *troetelkind* of yours. Joshua, you've called him." He turned to the Preacher. "You always wanted a Joshua, Dirk says."

Another uneasy silence followed his words. It was broken by the Bitch, speaking for the first time. "Then why – why have you come?"

He shrugged. "I suppose I wanted to see the place for the last time. It's quite a mess, isn't it?"

"Yes," she agreed quietly, "It's quite a mess." She hesitated. "You said you wanted to see the place 'for the last time'. Does that mean – ?" She left the question in the air.

He experienced a stab of surprise. Had he really used those words – *for the last time*? Yes, come to think of it, he had. He had formed no conscious decision to say them, but he was fully aware of all the implications now as he answered her.

"Yes, it means I'm giving up my fight for Jakkalsdrif." He smiled tautly at both of them. "You'll be glad to hear there'll be no more games from now on, no more tricks or threats. Dirk is welcome to Jakkalsdrif."

He heard her let her breath out in a long, uneven sigh. "You must be hungry," she changed the subject in a stilted voice. "Breakfast will soon be ready. Why don't you sit down at the table?"

He did as she'd suggested, and asked, "Where is Mwende?"

"She went with Koos to visit Suki and their children. The black people are talking to Mwende again now that Tina – " She stopped, apparently becoming engrossed in turning the eggs she had been frying.

"Oh yes, poor Tina," Abel said. "I was sorry to hear that she'd died. A fever, wasn't it?"

"Aai, but I was sorry too," the Preacher put in. "I was in ignorance of the matter until your mother told me this morning. Poor, sad Tina. And poor Mwende. For her there was suffering until the end because of what people called her mongrel child, her *basterkind*."

The Bitch again changed the subject. "I received a letter from Jakoba, Abel, telling me that you have been learning to read and write."

"But that is wonderful news!" the Preacher applauded. "Ah yes, Abel, you will surely become a good businessman because of the ability to read and write!" He paused, and then went on, "Perhaps you read the papers?"

"Sometimes," Abel exaggerated.

A sombre note entered the Preacher's voice. "Then you will have read how, in some countries in Europe, they have been burning shops and other property belonging to Jews. You will have learnt that there is hunger because Jews are prevented from carrying on their business, and that each day brings new dangers to their lives. People in other countries believe it will pass, but it will not." He added with what seemed to Abel to be pointed deliberation, "For a Jew living in a country like South Africa, it would be a most terrible thing to be sent back to his homeland in Europe."

Abel looked up in surprise, sensing that the Preacher had been trying to tell him, not about Jews in general but about one Jew in particular – himself. "I can't read complicated stuff like that yet," Abel admitted. "But why would a Jew living in South Africa be sent back to his homeland against his will?"

The answer came in a quiet voice which somehow served to lend emphasis to the words. "If he broke a law, Abel – even a minor law – and the authorities investigated and discovered that he was told, many years ago, that he could not live in this country because he was an undesirable alien . . . And if he had sneaked back and lived here all the same without permission – yes, then they would deport him to what they would consider to be his European homeland."

The Bitch had been putting breakfast on the table as the Preacher spoke, and the three of them began to eat in silence. Abel went over in his mind what the Preacher had been saying. He had been talking about himself, offering some kind of explanation for his long, stubborn refusal to admit that Abel was the first-born. Much had been left unexplained but it hardly seemed to matter any more. Abel ate quickly, wanting only to get this visit over with and leave.

He pushed his chair back when he had drained his coffee cup. "I must go and feed and water the horse I borrowed in Doornboomstad," he said.

The Preacher sprang up, pushing Abel back into his chair. "No, stay. Sit and digest your breakfast. *I* shall take care of the horse for you." There was something almost like pleading in his voice, as if he wished to do something, no matter how slight, as a gesture of atonement.

Abel found himself alone with the Bitch, facing her across the table. Distastefully, no longer caring about the answer, he asked again the question he had promised Susarah he would put to her. "Why did you hate me? What did I do?"

"Nothing." She looked down at her hands. "Except – you hated me first."

Memory stirred inside him, and with it curiosity. He found that he did, after all, want to be given answers to questions that had dominated so much of his life. "I remember now, you said that to me once before. But how can a *baby* hate?" When she didn't reply he went on, "Was it because I was in the way, because I took up time you wanted to spend with him?" He jerked his head towards the door, indicating the Preacher.

"A little," she admitted. "But at the very beginning – " He heard the catch in her voice as she paused before going on, "I thought you would look like a van Zyl. I thought you would make Mamma forgive me and love me again . . ."

He didn't know what she meant, but to his intense discomfort she began to weep silently, allowing the tears to roll down her cheeks, making no attempt to wipe them away. If she had wept in a dramatic way he could have looked on, scornful of her display of self-pity. But this was not self-pity, he sensed, and because he didn't know what else to do or say he found himself lying.

"That blue coat you talked about the other night – I remember it."

"Do you?" She seemed to be grabbing eagerly at the lie, because she was wiping her palms across her wet cheeks and going on, "It was a very complicated pattern. For a whole week – I sat up until midnight – struggling just to get the cutting-out right."

"I was proud of that coat, I remember." He listened to himself in amazement. Jesus, what was he doing, talking to her like this, telling lies about a stupid coat he couldn't remember at all? When she must *know* that he couldn't possibly remember it?

But she was going along with the lie, because she nodded and whispered, "I'm so glad."

"Yes, well," he said awkwardly, standing up. "I think I'd best be on my way back now. I only came to tell you – there'll be no more games, no more threats, from now on." He hadn't come to do any such thing, but as he said it he knew that it had become the truth.

He moved towards her and very hesitantly put out his hand, touching her shoulder. "Goodbye – " Once more he hesitated, and he was as surprised as she looked when he added, "*Ma*." It was the first time he had ever called her Ma.

"Goodbye – Abel," she returned unsteadily, and lifted a hand, placing it on his own.

He left her and went outside. The borrowed horse had been watered and fed and his father was brushing its coat. It struck Abel suddenly that he had thought of him as 'father' and not as 'the Preacher'. "Thank you," Abel said, and this time he added quite deliberately, "Pa."

They shook hands, and there was a shine of tears in his father's eyes. "I wish you all the happiness in the world, my son," he said.

Abel nodded his thanks, and spurred the horse on its way. He needed no one's good wishes. He already had all the luck and the happiness in the world.

If he could catch the noon train from Doornboomstad he would be in Newlands this evening, with Susarah, *his wife*. He would wait outside in the street until Tant' Jakoba's lights had gone out and then he would knock on the door of Susarah's house.

What would he tell her about the visit to Jakkalsdrif? What could he tell her? That his mother had cried, that both of them had told lies about a long-ago coat? How would he be able to explain that something indefinable had happened today, something that had brought him liberation and peace?

He didn't know. What he did know was that tonight he would be able to say, quite naturally and without the words sticking in his throat, "I love you, Susarah."

Petronella continued to sit by the kitchen table, because she did not believe her legs would be able to support her if she were to stand up. Now that the unexpected visit was over and Abel had said goodbye to her, calling her Ma, it was beginning to take on the unreality of a dream. Could it indeed be true that Abel had given up his fight for Jakkalsdrif, and that he would not be tormenting them again in the future?

She heard the baby yawning in his cradle. Yes, it must indeed be true, for there had been no doubt at all that Abel accepted Joshua as his youngest brother and nothing else.

She shuddered as she recalled her feelings of utter doom when Abel had appeared so unexpectedly in the kitchen, and again when he'd bent over Joshua's cradle and then held him. With what terror she had waited for him to hint that he resembled Tina. But it seemed certain now that if he did remember Mwende and Tina had told him the girl was carrying his baby, he must have decided later that it had been a false alarm. Clearly, Abel did not have the faintest suspicion that he was Joshua's father. Of that she was convinced.

She heard Marcus entering the house, and looked up when he came into the kitchen. "So," he said, "at last we have made a kind of peace with Abel."

"Yes." Was this, she wondered, the moment when she should tell him the truth about Joshua? While relief at the knowledge that Abel would not be hounding them in the future was still fresh and new in his mind? Her original plan had had to be scrapped, because Abel's unexpected arrival had prevented her and Marcus from setting out for Doornboomstad with Joshua, and by now it was far too late to leave for the service in the Tabernacle.

She gathered her courage, and opened her mouth to make her confession. But Marcus's attention had been drawn by the baby, who had just given another mighty yawn. He lifted Joshua from his cradle and held him high in the air. "So, my Joshua, we have deliberately kept you awake and now you wish only to sleep! What should your mother and your father do while you sleep, hmm? When the cows have already been milked, and it is too late to proceed to the Tabernacle, and there are no duties needing our attention until lunch-time? Is it your opinion perhaps, my son, that we should also go to bed while you sleep?"

I must tell him, Petronella thought desperately. *Now.* She stood up and went to him, but the only words she found herself able to form were an automatic warning. "Don't lift the baby up so high, Marcus, or he might be sick over you."

"So," Marcus laughed, "if he is sick, I shall wash it off. Eh, my Joshua, my son who will grow up to fill me with pride?" He gazed adoringly at the baby. "A doctor you will become one day, or a lawyer, or even perhaps a professor. Ah, I have such plans for you, my son!" With great tenderness he lowered the baby and placed him in his cradle, tucking the blankets around him. "Already his eyes are closing, Petronella; soon he will be asleep. And he fully agrees with me that you and I should also return to bed."

His blue eyes were glinting at her with love and desire, and once again the courage to tell him the truth deserted her.

Marcus moved away from the cradle and put his arms around her, leading her back to the bedroom where his hand began to remove the pins which held the hair in the nape of her neck, and then he pressed her gently down on to the bed so that her loose, silver-blonde hair fanned out on the pillow, and he bent his head to hers.

She had never meant to deceive Marcus. It had never even occurred to her that he might so thoroughly deceive himself. And now the truth would cause only harm and bitterness while the lie would bring nothing but happiness and joy.

The gods, Petronella decided suddenly and irrevocably, had offered her an unlooked-for second chance – and she was going to grab it with both hands.

Date Due
